O9-BUD-997

Richard Russo

EMPIRE FALLS

Richard Russo lives in coastal Maine with his wife and their two daughters. He has written five novels: *Mohawk, The Risk Pool, Nobody's Fool, Straight Man*, and *Empire Falls*, and a collection of stories, *The Whore's Child*.

Also by Richard Russo

Mohawk

The Risk Pool

Nobody's Fool

Straight Man

The Whore's Child and Other Stories

EMPIRE FALLS

EMPIRE
FALLS

Richard Russo

Vintage Contemporaries
Vintage Books
A Division of Random House, Inc.
New York

FIRST VINTAGE CONTEMPORARIES EDITION, MAY 2002

Grateful acknowledgement is made to the following for permission to reprint previously published material:

Acuff-Rose Music, Inc.: Excerpts from "Don't Let the Stars Get in Your Eyes" by Slim Willet, copyright © 1952, copyright renewed 1980 by Acuff-Rose Music, Inc. All rights reserved. International rights reserved. Reprinted by permission of Acuff-Rose Music, Inc.

Famous Music Corporation and Hal Leonard Corporation: Excerpt from "Magic Moments," music by Burt Bacharach and lyrics by Hal David, copyright © 1957, copyright renewed 1985 by Famous Music Corporation and Casa David. International copyright secured. All rights reserved. Reprinted by permission of Famous Music Corporation and Hal Leonard Corporation on behalf of Casa David.

Music Sales Corporation and *The Estate of Dick Manning:* Excerpt from "Hot Diggity," words and music by Al Hoffman and Dick Manning, copyright © 1956 (copyright renewed) by Al Hoffman Songs, Inc. (ASCAP) and the Dick Manning Music Company. All rights for Al Hoffman Songs, Inc., administered by Music Sales Corporation (ASCAP). All rights reserved. International copyright secured. Reprinted by permission of Music Sales Corporation and the Estate of Dick Manning.

The Library of Congress has cataloged the Knopf edition as follows:
Russo, Richard, 1949–
Empire falls : a novel / Richard Russo.—1st ed.
p. cm.
ISBN 0-679-43247-7
1. Restaurants—Fiction. 2. Restaurateurs—Fiction. 3. Working class—Fiction.
4. Fathers and daughters—Fiction. 5. Maine—Fiction. I. Title.
PS3568.U812 E4 2001b
813'.54—dc21   2001088568

Vintage ISBN: 0-375-72640-3

Author photograph © J. D. Sloan
Book design by Virginia Tan

www.vintagebooks.com

Printed in the United States of America

30

For Robert Benton

ACKNOWLEDGMENTS

As USUAL my debts are substantial. For space, I wish to thank Fitz-patrick's Cafe, the Camden Deli, and Jorgenson's. Thanks also to Perley Sasuclark, who told me a story I needed to hear, and to Allen Pullen at the Open Hearth, who reeducated me about restaurants. To Gary Fisketjon, who has labored over this manuscript so lovingly, I'd attempt to describe my gratitude in words, but then he'd have to edit them, and he's worked too hard already. To Nat Sobel and Judith Weber, who have been with me from the start, my love. To my wife, Barbara, who reads each book more times than anyone should have to read anything, more love. To my daughters, Emily and Kate, who have been the kind of girls, and now, young women, who have freed their father to worry about people who don't exist outside his imagination, more gratitude than I can express; this time, to Kate especially, for reminding me by means of concrete detail just how horrible high school can be, and how lucky we all are to escape more or less intact.

EMPIRE FALLS

COMPARED *to the Whiting mansion in town, the house Charles Beaumont Whiting built a decade after his return to Maine was modest. By every other standard of Empire Falls, where most single-family homes cost well under seventy-five thousand dollars, his was palatial, with five bedrooms, five full baths, and a detached artist's studio. C. B. Whiting had spent several formative years in old Mexico, and the house he built, appearances be damned, was a mission-style hacienda. He even had the bricks specially textured and painted tan to resemble adobe. A damn-fool house to build in central Maine, people said, though they didn't say it to him.*

Like all Whiting males, C.B. was a short man who disliked drawing attention to the fact, so the low-slung Spanish architecture suited him to a T. The furniture was of the sort used in model homes and trailers to give the impression of spaciousness; this optical illusion worked well enough except on those occasions when large people came to visit, and then the effect was that of a lavish dollhouse.

The hacienda—as C. B. Whiting always referred to it—was built on a tract of land the family had owned for several generations. The first Whitings of Dexter County had been in the logging business, and they'd gradually acquired most of the land on both sides of the Knox River so they could keep an eye on what floated by on its way to the ocean, some fifty miles to the southeast. By the time C. B. Whiting was born, Maine had been wired for electricity, and the river, dammed below Empire Falls at Fairhaven, had lost much of its primal significance. The forestry industry had moved farther north and west, and the Whiting family had branched out into textiles and paper and clothing manufacture.

Though the river was no longer required for power, part of C. B. Whiting's birthright was a vestigial belief that it was his duty to keep his eye on it, so when the time came to build his house, he selected a site just above the falls and across the Iron Bridge from Empire Falls, then a thriving community of men and women employed in the various mills and factories of the Whiting empire. Once the land was cleared and his house built, C.B. would be able to see his shirt factory and his textile mill through the trees in winter, which, in mid-Maine, was most of the year. His paper mill was located a couple miles upstream, but its large smokestack billowed plumes of smoke, sometimes white and sometimes black, that he could see from his back patio.

By moving across the river, C. B. Whiting became the first of his clan to acknowledge the virtue of establishing a distance from the people who generated their wealth. The family mansion in Empire Falls, a huge Georgian affair, built early in the previous century, offered fieldstone fireplaces in every bedroom and a formal dining room whose oak table could accommodate upwards of thirty guests beneath half a dozen glittering chandeliers that had been transported by rail from Boston. It was a house built to inspire both awe and loyalty among the Irish, Polish and Italian immigrants who came north from Boston, and among the French Canadians, who came south, all of them in search of work. The old Whiting mansion was located right in the center of town, one block from the shirt factory and two from the textile mill, built there on purpose, if you could believe it, by Whiting men who worked fourteen-hour days, walked home for their noon meal and then returned to the factory, often staying far into the night.

As a boy, C.B. had enjoyed living in the Whiting mansion. His mother complained constantly that it was old, drafty and inconvenient to the country club, to the lake house, to the highway that led south to Boston, where she preferred to shop. But with its extensive, shady grounds and its numerous oddly shaped rooms, it was a fine place to grow up in. His father, Honus Whiting, loved the place too, especially that only Whitings had ever lived there. Honus's own father, Elijah Whiting, then in his late eighties, still lived in the carriage house out back with his ill-tempered wife. Whiting men had a lot in common, including the fact that they invariably married women who made their lives a misery. C.B.'s father had fared better in this respect than most of his forebears, but still resented his wife for her low opinion of himself, of the Whiting mansion, of Empire Falls, of the entire backward state of Maine, to which she felt herself cruelly exiled from Boston. The lovely wrought iron gates and fencing that had been brought all the way from New York to mark the perimeter of the estate were to her the walls of her prison, and every time she observed this, Honus reminded her that he held the key to those gates and would let her out at any time. If she wanted to go back to Boston so damn bad, she should just do it. He said this knowing full well she wouldn't, for it was the particular curse of the Whiting men that their wives remained loyal to them out of spite.

By the time their son was born, though, Honus Whiting was beginning to understand and privately share his wife's opinion, as least as it pertained to Empire Falls. As the town mushroomed during the last half of the nineteenth century, the Whiting estate gradually was surrounded by the homes of mill workers, and of late the attitude of the people doing the surrounding seemed increasingly resentful. The Whitings had traditionally attempted to appease their employees each summer by throwing gala socials on the family grounds, but it seemed to Honus Whiting that many of the people who attended these events anymore were singularly ungrateful for the free food and drink and music, some of them regarding the mansion itself with hooded expressions that suggested their hearts wouldn't be broken if it burned to the ground.

Perhaps because of this unspoken but growing animosity, C. B. Whiting had been sent away, first to prep school, then to college. Afterward he'd spent the better part of a decade traveling, first with his mother in Europe (which was much more to that good woman's liking than Maine) and then later on his own in Mexico (which was much more to his liking than Europe, where there'd been too much to learn and appreciate). While many European men towered over him, those in Mexico were shorter, and C. B. Whiting especially admired that they were dreamers who felt no urgency about bringing their dreams to fruition. But his father, who was paying for his son's globe-trotting, finally decided his heir should return home and start contributing to the family fortune instead of squandering as much as he could south of the border. Charles Beaumont Whiting was by then in his late twenties, and his father was coming to the reluctant conclusion that his only real talent was for spending money, though the young man claimed to be painting and writing poetry as well. Time to put an end to both, at least in the old man's view. Honus Whiting was fast approaching his sixtieth birthday, and though glad he'd been able to indulge his son, he now realized he'd let it go on too long and that the boy's education in the family businesses he would one day inherit was long overdue. Honus himself had begun in the shirt factory, then moved over to the textile mill, and finally, when old Elijah had lost his mind one day and tried to kill his wife with a shovel, took over the paper mill upriver. Honus wanted his son to be prepared for the inevitable day when he, too, would lose his marbles and assault Charles's mother with whatever weapon came to hand. Europe had not improved her opinion of himself, of Empire Falls or of Maine, as he had hoped it might. In his experience people were seldom happier for having learned what they were missing, and all Europe had done for his wife was encourage her natural inclination toward bitter and invidious comparison.

For his part, Charles Beaumont Whiting, sent away from home as a boy when he would've preferred to stay, now had no more desire to return from Mexico than his mother had to return from Europe, but when summoned he sighed and did as he was told, much as he always had done. It wasn't as if he hadn't known that the end of his youth would arrive, taking with it his travels, his painting and his poetry. There was never any question that Whiting and Sons Enterprises would one day devolve to him, and while it occurred to him that returning to Empire Falls and taking over the family businesses might be a violation of his personal destiny as an artist, there didn't seem to be any help for it. One day, when he sensed the summons growing near, he tried to put down in words what he felt to be his own best nature and how wrong it would be to thwart his true calling. His idea was to share these thoughts with his father, but what he'd written sounded a lot like his poetry, vague and unconvincing even to him, and he ended up throwing the letter away. For one thing he wasn't sure his father, a practical man, would concede that anybody had a nature to begin with; and if you did, it was probably your duty either to deny it or to whip it into shape, show it who was boss. During his last months of freedom in Mexico, C.B. lay on the beach and argued the point with his father in his imagination, argued it over and over, losing every time, so when the summons finally came he was too worn out to resist. He returned home determined to do his best but fearing that he'd left his real self and all that he was capable of in Mexico.

What he discovered was that violating his own best nature wasn't nearly as unpleasant or difficult as he'd imagined. In fact, looking around Empire Falls, he got the distinct impression that people did it every day. And if you had to violate your destiny, doing so as a Whiting male wasn't so bad. To his surprise he also discovered that it was possible to be good at what you had little interest in, just as it had been possible to be bad at something, whether painting or poetry, that you cared about a great deal. While the shirt factory held no attraction for him, he demonstrated something like an aptitude for running it, for understanding the underlying causes of what went wrong and knowing instinctively how to fix the problem. He was also fond of his father and marveled at the little man's energy, his quick anger, his refusal to knuckle under, his conviction that he was always right, his ability to justify whatever course of action he ultimately chose. Here was a man who was either in total harmony with his nature or had beaten it into perfect submission. Charles Beaumont Whiting was never sure which, and probably it didn't matter; either way the old man was worth emulating.

Still, it was clear to C. B. Whiting that his father and grandfather had enjoyed the best of what Whiting and Sons Enterprises had to offer. The times were changing, and neither the shirt factory, nor the textile mill, nor the paper mill upriver was as profitable as all once had been. Over the last two decades there had been attempts to unionize all the factories in Dexter County, and while these efforts failed—this being Maine, not Massachusetts—even Honus Whiting agreed that keeping the unions out had proved almost as costly as letting them in would've been. The workers, slow to accept defeat, were both sullen and unproductive when they returned to their jobs.

Honus Whiting had intended, of course, for his son to take up residence in the Whiting mansion as soon as he took a wife and old Elijah saw fit to quit the earth, but a decade after C.B. abandoned Mexico, neither of these events had come to pass. C. B. Whiting, something of a ladies' man in his warm, sunny youth, seemed to lose his sex drive in frosty Maine and slipped into an unintended celibacy, though he sometimes imagined his best self still carnally frolicking in the Yucatán.

Perhaps he was frightened by the sheer prospect of matrimony, of marrying a girl he would one day want to murder.

Elijah Whiting, now nearing one hundred, had not succeeded in killing his wife with the shovel, nor had he recovered from the disappointment. The two of them still lived in the carriage house, old Elijah clinging to his misery and his bitter wife clinging to him. He seemed, the old man's doctor observed, to be dying from within, the surest sign of which was an almost biblical flatulence. He'd been turning the air green inside the carriage house for many years now, but all the tests showed that the old fossil's heart remained strong, and Honus realized it might be several years more before he could make room for his son by moving into the carriage house himself. After all, it would require a good year to air out even if the old man died tomorrow. Besides which, Honus's own wife had already made clear her intention never to move into the carriage house, and she lately had become so depressed by the idea of dying in Maine that he'd been forced to buy her a small rowhouse in Boston's Back Bay, where she claimed to have grown up, which of course was untrue. South Boston was where Honus had found her, and where he would have left her, too, if he'd had any sense. At any rate, when Charles came to him one day and announced his intention to build a house of his own and to put the river between it and Empire Falls, he understood and even approved. Only later, when the house was revealed to be a hacienda, did he fear that the boy might be writing poems again.

Not to worry. Earlier that year, C. B. Whiting had been mistaken for his father on the street, and that same evening, when he studied himself in the mirror, he saw why. His hair was beginning to silver, and there was a certain terrier-like ferocity in his eyes that he hadn't noticed before. Of the younger man who had wanted to live and die in Mexico and dream and paint and write poetry there was now little evidence. And last spring when his father had suggested that he run not only the shirt factory but also the textile mill, instead of feeling trapped by the inevitability of the rest of his life, he found himself almost happy to be coming more completely into his birthright. Men had starting calling him C.B. instead of Charles, and he liked the sound of it.

WHEN THE BULLDOZERS began to clear the house site, a disturbing discovery was made. An astonishing amount of trash—mounds and mounds of it—was discovered all along the bank, some of it tangled among tree roots and branches, some of it strewn up the hillside, all the way to the top. The sheer volume of the junk was astonishing, and at first C. B. Whiting concluded that somebody, or a great many somebodies, had had the effrontery to use the property as an unofficial landfill. How many years had this outrage been going on? It made him mad enough to shoot somebody until one of the men he'd hired to clear the land pointed out that for somebody, or a great many somebodies, to use Whiting land for a dump, they would have required an access road, and there wasn't one, or at least there hadn't been until C. B. Whiting himself cut one a month earlier. While it seemed unlikely that so much junk—spent inner tubes, hubcaps, milk cartons, rusty cans, pieces of broken furniture and the like—could wash up on one spot naturally, the result of currents and eddies, there it was, so it must have. There was little alternative but to cart the trash off, which was done the same May the foundation of the house was being poured.

Spring rains, a rising river and a bumper crop of voracious black flies delayed construction, but by late June the low frame of the sprawling hacienda was visible from across the river where C. B. Whiting kept tabs on its progress from his office on the top floor of the Whiting shirt factory. By the Fourth of July the weather had turned dry and hot, killing off the last of the black flies, and the shirtless, sunburned carpenters straddling the hacienda roof beams began to wrinkle their noses and regard one another suspiciously. What in the world was that smell?

It was C. B. Whiting himself who discovered the bloated body of a large moose decomposing in the shallows, tangled among the roots of a stand of trees that had been spared by the bulldozer that they might provide shade and privacy from anyone on the Empire Falls side of the river who might be too curious about goings-on at the hacienda. Even more amazing than this carcass was another mound of trash, which, though smaller than its carted-off predecessor, was deposited in the same exact area where a spit of land jutted out into the river and created in its lee a stagnant, mosquito- and now moose-infested pool.

The sight and smell of all this soggy, decomposing trash caused C. B. Whiting to consider the possibility that he had an enemy, and kneeling there on the bank of the river he scrolled back through his memory concerning the various men he, his father and his grandfather had managed to ruin in the natural course of business. The list was not short, but unless he'd forgotten someone, no one on it seemed the right sort. They were mostly small men of smaller means, men who might've shot him if the opportunity had presented itself—if, for instance, he'd wandered into their neighborhood tavern when they had a snoot full and happened to be armed. But this was a different quality of maliciousness. Somebody apparently believed that all the trash generated in Dexter County belonged on C. B. Whiting's doorstep, and felt sufficient conviction to collect all that garbage (no pleasant task) and transport it there.

Was the dead moose a coincidence? C.B. couldn't decide. The animal had a bullet hole in its neck, which could mean any number of things. Perhaps whoever was dumping the trash had also shot the moose and left it there on purpose. Then again, the animal could conceivably have been shot elsewhere by a poacher; in fact, an entire family of poachers, the Mintys, lived in Empire Falls. Maybe the wounded animal had attempted to cross the river, tired in the attempt, and drowned, coming to rest below the hacienda.

C. B. Whiting spent the rest of the afternoon on one knee only a few feet from the blasted moose, trying to deduce his enemy's identity. Almost immediately a paper cup floated by and lodged between the hind legs of the moose. The next hour brought a supermarket bag, an empty, bobbing Coke bottle, a rusted-out oil can, a huge tangle of monofilament fishing line and, unless he was mistaken, a human placenta. All of it got tangled up with the reeking moose. From where C. B. Whiting knelt, he could just barely see one small section of the Iron Bridge, and in the next half hour he witnessed half a dozen people, in automobiles and afoot, toss things into the river as they crossed. In his mind he counted the number of bridges spanning the Knox upstream (eight), and the number of mills and factories and sundry small businesses that backed onto the water (dozens). He knew firsthand the temptation of dumping into the river after the sun went down. Generations of Whitings had been flushing dyes and other chemicals, staining the riverbank all the way to Fairhaven, a community that could scarcely complain, given that its own textile mill had for decades exhibited an identical lack of regard for its downstream neighbors. Complaints, C.B. knew, inevitably led to accusations, accusations to publicity, publicity to investigations, investigations to litigation, litigation to expense, expense to the poorhouse.

Still, this particular dumping could not be allowed to continue. A sensible man, Charles Beaumont Whiting arrived at a sensible conclusion. At the end of a second hour spent kneeling at the river's edge, he concluded that he had an enemy all right, and it was none other than God Himself, who'd designed the damn river in such a way—narrow and swift-running upstream, widening and slowing at Empire Falls—that all manner of other people's shit became Charles Beaumont Whiting's. Worse, he imagined he understood why God *had chosen this plan. He'd done it, in advance, to punish him for leaving his best self in Mexico all those years ago and, as a result, becoming somebody who could be mistaken for his father.*

These were unpleasant thoughts. Perhaps, it occurred to C.B., it was impossible to have pleasant ones so close to a decomposing moose. Yet he continued to kneel there, the river's current burbling a coded message he felt he was on the verge of comprehending. In truth, today's were not the first unpleasant thoughts he'd been visited by of late. Ever since he'd decided to build the new house, his sleep had been troubled by dreams that would awaken him several times a night, and sometimes he found himself standing at the dark window of his bedroom looking out over the grounds of the Whiting mansion with no memory of waking up and crossing the room. He had the distinct impression that the dream—whatever it had been about—was still with him, though its details had fled. Had he been in urgent conversation with someone? Who?

During the day, when his mind should've been occupied by the incessant demands of two factories' day-to-day operations, he often and absentmindedly studied the blueprints of the hacienda, as if he'd forgotten some crucial element. Last month, his attention had grown so divided that he'd asked his father to come down from the paper mill to help out one day a week, just until the house was finished. Now, down by the river, his thoughts disturbed, perhaps, by the proximity of rotting moose, he began to doubt that building this new house was a good idea. The hacienda, with its adjacent artist's studio, was surely an invitation to his former self, the Charles Beaumont Whiting— Beau, his friends had called him there—he'd abandoned in Mexico. And it was this Beau, it now occurred to him, with whom he'd been conversing in all those dreams. Worse, it was for this younger, betrayed self that he was building the hacienda. He'd been telling himself that the studio would be for his son, assuming he would one day be fortunate enough to have one. This much rebellion he'd allowed himself. The studio would be his gift to the boy, an implicit promise that no son of his would ever be forced by necessity or loyalty to betray his truest destiny. But of course, he now realized, all this was a lie. He'd wanted the studio for himself, or rather for the Charles Beaumont Whiting thought to be either dead or living a life of poetry and fornication in Mexico. Whereas he in fact was living a life of enforced duty and chastity in Empire Falls, Maine. On the heels of this stunning realization came another. The message the river had been whispering to him as he knelt there all afternoon was a single word of invitation. "Come," the water burbled, unmistakable now. "Come . . . come . . . come . . ."

That very evening C. B. Whiting brought his father and old Elijah out to the building site. Up to this point he'd been secretive about the house without comprehending why. Now he understood. He and Honus sat his grandfather, who hadn't been out of the carriage house in a month, on a tree stump, where he instantly fell into a deep, restful, flatulent sleep, while C.B. showed his father in and around the frames and arches of the new house. Yes, he admitted, it was going to be some damn Mexican sort of deal. The detached structure, he explained, would be a guest house, which, in fact, he'd decided that afternoon, it would be. The river's invitation had scared him that badly. When they finished the tour of the hacienda, C. B. Whiting took his father down to the water's edge and showed him the mound of trash, which had grown since morning, and the moose, which had ripened further. From where they stood, C.B. could see both the moose and old Elijah still asleep but rising up on one cheek every now and then from the sheer force of his gas, and while C.B. couldn't reasonably hold himself responsible for either, he felt something rise in the back of his throat that tasted like self-loathing. Still, he told himself, the occasional flavor of self-recrimination on the back of the tongue was preferable to throwing away the work of his father's and grandfather's lifetimes, and he found himself regarding both men with genuine fondness, especially his father, whom he had always loved, and whose solid, practical, confident presence could be counted on to deliver him from his present funk.

"It's God, all right," Honus agreed, after C.B. had explained his theory about the enemy, and then they watched for a while as various pieces of detritus bobbed along in the current before coming to rest against the moose. The elder Whiting was a religious man who found God useful for explaining anything that was otherwise insoluble. "You better figure out what you're going to do about Him, too."

Honus suggested his son hire some geologists and engineers to study the problem and recommend a course of action. This turned out to be excellent advice, and the engineers, warned Whom they might be up against, proved meticulous. In addition to numerous on-site inspections, they analyzed the entire region on geological survey maps and even flew the length of the river all the way from the Canadian border to where it emptied into the Gulf of Maine. As rivers went, the Knox was one of God's poorer efforts, wide and lazy where it should have been narrow and swift, and the engineers concurred with the man who'd hired them that it was God's basic design flaw that ensured that every paper cup discarded between the border and Empire Falls would likely wash up on C. B. Whiting's future lawn. That was the bad news.

The good news was that it didn't have to be that way. Men of vision had been improving upon God's designs for the better part of two centuries, and there was no reason not to correct this one. If the Army Corps of Engineers could make the damn Mississippi run where they wanted it to, a pissant stream like the Knox could be altered at their whim. In no time they arrived at a plan. A few miles north and east of Empire Falls the river took a sharp, unreasonable turn before meandering back in the direction it had come from for several sluggish, twisting miles, much of its volume draining off into swampy lowlands north and west of town where legions of black flies bred each spring, followed by an equal number of mosquitoes in the summer. Seen from the air, the absurdity of this became clear. What water wanted to do, the engineers explained, was flow downhill by the straightest possible route. Meandering was what happened when a river's best intentions were somehow thwarted. What prevented the Knox from running straight and true was a narrow strip of land—of rock, really—referred to by the locals as the Robideaux Blight, an outcropping of rolling, hummocky ground that might have been considered picturesque if your purpose was to build a summer home on the bluff overlooking the river and not to farm it, as the land's owners had been bullheadedly attempting to do for generations. In the end, of course, rivers get their way, and eventually—say, in a few thousand years—the Knox would succeed in cutting its way through the meander.

C. B. Whiting was disinclined to wait, and he was buoyed to learn from his engineers that if the money could be found to blast a channel through the narrowest part of the Robideaux Blight, the river should be running straight and true within the calendar year, its increased velocity downstream at Whiting's Bend sufficient to bear off the vast majority of trash (including the odd moose), downstream to the dam in Fairhaven, where it belonged. In fact, C. B. Whiting's experts argued before the state in hastily convened, closed-door hearings that the Knox would be a far better river—swifter, prettier, cleaner—for all the communities along its banks. Further, with less of its volume being siphoned off into the wetlands, the state would benefit from the acquisition of several thousand acres of land that might be used for purposes other than breeding bugs. No real environmental movement in the state of Maine would exist for decades, so there was little serious opposition to the plan, though the experts did concede—their voices low and confidential now—that a livelier river might occasionally prove too lively. The Knox, like most rivers in Maine, was already prone to flooding, especially in the spring, when warm rains melted the northern snowpack too quickly.

A more practical obstacle to C. B. Whiting's alterations was that the Robideaux Blight had somehow been overlooked when previous generations of Whitings were buying up the river frontage. This parcel was owned by a family named Robideaux, whose title extended back into the previous century. But here, too, fate smiled on C. B. Whiting, for the Robideauxs turned out to be both greedy and ignorant, the precise combination called for by the present circumstance. More sophisticated people might have suspected the worth of their holdings when approached by a rich man's lawyers, but the Robideauxs apparently did not. Their primary fear seemed to be that C. B. Whiting would actually come inspect the land they were selling him, see how worthless it was for farming, the only use they'd imagined for it, and promptly back out of the deal.

Having no such intention, he purchased their acreage at what they imagined to be an extortionary price, and for years afterward they continued to believe they'd one-upped one of the richest and most powerful men in Maine, whose purchase of the Robideaux Blight just went to prove what they'd always known—that rich people weren't so damn smart. C. B. Whiting, himself again after coming out of his funk, came to a conclusion every bit as dubious: that he'd trumped not only the Robideauxs, who'd had him over a barrel and were too ignorant to suspect it, but also God, whose river he would now improve upon.

The dynamiting of the Robideaux Blight some seven miles upstream could be felt all the way to Empire Falls, and on the day in August when the blasting was complete C. B. Whiting knelt on the riverbank before his newly completed house and watched with pride as the freshly energized currents bore off what little remained of the moose, along with the ever-increasing mound of milk cartons, plastic bottles and rusted soup cans, all bobbing their way south toward an unsuspecting Fairhaven. The river no longer whispered despair as it had earlier in the summer. Reenergized, it fairly chortled with glee at his enterprise. Satisfied with the outcome, he lit a cigar, inhaled deeply of sweet summer air, and regarded the slender woman at his side, whose name, by no coincidence, was Francine Robideaux.

Francine was a bright, ambitious young woman, newly graduated from

Colby College, some ten years C. B. Whiting's junior, and until the day her family closed the deal to sell her future husband the Robideaux Blight, she'd never laid eyes on him, though of course she'd heard of him. C.B. himself had graduated from Colby, as had his father and grandfather, whereas Francine was the first Robideaux to continue her education beyond high school. Thanks to a scholarship, she had emerged from Colby no longer recognizable as a Robideaux in deportment, speech or mannerism, which disturbed and angered her family, who never would have allowed her to attend college had they known how contemptuous of them she'd be upon her return. A poor girl among rich ones, Francine Robideaux had carefully observed and then adopted their table manners, fashion sense, vocal idiosyncrasies and personal hygiene. At Colby she'd also learned to flirt.

In the soft light of his lawyers' book-lined offices, C. B. Whiting, who had not looked seriously at a woman since returning to Maine, liked the look of Francine Robideaux. He also appreciated that she was a Colby graduate and admired that she appeared to understand that he was snookering her family and didn't necessarily object. Every time he glanced at her, every time she spoke, he was more impressed, for the girl seemed able to convey, without contradiction, that she was observing him carefully, even as other of her mannerisms suggested that maybe, so far as she was concerned, he wasn't even in the room. Maybe he was there and maybe he wasn't, depending. To resolve the issue of whether he was there or not, he resolved to marry her if she would have him.

Well, as it turned out, she would. They were wed in September, leaving C. B. Whiting the rest of his days on earth to try to remember what exactly it was about the look of Francine Robideaux that had so appealed to him in the soft light of the lawyers' offices. In natural light she looked rather pinched, and in the manner of a great many women of French Canadian ancestry, she lacked a chin, as if someone had already pinched her there. He also came to understand that marrying Francine Robideaux would not answer as conclusively as he'd hoped the question of whether or not he was actually in the room. On that late afternoon in August when he lit a cigar in celebration, his wife-to-be at his side, C. B. Whiting studied his fiancée carefully. Whiting men, all of whom seemed to be born with sound business sense, each invariably gravitated, like moths to a flame, toward the one woman in the world who would regard making them utterly miserable as her life's noble endeavor, a woman who would remain bound to her husband with the same grim tenacity that bound nuns to the suffering Christ. Fully cognizant of his family history, C.B. had been understandably wary of matrimony. From time to time his father would remind him that he would have need of an heir, but then C.B. regarded his father and grandfather and wasn't so sure. Why not put an end to the awful cycle of misery right there? What was the purpose of producing more Whiting males if they were predestined to lives of marital torment?

And so C. B. Whiting scrutinized Francine Robideaux, trying to envision some future day when he might want to beat her to death with a shovel. Thankfully, he was unable to call such a scene into vivid imaginative life. About the best he could do was contemplate the possibility that it had been unwise to go to war with God. If He could deliver unto you an unwanted moose, what was to prevent Him from delivering something even worse. Say, for instance, an unwanted woman. This would have been a worrisome contemplation had he not wanted this woman. But he did *want her. He was almost sure of it.*

His bride-to-be had other thoughts. "That would be a fine place for a gazebo, Charlie," she observed, indicating with her thin index finger a spot halfway down the bank. When Charles Beaumont Whiting did not immediately respond, Francine Robideaux repeated her observation, and this time her future husband thought he detected a slight edge to her tone. "Did you hear what I said, Charlie?"

He had. In truth, though he had no objection to gazebos in general, he was not entirely taken with the idea of erecting one as an architectural companion to a hacienda. This aesthetic reservation was not, however, the cause of his hesitation. No, the reason he hadn't responded was that no one had ever called him Charlie. From boyhood he had always been Charles, and his mother in particular had been adamant that the fine name she'd given him was not to be corrupted with more common nicknames, like Charlie or, even worse, Chuck. For a brief time, in college, his friends had called him Beaumont, and in Mexico he'd been Beau. More recently, his business acquaintances mostly referred to him as C.B., but they did so reverentially and would never have presumed to address him as Charlie.

Clearly, the time to set the record straight was now, but as he considered how best to suggest his preference for Charles over Charlie, he became aware that "now" had already passed into "then." Strange. Had anyone else called him Charlie, he'd have corrected that person before his or her voice had a chance to fall, but for some reason, with this woman whom he had asked on bended knee to be his bride, he'd delayed. A beat passed, and then another and another, until Charles Beaumont Whiting realized that he was mute with a new emotion. At first he noted only its unpleasant sensation, but eventually he identified it. The emotion was fear.

"I said . . ." his wife-to-be began a third time.

"*Yes, dear. An excellent idea,*" Charles Beaumont Whiting agreed and in that fateful moment became Charlie Whiting. Later in life, he was fond of remarking, rather ruefully, that he always had the last word in all differences of opinion with his wife, and that—two words, actually—was, "*Yes, dear.*" Had he known how many times he would repeat that phrase to this woman, how it would become the mantra of their marriage, he might well have recollected the river's invitation and committed himself to its current then and there and followed the moose downstream, thereby saving himself a great deal of misery and the price of the handgun he would purchase thirty years later for the purpose of ending his life.

"*And would you mind putting out that awful cigar?*" Francine Robideaux added.

PART ONE

CHAPTER I

THE EMPIRE GRILL was long and low-slung, with windows
that ran its entire length, and since the building next door, a
Rexall drugstore, had been condemned and razed, it was now
possible to sit at the lunch counter and see straight down Empire
Avenue all the way to the old textile mill and its adjacent shirt factory.
Both had been abandoned now for the better part of two decades,
though their dark, looming shapes at the foot of the avenue's gentle
incline continued to draw the eye. Of course, nothing prevented a person from looking up Empire Avenue in the other direction, but Miles
Roby, the proprietor of the restaurant—and its eventual owner, he
hoped—had long noted that his customers rarely did.

No, their natural preference was to gaze down to where the street
both literally and figuratively dead-ended at the mill and factory, the
undeniable physical embodiment of the town's past, and it was the
magnetic quality of the old, abandoned structures that steeled Miles's
resolve to sell the Empire Grill for what little it would bring, just as
soon as the restaurant was his.

Just beyond the factory and mill ran the river that long ago had
powered them, and Miles often wondered if these old buildings were
razed, would the town that had grown up around them be forced to
imagine a future? Perhaps not. Nothing but a chain-link fence had
gone up in place of the Rexall, which meant, Miles supposed, that
diverting one's attention from the past was not the same as envisioning
and embarking upon a future. On the other hand, if the past were
razed, the slate wiped clean, maybe fewer people would confuse it with
the future, and that at least would be something. For as long as the

mill and factory remained, Miles feared, many would continue to believe against all reason that a buyer might be found for one or both, and that consequently Empire Falls would be restored to its old economic viability.

What drew Miles Roby's anxious eye down Empire this particular afternoon in early September was not the dark, high-windowed shirt factory where his mother had spent most of her adult working life or, just beyond it, the larger, brooding presence of the textile mill, but rather his hope that he'd catch a glimpse of his daughter, Tick, when she rounded the corner and began her slow, solitary trek up the avenue. Like most of her high school friends, Tick, a rail-thin sophomore, lugged all her books in a canvas L.L. Bean backpack and had to lean forward, as if into a strong headwind, to balance a weight nearly as great as her own. Oddly, most of the conventions Miles remembered from high school had been subverted. He and his friends had carried their textbooks balanced on their hips, listing first to the left, then shifting the load and listing to the right. They brought home only the books they would need that night, or the ones they *remembered* needing, leaving the rest crammed in their lockers. Kids today stuffed the entire contents of their lockers into their seam-stretched backpacks and brought it all home, probably, Miles figured, so they wouldn't have to think through what they'd need and what they could do without, thereby avoiding the kinds of decisions that might trail consequences. Except that this itself had consequences. A visit to the doctor last spring had revealed the beginnings of scoliosis, a slight curvature of Tick's spine, which worried Miles at several levels. "She's just carrying too much weight," the doctor explained, unaware, as far as Miles could tell, of the metaphorical implications of her remark. It had taken Tick most of the summer to regain her normal posture, and yesterday, after one day back at school, she was already hunched over again.

Instead of catching sight of his daughter, the one person in the world he wanted at that moment to see rounding the corner, Miles was instead treated to the sight of Walt Comeau, the person he least wanted to see—the one he could live happily without ever laying eyes on again—pulling into a vacant parking space in front of the Empire Grill. Walt's van was a rolling advertisement for its driver, who'd had THE SILVER FOX stenciled across the hood, just above the grill, and its vanity plates read FOXY 1. The van was tall and Walt short, which meant he had to hop down from the running board, and something about the man's youthful bounce made Miles, who'd seen this both in real life and in his dreams just about every day for the past year, want to grab an ax handle, meet the Silver Fox at the door and stave his head in right there in the entryway.

Instead he turned back to the grill and flipped Horace Weymouth's burger, wondering if he'd already left it on too long. Horace liked his burgers bloody.

"So." Horace closed and folded his *Boston Globe* in anticipation of being fed, his inner clock apparently confirming that Miles had indeed waited too long. "You been out to see Mrs. Whiting yet?"

"Not yet," Miles said. He set up Horace's platter with tomato, lettuce, a slice of Bermuda onion and a pickle, plus the open-faced bun, then pressed down on the burger with his spatula, making it sizzle before slipping it onto the bun. "I usually wait to be summoned."

"I wouldn't," Horace counseled. "Somebody's got to inherit Empire Falls. It might as well be Miles Roby."

"I'd have a better chance of winning the MegaBucks lottery," Miles said, sliding the platter onto the counter and noticing, which he hadn't for a long time, the purple fibroid cyst that grew out of Horace's forehead. Had it gotten larger, or was it just that Miles had been away and was seeing it afresh after even a short absence? The cyst had taken over half of Horace's right eyebrow, where hairless skin stretched tight and shiny over the knot, its web of veins fanning outward from its dark center. One of the good things about small towns, Miles's mother had always maintained, was that they accommodated just about everyone; the lame and the disfigured were all your neighbors, and seeing them every day meant that after a while you stopped noticing what made them different.

Miles hadn't seen much in the way of physical oddity on Martha's Vineyard, where he and his daughter had vacationed last week. Almost everyone on the island appeared to be rich, slender and beautiful. When he'd remarked on this, his old friend Peter said that he should come live in L.A. for a while. There, he argued, ugliness was rapidly and systematically being bred out of the species. "He doesn't really mean L.A.," Peter's wife, Dawn, had corrected when Miles appeared dubious. "He means Beverly Hills." "And Bel Air," Peter added. "And Malibu," Dawn said. And then they named a baker's dozen other places where unattractiveness had been eradicated. Peter and Dawn were full of such worldly wisdom, which, for the most part, Miles enjoyed. The three had been undergraduates together at a small Catholic college outside of Portland, and he admired that they were barely recognizable as the students he'd known. Peter and Dawn had become other people entirely, and Miles concluded that this was what was supposed to happen, though it hadn't happened to him. If disappointed by their old friend's lack of personal evolution, they concealed that disappointment well, even going so far as to claim that he restored their faith in humanity by remaining the same old Miles. Since they apparently meant this as a compliment, Miles tried hard to take it that way. They did seem genuinely glad to see him every August, and even though each year he half expected his old friends not to renew the invitation for the following summer, he was always wrong.

Horace picked the thin slice of Bermuda off the plate with his thumb and forefinger, as if to suggest great offense at the idea that onions should be in such close proximity to anything he was expected to eat. "I don't eat onions, Miles. I know you've been away, but I haven't changed. I read the *Globe*, I write for the *Empire Gazette*, I never send Christmas cards, and I don't eat onions."

Miles accepted the onion slice and deposited it in the garbage. It was true he'd been slightly off all day, still sluggish and stupid from vacation, forgetting things that were second nature. He'd intended to work himself back in gradually by supervising the first couple shifts, but Buster, with whom Miles alternated at the grill, always took his revenge by going on a bender as soon as Miles returned from the island, forcing him back behind the grill before he was ready.

"She's better than MegaBucks," Horace said, still on the subject of Mrs. Whiting, who each year spent less and less time in Maine, wintering in Florida and doing what Miles's long dead Irish maternal grandmother, who liked to stay put, would have called "gallivanting." Apparently Mrs. Whiting had just returned from an Alaskan cruise. "If I was a member of the family I'd be out there kissing her bony ass every day."

Miles watched Horace assemble his burger, relieved to see a red stain spreading over the bun.

Miles Roby was not, of course, a member of Mrs. Whiting's family. What Horace referred to was the fact that the old woman's maiden name had been Robideaux, and some maintained that the Robys and the Robideauxs of Dexter County were, if you went back far enough, the same family. Miles's own father, Max, believed this to be true, though for him it was purely a matter of wishful thinking. Lacking any evidence that he and the richest woman in central Maine weren't related, Max decided they must be. Miles knew that if his father had been the one with the money and somebody named Robideaux felt entitled to even a dime of it, he naturally would've seen the whole thing differently.

Of course, it was a moot point. Mrs. Whiting had married all that money in the person of C. B. Whiting, who had owned the paper mill and the shirt factory and the textile mill before selling them all to multinational corporations so they could be pillaged and then closed. The Whiting family still owned half the real estate in Empire Falls, including the grill, which Miles had managed for Mrs. Whiting these last fifteen years with the understanding that the business would devolve upon him at her passing, an event Miles continued to anticipate without, somehow, being able to imagine it. What would happen to the rest of the old woman's estate was a matter of great speculation. Normally, it would have been inherited by her daughter, but Cindy Whiting had been in and out of the state mental hospital in Augusta all her adult life, and it was widely believed that Mrs. Whiting would never entrust her daughter with anything more than her continued maintenance required. In truth, no one in Dexter County knew much about Mrs. Whiting's actual wealth or her plans for it. She never dealt with local lawyers or accountants, preferring to employ a Boston firm that the Whitings had used for nearly a century. She did little to discourage the notion that a significant legacy would one day go to the town itself, but neither did she offer any concrete assurances. Mrs. Whiting was not known for philanthropy. In times of crisis, such as the most recent flood of the Knox River, she occasionally contributed, though she always insisted that the community match her donation. Similar restrictions were applied to seed money for a new wing of the hospital and a grant to upgrade computers at the high school. Such gifts, though sizable, were judged to be little more than shavings off the tip of a financial iceberg. When the woman was dead, it was hoped, the money would flow more freely.

Miles wasn't so sure. Mrs. Whiting's generosity toward the town, like that she extended to him, was puzzlingly ambiguous. Some years ago, for instance, she'd donated the decaying old Whiting mansion, which occupied a large section of the downtown, with the proviso that it be preserved. It was only after accepting her gift that the mayor and town council came to understand the extent of the burden they'd been handed. They could no longer collect taxes on the property, which they were not permitted to use for social events, and maintenance costs were considerable. Similarly, if Mrs. Whiting did end up giving the restaurant to Miles, he feared that the gift would be too costly to accept.

In fact, now that the mills were all closed down, it sometimes appeared that Mrs. Whiting had cornered the market on business failure. She owned most of the commercial space in town and was all too happy to help new enterprises start up in one of her buildings. But then rents had a way of going up, and none of the businesses seemed to get anywhere, nor did their owners when they appealed to Mrs. Whiting for more favorable terms.

"I don't know, Miles," Horace said. "You seem to have a special place in that old woman's heart. Her treatment of you is unique in my experience. The fact that she hasn't closed the grill down suggests just how deep her affection runs. Either that or she enjoys watching you suffer."

Though Miles understood this last observation to be a joke, he found himself—and not for the first time—considering whether it might not be the simple literal truth. Viewed objectively, Mrs. Whiting did appear to cut him more slack than was her custom, and yet there were times when Miles got the distinct impression that she bore him no particular fondness. Which probably explained why he was not all that eager to meet with her now, though he knew their annual meeting could not be postponed for long. Each autumn she left for Florida earlier than the last, and while their annual "State of the Grill" meetings were little more than a pro forma ritual, Mrs. Whiting refused to forgo them; and in her company he could not shake the feeling that for all these years the old woman had been expecting him to show her some sign—of what, he had no idea. Still, he left every encounter with the sense that he'd yet again failed some secret test.

THE BELL JINGLED above the door, and Walt Comeau danced inside, his arms extended like an old-fashioned crooner's, his silver hair slicked back on the sides, fifties style. "Don't let the stars get in your eyes," he warbled, "don't let the moon break your heart."

Several of the regulars at the lunch counter, knowing what was expected of them, swiveled on their stools, leaned into the aisle, right arms extended in a row, and returned, in a different key altogether, "Pa pa pa paya."

"Perry Como," Horace said when he realized, without actually looking, that the seat next to him at the counter had been filled. "Right on time."

"Big Boy," Walt said, addressing Miles, "you hear the news?"

"Oh, please," said Miles, who'd been hearing little else all morning. Over the weekend a black Lincoln Town Car with Massachusetts plates had been reported in the lot outside the textile mill. Last year it had been a BMW, the year before that a Cadillac limo. The color of the vehicle seemed to alternate between black and white, but the plates were always Massachusetts, which made Miles smile. The hordes of visitors who poured into Maine every summer were commonly referred to as Massholes, and yet when Empire Falls fantasized about deliverance, it invariably had Massachusetts plates.

"What?" Walt said, indignant. "You weren't even here."

"Let him tell you about it," Horace advised. "Then it'll be over."

Walt Comeau looked back and forth between Miles and Horace as if to determine who was the bigger fool, settling finally on Horace, probably because he'd spoken last. "All right, you explain it. Three guys in eight-hundred-dollar suits drive all the way up here from Boston on a Sunday morning, park outside the mill, hike down to the head of the falls in their black patent leather shoes, then stand there for half an hour pointing up at the mill. You tell me who they are and what they're doing."

Horace set his hamburger down and wiped his mouth with his napkin. "Hey, it's clear to me. They came to invest millions. For a while they were thinking about tech stocks, but then they thought, Hell, no. Let's go into textiles. That's where the *real* profits are. Then you know what they did? They decided not to build the factory in Mexico or Thailand where people work for about ten bucks a week. Let's drive up to Empire Falls, Maine, they said, and look at that gutted old shell of a factory that the river damn near washed away last spring and buy all new equipment and create hundreds of jobs, nothing under twenty dollars an hour."

Miles couldn't help smiling. Minus the sarcasm, this was pretty much the scenario he'd been listening to all morning. The annual sighting was born, as far as Miles could tell, of the same need that caused people to spot Elvis in the local Denny's. But why always autumn? Miles wondered. It seemed an odd season to spawn such desperate optimism. Maybe it had something to do with the kids all going back to school, giving their parents the leisure to contemplate the approach of another savage, relentless winter and to conjure up a pipe dream to help them through it.

"Hey," Walt said, sounding hurt. "All I'm saying is something nice *could* happen here someday. You never know. That's all I'm saying, okay?"

Horace had gone back to his hamburger, and this time he didn't bother to put it down or wipe his mouth before speaking. "Something nice," he repeated. "Is that what you think? That having money makes people nice?"

"Ah, to hell with you," Walt said, dismissing both men with a single wave of his hand. "Here's what I'd like to know, though, smart-ass. How can you sit here and eat one greasy hamburger after another, day after goddamn day? Don't you have any idea how bad that junk is for you?"

Horace, who had one bite of burger left, put it on his plate and looked up. "What I don't know is why you have to ruin my lunch every day. Why can't you leave people in peace?"

"Because I care about you," Walt said. "I can't help it."

"I wish you could," Horace said, pushing his platter away.

"Well, I can't." Walt pushed Horace's platter even farther down the counter and took a worn deck of cards out of his pocket, slapping it down in front of Horace. "I can't let you die before I figure out how you're beating me at gin."

Horace polished some hamburger grease into the countertop with his napkin before cutting the deck. "You should live so long. Hell, *I* should live so long," he said, watching the deal, content to wait until he had his whole hand before picking up any cards. He always gave the impression of having played all these hands before, as if the chief difficulty presented by each one was the boredom inherent in pretending over and over again that you didn't know how everything would eventually play out. By contrast, when Horace dealt, Walt picked up each card on the fly, identifying it eagerly, each hand promising an entirely new experience.

"Nope," he now said, arranging the cards in his hand one way, then another, uncertain as to which organizing principle—suits or numbers—would be more likely to guarantee victory. "I'm your best friend, Horace. You just don't know it. And I'll tell you something else you don't know. You don't know who your worst enemy is, either."

Horace, who seldom seemed to move more than a card or two before his hand made sense, rolled his eyes at Miles. "Who might that be, Perry?" Horace asked, the way a man will when he already knows what's coming. It wasn't just these gin hands he'd played before.

Walt nodded at Miles. "It's Big Boy here," he said, to no one's surprise. "You keep eating his greasy burgers, you're going to look just like him, too, if you don't have a coronary first."

"You want some coffee, Walt?" Miles asked. "I always feel better about you undermining my business after I've coaxed eighty-five cents out of you."

"You *need* more customers like me," Walt replied, tossing a twenty on the counter. Among the many things Miles held against the Silver Fox was his compulsion to break large bills at every opportunity; even if his wallet was full of singles, he always paid for his coffee with a twenty or a fifty. Occasionally, he'd try to get Miles to break a hundred, enjoying the sport of Miles's refusal. "A cup of coffee costs you . . . what? A dime? Fifteen cents? And you get almost a buck for it, right? That's eighty-five cents profit. Not too shabby."

Miles poured each man a cup, then took Walt's twenty to the register. There was no point calling the Silver Fox on the intentional vagaries of his arithmetic. "After I refill it four or five times, how much have I made then?"

When the bell over the door jingled again, Miles glanced up and saw his younger brother enter, a newspaper tucked under his ruined arm. Noting where Walt Comeau was seated, he located a stool at the other end of the counter. When Miles poured him a cup of coffee, David, who had already unfolded the front section and begun reading, met his eye and glanced down the counter at Walt Comeau before returning to his paper. For the most part the brothers understood each other perfectly, especially their silences. This one suggested that in David's view Miles had not returned from his vacation any smarter than he was before he left.

"You're pretty well prepped," Miles said, referring to the private party David was catering that evening. "I brought you back a couple jars of that lobster paste for bisque."

David nodded, pouring milk into his coffee with his good hand. "Tell me something," he said. "Why do you allow him in here?"

"It's against the law to refuse service."

"So's murder," David said, picking up the newspaper again. "It'd be an elegant solution, just the same."

Miles tried to imagine it. Assuming he could get ahold of a hand-gun, what kind of man, he wondered, would walk up to another human being—even Walt Comeau—and squeeze another death into the world? Not Miles Roby, concluded Miles Roby.

"Hey," his brother said when Miles started back down the counter, "thanks for the paste. How was the Vineyard?"

"I think Peter and Dawn might be calling it quits," Miles told him.

David didn't look very surprised, or interested, for that matter. The idea of old college friends seemed to bore him, perhaps because David himself had never gone beyond high school, except for a single semester at the Maine Culinary Institute.

"I could be wrong," Miles continued. He hated the idea of Peter and Dawn divorcing, which, if true, would take some getting used to. In fact, he still wasn't used to the idea of his own divorce. "It was just an impression."

"You didn't answer my question," David observed, without looking up from the paper.

Miles tried to remember. Had there been a question? More than one?

"How . . . was . . . the Vineyard?"

"Oh, right," Miles said, aware that this was precisely the sort of thing his soon-to-be ex-wife always complained of: that he never really listened to her. For twenty years he'd tried to convince Janine that this wasn't the case, or at least wasn't precisely the case. It wasn't that he didn't hear her questions and requests. It was more that they always provoked a response she hadn't anticipated. "I'm not ignoring you," he insisted, to which she invariably replied, "You might as well be."

"Well?" his brother wanted to know. About the Vineyard.

"Just the same," Miles told him. Of all the places in the world he couldn't hope to afford, the Vineyard was his favorite.

"YOU KNOW WHAT you need in here, Big Boy?" Walt called from down at his end of the counter. Every time he lost another hand of gin to Horace, he thought of some further improvement for the Empire Grill.

"What's that, Walt?" Miles sighed, filling salt shakers at mid-counter.

"You need to stop with this swill and start serving Green Mountain Coffee." In his own opinion Walt was on the cutting edge of all that was new and good in the world. In his fitness club, which he was forever hounding Miles to join, promising washboard abs, he'd recently introduced protein shakes, and he thought these might prove to be a hot item at the grill as well. Miles, of course, had ignored all such suggestions, thereby reinforcing Walt's contention that he was a congenitally backward man, destined to run a backward establishment. Walt expressed this view pretty much every day, leaving unanswered only the question of why he himself, a forward man in every sense of the word, chose to spend so much time in this backward venue.

"I bet you couldn't pass a blind taste test," said Horace, who usually took Miles's part in these disputes, especially since Miles appeared reluctant to defend himself against the relentless assaults on his personal philosophy.

"You kidding? Green Mountain Coffee? Night-and-day difference," Walt said.

When the bell above the door tinkled again, Miles looked up and saw that this time it was his daughter, which meant that unless someone had given her a ride, she'd walked all the way up Empire Avenue from the river without his noticing. For some reason, this possibility unnerved him. Since he and Janine had separated, a separation of a different sort had occurred between himself and Tick, the exact nature of which he'd been trying for a long time to put his finger on. He wouldn't have blamed his daughter if she'd felt betrayed by his agreeing to divorce her mother, but apparently she didn't. She'd understood from the start that it was Janine's idea, and as a result she'd been much tougher on her mother than on Miles, so tough that simple fairness had required him to remind her that the person who wants out of a marriage isn't necessarily the cause of its failure. He suspected, however, that whatever had changed in their relationship had more to do with himself than with his daughter. Since spring he couldn't seem to get Tick to stand still long enough to get a good fix on her. She was maturing, of course, becoming a young woman instead of a kid, and he grasped that there were certain things going on with her that he didn't understand because he wasn't supposed to. Still, it troubled him to feel so out of sync. Too often he found himself needing to see her, as if only her physical presence could reassure him of her well-being; yet when she did appear, she seemed different from the girl he'd been needing and worrying about. The week they'd spent together on the Vineyard had been wonderful, and by the end of it he'd felt much more in tune with Tick than at any time since he and Janine had separated. But since they'd come home, the disconnected feeling had returned with a vengeance, as if losing sight of her might lead to tragic consequences. Even now, instead of relief he was visited by an alternative scenario—the screech of tires somewhere down the block, Tick's inert body lying in the street, an automobile speeding away, dragging her enormous backpack. Which had *not* happened, he reminded himself, quickly swallowing his panic.

As she did every afternoon, Tick gave Walt Comeau wide berth, pretending not to see the arm he stretched out to her. "Hi, Uncle David," she said, rounding the far end of the counter and giving him a peck on the cheek.

"Hello, Beautiful," David said, helping her off with her backpack, which thudded to the floor of the restaurant hard enough to make the water glasses and salt and pepper shakers jump along the lunch counter. "You gonna be my helper today?"

"Whatcha got in that pack, Sweetie Pie? Rocks?" Walt Comeau called the length of the counter.

Rather than acknowledge his existence, Tick went over to Miles and buried her face in his apron, stretching her arms around his waist and hooking her fingers at his back. "I've got Abba in my head," she told him. "Make them go away."

"Sorry," Miles told her, drawing his child to him, feeling the smile spread across his face at her nearness, at her confidence in his ability to dispel the bad magic of old pop groups. Not that she was a child anymore, not really. "Did you hear them on the radio?"

"No," she admitted. "They're *his* fault." Meaning Walt. And with this accusation she pulled away from her father and grabbed an apron.

The reason it was Walt Comeau's fault was that Janine, Tick's mother, played "Mama Mia" and "Dancing Queen" in her beginning and intermediate aerobics classes at Walt's fitness club, then hummed these same songs at home. Only her advanced steppers were deemed ready for the rigors of Barry Manilow and the Copa Cabana.

"Your dad says you had a good time on the Vineyard?" David said when Tick passed by on her way to the kitchen with a tub of dirty dishes.

"I want to live there," she confessed, like someone who saw no harm in confessing a sin she was never likely to have the opportunity to commit. "There's a bookstore for sale on the beach road, but Daddy won't buy it." The door swung shut behind her.

"How much?" David wondered, tossing down his paper, grabbing a clean apron and joining his brother at mid-counter. He still had partial use of his damaged hand, but not much strength and very little dexterity. "Save me half an hour and tie this, will you?"

Miles had already set down the salt shakers he was filling.

"So?" David said when the knot cinched.

"So what?"

"How much was the bookstore? God! How come you can recite twenty-five consecutive breakfast orders and not remember a simple question I asked you two seconds ago?"

"More like a book barn, actually," Miles said, since that was what it had once been. There'd been enough room downstairs to sell new books and set up a small café, since people seemed to think those belonged in bookstores now. The upstairs could be cleaned up and devoted to used books. There was even a small cottage on the property. The same couple had owned and run the business for about twenty years but now the wife was sick, and her husband was trying to talk himself into letting it go. Their kids didn't want any part of it after going away to college.

"How come you know all that and not the price?" David wondered when Miles finished explaining.

"I didn't actually see the listing. Peter just pointed the place out. I don't think he knew the asking price. He isn't interested in running a bookstore."

"They got a fitness club over there, Big Boy?" Walt wanted to know.

"I don't know, Walt," Miles told him, trying to sound neutral about the idea. If anything in the world could ruin the island for him, it would be Walt Comeau's presence. Of course, the idea of a blowhard like the Silver Fox anywhere outside of Empire Falls was absurd, but Miles didn't dare laugh. A year ago Walt had joked that if Miles wasn't careful he was going to steal his wife, and then he'd gone ahead and done it.

Walt scratched his chin thoughtfully, while contemplating a discard. "I figure my club here's doing pretty well. Practically runs itself. Now might be a good time to expand." He sounded as if his only obstacle was the matter of timing. The Silver Fox liked to imply that money was never a consideration, that every bank in Dexter County was eager to loan him whatever capital he didn't have. Miles doubted this was true, but it might be. He'd also doubted that his soon-to-be-ex-wife was the sort of woman to be taken in by Walt Comeau's bravado, and he'd certainly been wrong about that.

"Go ahead and split if you want," David told him. "He'll be wanting to arm-wrestle you in a minute."

Miles shrugged. "I think he just comes in to let me know there's no hard feelings."

This elicited a chuckle. "About the way he stole your wife?"

"Some sins trail their own penance," Miles said softly, after glancing toward the back room, where Tick could be heard loading dirty dishes into the ancient Hobart. One of the few things Miles and Janine had been able to agree on when their marriage came apart was that they wouldn't speak ill of each other in front of their daughter. The agreement, Miles knew, worked much to his advantage, since most of the time he had no desire to speak ill of his ex-wife, whereas Janine always appeared to be strangling on her wretched opinion of him. Of course, all the other agreements they'd arrived at—such as letting her stay in the house until it sold and the one that gave her the better car and most of their possessions—worked pretty much in Janine's favor, which left Miles staggering with debt.

"Tick really had a good time?"

Miles nodded. "You should've seen her. She was like her old self, before all the shit started raining down on her. She smiled for a solid week."

"Good."

"She met a boy, too."

"That always helps."

"Don't tease her about it, now."

"Okay," David promised, though it was one that would be hard for him to keep.

Miles took off his apron and tossed it in the hamper by the door. "You should take a week yourself. Go someplace."

His brother shrugged. "Why invite disaster? I'm down to one arm as it is. I ever let myself go someplace fun, I might start misbehaving, and then I'd have to flip your burgers with my toes."

He was right, of course. Miles knew his brother had been sober since the afternoon three years ago when, returning from a hunting trip up in The County, David, drunk, had fallen asleep at the wheel and run his pickup off a mountain road into a ravine. Airborne, the truck had hit a tree and there parted company with its unseatbelted driver, the vehicle careening a good hundred yards down the ravine and coming to rest well out of sight in the thick woods. David, thrown free of the cab, had gotten snagged by his hunting vest in the upper branches of a tree and hung there, some fifty feet above the ground, drifting in and out of consciousness, his arm shattered in several places and four ribs fractured, until he was discovered half frozen the next morning by a group of hunters, one of whom had stationed himself beneath the very tree David improbably dangled from, unable to utter a sound. If his bladder hadn't given way, as David was fond of remarking, he'd still be twisting there in the frigid wind, a sack of tough L.L. Bean outerwear full of bleached bones.

That lonely, hallucinatory night had proved more effective than all the therapies he'd undergone in the various substance abuse clinics he'd been admitted to over the previous decade. His old Empire Falls drinking buddies, most of whom were still roaring around Dexter County in beer-laden snowmobiles, occasionally sought David out, hoping to nudge him gently off the wagon by reminding him how much more fun the drinking life was, but so far he'd resisted their invitations. The year before, he'd bought a small camp in the woods off Small Pond Road, and he said that whenever he felt the urge to stare at the world through the brown glass of an empty beer bottle, all he had to do was walk outside on his deck and look up into the pines and listen again to the horrible sound the wind made in their upper branches. Miles hoped this was true. He'd been estranged from his brother at the time of the accident, and continued to observe David warily, not doubting his brother's intention to reform, just his ability. He still smoked a little dope, Miles knew, and probably even had a small marijuana patch out in the woods, like half his rural Maine neighbors, but he hadn't had a drink since the accident and he still wore the orange vest that had saved his life.

Miles surveyed the restaurant, trying to see what he'd left undone. One week away had been sufficient to make it all seem unfamiliar. He'd spent most of yesterday trying to remember where things went. Only when he got busy and didn't have time to think did his body remember where they were. Today had been better, though not much. "Okay," he said. "You think of anything you need?"

David grinned. "All kinds of stuff, but let's not get started."

"Okay," Miles agreed.

"You should think about it, Miles," David said from his knees, where he was checking stores under the counter.

"About what?"

His brother just looked up at him.

"What?" Miles repeated.

David shrugged, went back to searching under the counter.

"Number one, I can't afford it. At least not until I can sell this place. Number two, Janine'd never let me take Tick, and Tick is the one thing I won't let her have. And number three, who'd look after Dad?"

His brother stood, a mega-pack of napkins wedged under the elbow of his bad arm, a reminder that Miles had forgotten to fill the dispensers. "Number one, you don't know if you can afford it because you never found out how much it cost. The owner might be open to a little creative financing for the right buyer. Number two, you could win Tick in court if you were willing to go there and duke it out. You're not the one who has to worry about being found an unfit parent. And number three, Max Roby is the most self-sufficient man on the face of the earth. He only looks and acts helpless. So when you say you can't, what you really mean is that it wouldn't be easy, right?"

"Have it your way, David," said Miles, who didn't feel like arguing. "Give me those."

But when he reached for the napkins, his brother turned deftly away. "Go."

"David, give me the damn napkins," Miles said. It was an easy job for a man with two good hands, a hard one for somebody with only one, and it did not escape Miles's attention that this seemed to be his brother's point. It would be difficult, but he'd do it anyway. For a man who'd hung by his vest fifty feet up in a tree and nearly frozen to death as a result of his own stupidity, David had always been strangely impatient with the failings of others.

"Go on. Get out of here."

Miles shook his head in surrender. "Did he come in at all last week?"

"Max? Three afternoons, actually."

"You didn't let him near the register, I hope?" Their father could not be trusted around money, though Miles and David had argued for years about the boundaries of his dishonesty. In Miles's opinion, there weren't any. David thought there were, even if they were not always easy to locate. For instance, he believed Max would take money out of his sons' pockets, but not out of the restaurant's cash register.

"I did pay him under the table, though."

"I wish you wouldn't," Miles said.

"I know you do, but why not pay him the way he wants? What difference does it make?"

"For one thing it's against the law. For another, Mrs. Whiting would have a cow if she thought I was doing anything off the books."

"She'd probably prefer it, if she understood there'd be more money left over for her."

"Possibly. It might also start her wondering. If I play fast and loose with the government, maybe I'm playing fast and loose with her, too."

David nodded the way you do when you've been given an inadequate explanation and decide to accept it anyway. "Okay, I got another question for you," he said, looking directly at Miles. "What makes you think that woman is ever going to give you this restaurant?"

"She said she would."

David nodded again. "I don't know, Miles," he said.

ONLY ONE TUB of dirty lunch dishes remained, but it was a big one, so Miles lugged it into the kitchen and set it on the drainboard, stopping there to listen to the Hobart chug and whir, steam leaking from inside its stainless steel frame. They'd had this dishwasher for, what, twenty years? Twenty-five? He was pretty sure it was there when Roger Sperry first hired him back in high school. It couldn't possibly have much more life in it, and if Miles had to guess when it would give out, it'd probably be the day after the restaurant became his. He'd spoken to Mrs. Whiting about replacing it, but a Hobart was a big-ticket item and the old woman wouldn't hear of any such thing while it was still running. When Miles was feeling generous, he reminded himself that seventy-something-year-old women probably didn't enjoy being told that things were old and worn-out, that they'd already lived years beyond a normal life expectancy. In less charitable moods, he suspected his employer was shrewdly determined to time the obsolescence of every machine in the restaurant—the Hobart, the Garland range, the grill, the milk machine—to her own ultimate demise, thus minimizing her gift to him as much as possible.

Their arrangement, struck nearly twenty years ago now—another lifetime, it seemed to Miles—when Roger Sperry fell ill, was that he would run the restaurant for the remainder of Mrs. Whiting's life, then inherit the place. The deal had been struck in secret because Miles knew his mother would object to his dropping out of college in his senior year; for him to mortgage his future in order to be nearby during her illness would surely fill her with not just despair but also fury. Mrs.

Whiting herself had seemed aware that their fait accompli was necessary, that once Grace learned of the arrangement she would talk Miles out of this futile gesture and remind him that she was going to die regardless, that compromising his own prospects was so perverse as to render meaningless her sacrifices on his behalf. Miles knew all this too, and so he had conspired with Mrs. Whiting to give her no such opportunity.

His mother's illness aside, taking over the Empire Grill had not seemed like such a terrible idea at the time. As a history major, Miles was coming to understand that it was unlikely he'd be able to find a job without a graduate degree, and there was no money for that. He'd started working at the restaurant during his junior year of high school, returning summers and holidays after going away to college, so no aspect of the restaurant's operation was beyond him; and while the living it promised would be hard, its rewards meager by the world's reckoning, by local standards he would make out all right. Why *not* run the joint for a few years and save some money? He could always finish school later. Mrs. Whiting would just have to understand.

Of course, all that was before the textile mill closed and the population of Empire Falls began to dwindle as families moved away in search of employment. And Miles, being young, did not know, since there was no way he could, that he'd never love the restaurant as Roger Sperry had, or that the other man's affection for it had long been the primary engine of its survival. Despite his youth, Miles did understand that people didn't go to places like the Empire Grill for the food. After only two or three training shifts he was a far better short-order cook than his mentor. Roger proudly proclaimed him a natural, by which he probably meant that Miles remembered what customers asked him for and then gave it to them, something Roger himself seldom managed to do. If he intuited any of Miles's shortcomings, he was too fond of the boy to share them with him.

Only after taking over the restaurant did Miles begin to realize that his relationship to the patrons of the Empire Grill had changed profoundly. Before, he'd been the smart kid—Grace Roby's boy—who was going off to college to make something of himself, and thus had been the object of much gentle, good-natured ridicule. The men at the lunch counter were forever quizzing him about things—the operation of backhoes, say, or the best spot to sink a septic tank—they imagined he must be learning about at college. His complete lack of wisdom on these subjects led them to wonder out loud just what the hell they were teaching down there in Portland. Often they didn't speak to Miles directly, but through Roger Sperry, as though an interpreter already were necessary. After Roger's death, the food improved in inverse proportion to the conversation. The men at the lunch counter wouldn't have said as much to Miles, but in their opinion he spent too much time with his back to them, attending to their sputtering hamburgers rather than their stories and grievances and jokes. While appreciative of his competence, they began to suspect that he had little interest in their conversation and, moreover, was unhappy in general. Roger Sperry had always been so glad to see them that he botched their orders; half the fun of the Empire Grill had been razzing him for these failures. Under Miles's competent stewardship, the Empire Grill, never terribly profitable, had gone into a long, gentle decline almost imperceptible without the benefit of time-lapse photography, until one day it was suddenly clear that the diner was *un*profitable, and so it had remained for years.

Still, Miles often sensed regret in Mrs. Whiting's demeanor when she recalled her promise to bequeath him the restaurant. Sometimes she seemed to blame him for its decline and wondered out loud why she needed the aggravation of a business that produced so little revenue. But on other occasions—and there had been several of these—when Miles himself had become discouraged and offered the same argument to his employer, Mrs. Whiting quickly retreated and urged him not to give up, reminding him that the Empire Grill was a landmark, that it was the only non-fast-food establishment in town, and that Empire Falls, if its residents were to remain at all hopeful about the future, needed the grill to survive, even if it didn't thrive.

Even more mysterious was the feeling Miles had that Mrs. Whiting wasn't altogether pleased by recent signs that business was picking up. During the past nine months, thanks to a bold initiative by David, the restaurant was actually beginning to turn around, and for several months that spring had actually turned a small profit. When he expressed this optimistic view to Mrs. Whiting, expecting her to be pleased by the modest reversal of fortune, she regarded both the news and its bearer suspiciously, as if she either didn't believe the numbers with which she was being presented or feared that the Roby boys might be trying to put something over on her.

Miles knew Mrs. Whiting had put the bequest in her will, because she showed him the pertinent section of the document all those years ago. What he didn't know, of course, was whether, as David cautioned, she had ever amended it. That was possible, of course, but he continued to maintain, at least to his brother, that if Mrs. Whiting said she was going to leave him the restaurant, she'd do so. However, he had to admit it would be entirely in character for the old woman to ensure that the restaurant at the time of the transfer would be worth as little as possible. And in the meantime, it was his own responsibility to keep the Hobart running, with rubber bands, if necessary.

Tick was seated on the opposite drainboard, listlessly munching a granola bar, waiting for the machine to complete its cycle. "I had an Empire Moment on the way here," she said, without much enthusiasm. "Not a great one, though. The flower shop. Mixed B.O.K.A.Y."

This was a game they'd been playing for nearly a year, finding unintentional humor in the form of gaffes in the *Empire Gazette*, misspellings in advertisements for local stores, lapses in logic on printed signs like the one on the brick wall that surrounded the old empty shirt factory: NO TRESPASSING WITHOUT PERMISSION. They referred to the pleasure of these discoveries as "Empire Moments," and Tick was becoming disconcertingly adept at identifying them. Last month, down in Fairhaven, she'd noticed the sign outside the town's one shabby little rumored-to-be-gay bar whose entrance was being renovated: ENTER IN REAR. Miles was startled that his sixteen-year-old daughter had seen the humor in this, but he was proud too. Still, he wondered if Janine wasn't right. She'd disapproved of the game from the start, viewing it as yet another opportunity for the two of them to pretend superiority to everyone else, especially herself.

"Good eye," Miles nodded. "I'll look for it." By rule they always confirmed each other's sightings.

"I can do that," Tick said when she saw her father start scraping dishes into the garbage and stacking them in the plastic rack for the next load.

"Never doubted it," her father assured her. "How was school?"

She shrugged. "Okay."

There was precious little Miles would have changed about his daughter, but to his way of thinking far too many things in Tick's life were "okay." She was a smart kid, one who knew the difference between first-rate, mediocre and piss-poor, but like most kids her age she seemed bored by such distinctions. How was the movie? Okay. How were the french fries? Okay. How's your sprained ankle feeling? Okay. Everything was pretty much okay, even when it wasn't, even when in fact it was piss-poor. When the entire emotional spectrum, from despair to ecstasy, could be summed up by a single four-letter word, what was a parent to do? Even more troubling was his suspicion that "okay" was designed specifically as a conversation stopper, employed in hopes that the person who'd asked the question would simply go away.

The trick, Miles had learned, was not to go away. You didn't ask more probing questions, because they, too, would be met with this monosyllabic evasion. The trick was silence. If there was a trick.

"I made a new friend," Tick finally elaborated once the Hobart had shuddered to a halt and she'd raised the door to extract the tray of clean dishes.

Miles rinsed his hands and went over to where Tick was stacking the warm plates. He took one down from the shelf and checked it, relieved to find it squeaky clean. The Hobart would live.

"Candace Burke. She's in my art class. She stole an Exacto knife today."

"What for?"

Tick shrugged. "I guess she didn't have one. She starts all her sentences with oh-my-God-oh-my-God. Like, Oh-my-God-oh-my-God my mascara's running. Or, Oh-my-God-oh-my-God, you're even skinnier than last year."

This last, Miles suspected, was not a theoretical example. Tick, always stick-thin, was often accused of being anorexic. Last year she'd even been called into the nurse's office and questioned about her eating habits. In fact, Miles and Janine had been called in as well. This was before Janine herself lost so much weight, so she and Miles, sitting there in the school counselor's tiny office, did seem to suggest that Tick couldn't possibly have come by her reedlike body honestly.

Miles tried to think if he knew this Candace Burke. There were several Burke families in town. "What's she look like?"

"Fat."

"A lot or a little?"

"She's fat like I'm skinny."

"In other words, not very?" Miles ventured. In mid-adolescence his daughter was hard to compliment. The truth was that he thought her a heartbreakingly beautiful girl, and often tried to explain that it was her intelligence, her wit, that was keeping her from being more popular with boys. "Which Burke is she, I wonder?"

Tick shrugged. "She lives with her mother and her mother's new boyfriend down on Water Street. She says we've got a lot in common. I think she's in love with Zack. She keeps saying, 'Oh-my-God-oh-my-God, he's *so* good-looking. How can you *stand* it? I mean, like, he was yours, and now he's not.'"

"Did you tell her she's not missing much?" Even now, months after their breakup, the mere mention of Zack Minty, Tick's former boyfriend, was enough to make Miles grind his teeth. His fondest hope was that Donny, the boy Tick had met on the Vineyard, would free his daughter from any lingering attraction she might feel for a boy who, like his father and grandfather before him, bore more or less constant watching.

His daughter's pause did little to reassure him. "Here's the thing," she finally said. "Now that I'm not with Zack anymore, I don't have a single friend." Tick's two best friends had moved away in the last six months.

"Except Candace," Miles pointed out.

"Oh-my-God-oh-my-God!" she squealed in mock horror, "I forgot Candace!"

"And you forgot me," Miles pointed out.

Tick shrugged, serious now. "I know."

"And your uncle David."

A frown, a shrug, an apologetic "I know."

"And your mother."

Just a hint of a frown. When he didn't press further, she let him take her in his arms and surrendered limply to his awkward, overlarge embrace. Usually when Tick felt a bear hug coming, she'd position her body sideways, so one of her shoulders would dig under his breastbone. It was Janine who had explained what was going on, that their daughter's late-developing breasts were probably sore; her explanation made it clear that Janine herself hadn't cared all that much for his embraces. "I know we're not the kind of friends you had in mind," Miles told his daughter. "But we're not nobody."

A sniffle now, her nose buried deep in his chest. "I know."

"You going to write Donny?"

"What for? I'll never see him again."

Miles shrugged. "Who knows?"

"Me," she said, pulling away from him now. "And you."

He let her go back to unloading the Hobart. "You got homework?"

She shook her head.

"You want me to come back in a couple hours and run you home?"

"Mom said she'd come by," she said. "If she forgets, the idiot can do it."

"Hey," Miles said, and waited until she turned around and looked at him. "Go easy. He's trying. He just doesn't know how to . . . *be* around you."

"He could try being dead."

"Tick."

"Why can't you just go ahead and admit how much you hate him?"

Because he might not be able to stop there, was why. Because when David had suggested murder as a solution to the Silver Fox's daily visits, Miles had almost been able to imagine it.

"Big Boy!" Walt Comeau bellowed when Miles emerged from the kitchen. "Come over here a minute."

Walt had taken his outer shirt off now, Miles noticed. He always wore white T-shirts with the logo of his fitness club over the left pectoral, and he always wore them a size too small, so everyone could admire his still-rippling-at-fifty torso and biceps. David had been right, of course. The Silver Fox was about to plant an elbow on the Formica counter and challenge Miles to arm-wrestle.

"Be right there," he called, then turned to David, who was handing napkins to Horace to stuff in the dispensers. "You got help tonight?"

"Charlene," David said. "I think she just pulled in."

"You want me to stop by later?"

"Nope."

Miles shrugged.

David grinned at him. "You're out the back, aren't you."

"You bet."

Behind the restaurant, the first slot, beside the Dumpster, was occupied by Miles's ten-year-old Jetta, the next one by Charlene's even more dilapidated Hyundai Excel. He tried to make enough noise in his approach so as not to startle her, but Charlene's radio was on loud enough that she jumped anyway when he appeared at her door.

"Jesus, Miles," she croaked in the clenched-toothed manner of pot smokers, once she'd rolled down the window. Sweet smoke escaped along with an old Rolling Stones song. "Give me a coronary, why don't you? I thought you were that asshole cop." Meaning Jimmy Minty.

"Sorry," Miles said, though in fact he wasn't entirely displeased. Most women saw Miles coming and said so. Janine clearly had. "Don't imagine you snuck up on me, Miles, because you didn't," she'd told him after accepting his proposal of marriage. That proposal had certainly taken *him* by surprise, and he'd taken this as an indication that Janine might be surprised too, but she wasn't. The World's Most Transparent Man, she called him. "Don't ever consider a life of crime," she advised. "You decide to rob a bank, the cops will know which one before you do."

"How did things go last week?" he asked Charlene.

"Slow," she said. "Dinners picked up, though."

"They've *been* picking up."

"Some of the college kids are filtering back in."

Dinners were a relatively new thing. Until a year ago the restaurant was open only for breakfast and lunch, but David had suggested opening for dinner on weekends and trying to attract a different clientele, an idea opposed by Mrs. Whiting, who feared that they'd lose their old tried-and-true customers. Miles had managed to convince her that, for the most part, tried-and-true was done and gone. In the end she'd grudgingly consented, but only after being reassured that they wouldn't ask for an advertising budget or make any changes in the breakfast and lunch menus or pester her for expensive redecoration to accompany the newer, more sophisticated dinner service.

At David's suggestion they began by inviting students who wrote restaurant reviews for the college paper to a free meal. The college was seven miles away, in Fairhaven, and even Miles hadn't believed that many students would make the trek, not when their parents were already shelling out more than twenty-five grand a year for tuition, room and board. But apparently there was money left over. When students started frequenting the Empire Grill, the cars parked out front—some of them, anyway—were BMWs and Audis. Summer had slowed some after this luxury fleet returned to Massachusetts and Connecticut, but Friday and Saturday nights still did well enough to justify staying open. David's other brainstorm was also working out: during the week the restaurant now catered private parties.

"You and David think you can handle tonight okay?"

"In our sleep. Rehearsal dinner for twenty people."

"Okay," Miles said, not quite able to conceal his disappointment at not being needed.

Charlene, seeming to understand all this, changed the subject. "You and Tick have a good vacation?"

"Great," he said. "I wish I hadn't been so enthusiastic, actually. Now Walt's thinking about opening a fitness club on the island."

"I saw his van out front," she said. "You want me to go in there and wither his dick?"

"Feel free," Miles said, knowing that it was well within her power. Charlene, at forty-five, was still more than enough woman to produce the same effect among the smug jocks from the college. "I'm out of here, anyway."

"You shouldn't let him run you off, Miles."

"I'm grateful he shows up. Wasn't for him, I'd probably never leave the premises." Since he and Janine separated, Miles had been living in the apartment above the restaurant. The plan had been to fix it up, make it livable, but after six months he still hadn't done much. Half the available living space was still occupied by cardboard boxes from the storage room in the basement, supplies that had been moved upstairs years before when the river flooded. Miles also suspected something was wrong with the apartment's heating system, since in cold weather he often woke up with headaches, feeling groggy and half asphyxiated. Last April he'd even considered asking Janine if he could sack out in the back bedroom for a while until the headaches went away, but when he went over to ask her, he discovered the Silver Fox had all but moved in. Better to asphyxiate above the Empire Grill, he'd decided.

"Well, if you're going somewhere, I wish you'd leave and let me finish this joint," Charlene told him.

"Go ahead and finish. Who's stopping you?"

"You. You know I don't feel comfortable smoking dope around you."

Since this was a vaguely insulting thing to say, Miles felt compelled to ask why.

"Because you're the kind of man who can never quite manage to conceal his disapproval."

Miles sighed, supposing this must be true. Janine had always said the same thing. Odd, though, the way other people saw you. Miles had always thought of himself as a model of tolerance.

CHAPTER 2

FATHER MARK, returning late in the afternoon from visiting his parish shut-ins, found Miles around back of St. Catherine's staring up at the steeple. As a boy Miles had been a climber, so fearless that he'd driven his mother into paroxysms of terror. When it was time for dinner, she'd come looking for him, always searching at ground level, which delighted him—he loved to call down to her from the air, forcing her to look up and locate him among the blue sky's tangled branches, her slender hand rushing to cover her mouth. At the time, he'd concluded she lacked the gift of memory, always expecting him on the ground when time after time he was in the air. Now a father himself, he knew how frightened she must've been. She hadn't looked up because there were too many trees, too many branches, too many dangers. Only when Miles swung safely down and landed at her feet was she able to smile, even as she scolded him into a promise she knew he would never keep. "You're a born climber," she'd admit on their way home. "What heights you'll scale when you're a man! I don't dare even think."

Now it was Miles who didn't dare even think. Of climbing, anyway. Somewhere along the line he'd become terrified of heights, and the idea of painting the steeple made him weak in the knees.

"When I was a little boy," Father Mark said, "I used to think God actually lived up there."

"In the steeple?" Miles said.

Father Mark nodded. "I thought when we sang hymns we were calling to Him to come down and be among us. Which of course we were. But the literal proximity was reassuring." The two men shook hands.

Miles had changed into his paint-spattered clothes but hadn't started in yet, so he was still dry. The sky, in the time since Miles left the grill, had grown ominous. "God Himself, a couple stories up . . . so close."

"I was just thinking how far *away* it is," Miles admitted. "But then I was contemplating painting it."

"That does makes a difference," Father Mark said.

"Actually I wasn't contemplating painting so much as falling."

Interesting, Miles thought. Like himself, Father Mark, as a child, had been reassured by the imagined proximity of God, whereas adults, perhaps because they so often were up to no good, took more comfort from His remoteness. Though Miles didn't think of himself as a man up to no good, he did prefer the notion of an all-loving God to that of an all-knowing one. It pleased him to imagine God as someone like his mother, someone beleaguered by too many responsibilities, too dog-tired to monitor an energetic boy every minute of the day, but who, out of love and fear for his safety, checked in on him whenever she could. Was this so crazy? Surely God must have other projects besides Man, just as parents had responsibilities other than raising their children? Miles liked the idea of a God who, when He at last had the opportunity to return His attention to His children, might shake His head with wonder and mutter, "Jesus. Look what they're up to now." A dis-tractible God, perhaps, one who'd be startled to discover so many of His children way up in trees since the last time He looked. A God whose hand would go rushing to His mouth in fear in that instant of recognition that—good God!—that kid's going to hurt himself. A God who could be surprised by unanticipated pride—glory be, that boy *is* a climber!

An idle, daydream deity, this, Miles had to admit. In truth, when God looked down upon His mischievous children, they were usually up to far worse than climbing trees.

If there were such a deity, though, and if He'd ever feared that Miles would hurt himself, He could quit worrying anytime now. For all his early promise, Miles had scaled no heights, and now, at forty-two, he was so afraid of them that he cowered near the steel doors of glass elevators, reluctant to move back away from them and let others step on.

"I thought we agreed you weren't going to attempt the steeple," Father Mark said.

"We did, I guess." Originally, Miles had imagined that by painting the church himself, he could save the parish a lot of money, but both contractors he'd spoken to about painting just the steeple wanted to charge nearly as much for that as they would have for the entire building. Annoyed that he proposed to do the safe, easy part himself, they let him know that the part he didn't want was the part *nobody* wanted, and that was the part that cost you. The truth of this stung. "The trouble is," Miles told his friend, "every time I look up there, it's an accusation."

"So don't look up."

"Fine advice for a man of the spirit to give," said Miles, looking up and feeling at that moment a drop of rain.

Father Mark had also looked up and also felt a drop. "Let's go over to the Rectum and have a cup of coffee," he suggested. "You can tell me about your vacation."

Ever since Miles had confessed his boyhood confusion about the words "rectory" and "rectum," Father Mark—as delighted by the mistake as Grace Roby had been—had preferred this nomenclature, even though it sometimes slipped out when it shouldn't. Such as earlier that summer when at the end of Mass he invited the parishioners to join him and Father Tom for lemonade on the lawn behind the Rectum.

St. Cat's rectory was one of Miles's favorite places. It was bright and sunny in all seasons, warm in the winter, breezy in the summer, but probably it had more to do with the fact that Father Tom—now retired but still living in the rectory—had never allowed children there. Nor had Miles's mother ever been invited in, for that matter, so perhaps it was the exclusion that added to the attraction. All of the rooms on the bottom floor were large and high-ceilinged, with tall, uncurtained windows that allowed passersby a glimpse of the privileged life inside. The Rectum's dining room, which fronted the street, had an oak dining table long enough to seat twenty guests, though when Miles and his mother walked by late on Saturday afternoons after having had their confessions heard, the room was occupied only by Father Tom, seated regally at one end, and his housekeeper, Mrs. Dumbrowski, hovering in attendance. Back then there had been two, sometimes three, priests in residence, but on Saturdays Father Tom liked to take his evening meal early and would not wait for the younger priest, who invariably drew the late confessions. Miles's mother always remarked when they passed on how sad this seemed, but Miles didn't see anything so very odd in the practice and couldn't help wondering why it so upset his mother. By the time they'd returned home, his father would already have finished eating his sandwich and departed on foot for the neighborhood tavern.

To young Miles, the forbidden rectory, so full of warmth and light and wood and books, seemed otherworldly, and he imagined that a man would have to be very rich to be a priest. The romance of the profession had stayed with him for a long time. He'd seriously considered Holy Orders well into high school, and there were still times when he wondered if he'd missed his calling. Janine had wondered too. To her way of thinking, any man with no more sex drive than Miles Roby possessed might better have just gone ahead and embraced celibacy and been done with it, instead of disappointing poor girls like herself.

Father Mark and Miles never had their coffee in the dining room he'd admired as a boy, preferring instead the kitchen with its cozy breakfast nook, a booth not unlike those along the front windows of the Empire Grill. Father Mark put a plate of cookies on the Formica table, then poured each of them a cup of coffee. Though it was only the first week in September, already autumn was in the air, rustling the lace curtains of the open window. The drizzle had stopped as soon as they entered the Rectum, but the sky remained dark. The daylight was dwindling early, giving Miles less time to work on the church. Most afternoons he managed to leave the grill by three, but by the time he changed clothes and set up the ladder, it was at least three-thirty. By six, on cloudy days, the light was failing and it was time to quit. Of course the real culprit wasn't the abbreviated day so much as the lengthening coffee conversations with Father Mark, who now slid into the booth opposite Miles. "You look like your vacation did you some good," he observed.

"It did. And there's a nice chapel in Vineyard Haven. I drove in to Mass most mornings. Tick came with me, and that was even better."

The one good thing about her parents' breakup, Tick was on record as observing, was that at least she didn't have to go to church anymore now that her mother had replaced Catholicism with aerobics. In fact, Tick considered herself an agnostic, a philosophical position that allowed her to sleep in on Sunday mornings. Miles knew better than to force her to go, and had not done so on the Vineyard, which made him even more pleased when she dragged herself out of bed, still half asleep, in the mornings to accompany him. By the time Mass was over, she was fully awake and they would enjoy a muffin together at an outdoor café before heading out-island to Peter and Dawn's house and the rest of their lazy day at the beach. Back in Maine he'd asked whether she thought she'd start going to church again now that she' was back in the habit, but she didn't think so. It was easier to believe in God, she said, or at least the possibility of God, on Martha's Vineyard than it was in Empire Falls. Miles knew what she meant, understood the bitter irony. Half the cars in the Vineyard chapel's lot were either Mercedes or Lexuses. No surprise that their owners believed that God was in His heaven.

"And of course," Miles added, "Peter and Dawn spoiled her the whole time."

"Worse than you do?"

"By a mile," Miles said, chewing a cookie. Oddly, his appetite was never better than in the late afternoon here at St. Cat's. Surrounded by food all day at the restaurant, he often forgot to eat, whereas here, if he didn't pay attention, he'd finish the entire plate of cookies. "Or about as badly as I'd spoil her if I had the means. They spoiled us both, actually. Good food. A twenty-dollar bottle of wine with dinner every night."

"Must've been strange not having Janine there."

"She was invited," Miles said, surprised at the note of defensiveness in his voice.

"Never said she wasn't, Miles."

"There was plenty to occupy my thoughts without her. Their place is on a stretch of private beach, and every other woman was sunbathing in the nude. When we're not there, I suspect Peter and Dawn do too. If she had a tan line, I sure couldn't see it."

"How about Peter?" Father Mark asked. "Did *he* have a tan line?"

"Didn't occur to me to look," Miles said, smiling.

Father Mark smiled back. "Miles, you're a true Manichaean. You seek out Mass in the morning and your friend's wife's tan line in the afternoon. Anyway, what is it they do again?"

"Write television sitcoms. By next week they'll have shut everything up and flown back to L.A. You should see the house that just sits there vacant ten months out of the year."

Father Mark nodded but didn't say anything. Given the priest's political leanings, Miles knew that he didn't approve of personal wealth, much less conspicuous consumption.

"Peter said an odd thing, actually," Miles continued, even though he'd made up his mind not to tell anyone about this. "He said he and

Dawn were astonished Janine and I stuck it out as long as we did, considering how miserable we were together. They'd been admiring for years the way we kept trying to work through our problems."

Father Mark smiled. "Remember, though, people from L.A. have pretty minimal expectations when it comes to coping with marital difficulties."

Miles shrugged, conceding this. "I guess I was just surprised that people saw us that way."

"Mismatched, you mean?"

Miles considered. "Not really that so much. More that people saw us as unhappy. I *wasn't* all that unhappy . . . or I didn't know I was. So it's strange to have friends conclude something like that. I mean, if I was so unhappy, wouldn't I know?"

"Possibly," Father Mark replied. "But not necessarily."

Miles sighed. "Janine knew. I have to give her that. At least she knew how she felt."

At this point both men heard the shuffling of slippered feet in the hall. Father Mark closed his eyes, as if at the advance of a migraine. A moment later Father Tom, his gray hair wild, his collar askew, entered and fixed Miles with a particularly menacing glare.

"You want to join us, Tom?" Father Mark suggested, no doubt hoping to head off trouble. "I'll make you a cup of hot cocoa if you promise to behave."

Father Tom usually loved hot chocolate, especially when he didn't have to make it himself, but it appeared he was thirstier for a good confrontation. "Where did *that* evil bastard come from?" he growled.

Miles, also eager to placate the old priest, had been trying to get to his feet so he could offer to shake hands, but standing up proved no easy maneuver, since both the booth and the table were stationary.

"This is no evil bastard, Tom," Father Mark said calmly. "This is Miles, our most faithful parishioner. You baptized him and you married his parents."

"I know who he is," Father Tom said. "He's a peckerhead and his mother was a whore. I told her so too."

Miles sat back down. This wasn't the first time the old man, inspired by only God knew what, had taken one look at Miles and offered a poor opinion of his moral character, though he'd never before insulted the memory of Miles's mother. This was clearly an old man's dementia talking, but for the second time that afternoon Miles fleetingly considered how satisfying it would be to send another human being into the next world. This time, a priest.

"Look at him. Look at that face. He knows it's true," the old man said, taking in Miles's paint-spattered overalls. "He's a filthy degenerate is what he is. He's tracking his filth into my house."

Father Mark sighed. "You're wrong all around, Tom. First, it's not your house."

"Is too," he said.

"No, the house belongs to the parish, as you're well aware."

Father Tom seemed to consider the unfairness of this arrangement, then finally shrugged.

"And Miles isn't a degenerate," the younger priest said. "He's covered with paint because he's painting the church for us, remember? For free?"

The old man squinted first at his colleague, then at Miles. Always a frugal man in the extreme, Father Tom might have been expected to be mollified by this news, but instead he continued to glare fiercely, as if to suggest that no good deed could disguise the fundamental evil of Miles's heart. "I may be old," he conceded, "but I still know a peckerhead when I see one."

Father Mark, his patience exhausted, slid out of the booth and took him by the shoulders, rotating him gently but firmly. "Tom," he said, "look at me." When he continued to glare at Miles, Father Mark placed the tips of his fingers on the old man's stubbled chin, turning his head. "Look at me, Tom."

Finally he did, and his expression instantly morphed from disgust to shame.

"Tom," Father Mark said, "remember what we talked about before?"

If so, he showed no sign, as he studied Father Mark through red, rheumy eyes.

"I'm sorry you're not feeling well today, but this sort of behavior is intolerable. You owe our friend an apology."

To Miles, Father Tom resembled nothing more than a scolded child, convinced against his better instincts by a loving parent that he'd been a bad boy. He glanced back at Miles to see if it was possible to owe such a man an apology, then returned to Father Mark's stern gaze. The two men stared at each other long enough to make Miles squirm, but finally Father Tom turned to Miles and said, "Forgive me."

Miles didn't hesitate. "Of course, Father Tom. I'm sorry, too." And he *was* sorry. Satisfying or not, it wouldn't have been a good thing to kill an elderly priest, which also suggested it was not a good thing to wish for.

"There," Father Mark said, "that's better. Isn't it nicer for all of us when we're friends?"

Father Tom appeared to consider this extremely dubious, again studying Miles for several long beats before shaking his head and shuffling out of the room. Miles couldn't be sure, but he thought he heard one more "peckerhead" escape the old man's lips out in the hallway.

Father Mark continued to stare at the doorway as the sound of shuffling slippered feet receded. The expression on the younger priest's face wasn't quite as tolerant as one might have expected of a clergyman.

"It's okay," Miles assured him. "Father Tom and I go way back, you know. He's not himself."

"You think not?" Father Mark asked.

"It's not his fault that stuff comes out."

"True," Father Mark said. "Interesting that it's there to begin with, though. I understand why it's coming out, but how do you suppose it got *in* there?"

"Well . . ."

"I know." Father Mark grinned. "An eternal question, answered in Genesis. Still, I'm sorry he said what he did. I have no idea where he comes up with such things. He probably doesn't even remember your mother."

Miles forced himself to consider this possibility. True, the old man's mind was gone. The problem was, it wasn't completely gone, and Father Tom's eyes, especially when he was angry, often appeared to be ablaze with both intelligence and memory. "Actually, she's been on my mind lately," Miles said, adding, "I have no idea why." Though he did know. It was the Vineyard that had done it, just as it did every summer.

Outside, the rain had begun again, steadier now beneath the low sky. Miles pushed his empty coffee cup toward the center of the table.

"Well, it doesn't look like I'm painting anything today," he said, sliding out of the booth. Somehow the plate of cookies was empty, and Miles could feel the last of them lodged uncomfortably in his gullet.

Together, the two men went out onto the porch, where they stood listening to the rain.

"How many more days do you have on the north face?" Father Mark asked, contemplating the church.

"A couple," Miles said. "Maybe tomorrow and the next day if the weather clears."

"You really should stop right there," Father Mark advised. "I've been hearing more rumblings from the diocese. We may be out of business before long. I suspect poor Tom's the only thing that's saved us until now."

For more than a year now, rumors had persisted that St. Catherine's Parish would be combined with Sacred Heart, on the other side of town. Empire Falls, once sufficiently endowed with Catholics to support both, had been losing religious enthusiasm along with its population. Now the only reason for two parishes was simply that Sacré Coeur, as Sacred Heart was still known to most of its French Canadian parishioners, required a French-speaking pastor. Otherwise, the parishes could've been combined years ago. Father Mark suspected that Sacré Coeur would be the survivor and that he would be shipped elsewhere. He didn't speak French, whereas Father Tibideaux was bilingual.

What hadn't been resolved was what to do with Father Tom. While there were homes for elderly, retired priests, especially for those in ill health, his dementia, which vacillated between the obscene and the downright blasphemous, made the diocese cautious about placing him among elderly but otherwise normal clergymen, most of whom had served too long and too well to have their faith tested further in their final years by a senile old man whose favorite word was "peckerhead." Besides, Father Mark was able to handle the old priest, who had lived in St. Cat's rectory for forty years and was comfortable there. In a sense it *was* his house, just as he maintained. Also, there were words worse than "peckerhead," and if the diocese tried moving Father Tom he might start using them. Hearing him carry on had already converted several of St. Catherine's Catholics, some to Episcopalianism, a few others to fearful agnosticism, and the bishop didn't want to risk his contaminating other priests. No, the diocese seemed to believe that they had the Father Tom situation under control, and until recently they'd shown no inclination to break containment.

"Have you gotten any sense of where you might be assigned?" Miles asked.

"Not really," Father Mark said. "I suspect they're not through punishing me, though." He had a doctorate in Judaism, and the perfect position for him would be at the Newman Center of a college or university. That was the sort of post he'd held in Massachusetts before he made the mistake of joining a group of protesters who climbed the fence of a New Hampshire military installation and got arrested for whacking away at the impervious shell of a nuclear sub with ball peen hammers—an act that Father Mark had considered symbolic but that the base commander, a literalist, had interpreted as an act of sabotage and treason. Not that this protest had been Father Mark's only offense. In addition to teaching and pastoring at the university's Newman Center, Father Mark had also hosted a Sunday evening radio show, during which he had drawn his bishop's ire by counseling loving monogamy for a young male caller "regardless of the boy's sexual orientation" and further advising him to trust God's infinite understanding and mercy. Apparently, what happened to young, overeducated, rumored-to-be-gay priests who'd landed cushy campus gigs and doled out liberal advice was that they got packed off to Empire Falls, Maine, probably in hopes that God would freeze their errant peckers off.

"I hope they don't have any worse duty in mind for you," Miles said, trying to imagine what such a thing might be.

Father Mark shrugged, studying the half-painted church. "They can't really hurt you unless you let them. I certainly don't regret coming to Saint Cat's. She's been a good old gal. And I wouldn't have missed out on our friendship."

"I know," Miles said. "Me neither." Then, after a moment, "I wonder what will become of her?"

"Hard to say. Some of these beautiful old churches are being bought up and renovated into community theaters, art centers, things like that."

"I don't think that would work here," Miles said. "Empire Falls has even less interest in art than religion."

"Still, you'd better quit when you finish the north face. You could be painting Empire Falls's next Baptist church."

THE HOUSE HE GREW UP IN on Long Street had been on the market for more than a year, and Miles was parked across the street, trying to imagine what sort of person would purchase it in its present condition. The side porch, dangerous with rot even when he was a boy, had been removed but not replaced; visible evidence of where it had been wrenched away remained in four ugly, unpainted scars. Anybody who left the house by the back door, the only one Miles had ever used, would now be greeted by a six-foot drop into a patch of poisonous-looking weeds and rusted hubcaps. The rest of the structure was gray with age and neglect, its front porch sloping crazily in several different directions, as if the house had been built on a fissure. Even the FOR SALE sign on the terrace tilted.

Several different families had rented the house since his mother's death, none of them, apparently, interested in preventing or even fore-stalling its decline. Of course, to be fair, Miles had to admit that the decline had begun under the Robys' own stewardship. On what had once been a tidy, middle-class street, theirs and the Minty place next door were the first houses to prefigure the deterioration of the whole neighborhood. Miles's father, though a sometime house painter, had been disinclined to paint any house he himself happened to be living in. Summers he was busy working on the coast, and by October he would pronounce himself "all painted out," though he sometimes could be induced to work for a week or so if the landlord—with whom they had a reduced-rent arrangement contingent upon Max's keeping the house painted and in good repair—complained or threatened evic-tion. Resentful of such a strict literal interpretation of their agreement, Max retaliated by painting the house half a dozen different, largely incompatible colors from the numerous leftover, half-empty cans he'd appropriated from his various summer jobs. The Roby cellar was always full of stacked gallon cans, their lids slightly askew, the damp, rotting shelves full of open mason jars of turpentine, the fumes from which permeated the upstairs throughout the winter. Miles was in fourth grade when one of his friends asked what it was like to live in the joke house, a remark he passed along not to his father, who was respon-sible for its harlequin appearance, but to his mother, who first flushed crimson, then looked as if she might burst into tears, then ran into her bedroom, slammed the door and did. Later, red-eyed, she explained to Miles that what was on the inside of a house (love, she seemed to have in mind) was more important than what was on the outside (paint, preferably in one hue), but after Miles went to bed he heard his parents arguing, and after that night Max never painted the house again. Now its motley color scheme had weathered into uniform gray.

Miles hadn't been parked across the street for more than a minute, staring up at the dark, shadeless window of the room where his mother had begun her death march, before a police car wheeled around the corner two blocks up Long and came toward him, swerving across the street and rocking to a halt so close that its bumper was mere inches from the Jetta's own grill. A young policeman was at the wheel, one Miles didn't recognize, and when he got out of the cruiser, putting on sunglasses that the gloomy sky didn't warrant, Miles rolled down his window.

"License and registration," the young cop said.

"Is there a problem, officer?"

"License and registration," the cop repeated, his tone a little harder this time.

Miles fished the registration out of the glove box and handed it out the window along with his license. The policeman attached both to the top of his clipboard and made a couple notes.

"You mind telling me what you're doing here, Mr. Roby?"

"Yes, I do," said Miles, who would have been reluctant to even if he'd had an explanation that made any sense. That a demented priest had called his mother a whore, thereby compelling him to visit the house he'd grown up in, as if his mother, dead these twenty years, might be rocking on the porch, did not strike Miles as the sort of story that would satisfy a man who felt compelled to wear sunglasses on dark, rainy afternoons.

"Why's that, Mr. Roby?"

To Miles, this didn't sound like a serious question, so he didn't answer it.

The young policeman scratched some more on his form. "Maybe you didn't hear the question?" he finally said.

"Have I done something illegal?"

Now it was the cop's turn to fall silent. For a full minute he ignored Miles, apparently to prove that he too could play this silence game. "Are you aware that you're driving an unregistered vehicle, Mr. Roby?"

"I believe you have the registration in your hand."

"Expired last month."

"I'll have to take care of it."

The cop didn't register this remark, instead pointing at the inspection sticker on the windshield. "Your inspection's also past due."

"I guess I'll have to take care of that, too."

No opinion on this either. "So what are you doing here, Mr. Roby?" the officer said, as if he were asking this question for the first time.

"I used to live in that house," Miles said, indicating which one.

"Used to. But not now."

"That's right."

Miles then caught a glimpse of something red in his rearview mirror and turned in time to see Jimmy Minty's red Camaro pulling up behind him. Jimmy, who'd grown up next door, was about the last person Miles would have wanted to catch him parked just here. When Jimmy rolled down his window, the young cop abruptly walked back to the Camaro. Miles watched their conversation in the mirror, smiling when the officer took off his dark glasses. In such situations, apparently only the ranking officer got to keep his glasses on. The conversation was short, then Jimmy Minty did a U-turn and headed back down the street in the direction he'd come from. The young officer, clearly disappointed, watched him go, then returned to Miles and handed back his license and registration. "Might be a good idea to take care of these today," he said, the confrontational edge gone from his voice now.

"You're not citing me?"

"Not unless you think I should, Mr. Roby."

Miles put the license back in his wallet, the registration back in the glove compartment.

Now that they were pals, the cop seemed anxious that there should be no hard feelings. "You lived in that house there?"

Miles nodded, slipping the Jetta in gear.

"Huh," the young cop said. "Looks haunted."

THE MOTOR VEHICLES DIVISION office was being run out of the Whiting mansion, or rather "the Cottage," a large outbuilding nestled in a grove of trees behind the main house. This arrangement was only temporary, until renovations at the courthouse, whose domed roof had partially collapsed after last winter's ice storm, were completed. Since then, justice—never swift in Empire Falls—had ground to a virtual halt. Except for traffic court, most legal matters were being processed out of nearby Fairhaven, whose docket had grown so crowded with the legal business of both towns that everything from building permits to property disputes to small claims to assessments was backed up for months. Even the simplest legal transactions, like Miles's uncontested divorce, seemed endlessly bogged down. Since he hadn't wanted the divorce to begin with, he wasn't terribly troubled. In fact, last spring he'd hoped the holdup might cause Janine to reconsider, though by now he knew that she was determined to marry the Silver Fox, and that somehow she held this legal delay, which had ruined her plans for a summer wedding, against Miles. So determined was she to marry Walt Comeau the moment her divorce became final that Miles had begun to suspect that in some part of her brain, the workings of which still mystified him, Janine realized that this second marriage was some pure folly she needed to commit quickly, lest she come to her senses first.

Miles parked in the small lot between the main house, now headquarters of the Dexter County Museum and Historical Society, and the cottage, which housed, in addition to the temporary DMV, the permanent offices of the Empire Falls Planning and Development Commission, which over the last decade had become something of a joke, since no one had developed anything in Empire Falls during that period, nor was anyone planning to. Mrs. Whiting, as director of the board, kept an office there, however, and when Miles saw her Lincoln parked in the lot, he hurried across the lawn, head down, in the hope that she wouldn't spy him out her window. He'd been avoiding "the State of the Grill" since his return from vacation, and despite the restaurant's improved business, he was even more reluctant than usual to spend an afternoon going over receipts and making projections.

Safely inside, he joined a short line and awaited his turn at a window marked AUTO REG. The entire mahogany counter, he realized, had been transported from the courthouse, and would no doubt be ferried back again. The other furnishings, including the paintings and photographs of Whiting males that decorated the walls, all belonged to the museum collection. Miles studied these men while he waited. For direct lineal descendants they didn't look all that much alike except, Miles decided, for one feature. Even as young men, they appeared prematurely old, or maybe just distinguished, their hair white, their brows chiseled in cogitation. Or perhaps they were reflecting with satisfaction that the history of Empire Falls, indeed of Dexter County, was little more than the history of their own family.

After a few minutes, he noticed Jimmy Minty's red Camaro pull into the lot. Leaving the car idling, the police officer got out and came toward the cottage, angling off the walkway that led to Motor Vehicles and proceeding across the lawn to the back of the building. Miles followed his progress until a man behind him in line tapped him on the shoulder and pointed out that it was his turn. At the window he wrote out the check for his new tags and slipped it through the opening. When the woman on the other side of the glass smiled and said, "Hello, Miles," he recognized her as a girl he'd gone to high school with. Marcia, according to her name tag. Which was more likely, he wondered, that he and Marcia should have lived so long in such a small town without running into each other, or that he and Jimmy Minty would cross paths twice in half an hour?

"You keep this car another year or two and we'll have to pay *you* to register it," the clerk observed when she saw the amount of the check he'd written out.

"That would be fine with me, Marcia," Miles told her, hoping she'd conclude that he'd remembered her name across the long span of years.

"Here's your new chickadee plates," she said, pushing a pair through the opening.

"What was wrong with the lobster ones?"

"People from out of state made fun of them. Said the lobsters looked like cockroaches."

Miles studied the new plates, which didn't strike him as much of an improvement, though the lobsters *had* looked like cockroaches. "I hope this doesn't mean we have to start eating chickadees."

"It may come to that, if things don't start looking up," she said. "I hear there might be a buyer for the mill, though."

Miles considered asking where she'd heard this. After all, the Planning and Development Commission office was only a few feet away, so it was possible she might have overheard something genuine. More likely, however, was that she'd overheard somebody standing in this very line, somebody who'd had coffee that morning at the Empire Grill.

Through another window Jimmy Minty could now be seen standing on the doorstep of the Empire Falls Planning and Development Commission office, conversing with someone who, because of the angle, wasn't visible, though Miles immediately concluded that it had to be Mrs. Whiting. The policeman's body language told the story; he was listening with much the same attitude as the younger policeman had listened to *him* half an hour earlier, and this time it was Minty who removed his dark glasses. Miles watched as he nodded once, twice, three times, apparently at specific instructions. Was it Miles's imagination, or did Minty glance quickly into the Motor Vehicles office and then away again, as if he'd been told not to?

"Don't you think?" Marcia was saying.

"I'm sorry," Miles said, returning his attention to her. "Don't I think what?"

"I said it's about time our luck changed around here."

"It sure is," Miles agreed. Assuming it's luck that's the problem, of course. Which he privately doubted. The problem with trying to gauge mathematical probability was that it presupposed the circumstance you were observing was governed by chance.

Outside, Jimmy Minty nodded one last time before recrossing the lawn to his idling Camaro and pulling back out onto Empire Avenue. Miles waited until he'd turned the corner before tucking his new license plates under his arm and heading for the door. Before he could complete his escape, though, Marcia's phone rang and he heard her say, "Yes, it is," and then call his name. He thought he might just keep going, pretending not to hear. Then he thought again.

MRS. WHITING was on the phone when he knocked and entered, but she acknowledged his presence by pointing to a chair. Miles, however, was reluctant to sit down before scanning the room for the old woman's frequent companion, a vicious black cat named Timmy. Miles was allergic to cats in general and Mrs. Whiting's in particular. It was a rare encounter between the two that didn't leave Miles striped and puffy.

Mrs. Whiting smiled and put her hand over the phone. "You can relax," she assured him. "I left Timmy at home."

"Are you sure?" Miles wondered, still far from at ease. The cat in question, in Miles's opinion, possessed many borderline supernatural abilities, including a talent for materializing at will.

"That's hilarious, dear boy," she replied, then resumed her conversation on the phone. Their twenty-year relationship, Miles often thought, could be summed up in those four words. From the beginning, when Miles and her daughter, Cindy, were in high school together, Mrs. Whiting had referred to him as "dear boy," though Miles doubted he was particularly dear to her. And she was forever pronouncing things he said "hilarious," despite a demeanor that suggested she didn't find them even remotely funny.

The Planning and Development Commission office, which Miles had never entered before, was large, and along one whole wall sat a scale model of downtown Empire Falls, so obviously idealized that he didn't immediately recognize it as the town he'd lived his whole life in. The streets were lined with bright green toy trees, and the buildings so brightly painted, the streets so clean, that Miles's first thought was that this was an artist's notion of what a future Empire Falls might look like after an ambitious and costly revitalization project. Only closer inspection revealed that the model represented not the future but the past. This, Miles realized, was the Empire Falls of his own childhood, and he noticed several businesses along Empire Avenue that had been razed over the last two decades, leaving in real life a rash of excess parking lots. The Empire Grill, neglected in real life, in miniature looked as if Mrs. Whiting had given Miles every penny he'd ever asked for.

A small silver plate on the base read: "EMPIRE FALLS, CIRCA 1959." The actual town, of course, had never looked quite so prosperous. Even in 1959 the brick walls of the textile mill and the shirt factory—bright red on the model—had gone rust brown, even black in some places, with weather and soot. And the river that ran past them on the model had been rendered sky blue. Now *that's* hilarious, Miles thought. Surely the only time in the last hundred years that the Knox had run blue was when the textile mill was dumping blue dye into it. Even more hilarious was the idea that such a nostalgic past should have found a home in the town's planning and development office. Evidently the commission's plan was to turn back the clock.

Elijah Whiting, whose stern portrait overlooked the model, failed to see the humor in any of this. Like the Whitings in the other room, old Elijah wore a grim expression, and he had the same weakness about the mouth. They all reminded Miles of someone, though he couldn't imagine who.

When Mrs. Whiting said good-bye and hung up, she did it so perfunctorily that Miles couldn't help wondering whether she'd really been on the phone or was just using the pretense to study him. Around her, this feeling of being scrutinized was not unusual. She now rotated in her chair, leaned back and regarded Elijah Whiting. "They were all mad as hatters, you know. In one way or another. You can see it lurking behind the eyes, if you look."

Miles did look, though he didn't see what he was supposed to. There was a quality of zealousness perhaps, of bigotry maybe, but not of insanity.

"You probably heard the stories about this distinguished ancestor when you were a boy?"

"I don't think so."

"He's said to have chased his wife around this very room with a shovel, intent on bashing in her skull."

"Surely nothing like that ever happened *here*," Miles said, indicating the model, in which only the Whiting estate didn't look different in quality from its appearance in real life. It suddenly occurred to Miles that Mrs. Whiting herself must have commissioned it. By idealizing the rest of the town, she had successfully obscured the truth—that its wealth and vitality had been bled dry by the generations of a single family. A cynical interpretation, perhaps, but it also explained why the house C. B. Whiting had built across the river was not represented on the model at all. Across the Iron Bridge was virgin wilderness, all lush trees and rolling hills.

"Seeing you standing there gives me an inspiration," the old woman said, though Miles doubted, even before she continued, that her sudden intuition would be anything like his own. "You should be mayor."

"Of the model?" Miles smiled. "I could just about afford that." Being mayor of Empire Falls was a full-time job with a part-time salary, though it was often remarked that past mayors had found ways to supplement their income.

"You're too modest, dear boy. I've often thought you should run for political office."

Miles decided not to remind her that he'd run for school board twice and been elected.

"Are you offering me the job?"

"You overestimate the extent of my influence, dear boy." She smiled. "You're rather like your mother in that respect. But then, people are forever confusing will with power, don't you find? I have a theory about why, if you're interested."

"Why I'm like my mother," Miles asked, finally taking his seat, "or why people confuse will with power?"

"The latter," she said. "After all, there's nothing very mysterious about why you take after your mother, is there. Your father isn't exactly the sort of man who inspires imitation. No, people confuse power with will because so few of them have the foggiest idea what they want. Absent any knowledge, will remains impotent. A limp dick, as it were." She regarded him, eyebrow arched. "The lucky few who happen actually to know what they want are said to have will-*power*."

"That's all it takes?"

"Well, let's call it a necessary beginning."

Miles allowed himself to settle into his chair. More than anyone he knew, Mrs. Whiting had the ability to draw him into conversations he otherwise would have avoided. The reason seemed to be that her conclusions were invariably antithetical to his own. "So you think human beings are meant to know what they want?"

Mrs. Whiting sighed. "That word 'meant' suggests you're up to your old tricks, dear boy, casting everything in a religious light. That won't do if you intend to be mayor."

"I don't," he pointed out. "Certainly not of Empire Falls in 1959."

"But that's where you're foolish, dear boy. Most Americans *want* it to be 1959, with the addition of cappuccino and cable TV."

"That's what they want, or what they *think* they want?" The person he was thinking of was Janine. His soon-to-be-ex-wife was never uncertain about what she wanted, just disappointed by its eventual acquisition. Miles himself had been an example. The Silver Fox, though he didn't yet suspect it, would be another.

"That's not a particularly helpful distinction, is it? What is wanting but thinking? But for the sake of argument, let's accept your terms and begin at the beginning. Adam and Eve. They knew what *they* wanted, did they not?"

"I doubt it," Miles said, also for the sake of argument. "Until it was forbidden."

"Precisely, dear boy. But once it was forbidden, they suffered no such doubts—am I correct?"

"No. Just regrets."

"Do you imagine that refusing the forbidden fruit would've made them happier? Would *that* have eliminated regret or merely redefined it?"

She had a point. "I guess we'll never know."

"*I* certainly won't, dear boy, but like our progenitors, I've not resisted many temptations. *You*, on the other hand . . ." She dangled the thought. Mrs. Whiting had never made any secret that she considered Miles a case study in repression. "Did you have a nice vacation?"

"Wonderful," he said, eager for the old woman to understand that fine times could be had by others.

Mrs. Whiting studied him carefully, as if suspicious that his enthusiasm masked a falsehood. "You return there every summer, don't you."

"Just about."

"Has it occurred to you to wonder why?"

"No," he told her. When not insinuating that he was repressed, the old woman liked to imply that despite his intelligence, his views were parochial, the result of his having traveled and seen so little. Like many rich people, she seemed not to understand why the poor didn't think to winter in Capri, where the weather was more clement. Nor did it strike her as unfair to suggest as much to a man who for twenty years had tended one of her businesses while *she* traveled. "I've got friends who have a house there," he continued, leaving unsaid what Mrs. Whiting no doubt understood perfectly well—that only charity made even so modest a vacation possible.

Actually, it was Miles who had introduced Peter and Dawn to the Vineyard all those years ago, during college. They'd all been poor then, and when they pooled their resources that fall they'd had just about enough to pay for the ferry crossing. They'd slept on the beach, illegally, beneath the cliffs at Gay Head, confident that after Labor Day they wouldn't be rousted by the island police, who probably numbered no more than half a dozen. It was during this weekend on the island, Miles suspected, that Peter and Dawn had fallen in love, first with the island and then with each other. Since then they'd considered Miles instrumental to their happiness and were grateful to him for it. Even if their affection for each other had begun to wear thin, as he feared, clearly they both still loved the Vineyard. He couldn't imagine either one of them conceding the house in a divorce settlement.

"Yes, well, that makes sense," Mrs. Whiting grudgingly acknowledged. "And yet—"

"And yet what?"

She appeared to lose her train of thought, but only momentarily. "And yet 'we beat on, boats against the current, borne back ceaselessly into the past.'" The old woman was smiling at him knowingly, and Miles, who recognized the final line of *The Great Gatsby*, felt an intense obligation to reveal neither this nor the slightest curiosity about her intention.

When the phone rang, both were visibly relieved. Mrs. Whiting picked up the receiver and waved good-bye in one efficient motion, dismissing Miles without further ceremony.

A hell of a way, Miles thought, to treat someone you'd just encouraged to run for mayor.

[CHAPTER 3]

WHEN JANINE FINISHED her last aerobics class, she showered quickly and drove over to the Empire Grill, circling the block to make sure Miles wasn't there. Even though the divorce was dragging on forever, the whole thing had been amicable enough. In fact, she'd liked Miles better these last nine months since they'd decided to separate than at any time in the previous twenty years. Still, she had no desire to see him right now, especially not in the company of her fiancé. It was genuinely weird the way Walt had begun hanging out at the grill, a place he'd totally avoided when they were sneaking around.

Pulling in and parking next to Walt's van, she made a point of not looking at the stenciled logo, not wanting to admit that it was beginning to irritate her. THE SILVER FOX. What sort of man would write that on his car? For Janine this question was neither idle nor rhetorical. She was going to marry Walt Comeau as soon as the divorce was final, and part of her wanted to know the answer to that question before she became half owner of the vehicle and sole owner of the driver.

Then again, some questions were better left unanswered. She knew Walt pretty well, certainly better than she'd known Miles. Back when they got married, she hadn't even known who *she* was, her own self, never mind her intended. At least now Janine knew who Janine was, what Janine wanted, and, just as important, what Janine didn't want. She didn't want Miles, or anyone who reminded her of Miles. She didn't want to be fat anymore, either. Never, ever, again. Also, she wanted a real sex life, and she wanted to act young for a change, something she hadn't been able to do when she actually was young. She wanted to dance and have men look at her. She liked the way her body felt after dropping all that weight, and by God she liked to come. For Janine, at forty, orgasms were a new thing and she damn near lost her mind every time she had another, or when she contemplated how close she'd come to going her whole life without experiencing that singular, incomparable, tingling, explosive, mind-bending thrill. The first one had so caught her by surprise that at the height of the wave she went someplace very far away, then returned, sobbing in Walt's arms, having concluded she'd never get to go there again, though he assured her she would and then made sure that she did. Damn, she remembered thinking. I mean, *DAMN*.

It was Walt Comeau who'd taught her about herself and her body's needs, though she was beginning to realize that even Walt's views on the matter were oversimplified. To his way of thinking, what her body needed was lots of exercise and lots of Walt. Janine herself was wondering if her body might not benefit from a little travel. She didn't mind working out at Walt's own club, but she'd read somewhere about a spa out in the desert near Tucson, Arizona, that specialized in women's bodies. "Luxurious" was the word the brochure used, and now that Janine was beginning to feel luxurious about her body she thought she deserved a week or two at a place like that. It was expensive, sure, but Walt was always going on about all his money, and she kept hoping to talk him into honeymooning there. And once Tick graduated from high school, what would prevent them from relocating to a warmer climate? After living in Maine all her life, it'd be nice to be someplace where the sun came out and stayed out. Walt was always talking about opening up a new health club, so why not Sedona or Santa Fe? If what she heard was true, the desert Southwest was like California. People kept fit and healthy and wore bathing suits that were basically symbolic of clothing. If Walt didn't want to at least check it out, Janine wouldn't mind going by herself for a week. She'd liked the look of the Latino masseurs in the brochure. Which seemed a little ungrateful, she had to admit. After all, Walt had been the one who woke her up, who helped her locate herself, the person she really was. And he also located that wonderful spot, found it right away, the one Miles never suspected the existence of. Now here she was thinking about Latino masseurs.

If only he just hadn't stenciled those stupid words on the side of the van, Janine thought as she got out of her Blazer. Probably "stupid" wasn't the right spin. They weren't stupid so much as boastful, she decided, heading for the front door of the restaurant. Besides, wasn't it Walt's cockiness that had attracted her in the first place? The fact that he was so different from Miles, who was so docile? Her mother, of course, still loved Miles and sided with him on all occasions, referring to Walt as "that little banty rooster." "Miles is modest for good reason, Ma, believe me," she assured her mother. A mean thing to say, maybe, but true, and it hinted at what there was no way to discuss with Bea— the whole sex thing. Her mother, Janine felt certain, was one of those poor women who'd managed to do what Janine herself had damn near done. She'd lived her entire adult life from one end to the other without a single orgasm. When Bea died, it would be possible to say truthfully that she went before she came. Not Janine. If she'd been the sort of person to stencil anything on the side of a van, it'd be something more like, SHE CAME BEFORE SHE WENT. Which meant, she supposed, that she and Walt Comeau were made for each other, and she ought to quit thinking about the strong hands of Latino masseurs.

"Hey, babe," she said, sliding onto a stool next to the man she'd be married to next month, if her idiot lawyer was to be believed. Unless the roof of the Fairhaven courthouse fell in too, which wouldn't surprise Janine one bit, not the way everything had been conspiring against her right from the start, when she made the mistake of telling that priest with the Alzheimer's all about herself and Walt, figuring he'd forgive her and then forget all about it. Everyone said he couldn't remember twice around, which was why they'd finally had to hire the younger priest. Except that this time the old guy remembered three or four times around. He told Miles everything she'd said in the confessional and then, forgetting he'd told him, told him again the next day.

Still, now that it was almost over, Janine figured it was probably just as well the old nitwit had squealed on her. At the time she'd been confused about what she wanted, or else she wouldn't have gone to a priest at all. Once everything was out in the open, it occurred to her that what she wanted was Walt and for the two of them to make up for all the sex she'd been cheated out of. If that meant everybody thought she was a slut, including her daughter and her own mother, then they could just think whatever they wanted. In a sense it was good she and Walt got caught, because if they hadn't, Walt, being a man, probably would've been just as happy to keep on with the hanky-panky. It was Janine who hadn't liked all the sneaking around, and getting caught had at least set the legal ball rolling, which was something. Keeping it rolling had required all her energy, except for what she kept in reserve for sex and the Stairmaster. The last nine months had proved one thing beyond a shadow of a doubt: you can't beat city hall the same year its roof falls in.

Walt was intently playing gin with Horace, so he didn't notice when she came in. Another thing that was beginning to bother Janine was the way Walt knitted his brow over anything that taxed his intellect. Quite a lot did, Janine had to admit, so she had plenty of opportunity to study her least favorite expression. Walt was wearing it now as he looked up from his hand to study his opponent, as if the solution to whatever perplexed him might scroll across Horace's broad forehead, disgusting cyst and all. At moments like this, his brow tightly knit, his eyes narrowed, Walt Comeau always looked like he was trying to figure out not how his opponent happened to be winning so much as how he was cheating, and Janine wondered if this sly, distrustful expression might be responsible for his nickname. Certainly it always made Janine want to take him aside and explain exactly how he was being cheated. "He's smarter than you, Walt," she'd have liked to tell him. "He's cheating you by remembering what cards you've played and what cards he's played. That's how he knows what's left in the deck. He pays attention to what you're doing, and to what it means. It's not a damn marked deck, and he doesn't have an accomplice, and there's no mirror behind you reflecting your cards. He's just smarter than you. It might not be fair, but he is."

Miles, bad as *he* was, had been a far better card partner. He had no poker face at all, and he couldn't help looking surprised when Lady Luck smiled on him and disappointed when she didn't, but at least he was more often a step ahead of the game than a step behind, like the Silver Fox. To Janine, one of life's crueler ironies was that Miles, who often could locate the Queen of Spades two tricks into a game of hearts, hadn't been able to find her spot in twenty years of marriage.

Janine counted Mississippis and got to ten before Walt decided what to discard, which ginned Horace nicely. Walt, ever curious, turned over the card Horace had laid facedown, groaning when he saw what it was. "You lucky bastard," he said. "That was *my* damn gin card."

"I knew that, Mr. Comeau," Horace explained, totaling up the points he'd caught Walt with. "Why do you suppose I wouldn't give it to you?"

Thus released from his torment, Walt rotated on his stool and took in the woman who would soon be his wife, breaking into a wide grin.

This, Janine realized as Walt looked her over, was why she was marrying the man. He might be a beat slow—all right, several beats slow—but damn if he wasn't always glad to see her. He always drank her in with what seemed to be fresh eyes, and she didn't really care if the reason for this might be short-term memory deficiency. Walt's appreciation made her glow inside, opening her up, allowing her spot to unfold like the soft petals of a flower so obviously that even Miles could have found it, not that he'd ever have the opportunity again. "Hey, goodlookin'," Walt said. "Good thing Big Boy isn't here. He'd commit harikari seeing how good you look."

Having given voice to this pleasantly dark thought, Walt turned to Horace for a second opinion. "How'd you like to go through the rest of your life knowing you had a woman this beautiful and lost her?"

Horace was either still totaling up their score on his notepad or pretending to, forcing Walt to rotate back on his stool. "Let me guess," he said. "One twenty-two."

Well, sure, okay. Here was another thing that irritated Janine, this constant public guessing game about her weight. Not that she wasn't proud of having dropped the fifty pounds. And she knew, too, that Walt did it because he was proud of her. Still, it reminded her a little of that midway trick back when she was a girl, the booth where they guessed people's weights. "One twenty-three." Pleased in spite of herself, she grinned at him. "But can we *not* have this conversation in public?"

"One twenty-*three*?" Walt bellowed. "I'm going to get that scale in the women's locker room checked out." Again he rotated on his stool and nudged Horace. "How about it, though? One twenty-three. Guess how much she weighed when we met."

"I'd be *real* careful," Janine advised Horace, who looked like he didn't need to be warned.

"Don't be like that," Walt said. "You should be proud." Then, rotating back to Horace, "Mid one-eighties."

"You want anything, Janine?" David called over his shoulder from where he was browning a roast. Without, of course, actually looking at her.

"No, I'm fine," she told him. "Tick almost done back there?"

"Pretty close." Still not looking up from his work, the prick.

"Tell her I'm here, okay?"

"She knows you're here."

The implication being what—that the kid could smell it when she came in? Or that Janine's appearance altered the whole atmosphere?

"Can you believe this woman?" Walt now asked. "No, I sure wouldn't want to be that brother of yours, knowing I let a woman this good-looking get away from me."

"She's a beauty, all right," David agreed.

"Hear that?" Walt said, nuzzling Janine's neck. "Everybody says the same thing."

Janine had heard what her brother-in-law said—heard it a lot clearer than the Silver Fox had, and she leaned away from his cold nose. At home she might've enjoyed the affection, but not here, especially with people making sarcastic remarks. To show David who was boss, she got up and went around the counter to the register, hit No Sale, and the drawer flew open.

"I'm changing a fifty here, David," she called. "That all right with you? Since I'm a former employee and all-around beauty queen?"

"If it's all right with Miles," he said. "I just work here."

Which pissed her off even more. "You can come over and watch if you want."

Charlene stepped up just then, snatched the fifty, and quickly made change out of the drawer, then slammed it by way of punctuation. "How you doin', Janine?"

"Just fine, Charl." She wadded up the bills and stuffed them in her purse, feeling robbed of some vague satisfaction. She hadn't needed change for the fifty to begin with. The good news, she thought, watching Charlene arranging tables for tonight's private party, was that, at forty-five, Charlene was finally showing her age. Since her operation she looked tired, and a little fan of lines had appeared at the corners of her eyes and was deepening there. By the look of her, she'd also put on about ten pounds, which made Janine wonder how much longer her soon-to-be-ex-husband would continue mooning over her. That would be a hard habit for him to break, having been at it his entire married life. In matters of the heart, Miles was even more transparent than when he was playing cards. When it came to what he was holding close to his vest, he'd just hang on to it, tight as grim death, and deny it was there, no matter how hard you tried to pry it out of him.

When Charlene finished rearranging tables, Janine couldn't help but smile. Another year or two and that's going to be one fat ass, lady, she thought. Drape it with a sheet and show home movies. This last weekend, Janine had noticed, the college boys returning for the fall semester hadn't been quite as flirtatious, and this year they actually seemed more interested in their own dates than in peeking down Charlene's shirt. Next year, even the salesmen who pushed dollies full of canned goods into the back, calling out mock invitations for her to join them in the walk-in cooler for a minute, would stop treating her like she was sex on the hoof. And then that would leave just Miles in love with her—and not really her, either, but the woman she was before she wore out, the woman he still believed her to be, against the testimony of his own eyes.

There, Janine thought. Now I've thoroughly depressed myself. Because the truth was, she liked Charlene, who'd had four bad marriages and her own share of heartache, and never once during the years that Janine and Miles were married had she encouraged his crush, any more than she encouraged the college boys. It was her body that drew them, and she couldn't help that. While it was pleasurable to consider that Janine was winning her own body war at about the same rate that Charlene was losing hers, Janine was too smart not to see the end of all this, which was that they would both lose. The competition for the love and admiration of men like Walt and Miles would be passed like a torch to some other girl, some kid, really, who'd look at Janine and Charlene and never even suspect that they'd been there and done that. The sad, fucking truth was that no matter who you are, you never, ever, will get your fill.

In full possession of this wisdom, Janine slipped her left hand beneath the counter and into the front trouser pocket of the Silver Fox, who smiled slyly and slowly rose to the occasion. That Walt was fifty *did* worry her a little. She was getting started late, orgasm-wise, and it'd be just her luck for Walt to shut down early. He wasn't exactly leaping to attention at the moment, but he was getting there.

Down at the other end of the restaurant there was a table full of young women from the Dexter County Academy of Hair Design who came in most afternoons a few minutes before closing and hunkered down in the far booth, chattering and whispering and eating pie. Studying these girls, she wondered if one of them might be the next Charlene, the next Janine. A couple were almost pretty if you imagined them without the big hair and the extra pounds that already, in their early twenties, were weighing them down. No, maybe Janine's days, like Charlene's, were numbered, but at least there didn't seem to be much competition on the immediate horizon, which meant that for a while she'd have the field, such as it was, to herself.

Janine was smiling when the door to the kitchen swung open and her daughter appeared, announcing that she was ready to go home.

Walt, apparently forgetting there was a friendly hand in his front trouser pocket, damn near leapt off his stool, twisting Janine's wrist in the process. "*There* she is," he cried, ignoring his fiancée's distress. "There's our little beauty."

CHAPTER 4

IN ART CLASS, the five long, rectangular tables are all color-coded, seven or eight students at each, and Tick has been assigned to Blue. Mrs. Roderigue, the art teacher, is a large woman with a massive shelf of a bosom, of which she appears to have no knowledge. When she enters the classroom and one of the boys says, all too audibly, "Bah-zooooom!," she never seems to connect her own appearance with this too predictable utterance. Though Mrs. Roderigue is about Tick's father's age, she seems older, perhaps because she wears her hair in a style that Tick associates only with elderly women.

As a teacher, what Mrs. Roderigue prides herself most on is her organization. "There are forty of you," she told the class after they were all seated that first day, "and so it will be imperative that we *get* organized and *stay* organized." Normally classes are not allowed to grow so large, but an exception is made for art—unspoken acknowledgment, Tick suspects, that nobody considers art to be a real course, like history or math. Mrs. Roderigue isn't even full-time, teaching afternoons at the high school, mornings at the middle school, her teaching strategies identical regardless of her audience.

For Tick, the interesting thing about Mrs. Roderigue's color coding is that the tables themselves are all steel gray, so the only way to differentiate Blue from Red that first day was to read the signs—BLUE, GREEN, RED, YELLOW and BROWN, carefully lettered in black ink—taped to each. On the second day all the signs came down and were slipped into plastic baggies before they could be dirtied or wrinkled. Art, she told her students, was the study and practice of order. There was no such thing as Sloppy Art. Artists, she claimed, first had to know where they were, and in Mrs. Roderigue's class the first thing you learned was whether you were Blue or Green and so forth. If you were Blue, you were supposed to remember where Blue was, though *why* Blue was Blue, and not, for instance, a number, like "one" or "two," remained a mystery.

Nonetheless, at the Blue table, Tick sits next to Candace Burke, who favors trendy, girlie clothes—baggy jeans, tight shirts, pink Adidas shoes. Also, white eye shadow and lots of mascara. Today she's wearing her unicorn T-shirt. Either she's got two of these or she washes the one right after she's worn it. She'd worn it the first day of school and now, Thursday, she's wearing it again. "Oh-my-God-oh-my-God!" she exclaims, looking at Tick's painting. "You're almost done. I haven't even started. Help me, okay? What's my most vivid dream?"

"I don't know *any* of your dreams," Tick points out.

Candace shrugs, as if to suggest that that makes two of them, but this problem occupies her for no more than a split second. "So how come you're in here with the morons?" is what she'd really like to know. Though Candace has asked this every day, and been answered too, she either keeps forgetting or else is suspicious of the answers she's been given. Her persistence reminds Tick of a movie she saw once in which a man was interrogated for hours, asked all sorts of things, but one question, in particular, over and over. His answer was always the same, but his questioners must have suspected something, because they kept coming back to that one question. Finally, they killed him— out of frustration, apparently. You never found out whether the man was telling the truth or not.

Candace is openly using an Exacto knife she stole during the first day of class, carving the name of her boyfriend, Bobby, into the back of the wooden chair she's turned around and is sitting in the way older men sometimes do in the Empire Grill. Tick's proximity to this dangerous- looking instrument and the use to which it is being put are making her more than a little nervous, especially when Candace stops carving and gestures with the blade for dramatic emphasis. Tick half expects her to put the knife to her throat and hiss, "Why are you *really* in here with the morons? Who sent you? Tell me the truth or I'll—"

What Candace is trying to reconcile is that Tick is a high-track kid, whereas she herself and all the rest are "Bones," kids who take the lower-track versions of required courses like biology along with guar- anteed GPA boosters like art. One reason Candace has befriended her, Tick suspects, is that she enjoys showing strangers around Bone

World, an academic sphere populated by those who can't learn grammar or solve math problems and see no reason why they should. The majority are boys, who don't at all mind being referred to as "Boners."

Candace herself prefers "moron." She confessed to Tick that it's also her mother's favorite word, one she applies to Candace on a wide variety of occasions, such as, "What's up, Moron?" or "You learn anything in school today, Moron?" or "Hey, Moron, you didn't walk off with my goddamn car keys again, did you?" or "I swear to fucking Christ, Moron, I catch you in the damn liquor cabinet again, I'm going to take you out of where you are and put you in Mount Calvary with the damn Christians, let you drink the Blood of the Lamb for a while and see how well you like that shit, and I can tell you right now you won't, so just stay *out* of my fucking vodka." As far as Tick can tell, Candace has concluded that the word is a term of endearment applied to kids like herself who happen, everyone seems to agree, to have no future.

Still, Tick wonders if she should voice her objection to the "moron" label before explaining why she happens to be among those thus classified. But since Candace doesn't appear to expect this, she decides not to. "I like art," Tick says weakly, just as she has every day this week, aware, as always, that the truth isn't much of a substitute for a good answer.

Tick almost didn't take art because it wouldn't fit into her schedule, being offered only at times when the high-track kids had required courses, like chemistry and calculus, or were at lunch. When Tick proposed that she could take art if she were allowed to eat lunch in the cafeteria during sixth period, the idea was vetoed until her father went with her to see the principal, Mr. Meyer, who pointed out that the cafeteria closed after fifth period. Even if Tick brought a sandwich with her and got a soda out of the machine, she'd have to eat it all by herself in the big, empty cafeteria, which would be locked after she entered, and she'd be on her honor not to let anyone else in, because there would be no monitor.

When Mr. Meyer asked Tick if she could live with these provisos, she wondered, as she so often did, at the strange world adults seemed to inhabit. Did they all suffer from some sort of collective amnesia? You had only to look at Mr. Meyer to know that he'd been the kind of fat kid everybody made fun of and that lunch had surely been a torment to him. He'd either gravitated naturally to the leper table or sat by himself at a table designed for sixteen, a target for all the kids overcrowding the cool tables, the tables that were identified as cool by who had a right to sit at them, codes established the first day of school, the rules clear to everyone, no need for color-coding. You had only to look at Mr. Meyer to know he'd spent all his high school years getting hit in the back of the head with all manner of throwable food, yet here he was worried that Tick was going to miss out on the important "socialization" aspects of a good secondary education. Some damn thing must have hit him in the back of his pointed head pretty hard during one of those lunches, Tick decided, because the man honestly seemed to have no recollection of them.

Therefore, he had no idea how thrilled Tick was at the prospect of eating lunch by herself. She didn't mind in the least waiting until sixth period to eat her sandwich. School twisted her stomach into knots anyhow, and this way at least she wouldn't have to endure the humiliation of not having a place to sit. Which certainly would have been her destiny. She'd broken up with Zack Minty over the summer, meaning she would no longer be welcome at the table dominated by his circle. And she knew better than to try to crash one of the cliques at the popular girls' table. Far better to be alone in an empty cafeteria, Tick thought, than to be alone in a full one.

"Did you know Craig was going to buy me *The Beatles Anthology* for my birthday?" Candace wants to know now. "Before I broke up with him, I mean?"

Tick tries to ignore her. The first assignment is to paint your most vivid dream, and Tick's is the one where she's clutching a snake in her fist. The painting is going pretty well. The snake started out looking like an eel, but now it's less flat, more serpentine, except it's not as scary as the snake in her dream, which, no matter how tight her grip, manages to squirm up to where it can turn and look at her. In the dream she's safe as long as she can hold the snake up near its head, but each time it manages to slither through her grip. When it turns to look at her, she wakes up with a start. From this dream Tick concludes that she's learned something useful: whatever means you harm will look you over first.

"Are you listening to me?" Candace says.

"Who's Craig?" Tick asks, suspecting she's supposed to know, that he's somebody Candace has mentioned before, probably more than once. The good news is that Candace never minds repeating boyfriend stories.

"He's the one I broke up with for Bobby," she explains, preferring this subject to the task of beginning her thumbnail sketch, which she will later be required to transfer to a large piece of paper and then, finally, to paint. It doesn't appear to bother Candace that she's behind everybody in the class. More interesting, it doesn't seem to bother Mrs. Roderigue, either. All week long Tick has been expecting the woman to come around to the Blue table, see that Candace has done exactly nothing, and read her the riot act, but so far she's stayed strictly away, as if she's already determined that Blue is trouble and therefore doesn't exist.

Most teachers, Tick has learned, feel no great compulsion to confront trouble. They're never around when drugs are being bought and sold, for example. The mystery of the Exacto knife stolen after the first art class, its theft announced over the loudspeaker during homeroom, would be solved if Mrs. Roderigue ever visited Blue, where Candace openly uses it on her "Bobby" carving. Tick can't help but wonder if Mrs. Roderigue is as afraid of the knife as she is. Fear, often irrational, of the sort that paralyzes Tick, is something she'd like to think she'll outgrow. Adults, by and large, seem free of it. Even her Uncle David, whose car wreck nearly severed his arm at the elbow, seems almost carefree when he gets behind the wheel. No, most adults are more like her father, whose fear, if he feels any, has been replaced by a kind of melancholy. Her mother's a different story, though. Sometimes Tick sees a fleeting look of panic on Janine's face when she doesn't know she's being observed, but then she swallows hard and subdues whatever it is by sheer force of will. That's a trick Tick would be glad to learn, because dread is her more or less constant companion.

"So, should I wait for my boyfriend," Candace wants to know, "or go back with Craig for a couple weeks?"

Bobby, the one Candace may or may not wait for, is in jail. He was arrested at Fairhaven High, according to Candace, and it was not a righteous bust. Why she thinks this is not clear to Tick. Candace actually seems to believe the cops came for him because he took a dollar from his mother and only paid back seventy-five cents. Supposedly he'll be released in a couple weeks, in time for homecoming. Tick doesn't know how much of what Candace tells her is true. She's not sure, for instance, if the boy is really in jail. Or if he exists at all. Or if the other boy, Craig, ever really promised to buy her *The Beatles Anthology*. Vagaries of this sort make it hard to give good advice.

If she's to be believed, Candace has a very dramatic love life, which is fine with Tick, except that when she has finally exhausted the subject of her own romances she'll want to know about Tick's, which are singularly lacking in drama. Or maybe just singularly lacking. On Martha's Vineyard she'd met a shy boy from Indiana who was visiting friends with his mother while her divorce from the boy's father became final; if Tick were to steal an Exacto knife and carve a boy's name in the back of her chair, the name would be "Donny." When he told her about his father, who was moving to California, his eyes filled with tears. His father was moving right then, that very week, and Donny had been packed off to Martha's Vineyard, he'd confided, so he wouldn't have to watch him leave home. Donny also told her he'd have preferred to live with his dad, even though he was the one at fault, for falling in love with another woman.

Tick told him that this had been pretty much her experience, too; after her parents split up, nobody had asked her who she wanted to live with. Of course, in her case nobody was moving to California, and although she technically was living with her mother, she spent almost as much time with her father. Donny found it hard to believe that Tick's mother and father still lived about three blocks from each other; his father, apparently, had selected San Diego as his new home because it was as far from Indianapolis as you could get without leaving the continental United States. Tick explained that her parents probably just didn't have enough money to put much distance between themselves.

This intimate conversation had taken place on the beach on their last night together, and Donny had taken her hand as they watched the orange sun plunge into the ocean. They hadn't even found the courage to kiss, and early the next morning when they'd said their good-byes, they'd shaken hands there in front of Tick's father and Donny's mother, unsure that anything more would be allowed them, their fingers icy-cold with disappointment.

Anyway, it wasn't much of a story to tell someone like Candace, even if Tick was inclined to share it. She suspects it's mostly evidence of her own stunted emotional and romantic development, as is the fact that she can't seem to stop thinking about how good it was to sit there on the warm sand in the gathering dusk and just hold hands with a boy she liked. Sure, she wishes now that they'd found the courage to kiss, but at the time they'd both been content. Their mutual understanding, even though it was an understanding of grief, had at first been thrilling, then quietly reassuring, though she doubts Candace would see it that way. She's already made several references to going down on Bobby. Tick is almost sure she knows what going down on a boy means, and if she's right, Candace won't be impressed by an encounter that climaxed with hand-holding.

"I mean, Craig's not so bad, and he loves me and everything . . . and he really wants to buy me *The Beatles Anthology*, so, like, what should I do?" Candace wants to know.

Before Tick can say anything, they're interrupted by a boy named Justin who's sitting at the far end of their table.

"What, Candace?" he says, pretending she'd spoken to him. "You say you want to make out with John?"

John Voss, also at the Blue table, never even looks up. Of all the kids at Empire High, he seems to Tick the most unknowable, and for this reason he scares her a little. It isn't so much his strange, thrift-shop clothes or his hair cut in patches, as if he'd done the job himself. It's his silence. So far this week, he hasn't spoken a word. Were he not referred to every now and then by Justin, who pretends to narrate the comatose boy's thoughts, everyone would forget he is even there. John Voss is painting something elaborately filigreed in the shape of an egg, which is also confusing and frightening Tick. Who dreams of eggs? Watching him work makes Tick think of analogies of the sort she encounters on standardized tests. This one would read: *John is to Justin as* BLANK *is to Candace*. The answer would be *Tick*.

"John says you should come over to his house today after school, Candace. He says he's got something he'd like to show you."

"Shut up, you asshole!" Candace shouts, startling Tick. The panic in her voice results, Tick knows, from Justin's attempt to link her romantically with this boy who is at the very bottom of the high school's social hierarchy. Since Candace isn't so far from the bottom herself, she must guard against any misunderstanding of this sort. "I'm sorry, Mrs. Roderigue," she says when everyone from Red, Green, Yellow and Brown turns to look at her, "but Justin is always embarrassing me."

Mrs. Roderigue has indeed straightened up and is now glaring at Blue, as if everyone at the table were equally responsible for Candace's outburst. Her disappointment and displeasure seem to include, for instance, Tick herself and John Voss, who still hasn't even looked up from his egg. "I hope," the teacher intones, "that we will have no more outbursts from the Blue table."

"I *said* I'm sorry," Candace responds audibly, rolling her eyes as if to suggest that it's hard for her to imagine what the woman could possibly want from her that she hasn't already given.

"If you require a model for acceptable behavior," Mrs. Roderigue continues, as if she imagines that this might truly be the problem, "you need look no further than Green."

The Green table, Tick notes, is decimated by absenteeism today. Normally it has eight students, but four are missing; two of those present are reading their algebra books in preparation for a test next period, and another is fast asleep with his head on the table. If she didn't know better, Tick would like to raise her hand and ask Mrs. Roderigue precisely what it is about the Green table that's so worthy of emulation. Even Candace, using a stolen Exacto knife to carve her jailed boyfriend's name in ornate letters, memorializing her affection for a juvenile delinquent and thereby defacing school property, comes closer to fulfilling the implied objectives of an art course.

"So, how come you broke up with Zack Minty?" Candace asks, once Mrs. Roderigue has returned her attention to the creative efforts of the favored Red table.

"We kind of broke up with each other," Tick says, which is true in a way. When she'd told Zack she didn't want to go out with him anymore, he'd said fine, that he didn't want to go out with her anymore either. Like, who did she think she was, anyway? He'd called the next day to tell her he already had a new girlfriend, naming a girl who seemed to hate Tick, despite their never having exchanged a word.

"I think you should get back together with him," Candace says, apparently uninhibited by knowing virtually nothing about the relationship. "I mean, he still really loves you."

Tick swallows hard, tries to concentrate on her snake, which suddenly feels wrong in some way she can't exactly put her finger on. True, it *is* looking less like an eel, which is good, but there's something definitely wrong about its proportions, as if the lower part of its body were drawn to one scale and the upper, including its head, to another. She wishes she could justify this as perspective. A lot of bad art, it seems to her, gets excused as intentional.

"I doubt it," Tick says, resorting to the absolute, unadorned truth this time.

The odd thing was that before she went to the Vineyard, she hadn't known what to do about Zack. Summer was one thing, but it was much harder to be friendless during the school year when as a friendless person you were constantly on display. Losing Zack wasn't so bad in itself. At least she didn't have to wonder every day what kind of mood he was in, whether he'd be nice or mean, his behavior about as predictable as the wind. So being without a boyfriend was okay, even though she doubted she'd find another anytime soon. What worried her more than losing Zack was losing his friends, the whole Zack network. While they were together, *his* friends had been *her* friends, but as soon as they broke up, she discovered the truth: that they were *his* friends, every one of them. Not that they disliked her. She suspected that a couple of them actually liked her better than they liked Zack, or would've been happy to remain neutral, had the rules permitted any such thing. But they didn't, and Zack wasn't someone you wanted for an enemy. Right away she'd started getting calls from his friends urging her to get back together with him, hinting that she wouldn't be welcome in their group otherwise. A couple of the boys sounded almost afraid, like they couldn't imagine the kind of recklessness she was contemplating. One of the girls even volunteered that Zack might be willing to break up with this new girlfriend if Tick came back, maybe, though it wasn't for sure.

Until Martha's Vineyard she'd seriously considered doing so, but now she was pretty sure she couldn't. After being with a boy who actually liked her, she was willing to be friendless, at least for now. What saddened her was the cost of this new knowledge. Could it be that getting the taste of affection, so sweet and new, from somebody who wasn't your father or mother, meant that she'd have to forgo other companionship entirely?

"I mean, he totally does *not* care about Heather," Candace is saying. "You should, like, see the way he treats her."

"I know how he treats her," Tick says, studying her snake critically. What it needs, she decides, is a tongue. "It's how he used to treat me."

"He's changed," Candace says, looking at her now. She's stopped carving entirely and is gathering up her things in anticipation of the bell. Her sudden interest in Tick's romantic life confirms what Tick has been fearing: that Candace is befriending her because she was specifically commissioned by Zack to sound her out on the subject of a possible reconciliation. Tick has seen blessedly little of him since school began, but that's because of football practice, which he has to attend every day after classes. If it weren't for that, he would have been tormenting her nonstop. The other thing saving her is that Zack screwed up so badly last year that he was booted out of the high-track courses. Otherwise he'd be sitting right behind her in chemistry and

American lit, and she'd be feeling the weight of his wounded, angry eyes all day long.

Now that Tick is sure about Candace's motives it angers her, and before she can consider the wisdom of doing so, she says, "I've changed, too. The biggest change is that I don't like him anymore."

Candace's response to this is to let loose the loudest scream Tick has ever heard. John Voss, at the other end of the table, actually looks up from his egg. Something metallic rattles onto the floor next to Tick's clog, and Candace, howling oh-my-God-oh-my-God, holds up her hand, which is gushing blood from a deep gash that extends from her thumbnail almost to her palm. The blood is everywhere—down her arm, in the elaborate grooves she's been carving in the back of her chair, even a small pink drop on Tick's snake. Looking at all the blood, Tick feels her own left arm begin to throb the way it always does in anticipation of hypodermic needles at the doctor's office, and at horror movies when somebody gets slashed.

Candace, still screaming, wraps her thumb in the palm of her other hand and bends rapidly back and forth at the waist like one of those mechanical birds sipping water at an imaginary pool. There's blood down the front of her unicorn shirt now, and the cowards at the Green table have all gotten up and moved away to the back wall.

Tick's left arm now hurts so bad that she's beginning to feel lightheaded, and the whole room takes on an odd sheen, blurred at the edges like a television dream sequence. She leans forward, resting her forehead on the cool metal table and listening to Candace shriek until another voice, sounding far off, joins in and a new pair of feet appear next to Candace's. Tick identifies them as Mrs. Roderigue's, and way off she hears the woman shouting, "Take your hand away so I can see, child." And then, "Who did this to you?"

Now Candace is screaming, "I'm-sorry-oh-my-God-I'm-so-sorry." Tick, confused, concludes that Candace must be talking to her, apologizing for acting as Zack Minty's go-between. "It's okay," Tick says, or imagines saying, probably, since she's unable to lift her head from the table to speak. In any case, it's what she would like to say, because she's the kind of person who forgives easily, who in fact cannot bear to think of a person wanting to be forgiven and having that forgiveness withheld, and so the words "it's okay," spoken or unspoken, ring in her ears along with the rush of her own blood. When it seems the pain in her left arm can't get any worse without the arm itself exploding, the pain

peaks and then everything gradually becomes vague. Tick, now sweating and shivering, fears that for things to right themselves again, she'll
have to cross back through that territory of pain, and the truth is she'd
rather not. She'd rather pass out.

Only when she opens her eyes does she realize she's been clenching
them tightly shut for some time. With her forehead still on the cool
edge of the table, she has a view of the floor at her feet. There, between
her right foot and her backpack, is the bloody Exacto knife. Candace's
screaming has stopped, and there's no sign of her pink Adidases. Mrs.
Roderigue, who seems to have gone away somewhere and come back
again, is urging Tick to raise her head, and this time she discovers that
she can. She's even more surprised to see that the room has emptied
and that all the kids are clustered out in the hall, peering in at her.
According to the clock on the wall, ten minutes have passed. Mrs.
Roderigue is running her thumb along the metal edge of Candace's
chair, apparently trying to locate a surface sharp enough to slice a kid's
thumb open to the bone. The principal, Mr. Meyer, elbows his way
into the room, then comes over and puts his hand on Tick's forehead.

"I wouldn't get too close," Mrs. Roderigue says. "She looks like she
might puke."

Mr. Meyer reacts visibly to this intelligence, though Tick can't tell
for sure whether he's startled by that possibility or by his teacher's
crudeness.

"I think I'm okay," Tick says, in case it's the former that's worrying
her principal. "What happened?"

"You fainted, angel," Mr. Meyer said, making her like him for the
very first time. "The sight of all that—"

He breaks off his thought, worried perhaps that the word "blood"
might have the same effect as the sight of blood. "You want me to call
your mom and dad?" He catches himself as soon as he says this, probably remembering that her parents are separated.

Tick, wiggling the fingers of her left hand, repeats that she thinks
she's going to be all right. The fingers now feel like they're being
poked by a thousand needles, but otherwise there's no pain, which
means she's going to come out of this in a new place, which is a relief,
not having to enter that same dark tunnel of pain again.

After instructing her to remain where she is, Mr. Meyer takes Mrs.
Roderigue aside. Tick is still able to overhear small snatches of their
conversation, Mrs. Roderigue explaining how Candace told her she'd
sliced her thumb open. Now it's Mr. Meyer's turn to examine the back

of the chair, turning it upside down, running his own thumb along the metal surfaces tentatively, as if he isn't sure whether he really wants to solve this mystery or not. Tick reaches under the table, as if for her backpack, picks up the Exacto knife, and slips it into one of the open side pouches.

When she straightens up, shouldering her backpack, Mr. Meyer takes her gently by the elbow and guides her toward the door. There she catches a glimpse of Zack Minty out in the corridor and a wave of nausea passes over her quickly, her knees wobbly for a second, and Mr. Meyer catches her around the waist. Normally Tick hates being touched, especially by adults, but this time she's grateful.

"The nurse's room for you, young lady," Mr. Meyer says, steering her in the right direction. It occurs to Tick then that she and Candace have sink duty this week and they haven't done their cleanup, which Mrs. Roderigue has made clear is the most important part of the whole artistic process. When she glances back into the room, she sees Mrs. Roderigue standing at the Blue table, as if to suggest that it's safe to visit Blue now that its artists are all gone. She's looking at Tick's snake with an expression of extreme distaste.

CHAPTER 5

THE DONUT SHOP in Empire Falls had always been one of Max Roby's favorite places because of its smoking policy, which was, "Go ahead. See if we care." Miles wondered what his father was going to do next year when all Maine restaurants would by law become smoke-free. For the present there was still a cigarette machine by the door, and with only eight booths and a counter with half a dozen stools there could be no nonsmoking section, which pleased the old man even more than being allowed to light up. Max was the kind of guy who created his own atmosphere, and he took particular pleasure, it seemed to Miles, in knowing that other people had to breathe his air when he was done with it. Actually, smoking was only one manifestation of this phenomenon. Max had always enjoyed breaking his own containment. He liked to stand close to people when he talked; and when he was eating, food had a way of becoming airborne. Now, at seventy, he'd developed a sweet tooth. He would've eaten chocolate bars if his teeth had allowed it, but half of them were gone and the other half loose, so he settled for sugar donuts. By the time Max was finished with one, Miles, who usually just drank coffee, often found his entire shirtfront dusted with confectioners' sugar.

Many years ago, Miles had asked his mother what had attracted her to a man with such disgusting personal habits, and she'd replied that his father hadn't always been this way, certainly not as a young man. Miles loved his mother and would've liked to believe her, but it wasn't easy. All her life she'd been a woman who, once she gave her heart, would ignore anything dismaying, but Miles suspected she'd learned to overlook Max entirely in order to stay married to him. Still, by the time Miles asked, she was clearly mortified by her choice of a mate. "You'd never guess it to look at him now," she told her son, "but your father had the most infectious smile."

Infectious Miles could believe. Like most kids, when Miles and his brother were growing up, they brought a great variety of illnesses home from school—chicken pox, mumps, measles, routine colds and flus. David proved particularly susceptible to whatever was going around, and stayed sick longer than Miles did, but neither boy could be described as sickly, except when their father brought something home and shared it with them. Then everyone but Max himself went down for the mandatory eight count. Whatever the virus, it became several degrees more deadly in his pulmonary system until he finally reintroduced it into the atmosphere by means of his explosive sneezes. Max regarded covering his mouth as irrational behavior. The way he looked at it, you might as well cover your ass with your hand when you farted. See how much good that did.

Miles watched his father light a fresh cigarette with his old one before crushing out the butt in the ashtray he'd managed to half fill in twenty minutes. Miles studied his father's mouth, trying to imagine a full set of white teeth and that infectious grin, but it was no use. One of the great unsolved mysteries of the universe, Miles had long believed, was what women found attractive about certain men. Apparently women all over the world wanted to have sex with Mick Jagger, or at least had wanted to once upon a time. Others had not found Max Roby repulsive. Miles couldn't help admiring women for their ability to dismiss the evidence of their senses. If that's what explained it. If it wasn't simply that from time to time they were unaccountably drawn to the grotesque.

Outside, it was drizzling again, as it had the day before, just hard enough to make painting impossible. Half an hour earlier, Miles, heading back to the restaurant, had seen his father sitting on one of the benches outside the Empire Towers, talking to an old woman who seemed to be wondering what she'd done to deserve his company and how she might avoid making the same mistake in the future. "Just keep driving," Miles had said out loud, even as he pulled the Jetta over and tooted the horn. No good deed, he reminded himself as Max hopped up from the bench and came toward him across the newly seeded lawn, goes unpunished.

Nor would this one, Miles added to himself, studying his father across the booth. "You've got crumbs in your beard, Dad," he pointed out. "Did you know that?" Max shaved only every third or fourth day, and he never ironed the clothes he abandoned in the communal dryers of the Towers complex until one of the other residents removed and returned them. The result was a web of crazy pleats and wrinkles in everything he wore.

"So what?" the old man wanted to know, drawing in another lungful of smoke, then expelling it off to the side in deference to Miles, who didn't smoke. As if the air weren't blue all around them. As if Miles and David hadn't smoked the equivalent of a pack a day since they were babies whenever their father was around.

"You look like an idiot is what," Miles told him. "People are going to take one look at you and conclude you're as senile as Father Tom." Actually, next to Max, Father Tom looked positively elegant.

Max appeared to consider this possibility for a full beat before dismissing it. "You should let me help you out with the church," he said, reminded of this desire by Miles's reference to the old priest. Painting the church was a subject Miles considered closed and Max considered wide-open. "I did paint houses for forty years, you know. I'm supposed to go down to the Keys in another month. How do you expect me to do that if I don't have any money?"

"I don't think helping me paint is a good idea, Dad," Miles said. "Last month you fell off a barstool. I don't want you falling off any ladders."

"That's different," his father explained. "I was drunk."

"Right," Miles said. "As I'm sure you'll be when you fall off the ladder."

His father nodded agreeably, and if Miles hadn't known better he'd have sworn Max had given in.

But when the old man exhaled this time, he didn't turn his head.

"If I had a few bucks in my pocket, I wouldn't have to hit you up all the time, you know."

The waitress appeared, refilled their coffee cups, and departed again in one fluid motion, suggesting to Miles that she was dead set against lingering in Max Roby's proximity.

"Did you hear what I said?" his father wanted to know.

"I heard you, Dad," Miles answered, emptying a packet of sweetener into his coffee. "But you keep forgetting that I'm painting St. Cat's for free."

His father shrugged. "That doesn't mean *you* can't pay me."

"Yes, it does, Dad," Miles said. "That's precisely what it means."

The last thing Miles wanted was Max working alongside him at the church. Every time Max saw Father Mark, he'd rag him about how cheap Catholics were; he reasoned that since the Vatican was rich, all priests, by virtue of being employed by the Vatican, could write checks at will. How could the church have all those millions stashed away and not be able to afford to pay two poor house painters in Empire Falls, Maine? That's what he'd want Father Mark to explain. Actually, the question would be rhetorical, since Max would allow Father Mark about two seconds before explaining how the church operated this scam. Every week, he'd argue, you collect money from people who don't know any better than to give it to you, then you put it in a bank halfway around the world where nobody from Empire Falls, Maine, is likely to look for it, much less find it. If anybody ever asks you for part of it back—say, to have your own damn church painted—you tell them the money's all gone, that you're as poor as they are, that you gave the money in question to the bishop, who gave it to the cardinal, who gave it to the pope. "In my next life," Max would conclude, "that's who I want to be. The pope. And I'll do the same thing he does. I'll keep all the goddamn money." Miles enjoyed scripting scenes like this, mostly because doing so helped him to avoid them in reality.

"If you paid me for work," continued Max, whose rhetoric was more sophisticated than you might expect from a man with food in his beard, "I wouldn't have to feel worthless. There's no law says old people have to feel worthless all the while, you know. You paid me, I'd have some dignity."

Now it was Miles's turn to nod and smile agreeably. "I think the dignity ship set sail a long time ago, Dad."

Max grinned, then finished stirring his coffee and used his spoon to point at his son, who felt a couple stray drops of coffee fleck his shirt-front. "You're trying to hurt my feelings," his father said knowingly, "but you can't."

Miles dabbed a wet paper napkin on the spots. "Besides, Dad," he said, "anytime you feel like an infusion of dignity, you can come down to the restaurant and wash dishes for a while."

"That's your idea of dignity? Coop your old man up in that little room with no windows for hours, washing dishes for minimum wage? Half of which goes to the government?"

Which Max would do, eventually, when he got needy enough. Miles was in no hurry to have him give in, either, since the old man was a careless, resentful worker. In his opinion any dish that came out of the Hobart was clean by definition, no matter if it was stained yellow with egg yolk. He hated, even more than the claustrophobic room, Miles's refusal to pay him under the table. He reckoned that if you could paint a whole house under the table—and he had, all his working life—then you ought to be able to wash a few dishes under there too. In Max's view, Grace had raised their son to be morally fastidious just to spite him. Had he foreseen such moral inflexibility, he'd have taken more of a personal interest in the boy's education, but unfortunately he hadn't noticed until it was too late. His other son, David, had more give to him, thank God.

"I'd let you hire me at the restaurant if I could come out and work the counter now and then," Max said. "There's nothing to flipping a burger, you know. And I like talking to people."

"I'd have to run you through the Hobart first," Miles told him. "Rinse some of the crumbs out of your beard. You don't seem to understand that people come into the Empire Grill to eat, and you're a walking appetite suppressant."

"I may be sempty," his father continued without missing a beat, "but I can still climb like a monkey."

Back to painting the church again. The old man *was* nimble, Miles had to admit, both of foot and of conversation. Miles had given up trying to corner him long ago.

Max's persistence about the church was curious, though. Thirty years ago, when Father Tom had hired another contractor to paint St. Catherine's, his father had vowed never to set foot on the grounds again. Of course he hadn't set foot inside for a decade anyway, leaving his wife and son (David wasn't yet born) to attend services. The way Max saw it, though, was that everything his wife and son did, they did under his aegis, and the contractor Father Tom had hired was a damn Presbyterian, not even remotely connected to the parish. Maybe Max wasn't a practicing Catholic himself, but he was married to one who practiced every minute of her life, even though she had it all down pat. Also, he'd bred another little Catholic, and that should have counted, too.

Still, Max had been true to his pledge, which now caused Miles to wonder. Was his desire to help paint the church some kind of oblique regret? Miles had never known his father to indulge regret in any form, though he'd had more than his fair share of opportunities. After all, Max had made a poor effort at being a father and an even poorer one at being a husband. In truth he wasn't even much of a house painter. He didn't like to scrape, and he laid the paint on thick and sloppy. He preferred sitting in bars to painting houses, and so, to proceed from the former to the latter, he liked to work fast, even in circumstances that cried out for deliberation. He painted windows shut and couldn't be bothered to wipe the glass off with a rag if he'd managed to swipe it with a brush.

In any other man his age a desire to paint the church might have represented nothing more than a longing to spend some time with his neglected son, but Miles doubted this was the case with Max, who'd never given much evidence of enjoying the company of either of his sons, though he did appreciate anyone who'd spring for a donut so he could put the price of the donut toward a pack of cigarettes. No, the only conclusion that Miles could come to was that old age generally played havoc with your personality. Father Tom, for instance, who had always assigned the hearing of confessions to the junior priests, now, in his dotage, pleaded with Father Mark to let him hear just a few. If the younger priest wasn't vigilant on Saturday afternoons, he'd look up and find the old priest had disappeared and then would have to hurry across the lawn between the rectory and the church to the dark confessional, where the old man would be patiently awaiting further revelations from his parishioners, curious now, in his old age, about what people were up to, and eager to share what he'd learned. It was from Father Tom that Miles first learned his wife was carrying on with Walt Comeau.

"I'll tell you another thing, too. Once I'm up on a ladder, I don't get scared like some little girl."

"Works both ways, Dad," Miles reminded him. "You can't hurt my feelings either."

"Never meant to," the old man said, exhibiting a kind of straightforward insincerity that was, in its own way, endearing. "When did you become such a damn sissy about heights, is what I'd like to know? I'm sempty and I can still climb like a monkey. And you're what?"

"Forty-two."

"Forty-two." Max stubbed out his cigarette, as if at least the question of his son's age had been established beyond question. "Forty-two and afraid to climb a stepladder. I fell two damn stories once and *I'm* not scared."

"Finish your coffee, Dad," Miles said. "I need to get back to the restaurant."

"I fell off a scaffold over on Division Street—two damn stories— and landed on my ass in the middle of a rosebush. Try that sometime. That don't mean I'm afraid to climb a ladder anymore."

Outside, a police cruiser pulled into the parking lot, and Miles saw it was Jimmy Minty at the wheel. He could feel the cruiser's front bumper actually nudge the side of the building, causing the Formica booth, as well as its ashtrays, to shudder. Instead of getting out, Jimmy—in uniform today—just sat there, his lips moving as if in conversation with an invisible companion. Only when he leaned forward to hang up the receiver did it dawn on Miles that he'd been talking into his radio. This made three times in two days that their paths had crossed. Coincidentally. Well, it *was* possible.

"I could help you rig the platforms at least," his father was saying. "That way you'd know you were standing on something solid."

"I know how to rig scaffolding, Dad."

"I should hope so," Max said. "I'm the one taught you how, in case you forgot."

"I didn't forget."

"I let *you* help, if you recall. If your mother'd known she'd have had a fit, but I let you help anyway. Now I need some traveling expenses and you tell me to take a hike."

"I never said—"

"I gotta pee," his father said disgustedly, sliding out of the booth, as if the conversation, not the coffee, had caused this unfortunate need to relieve himself.

The restroom door had no sooner closed behind Max than Jimmy Minty slipped into the booth, setting his shiny black hat on the table. His red hair was going a little gray at the temples, Miles noticed.

The waitress set a cup of coffee in front of him. "I wish you wouldn't run into that wall every time you pull in, Jimmy," she said. "You scare the hell out of people. One minute they're drinking coffee and minding their own business, and the next minute you're parkin' in the booth with them. It's not like the side of this damn building's invisible. The idea is to stop before you get to it."

"You need to get a couple of those concrete curbs out there." Minty smiled. "I bet I'm not the only one who taps that wall, Shirley."

"No," she admitted. "You're just the only one who hits it every time."

When she stepped away, the policeman shrugged. "Hey, Miles. I thought that was your Jetta out there. You should've spent the extra for the undercoating. What would it have run you—couple hundred?"

It never took Jimmy Minty long to turn any conversation to one about money. He particularly liked to draw Miles's attention to whatever was wrong with any of his possessions, such as rust on the Jetta, of which there was plenty. Miles had long suspected that Jimmy Minty considered him some kind of yardstick by which he might measure his own economic well-being. The oddest thing about this, Miles thought, was that it seemed a direct extension of their childhoods on Long Street. Jimmy Minty had always taken careful inventory of Miles's belongings, wanting to know how much everything cost and where it was purchased. If they got similar Christmas presents, Jimmy liked to explain why his was better, that it had been purchased smarter and cheaper because *his* dad knew where to go—even if the toy in question was obviously a cheap knockoff. After detailing the advantages of his present, he'd suggest they switch, just for a while; often, before Jimmy returned it, Miles's toy would get broken.

Even thirty years later Miles could still remember the relief he felt when his mother took him out of the public grade school and enrolled him at Sacred Heart, where Jimmy—the family was not Catholic—could not follow. Gradually, though they remained neighbors, the boys' lives began to drift apart, and by the time they were thrown together again in high school, they had different lives, different friends. Of course, Jimmy's, as he explained to Miles, were better. After graduation he did a stint in the service while Miles was away at college, and by the time Miles returned to Empire Falls, Jimmy was newly married and living in Fairhaven. He visited his parents, though, and after Miles and Janine got married he made overtures about striking up their old friendship, something Miles didn't particularly desire, since the grown-up Jimmy Minty had the same way of taking inventory behind his eyes, only now he was comparing wives. For the last decade, they had seldom seen each other, except in moving vehicles or when Jimmy had a new toy he wanted to show off in the Empire Grill. The last time—a year ago—he'd ordered a steak and then lingered at the counter drinking coffee until Miles deigned to notice the red Camaro parked out front. On any such occasion Jimmy would assure Miles that he was doing all right for himself, despite having been denied opportunities like college. If he kept his nose clean, he didn't see any reason he shouldn't be the next chief of police of Empire Falls. His son, Zack, though—*he* was going to have it made.

"That your dad I saw with you?" Jimmy wondered now, nodding toward the men's room.

"You know it was. You sat right there"— Miles nodded through the window at the cruiser—"staring at us."

"The light was reflecting off the glass," Minty said. "It could've been anybody."

"Hell of a guess, then."

"Sorry about yesterday," he said, apparently in reference to the young police officer who had interrogated Miles on Long Street. "New kid. Still learning the ropes. Good thing I happened by, though. You talk back to him or something?"

"Not even remotely."

Minty shrugged. "Well, you pissed him off somehow. Good thing I turned up when I did."

This second reference to his good fortune, Miles realized, was intended as another chance for Miles to express his gratitude. That he should fail to take advantage of it was visibly disappointing, but Jimmy seemed determined to get over it.

"Breaks your heart, doesn't it?" he said. "The old neighborhood?"

Miles tried to navigate their talk into the calmer waters of generality. "The whole town, for that matter."

Jimmy Minty's surprised, even hurt expression suggested that he considered this indictment of Empire Falls far too sweeping. "I still like it here," he said. "I can't help it, I just do. People say there are better places, but I don't know." He paused in case Miles wanted to rattle off a list of supposedly better places. "Long Street, though. That's different. I get called up there all the time these days. Nothing but wife beaters and drug dealers anymore."

"Wife beaters aren't anything new," Miles reminded him, since Jimmy's own father, William, had been known to settle marital differences in this fashion.

Jimmy ignored him. "Hell, the place you were parked out front of is the biggest drug house in town." He lowered his voice now. "We've been monitoring who goes in and out for a while. I guess Officer Pollard thought you were there to make a score."

Miles couldn't help smiling. "Somebody should tell him he'll have better luck, evidence-wise, if he waits until suspects come out, instead of busting them on the way in."

"That's what I told him. You gotta admit, though, that Jetta of yours does look like a drugmobile."

"Really? How's that?"

Minty shrugged. "No offense, but it's the kind of vehicle the owner won't mind that much if it's impounded."

"I'd mind. It's the only car I own."

Jimmy Minty looked like he could just kick himself. "Damn. I guess I hurt your feelings."

"Not at all." Miles smiled.

The other man puzzled over how this could be for several full beats. "You want to know a secret?"

The honest answer to this was no, so Miles said nothing.

"What you were doing over there yesterday? I do the same thing, sometimes."

"What's that?"

"You know. Just drive over, sit in the car and try to figure it all out."

"All *what* out?" Miles asked, genuinely curious.

Minty shrugged. "Life, I guess. The way things turn out. I guess some people would think it's pretty weird, me ending up a cop."

"Not me, Jimmy."

Minty studied him carefully, perhaps suspecting an insult. "My dad and all, is what I meant. It's true. He did slap my mom around a little. That's what you meant a minute ago, right? And I guess we did have a freezer full of meat out back that wasn't always taken in season. Shit like that. But I miss him anyway. You only get one father, is the way I look at it, even though now, looking back, I can see where he crossed the line. Anyway, a cop's what I turned out to be, weird or not. God probably had a hand in it, I guess."

"I suppose it's possible."

Jimmy nodded. "Take you. If your mother hadn't got sick when she did, you probably never would have come back here at all, am I right?"

Miles allowed that this, too, was possible.

"That's what I mean. Sometimes I drive over to the old neighborhood and just sit there." He paused. "I always think about your ma. Pretty awful way for anybody to die."

"Can we change the subject?" Miles said.

"Hell, yeah." Jimmy Minty straightened up and shook his head. "I don't know what got me started on all this. Seeing you just sitting there yesterday, I guess, and thinking how we used to be friends. All that water over the dam. How's that cute little girl of yours?"

"Good," Miles told him. "Happier than she's been in a while." Since she stopped going out with your son was what Miles *didn't* say.

If Jimmy Minty intuited the omission he gave no sign. "Want to know another secret? I gotta think my Zack's still a little sweet on her," he said, letting the words hang in the air between them, as if inviting Miles to betray either enthusiasm or aversion. "Of course, with kids you never know. I told him at the time he should have let her down gentler. Treat people the way you want to be treated, is my motto. You can't go too far wrong. Not that you can tell kids their age anything."

Hearing the men's room door open behind him, Miles allowed himself a half smile. Few social situations were improved by Max Roby's participation, but this was one of them.

"I keep telling him if he doesn't start paying attention to his grades, no college is going to want him, but no, he's got all that figured out, just like they all do. Not that I blame him, exactly. He looks at me, and I'm doing all right without college—hell, better than all right, really—so he figures what the hell."

Jimmy Minty paused again. "What our kids don't understand is we want even *better* for them, not just as good. Am I right?"

Max's return spared Miles the necessity of agreeing with him.

"Jimmy Minty," said Max, sitting down on the bench seat and forcing the policeman to slide down next to the window. Max looked at him with what appeared to be total bewilderment. "My *God*, what a stupid kid you were growing up."

"Go easy, Dad," Miles said. "He's carrying a gun these days."

"I just hope he's smarter than he was back then," Max said, offering a paw to the policeman. "How the hell are you, Jimmy?"

Minty looked at the proffered hand as if he doubted Max had washed it in the men's room, but shook it anyway. "How you doin', Mr. Roby?"

Speaking to Miles now, as he and Jimmy Minty shook, Max said, "You remember what a stupid kid he was? My *God*, it was pitiful. I don't think I can remember another child so untalented."

Minty seemed to want his hand back now, but didn't know how to get it, and Miles shrugged at him as if to suggest he had no idea what possessed his father to act the way he did.

"It was enough to make you cry," Max said, finally letting go of the man's hand.

Minty seemed to be weighing the dangers and benefits of asking just what he'd done to warrant such a low opinion.

"I suppose it should be a lesson to us all," Max observed. "Never give up on a child. 'Cause even the ones you have to tie their shoes for on their wedding day could surprise you and end up gainfully employed."

Max, with a face almost beatific, delivered this lesson as if to suggest he meant the whole thing as a compliment, causing the officer to knit his brow in confusion. He was *almost* sure he was being insulted, but not quite.

Miles, of course, had often seen his father smile and chuckle and slap men on the back, continuing to insult them until they finally had no choice but to punch him. Only the smartest popped him right away. Once Max had established that whatever he said was all in good fun, it was hard to break free of that context. Miles also knew that the target of his father's ridicule often turned on a dime, so he wasn't surprised when it did so now.

"My son here is the opposite," Max explained. "Always at the top of his class . . . straight A's right through school. You'd have sworn he'd go places."

Miles sighed, resigned to his inevitable drubbing. Before, Max had insulted Jimmy Minty while looking at Miles. Now, insulting his son, he was, of course, speaking directly at the previous object of his scorn.

"There's nothing harder to figure than a kid," Max was telling him, as if he'd spent the better part of a long, largely contemplative life studying this question. "I'd have bet that Miles here would have grown up to have a good heart. If his father was on his uppers and needed a hand and asked his own son for a job, he'd help pronto. But apparently not."

"You about ready to go, Dad?"

"No, I'm talking to Jimmy Minty. Go ahead if you want."

Miles caught the eye of the waitress and signaled for the check.

"Jimmy here may not have been gifted like you, but I bet you he understands what I'm saying."

Minty's brow furrowed even deeper at this second reference to his intellectual limitations, even though Max had safely located these in the past.

"You see, Jimmy, I asked my son to let me help him paint our old church, so I'd have the money to go down to the Keys, but for some reason he won't hire me. I can still climb like a monkey, too."

Having slid a five-dollar bill onto the table, Miles stood to go. "You're sure you don't want a lift home, Dad? I'm not coming back for you, so don't bother calling me at the restaurant."

"I don't intend to call you," his father assured him. "Besides, Jimmy Minty here can give me a lift in the cruiser."

"Actually, that's against the rules," Minty said. He was looking even more boxed in now that Miles had vacated his side of the booth. That left him and Max sitting way too close, and he knew how this would look to other people, two men crammed together like that on the same side of a small booth, one of them with crumbs in his beard.

"Hell, I can understand that," Max conceded, waving good riddance to Miles and looking like a man who had no intention of moving. "Rules are rules. They may be dumb, and the people you hire to enforce them may be dumber yet, but what can you do? The law's the law. There's no law says a man's own son can't help him out when he needs it, that's all I'm saying. Ain't no law against that."

OUTSIDE, Miles got into the car and turned the key in the ignition, determined to ignore the knocking on the window of the donut shop. His father, having made his point, now decided to unmake it, since the truth was that he probably *did* want a lift somewhere. Besides, he hadn't hit Miles up for a loan yet. Sitting in the Jetta, pretending not to hear the frantic knocking, Miles supposed he understood his father's thinking better than Max did himself. The thing to do was put the car in reverse, back out of the parking space and drive off. Teach the old man a lesson. Maybe because he was grateful to Max for giving Jimmy Minty such a hard time, he gave up the pretense and acknowledged hearing the knocking on the window. He was immediately glad that he did, for the scene framed in the window was priceless. In order to rap on the glass, Max had to lean across the booth in such a way that his moist, fragrant armpit was practically covering the policeman's face. Miles couldn't help but smile. He *was* grateful for his father's existence, just as Minty had told him he should be. Sighing, he waved for Max to come along, which the old man would do, Miles knew, in his own sweet time.

His feet flat on the floor beside the Jetta's pedals, Miles felt some give in the metal beneath the worn carpet, which suggested that the rust was eating away at the chassis. Minty was right about that, too; he should've sprung for the undercoating. As he watched the two men slide out of the booth, he realized that Jimmy Minty hadn't been telling the truth about light reflecting off the donut shop window. Everything on the other side of the glass possessed the stark clarity of an Edward Hopper painting, which meant that Jimmy had pretended to be unable to see what had been plainly visible. A silly lie. A lie so small and to so little purpose that it suggested to Miles a way of life, a strategy for confronting the world, and this was further reason—if any was needed—to doubt the truth of everything the man had said inside. As Minty paid the bill at the register and Max bought a pack of cigarettes from the machine, Miles tasted something on the back of his tongue. Too much coffee mingling with stomach acid, probably. Either that or anger mingling with fear. Miles swallowed hard, forcing down whatever it was.

The two men pushed through the door onto the sidewalk, and Miles noticed that both had acquired toothpicks. "You're okay, Jimmy," Miles heard his father say. "I'll tell you the God's honest truth. I'd rather have a complete idiot for a son than an ingrate."

Instead of getting into the cruiser, Minty came around the Jetta and motioned for Miles to roll down the window. "Take a little walk with me," he suggested, his voice low, confidential.

"I really need to get back to the restaurant," Miles told him.

"Won't take a minute."

"Go ahead," Max said. "I'll just sit here by myself and wait. You go with Jimmy Minty and swap secrets."

Miles followed the policeman over to his patrol car, where he rolled the toothpick in his mouth as if considering how to begin. "I shouldn't be doing this, but we go back a long ways," he said. "I was going to mention it back inside, but then your old man came back and I didn't want to worry him."

"What is it, Jimmy?"

"Here's the deal," Minty said, working his toothpick. "There's a lot of dope around town right now. Tell your brother to be careful."

Miles felt himself instantly bristle, more at the presumed intimacy than the implied accusation. "Why should David be careful?"

"Hey. I understand. He's your brother. I'm just saying."

"No, Jimmy. *What* are you saying?"

"I'm just . . . nothing. Forget it. I'm just saying. Word to the wise is all."

The toothpick still twirled thoughtfully. Miles considered grabbing it and running it through the man's bottom lip and tying it there in a splintered knot. "And I can't help thinking how bad your ma would feel if—"

Rather than punch an armed cop in broad daylight in the middle of Empire Avenue, Miles turned on his heel and strode back to the Jetta. The suddenness of this movement apparently caught his father by surprise as he was rummaging through the Jetta's glove box. This discovery had the unintended effect of sending Miles back to Jimmy Minty, who hadn't moved. "Look," he said, "you don't know the first thing about my mother, okay, so don't bring her up in any more conversations."

"Hey—"

"No. Shut up and listen, Jimmy," Miles said, feeling his fury rise in his throat—the taste was anger, after all, not fear—and the blood pounding in his cheeks. "You . . . didn't . . . know . . . her. Say it for me, so I know you understand."

Jimmy Minty's face had gone pale. "Hey, okay. I didn't really know your mother."

"Fine," Miles said, some of the rage draining out of him, replaced by the knowledge that he'd overreacted. "Terrific."

"You shouldn't tell me to shut up, Miles," Minty said. "Not out here in public like this. This uniform entitles me to some respect."

"You're right," Miles admitted, flushed with shame yet unwilling to surrender his anger. "You're right, and I'm sorry. Just don't pretend you knew my mother."

"Hey, I thought she was a great lady. That's all I was saying—" But he must have seen Miles's color rising again, because he stopped. "Your brother should be careful is all I'm saying, okay? Everybody knows he's growing marijuana out there in—"

"See?" Miles said. "That's where you're wrong. Everybody does *not* know that. *I* don't know that, for instance." Which was true. He didn't know it, not for sure.

"How come you're getting so bent outta shape, Miles? I try to do you and your brother a favor—"

"No," Miles interrupted him, feeling suddenly calm. "I don't believe that. I have no idea what you're trying to do, Jimmy. I don't know why I'm suddenly seeing you everywhere I turn lately. I don't know why my name should come up in your conversation with Mrs. Whiting at the courthouse, either . . . "

Minty squinted at this, then glanced away.

"But I do know you aren't looking out for my well-being. That much I'm sure of. So from now on, if you want to do me a favor, stay away from me and my family. That goes for your kid too. There are lots of girls in Empire Falls. As far as I'm concerned he can choose any one he likes. There's just one he can't have, and that's Tick."

A sly smile began to steal over the policeman's features, and Miles turned away, fearing the temptation to remove it.

"How come you don't like me, Miles?" Minty called after him. "I've always wondered why."

Miles answered without turning around. "Call it the habit of a lifetime."

Back in the Jetta, Miles waited to turn the key in the ignition until Minty's cruiser disappeared down the avenue.

"*God*, what a prize dunce he was," Max recalled fondly.

"He wasn't stupid, Dad. He was sneaky and mean and envious and dangerous. He still is."

"Don't get mad at me," his father said. "It's Jimmy Minty you're mad at. I'm just a useless old man."

Miles put the car in reverse. "Did you find what you were looking for in the glove box?"

"I borrowed ten dollars," his father said sheepishly. "I was going to mention it, but you never gave me the chance."

"Right."

"I was," Max insisted, perhaps truthfully. He did sometimes tell the truth if it suited his purpose. "If you'd hire me, I wouldn't have to be broke all the while. If I could make some money, you'd get rid of me for the winter."

Before pulling out, Miles craned his neck forward to look down Empire Avenue, to make sure no traffic was coming. When he and his mother used to walk downtown for a Saturday matinee at the old Bijou Theater, the sidewalks had been so crowded, the street so clogged with vehicles, that pedestrians had to turn sideways to pass by one another. They crossed the street between cars backed up for blocks from the traffic light. Now Empire Avenue was empty all the way down to the old shirt factory (NO TRESPASSING WITHOUT PERMISSION) where Miles's mother had worked so they could afford the rent on the little house on Long Street, in the dark upper bedroom of which, after her cancer returned the final time, she'd screamed her agony so loudly the neighbors could hear her. Of *course* Jimmy Minty had heard those screams.

Miles himself had heard them all the way down in Portland, in his small Catholic college, and hearing them he'd hurried home, even though she'd begged him not to.

Looking down the deserted street, Miles couldn't help feeling that everyone in town must have heard her terrible screams. His brother, a mere boy, had fled into the bottle, his father to the Florida Keys. It was almost possible to believe her screams were responsible for the mass exodus that by now had lasted more than two decades, a panicky flight from her pain that emptied out the town.

"You can drop me off at Callahan's," Max suggested.

Miles blinked, then turned to stare at his father. "You mean Callahan's right there?" he said, pointing at the red-brick tavern across the street, his mother-in-law's place.

"Right."

"For *that* you wanted a lift?"

"Maybe I wanted to spend some time with my son. Or is there some law against that, too?"

Miles sighed. The old man was truly without conscience.

"How come you've got a Martha's Vineyard real estate guide in there?" his father wondered, pointing at the glove box.

"Is there a law against that?" Miles said.

Max ignored this. "Be just like you to move to some island and leave me here without a job. I ever wanted to see you, I'd have to swim."

"I'm not going anywhere, Dad. You said so yourself," Miles reminded him. "It was just a week's vacation."

"You *could've* taken me along, you know. I might like a vacation myself. Did that ever occur to you?"

Miles pulled across the street into Callahan's parking lot

When his father started to get out, Miles said, "Dad, you've still got crumbs in your beard."

"So what?" said Max, closing the door on the possibility of enlightenment.

CHAPTER 6

"I DON'T THINK Mrs. Roderigue likes my snake," Tick confessed to her father.

It was a Thursday in mid-September, and on Thursday nights she and Miles always had dinner together, since Janine usually worked the desk at the fitness club until eight and Tick refused to eat with the Silver Fox. At the Empire Grill, Thursday nights also meant Chinese. Tonight David had on special something called Twice-Cooked Noodles with Scallops in *Hoisin* Sauce. His brother's more adventurous concoctions always made Miles smile in memory of old Roger Sperry, whose favorite special had always been Deep-Fried Haddock with Tartar Sauce, Whipped Potatoes with Beef Gravy, a side of Apple Sauce and Parker House Rolls. His theory of noodles, which Roger didn't often put into practice, was to leave them in boiling water until you were sure they were cooked; then you wouldn't need to cook them again. It was also his firm conviction that there wasn't much point in fighting a world war if you were going to come home and start serving things in *hoisin* sauce—whatever that was. That was the sort of thing you'd do if you lost the damn war. (Roger would never have made a distinction between the Japanese, with whom we'd been engaged in armed conflict, and the Chinese, with whom we had not.)

Miles himself had had some doubts about International Nights when his brother first proposed them as part of his plan to attract out-of-town business—something they'd have to do if the restaurant were going to survive the local economy. For a while Friday and Saturday nights didn't show a profit, but David had correctly predicted that good, cheap ethnic food would eventually attract students and junior faculty from Fairhaven, who would consider the grill's worn-out, cigarette-burned countertop and wobbly booths "honest" or "retro" or some damn thing. Tonight was only the second Thursday they'd served Chinese—to augment their Friday Italian and Saturday Mexican—and Miles was pleased to see the restaurant nearly full of people, many of them new faces, who seemed willing to entertain the possibility that noodles might benefit from a second cooking. When a brief lull occurred, David turned away from the stove, leaned on his spatula and searched out Miles's eye, raising an eyebrow. Not bad? Miles nodded. Not bad.

In fact, tonight it all seemed better than "not bad." Granted, his first week back from the Vineyard had been tough, but it usually was. Every year he left the island haunted by a profound feeling of personal failure. Was it the island itself that inspired this? Perhaps. More likely it had something to do with Peter and Dawn, who, without intending to, reminded him of who he'd wanted to be when they had all been students together. Of course it was possible that they too were haunted by similar regrets. After all, back when they were undergraduates, Peter had wanted to be a playwright, Dawn a poet. Certainly the way they talked about their profession in television suggested they also wondered if they hadn't betrayed their original, deeper purpose. Maybe they even indulged the feeling, as Miles sometimes did, that they each must have a double in some parallel universe, happily living the life they'd imagined for themselves in their youth.

But such self-indulgence was fraudulent. For one thing, Miles couldn't even be sure anymore if this alternate life was one he'd imagined or just one he'd inherited from his mother's hopes and wishes. From the time he was a boy, he would look up from a book he was reading to find her quietly studying him. "My little scholar," she'd say, smiling. Later, in college, he'd been greatly attracted to the exciting life his professors seemed to lead, richly furnished with books and ideas worth arguing over, and he'd thought that maybe his mother was right, that the life of the mind was his own truest destiny. One thing was for sure. He'd never aspired to feeding other professors twice-cooked noodles for a living.

Over at the counter Charlene was balancing plates up her forearm, and at this distance she might almost have been the girl he'd had a crush on in high school, a girl so womanly at age eighteen that she made Miles, at fifteen, feel about eleven. Looking at her now made it hard for him to claim he'd been an entirely unwilling participant in his own foiled destiny. Yes, he'd been attracted to the life of the mind, and no doubt his mother's idea of the man she thought he would become had shaped his own image of himself, but when she'd fallen ill and he'd left school to return to Empire Falls and manage the grill for Mrs. Whiting, his doing so had not been entirely altruistic. True, he'd wanted to be near his mother; and yes, his brother was already exhibiting signs of trouble. But he'd also thought of Charlene, calculating that the three years' age difference wouldn't matter so much now, at twenty-one and twenty-four. Though he told Mrs. Whiting he wanted to mull over her offer, by the time he'd hung up the phone he'd already decided. That summer Charlene's first husband had run off and left her, and Miles had thought maybe . . . just maybe. What he had no way of knowing then was that by the time he returned to Empire Falls, Charlene would already be engaged to husband number two.

No, he certainly had not been an unwilling participant. And, more to the point, if given an opportunity to rewrite the script, he would not be inclined to do so. At least not tonight, in this restaurant that would one day be his, sharing a booth with his daughter, whose destiny would *not* be tied to Empire Falls—not if he had anything to say about it. That his mother had believed the same thing about his own destiny was vaguely disconcerting, but tonight he couldn't help feeling fortunate. For the first time in a decade, business was looking up. David appeared to have banished the worst of his demons. Tick, it seemed, would survive the divorce. There was much to be thankful for, even if the balance of things remained too precarious to inspire confidence, so on nights like this one his life seemed almost . . . almost enough.

"BUT HERE'S THE THING," Tick was saying, using her fork as a baton to emphasize a point about her art teacher. Miles, studying the fork, was grateful that, unlike her grandfather, Tick was able to demonstrate ideas without flinging food. "What if she *did* like it? That'd be even worse. I mean, if she *liked* it, then I'd wonder what was wrong with it."

Miles tried to suppress a smile but couldn't. His daughter's grasp of adult situations often staggered him. In this instance, she understood completely what the endorsement of a fool was worth. Miles had gone to high school with Doris Roderigue—Doris Flynn, back then—and he knew her mind had fused shut sometime during Catholic grade school. Nothing had happened since she was twelve that did anything except reinforce the convictions she already held. As a condition for keeping her job, the school district insisted that she attend summer school in Farmington, but these classes did little to shake the woman's defiant convictions, which she proudly maintained were uncorrupted by the university.

In Bill Roderigue, a local insurance man, she'd found her ideal mate, an infinitely patient fellow who never seemed to weary of her sense of thwarted superiority. Miles, after serving several terms on the school board, knew most of Tick's teachers and made it a matter of policy not to speak ill of them, regardless of how ignorant and narrow-minded they were, but with Doris Roderigue he was often tempted to make an exception. During the last five years he'd run up against her on numerous occasions—about curriculum, about books held in the library, about staffing—but since the day he'd invited her, in public meeting, to explain a single difference between the work of Andrew Wyeth and Jackson Pollock and then used her startled confusion to suggest an explanation for why art history was not included in her courses, she'd steered clear of him. According to Tick, the woman was steering clear of her as well, by putting her at the table composed of the least motivated students in the class and then pretending the table didn't exist.

"Keep in mind," Miles reminded her, "it's not you she objects to, it's me. She probably thinks I'm trying to get her fired."

"Are you?"

"Teachers can't be fired unless they molest their students," Miles told her. "Doris hasn't been molesting anybody, has she?"

But Tick had turned her attention back to her dinner, pushing the ingredients around on her plate thoughtfully, as if considering a better, more artistic use for food.

"Has she made any specific criticisms of your snake?"

"*That's* the thing," Tick said happily, again wielding her fork as a baton. Lately all her statements were preceded by variations on "the thing." Here's the thing. That's the thing. The thing is. "I think what she doesn't like about *my* snake is that it reminds her of *real* snakes."

"That's one possibility," Miles agreed. The other that occurred to him was more Freudian, though he didn't think his teenage daughter needed to start worrying about sexual repression just yet.

"Which is interesting," Tick went on, "because it means that the better I draw the snake, the more it will remind her of what she hates, and the worse grade I'll get. Hence"—this word was another of Tick's new rhetorical devices—"if I want a good grade, my strategy should be to draw the snake *badly*."

"Or not draw a snake," Miles felt compelled to point out.

"Except our assignment was to draw our most vivid dream, and that's my most vivid dream."

"I understand," Miles said. "But you mistrust your teacher's judgment about the merits of your snake, correct?"

"Correct."

"Hence"—Miles grinned—"you might as well distrust the wisdom of the assignment, right? Draw her an angel. Mrs. Roderigue would be cheered to think you're dreaming of angels." This was no guess, either. Doris Roderigue, who'd never seen the sense of separating church and state, openly encouraged work with religious themes.

"But I'm dreaming of snakes."

"What you're dreaming about is none of her business," Miles pointed out, a little surprised by his growing anger at the thought of trusting the development of his daughter, or any smart kid for that matter, to the likes of Doris Roderigue.

"Want to know what your real problem is?" said Charlene, who had passed their booth several times during this conversation and apparently overheard enough to feel qualified to contribute. Charlene hadn't been a small-town waitress all her life for nothing. She entered into the conversations of diners with both confidence and a sense of entitlement. Last spring David and Miles had each suggested this might not be a good idea with their new evening clientele, especially with the professors, who probably weren't accustomed to having their thinking clarified by waitresses. Nor were they likely to tip anyone who'd belittled their logic. Charlene had briefly considered the wisdom of this advice, but in the end rejected it. For one thing, she said, having listened to their conversations, many of the professors badly needed a little clarification. For another, she was confident that despite their carefully trimmed beards, their pressed chinos and tweed jackets, college professors tipped in the same fashion as other men—according to cup size. She was doing very well by them, thanks all the same. "Your *real* problem," she told Tick, "is that you're dreaming instead of eating. Shall we let your father in on your secret?"

"The thing is"—Tick began, pointing the tines of her fork at Charlene, who surprised both father and daughter by snatching the fork and pointing it back at Tick, who leaned away in mock fear.

"And don't give me 'the thing is.'"

"What secret?" Miles said.

Charlene handed the fork back to Tick, then put her hands on her hips and regarded him as you would a favored pet, perhaps a dog that's found a place in your heart even though you've owned other, smarter dogs. "The purpose of this whole conversation has been to distract you from the obvious fact that Tick isn't eating her dinner. Again."

In addition to feeling free to enter into the conversations of her customers, Charlene, a full-service waitress, never shirked from reminding people that there was no excuse for wasting good food when other people were going hungry. She was particularly vigilant with Tick, who after her checkup last spring was declared underweight. Not that Tick was the only one whose eating habits drew Charlene's notice and comment. She'd been on Miles's case for years, pointing out his tendency to pick listlessly at things instead of sitting down to a proper meal. Over the years he'd fallen into the classic restaurateur's trap of eating his mistakes—the extra order of fries, the under- or overcooked burger—and not just when he was hungry but whenever they occurred. Tonight, for instance, that bowl of David's bisque, simply because it finished off the pot. It was Charlene's opinion that if Miles could bring himself to toss out every stray french fry that fell onto the counter, he'd weigh no more than his brother, David, who was gaunt and sinewy.

"It's not nice to tell a person's secrets, Charlene." Tick frowned. "I don't go around telling your secrets."

"That shows you're smart," Charlene said.

"She hasn't done that bad a job," Miles said weakly, indicating Tick's plate. True, she'd flattened out her food, artfully carving out an area in the middle to suggest that where there had once been food, there now was none. Still, Miles guessed that at least a third of the portion David had served her was gone.

"No, Miles," Charlene said. "*You're* the one who hasn't done such a bad job. You ate your own bisque and for the last fifteen minutes you've been picking at Tick's dinner. Don't tell me you haven't, either, because I've been watching you."

Well, it was true Miles *had* been picking at his daughter's food a little—surprised, as always, by how tasty David's specials were.

"I can't help it if I'm not hungry, Charlene," Tick said, pushing her plate away now that there was no point in continuing the charade. "It's not a person's fault if they're not hungry."

Charlene pushed the plate back in front of her. "Yes, it is," she said. "That's exactly whose fault it is. Kate Moss is yesterday's news, kid. Eat."

When she was gone, Tick speared a small *hoisin*-covered scallop and bit it in half, surrendering a half-guilty grin to her father.

"Charlene has secrets?" Miles said hopefully. It pleased him that she'd been watching him, hinting as it did at the possibility—admittedly remote—of an affection that transcended their long friendship. She'd been between boyfriends for some time, and Miles's divorce would soon be final, so maybe. And for years she'd been claiming that Miles was exactly the *sort* of man she'd fall in love with if she had any sense at all—a good man, straight and true, who, with the slightest encouragement would love her all the days of his life. So again, maybe.

Unfortunately, Charlene had also admitted, even after four failed marriages, her abiding preference for bad men whose insides were all twisted up in knots, and who cleared out the minute the going got tough. They had fast cars and drove them recklessly, and this was something she actually liked about them. There was no telling what would happen if she ever hooked up with a man like Miles, but she suspected she'd end up being mean to him, probably even meaner than Janine had been, which was going some. "I just don't think I could go through life at your speed, Miles," she told him once. "Don't you ever want to just put the pedal down to the floor and just see what it feels like?" Therefore, probably not.

"Everybody has secrets except you, Daddy," Tick was saying.

Miles considered this, then said, "What makes you think I don't have a few?"

His daughter didn't answer right away. "It's not like you don't have any," she explained, for once leaving her fork at rest. "It's just that everybody figures them out."

"I think you're just repeating what your mother always says about me."

"I'm repeating what *everybody* says about you. Because it's true. I'm more like Mom," she added somberly, as if this were something she wasn't particularly proud of. Since he and Janine had filed for divorce, Tick had begun cataloging her differences and similarities to each of her parents, perhaps thinking this genetic road map might make her own destiny more navigable. "I'll be good at keeping secrets. If I cheated on my husband, nobody would ever know."

Miles opened his mouth, then shut it again, wondering as he often did if there was another sixteen-year-old like this one anywhere else in the world. "Tick," he finally said.

"I didn't say I'd cheat on my husband," she added. "I just said I can keep a secret."

Before Miles could respond, the bell above the front door tinkled and Janine materialized in the doorway, as if summoned by her daughter's allusion. Without pausing for a moment, she headed right for them through the crowded restaurant. Tick, also without turning around in the booth, seemed to know that her mother had appeared, and she slid over next to the window to make room.

"We weren't expecting you for another hour, at least," Miles said when Janine slid into the booth, pulled her sweatshirt over her head and revealed a hot-pink exercise leotard underneath.

"Yeah, well, here I am, anyway," she said. "And don't be staring at my breasts, Miles. We were married for twenty years, and they never interested you that whole time."

Miles felt himself color, because he *had* been staring at them. "That's not true," he said weakly. Actually, he wasn't really all that interested in them now, except for the fact that they were so completely on display beneath her leotard—though this wasn't a subject he was keen on pursuing in front of their daughter.

"I just finished up at the club," Janine explained, "and I'm hot and sweaty and I haven't even had a chance to shower." She turned toward Tick. "You ready to go home?"

"I guess," Tick said.

"You guess," Janine repeated. "Is there somebody who'd know for sure? Somebody we could consult for a definitive answer?"

"I have to get my backpack," Tick told her. "You don't *have* to be such a bitch every minute, do you?"

"Yes, I do, little girl," Janine said, sliding out of the booth so Tick could get out. "You'll understand why when you're forty."

"You're forty-one," Tick reminded her. "Forty-two this January."

Miles watched his daughter all the way into the back room, feeling, as he always did these days, a terrible mix of irreconcilable emotions— the shame of his failed marriage, anger at Janine for her part in its dissolution, anger at himself for his own part, and gratitude that they'd managed to be faithful to a bad idea long enough to have this child. He would've liked to know if Janine felt any of this, or whether she'd managed to simplify her emotional life by indulging only the regret. Turning back to Janine, Miles caught her sneaking a scallop off Tick's plate.

"Damn," she said, aware that she'd been witnessed. "*Damn*, that's good."

"I could order you some, Janine," Miles offered. "It wouldn't kill you to eat something."

"That's where you're mistaken, Miles. That's exactly what it would do. I'm *not* going to be fat again, not ever."

Charlene happened to be passing by at that moment, so Janine handed her the plate. "Do me a favor and get this away from me, will you?" she said, then turned back to Miles. "There's a word for people like you," she continued. "'Enabler.'"

There was a word for people like Janine, too, Miles thought, and her own daughter had already applied it.

"You're through feeding me, buddy boy. I've assumed control of my own body."

"Good," Miles said. "I'm happy for you."

If Janine heard any sarcasm in this, she didn't react to it. In fact, some of her anger seemed to leak away, and when Tick reappeared with her backpack, Janine said, "Why don't you go on out to the car for a couple minutes. Since I'm here, I want to talk to your father."

Tick leaned into the booth to give Miles a kiss. "See you tomorrow, Daddy. Will you have time to proof a paper?"

"I'll make time," Miles said. "It wasn't very nice to fool me about eating your dinner, though."

"I know," she said without the slightest indication of remorse. "You're just so easy."

Once she was safely through the door, Miles turned back to Janine. "You sure are tough on her lately." He knew, as soon as he spoke the words, that they were a mistake. For Miles, one of the great mysteries of marriage was that you had to actually say things before you realized they were wrong. Because he'd been saying the wrong thing to Janine for so many years, he'd grown wary, testing most of his observations in the arena of his imagination before saying them out loud, but even then he was often wrong. Of course, the other possibility was that there *was* no right thing to say, that the choice wasn't between right and wrong but between wrong, more wrong, and as wrong as you can get. Wrong, all of it, to one degree or another, by definition, or by virtue of the fact that Miles himself was the one saying it.

"Well, *somebody* has to be," Janine said, her hackles now as fully raised as her nipples. "Since she can do no wrong with either her father or her uncle."

Miles opened his mouth to object, but his wife—no surprise—wasn't finished.

"Walt's no better, either. The worse she treats him, the more he fawns over her."

"She's just a kid, Janine." Ours.

Janine picked up an unused spoon, held it like a knife at her temple and made as if to drive it home. "Miles. You're wrong. First, she's not a kid. You don't believe me, just look at her. Try using the eyes you look at other people with. Second, so what? I was never a kid and neither were you. From the time I was old enough to manage it, I was changing diapers. Tick's led a charmed life, and you know it."

"Wasn't that the idea?" Miles said. "I thought that's what we meant to do."

"Not forever, Miles."

What Miles was imagining right now was their daughter watching them, their heads bent forward toward the center of the table so they could lower their voices and still yell at each other. No, this last year of their daughter's life had been anything but charmed. Maybe the others hadn't been so wonderful either. "Janine," he said, feeling suddenly exhausted, "could we not fight?"

"Nope. That's what the last twenty years have been about, in case you missed it. Also, every time there's a problem and the damn school calls somebody, they don't call you, they call me. I'm the one who has to leave work to deal with it, not you."

"I'm not sure that's fair," Miles said. "I wish they *would* call me. If you'd let me have primary custody—"

"Right. And where would she live? Upstairs? Move the pallets of fryolator grease down to the basement to make a little room for her?"

"You have a point," Miles said, trying to keep the bitterness out of his voice. "I *am* left without a house in all this. Speaking of which."

"Don't." Janine pointed the spoon at him. "Don't go there."

"Okay," he agreed, since he'd already gone there and Janine knew it.

Janine had promised to talk to Walt about the house. The sensible, fair thing, she agreed, would be for Walt to buy out Miles's share—or what would have been his share if he had one. The settlement would award Janine the house and Miles had been instructed to continue paying half of the mortgage until such time as the property sold or she remarried. Privately, he and Janine had agreed that when the house did sell, they would divide what was left of the equity. The money they'd used for a down payment had been his, but it didn't amount to that much, and he'd decided not to make an issue of it, or anything else. His instructions to his lawyer had been simple: let her have what she wants. In truth, there was embarrassingly little to quibble over, and even if he'd felt like it, he couldn't be small with Janine without being small with Tick. Not an option.

However, the divorce would soon be final, allowing for Janine's long postponed nuptials, and Miles was beginning to wonder if he should have listened to his lawyer's advice. Walt Comeau, the lawyer had correctly predicted, would rent his own house and move in with Janine. "Is that what you want? For the man who stole your wife to live with her in *your* house, sleeping in *your* bed, all of it rent-free?" Well, of course Miles hadn't wanted that, but at the time such a scenario seemed far-fetched. What sort of man would behave that way? But then Miles wouldn't have predicted that Walt Comeau would also become a regular at the grill, dropping in every afternoon to drink coffee and play gin with Horace and offer Miles business tips. Just today he'd suggested that Miles add an "e" to the word "Grill" to make the place sound classier. Every time Walt made one of his proposals, two things occurred to Miles. First, strange as it seemed, was that Walt's purpose was *not* to inspire Miles to homicide. Walt Comeau truly believed his suggestions to be valuable. And second, he was probably offering them in lieu of rent. Most people, Miles had come to understand, went about their business logically enough if you granted them a couple fundamental assumptions. No court had ordered Walt to pay rent on Miles's house, so he wouldn't. Still, he couldn't help but feel sorry for the man whose wife he'd stolen—fair and square, Walt would consider it, the better man having won—and so, even without obligation to do so, he would continue to look for little opportunities to make it up to Miles. In fact, he seemed increasingly determined to help out in any way he could. No doubt he thought his free advice was worth thousands of dollars, yet Miles stubbornly refused to implement any of it. What could you do? Talk about leading a horse to water. No, if Miles were to die in his sleep tonight, Walt would tell every last mourner that he'd tried everything he could think of to turn the Empire Grill into a profitable enterprise. Miles was a hell of a nice guy, he would conclude, but he had no head for business. Nothing about any of this would strike the Silver Fox as outrageous.

"I *did* speak to him about it," Janine finally said, staring at her reflection in the window. "He said . . ." Here she paused again, as if she herself could hardly credit what she was about to report. "He said he's not sure that real estate here is that good an investment right now."

"Really," Miles said. "He figured that out?"

"He says he doesn't want to tie up his money until he's sure about his next move."

"When will that be?"

"I don't know, Miles. I really don't," she admitted, suddenly dropping the pretense of being angry. "Have you ever noticed the way he scratches his chin when he plays cards? When he's trying to figure out what Horace is holding? It's almost like time stops. Like you're watching a still life."

"Janine—"

"I mean, who knows? One minute he's talking about expanding the club, putting in more indoor tennis courts, then the next he's saying we should build a place out by the lake. There's a half acre of waterfront property he's had his eye on, but when I ask him where exactly, he gets all secretive, like I'm going to blab to somebody who'll buy it out from under him. Every time I try to pin him down about anything, he gets that sly expression, you know? The one he always gets right before Horace gins him."

"Janine."

She continued staring at her reflection, as if meeting his eye would amount to some terrible admission. When she finally did, there were tears, and it occurred to Miles that there might be something she wasn't telling him. Something she wasn't sure of herself.

"What, Miles?"

"Are you having second thoughts?"

She wiped the corner of one eye with the strap of her leotard and gathered her defiance again, causing Miles to wonder, as he had on and off for two decades, what there was about this combative stance that Janine found so attractive.

"No. Don't worry," she assured him. "I'm going through with it. I promise. This time next month all you'll owe is child support."

"I never said I wanted you to go through with anything," Miles reminded her, suddenly feeling the kind of tenderness toward his ex-wife that occasionally crept up on him when he wasn't paying strict attention.

"It's not Walt and me I'm worried about. What I still don't even begin to understand is us."

"You mean how we managed to make such a mess of everything?"

Janine made a face at him. "Hell, no, Miles. That part's easy. We messed things up because we didn't love each other. What I'd like to know is why. I mean, I told you why I didn't love you. Everything you did during the last twenty years that pissed me off, I told you about."

Miles couldn't help but smile. True, Janine's list of his shortcomings was long, comprehensive, and subject to constant revision.

"Now here we are almost divorced and I'm getting set to marry somebody else, and you still haven't told me why you didn't love me. Does that seem fair? I mean, if you were ever inclined to get married again—which I don't recommend—*you'd* at least know what to do different, right? Because I was honest with you."

"What do you want, Janine? A list of marital grievances? You took up with Walt Comeau, for God's sake."

"Well, sure, throw that in my face."

Now it was Miles's turn to study his reflection in the glass. The man who stared back at him looked exasperated.

"It's not fair, and you know it," she continued. "I mean, sure, fine. I took up with Walt, so you've got a gripe. But I took up with Walt because *you* didn't love me. I know it hurt your feelings, me falling in love with him, but you shouldn't pretend you were in love with me, Miles, because we both know you weren't."

"What's my part in this conversation? If you're going to speak for both of us—"

"Are you telling me you loved me, Miles? If that's what you want to tell me, say it. I'll shut up so you can." When he looked down at his hands, she said, "I didn't think so."

She was right, of course. In the deepest sense, he hadn't loved her. Not the way he'd intended to. Not as he'd sworn he would before God and family and friends, and this simple truth embarrassed him too deeply to allow for anything like analysis. No, he hadn't loved her, and he didn't know why. He also didn't know what to call whatever it was that would've prevented him from telling her, even if he had known. If you didn't call it love, what did you call the kind of affection that makes you want to protect someone from hurt? What was the name of the feeling that threatened to swamp him now, that made him want to take her in his arms and tell her that everything would be all right. If not love, then what?

Still, she was right. Because whatever it was he felt for this woman whose life had been joined to his for so long, whatever it was certainly couldn't be confused with desire and need and yearning. Miles knew that much, if only because he'd tried his best to confuse them.

"Why are you tormenting yourself, Janine?" he said. "If Walt makes you happy, what else matters?"

She studied him for a minute, then gave up. "Beats the shit out of me," she admitted, forcing a smile. "I guess I'd just like to hear you say I'm not a horrible person."

"I never said you were a—"

"That's what I'm trying to tell you, Miles," she said, sliding out of the booth. "You never said anything."

"HE KEEPS SAYING he can climb like a monkey," Miles told his brother. They were upstairs in his apartment above the restaurant, and it was nearly eleven o'clock. Miles, a lifelong insomniac, would be awake by five anyway, but he couldn't help resenting that if he *should* ever be visited by a decent night's sleep, he'd have to interrupt it to open the restaurant. David, who'd taken a small club soda from the mini-fridge, set it down on the floor and moved a huge box of toilet paper off the sofa so he'd have a place to sit. The Sox were on TV, a late game from the West Coast.

Janine had been right, of course. As things stood, there was no room for Tick here, even though he'd been toying with the idea earlier that evening, trying to make it work. He could move all the grill supplies back down into the basement until the river flooded again and the restaurant started taking on water. If he cleared out all that stuff, there would be room for both of them, except that a girl Tick's age needed more than space. She needed a room of her own with a door she could close, even slam, when necessary. Miles's apartment, which hadn't been occupied since Roger Sperry died, was basically one big room. Except for the door you entered by, there was only one other, to the bathroom, and even that didn't close tight. Tick deserved better. Sure, with a little work and expense he could make it nicer, but it would still be a shabby second-floor flat above a place of business.

For all of that, he knew that his daughter would jump at the chance to get out of her mother's house. She despised living under the same roof as Walt Comeau. Though it wasn't a whole lot bigger, the little cottage behind the bookstore on Martha's Vineyard would be plenty big for the two of them, if he could ever figure out how to afford it.

"Everything he does," David remarked from the sofa, "he does like a monkey." Regarding their father, David was unsentimental. "You're right not to let him on any ladders, though. Don't let him con you into feeling sorry for him."

"I'll try. But he's pretty good at getting to me. I guess I don't want to be sold short when I'm old," Miles said, trying to explain away the foolish emotion. Feeling sorry for Max Roby was certainly all of that.

"Pretty good night," David said, shaking his longish hair. The effect of wearing a hairnet through an eight-hour shift was that you looked like you were still wearing one even after you took it off.

"Better than pretty good," said Miles, who'd rung out the register. "Looks like Thursdays might fly."

"I'm not sure we've got our costs in line."

"I doubt we're too far off."

"You *do* know the next logical step, don't you?"

"Yes, I do," Miles said. This was an old conversation. Pointless, too, like so many of his conversations with his brother, going all the way back to when their mother was still alive. Strange. He and David were closer now, since his brother's crippling accident, than ever. Before, both men had pushed their conversations until their words burst into flame, rekindling age-old resentments, reopening old wounds. There was nearly a decade's difference in their ages, and their life experiences were radically dissimilar. Miles had grown up before their mother became ill, David after. Perhaps just as important, they'd always been temperamental opposites: Miles careful and thoughtful, like their mother; David energetic and restless, like Max. Since the accident, though, all this seemed to matter less, though it troubled Miles that their newfound intimacy seemed to depend on their having so little to say to each other. They passed the baton of the restaurant back and forth with an almost effortless minimum of talk. Often their communication seemed almost ritualistic. David would report to Miles that he'd locked up, understanding that Miles already knew this, but also that he expected to hear these words, probably was waiting to hear them, needing them to provide some kind of closure that the day wouldn't otherwise have.

"Wouldn't need to be a full liquor license," David said. "Beer and wine would do it."

"Mrs. Whiting won't go for it, though."

"She'd rather lose money?"

Odd, but Miles had the feeling this might be the precise, literal truth. It violated logic, of course. Why be content to squeak by on the slenderest of profit margins when there was an opportunity for more substantial gain? Mrs. Whiting was a practical and ruthless business-woman who had recognized the exact moment at which to sell each of the three Whiting mills, who had never before exhibited the slightest patience with borderline businesses. Yet for more than a decade she'd seemed content to let the Empire Grill limp along toward its inevitable extinction. In the absence of any other rational explanation, Miles had almost concluded that it must be a matter of affection. But for whom? Miles himself? It was possible, he supposed. Horace, as clever and cyn-ical an observer as the local scene offered, had concluded as much, so maybe. If not for Miles, for the Empire Grill itself? Unlikely, since the old woman hadn't set foot in its shabby premises in twenty years. The other possibility, which Miles kept returning to, was the old woman's fondness for Miles's mother, who had worked for Mrs. Whiting until she fell ill. So again, maybe.

"Reason with her," David urged him. "Tell her people won't eat spicy Mexican and Asian food without beer. And they like wine with Italian."

"I'll try," Miles said. "But don't get your hopes up. She's not stupid, but for some reason she doesn't like change. Maybe it's just old age. Maybe she doesn't want to be bothered. Anyway, it's her business."

David pondered this obvious truth while a Red Sox batter hit a tow-ering fly ball that was caught on the warning track. Then, studying his empty club soda, as if trying to recollect why a man like himself would drink soda water instead of beer, he said, "Want to hear another idea?"

No, was the simple truth. It had been a long day, and Miles was too tired and dispirited by his conversation with Janine to think. "Sure," he said. "What?"

"Go talk to your mother-in-law."

"Bea? Why?"

"Think about it, Miles. It makes sense."

"It's a thought," Miles said. Janine's mother owned not just the dying tavern, Callahan's, but the building in which the tavern was housed, which meant that Mrs. Whiting, if she felt betrayed and decided to be vindictive, would have little recourse. No, there was no need for David to explain his thinking here. If Mrs. Whiting didn't want to spring for a liquor license and give them a fighting chance, move the whole kit and caboodle across town. Bea's place was bigger, too, which meant they'd have room to grow.

"You'd be doing Bea a favor. She's going under by degrees. You could save her and yourself at the same time."

"I don't have the money to buy her place, David."

"Offer to go partners. She provides the liquor license, you provide the food service."

"And what do I do when you leave?"

"Am I going somewhere?"

"Well."

"Don't 'well' me, Miles."

"You get bored with things. And then you split. I don't mean that as a criticism. There's no reason you shouldn't. You don't have a family. I just don't have the luxury, is all."

"So you're saying I'm the reason you won't consider Bea's place?"

"I'm not saying I won't consider it," Miles said. "I admit, it's a thought."

"I wish you wouldn't say it like that," David told him. "It sounds dead already."

Miles didn't respond right away, not until he could speak without irritation. When the last Red Sox batter of the inning finally struck out with men on first and third, Miles said, "I owe her, David."

"Owe who?"

"Mrs. Whiting. Isn't that who we were talking about? Maybe Janine and Tick and I haven't had a terribly prosperous life, but it hasn't been bad, either. The restaurant has struggled, obviously, and God knows we've struggled right along with it, but we've kept our heads above water, and that's more than you can say for a lot of people around here. Mrs. Whiting could've closed the place down years ago, and where would that have left us? You want me to thumb my nose at her? And there's something else, too. I was away at college for three years, and every time I really needed money, Mom sent it. Where do you think Mom found five hundred dollars every semester for books and fees?"

David considered this. "You think it was from Mrs. Whiting?"

"She didn't get it from Max. Who else was there?"

"I don't know," David admitted, "but at least we're finally talking about the right person."

"What's that supposed to mean?"

"It means when you said you owed her, that's who I thought you were talking about. Mom. If you were saying you owed *her*, that would have made some sense."

"I don't need you to tell me how much I owe her, David."

"Yeah? Well, there's only one way to pay off that debt, big brother. And I'm sorry, but you *do* need reminding about the way things were. Mom never wanted you to come back. Your getting out of here was her life's work. You know that better than I do. If she borrowed money from Mrs. Whiting, you can bet she paid it back in full. Services rendered. She practically raised that woman's daughter. And if she knew you'd ended up forty-two and running the Empire Grill, she'd turn over in her grave."

Miles rubbed his temples with his thumbs, feeling the first aura of a headache coming on. "I'm sure you're right that she'd be disappointed," he conceded, knowing too that "disappointed" was too lame a word for it. "Brokenhearted" was more like it. "No doubt I've shamed her. I feel like I have, believe me. But the one thing I don't think I'd have to explain to Grace Roby is that a kid comes first. Maybe I was wrong to come back, but I've got Tick now, and I can't put her in jeopardy. I won't."

"And you imagine I would? You think I'd advise you to?"

"Isn't that what you're doing? Last week you were all for that bookstore I can't afford on Martha's Vineyard. Now you want me to make Mrs. Whiting my enemy by going into business with Bea. Have you ever looked at that kitchen? Do you have any idea how much fixing it up would cost?"

"Between us we could—"

Miles couldn't listen. "David, if you want to go into business with Bea, then *go*. I give you my blessing."

His brother nodded slowly, as if this whole conversation had already taken place numerous times and there were just one or two minor details he'd failed to memorize. "All right," he said finally. "Since I've already pissed you off, I'll try this one more time and then give up. I *know* you've got Tick, Miles. And I know you're in a tight spot. In fact, I'm even more worried about the spot you're in than you are, because it's worse than you think. What I'm trying to say is that it isn't going to get any better. That woman's got you on a treadmill, Miles. You're running so hard all the time just to keep up that you can't see it. It's what Mom feared. It's what she knew would happen if you—"

"Tell me something," Miles interrupted. "Why do you hate Mrs. Whiting so much?"

"Look," he said, "it's not a question of hating her. You think she'll give you the restaurant like she promised, and then you'll sell it and get out, right?" When Miles didn't say anything, he continued, "Except Mrs. Whiting isn't dying, Miles. You know what she's doing instead? She's living. In Italy for a month when it suits her. In Florida during the winter. Santa Fe in the late spring. You're the one that's dying, Miles, a day at a time. Do you have any idea how old Mrs. Whiting's mother was when she died?"

"None," Miles confessed.

"That's because she's still alive," David told him. "She's in a nursing home in Fairhaven, in her nineties. If Mrs. Whiting lives that long, you'll be sixty-five when you inherit the grill. That's *if* she gives it to you. And that's not even the worst part, Miles. You claim you're sticking it out for Tick, but do you know what that kid's going to be if you aren't careful? She'll be the next manager of the Empire Grill."

"Over my dead body," Miles said.

His brother got to his feet and smiled, clearly having seen this coming. "Good. Now we've come full circle. That's what Mom always said about you."

David tossed his empty soda bottle into the trash can by the door. "Look, I'm sorry I said anything. I should go home. I already know how this is going to end."

For a moment Miles thought that he was referring to their discussion, but then he realized that David probably meant the ball game. The Sox held a slender one-run lead in the seventh, and history, both recent and not so recent, suggested it wouldn't hold up. September was a bad month for New England baseball fans. You could spend most of it searching in vain for reasons you were so optimistic back in April. Next April was when you'd remember them.

"When's Buster coming back?" David wondered, referring to the grill's other fry cook, who'd commenced his bender the day Miles returned from Martha's Vineyard.

Miles doubted his brother really cared about Buster. David was just anxious that they not part angry. His question was designed to restore the usual equilibrium. "I'll see if I can hunt him down tomorrow."

"We're going to need another waitress and busboy, too."

"I know. I'll get on it."

"Okay," David said, starting out, then stopping, one hand on the doorknob. "What was Janine all upset about tonight?"

"I don't know," Miles said, meeting his brother's eye. The simple truth. "Cold feet, probably."

David nodded. "I should hope. Given the man she intends to marry, she ought to be cold all the way up to her barrettes."

"I don't think women wear those anymore, do they?" It'd been so long since Miles had loosened a woman's hair that he'd lost track.

"Funny thing, though," David said, still standing in the doorway.

Miles studied him, dead certain that what came next would not be funny in the least.

"The two of you sitting there in that booth tonight looked more like lovers than you ever did when you were married."

"Funny?" Miles said sadly. "That's hilarious."

Mrs. Whiting's refrain, he realized.

David was all the way down the back stairs when Miles remembered something and hurried after him. His brother was backing his pickup out of his space behind the restaurant, a complicated maneuver for a man with only one good arm, when Miles rapped on the window.

"Listen," Miles began, "tell me to mind my own business . . ."

"Okay, I will," David promised.

"Are you growing marijuana out there at the lake?"

His brother snorted. "Why, Miles? Do you want some?"

Miles didn't see why this seemed so damned funny, but he let it go. "Jimmy Minty thinks you are, is the reason I mention it."

"Jimmy Minty *thinks*?"

"Apparently."

"Why tell you?"

"He characterized it as a friendly warning, since we're all old friends. I sort of told him to fuck off. I also told him I didn't think you were."

David nodded. "You see him, tell him I said thanks for the tip."

When his brother started rolling the window back up, Miles rapped on it again. "You didn't answer my question," he said. "*Are* you growing marijuana out there?"

David smiled. "Mind your own business."

"You always talk about Mom as if I was the only one she had plans for. That's not true, you know."

David nodded. "I know exactly what she wanted me to do, because she told me before she died."

Something in Miles sensed a trap, but since it was his brother who'd set it, he decided to walk right in. "What was that?"

"Look after your brother," David said, backing out.

CHAPTER 7

"WHO'S THAT just came in?" Max Roby wanted to know when he felt the air change in the tavern. Sitting at the far end of the bar, he heard the front door swing shut with a dull thud. Whoever it was had stopped at the cigarette machine, a promising sign. Max leaned back on his stool, squinting across the dark room, trying to make out who it was. Since he'd turned seventy, his eyes weren't as good as they used to be. Fortunately, he could still climb like a monkey.

"It's Horace Weymouth," Bea Majeski told him from behind the bar. "Leave him alone."

Bea was just now pondering whether to close Callahan's for the night. It was going on midnight, and her only customer was Max Roby, who you couldn't really call a customer because he perpetually hovered at his hundred-dollar credit limit. Truth be told, most of Bea's customers were the same. They'd pay down their tabs by ten or twenty bucks in the afternoon, then drink them back up to a hundred by closing time. Unless she got lucky and one of them handed her a twenty and keeled over on the spot, every goddamn one of these deadbeats was going to die owing her a hundred dollars. Even the stiff that had handed her the twenty would owe her eighty. About the only trade Callahan's got anymore was from the Empire Towers, the subsidized senior citizens' housing facility down the block. First of the month, after they got their checks, the geezers would stream in. They'd drink old-fashioneds and sidecars for a few days, but by the tenth or so, they'd have blown their booze allotment and Bea wouldn't see any of them again until the first. Except for Max Roby. He also lived over at the Towers, but he turned up regardless. At least the geezers didn't start fights, she told herself. Again, except for Max Roby.

"In fact," Bea told him now, suspecting that her previous instructions might be interpreted too narrowly, "leave everybody alone."

"Invite him down here," Max suggested. "I could use some company."

Bea glared at him. "What'd I *just* say?"

"How's that bothering anybody? I like Horace."

"Me too," Bea said, studying him in the entryway hunched over the cigarette machine, madly pulling at the levers now. He'd clearly abandoned his own brand for whatever the machine might deign to give him. "Which is why I told you to leave him alone. A man ought to be able to come in here without you bumming cigarettes and draft beers."

Out in the entryway, the machine surrendered a pack of some brand or other, which Horace bent down to scoop out of the trough. When he raised up again and turned toward the bar, he caught sight of Max, the only customer, seated at the far end, where Bea always parked him because he smelled rancid and was a pain in the ass. This sight occasioned a small hitch in Horace's giddy-up, a split second's hesitation, during which a man might consider his options. Like leaving. Other men had been known to turn promptly on their heels upon spying Max, but all his life Horace had been victimized by his own good manners. A reporter for the *Empire Gazette* for going on thirty years, he'd seen humanity from every angle. Most people, he concluded, were selfish, greedy, unprincipled, venal, utterly irredeemable shit-eaters, but he'd also observed that these same people were highly sensitive to criticism. Max Roby was an exception, but Horace nonetheless couldn't bring himself to hurt the man's feelings. Which meant he also couldn't plop down at the opposite end of the bar. That strategy wouldn't work anyway, since the exact same conversation would ensue, with Max shouting it.

"What'd it give you this time?" Max said in an idly curious tone when Horace slid onto a nearby stool, leaving one between them as a buffer zone, however inadequate. Horace tried to imagine the situation whereby someone would come in and fill *that* vacancy. It'd have to be a stranger. A blind stranger. No sense of smell, either.

"Chesterfields," Horace said, examining the pack before placing it on the bar alongside a twenty-dollar bill. Bea poured him a draft and slid an ashtray in front of him, leaving the twenty where it was, for now. "You want one, Max?"

"Sure," he said, leaning over to snatch the pack, then deftly peeling off its slender ribbon, thumbing up its flip top, discarding the foil and removing two cigarettes.

Horace noted that Max had taken two, not one, but said nothing, just as Max had known he wouldn't. "You might as well draw one for my friend here," he told Bea. "He's got that thirsty look."

Bea did not approve of Horace's generosity, but she complied with his request. "Working late?" she asked.

Horace nodded. Tonight had been a beaut. For starters he'd had to cover the school board meeting in Fairhaven, one of his least favorite assignments; this one had progressed rapidly from civil to uncivil to angry to plain insulting, stopping just short of fisticuffs. Then, on the way home, his car had broken down on a seldom-used back road out by the old landfill. There was only one house within a radius of about a mile, and Horace, hoping to use the phone to call for a tow, had walked up the long dirt driveway and there, around back of the dark old house, had secretly witnessed something that had rattled him to the core, something that went far beyond the selfish, greedy, unprincipled, venal, utterly irredeemable shit-eating behavior he was used to and sent him stealing back out to the road, as if he himself and not that sad, alarming boy had been the guilty party. As he walked nearly three miles into town, what he'd witnessed was with him every step, and it made him glad of companionship now, even if one of his companions was Max Roby.

"You should get that thing removed," Max suggested, glancing at the fibroid cyst on Horace's forehead.

"What thing?" Horace said, his standard reply to such comments, which were more frequent than anyone would imagine.

"I'm always afraid it'll explode when I'm talking to you," Max said, draining half of his beer in one sudden motion. It hadn't been Max's intention to gulp so much, but he'd been perched there on his barstool, dry, for a hell of a while. A bar could become a desert when you were broke, its beer spigots a mirage. When you finally arrived at the oasis you could tell yourself not to drink too deeply, but a body parched so long by the desert sand has its own needs, its own devices, and Max was just glad his body hadn't demanded the whole glass Horace had bought him. The idea now was to be patient and adjust himself to the pace of the man he hoped to continue drinking with. If he tried to push Horace by draining his own glass too quickly, the other man would feel pressured and leave, then Max would be smack-dab in the middle of the desert again. Horace had a car and, if so motivated, could just get up and walk out and drive to the Lamplighter, a place where Max wasn't welcome—even if he had a way to get there, which he didn't, unless he walked or hitched. The first he refused to do, the second he never had much luck at, owing, if his son Miles was to be believed, to his personal appearance.

This lack of transportation was beginning to get Max down. They'd taken away his license three years ago when he ran over the mayor's daughter's dog, strengthening his conviction that a man's prospects in life were determined by luck and politics. In a town overrun by mangy curs, it was a damned unlucky man who ran over a purebred fox terrier owned by the mayor's eight-year-old brat. Any other victim wouldn't have had the political wherewithal to pull Max's records and get him declared a public menace. A luckier fellow would've run over a stray mutt and been proclaimed a public benefactor—they'd have probably given him a job at the humane society, where they allowed animals a week, two at the outside, to get claimed, after which they got the needle.

No, Max knew all about luck. He knew, for instance, what bad luck was always followed by. Worse luck. Not a month after losing his license, he'd left Callahan's around closing time one night and, nodding off at the wheel, had driven into a ditch, where the car's frame snapped in half, leaving him no choice but to walk back to Callahan's and report the vehicle stolen. Also leaving him in the condition in which he now found himself—a man not only without a license, which was inconvenience enough, but also without a car, which made it a full-blown dilemma. An old man without wheels was a pitiful thing. People could get up and leave and you couldn't follow them, and they knew you couldn't, which meant they were more likely to do just that. Winter was just around the corner, too. High time he got himself down to Key West, where you didn't freeze your ass off and you didn't need a car, since the bars were all lined up one right after another, and almost everybody either walked or rode bicycles.

Max sighed, staring at his now empty glass, considering the unfairness of it all. "What would it cost you to have it removed?" he wondered out loud, touching his forehead where his own cyst, if he'd had one, would have been located. Horace was sitting there nursing his beer, which made Max even more resentful. "A couple hundred bucks?"

Horace shrugged, exchanging a glance with Bea, who was getting ready to give Max the boot, he could tell. "Hard to say."

Max stifled a bitter laugh. "Why? You never looked into it?"

"Never did."

"I sure would've," Max said. "That son of a bitch was growing out of the middle of *my* forehead, I'd have looked into it pronto."

"I think it might be the source of my intelligence," Horace told him, winking at Bea. "What if I let somebody cut it off and then discovered it was responsible for all my best ideas?"

"That's something Max wouldn't have to worry about," Bea said. "Not having a brain."

Max treated this insult the way he treated all insults, by pushing his glass forward for a refill. In his experience, after insulting you, people generally felt guilty. It occurred to them that maybe they were selling you short. They wondered if they could do something to make it up to you. This impulse never lasted long, though, so you had to take advantage swiftly. Max had been offering Bea opportunities to insult him all night long, but until this very moment she'd resisted, which meant she hadn't owed him anything and his glass had remained dry. Now she had no choice but to fill it and grudgingly slide it back in front of him. This time he drained off only a third, which put him in stride with Horace, right where he wanted to be.

"You ever been to Florida?" Max asked.

"Once," Horace admitted. "Back when I was married."

"Before that thing started growing out of your forehead, I bet," Max said, abruptly scooting off his stool. "I gotta pee."

Bea sighed when the men's room door swung shut behind him. "You want me to run his sorry ass?" The only reason she hadn't eighty-sixed the old fart before now was out of affection for his son Miles, who was about the nicest, saddest man in all of Empire Falls, a man so good-natured that not even being married to her daughter, Janine, had ruined him. What Janine was thinking in trading in a man like Miles for a little banty rooster like Walt Comeau defied imagination. Or at least Bea's imagination. True, Miles wasn't sexy and never had been— unless you considered kindness sexy, which Bea always had. Granted, there were men you wanted to sleep with, some men because they got you all hot and bothered, but others, like Miles, you just kind of wanted to do something nice for because they were decent and deserved it and you knew they'd be appreciative and wouldn't hold it against you for maybe not being so damn beautiful yourself. Bea had tried to explain this to her daughter once, but it had come out all wrong and Janine had misunderstood completely. "That's mercy-fucking," she'd said, and Bea hadn't bothered to argue because her daughter, lately, considered herself an authority on all matters sexual. In fact, she'd grown tiresome on the subject, especially since Bea was just as happy to have that part of her life safely behind her. Saying good-bye to sex was like waking up from a delirium, a tropical fever, into a world of cool, Canadian breezes. Good riddance.

Miles, though, was the sort of man you could love without completely losing your self-respect, which couldn't be said for most of them, and certainly not for Walt Comeau.

"Nah, leave him be," Horace said. "Max just says what he thinks whenever he thinks it. It's the people who always pause to consider that I worry about."

"He's an asshole, is what he is."

"Well, yeah, there is that," Horace admitted, as the men's room door swung open to announce Max's return. That a man could relieve himself so quickly didn't seem possible, and both Horace and Bea regarded him curiously as he slid nimbly back onto his stool. The front of his trousers bore traces of urinary haste.

"Jesus," Bea said, shaking her head in disgust. "You're a foul, vulgar old man. When you're done, give it a shake at least."

"You ever been to the Keys?" Max asked Horace, ignoring Bea entirely.

"Never."

"Where were you in Florida?"

"Orlando."

"You'd like Key West," Max assured him. "Hemingway lived there."

Horace took a swig of beer and watched Max do the same. The Hemingway tidbit was interesting coming from this particular old man.

"Hemingway."

"Right," Max said, glad to see he'd set the hook properly. Horace, he knew, wrote for the newspaper and might be drawn to another writer the way a normal person might be drawn to beer and warm weather. "Hell of a guy."

"You met him?"

"Everything's named after him down there. Hemingway this, Papa that. His pals called him Papa, you know."

"What I asked was, did you ever meet him?"

"Who knows?"

Horace couldn't help but chuckle. "What do you mean?"

"I mean, who the hell knows? I drank a lot of beer down there over the years. He could've been sitting on the next stool one of those nights. How would I know?"

"I bet there was at least one stool between you," Bea said.

"When did you start going down there?" Horace asked.

"Winter of 'sixty-nine."

"Then you didn't sit next to Hemingway," Horace said. "He killed himself in 'sixty-one."

Max tried to remember if he'd heard this. He was pretty sure he already knew Hemingway was dead. He'd snuck into the writer's house with a group of tourists—what, twenty years ago?—and he seemed to recall there'd been some mention of Hemingway being dead. He wasn't home, at any rate. What had impressed Max most about the house was all those cats, most of which had an extra digit that looked like a thumb on their front paws. He didn't think a thumb was all that attractive on a cat, though these old toms looked like they could pick up a glass of beer just like a human being did, the way that damn thumb curled around. According to the tour guide, the great writer's cats were much revered; at any rate, they sure had the run of the place. That was what Max liked about the Keys, that pretty damn near everything was tolerated, including Max himself, whose decrepit state, much derided up North, was considered down there the natural, indeed, the inevitable, state of man. In Key West Max was often taken for a local, the ones they called Conchs, and such misguided tourists would happily buy him drinks. Hemingway, being famous, probably never had to buy his own drinks. Which raised an interesting question.

"Killed himself? Why would he do that?"

"Probably just woke up one morning and felt the futility of the whole thing," Horace guessed.

"What futility?"

Horace studied his companion. "People have been known to come to that conclusion about their existence, you know. Hell, not all that long ago, the richest man in central Maine blew his brains out right here in Empire Falls."

C. B. Whiting, he meant. Charles Beaumont. Charlie. "Twenty-three years ago March," Max said, aware as soon as the words were out of his mouth that both Horace and Bea were staring at him.

"How in the world would you know that?" Bea said.

Max shrugged, as if to suggest that people had a right to know anything they wanted to, this being a free country. Anyway, C. B. Whiting's killing himself wasn't even the weird part, to Max's way of thinking, and he'd thought about it plenty during the past two-plus decades. No, the weird part was that Whiting had taken the time and trouble to come all the way back to Empire Falls when he could have just shot himself in Mexico, where he was living at the time. On the other hand, Max allowed, draining the rest of his beer, a man who'd decided to shoot himself in the head probably wasn't thinking too clearly in the first place.

His glass empty again, Max looked over at Horace's, which was still half full. Max supposed he could try pushing his glass at Bea again, but he knew it wouldn't do any good. You only got one insult-beer per night with Bea, who afterward could insult you for free. Talk about futility.

"You and I should go down there someday," he suggested to Horace. "The women all walk around half naked. They don't mind if you look, either. There's this one bar down there where the girls take off their bras and panties and nail 'em to the ceiling. You should see it. I'm free, anytime you want to go."

"I don't think so," Horace said, pushing the twenty toward Bea and signaling to Max Roby his intention to make this a one-draft night. "I might get depressed. Shoot myself in the head."

Max saw the gesture and was gravely disappointed. Miffed, too. "Try to miss that thing on your forehead," he advised. "What a hell of a mess *that* would make."

AFTER HORACE LEFT, Max downed the last swallow of beer in the other man's glass and then, annoyed with himself for indulging morbid thoughts, gave himself over to the problem of whom he might entice to accompany him southward. The ideal candidate would own a car and not expect much in the way of gas money from Max. Once in Florida, things would be easier. Once he found a place to stay, he'd get somebody at the Empire Towers to send him his government check at the first of each month. It worried Max a little, the way money evaporated in the Keys. Sun, Max supposed—shining all the while, making you sweat, and it was the sweating made you thirsty. Beer was more expensive down in Florida, but Max much preferred how they served it, with a fresh slice of lime wedged right into the mouth of the sweating bottle. If a man wasn't careful, he could drink the bottom right out of a Social Security check by mid-month, and then he'd have to scam like mad till the first.

What Max needed was an honest-to-God live one—somebody with a little dough who was looking to have a good time and didn't know how. Horace, whom Max had initially cast in this role, wasn't right, the more he thought about it. Just as well he hadn't warmed to the idea. He couldn't imagine trying to explain that damned knot on the man's forehead everywhere they went. Women, especially, would want to know the story of that purple veiny son of a bitch, at least enough to be reassured it wasn't contagious.

Ten years ago there were any number of people Max might've talked into making the trip, but the years had taken a heavy toll. Many of Max's favorites were dead, others were in nursing homes, still others had just gotten too damned old in spirit, which Max flatly couldn't understand; he'd just turned seventy, he felt about fifteen, and had all his life.

A woman might make an interesting traveling companion, and here again, ten years ago he wouldn't have had to go looking very far. In a town like Empire Falls, somebody's wife was always ready and willing to fly the coop if approached in the right way, and Max found himself wondering what in hell had happened to all the good women. Most of the old ones had got religion, and the younger ones could do better than Max Roby and let him know as much, in case he had any doubts. Which was also probably just as well. Women, generally speaking, had a lot of needs. They needed to stay in nice places, and needed to pee every time you turned around, and needed to keep you abreast of what they were thinking pretty much constantly. But they didn't understand money needs at all. Like when you ran out. Then there was the philosophical issue of why you'd even want to bring one someplace when there'd be plenty of women already there when you arrived. Coals to Newcastle, if you thought about it. Max liked the women in the Keys. Life seemed to have made them realists, not dreamers. Also, they seemed to grasp instinctively how men like Max ended up men like Max, and not to hold it against them.

"Wake up, Max," Bea said, interrupting his reverie, and for a moment he concluded that she'd been eavesdropping on his thoughts. On the TV above the bar he was surprised to see that the ball game had been replaced by the postgame show. Yet again the Sox were losers. "Go home," Bea told him.

"What time is it?" Max asked, squinting at the clock positioned halfway down the bar. If there was one thing he hated, it was a bar that closed early.

"One o'clock," Bea told him. "You've been asleep for an hour."

"I wasn't asleep, I was thinking," Max said.

"Yeah? Well, you're the only man I know who snores when he's thinking." She switched the TV off, leaving Max just enough light to make his way to the front door. "You drank those last two beers too fast, old man. They did you in."

"I drank them just right," he assured her. There was only one wrong way to drink beer, in Max's opinion, and that was the way Horace had done it, letting it get warm and then leaving some of it in the glass. When Max left beer, it was in the urinal. "I gotta pee," he said, heading for the gents'.

"Then do it in your own place," Bea told him, steering him toward the front, hard and heartless woman that she was. "You only live down the block."

True, perhaps, but down the block was too far. The Empire Towers were set way back off the street, Max's studio apartment was on the sixth floor, and the elevator was slow; he knew from experience that when it was most urgent that he do so, he sometimes couldn't slip his key into the lock cleanly.

Fortunately, the alley alongside Callahan's was unoccupied, and Max used the brick wall of the tavern to excellent advantage. When he finished, he felt energized, suddenly unwilling to call it a night. A fine, almost foglike mist hung in the air, and Max decided it was a good night for a stroll, so he set off across town, the whole of Empire Falls rolled up and quiet. He didn't run across a single car or pedestrian the entire way to the cemetery, where he located without difficulty, even in the dark, his wife's grave. He stood at the foot of it without moving for so long that anyone passing by on the other side of the tall, wrought-iron fence could fairly have concluded he was a statue. Gradually the gentle mist turned to rain, and still the old man, hatless, remained at the foot of the stone marked GRACE ROBY, the stone his sons had placed there when she died, when Max was down in the Florida Keys consorting with a different sort of woman entirely, the sort he should've found right at the beginning. Strange that he should feel so content and peaceful in Grace's company now, since he never had when she was alive, so full of hopes and dreams it hurt to look at her. Max catnapped on his feet a while longer, then woke up feeling refreshed, if soaked through. Also, he had to pee again, which necessity he announced aloud to his wife and the other silent sleepers. One of these was Charles Beaumont Whiting, who, like the great Hemingway (if Horace was to be believed), must have woken up one morning impressed by the futility of his existence, a feeling Max doubted he'd ever understand. Life was a lot of things, including disappointing from time to time, but still.

Atop C. B. Whiting's nearby grave, his widow had placed a monument to ensure that her husband stayed right where he was. Max unzipped there and reflected that a good, long, soul-cleansing pee was something many men his age were incapable of. Once they turned seventy, they became leaky faucets with slow, incessant drips. Not Max, whose prostate ought to be willed to science. "I hope you're good and thirsty," he told old Charlie, then let go.

Only when he was finished did he look up and notice, perched atop the monument, a stone cat. Odd that he hadn't noticed this on any of his previous homages to C. B. Whiting, of which there'd been many. The animal looked so lifelike that it gave Max a scare, though not as big as the one he would've gotten had he looked closer and seen it was breathing.

CHAPTER 8

THE SUMMER MILES TURNED NINE, *he played second base for the Empire Paper Giants. One of the younger boys on the team, he spent most of the season on the bench watching the older boys, the fearless ones who stayed in front of ground balls no matter how hard they were hit. Coach LaSalle wouldn't put him in until the late innings, by which time the game was either won or lost—for which Miles was grateful, terrified that the team might lose because of him. When he did finally enter the game and the boys on the opposing team saw him loitering around second base with his too large glove and fearful expression, they'd turn around and bat left-handed, knowing that a ground ball in his direction was as good as a hit.*

All of which changed the last week in July when Miles made a miraculous catch. Actually, he'd been daydreaming at his post when he heard the crack of the bat, and the ball was on him so fast he hadn't time to duck out of the way, as was his custom. The ball hit his open glove so hard that it lodged in the webbing, spinning Miles completely around and landing him on the seat of his pants. Somehow the glove managed to stay on his hand and the ball in the glove. "Look what I found," Coach LaSalle said when he trotted in, his tone not so much mean as pleased, and the backslapping congratulations of his teammates gave Miles heart. Though to this point it had been a consistent source of humiliation, Miles purely loved the game of baseball, and he loved even more the idea that he might be an asset to the team instead of a liability. Having caught one ball by mistake, he saw no reason why he shouldn't start catching others on purpose.

When his mother announced that they were going away for a week's vacation, Miles agreed only on the condition that he be allowed to bring his glove. Grace assured him there'd be no place to play on Martha's Vineyard, but he was determined to practice every day, even if only by throwing himself pop flies on the beach. Besides, his mother admitted she'd never been there herself, so Miles harbored a secret hope they'd be surprised by what they found there. To his way of thinking, if the island was full of rich people, as she claimed, there just might be baseball diamonds everywhere, more than enough for everyone who wanted to play. There were probably leagues set up just for boys like himself who were dragged away against their will, at the worst possible moment, on hastily conceived vacations.

It turned out his mother was right, though, as Miles could tell from the deck of the ferry as they steamed into Vineyard Haven. But it was clear that his mother hadn't known exactly what to expect either, because when they docked and she got a good look at the crowds of well-dressed people in expensive-looking cars who'd come to meet the ferry, Miles saw her hand steal to her mouth, as it did when she was afraid or became aware that she'd made a mistake. In fact, she looked like she was considering just remaining there at the railing of the ferry and returning home without even disembarking. It was Miles who spotted the man on the wharf below, waving either at them or at someone near them. Miles had never seen him before, but when he pointed the man out, his mother waved back. "How did you know us?" she asked when the man, who introduced himself as Mr. Miller, met them at the bottom of the ramp.

"This fella here was the tip-off," Mr. Miller said, smiling at him. "Ballplayer, eh?"

Now it was Miles's turn to admire the man's apparent prescience—until he remembered he was wearing his mitt, which the soft sea air and salt spray on the lower deck of the ferry seemed actually to be softening. For the first time since his father had given it to him, he was able to close it with one hand.

"We sure appreciate your making an exception for us," his mother said as Mr. Miller gathered their bags from the train of luggage bins being off-loaded from the ferry. He seemed to know which ones were theirs without asking, which made Miles wonder if this was because they were shabbier than the others. "I know you don't normally take children."

"Well," Mr. Miller said, loading the suitcases into the back of a station wagon whose engine had been left running, "you had a friend in high places." Then he quickly added, "Besides, this young fella's mostly grown up anyhow, right?"

It happened they were staying on the other side of the island, near a fishing village, and when Mr. Miller pulled the station wagon into the long, narrow drive that led to Summer House, which sat on a bluff overlooking the ocean, the fear Miles had noticed before on the ferry crept again into his mother's eyes, and he wondered if she might instruct Mr. Miller to turn around and take them back to the dock.

In addition to the main inn there were a dozen or so cottages, which Mr. Miller told them were sometimes rented by artists and movie stars. The one Miles and his mother were to occupy was set slightly apart from the rest and had a rose trellis up one side. Miles liked it the best of all the cottages because it was closest to the path that led down the bluff and over the dunes to the beach. They were warned not to stray from the path because of the poison ivy.

What Grace liked best about the cottage was that in the early morning when the wind shifted, they awoke to the sound of pounding surf. Miles knew how far away the water was, but the waves crashed so hard that every morning he went to the front window to make sure the world hadn't tilted during the night. He half expected to look out and see the waves foaming right up to the porch steps.

They stayed out of the inn's dining room because Grace had gotten a quick glimpse of it when they checked in, enough to know that it would be very expensive and to suspect she didn't have anything nice enough to wear. The cottage's galley kitchen was equipped with a small refrigerator, and Grace bought a box of cereal and a quart of milk in the village for their breakfast. By ten o'clock each morning someone from the inn appeared with a wicker basket full of sandwiches, fruit and soft drinks for them to bring to the beach. Only there, among the dunes, did his mother seem truly to relax and enjoy herself.

At thirty, Grace was an attractive woman, and even in the company of a nine-year-old boy, she was regarded by many of the male guests with admiration open enough to be noted by their wives. One man stopped by their blanket and introduced himself, wondering why the two of them never appeared in the dining room in the evening, even offering to buy Grace a cocktail later that afternoon if she felt like it, and if her young companion could find a way to amuse himself for a while. Grace rested her chin on the knuckles of her left hand, pretending to consider this proposal, while her wedding ring reflected the sun, until the man shrugged and said, "Well, you can't blame a guy for trying." She offered no opinion as to whether you could or you couldn't.

Evenings, the day's sun still glowing on their skin, they showered off the sand and salt at their cottage, dressed in shorts and tops and sandals, then strolled down the dirt road into the village for dinner at the least expensive restaurant they could find, a place called the Thirsty Whale, which specialized in takeout but also served food on a small deck under beach umbrellas. A college-girl waitress took a shine to Miles and taught him how to eat steamer clams, which were served in wire baskets along with two cups of liquid. In the first was a hot broth containing juices of the clams themselves, but this, she explained, was really for cleansing them of sand. The second cup contained drawn butter for dipping. The clams were accompanied by a big bowl of oyster crackers. They were expensive, but Grace said it was okay, and Miles ordered them every night, working through the big wire baskets greedily.

The early-evening sun was usually still strong when they sat down to eat, but by the time they finished, a cool breeze would begin to ripple the umbrella above them, and Miles, full of buttery clams, would become deliciously drowsy, so the walk back to Summer House seemed impossibly long. The few stores in the village stayed open late, and one evening Grace stopped in one to look at a summer dress in the window. By the time she'd tried on one in her size and decided to buy it, Miles had fallen asleep in a chair by the door. On the way back to the cottage in the pitch-dark night, Miles asked a question that, perhaps during his nap, had arisen in him from somewhere. "Mom," he said, "are we waiting for somebody?"

He felt his mother stop walking and regard him in the darkness. "What gave you that idea?"

PERHAPS BECAUSE THERE WAS *no one else, the person Miles thought they must be waiting for was his father, even though his mother and Max had had a huge fight earlier in the week before her surprise announcement that she was going to Martha's Vineyard. In fact, after the argument Miles hadn't even seen his father before they left Empire Falls, though this was not terribly unusual. Max often disappeared without notice after such disputes, possibly imagining that his absence would teach Grace a lesson. Sometimes, though more often in winter than in summer, he'd disappear for months, heading down to the Keys, where the weather was warmer and he could pick up work painting houses or crewing on the schooners that took tourists on sunset sails. He didn't send money home when he was gone, nor did he consider this an abandonment of his wife and child. To Max's way of thinking, his being gone meant Grace had one less mouth to feed and, more significant, no bar bill to pay out of her salary at the Empire Shirt Factory. This, far from abandonment, was something of a financial windfall, and he was not shy about reminding her of that whenever she might be tempted to feel herself ill-used.*

Of course, Max would disappear in the summertime, too. The best prospects for house painters were on the coast in places like Camden and Blue Hill and Castine, where rich people from Massachusetts had summer homes and the money to repaint them at the first sign of flaking. Even better, these people, not being local, wouldn't necessarily know of Max's aversion to scraping—indeed, to all of the more time-intensive aspects of any task. Nor were they likely to discover he'd painted their windows shut until after he was long gone. By the time they'd discovered his shoddy work in Boothbay, he'd be painting someone else's windows shut in Bar Harbor. To fire an unreliable painter in season on the coast of Maine was hard, because chances were good he'd have to be replaced by an even shoddier one. During July and August, poor Mainers held a distinct advantage over the rich, which was why these two months were particularly satisfying to Max Roby.

So when Max disappeared the day after the most recent blowup, Miles assumed he'd simply hitched a ride to the coast. He'd earn some money, get himself fired when the time was right, then join them here on the island for the last few days of their vacation. They had never gone on a vacation without Max before, which was why Miles expected his father to turn up eventually. His mother twice went up to the main house to make phone calls, and she had to be calling somebody. When she returned, she seemed downcast, which Miles took to mean that his father was either tied up with work or still miffed. Miles himself was relieved. His mother had instinctively understood that they didn't belong at Summer House, but his father felt welcome everywhere, even when he clearly was not. If Max were to join them, he'd set up shop at the end of the bar and make fun of the gold-buttoned, blue-blazered men and their hefty, lilac-scented wives until he got eighty-sixed. On his way out he'd likely drop his pants and moon the lot of them.

Late one afternoon, just two days before Miles and his mother were to leave, Miles was showing off in the surf and ignoring his mother's pleas to come in and dry off for dinner, when he noticed that she wasn't really paying attention, even when he called to her. These last few days he'd learned to enjoy her alarm when a particularly demonstrative wave would crash over him and wash him up on the beach. In fact, since arriving on the island, she'd been a ready audience for all his foolishness, but at the moment she had her back to him, shading her eyes against the sun, and when he followed her gaze he saw a solitary figure up on the bluff, backlit by the late-afternoon sun, staring down at the beach. Almost everyone else had already packed up their things and headed up the twisting, sandy footpath, and when the man on the bluff appeared to wave, Miles looked around and found no one else he might be waving to. He looked back at his mother just as she dropped the hand that had been shading her eyes. Had she waved back at the man? Probably not, he decided, when she turned away from the bluff and called again for Miles to come in.

"*Who was that?*" *he asked when his mother began toweling him off.*
"*Who was who?*"

Back at the cottage, she insisted that he shower before they went out to dinner, and when he emerged, dressed in shorts and a T-shirt, Grace told him to go back and put on a nicer shirt and a pair of long pants and real shoes, not sneakers. Tonight they were going to eat in Summer House's main dining room. She herself was going to wear the new white dress she'd bought in the village.

MILES LOOKED IN VAIN *for steamer clams on the menu at the Surf Club. In fact there was nothing he recognized, including the language many selections were written in, which his mother informed him was French. To Miles, none of this boded well. There was no advantage that he could see to dressing up in long pants and a stiff shirt and shoes to eat indoors on a white tablecloth, when they might've been dressed comfortably and seated under one of the colorful umbrellas outside the Thirsty Whale and eating steamer clams in English. He especially resented the long pants, because he was itchy on his calves and thighs. The day before, on the way up the footpath from the beach, he'd tossed himself a pop fly and had to chase it into the thicket, and this afternoon in the shower he'd noticed patches of rough red skin. When he got out, he rubbed them with one of the rough white towels that were delivered to the cottage each day, rubbed the dry skin past the point of ecstasy to where it began to glow and hurt. Now these same patches were itching again, and he couldn't get at them. Even worse, his mother had given him a long list of dos and don'ts, saying this was an adult dinner. It was going to last a long time, which was a good thing. He wasn't to fidget or scratch. He hadn't even been allowed to bring his mitt along.*

Miles had to admit that he'd never seen his mother look more beautiful than she did tonight. Her skin had darkened during their week on the beach, but she'd been careful not to burn, and her new white dress made a fine contrast of fabric and skin, and the fact that she was wearing perfume made him wonder if maybe his father would be joining them after all, though that didn't make sense, not with only one more day on the island.

The dining room was nearly full, yet strangely quiet. Miles couldn't remember ever seeing so many people in one room making so little noise. Piano music was coming from somewhere, barely audible, and over it you could hear the noise of cutlery. When Miles examined the menu and observed that there were no steamer clams, Grace leaned forward and whispered that he would have to keep his voice down. At the next table was seated a man with white hair and sad eyes, sipping a cocktail and looking at his own menu. Like half the men in the dining room, he wore a navy blue blazer with gold buttons, and he had smiled at Miles and his mother when they sat down. In fact, every man in the room had managed to turn and look at Grace, though most immediately pretended it was something else that had caught their attention. When the white-haired man heard Miles remark on the absence of steamer clams, he lowered his menu and leaned toward them. "I hope you'll forgive the intrusion," he said, "but I suspect your charming companion might like the Clams Casino. They're excellent here."

Miles studied the man as he spoke, trying to judge his age. Because of his fine white hair, Miles at first thought he must be old, but his face was smooth, and the longer Miles looked at him the younger he seemed. He was older than Grace, of course, though Miles couldn't tell how much older. The way his mother returned his smile also suggested that he wasn't just some old man. "What do you think, Miles?" she said. "Do you trust this gentleman?"

Miles weighed this question carefully. It should've been an easy one but somehow wasn't, and before he could decide, the man got the attention of a passing waiter and ordered half a dozen of the Clams Casino, telling Grace, "Don't worry. If he doesn't like them, I do."

To Miles's surprise, his mother entered into a conversation with the man, explaining that clams of any sort were a new experience for her son and that since discovering them he didn't want to eat anything else.

The man smiled. "Sounds like he's going to have a taste for the good things in life."

"Well, we're on vacation," Grace said, introducing herself and Miles, then hesitating. "Do you mind my asking if you're eating alone?"

"Alas."

"Maybe you'd like to join us?"

"I'd be delighted," the man said, "though I seem to have the larger table. Why don't you and Mr. Miles join me at mine?"

This suggestion was no sooner made than two waiters appeared to put the plan into effect. Miles, at first, was not thrilled with the idea, until the man asked what his favorite sport was. Since arriving, Miles had been acutely aware of how many men would have introduced themselves to his mother if Miles himself had not been there to dissuade them. But this appeared to be a different sort of fellow altogether, and so, when asked about his favorite sport, Miles said baseball and then, without further encouragement, launched into the story of his amazing catch the week before. When he finished, he told the story all over again, in case the man had missed any of its nuances. The tale *carried them through their appetizers quite nicely, he thought. As predicted, Miles liked these new clams a lot, though he was disappointed not to get a whole bucket of them like at the Thirsty Whale.*

The man's name was Charlie Mayne, and he spelled it out loud so as to differentiate it from the state where Miles and his mother resided. For some reason Miles's mother seemed surprised by the name, though Miles thought it suited him well enough. While Miles had been devouring his clams, Charlie Mayne busied himself with expertly extracting what looked like large pencil erasers from inside curved shells that reminded Miles of something, though he couldn't think what. During the week he'd spent hours combing the beach for shells, but he hadn't found any that looked like these.

"Like to try one?" the man said when he saw Miles studying them.

The pencil erasers didn't look all that appetizing, but then again they didn't look any worse than steamer clams with their little sheathed black penises, so Miles tried one. The thing turned out to taste pretty much as he would have predicted—a chewy little devil but tasty too—and when he was offered another, he promptly accepted, though Grace protested that the first gift was more than sufficient. "Not at all," Charlie Mayne insisted. "I'm enjoying this as much as he is. Should we tell him what he's eating?"

He was grinning at Miles's mother now, and Miles noted that his eyes remained sad even when he smiled, and when his mother returned his sad smile with one of her own, it occurred to Miles that they made a couple in some strange way that Grace and his father did not.

"Some secrets are best kept, Mr. Mayne," his mother said. "At least for a while."

But Miles, who sensed that Charlie Mayne was a man who'd cave under tough cross-examination, kept after him to say what the pencil erasers were until Charlie gave in and told him he'd eaten an escargot. This was such a disappointing revelation that Miles suspected he was being lied to and, moreover, that his mother was in on it. If that was true, it was all in good fun, of course, but to think that his mother might take Charlie Mayne's part against him was still disquieting. But it turned out not to be a lie after all; when their menus were returned so they could order a main course, Miles saw the item in question listed under appetizers: Escargot du maison, *served in their shells, with garlic butter. And it occurred to him that Charlie Mayne had been right, having taken one look at Miles before and concluding that here was a boy who'd grow fond of the finer things in life.*

After they finished their dinner and Charlie Mayne made the bill simply disappear, with no money changing hands, he asked if they'd seen the rest of the island. Grace explained they hadn't left the grounds of Summer House except to walk to the village, and Charlie (as Miles now thought of him) consulted his watch and then proclaimed there might still be time if they hurried. When they asked what he was referring to, he just smiled and said they'd see.

They hurried. Or, rather, Charlie hurried. He drove a little bright-yellow sports car with just enough room for himself and Miles's mother in the two front seats, a stick shift between them, and Miles squeezed into a narrow space behind them. They flew across the island, Charlie taking the curves at thrilling speed. With the top down, his longish hair flowed out straight behind him like a wild white mane. He offered Grace a canvas sailor hat, which she managed to keep on only by clamping it down with one hand. Miles kept expecting her to ask Charlie to slow down. She had a fit whenever Max sped, but for some reason she didn't object now. At least Miles didn't think she did. With the top down, the wind was roaring so loudly that he couldn't hear anything being said in the front seat. It felt like the corners of his eyes were actually being drawn back along his cheeks by the speed, and he wondered if he'd look Chinese by the time they arrived at wherever they were going.

Eventually the pavement came to an end, and Charlie Mayne pulled the little car onto a dirt road that ended a hundred yards farther on in a sandy lot, where he parked by a log fence at the very edge of a sloping beach. The sun, incredibly large and orange, sat inches above the calm waters of Vineyard Sound, and when the engine died, Miles heard his mother say, "Oh, Charlie, look!" And when Miles asked what it was that they'd hurried to see, both she and Charlie laughed, making him feel foolish, though he noted that he wasn't the only one not paying strict attention to the sunset. Half a dozen other cars were in the lot, and Miles could see a couple kissing in the nearest one. To his surprise, when he asked his mother if he could go down to the beach, she said sure, so long as he took his shoes and socks off and rolled up the cuffs of his pants and promised not to wade in the surf. "And no more than ten minutes," she warned him. "It's going to get dark fast."

It did, for which Miles was grateful. The patches of rough skin he'd scratched raw in the shower were now pulsing, and he'd been too cramped in the backseat to really get at them. Once he got out of sight, he intended to scratch himself into ecstasy. So when he scrambled over the dunes he was both surprised and discouraged to discover that the beach wasn't deserted, as he'd expected. Spaced evenly, as far into the distance as he could make out, were fishermen casting way out into the gentle waves, then furiously reeling in, then casting again. Miles watched them for a few minutes, trying to make sense of it. Max had taken him fishing on the lake once, but there you just dropped a line over the side of the boat and waited for something to pull on it.

These men seemed almost to be in a competition to see who could cast the far-thest into the waves, and since every cast was a disappointment, they reeled in and tried again. The closest one called out a warning, and Miles saw why a second later when the man drew back his long rod and something silver flashed and whistled through the air behind him and then shot far out into the waves.

Keeping what he hoped was a safe distance behind the casters, Miles trudged up the beach until he came to a secluded spot among the dunes and the tall sea grass. There he lowered his pants down around his ankles and began scratching. It was too dark to tell for sure, but the splotches of rough, red skin seemed to have doubled in size since his shower. Digging at them with his fingernails was midway between intense pleasure and pain, and he would have kept at it until he bled had he not heard a sound nearby, and then low voices. He quickly pulled up his trousers and hurried away.

Back up the beach he heard another sound, more like flapping this time, and when he looked down he was surprised to see a large silver fish, bloody at the gills, flopping in the sand at his feet. "Careful," said a voice a few feet away, where a man crouched, tying a silver lure onto his line. "They got teeth."

It was almost completely dark by the time he arrived back at the parking lot, where he found Charlie Mayne's little car more by the size and shape of its silhouette than anything else. He fully expected his mother to scold him for staying too long on the beach, but he was wrong. There'd been just enough light to see his mother's head resting on Charlie Mayne's shoulder before they heard him coming.

The next morning, aware that he'd been dreaming vividly all night long, Miles awakened to the sound of his mother retching into the toilet of the cottage's tiny bathroom. This was actually the second or third morning he'd heard this, and today he was angry with her, though he hadn't been when he went to sleep. It seemed to have something to do with catching that glimpse of the two of them in the car, but even more he sensed that during the night things had somehow realigned themselves. His mother's asking a stranger to join them at dinner did suggest that his own company left something to be desired. Not that he didn't like Charlie—he did. But Miles found himself angry with the man, too. Charlie, who'd been so attentive during dinner, hadn't seemed particularly interested in hearing about the gasping silver fish Miles had seen on the beach, and when he exaggerated his peril by telling them he'd nearly been snagged by the lure of one of the surf casters, neither his mother nor Charlie seemed as frightened as he might have wished. Worse, he woke that morning almost nauseous with the understanding that the night before he'd actually eaten a snail.

He discovered, however, that it was hard to stay mad at someone you love when she's throwing up in the next room, and so, to preserve the satisfaction of his righteous anger, he went outside with his glove and ball to throw himself pop flies and await the picnic basket from the main house. When it arrived, it was heavier than usual, and he lugged it inside and set it on the breakfast table, where his mother, still in her nightgown, sat with her head in her hands. When she looked up at him, pale and discouraged and clearly exhausted, the anger he'd been trying to protect drained out of him completely.

"Are you sick?" he asked, suddenly afraid.

"I wish I were," she said, with a rueful smile. "Then I could look forward to getting well."

He noticed that as she spoke, she was idly scratching a patch of red skin on her forearm.

"Don't worry," she added. "I'm not dying or anything."

Miles was going through the picnic basket. The instant she told him not to worry, he'd taken her advice and quit. "There's a lot more stuff today," he informed her, holding up a small jar of what appeared to be inky little ball bearings.

This news seemed to cheer her, and Grace rose from the table and threw open the curtains over the kitchen window and stood in the bright sunlight that flooded the room. She stood there for a long moment, her eyes closed, seeming to soak in the sun's rays with something like a smile forming on her lips. For a woman who'd spent the last hour on her hands and knees in front of the commode, Miles thought she looked very beautiful, and he decided to forgive her for last night.

After all, it was their last day on the island.

THEY'D NOT BEEN at the beach for more than half an hour, though, when Charlie Mayne showed up. Miles was pleased to note that he had scrawny, white, almost hairless legs, and when he pulled his sweatshirt over his head Miles saw a pale, concave chest with a few strands of coarse black hair encircling his nipples. Though his mother was not a large woman, Miles now realized, seeing them side by side, that she was a full size larger than Charlie. Last night, especially in the sports car, he'd seemed average-sized, but today, as he settled onto a corner of their blanket, he looked downright puny. Surely, Miles thought, his mother would notice this and send him packing.

"Didn't they make you a lunch basket?" she inquired.

"Alas, they did not," said Charlie, who didn't look concerned.

"Then you'll share ours," Grace told him. To look at her now, you'd never guess how sick she'd been an hour earlier. Nor did she display any inclination toward sending Charlie Mayne away.

"You'll be pleased to learn, however, that I've not come completely empty-handed." And from the pocket of his swimming trunks he took out a long white tube, showed it to Grace, and then tossed it to Miles, who fielded it with his mitt.

Grace clapped her hands in delight. "Oh, Charlie, you're a lifesaver!"

"That's me," he agreed.

"They told me up at the main house that they were all out," she said, motioning for Miles to bring her the tube of ointment.

"I drove in to Edgartown this morning," Charlie explained while Grace applied the poison ivy cream to Miles's legs and stomach, then to her own forearms and a patch Miles hadn't noticed before, on her upper thigh. "In fact, I got the last tube at the drugstore. Apparently this is a banner year for poison ivy all over the island."

Charlie Mayne watched her massage the cream into her thigh until he noticed Miles, who had yet to say hello, staring intently at him, and then turned his attention to the picnic basket. When he found the inky-looking jar, he held it up for Miles's inspection. "Ever tasted caviar, big guy?"

Miles shook his head, still feeling tricked on the subject of specialty foods by last night's snail. He made a mental note to refuse the caviar when it was offered, not because it wouldn't be good, probably, but because Charlie Mayne would be doing the offering. Last night he'd been pleased to be recognized as a person who appreciated the finer things. This morning, everything had changed. In fact, he now wished he'd refused the ointment, because he could already feel it cooling the patches of infected skin, and stubbornly pretended that he preferred the itching.

"I also found us a great place for dinner," Charlie was saying to his mother. "But you have to promise to wear that white dress again."

His mother had put on sunglasses and rolled onto her back. "It's the only one I have." She laughed, and Miles could feel his anger returning. Without even discussing it with him, she was letting Charlie Mayne come to dinner with them.

"I want to eat at the Thirsty Whale tonight," Miles said, nudging her foot with his. "I want steamer clams."

His mother sighed contentedly. "Just feel that sun," she purred.

Miles nudged her foot again. "Did you hear me?" He could tell, even through the sunglasses, that her eyes were closed.

She didn't open them when she spoke. "No, I didn't hear you," she said. "And if you continue to be rude, I won't hear you then, either."

Charlie Mayne didn't seem to understand they were having an argument. "So, it's steamer clams you want?" he said cheerfully, stretching out on his stomach. His back also sported random curly black hairs. About a dozen of them. Ridiculous. "Look at his back," Miles would've liked to tell his mother. Her problem, he was certain, was that she wasn't paying attention.

"Then it's steamer clams you'll get," Charlie finished.

LATE THAT AFTERNOON, when Grace came out of the bathroom freshly showered and dressed in her robe, Miles told her he didn't want to go out to dinner with Charlie. He wanted for it to be just the two of them. They'd been having fun, he told her, before Charlie Mayne showed up.

"Yeah?" Grace said, angry so instantly that it scared Miles, as if she'd been just waiting for him to say something like this. "Well, I've been having fun since he showed up. What do you think about that?"

Miles didn't answer immediately. "Dad wouldn't like it," he said, looking right at her.

"Tough."

"I'll tell."

"Fine," she said, surprising him again, increasing the sensation he'd been feeling all day that everything was adrift. She'd taken out the ointment and was applying cream to her skin. "Then tell."

"I will," he said, knowing it was the wrong thing but saying it anyway.

"You'll have to wait till he gets out of jail, though," she said, her eyes suddenly harder than he'd ever seen them. She hadn't so much spoken the words as let them out of their cages, and she watched him now as if purely curious as to the effect they'd have. If necessary, she had more of them to turn loose. "You didn't know that, did you? That your father was in jail."

She'd propped one foot up on the kitchen chair to apply the ointment, and when she put that one down and the other one up, her robe gaped and Miles caught a dark glimpse of what he knew he was not supposed to see, what he didn't see, not really, because his eyes were already filling with tears.

"You want to know why, Miles? Because last week he was arrested as a public nuisance, that's why. Not for the first time, either. He becomes a public nuisance every now and then when he tires of being a private one. And I'll tell you something else, too. You think Max Roby would care if you told him about Charlie Mayne? Think again. Your father cares only about your father. I wish that weren't so, but it is, and you're old enough to know it. The sooner you understand it, the better off you'll be."

Finished with applying the ointment, she stood facing him. *"And I'll tell you one more thing while I'm at it. When we get back home, things are going to be very different, so you can prepare yourself for that too."*

To punish her, when Grace went to change into the white dress, Miles, instead of getting into the shower as instructed, slipped out the back and returned to the now deserted beach beneath the bluff, where he threw towering pop flies as high as he could until an errant, angry throw sent the ball into the waves. Then he just sat down in the sand, pounding the palm of his glove and wishing they'd never come to Martha's Vineyard. Suddenly he was no longer afraid of ground balls, no matter how sharply struck. If he got hit by one, so what? He understood now what Mr. LaSalle had been trying to teach him all summer. It didn't matter if you got hit. It didn't matter if it hurt.

After a while he heard someone coming down the footpath behind him. When he turned around, he thought it would be his mother, furious, coming to fetch him, but it was Charlie Mayne walking across the sand in a pair of shiny black shoes. He had on a pair of nice pants, and Miles didn't expect him to sit down, but he did.

"What happened to the ball?"

Miles pointed at the waves.

Charlie Mayne nodded. *"You and your mother had an argument?"*

Miles didn't say anything.

"She's an awfully nice person, you know," Charlie finally said.

"I know she's nice," Miles said angrily, not wanting to be told something he already knew, not by somebody who'd only known his mother for two days.

"She loves you."

"I know," Miles said.

"She said for me to tell you she's sorry about the things she said about your dad. That wasn't such a good thing to do."

Miles shrugged.

"The thing is," the man went on, *"everyone deserves a chance to be happy, you know?"*

"She is happy."

"And there comes a time in your life when you realize that if you don't take the opportunity to be happy, you may never get another chance again."

"She is happy," Miles insisted.

"Actually," he said, "I was talking about me. Your mother is the kind of woman who—well, she's like the sun suddenly coming out from behind a cloud."

Miles didn't say anything to this, but it did remind him of how she'd looked that morning when she'd thrown open the kitchen curtains.

"She makes everything look new, sort of." When Miles didn't say anything to this either, Charlie added, "Anyway, it'd make me happy if I might join the two of you for dinner this evening, but it's up to you."

Miles shrugged.

Charlie Mayne nodded and waited. Finally he said, "What's that mean? That shrug?"

Another shrug.

"Well," he said, "I guess it could mean that it's okay for me to come to dinner. Or it could mean you'd prefer I didn't. Or it could mean you wish the whole world were different from the way it is, right?"

Shrug.

Charlie Mayne nodded again. "Right," he said. "Gotcha."

THEY ATE IN A RESTAURANT called Cock of the Walk, and like the evening before, the man paid more attention to Miles than to his mother. Though steamer clams were not on the menu, Charlie suggested Miles order them anyway, and then winked at the waiter. When they came, it was a mound of clams that no three grown people could've eaten, though Charlie seemed to enjoy watching Miles try. "Look at him go," he said to Grace, who was trying not to be mad at Miles anymore. When she smiled and told him not to eat himself sick, he said not to worry and besides, he wasn't the one getting sick every morning. Charlie blanched when he said this, and for a few minutes there was only the sound of empty clamshells rattling into the bowl the restaurant had provided for this purpose.

A couple of times Miles considered that they were enjoying themselves in an expensive restaurant with a man who drove a fancy sports car while his father was sitting in an Empire Falls jail cell, but this thought was only momentarily disconcerting. Whenever he decided he should take his father's side, he remembered what Charlie Mayne had said about everybody deserving the opportunity to be happy and concluded this was probably true. He understood, too, why his mother might prefer, at least for a day or two, the company of a man who made nice things happen, as Charlie Mayne seemed able to do by mere whim, to that of a convicted public nuisance. At first the news of his father's being arrested had mortified and humiliated him; but the more he thought about it, the more comforted he felt. Until this afternoon he'd always known that his father was a different sort of man from other boys' fathers, but he'd had no way of summing him up. Now he did. Max Roby was a public nuisance. Having this short phrase to describe him was better than suspecting that his father was so different and unnatural that nobody had yet invented a way to describe him.

Only later that night—just before dawn, in fact—did the sadness of all this hit him, and he woke up frightened for reasons he couldn't name. He seemed to have been dreaming about his father, though he couldn't remember any details, and now, lying alone in bed, he felt guilty. Surely his father deserved a better summation than "public nuisance." He wondered if Max would be mad when he got out of jail and found them gone, which got him thinking that maybe he'd already been released and found out, somehow, where they'd gone. Maybe he was on his way right now to gather up his family, to seize them by the wrists and yank them back to Empire Falls where they belonged, with orders to behave themselves and quit eating snails. Miles had just about convinced himself that all of this was possible when in the perfect stillness outside the bedroom window he heard a noise.

A milky mist had rolled in off the ocean, amplifying sounds, including the far-off ringing of a buoy. Through the parted curtains next to his bed Miles squinted into the mist until he was certain that he'd imagined the sound, but then there came another, a footfall on the gravel path, and then the mist gathered itself around a dark shape coming toward him, and finally the mist became his mother, making her way along the grassy edge of the dirt path, carrying her shoes in one hand and concentrating on her footing. The sight so startled Miles that before he could reconcile seeing his mother outside with his belief that she was asleep in the next bedroom, she looked up and stared right at him, and only then did he let the curtains fall back into place.

CHARLIE MAYNE DROVE THEM to the ferry in silence and helped them load their bags onto the luggage trolley. Then he got the man at the ramp to let him come aboard without a ticket so he could see Miles and his mother off. It was the thing about him that amazed Miles most, that he would remember longest: the way he could make things happen and get people to do things for him that they never would've dreamed of doing for anyone else. If you *happened to be with Charlie Mayne, you could eat steamer clams in a restaurant that didn't even serve them.*

Yet despite his amazing talent, there were clearly limits to his powers, and as Charlie stood there on the upper deck of the Vineyard ferry, one of the things he couldn't seem to do was find the words to say whatever it was he wanted to say to Grace. Miles watched him struggle, unaware at the time that his own presence stole half the words away and that the other half were inadequate to the message. His mother, so radiant by candlelight in her white dress the night before, looked pale and fragile in the harsh morning light, and Charlie himself looked haggard and unsure, and for the first time his clothes seemed to hint at the awkward, concave-chested body they contained. He looked, Miles thought, plain old. Which was strange, because that had been his first impression two nights ago, before he'd looked more closely.

Below them the final passengers were moving in line up the plank, the last of the automobiles being loaded into the belly of the ship. In a moment, Miles could tell, the ramp would be detached and the ferry would pull away from the slip. Finally, Charlie Mayne took Grace by the hand and said, "Look. The thing is, it's going to take a while."

"I know," she said, looking away from him, off toward Vineyard Haven.

"Think of Puerto Vallarta."

"I will."

"Promise me you won't lose heart."

"You need to go," she said, pointing to the dockworkers below, who had begun to detach the foot ramp.

He saw that this was true, but took a moment to address Miles. "Maybe we'll meet again," he said, offering the boy his hand to shake, and when Miles did, he noticed a big blotch of poison ivy on Charlie's forearm.

"Charlie," Grace said. The ramp was being pulled away now.

They faced each other. "Grace."

"I know," Grace said. "I know. Go."

And then he was off, waving and hollering to the workmen below as he hurried down to the lower deck. Without protest, they wheeled the ramp back into place, and when he'd safely descended, Charlie shook hands with each man, as if, collectively, they'd managed to pull off some complex and wonderful feat. Then, as the whistle blew and the ferry began to push back from the slip, Charlie Mayne continued to stand there at the very edge of the dock, waving to them. He continued to wave until he was small, pausing only, Miles could tell, to scratch his forearm. Miles couldn't help feeling sorry for him, left behind on the island without any ointment, with nothing to relieve his suffering. Eventually, then, he realized his mother was no longer at his side.

The island had disappeared entirely and the thin line of the Cape Cod coast was becoming visible on the horizon when Grace returned to the deck. Miles could tell she'd been sick again, and as she came toward him, wobbly and weak, she looked so little like the figure who had materialized out of the morning mist that he wondered if maybe he'd dreamed it. In case he hadn't, when she sat down next to him, he said, "I won't tell Dad. I promise."

He knew she'd heard him, but it was as if she hadn't. She took his hand, and neither of them spoke until the ferry pulled into the harbor at Woods Hole and bumped roughly against the sides of the slip before coming to rest.

They were standing at the rail, Grace gripping it with white fingers, until she took a deep breath and said, "I was wrong."

He started to say something, but she shook her head, stopping him. "I was wrong when I said things were going to be different when we got back home," she said. "Nothing's going to change. Not one thing."

He hoped she was right, but feared she wasn't. On the dock below there was a man wearing a Red Sox cap, and seeing this caused Miles to remember that he'd forgotten his mitt. He could see it on the nightstand next to his bed back at the cottage. Right where he'd left it.

PART TWO

EVEN BEFORE Miles crossed the Iron Bridge on his way to Mrs. Whiting's, he was not in the best of moods. The last several days had been gray and drizzly, too wet to get any painting done at St. Cat's. This morning the skies had finally cleared, offering the prospect of a long, brilliant afternoon under a high sky the color of a robin's egg. On a day such as this, Miles thought, a man frightened of heights might just surprise himself and find the courage to paint a church steeple. Or might have if he hadn't gotten a call from his employer saying she had a surprise for him if he cared to drop by that afternoon. Though he knew better than to get his hopes up, Miles briefly considered the possibility, as he turned between the two stone pillars and into the circular drive, that the old woman had changed her mind about the liquor license. Or maybe she was still thinking he should be mayor and wanted to inform him that she was funding his campaign.

But no sooner had he parked in front of the main house, climbed out of the Jetta, and started toward the front door than the precise nature of Mrs. Whiting's surprise became clear, and it stopped Miles dead in his tracks. The far door of the two-car garage, the one that usually remained shut, now stood wide open, revealing in its bay the old beige Lincoln with its wheelchair license plate. At this sight, Miles Roby, a grown man, had to summon every ounce of intestinal fortitude he possessed to mount the steps and ring the bell instead of getting back in his car and leaving a thick patch of burning rubber on the asphalt. Which was precisely how Max would've handled the situation, Miles knew, and standing dutifully at the front door, he wondered, as he often had throughout his adult life, what it was in his character that prevented him from embracing his father's cheerful, sensible cowardice in the face of unpleasantness. Max had exactly zero desire to suffer himself, and even less to share the suffering of others. To his way of thinking, this reluctance required neither excuse nor explanation. It was the people who enjoyed suffering who had some explaining to do.

Before Miles could come to any conclusion as to why his father's excellent instinct for self-preservation had been left out of him, the door grunted open and there was Cindy Whiting, struggling as she always had struggled from the time she was a child, to get out of her own way, to wrestle into compliance the mangled body that had thwarted her so relentlessly. She'd graduated, Miles noted at once, from the canes she'd been using the last time he saw her—maybe five years ago?—to a sturdy, four-legged aluminum walker. She must have made the transition fairly recently, because she didn't seem to have mastered the contraption yet. Either that or opening a door from behind such a device was sufficiently difficult that you could spend a lifetime getting the hang of it. In order to reach the doorknob you probably had to place the walker right up against the frame, but then the walker itself would prevent the door from opening, except in short, clumsy, humiliating stages, one thump at a time.

"Cindy," Miles said through the half-open doorway, feigning surprise and delight. "I had no idea you were home."

Her eyes were already full of tears. "Oh, Miles," she exclaimed, covering her mouth with her free hand, overcome with emotion. "I *so* wanted to surprise you. And I *have*, haven't I?"

"You look wonderful," Miles said—an exaggeration, perhaps, though she did look surprisingly healthy. She'd put on about ten pounds, and the weight had heightened her color. Cindy Whiting would never be beautiful, but she could've been attractive if she'd had good advice and not been drawn to dowdy clothes and hairstyles at least a decade too old for her. At twenty she'd already begun to resemble the spinster. At thirty she'd settled into the role. Now, at forty-two—Miles knew because they were born on the same day in the Empire Falls hospital—she seemed to have discovered some hint of womanliness, or even forgotten girlishness.

"Come in," she said, "and let me get a *look* at you." But when he stepped forward, he stubbed his toe against the walker, causing Cindy once again to grab hold with both hands.

"I'm still the picture of grace, as you can see," she said, illustrating

her point by pretending to lose her balance, and Miles, who throughout his life had practiced a necessary hard-heartedness toward her, felt
something in him soften. Since she was a teenager she'd tried to deflect
her tragic awkwardness with self-mockery, chiefly pratfalls, which she
never seemed to realize didn't make a very good joke. For one thing,
these make-believe spasms were indistinguishable from her real ones,
and they invariably sent people lunging to catch her. Worse, her
feigned stumbles sometimes resulted in actual ones, and then she often
fell even more violently than she would have had it occurred naturally.
Her wrists, Miles knew, were full of surgical pins, but apparently her
need to mock herself was greater than her fear of broken bones.

In a similar circumstance Miles would've given another woman a
hug, but then, another woman would've understood that she was supposed to let go, that the hug meant nothing more than "Hello, it's been
a long time." This woman would have used the opportunity to clutch
him like grim death, sobbing moistly, her makeup dissolving into his
shirtfront, "Oh, Miles. Oh, dear, dear Miles." The last time he'd seen
her, she'd raised her two canes into the air like a TV cripple at an evangelical revival, and pitched forward into his terrified embrace, forcing
him to hug her almost as tightly as she was hugging him to keep her
from slithering down his trunk to the ground. Which was why he was
grateful—God forgive him, he *was!*—for this new aluminum contraption that allowed him to lean forward and give her a chaste peck on the
cheek, to him a more successful greeting than he might've expected
from someone who'd been in love with him since grade school and, as
proof, had twice attempted suicide, citing Miles as the reason.

"So," he said clumsily, in the throes of a rhetorical dilemma that not
many people, he suspected, had ever faced: what precisely to say to a
woman who has attempted to end her life on your behalf. "How are
you, Cindy?"

"*Well*, Miles," she replied. "I'm *so, so* well. The doctors are amazed,"
then adding, as if aware of the implausibility of this, "They say it's a
miracle. It's as if my psyche just suddenly decided to heal. I haven't had
any setbacks in . . ."

Here she stopped to think, apparently doing the math in her head,
though Miles had no idea what numbers she might be adding or sub-
tracting, whether they were large or small, representing days, weeks,
months or years. While she calculated, Miles took in the entry hall
and living room of the Whiting home and felt, as always, vaguely
uncomfortable. While the rooms were spacious, the ceilings were low,

creating in Miles, a large man, not so much a sense of claustrophobia as of a great weight bearing down. Mrs. Whiting was a collector, and the walls were covered with original art, but most of the paintings, he thought, were not well displayed. The larger pieces overpowered the walls on which they hung. Even his own favorites, some smaller John Marins, looked out of place, outdoor Maine scenes held captive indoors against their will. Conspicuously missing were family photos, all of which Mrs. Whiting had donated to the old Whiting mansion downtown. Neither Whitings nor Robideauxs were anywhere in evidence.

"Anyway," Cindy Whiting said, apparently having given up, "it seems I'm to begin life again, like a normal person, at age thirty-nine. You may congratulate me."

"That's wonderful news, Cindy," Miles said, swallowing this outrageous lie whole. Miles, having been born on the same day, was the one person in the world not likely to forget how old she really was. On the other hand, her desire to be thirty-nine instead of forty-two might, he supposed, be evidence that what she'd told him was true, that something in her psyche had healed. After all, shaving off a few years was something normal women were known to do. Maybe Cindy had learned to replace big lies—for instance, that Miles Roby was in love with her, or one day would be—that had compromised her sanity with smaller, more harmless and optimistic ones. Like imagining that one sunny day you'll wake up able to climb a ladder and paint a church steeple, right up there in the middle of the blue sky. It could happen.

"Where will you live?"

These words were no sooner out than Miles realized they formed a hurtful question, which he hadn't intended.

"Why, right here, of course. Where else?"

"Of course. That's not what I meant," he quickly lied. "I guess I was wondering if you'd live with your mother or—"

"Only until I can find a place of my own," she said, smiling at the thought. "A grown woman should be able to come and go as she pleases, don't you think? Entertain who she pleases?"

Before Miles could offer an opinion on the conduct of grown women, there was a loud hissing sound behind him, and he didn't need to turn around to know that his nemesis had joined them. The cat had been called Timmy from kittenhood, when, despite her actual gender, she was still thought to be male because of her aggressive viciousness. The tiny animal—soaking wet, its fur matted, its yellow eyes wild with fright and rage—had appeared one morning on the Whiting patio, where it howled so balefully that Cindy Whiting, home on a furlough from the state facility in Augusta, had taken it in and nursed it to health. Someone presumably had tossed the kitten into the river somewhere upstream, expecting it either to drown or be dashed on the rocks at the falls. A scrap of burlap had been attached to one of its talons, suggesting that Timmy had started her river journey in a sack—perhaps, to judge from the depth of her psychosis, in the company of her siblings. At any rate, once she got her strength back, Timmy was one pissed-off little critter, whose single ambition in life seemed to be to shred the world around her. Neutering seemed a good idea, though, the vet she was taken to for castration had quickly pointed out, an impractical one, given her gender.

To Miles, Timmy's gender seemed less the issue than her metaphysical nature, which appeared to be less feline than demonic. Horace Weymouth, who in his capacity as an *Empire Gazette* reporter had interviewed Mrs. Whiting at her residence more than once, swore that Timmy was the old woman's familiar, and Miles, who noted that the cat's sudden appearance often coincided with the mention or advent of Mrs. Whiting, was inclined to agree.

Since Timmy had no testicles to snip, she'd been returned home intact and relegated to the basement with her litter box and a week's supply of food, to see if this dark confinement might provide her an opportunity to reflect that her new owners weren't to blame for any past inhumane treatment. It did not. In fact, the animal did not take kindly to imprisonment, which might have reminded her of the inside of the burlap bag. There was a small gap between the floor and the bottom of the basement door, and from the top step Timmy was able to reach underneath and rattle the ill-fitting door about as loudly as a full-grown man would have been able to do with his hand. At first no one had been willing to believe that a small, angry cat could make such a racket all by herself, but every night Timmy shook the door until she was let out; then, to celebrate her freedom, she began shredding the upholstery on the dining room chairs. At the end of a week, Mrs. Whiting instructed the housekeeper to go to the drugstore and buy herself and Cindy and Mrs. Whiting earplugs. Good ones.

That night, even with the earplugs, they'd heard Timmy screaming and rattling the door to the basement, but sometime after midnight the noise ceased, and the three congratulated themselves that the animal's spirit was finally broken. The next morning, when the housekeeper came into the kitchen to release the—she imagined—now tame and chastened cat, she got the shock of her life. Indeed, she could not quite believe what she was staring at. The animal's head, blood-fanged, was upside down on the tile floor under the bottom of the cellar door, its two front paws seemingly pinned to the floor when the door had come crashing down. That was the conclusion the poor housekeeper came to, based on the evidence of her senses. She knew, of course, that the door *couldn't* have come crashing down. This door swung open and shut on two copper hinges just like all the others. But with the cat's bloody head and paws motionless underneath it, the door appeared to have operated like a garage door, rising into and descending from the ceiling. It had apparently come slicing down like a guillotine when Timmy had attempted to cross the threshold. So powerful was this optical illusion that the woman's reason was unable to conquer it until Timmy moved. Alas, the resulting apparition of a now squirming, bloody, disembodied, undead cat head sent the woman shrieking from the house.

What had happened, it was later deduced, was that the poor woman had interrupted Timmy's escape. Since midnight the cat, ignoring her bleeding gums, had methodically chewed her way through the bottom of the door. The housekeeper had entered the kitchen just when the hole had gotten large enough for Timmy, squirming on her back, to poke her horrible head and part of one shoulder through. At the housekeeper's sudden appearance, she'd frozen in surprise.

It had been, no doubt, a ghastly sight, though only slightly more ghastly than the one Miles was treated to now. Timmy's teeth were not bloody from having chewed through a door, but she'd pulled her lips back and was making sure Miles could see every razor-sharp tooth. Her fur was standing straight up, and her back was arched in the manner of B-movie cats when a ghost, visible to pets but not humans, has just entered the room. Miles, no ghost, instinctively backed away.

"Oh, Timmy," Cindy Whiting said, risking her precarious balance to bend down and stroke the beast. "Quit that. Can't you see it's only Miles?"

At this, Timmy proceeded to hiss and spit even more emphatically. As Miles, who knew from experience that the owners of savage pets seldom offered much in the way of protection from them, began looking around for a weapon, he heard a distant bell ringing somewhere in the rear of the house. When he turned back toward Timmy, the cat had vanished.

"That's Mother," Cindy said, nodding in the direction of the bell. "She must've heard you pull up, and now she's impatient."

Miles was still scanning the room for Timmy the Cat.

"She's waiting out in the gazebo," Cindy explained. "She made me promise to bring you *straight* out, so you go along." She began to negotiate a slow, awkward turn with her walker. "I'm slow."

"That's okay," Miles said, taking her by the elbow, rattled by both the cat and his embarrassing fear of it. The bell continued to ring as they made their slow progress, and when they arrived at the patio door, Miles saw the cat splayed across the inside of the sliding screen, about halfway up, purring loudly, her claws gripping the mesh. The screen was rent in several places, suggesting that this was not the first time Timmy had performed such an acrobatic feat.

"She just loves the sound of Mother's bell," Cindy said sweetly.

Outside, Miles could see the old woman sitting in the gazebo, facing the river with her back to them and ringing her bell as if she expected the sound to make fish jump at her command. Everyone else certainly did. Why not the fish? Grace Roby had claimed she could hear her employer's bell ringing in her sleep. Miles again felt his heart soften, considering the saddest truth of Cindy Whiting's existence: her choice in life was between living at home and answering that bell and remaining at the state hospital in Augusta.

Miles took a deep breath and turned toward her before heading outside. "Cindy," he said softly.

A mistake. Clutching the walker with her left hand, she made a grab for Miles with her right, snagging his shirtsleeve and holding on with amazing strength. "I heard about you and Janine," she said. "Your divorce. I'm *so* sorry, Miles."

He decided on the simple truth. "Me too."

But Cindy didn't seem to register his tone.

"You never loved her, Miles," Cindy told him. "I know you didn't."

"That's what she claims, too," he admitted, sad that two women as different as Janine and Cindy should have arrived at the same depressing conclusion.

Letting go of his shirt, Cindy now caught his fingers in her viselike grip. "I lied, Miles," she told him, tears starting to spill now. "I'm *not* sorry about your divorce. It gives me a slender thread of hope—"

"Cindy—" he said, trying to pull away without upsetting her fragile balance. The bell outside was ringing louder now.

"I still love you, Miles. You see that, don't you? It's the one thing the lithium can't touch. Did you know that? The drugs wash into your brain and make things easier to bear, but they can't touch your heart! They can't alter what's already there, Miles."

She clasped his hand to her breast so he could feel the truth of what she was saying. Now it seemed to Miles that Mrs. Whiting's bell was playing through a bullhorn inside his head. He tried to withdraw his hand but could not, at least not without toppling Cindy. "I should go—"

"Don't, Miles."

"Cindy," he said, more harshly than he'd planned, as he finally broke free and she again grabbed hold of her walker. "Cindy, please."

When the walker wobbled, he caught her by the wrist, the same one she'd slashed twenty years ago. "It's okay," she said, visibly gathering herself. "Go."

There can't be a God, Miles thought. There just can't be. "Cindy," he repeated.

"No, go," she said, backing away now, dragging the walker. "I'm fine."

Miles took a deep breath, then heard himself say, "How about I give you a call sometime this week?"

At this suggestion her face lit up so quickly that Miles briefly suspected he'd been tricked. "Really, Miles? You'll call me?"

Now the task was to swallow his annoyance. "Why wouldn't I?" he asked, a man with more reasons than he could count.

"Oh, Miles." Her hand again went to her mouth. "Dear, dear Miles."

Dear, dear God.

He got as far as the sliding patio door before she called after him. Her expression had darkened into the one he remembered from when she was a girl, a look of terrible recognition. "Miles?"

"Yes, Cindy?"

"Outside? When you got out of your car? You stopped and just stood there for a minute. You looked . . . like you wanted to run away."

Miles located the lie he needed. "I realized I'd forgotten some stuff I needed to give your mother. You know how she is—receipts for all expenditures."

She studied him for a long moment. "I had this terrible thought," she said slowly, "that maybe you'd noticed my car and realized I was home."

"Cindy—" Miles began.

"I can bear it that you don't love me, Miles," she said. "I've borne it all my life. But if I thought I made you want to run away . . ."

"We're old friends," he assured her. "I don't want to run away from you."

She gave him a smile in which hope and knowledge were going at it, bare-knuckled, equally and eternally matched. No, there *was* a God after all, Miles concluded, as he took his leave of her. This misery was His plan for us.

Instead of thinking about God, what Miles should have been doing was paying attention to Timmy the Cat, because when he reached to slide the screen door open, Mrs. Whiting chose that moment to stop ringing her bell, thus releasing Timmy from her trance. In that same instant her deep, throaty purring stopped, and she reached for Miles, striping the back of his hand.

"Oh, Timmy," Cindy Whiting said when she saw what the cat had done, "you're *such* a little pill!"

"HAS IT EVER occurred to you that life is a river, dear boy?" Mrs. Whiting said when Miles sat down opposite her in the gazebo. In asking this question the old woman managed to convey, as with all such queries, that she was not anticipating a response that would enlighten her. Whereas some people's attitude suggested that perhaps they knew something you didn't, Mrs. Whiting's implied that she knew *everything* you didn't. She alone had been paying attention, so it was her duty to bring you at least partially up to speed.

She was elegantly dressed, especially for the backyard. If Cindy was already beginning to look dowdy, Mrs. Whiting herself—her hair cut and styled expertly, her tweed jacket and moleskin slacks smartly tailored, her wrists alive with jewelry, not scar tissue—looked like a woman who'd been enough of a good sport to give old age a try but then decided against it, much preferring youth. Somehow she'd negotiated for its return, not all at once, of course, but rather gradually, a minute, an hour, a day at a time, the clock hands ticking backward until, presumably, she arrived at a satisfactory vantage. Even spookier, Mrs. Whiting also radiated—Miles had no idea how—a sexuality that was alive and ticking. Something about her knowing smile hinted that she'd gotten laid more recently than Miles had, and that she knew it. As if she might even have considered him, briefly, as a sexual partner, then rejected the notion.

At the moment she had positioned herself in a patch of weakening September sun, leaving Miles the chilly chair in the shade. Taking note of the arrangement, he couldn't help recalling his brother's observation that, far from dying, Mrs. Whiting was living, while those around her were relegated to a kind of limbo. With his back to the river, Miles's view was of the sloping lawn and gravel path, bordered in white brick, that wound its way up to the house. Had she wished to, Mrs. Whiting might have widened the path, perhaps even paved it, so her crippled daughter would also have access to the gazebo. After all, it was the nicest architectural feature of the property, especially on a sunny after-noon, although today he thought he caught a whiff of something rancid in the air.

"I suspect that's occurred to anyone who's ever seen a river, Mrs. Whiting," he said. After his conversation with Cindy, Miles was in no mood for abstract philosophy. The silver bell sat on the table between them, and Miles had to suppress a strong impulse to toss it into the river. Not the River of Life, either. The old woman must have read his thought, because she picked up the bell and set it down again on her side of the table, well out of his reach.

"My late husband . . . ," Mrs. Whiting began, then stopped. "Did you ever meet him?"

"I don't think so." Miles had been away at college when C. B. Whiting had put a bullet in his brain. In this very gazebo, they said. In fact, whenever he met Mrs. Whiting out here, he made a conscious effort not to look too closely for evidence of the gunshot, a small piece of missing latticework, perhaps, or a bullet-splintered rafter.

The old woman studied him for a moment, then shrugged. The ease with which she summoned the memory of a man who'd taken his own life—her husband, for God's sake—always amazed him. It was almost as if she expected *other* people to be made uncomfortable by such recollections of him, not herself. "You probably did without knowing it. He wasn't the sort of man you'd notice unless you knew he had money."

"*You* noticed him," Miles couldn't help pointing out.

"True"—she chuckled—"and I just explained why. At any rate he was no more foolish than most men, I suppose, and yet you'll never guess what he was up to when I met him. He was actually engaged in altering the flow of this very river. Spent a small fortune dynamiting channels and building guide walls and levees upstream, not to mention bribing state officials to allow all of this, simply so trash wouldn't collect along our bank. He died imagining he'd succeeded, too, so how's that for folly?"

Miles shrugged, far too miffed with the old woman to pretend much interest in the arrogance of the rich.

"But now the river's gone back to doing what it wants, and what it wants is to wash up dead animals and all manner of trash on my nice lawn. That's the lovely odor you noticed when you sat down. Which is my point. Lives are rivers. We imagine we can direct their paths, though in the end there's but one destination, and we end up being true to ourselves only because we have no choice. People speak of selfishness, but that's another folly, because of course there's no such thing. It's a point I could never make your dear mother comprehend. In her own way she was like my late husband, except it was always human rivers she was trying to redirect."

Miles pretended to examine the scratch Timmy had given him on the back of his hand, a ragged tear that had already puffed up along its length, stinging and itching at the same time. It was probably true that Grace Roby had been foolish enough to believe she could change lives. No doubt she'd married Max with this very idea in mind. There was a difference, though. Her purpose was never to change the course of rivers so the garbage wouldn't wash up on her shores. He considered making this distinction to Mrs. Whiting and immediately thought better of it. "You might've mentioned that Cindy was home," he said.

"She wanted to surprise you," the old woman said, bending down to pick up something underneath the round table. To Miles's astonishment, it was Timmy the Cat. There were times when he suspected there must be two of the little beast, since she never seemed to pass from one place to another but simply materialized in the middle of things. The screen door, Miles noted, was still shut. How had she gotten out, then crossed the wide expanse of manicured lawn without his noticing?

Miles wiped away the blood with his handkerchief, eyeing Timmy warily and wondering, as he always did, why anyone would keep such a homicidal animal when there was a perfectly good river right out their back door. Timmy's previous owner had had the right idea. At the moment, however, Timmy looked anything but homicidal. She burrowed under her mistress's bosom and began to purr loudly, studying Miles with feline indifference, her eyelids closing slowly, as if heavy with sleep, then opening again to reveal urine-yellow orbs. "Which of them scratched you, my daughter or this one?"

"I wish to God you'd put her down," he said, having offered on numerous occasions to attend to the task himself. "And I don't mean on the ground, either."

"Dear boy"—the old woman smiled—"when you're upset, you're careless with your pronouns. I assume you're referring to the cat. Do correct me if I'm mistaken."

Miles sighed. "I'm afraid I've upset her. I didn't mean to—"

"Poor Miles," Mrs. Whiting said. "You have an overdeveloped sense of responsibility. Surely you know you're not responsible for my daughter's sad life. You were just a little boy when she had her accident."

In fact, that terrible event was one of his earliest and most vivid memories. Miles hadn't seen the child run over, but people had talked about the accident for weeks, and the images lingered much longer in his horrified mind. The car had struck and then dragged the little girl, crushing both of her legs and fracturing her pelvis. She'd sustained serious head trauma as well, slipping into a coma shortly after she was hospitalized, and for several weeks it had appeared that she would surely die.

The authorities conducted a frantic and prolonged search for the bright green Pontiac that had been reported speeding away from the scene. Miles still remembered how everyone in Empire Falls who owned a Pontiac had fallen under suspicion. At first it was assumed that the driver was probably local, because the accident took place on the Whitings' side of the Iron Bridge. Back then there hadn't been much on that side of the river except the Whiting property and the country club. Jimmy Minty's father had owned a beat-up old red Pontiac at the time, and he always parked it in the shared driveway between his house and the Robys', a reminder that he owned a car and they did not, at least most of the time. Max was always buying cars, but he seldom made payments on them, so they were invariably repossessed. When Miles was a boy he figured it was these repossessions that caused his father to disappear, and when he asked his mother if Max had been repossessed along with the car, the remark had delighted her and made him feel foolish for having made a joke he couldn't understand.

From his bedroom window on the second floor Miles had looked down at the Mintys' red Pontiac, certain, despite the fact that it was the wrong color, that it must be the car that had run over the Whiting girl. Mr. Minty was a big man with a terrible temper, and he seemed to Miles just the sort to run over a little rich girl. He was forever appearing at their back door—though never when Max was home—and offering meat from his freezer. Grace, who usually invited people in, never did with Mr. Minty, who had a way of looking his mother over that made Miles uncomfortable. In fact, Grace always made sure the screen door was locked when she saw him coming. And here was the murderous vehicle right outside, probably waiting for Miles to cross carelessly behind it. But even as a boy he understood instinctively that *his* being run over wouldn't cause nearly the sensation that Cindy Whiting's accident had.

And he was right. The fact that it was the Whiting girl had, of course, captured the imagination of everyone in Dexter County. That such a tragedy should visit a family historically shielded from misfortune had occasioned a wave of philosophizing, especially in the millworkers' neighborhoods. It just went to prove, people said, that God didn't play favorites. He didn't love the rich more than the poor, not really, and it took something like this to demonstrate this oft-doubted truth.

Grace had not been sympathetic to such talk, which surprised Miles, because she'd always told him that God's hand could be seen in all things. But she was adamant that it wasn't God behind the wheel of that Pontiac, which caused Miles to wonder if she was taking God's side in hopes that when He next decided to loose a little more misfortune upon the world, He'd remember who His faithful were.

If Mrs. Whiting was right and Miles's feeling of responsibility for Cindy was exaggerated, he came by it rightly, for in retrospect it seemed to him that his mother had been genuinely unhinged by the accident, as if it had somehow confirmed what she'd always feared—that the world was teeming with dangers. She was forever trying to use the accident to frighten Miles out of his tree-climbing, describing what would happen if he fell and asking if he wanted to be crippled for the rest of his life, like little Cindy Whiting. Of course, this argument made less than perfect sense to Miles, who saw being up in a tree as reducing his chances of being run over by a car. But Grace was determined and inflexible. Because she and Mrs. Whiting had given birth on the same day, in the same hospital, in his mother's imagination he and Cindy Whiting had become psychic twins, or so he supposed. Right from the start Grace had sent the little Whiting girl birthday and Christmas cards, though Mrs. Whiting, to Miles's knowledge, never reciprocated. After the accident Grace made sure that he understood they had a special duty toward the crippled child. If Miles had a birthday party, Cindy Whiting had to be invited. If they saw her in town with her mother, Miles was always instructed to go over and say hello. Cindy Whiting, she reminded him over and over, was a brave little girl who'd endured one operation after another. A terrible thing had happened to her, and that meant *other* people had an obligation to make nice things happen. This, Grace Roby believed, was a person's duty on earth, God's plan—spelled out in the Bible, to make life a little more fair—was for us to feed the hungry, to give warm clothing to those who were cold and drink to those who were thirsty. (Max, on his way out the door to his favorite tavern, always seconded this one.) And most important, it was our duty to give love to those who needed our affection. (Max was usually gone by the time his wife got around to the *most* important point.) In Grace's opinion it was love that people needed most—more than food and shelter and warmth—and the best part was that love didn't cost anything. Even poor people could afford to make a gift of it to the rich.

Though his mother never actually told him so, Miles suspected that something, or maybe a cluster of things, had happened at the hospital when she and Francine Whiting were delivering their babies, something that caused his mother to forge her belief in the psychic link between the newborns. Her logic was not so hard to reconstruct. Two children born within hours of each other into such different circumstances, one rich, the other poor. No doubt the hospital staff would've made clear to Grace in a hundred small ways which was the *important* baby, and such a quiet and thoughtful woman couldn't have failed to contemplate the very different destinies in store for her child and the child of a woman whose last name was Whiting, even if not so long ago it had been Robideaux. She might even have considered the unfairness of it all and wondered if babies were ever mistakenly switched in their bassinets, fate thwarted by incompetence. Not that such a switch was likely when one child was a boy, the other a girl, but still. How could a woman in Grace's position *not* ponder such questions?

Yet this explanation had never felt terribly compelling to Miles. For one thing, if memory served, even *before* Cindy Whiting's accident,

Grace seemed to consider her own infant the lucky one, the one God had blessed. Why? Miles had no idea. He didn't know if his mother had been acquainted with Francine Robideaux before she married the richest man in central Maine, but he doubted it, which meant that Grace had no prior reason to suspect that Francine would make a poor mother. Any knowledge she had about the other woman would've sprung from their acquaintance at the hospital. Still, Grace had been a close and intuitive observer, and perhaps she'd simply seen the baby girl struggling at her mother's meager breast and thus projected for her a hungry future. Whatever her reasons, Grace had always pointed the little Whiting girl out as someone important, someone for him to be especially kind to. The accident had not occasioned the connection but merely amplified it, so when the senior prom rolled around and Cindy Whiting didn't have a date it fell to Miles to invite her—though by then his heart had been lost to a pretty girl named Charlene Gardiner, who was three years older than he and a waitress at the Empire Grill, where Miles had an after-school job busing dishes and washing pots, a girl who seemed to understand how devoted he was to her, who was unfailingly kind and affectionate and never allowed her many boy-friends to joke about him too harshly in his hearing, who sometimes even appeared to take his affection seriously.

Unfortunately, according to Grace, Miles had no duty to love the Gardiner girl. True, Charlene was about as pretty as girls got in Empire Falls, Grace conceded. Still, she was careful to explain some-thing she said he was too young to comprehend just then, though one day he would. "Charlene Gardiner isn't really a girl," she said, causing Miles's jaw to drop. "I know she's not that much older, but she's already a *woman* and you're still a boy."

Grace might've been right about the latter, but she'd been dead wrong about his not understanding that Charlene was a woman. That was what he liked best about her, and his favorite fantasies concerned the various ways in which she might make him a man. Whereas Cindy Whiting, he suspected, would never make him anything but miserable, a prediction that had been borne out over the next thirty years, right up to the present moment.

When Timmy the Cat raised her head, Mrs. Whiting obliged by scratching her neck. "I suppose I *should* put you down," she allowed. "You're a truly hateful little beast. Still, one does have to admire the intensity of your feelings."

"I don't," Miles said. "She either scratches or bites me every time I come here."

"Oh, it's not just you, dear boy. She treats everyone who isn't family with the most exquisite malice. She dug a furrow the length of the mayor's forearm just last week—didn't you, sweetheart?"

"You should hold a raffle," Miles suggested. "Ten dollars a shot and the winner gets to beat her to death with a baseball bat. We could use the proceeds to help finish off the new wing of the hospital."

The old woman clapped her hands in delight. "I don't know why I'm always so surprised to be reminded of your sense of humor, dear boy."

"Did I say something funny?" Miles inquired.

"You see? There it is again. You must get it from that reprobate father of yours. He called me again when you were gone, by the way. I had to threaten him with the police."

"I'll speak to him."

"Does he have any clue what a funny little man he is?"

"I don't think so. A lot of it's lost on me, actually."

"And your mother, as well, dear woman. Poor Grace was not blessed with a sense of life's grand folly." At this, Timmy shook her head, piston fashion, and studied her mistress in a way that suggested she was following this conversation with interest.

"Actually, my mother loved to laugh." Miles hated talking about his mother with Mrs. Whiting almost as much as with Jimmy Minty. "Life may be a grand folly, as you say, but it's harder to appreciate the joke when you're always the butt of it."

"Yes, I *am* aware that life is hard for some people," Mrs. Whiting conceded, as if she'd heard this sentiment expressed somewhere before and supposed it might be true. "Still, I've always believed that people largely make their own luck. And you needn't smile at that, Miles Roby." For once she sounded almost sincere. "You think I married my luck, but that conclusion is both unkind and unthoughtful, and it does you no credit. There's a world of skill and timing involved in marrying the right person. Especially when the girl in question comes from the Robideaux Blight."

"By way of Colby College," Miles felt compelled to add, since being reminded of this was likely to annoy her. People who imagine themselves to be self-made seldom enjoy examining the process of manufacture in detail.

"Dear me, yes," Mrs. Whiting agreed, missing only half a beat. "Let us *not* forget Colby and the liberating effects of higher education. Though it doesn't liberate everyone, does it?"

Meaning himself, Miles understood. One of Mrs. Whiting's great skills was rolling with the punches. Whenever she absorbed a blow, she came back out swinging. Miles settled in, prepared for his drubbing.

"Still, a wise marriage is a rare thing, don't you think?" she asked. "Most people make a complete hash of it. They marry the wrong people for all the wrong reasons. For reasons so absurd they can't even remember what they were a few short months after they've pledged themselves forever. To the unhappily married, what it was that possessed them remains a lifelong mystery, though to observers their reasons are often painfully obvious. For instance, I'd wager you have no idea why you married."

Miles nodded. "You mean you'd bet if you could find somebody to bet with."

"So you admit you have no idea!" she cried. "Lovely. Now then, shall I tell you?"

"No thanks."

"Come, come, dear boy, aren't you the least little bit interested?"

In truth, he was. Or would've been, had he believed Mrs. Whiting possessed any genuine insight. What she wanted to share with him, he felt sure, was her mean-spiritedness. "So, why *did* I marry, Mrs. Whiting?"

"Oh, good," she said. "I thought for a moment there you were going to be a party pooper. You married out of fear, dear boy." Timmy again shook her head violently, as if to suggest she wasn't sure she'd heard right. "Shall I go on?"

"I thought fear was the reason men *didn't* get married."

"Don't be absurd. Just because people are forever saying silly things, that doesn't make them true."

"So what was I afraid of?" Miles heard himself ask.

"You really don't know?" She smiled. Timmy yawned widely, as if to suggest that even *she* could answer this one. "Oh, my, it's true. You don't, do you? Well, then. This gives us the opportunity to test the old adage that the truth will set you free. I've never quite believed it myself, but—"

"Mrs. Whiting—"

She leaned toward him and lowered her voice conspiratorially. "You married, dear boy, to escape an even worse fate. I suspect you're ashamed of this, but really, you shouldn't be. You may not know this about yourself, but what I'm about to reveal to you is quite true, I assure you. By nature you instinctively seek out the middle road, midway between dangerous passion and soul-destroying indifference. Your whole adult life has been a study in deft navigation, and I don't mind telling you I've long admired the way you've charted your course. You chastise yourself—and don't pretend you don't, because I won't believe you—for making a poor marriage, but that's foolishness. You merely saved yourself, and self-preservation is the design feature we all have in common. Bravo, is what I say."

"Saved myself from what, Mrs. Whiting?"

"Oh, surely you suspect, given so immediate a reminder. Think, dear boy. Remember. You willingly entered a bad marriage to save yourself from a worse one. You feared that if you didn't marry soon, you'd find yourself at the altar with my daughter, because you were certain those were your mother's wishes. You had enough of your father in you to cut yourself the best deal you could that didn't involve the more elegant solution of simply running away. The Greyhound terminal was still operating in Empire Falls twenty years ago, but that would never have been an option for Grace Roby's son. All those catechism classes convinced you that no one gets away scot-free. So you attained that safe middle ground. Maybe you couldn't have what you wanted most, which was that girl with the knockers who still works for you at the restaurant—am I right?—but you were clever enough to avoid what you feared most, which was a poor crippled young woman, who was suicidally in love with you and whose pitiful devotion would've made your life one long, hellish exercise in moral virtue."

Mrs. Whiting was brushing her lap off now, Timmy apparently having jumped down at some point, though Miles didn't recall seeing her do it.

"So, here you are, moping about, doing your duty in daily penance instead of celebrating your achievement, as any sensible person would. And I *do* wish you'd say something instead of just sitting there looking gut-shot. Believe it or not, it was not my intention to hurt your feelings."

"What *was* your intention?"

"To give you a badly needed heads up, dear boy. To point out that despite your considerable skill, you're back in the soup. You're about to become a bachelor again, are you not? Surely you don't imagine that this . . . situation and my daughter's return to beautiful Empire Falls are entirely coincidental?"

No, now that he thought of it, he didn't.

"To be frank, I'm more than a little curious to see how you'll handle this business the second time around."

"Curious."

She looked at him over the rim of her glasses. "Oh, please, spare me that tone of moral superiority. *That* you get from your mother. Frankly, it was the one tiresome, disagreeable trait in an otherwise charming woman. She couldn't bring herself to be openly critical, but she was forever using that very same tone. No doubt she shared your mistaken opinion that my intellect is cold and uncaring, whereas in fact it is simply lively. A lively intellect, so much admired in a man, is seldom tolerated in a woman—or am I mistaken?"

"Am *I* mistaken, or is this your daughter we're talking about?"

"Actually, I thought we were speaking about you. I feel my daughter's plight, dear boy, and have done so all her life. Believe this or not, as you choose. But forgive me for speaking the truth here and pointing out that her predicament, though poignant, is not—compared to your own—terribly interesting. Fate intervened at an early age, and since her accident, my daughter's life has been largely determined by forces beyond her understanding and control. Pity and fear, if I recall correctly, are the appropriate emotional and moral responses. But once fate takes the reins and free will is thrown from the saddle, there's really little to be said, is there? You, on the other hand, are an actor, however reluctant, on life's stage. Not everyone gets to choose, as you once did. And now you get to choose again. Don't tell me you don't find that extraordinary. I'm not saying I envy you, but I am curious. Will you choose the same, or differently? Most of your original options remain open. You could marry again—for instance, that girl with the knockers. After all, there's that tiny voice in your head, the one you always turn a deaf ear to, which is forever asking, 'Don't I deserve a little happiness? Haven't I been a good boy long enough?' But then there's the other voice, the one your mother was so instrumental in forming, that accuses you of selfishness, of not thinking of others . . . like poor, crippled Cindy Whiting. Doesn't *she* deserve a little happiness? And this time around, you might just listen to that voice, because it's the one that feels moral, or would if it didn't trail those nagging considerations of self-interest—because of course the money that would accompany such a marriage would be nice and you're tired of straining to make ends meet. Who wouldn't be? If you started feeling *too* guilty, you certainly could tell yourself you were doing it for your daughter, who'll soon be ready to go off to college, and isn't she the one who really matters? Oh, dear me, it *is* complicated. No surprise that people are always trying to simplify life. What's that question our evangelical brethren are always asking? 'What Would Jesus Do?' What, indeed?"

The breeze shifted then, and Miles caught another rancid whiff off the river, whether from the near bank or from the Empire Falls side he couldn't tell.

"Something tells me you have some advice for me."

She sighed. "I fear not, dear boy. Beyond clarifying your dilemma, I'm afraid I can offer very little indeed. Alas, there's only one thing I'm quite sure of."

"And that is?"

"My daughter may have suggested to you that her doctors believe her to be well?"

Miles nodded.

Mrs. Whiting, eyebrows arched, shook her head.

IT WAS NEARLY THREE in the afternoon before Miles drove back across the Iron Bridge into Empire Falls. The day had gone gray by the time he pulled in behind the Rectum, the clouds framing the accusing steeple now heavy with rain. Which was not the worst of it. Seated on the porch steps, in apparently pleasant conversation, sat the old priest, Father Tom, and Max Roby, who looked up and grinned when his son switched off the Jetta's ignition. After a few minutes, Miles having made no move to get out of the car, Max shuffled over and motioned for him to roll down the passenger-side window. Evidently Max felt safer with the entire width of the car between them.

"What are you doing here, Dad?" Miles said, rubbing his temples with his fingertips.

"Waiting on you."

"What for?"

"I've *been* waiting on you for two hours."

Old Father Tom was still sitting where Max had left him, but he now fixed Miles with his baleful gaze. Though the old man's lips were moving, he was too far away for Miles to guess whether any of the words they were forming might be "peckerhead."

"Let's go to work," Max suggested.

"It's about to rain," Miles said, pointing at the sky.

"Maybe not," Max said.

"It's going to rain," Miles assured him.

"You should've come earlier," Max said. "The sun was out."

"I know."

"You don't need to pay me for the two hours I was waiting."

"I don't have to pay you for anything."

Max considered the unfairness of this, then stared down at the Jetta. "What happened to your car?"

"None of your business," Miles told him, preferring not to explain. When he'd walked up to the Jetta in the drive outside the Whiting house, he saw a darting movement and suddenly remembered that he'd left the passenger-side window partway down. The car's interior was now full of tiny floating particles of foam from the shredded passenger seat.

"Don't get mad at me," Max said. "I didn't do it."

"I know that."

"I didn't make those clouds, either. I didn't do anything. I'm just an old man."

Miles studied his father, whose stubble had a strange orange tint. "Your beard's full of food. Cheetos?"

"So what?"

He had a point, and Mrs. Whiting, Miles sadly reflected, was probably right. People were just themselves, their efforts to be otherwise notwithstanding. Max was just programmed to be Max, to have food in his beard. Looked at from another angle, it probably *was* admirable that his father never battled his own nature, never expected more of himself than experience had taught him was wise, thereby avoiding disappointment and self-recrimination. It was a fine, sensible way to live, really, much more sensible than Miles's manner as he went about his business, disappointed by his failure to scramble up ladders, blaming himself for his wife's infidelity, perversely maneuvering himself into situations that guaranteed aggravation, if not outright distress. Maybe, as the old lady had suggested, it *was* all that catechism, its rote insistence on subordinating one's will to God's, so many of these lessons administered by the now senile priest who was seated a few yards away and giving him the evil eye. What in the world could these old goats have been discussing, Miles wondered.

"Mrs. Whiting says you called her again," Miles said.

Max shrugged. "So what?"

"You said you wouldn't."

"No, I didn't," he said with breathtaking dishonesty. Max firmly believed there was a brief statute of limitations on all promises. "Her and I are related, you know. The Robys and the Robideauxs. Same family."

"You don't know that," Miles said. "You just wish it. Besides which, it doesn't give you any right to call her up late at night begging for money."

"She never answers during the day," Max explained. "She lets her machine pick up."

"People like you are the reason other people get answering machines to begin with," Miles told him. "In fact, people like you are driving a lot of modern technology."

"All I wanted was enough money to get down to the Keys. If you'd cough it up, I wouldn't have to ask her. You're a closer relative than she is, you know."

"She says if you call again, she'll sic the cops on you."

Max nodded thoughtfully. "They'll probably send that Jimmy Minty. My *God*, he was a stupid kid."

Not as stupid as yours, Miles would've liked to confess. Leaning over, he rolled up the window, effectively concluding the conversation, and got out. At least outside the air wasn't drifting with foam particles. Miles walked around and opened the passenger-side door to study the shredded seat, then wisely turned and walked away from the whole mess. After all, the destroyed cushion wasn't the worst of it. Because leaving the Whiting house he'd done something so perverse that even now, fifteen minutes later, it nearly took his breath away. *What*, he wondered, had he been thinking?

What he'd done was stop back in the house on his way out and invite Cindy Whiting to accompany him to next weekend's high school football game. Homecoming, it was. Dear God, he thought now, staring up at St. Cat's flaking steeple. Why didn't he just climb the ladder all the way to the top, step off the son of a bitch, and be done with it? The truth was, Mrs. Whiting's cynical assessment of his character had rattled him. Maybe the old woman didn't know everything about him, but she knew enough—which made him want to do something to prove her wrong, not just about human nature, but about *his* nature. He'd wanted to demonstrate that it was possible to act unselfishly, thereby validating his mother's belief in the necessity of sacrifice. Except he now suspected that by asking Cindy out on what she'd no doubt consider a date, he'd proved the very point he hoped to challenge. The middle road. He'd permitted guilt to maneuver him into offering a weak, hypocritical gesture he was pathetically unprepared to follow through with. Twenty years ago, at his mother's request, he'd asked Cindy to the prom, and now he'd done almost the same identical thing again, and he could imagine Mrs. Whiting sitting across the river in the gazebo and having a good chuckle at his expense. Once again, she'd played him like a fiddle.

And the subject of the beer and wine license, which he'd promised his brother he would raise, had never come up.

CHAPTER 10

THREE WEEKS into the fall semester, Tick looks up when the cafeteria door opens, and the principal, Mr. Meyer, enters with the virtually comatose John Voss in tow. Dressed as usual in a too large black T-shirt with a stretched-out neck, thrift-store polyester golf slacks, and tennis shoes with broken laces, the boy is carrying before him, with both hands, a lumpy, crumpled paper bag, from which Tick deduces that she's to have a luncheon companion. If "companion" is the right word for a boy Tick has never heard speak. Had Justin not featured John Voss in his constant heckling of Candace, Tick wouldn't even know what to call him. The guys on the football team, who take special glee in tormenting him, just call him Dickhead. After materializing in their midst—what, two years ago?—John Voss has remained a mystery. Tick has no idea where he lives, why he's silent, why he dresses as he does, why he doesn't respond to external stimuli. Obviously, he doesn't have a single friend, which makes him unique, since the school's other pathetic social outcasts have formed a loose society. Actually, the person John Voss most resembles, now that Tick thinks about it, is Tick. At least now that she's no longer part of Zack Minty's crowd. If it weren't for Candace pumping her for information during art class, Tick herself would probably go all day without speaking a word to anyone. For all she knows, in the eyes of the other kids at school she might look as pathetic as this silent boy now standing before her.

At the moment, he's staring at the floor, awaiting a command from Mr. Meyer, who, lacking one, studies the boy for a moment as you would a uniformed guard at a wax museum, waiting for him to move so you can be sure he isn't part of the exhibit. Is it possible, Tick wonders, for a boy to possess less natural grace? He looks like he's been taking lessons in the art of human movement from a Disney World robot. When Mr. Meyer tells him to take a seat anywhere he wants, he shuffles to the other side of the cafeteria, sits down, and stares at his brown paper bag for an exaggerated beat before opening it and peering inside. Whatever is inside does not immediately motivate him to further action.

Mr. Meyer continues to watch for a minute, looking especially clueless even for a high school principal. To Tick he resembles a soldier who's been parachuted into the middle of a battlefield and instructed to make weapons out of whatever materials are at hand. When he motions for her to join him outside in the hall, she reluctantly complies.

"I've found someone to have lunch with you," Mr. Meyer reports once the door is safely shut between them. Tick can't help but stare at him. The fundamental dishonesty of adults never fails to amaze her, their assumption that you'll believe whatever they say just because they're grown-ups and you're a kid. As if the history of adults' dealings with adolescents were one long, unbroken continuum of truth-telling. As if no kid was ever given a reason to distrust anyone over the age of twenty-five. In this instance Mr. Meyer would apparently have Tick believe that in the two weeks since allowing this solitary lunch privilege, he's been thinking of nothing except finding her a companion. Whereas Tick doubts that she's crossed his mind until provoked by the larger problem of what to do with this wretched boy, who by virtue of being friendless, voiceless and graceless has become the target of lunchroom bullies who consider it fine sport to hit him in the back of the head with empty milk containers, broken pencils, thumb-shot rubber bands and any other handy missile, launching these objects from all the way across the cafeteria for maximum impact.

Tick's strategy for dealing with lying adults is to say nothing and watch the lies swell and constrict in their throats. When this happens, the lie takes on a physical life of its own and must be either expelled or swallowed. Most adults prefer to expel untruths with little burplike coughs behind their hands, while others chuckle or snort or make barking sounds. When Mr. Meyer's Adam's apple bobs once, Tick sees that he's a swallower, and that this particular lie has gone south down his esophagus and into his stomach. According to her father, who's an old friend of Mr. Meyer's, the man suffers from bleeding ulcers. Tick can see why. She imagines all the lies a man in his position would have to tell, how they must just churn away down there in his intestines like chunks of undigestible food awaiting elimination. By their very nature, Tick suspects, lies seek open air. They don't like being confined in dark, cramped places. Still, she likes Mr. Meyer better for being a swallower. Her father, who lies neither often nor well, at least by adult standards, is also a swallower, and she approves that his lies go down so painfully. The snorters, like Mrs. Roderigue, and the barkers, like Walt Comeau, are the worst.

"John has the same scheduling difficulty you had because of art class," Mr. Meyer continues, studying her to see how this second lie will play, his Adam's apple bobbing again. John Voss has no such scheduling difficulty, Tick knows. Except for computer studies, at which the boy is reportedly brilliant, he's in all low-track classes, and art fits this program like a glove.

When Tick remains silent, Mr. Meyer breaks into a nervous sweat. What is this—*two* comatose kids? If coming to the aid of floundering liars weren't against Tick's religion, she'd be tempted to toss him a rope. She hasn't forgotten his kindness the afternoon that Candace sliced her thumb open with the Exacto knife, and she hasn't forgotten that she repaid his kindness and concern with duplicity by slipping the knife into her backpack, where it has remained ever since.

"Actually, I have a favor to ask you, Christina," Mr. Meyer continues, his Adam's apple stationary now, so this part of it must be true. He nods at the door. "John Voss is a very unhappy boy. More unhappy than anyone suspects, I fear."

He's lowered his voice another notch, perhaps worried that the unhappy boy might find out about his unhappiness and be unhappier still. "There is an *element* in our school that finds in this unfortunate young man an excellent candidate for ridicule and even worse forms of cruelty."

He pauses to study Tick here, hoping maybe that she'll contradict him by testifying that no such element exists. About this, he would very much like to be wrong. "We have a *good school* here," he quickly adds, as if fearful that his criticism has gone too far. "But not everyone . . ." As his voice trails off, his Adam's apple starts bobbing again, confirming Tick's belief that omissions, too, can be lies, perhaps the most dangerous ones.

"What John Voss needs," Mr. Meyer says, placing a hand on her shoulder, "is a friend."

Tick would like not to, but she takes an involuntary step backward anyway. She doesn't like being touched by adults. The Silver Fox, who is forever dragging a paw across the top of her head when he passes by, has no idea how badly this gesture makes her want to shower and wash her hair.

Mr. Meyer notices the reflex and quickly removes his hand. "I don't mean . . ."

Tick waits patiently for the man to explain what he doesn't mean.

"It's not that you should be best pals or anything like that," he says, mopping his glistening forehead with a cloth handkerchief. "I'm just thinking how . . . *nice* it would be for that boy to know there's some-body his own age who doesn't . . ."

Consider him a maggot, Tick thinks, since completing the sentence isn't all that hard. She completes it a few other ways, too, substituting snail, rodent, cockroach, lizard, toad for maggot, while Mr. Meyer continues to wrestle mightily with the dilemma of teen cruelty.

"You may have heard that some boys assaulted him in the cafeteria yesterday," he says, abandoning completely his lie about having at long last found Tick a suitable lunch companion. When Tick nods, almost imperceptibly, he continues. "This is the second such incident in recent . . ."

Now even common words used to denote time—days? weeks? months? what?—seem to have deserted him. Mr. Meyer looks hopefully at Tick, as if she may be able to supply the needed infor-mation. Or perhaps he is awaiting her promise that, should he entrust the unfortunate John Voss to her company, she herself will be able to withstand the apparently universal impulse to beat the boy up.

Or else, just possibly, the principal is aware how big a favor it is that he's asking. He's been trying to pretend it's a small, good thing, but they both know better. He's asking someone on one of the lowest rungs of the high school's social ladder—a person nearly as friendless as the boy she's to befriend—to descend to the very bottom of the ladder itself, into the damp darkness where those dwell who have no hope or recourse but to wait patiently for their eventual rescue in the form of graduation (if applicable), college (ditto), a job (in Empire Falls?), mar-riage (implausible) or death (finally).

"Maybe you could elicit the help of one or two of your friends," Mr. Meyer suggests, as if it's suddenly occurred to him that this job is too big for a skinny, already unpopular kid. "Maybe the girl from Mrs. Roderigue's art class? The one who cut herself?"

Tick can't help but smile at this, recalling Candace's horror at being jokingly linked with John Voss. "Candace?"

"Yes, Candace," Mr. Meyer agrees quickly, thrilled that Tick should recognize the very girl he is referring to, or perhaps simply relieved that Tick has at last uttered a sound in his presence. "Or whoever," he adds just as quickly, so as not to seem like he's telling her how to do her job.

"Okay, I'll try," Tick hears herself promise, feeling her heart plummet. Nor does it cheer her to see the weight of moral responsibility lifting off Mr. Meyer's thick, round shoulders and descending onto her own slender, bony ones. The man seems to stand straighter, having set this responsibility down, and suddenly looks as if he'd like to skip down the corridor, whistling all the way. But then his face clouds over again and Tick suspects that she's misjudged him. "The Minty boy . . . ," he begins.

"Zack?" Tick says. There's only one Minty boy.

"Is he a friend of yours?"

"He used to be."

Mr. Meyer nods thoughtfully, then glances toward the cafeteria. "That boy's suffering . . . I don't mean to say that Zachary Minty participates directly, but I don't think any of this could happen without his encouragement. But perhaps I'm being unfair to him."

"I wouldn't worry about being unfair to Zack." Tick regrets these words as soon as they're out, perceiving that they amount to an implied alliance or, worse, a shared worldview between herself and the principal. She senses, too, that going into battle with Mr. Meyer at her side would be a lot like going into battle alone.

Clearly, though, her remark has restored the man's happiness. "How are you and Doris getting along these days?" he asks, using Mrs. Roderigue's Christian name as the gesture of intimacy that seals their deal.

"Great," Tick says, swallowing hard, since she can see no advantage in telling the truth: that she'd as soon the woman were dead.

BACK INSIDE THE CAFETERIA, Tick decides that the most attractive of her options is to pretend the conversation with Mr. Meyer never took place. For one thing, the principal will quickly forget that he has asked this favor of her, if he hasn't already. He'll likely remember their agreement only if he runs into her in the next day or so, and she's confident of her ability to steer clear of him, given her anonymity in the halls of Empire High. Unless their eyes actually meet, he won't notice her; if their eyes *should* meet, the worst that can happen is that he *will* remember, in which case he'll ask what kind of progress she's made. And Tick knows how easily adults are satisfied with vagaries. A shrug of the shoulders and a "Not bad, I guess" will usually do the trick.

Almost as attractive as this scenario, which risks little and requires less, is another. She can go over to the boy and say, "So, you want to eat lunch together?" She can make clear from the tone of her voice that she's been put up to this by Mr. Meyer and is merely making good on a promise extracted under duress. This second option has the added advantage of being the truth, assuming that's ever an advantage. The point is, the boy will want no part of her charity, and that will be the end of it. After all, he did select a table on the other side of the cafeteria, and if that gesture wasn't clear enough, he chose a chair facing away from her. In all probability he wants no more to do with her than she does with him.

By far the least attractive possibility is to make an honest effort, and at first Tick thinks that she won't, that it's simply too much to ask. The only problem is that while John Voss has aimed himself away from her, she, unfortunately, is facing him, and she does not relish the idea of spending the rest of her lunch period staring at the victim's accusing back. Having eaten half the chicken salad sandwich her father made for her at the restaurant that morning, she has no interest in the rest. What she'd planned to do with the last twenty minutes of the period was read another chapter of her Picasso book, which she'd finished last week and which so inspired her that she'd immediately begun again. She simply marveled at how content the man was to be different, to go his own way, self-reliantly, as Emerson said you should in that essay they'd read back in the first week of English class. It's a pretty neat trick, that, and Tick would like to learn how it's done, though she knows the book doesn't reveal the how of it, at least not on first reading. Still, just knowing that such self-confidence is possible is reassuring to her, and reading a few pages during lunch would help her make it through the afternoon.

But in order to concentrate, she'd have to get up and change seats so that *her* back would be to John Voss's back. When she gets up from her chair to do precisely this, she's surprised to discover herself shouldering her backpack, picking up her lunch leftovers, and making her way across the cafeteria. At the boy's table, when she sets her backpack down with a thud on one of the plastic chairs, he looks partway up, maybe to chin level, then back at his food. He's eating what looks like tuna fish from a plastic container; whatever it is, its odor is particularly strong. Tick herself is well on her way to becoming a vegetarian, and most meat and fish smell rancid to her.

"I liked your egg," she offered, an awkward opening gambit.

"You don't have to talk to me," the boy says quickly and rudely, so rudely, in fact, that Tick considers herself absolved of further moral obligation. Where *he* gets off offering *her* an attitude she can't imagine. No wonder he gets the shit kicked out of him every other day. But instead of retreating, she pulls out a plastic chair, then sits and stares until he looks up again, almost, but not quite, meeting her eye. Already she's made progress, it occurs to her. The boy has actually spoken, which means he's not a mute.

"Maybe I want to," she says, quickly swallowing the lie, Meyer-fashion, and allowing just a touch of rudeness to edge into her own tone. "Maybe I feel like telling you I liked your egg."

"Uh-uh," he responds, shoveling the oily, stringy lunch substance into his mouth, causing Tick to wonder what it would be like to kiss a boy after he'd eaten something so disgusting. "*He* told you to." The boy allows the pronoun to hang there in the air. It's as if, for John Voss at least, Mr. Meyer is still in the cafeteria with them. Spooky. Also, each time the boy glances up, his eyes hesitate for a split second on Tick's sandwich before dropping again to his own ghastly fare.

"So how come you dream about eggs?" she finally decides to ask.

"I *don't* dream about eggs." What a dumb thing to dream about, his tone of voice seems to suggest. Each time he speaks, the shock of hearing his voice at all takes her by surprise: it's a perfectly normal, if somewhat angry-sounding, voice, and there's nothing so very odd about it except that before now she's never heard him use it. His voice, Tick concludes, is the one normal thing about this otherwise deeply weird boy.

"Well, the assignment was to paint your most vivid dream," she reminds him.

"I never dream," he says. "So I couldn't *do* the assignment."

"Everybody dreams."

He meets her eye for the first time now, reminding her of something she can't quite think what. "You're one person," he says, as if to suggest that's just as well, that he wouldn't have wished her to replicate.

"True," she allows. "So?"

"So how does that qualify you to know what everybody in the world does or doesn't do?"

Tick, having already had this conversation with her father, feels pretty confident of the intellectual terrain. "It's called an inference," she says. If she were certain she could speak with such authority in class, she wouldn't be so quiet. "I infer that no two snowflakes are alike. I don't have to examine every one."

The boy doesn't miss a beat. "That's not a very good example," he says, as if he, too, may have had a similar conversation before. "When you say that I must dream because you do, you're inferring that nobody can be *different* from you, not that everybody must be similar." His eyes fall on her Picasso book. "Wasn't he different?"

This she'd have to think about. "In degree," she decides, pleased to discover that this is what she actually believes, not just something she's saying to keep from losing an argument. She's even more pleased to see her companion shrug as if it didn't matter. Tick herself has shrugged enough to know that this is what you do when it *does* matter. Or, more precisely, she *infers* that one of his shrugs means more or less the same thing as one of hers. "So how come you're *thinking* about eggs?"

He shrugs again, as before, so Tick pays particular attention when he says, "It's just something my mom said once. If chickens had any idea what was in store for them, they'd stay where they were in their eggs."

Ah, a philosophical position.

"She was actually frying eggs at the time," the boy continued. "I'm not sure she understood that those particular eggs were never going to become chickens. My mom wasn't all that smart—according to Grandma, anyhow."

Tick hesitates, then decides to ask. "Is your mother dead?"

"That's a possibility," he says, as if it were a matter of scientific curiosity only.

Tick tries to puzzle this out. She likes to understand things, hates to admit when she doesn't, especially if she suspects she's missing something obvious. Another leading question just might result in ridicule, however, so she waits until it becomes clear that John Voss has said all he intends to say on this subject. "I don't get it," she finally admits.

"*You* don't get it," he snorts, the contemptuous kind of response that keeps people from even bothering.

Angry now, Tick takes the bit in her teeth and says, "No. I *don't* get it."

Finally the boy says, "My dad left first. Then my mom remarried, and they left. After that I came here to live with my grandmother. *Now* do you get it?"

He's finished his lunch by now, the smell of it still thick in the air between them. When his eyes pause again on Tick's half-eaten sandwich, she says, "I can't finish this. You can have it if you're still hungry."

"I'm full," he says, but he doesn't look even remotely full, so Tick watches his Adam's apple, expecting to see it bob. The boy has a long, thin neck and an Adam's apple that juts out from beneath his pale skin like the edge of something foreign and jagged. Tick can tell from the rash on his neck that he's recently begun to shave and doesn't really have the knack yet. He can handle his upper lip and his chin, but not the less regular topography of his pimply neck, where the hair is tougher and grows at unpredictable angles. There are individual hairs he's apparently been missing for weeks, because they have begun to curl.

When the boy's eyes flicker at something over her shoulder, Tick glances at the cafeteria door, where Zack Minty's face is framed, motionless, in one of the small rectangular windows. She nearly flinches, since something about the stillness of the face in the tiny window suggests that it's been there for a long time, observing them. She's just about to tell her companion not to worry, that the cafeteria door is always locked after fifth period, when Zack flings it open and saunters inside. Some people, Tick thinks, should never be entrusted with keys, and Mr. Meyer is one of them. Having unlocked the door to let John in, he's forgotten to lock it back up again, this after lecturing Tick at the beginning of their solitary lunch arrangement that this door must remain locked, that she wasn't to open it for any of her friends.

As the door clangs shut, Zack Minty pauses dramatically, as if to give both his former girlfriend and Empire High School's favorite object of derision time to consider the absurdity of imagining that he of all people could ever be kept out of anyplace he wanted into. In no apparent hurry to join them, he wanders over to the bank of vending machines, hitting each button on the soda machine with the heel of his palm and waiting for something to drop. When nothing does, he places a hand on each side of the machine and leans on it, as if the effort of having made so many simple requests and the disappointment of having been refused have been too much for him. He rests his forehead against its smooth surface for a long beat, then begins to rock the whole thing back and forth until it slams into the wall and there's the sound of breaking glass inside. Letting the machine fall back into place, he waits. Still nothing.

Tick watches this entire exhibition with more fascination than fear. Meanwhile, John Voss seems to have slipped back into his coma. When Zack gives up on the machine and comes over, pulling out a chair next to Tick, she digs three quarters out of her pocket and slides them in front of him. Zack hasn't looked at her yet, but is staring at John Voss as if searching in vain for a reason for this kid's existence. Eventually he notices the quarters, though he can't seem to compute a reason for them either.

"What's this?"

"I thought you wanted a soda," Tick says.

"Nooooo," he replies, fingering one of the coins and walking it across his knuckles. He once tried to teach Tick this trick, and she knows how proud it makes him. Sitting so close, it's clear that he's grown a couple inches over the summer, but more than that, he's bulked up, causing Tick to wonder if he's on steroids. He's definitely dumb enough, but last spring he swore to her he wouldn't, though their breaking up might've absolved him of this promise.

He's still good-looking, though, she has to admit, good-looking enough to make her wonder, as she did all last year, what he wants with her. He could have a really cool girlfriend if he wanted one. Candace isn't the only one who considers him a major hunk.

"I didn't want a soda," he explains. "What I wanted . . ."

The quarter continues to dance over his knuckles.

". . . was a free soda."

And with this the quarter, which had come to rest between his thumb and forefinger, shoots across the table and hits John Voss in the forehead, hard, just above the left eyebrow. The boy barely flinches, though it had to hurt. When Zack reaches for a second quarter, Tick sweeps both remaining coins into a side pocket of her backpack, where she hears them click against the Exacto knife she keeps meaning to slip back into the supply cupboard in art class the next chance she gets.

"So," Zack says, "who's this? Your new boyfriend?"

"No," Tick says, maybe just a little too quickly, since Zack is quick to smirk. "We were just talking. And you're not supposed to be in here."

Zack shrugs and goes back to staring at John Voss. A red spot has appeared where the quarter struck the boy's forehead, and Zack may be wondering, as Tick is, how he can keep from rubbing it.

"The door wasn't locked," Zack says. "And I have a hall pass." He shows her the pass, signed by Mrs. Roderigue, which in itself is a minor mystery, since he doesn't have a class with her. But then, Zack always has whatever is required. It's one of the more amazing things about him, actually, and Tick is surprised to have forgotten this over the summer. Last year, whenever they went to a movie, he'd have two tickets without having to go to the box office. If one of his friends showed up unexpectedly, he'd produce a third ticket. Or a fourth. Always secretive about how such things came to him, he'd just smile under direct questioning. He apparently liked to foster the impression that people who were loyal to him would be taken care of.

Sliding the pass back into his pocket, he turns to the boy. "Why don't you go away?" he suggests.

John Voss treats this as one of the best ideas he's heard in ages, practically jumping to his feet and gathering his things.

"My old girlfriend is going to explain why she doesn't like me anymore."

The strangest part of this statement is that it appears heartfelt. Zack's point, if she understands him correctly, is that big, stupid, cruel people have feelings too, and she's hurt his.

Tick watches the boy walk to the far corner of the cafeteria and sit down with his back to them. She hadn't expected much in chivalry from this kid, but she's still surprised by such unapologetic cowardice. He's apparently come to accept humiliation as his lot in life, perhaps even made it his friend.

"Billy Wolff sprained his ankle in practice," Zack says. "That means I'm starting outside linebacker this weekend. You going to the game?"

"I don't know," Tick says. The stench of the boy's food has departed with him, mostly, though the plastic container is still there on the table, its lid sealed shut. The fishy smell has been overpowered by Zack's cologne, and Tick notices that during the summer he, too, has taken to shaving daily. Either his stubble is less resistant, or else he's mastered the technique that has eluded John Voss. "The gang's going to hang out afterward," he says. "You want to come?"

Tick wishes she didn't, but the truth is she does. Only three weeks into the fall semester and she's already tired of being friendless. She misses her friends, if that's what they really are, or at least being part of something. Maybe someday she'll be self-contained like Picasso, but not yet. After meeting Donny on Martha's Vineyard she vowed she'd never fall back in with Zack Minty, because it wasn't worth it. And she's no fool. She knows it won't be long before he'll start belittling her again, undermining her slender confidence, making fun of the things she cares about, saying Picasso was a fag. Worse, he'll be trying to make her jealous by flirting with prettier girls. Tick understands herself well enough to know she's prone to jealousy. She doesn't like this about herself and would change it if she could, but she doesn't know how. After a while, Zack won't be content to belittle her and make her jealous. He will begin to treat her like shit, and there won't be any way out, because by then she'll begin to believe the things he's saying. And even that isn't the worst. Tick doesn't even like to think about the worst, though last spring before they broke up Zack promised nothing like that would ever happen again.

"Candace is going," Zack adds, as if—who knows—this might be just the enticement needed.

"I don't know," she says. "Maybe."

"Maybe," he repeats after taking a deep breath, as if the concept of "maybe" needed to be mixed liberally with oxygen before being swallowed. He picks up the plastic lunch container and pries up the corner with his thumb, and the air is suddenly rancid again. "I've changed a lot since last spring," he says.

"So Candace tells me," she says, in case he's wondering if his message was conveyed. The smell makes her want to gag, though Zack doesn't seem to notice.

"It just makes me really angry that you won't give me another chance," he blurts out. They've had this conversation before, of course. Zack believes fervently, devoutly, in second chances. Also third and fourth chances. Tick suspects this issues from his devotion to sports, where repeated losses and even the most grotesque behavior never prevent you from playing again. You can get suspended for a game or two, but there's no such thing as a lifetime ban; so to his way of thinking, he's served his suspension and now it's her fault for trying to impose a greater penalty than the league has the authority to enforce. When he says it makes him angry, he isn't kidding. She can tell. Nor does his anger strike the boy as evidence against him. Who *wouldn't* be angry, is what he'd like to know. This is *some* kind of unfair, after all. A guy made you this angry, you'd knock him on his ass, and if he got up, you'd go at it. Later, you'd shake hands and it'd be over. With girls you never get anywhere because nothing ever really gets settled. They say *maybe*, which might as well be *fuck you*.

Frustrated, he now wishes he hadn't sent John Voss away, Tick can tell. "I got an idea," he says. "Let's invite your new boyfriend to come along. Hey, Dickhead!"

No response from the boy.

"Is he deaf," Zack says, almost pensively, "or does he think there are two dickheads in here?"

There *are* two, and Tick comes very close to saying so. Instead she says, "Don't, Zack. Leave him alone."

"Hey, Dickhead," Zack calls again. "Don't pretend you don't know who I'm talking to. Turn around."

The boy rotates in his chair without looking at them. As always, he studies the floor.

"That's better," Zack says.

"Zack," Tick says, wishing that the sound of her voice didn't contain so much pleading, "don't be mean."

"What's so mean about asking him if he wants to hang out after the football game? How's that mean?"

"That's not what you're doing."

"It isn't?" he says. "You're telling me I don't know what I'm doing? You know what I'm doing better than me?"

"Just leave him alone."

"Listen up, Dickhead," Zack says. "No hard feelings, okay? What's your name, anyway?"

The boy glances up briefly, then down again.

"His name," Tick says softly, "is John Voss."

"Hey, John Voss! You want to hang with us after the game?"

Does the boy make a sound? Tick can't tell. Apparently Zack Minty can't either, because he looks at her, then back at the boy. "Hey, John Voss. Was that a yes, or what?"

This time they both hear him say, "Okay."

"You hear that?" Zack says to Tick. "It's okay with John Voss."

"If you leave him alone," Tick says, "I'll go, okay?"

Zack is about to call something else to the boy, but when he hears this he stops and looks at Tick with the kind of smile that almost dispels her misgivings. A smile full of . . . what? Something she needs. She'd like to think it's love, and maybe love is in there somewhere, though she suspects it's not the major ingredient. What, then? Gratitude? Relief that on third and long, things were going to work out after all?

"Hey, Dickhead—I mean John," he shouts. "You hear that? Tick's going too! What a great time we'll all have, right, John?"

Nothing.

"You aren't mad at me now, are you? About that quarter? That was a shitty thing, John, I admit. We're still buddies, though, right?"

Again, nothing.

"Just nod your head if we're still buddies, okay, John Voss?"

He nods.

Zack doesn't even see this because he's looking back at Tick. He takes her hand and she doesn't resist. "That's great, John," he calls, still looking at her. "Thanks for the second chance, John. I mean it."

"Let's just go, okay?" Tick whispers, not wanting to look over at the other boy. Getting to her feet also gives her an excuse to draw back her hand. As if to second the motion, the bell rings, ending sixth period.

"Okay, then, John," Zack calls, picking up the plastic container. "See you Saturday."

Together, he and Tick start toward the cafeteria's double doors. Hoping to prevent him from stopping at John's table, she reaches out and tugs at his sleeve, but he easily pulls free.

"I just got one question, okay?" Zack says, tossing the lunch container onto the table in front of the other boy. "Just what the fuck have you been eating?" And suddenly he's laughing so hard he's unsteady on his feet. "Because I have to tell you, it smells like something somebody already ate before you got to it, buddy," he says. "I'd watch out for that in the future, John Voss. No pre-chewed food, okay? That's my advice."

Outside in the corridor, which is already full of jostling students, Zack slumps against the wall. He's laughing so hard that tears are rolling down his cheeks. Several kids witness this and begin laughing too, though they have no idea why. Which leaves Tick, solemn-faced, in the minority. She's seen Zack in these moods before, though, and she knows the real danger has passed. He'll stay manic now for a while, which means she can ask her question without fear.

"Why do you always have to be *such* an asshole?" she says.

Which Zack considers the funniest thing yet. He doubles over, laughing so hard he can barely answer. "I have *no* idea," he wheezes, putting his arm around her so they can merge into the stream of bodies. She wishes it weren't so, but it feels good to have his arm around her, good to be so close to so many kids all headed in the same direction. She knows better than to glance over her shoulder at the small rectangular windows of the cafeteria doors, but she does so anyway and regrets it immediately, wishing she hadn't glimpsed John Voss taking a hungry bite out of her leftover sandwich.

CHAPTER 11

JANINE ROBY SAT at the end of the bar at Callahan's drinking seltzer water with a squeeze of lime and practicing her new signature—*Janine Louise Comeau*—on a stack of cocktail napkins, while her mother changed a beer keg. Unless the damn courthouse in Fairhaven fell down, which it might, just to thwart her, Janine and the Silver Fox would be marrying soon, and she wanted her signature to be second nature when the time came, not like at the end of the calendar year when you kept writing the wrong year on your checks halfway through January. Or, if you were like her husband, Miles—correction: soon-to-be-ex-husband, Miles—halfway through March. Which made her smile. It was just as well he wasn't the one who had to adopt a new name and signature, because she doubted he was up to it. If there was a worse creature of habit than her husband—correction: her soon-to-be-ex-husband—Janine sure hadn't met him. A human rut was what he was, bumping along in his groove from home to the restaurant, from the restaurant to the damn church, from the church back to the restaurant, and from the restaurant back home (back when it *was* his home). One night, weeks after they'd separated and Miles had moved into the apartment above the restaurant, he'd turned up in her bedroom. It had given her a start, waking up like that and seeing him there at the foot of the bed, looming over her and Walt, and her first thought had been that Miles had come to kill them. Then she saw him pull his shirt over his head and toss it on top of the hamper, and she knew he'd closed the restaurant and made his exhausted way home by rote. He must've come to when Janine turned on the end-table lamp, because the light sent him scurrying after his discarded shirt like a burglar. Where another man might have taken advantage of his mistake by acting on the impulse to slit their throats, Janine could tell from the expression on his face that if he'd had a knife, the only throat he'd have slit would have been his own.

Actually, what Miles reminded her of was the plastic figures of her brother's hockey game, back when they were kids. The surface of the board represented the ice rink and was full of slots, each one occupied by a stick-wielding plastic figure who moved forward or backward in his slot. This hadn't been a terribly successful gift. Their parents had concluded that Billy wasn't old enough for it, because the first thing he did was rip the plastic figures out of their slots, thinking, perhaps, that the game would be more fun if the players could go where they wanted, like real hockey players. How was the kid to know that under-neath the board were big, bulging discs that kept the plastic men stable? Once liberated, they looked ridiculous, like a miniature platoon of clubfooted soldiers who happened, incidentally, to be armed only with hockey sticks. Worse, they simply could not be induced to stand up like men. Janine had understood long ago that if you somehow managed to extract her soon-to-be-ex from his ruts with the idea of setting him free, you'd have the same result. Free Miles Roby and he wouldn't even be able to stand upright.

"Those cocktail napkins cost money, you know," Bea said when Janine had gone through about half the stack. Janine could fit about three *Janine Louise Comeau*'s on the back of each napkin, but only two on the front, thanks to Callahan's leprechaun logo. "What the hell's the matter with you, anyhow?"

Janine took a fresh napkin and signed her new identity on it below the little Irish freak. "I was just thinking of Billy," she explained. "Remember that hockey game you and Daddy bought him for Christmas?"

"Yes, I remember it," Bea said, leaving about half a dozen napkins there on the bar by her daughter and moving the others out of harm's way. "I remember every toy that child destroyed, which was every single one he touched. It took him about a New York minute to yank those little bastards out of where they belonged. Then he cried until we promised to buy him another one."

Janine tuned out most of her mother's nostalgic recollection. Her little brother had been killed at the age of nineteen when a car he'd jacked up crashed down on him, and she hadn't meant to think about Billy at all. She'd been happily reflecting on the shortcomings of her husband—correction: soon-to-be-ex-husband, the Human Rut—when Billy just crept in. So, since thinking about her brother had made her sad and depressed, she went back to thinking about Miles, which made her happy and depressed. Depressed because he'd always be Miles, happy because she'd soon be shut of him.

When she'd finished autographing the rest of the cocktail napkins, Janine consulted her watch. Her afternoon aerobics class was just shy of half an hour away, if she could last that long. For Janine, late afternoon was always the worst part of the day, the stretch she couldn't handle alone, which was the only reason she visited her mother, who drove her nuts. She knew from experience that once she got back to the gym and got Abba pounding on the big speakers ("Mama Mia! How can I resist him!"), she'd be fine. There was no better appetite suppressant than vigorous exercise, and by the time she finished the high-impact aerobics session at four, and then the low-impact one at five, the worst of her inner demons would be back on the leash. She'd be able to sit down to a reasonable dinner with Walt, who'd taught her how to quit eating when she started to feel full instead of plowing on through until she was sated. After a sensible dinner she'd be content until bedtime, when the hunger dogs would start baying again, but by then she could make them heel because she'd be exhausted from the workouts. And as Walt was always reminding her, exhaustion trumps hunger. There'd also be sex, another excellent distraction.

Right now, though, she was hungry enough to eat the soggy lime wedge floating in her seltzer. The disgusting pickled pigs' feet swimming in brine in a gallon jug halfway down the bar actually looked delicious, and Janine could imagine herself getting down on the floor and gnawing on one like a dog, cracking the bone with her back teeth and sucking out the marrow. Her mother, intuiting her misery, put a bowl of beer nuts in front of her, munching a small handful herself to demonstrate how good they were. "Mmmmm," she said.

Janine was able to identify only three primal urges: to eat, to fuck, and to kill your pain-in-the-ass mother. She wasn't sure which of these was the most powerful, but she knew the last was the most dangerous because there was so little to counterbalance it. "You know what, Beatrice?" Janine said. She never used her mother's full name except to suggest her proximity to actual matricide. "You're just jealous." Of her weight loss and relative youth and sexual activity, it went without saying.

Standing up, Janine carried the bowl of beer nuts down the bar and handed them to the only other customers, two morose-looking unemployed millworkers who were nursing cheap draft beers and patiently awaiting happy hour. On the way back she snagged another short stack of cocktail napkins.

"I am," her mother agreed. "I really do wish I could go through life blind and selfish. Did it ever occur to you that I'm sixty years old? That maybe I could use a hand changing these damn kegs?"

Janine Louise Comeau, wrote Janine Louise Roby on the back of the first new napkin. Beneath her signature, the same thing, twice more. "Don't tell me after all these years you finally decided you don't like mule work," she said.

"I like it fine," Bea said, which was true. Until recently she used to pick *up* the damn kegs. Now she rocked them gently on and off the hand truck she kept out back, wheeling the full kegs in and the empties back out. "Nolan Ryan still likes to throw fastballs, too."

Having tended bar for forty years, Bea had watched several thousand ball games she had no interest in, only to discover at this late date that she'd picked up so damn much knowledge about baseball that she halfway enjoyed it. And she'd come to believe life was like that: you could enjoy almost anything if you gave it enough time. "Including a man," Bea always concluded. Meaning Miles, Janine understood. Her mother had little patience on the subject of her marriage. "If I could learn to love your father," Bea never tired of reminding her daughter, "you could learn to love a man as good-hearted as Miles." Which was a damn lie, Janine knew. Bea had loved her father from the start and continued loving him until the day he died. The fact that her father was no damn good was beside the point.

"You think Nolan Ryan likes pitching ibuprofen after pitching fastballs?" Bea wanted to know.

Janine Louise Comeau, Janine wrote above another leprechaun. According to her watch, a minute and a half had passed. "I don't have any idea, Mother. I don't even know who Nolan Ryan is."

"What I'm saying is, I could use a hand sometimes," Bea told her. "If it's an aerobic workout you're after, I can help you out."

Janine knew where this was heading, of course. What Bea was hinting at was getting her to work at the tavern, which wasn't going to happen. Lately her mother had been thinking about reopening the kitchen for lunch. Back when Janine's father was alive, Callahan's had served sandwiches and done a decent lunch trade. Janine could make it work, too. She knew food from all those years wasted on the Empire Grill—

but it was working around food all the time that had put an extra fifty pounds on her. Walt had come along and talked her into working at the club just in time. Another year or two and she would've looked just like her mother, who was built like a thumb, except not so flexible in the middle. The thing Janine couldn't figure out was why her mother would *want* her at the bar. They'd just fight like cats the whole time, unable to agree on anything.

"Give it up, Beatrice," Janine advised. According to her watch, only twenty-two minutes to go. "I got a job at one of the few successful businesses in Dexter County. I've lost fifty pounds and I feel good about myself for the first time in my whole damn life. You aren't going to bring me down, so don't even try, okay?"

The two mopers at the other end of the bar had stopped pretending they weren't eavesdropping, so Bea switched on the TV to a talk show, loud enough that she and her daughter could continue their conversation in private. The men were clearly disappointed. "If we got to listen to a fat woman talk, can't she at least be the white one?" one of them complained.

Reluctantly, Bea did as requested, though in her opinion these particular men would've benefited more from watching Oprah than Rosie. "Oprah's smarter than any five white men you can name, Otis."

"She ain't smart enough to be white, though, is she?" he countered, eliciting a bitter chuckle from his companion.

The argument Bea wanted was with her daughter, not these two reprobates, but she couldn't let Otis have the last word, either. She considered herself one of the few unprejudiced people in Empire Falls by virtue of the fact that she took a dim view of practically everyone, regardless of their race or gender. "Unlike some people," she said, "Oprah's content in her own skin."

"I'm plenty content in my own skin too," Otis said, not understanding that her remark was directed at her daughter.

"Now *that's* a tragedy," Bea replied, then turned away to face Janine. "And I'm *not* trying to bring you down, little girl. You're always accusing people of that, as if everybody in the world's only got one thing on their mind. You. It's a mother's duty to point out when her child is acting dumber than usual, and that's all I'm doing."

Janine tore the napkin with a vicious stroke of the "u" in *Comeau*. "Can we just drop the whole thing, Ma?" she suggested, wadding up the ruined napkin. "There's no point in us discussing what isn't any of your damn business to start with. If you can't understand why I might want something better than going through life fat and miserable, then that's too damn bad. Maybe someday I'll give up—like you—but not today, all right? People can change, and I'm changing."

"You aren't changing, Janine," her mother said. "You're just losing weight. There's a difference. If you woke up one morning thinking of somebody but yourself, *that* would be a change. If you thought for two seconds about the effect of all your foolishness on your daughter, that'd be another."

"Like I said, Ma," Janine replied, grabbing the last of the napkins, "you're just jealous, so let's drop it before one of us says something they'll regret, okay?"

"I'm not even close to saying anything I'll regret," Bea assured her. "What I'll regret is holding my tongue."

"How would you know? You've never even tried."

Down the bar, Otis snorted at that one. Which meant that the television's volume wasn't up high enough. Which Bea remedied.

"What I'm trying to tell you," she continued, "is that all you're doing is shoveling shit against the tide. A person is what she is."

Janine was tempted to tell her mother about all the orgasms she was having now, how Walt had found the spot whose existence Miles had never even suspected, how *nice* it felt to be desired for once. Except what was the point of trying to explain this to a woman who wouldn't even know orgasms existed if Oprah didn't tell her? "I don't need you to tell me who I am, Beatrice. For the first time in my life I have a pretty good idea."

"You do?" Her mother was grinning now in that superior way of hers.

"You're damn right I do," Janine said, autographing the last of the napkins. After all, there was no point in getting angry. The argument had done exactly what she'd hoped, distracting her from her hunger. According to the clock over the register, it was now ten till four, time to head back to the club.

"Well, I don't believe you," her mother said. "And what's more, I can prove you're full of it."

Sliding off her stool, Janine shouldered her tote bag and pushed her glass, now empty except for the soggy lime wedge in the bottom, toward her mother. "Yeah, well, I'm not interested in your proof, Beatrice. I'm going to work."

"*Who's* going to work?" Bea said, covering the napkin with her rough hand. "The woman whose name is on this napkin?"

"That's right, Ma," Janine said, heading for the door. It was her mother's chuckle that stopped her.

"Read it and weep, little girl," Bea said, holding up the napkin between her thumb and forefinger for her daughter's inspection.

Suddenly Janine didn't want to look, aware from her mother's triumphant expression that somehow she'd managed to betray herself. And there in plain sight was the evidence, scrawled in triplicate in her own hand.

Janine Louise Roby.
Janine Louise Roby.
Janine Louise Roby.

"THERE *have* been times," Father Mark admitted, "when I feared that God would turn out to be like my maternal grandmother."

Late in the afternoon, he and Miles were sitting in the rectory's breakfast nook, drinking coffee, Miles having just confessed a petulant doubt about God's wisdom. Earlier that afternoon, at his daughter's behest, he'd hired a new busboy. They needed one, so that part was fine, and one thing Mrs. Whiting was good about was giving him free rein with regard to personnel, for which he was particularly grateful in this instance, because he couldn't imagine how to explain today's hiring to his employer. In fact, he wasn't even sure how he was going to explain it to David and Charlene, who'd both looked at him as if he'd lost his mind when he introduced John Voss. What?—they clearly wanted to know, when the boy seemed equally incapable of speech and meeting any adult eye—you hired a mute? Miles could tell from his brother's body language that he considered this merely the tip of the iceberg when it came to Miles's bizarre behavior since returning from Martha's Vineyard. David hadn't raised the issue of the liquor license after Miles returned from his meeting with Mrs. Whiting, but Miles knew the subject wasn't dead. Nor was the necessity of hiring a replacement for Buster, whom Miles could find neither hide nor hair of. While they did need another busboy, hiring a backup fry cook was far more urgent if Miles didn't intend to continue opening the restaurant himself every day of the week, which he'd done now for nearly a month. If he got sick, that was that, since David only worked evenings and seldom rose before noon. So at the sight of John Voss, David shook his head as if Miles had sent in a flanker to replace an injured interior lineman.

"Ours was a large family," Father Mark was explaining, "and every Christmas my grandmother gave gifts of cash in varying amounts, claiming she was rewarding her grandchildren according to how much they loved her. She swore she could look right into our hearts and know. One child would get a crisp fifty-dollar bill, the next a crumpled single. No two gifts were ever the same amount."

Miles nodded. "Well, maybe there's a hell."

Father Mark smiled. "It's pretty to think so. Of course, none of this had anything to do with the grandchildren at all. She was punishing and rewarding her own grown children according to her own mean-spirited sense of justice. Those who stopped by to see her during the week, who did her bidding and fawned over her, were rewarded. Those who didn't got coal in their stockings. My Aunt Jane was among the favored until her husband took a job in Illinois. My grandmother warned her not to move, and when they did anyway, she wrote Jane out of the will."

Miles nodded. How did the world come to be run by power-mad old women? he wondered.

"Driving all the way back to New Jersey for the Christmas holidays didn't win Janey any points, either. With my grandmother, when you were out, you were Old Testament out, buried like Moses in a shallow grave. But it was her kids who took the worst of it. I can still see my cousin Phyllis's face when she opened her Christmas card and saw that crumpled dollar bill. I don't think she cared about the money, but she believed what my grandmother had said about being able to look into her heart. How she sobbed, poor child."

Naturally, Miles was curious. "How did *you* do that year?"

"Me?" Father Mark smiled. "Oh, I got that crisp new fifty. You could still smell the ink on it."

"Did you share it with your less fortunate cousins?"

"No, as you might expect, sharing was strictly forbidden. I did tell my cousins the truth, though."

"Which was?"

"That I hated my grandmother with a fierce passion, which proved that she was lying about being able to look in our hearts. I told little Phyllis that if Grandma'd ever seen into mine the old bat would've seen someone just waiting for her to die." When Miles didn't say anything right away, Father Mark became sheepish. "In telling that story, it occurs to me that I've never forgiven her."

"I'm not sure it'd work as a homily without some retooling," Miles conceded, though he himself had instigated the story by trying to explain why he'd hired the new busboy. If what Tick had told him was true, the boy's parents had abandoned him, one after the other, and he was now the butt of practical jokes at the hands of the school's lunchroom bullies. Which had caused Miles to question God's wisdom, if He arranged things so that children so often were given burdens far too heavy for them to bear.

As his "date" with Cindy Whiting approached, Miles had been thinking a lot about life's inequities and his mother's tendency to take them to heart and to act upon her belief that we were all put on earth to make things a little more fair. It was Tick who'd made the request to hire that hopeless, bedraggled boy, but it was his mother, no doubt, . who'd whispered in his ear when his instincts had argued against doing so.

"It's a good story with a bad lesson," Father Mark admitted. "Maybe I'll work on it. I *do* get some of my better homilies from our afternoon chats. I always feel guilty after we've talked, like maybe I should pay you back with a recipe for the restaurant. Actually, I don't really think God's anything like my grandmother, but I can't help wondering if the situation isn't instructive, seen from the child's point of view. I mean, what if we assume our relationship to God to be one thing, and it's really something else? What if there's something central to the equation that we're leaving out? Maybe, like children, we assume ourselves to be of central importance, and we're not. Maybe the inequities that consume us here on earth aren't really the issue."

"So feeding the hungry isn't important?"

"Not exactly. Maybe it's important, but not quite in the way we think. Maybe, to God, it's our way of expressing the 'something else' that passeth beyond all understanding. Something we aren't meant to understand."

"Nonsense." Miles grinned. "I understand your grandmother perfectly, and so do you. You're trying to make a mystery out of selfishness."

Father Mark chuckled. "Yeah, I guess. She *was* a mean, self-centered old harridan. Still, we're attracted to a good mystery. Explanation, no matter how complete, isn't really that satisfying. Take those two, for instance." He pointed out the window at Max and Father

Tom, who were seated in the gathering dusk beneath a big weeping willow. To Miles they looked like a pair of old hobos who couldn't decide whether to get up and catch the night freight south or let it go and hop a train in the morning. With each gusting breeze the thin brown willow leaves swirled down upon them, some settling in their hair. Neither man seemed to notice. "Part of me wants to know what in the world they find to talk about, yet I doubt I'd feel much wiser for knowing."

In the week since Max had started helping Miles with the church, he'd struck up a surprising friendship with the old priest. At first Miles had thought that Father Tom, slipping ever deeper into his dementia, didn't recognize Max as someone he'd long known and despised utterly, but this was apparently not the case. When questioned, he recalled quite well that he'd always held Max Roby in the lowest possible esteem as a blasphemer, a shiftless charmer, a drinker and general ne'er-do-well. What he seemed less clear about was why he'd objected to these qualities. While neither Miles nor Father Mark wanted to deny the codgers their friendship, both agreed they bore watching.

And on Miles's advice, Max was still not allowed in the Rectum, as the old man was notoriously light-fingered; if Father Mark didn't want the church's valuables turning up for sale at Empire Music and Pawn, Max had best be kept outside.

"He'd steal from God?" Father Mark had wondered, the question tinged with the priest's usual irony.

"He's pretty fearless where God is concerned," Miles answered. "I can't tell whether he's a genuine atheist or simply believes in a God who's lost His grasp of the details."

"A God you could bullshit?"

"Exactly," Miles agreed, shrugging. Bullshitting God would be Max's plan in a nutshell. Miles could even guess his father's opening gambit. He'd point out to God that if He expected better results, He ought to have given Max better character to work with, instead of sending him into battle so poorly equipped.

However, as much as Miles hated to admit it, the painting *was* going a lot faster. Probably it had something to do with the fact that they got to work right away, instead of Miles wasting an hour with Father Mark over coffee. And it was also true that even at "sempty" Max *could* still climb like a monkey. He also could paint from either the ladder or the platform, and being twenty feet off the ground didn't rattle him at all, whereas Miles was distrustful of his footing and unwilling to lean.

Max's fearlessness worried him at first, but the truth was that the old man never fell unless he was drunk, so Miles just checked his breath before letting him set foot on a ladder. As a result, the west face of St. Cat's was nearly finished, thanks to a stretch of bright, sunny late-September days. If he and Max were smart, they'd let it go at that, then pick up the work again in the spring, assuming that St. Cat's hadn't turned into an art gallery or a music hall by then.

One thing Miles had decided for sure was that he wouldn't attempt the steeple, nor would he allow his father to, though the old man was game. Miles *had* hoped maybe he might summon the courage to do it himself if he went slow, and earlier that week, after sending Max home, he'd borrowed the key from Father Mark and climbed up the narrow stairs into the belfry. Miles could feel the dread welling up as he climbed, but he was okay as long as he remained in an enclosed, windowless space. Once he pushed open the trapdoor and tried to stand in the belfry, though, he knew that painting the steeple was flatly out of the question. He knew he'd never be able to climb a ladder this high, or stand on a platform either, not without hanging on to whatever was handy with both hands. In fact, he'd not been able to rise further than his knees there in the steeple, knowing that if he stood it would be possible to tumble over the waist-high railing. Even from this penitent posture he'd caught a quick glimpse of the landscape below, extending all the way across the river to Mrs. Whiting's house and beyond, and suddenly he wondered whether Cindy Whiting, if she could see him frozen in this cowardly posture, clutching the railing with both hands, might not be able to rid herself of her lifelong affection. It had taken him half an hour to find the courage to back down into the hole and pull the trapdoor shut over his head.

"Max is the one doing most of the talking," Miles observed in response to his friend's question about what the two old men could possibly be talking about.

"Confessing his sins, do you think?"

That possibility hadn't occurred to Miles, though it made immediate sense. Max was a terrible braggart, and the old priest deeply resented being barred from the confessional. The one would prove a treasure trove of stories of the very sort the other seemed to hunger for. Max's confessions would be colorful, dramatic, various and educational, lacking little save repentance, but, Miles wondered, were demented priests still vested with the power to forgive sins anyway? Max had always been blessed in his ability to pass through life without ever suffering consequences, and it'd be just like him to find a loophole now in the form of a priest willing to forgive his myriad sins without requiring contrition.

"You may be on to something," Miles admitted, now studying the old men more carefully. Max was talking and gesturing, the priest nodding enthusiastically.

"Well, I wouldn't worry about it. I suspect your father is heavensent. Just what Tom needs."

"Max Roby? On a mission from God?"

"Think about it. Tom's always been an old-school pastor. The emphasis for these guys has always been avoiding sin."

"That's old-fashioned?"

Father Mark shrugged. "To the extent you never have to come to terms with your own humanity. What wisdom would a truly blameless man have to offer us sinners? What comfort could he provide?"

"Something tells me this isn't party-line Catholicism you're espousing here."

"Depends on who's throwing the party," the other man admitted. "You know what I mean, though. Tom's never exactly been a warm, understanding presence among his flock. Like a lot of the old-timers, he's always seen himself as an enforcer. Dirty Harry with a collar. On your knees, punk. Fifty Our Fathers and fifty Hail Marys—and don't let me catch you even *thinking* about that again or I'll have to get really rough."

"People used to like that," Miles pointed out. He remembered liking it himself, as a boy, thinking there was someone out there who was above it all, who knew what was right and whose job it was to see to it that you did too.

"Maybe," Father Mark said. "My point is, Tom could stand some humanizing."

"In that case," Miles allowed, "he's talking to the right man."

"Cheap bastard," Max said, counting the bills Father Mark had given him before stuffing them into the front pocket of his paint-splattered pants. The passenger seat and floor of the Jetta were now paint-flecked, thanks to Max's refusal to change into clean clothes when they quit for the day. He made no distinction between work clothes and other clothes, and since he had started helping Miles at St. Cat's, the old man's shirts and pants and shoes were all paint-smudged.

When people pointed this out, he offered his customary "So what?" Few men, Miles reflected, lived so comfortably within the confines of a two-word personal philosophy.

"Did you even say thank you?" Miles asked as they pulled out of the driveway.

"Why should I?" Max said. "I worked, didn't I?"

"I told you we were working for free and you agreed."

"That doesn't mean he can't give me money if he feels like it. You're the fool, not me."

Miles turned toward the restaurant. Tick was working in the back room tonight, so he'd give her a hand. He also wanted to check in and see how John Voss was doing, and made a mental promise not to fire the new kid no matter how big a mess he was making of his new responsibilities.

"Of course I can see where *you'd* be embarrassed to take money," Max said. "You climb up two rungs onto a damn ladder and you're hanging on for dear life."

"You want me to drop you off somewhere, Dad?"

"He's a queer, you know," Max said. "That young one?"

"Where did you get that idea, Dad?"

"That's what the geezer told me," Max added hastily. "I wouldn't know myself one way or the other."

"Father Tom's senile, Dad. In case you hadn't noticed."

"Oh, I noticed right away," Max said. "I like him better this way. But knowing you, you probably approve."

Miles squinted over at his father. "Of senility?"

"No, of queers," Max clarified. "We were talking about queers."

"No, *you* were saying you thought Father Mark was gay, and *I* was saying you don't know what you're talking about. As usual."

"Queer's what I said, not gay. You're just mad because you didn't get paid and I did."

"No, Dad, I'm not. I'm thrilled, in fact. Maybe you can make it through the weekend without hitting me up for a loan."

"Everybody's got needs," Max said, leaning forward to push the button on the glove box. "Just because I'm sempty don't mean I've stopped eating, you know."

"You should remember those end-of-the-month needs when you're sucking down beer at the beginning of the month," Miles suggested. "You mind telling me what you're doing?"

"Your glove box won't open."

"You know why, Dad? Because it's locked."

"Locked?" Max looked flabbergasted. Just yesterday it *hadn't* been locked when he went through it and removed the sawbuck that had gotten him through until payday. He clearly regarded finding the glove compartment locked now as a disappointing development. Like arriving someplace for dinner, assuming you'd be welcome, and finding your place setting in the cupboard.

"It's locked to keep out people who have no business being in there," Miles explained.

If Max was offended by this inference, he didn't show it. Instead he leaned forward, feeling under the dash. "That little lock wouldn't keep anybody out," he said. To illustrate, he thumped a spot underneath with the heel of his hand and the glove box popped open. "A guy down in the Keys taught me that," he said, clearly pleased that he'd been such a good student. "I could show you if you want."

Miles pulled over to the curb, put the car in Park, leaned across his father and rummaged through the sprung compartment until he located the twenty he'd put there in the morning as a hedge against emergency. The bill safely in his shirt, he pulled back into the street.

Max studied his son's shirt for a moment, as if to memorize the exact location of the pocket for future reference. "You never take advantage of all the things I've learned in life," he said. "A man doesn't get to be sempty without learning a thing or two, you know." When Miles failed to respond, he added, "Or maybe you think you know everything already."

"I know you're not going to get this twenty-dollar bill," Miles said, glancing over at him. Max shrugged, as if to suggest that only time would tell. He reminded Miles a little of Harpo Marx, who wouldn't dispute the ownership of a twenty because he knew something you didn't when you put it in your pocket—that the bill was on a string. In fact, the resemblance between his father and Harpo was so uncanny just then that Miles patted his pocket to make sure the bill was still there. "You'd have swiped it, too, wouldn't you? Even though you got paid five minutes ago and the money's still warm in your pocket, all you can think about is what might be in my glove box since the last time you looked."

Max ignored this. He'd taken out the real-estate booklet again and was leafing through the pages of million-dollar houses on the Vineyard like a prospective buyer. "Wasn't it you who was just telling me I should remember my future needs?"

At the red light, Miles stopped, grabbed the pamphlet, stuffed it back in the glove compartment and slammed the door shut. No doubt about it. Max could bullshit God Himself. In fact, Miles wondered if God would even know what He was up against. When the time came, he hoped He would attend to the matter first thing in the morning, because at the end of a long day, Vegas odds would make Max the runaway favorite.

"If I was you," Max offered, "I'd start courting that crippled Whiting girl."

"And you wonder why I never come to you for advice," Miles said. He had absolutely no intention of revealing that he and Cindy Whiting were going to the homecoming game tomorrow. Perhaps Max would forget about the game and not go. Perhaps no one would see them there together and report back to the old man. Perhaps pigs would fly.

Max didn't say anything until Miles failed to dodge a pothole and the glove box door dropped open again. "If all I had to do to get my hands on ten million dollars was marry a cripple, I'd marry her."

"I know you would, Dad. Then you'd leave her."

"No, I wouldn't," Max said, fiddling with the lock mechanism. "I might take a vacation or two when I felt like it, though." He closed the door again, but it immediately popped open.

Miles just looked at him until the light turned green.

"You had a screwdriver in there, I could probably fix that for you," Max offered.

"You already fixed it great, Dad," Miles said, accelerating through the intersection and recalling that Mrs. Whiting herself had pointed out how much easier his life would be if he married Cindy. "Just do me a big favor and don't fix anything else, okay?"

Max crossed his legs and stared out the window, the sprung door of the glove box resting on his knee. He contented himself with this view for about a minute, then pulled out the real-estate guide again. "You married that cripple, you could buy this place you want so bad."

"Dad?" Miles said. "Could you not refer to her that way?"

"What way?"

"As a cripple. Could you not do that?"

"What should I call her?"

"How about this? Don't call her anything. In fact, I can't think of any reason for you to refer to her at all. She's nothing to either one of us."

Max paused. "Same family. The Robys and the Robideauxs."

"Don't start in again," Miles warned him. "You've got even less chance of getting your hands on their money than you have of getting the twenty in my shirt pocket."

When Max didn't say anything to this, Miles again discreetly checked his shirt pocket to make sure the old man didn't have it already. The bill crinkled reassuringly against the fabric.

"I knew a guy in the Keys used to call himself a cripple all the time," his father said. " 'Max,' he'd say. 'Don't ever be a cripple.' "

"Good God," Miles said.

"Don't get mad at me, is all I'm saying," his father said. "It wasn't me that ran over her."

"No," Miles agreed, "you were lucky. All you hit was the mayor's little dog."

"Unlucky, you mean," Max said. "It was his daughter's, not his. Ran out right in front of me—couldn't have been helped even if I was sober. Happened right over there." Max pointed at a quiet, shady neighborhood of once elegant homes, most of which, lately, had gone slightly to seed. One of them, Walt Comeau's, had a For Sale sign out front.

"No, I meant lucky," Miles insisted. "If it *had* been a child, you wouldn't have been able to help that, either. You got off easy."

"Would've been less fuss over a lot of kids," Max recalled. "You'd think I *had* run over a child the way everybody carried on."

"I don't—"

"If your mother was still with us, she'd tell you to marry that crippled girl, same as me. And if *she* told you to . . ."

Miles couldn't help smiling at this. Mrs. Whiting had used the same tactic.

". . . you'd do it. Then we'd have ten million to split up."

"That's what you think," Miles said. "If Mom was still alive, she and I would have ten million. You'd be shit out of luck."

Max considered this possibility. "You know, the way you don't like me, I'm surprised you won't pay me to go away. I *would*, you know. I had five hundred dollars in my pocket, I'd head down to the Keys right now. That's all I'd need."

"Then how come you're always calling me for money when you're there?"

"You're my son. You're supposed to help me out a little every now and then."

Again, Miles couldn't help smiling. "Did it ever occur to you that you've got it backward, Dad? Aren't parents the ones who are supposed to help their kids?"

"Works both ways," Max said.

"Not in this family," Miles assured him. "In *this* family it only works *one* way and we both know which way that is."

Max managed a ten-count silence. "Five hundred is all I'd need," he finally said. "Once I get down there, I'm fine. All the tourists think I'm a Conch. You know what a Conch is?"

"Yeah. It's the local term for a bum who won't bathe, right? An old reprobate who wears food in his beard and goes around sponging off strangers."

This time Max was quiet for a good twenty beats, causing Miles to look over at him. Experience had taught him that it was impossible to hurt his father's feelings, but sometimes he worried that one day he'd go too far.

Finally his father chuckled. "Funny you should mention sponges," he said. "That's what they called the old sponge divers. Conchs. They were Greeks, most of 'em. I could maybe swing it on four hundred."

Miles had to admit that getting rid of his father for an entire Maine winter for four hundred dollars was tempting—not to mention a bargain. The first problem was that Miles didn't have it; the second was that he knew Max. You could pay him to go away, but that didn't mean he'd *stay* away. No, paying Max to go away would be like giving money to a blackmailer; once he'd determined your ability and willingness to pay, he'd be back. Eventually you'd have to murder him or go broke.

"Bookstore and café with adjacent two-bedroom cottage. Idyllic setting. Bicycle to town and beaches," Max read from the ad Miles had circled.

"Eye-dill-ick," Miles said slowly, correcting his father's pronunciation. After returning from Mrs. Whiting's house earlier in the month, the horror of having asked Cindy out still burning in his mind, he'd made two mistakes, the first out of fear, the second out of carelessness. He'd called the realtor to find out the asking price of the property, and then he'd written it down above the listing. Actually, he'd written only the first three digits, which may have been what was now confusing his father. He hadn't intended to write anything down, of course, but the figure the realtor had quoted him had taken his breath away, and he'd written down those first three digits to make it seem real. By the time he stopped writing, he'd already known the truth—that even if Mrs. Whiting were to will him the restaurant, and even if he managed to sell the grill and Janine turned their house at a profit, the sum realized from both sales wouldn't make the down payment on the Vineyard property. And even if he *could* finagle the down payment, he'd be saddled with a mortgage he could never meet by selling books and espresso. The broker had offered to put him in touch with the current owners to discuss the whole issue of profitability, but Miles had thanked him anyway and hung up, gut-shot by those first three digits.

Unfortunately, Miles Roby was not like Walt Comeau, who could easily indulge such a fantasy. Over the last few weeks, the idea of opening a health club on Martha's Vineyard had actually grown on Walt, who, the more he thought about it, didn't see any reason why he shouldn't. If the new club made money, maybe he'd open another on that other island, Nantucket, or whatever. Miles couldn't keep from admiring the other man's ability to sustain such pleasant fantasies in the complete absence of plausibility. Walt seemed to know better than to do the numbers and study the odds; such things only squeezed a man's heart, as surely as a tightening fist.

"What's that mean? Idyllic?"

"It means not a Conch in sight," Miles told him. "Do me a favor and put that away."

To Miles's surprise, Max complied without comment, even getting the glove compartment door to stay shut somehow. If Miles hadn't known better, he'd have sworn his father had intuited the significance of the listing and those numbers and what it all must have meant to his son.

But then Max began to whistle. It took Miles a minute to recognize the bouncy tune, which he hadn't heard since he was a kid. When Max got to the chorus, he stopped whistling and mouthed the words, just loud enough to be heard, and anybody who didn't know Max Roby would've sworn his mind was drifting elsewhere:

> *Git along home, Cindy, Cindy*
> *Git along home, Cindy, Cindy*
> *Git along home, Cindy, Cindy*
> *I'll marry you someday.*

THERE WERE NO parking spaces in front of the Empire Grill, so Miles parked in back behind the Dumpster, next to Charlene's

Hyundai. People were waiting in the entryway for tables when they drove up, and Miles could tell at a glance that the place was full up. Friday-night Mexican. Shrimp *flautas* on special.

"They could probably use some help inside," Miles told his father, fully expecting Max to take a powder. The old man had money in his pocket and he probably was eager to head over to Callahan's or the Olde Mill Pub. "We've got a new busboy on tonight, but he won't be up to this crowd."

"I could use the extra scratch," Max said, falling in step and causing Miles to make a mental note to keep an eye on him tonight. His father hated work but loved crowds, probably because chaos created many more opportunities than order.

"Put on a clean shirt before you go out front," Miles reminded him.

"I've worked here before, you know."

"And an apron," Miles said. "And wash your hands."

"Wash my hands so I can bus dirty dishes?"

The back room was thick with steam, and Tick was stacking dishes when her father and grandfather entered.

"How's it going, darlin'?" Miles said.

"Okay," she told him. "The Hobart's acting up."

Miles smiled and gave her a kiss on top of the head, breathing her in, this kid who wasn't a kid anymore but still smelled like one. Everything about his daughter seemed just about right, including the way the second thing she said often contradicted the first. Things were going okay. Except they weren't.

"Do the best you can and I'll look at it later. How's your friend John doing?"

"Okay," she said. "A little slow. You shouldn't have started him on a weekend night."

"Grandpa's going to give him a hand," Miles said as Max stepped out from the storeroom buttoning a starchy white shirt two sizes too big for him. Coming up behind her, he circled his arms around her tiny waist and pulled her against him. Tick, Miles knew, was fond of her grandfather, but not his embraces, and would've told him so if she could've devised a way of doing it without hurting his feelings. Miles had tried to explain that Max probably didn't *have* feelings in the conventional sense, but she couldn't quite accept that, preferring to believe that he kept them hidden away somewhere. And who knew? If Max did harbor genuine feelings for anybody, Miles conceded, they were for his granddaughter.

"How's my girl?" Max wanted to know.

"Your beard's scratchy, Grandpa. Plus you smell."

"So do you," Max said. "The difference is you're young and you smell good. When I was your age, all the girls used to tell me I smelled like a ripe apple."

"Ripe I can believe," Miles said, handing his father a rubber dish tub. "Just the dishes. Charlene catches you swiping her tips, she'll gut you like a fish."

Max followed him out through the swinging door. "Down in the Keys, waitresses share their tips with the busboys."

"Suggest that to her, why don't you?" Miles grinned, knowing full well that Max was neither so brave nor so foolhardy.

"All right, then," David said when he heard their voices. "The cavalry has arrived."

"What do you need?" Miles asked.

"Help Charlene," David suggested. "She's trying to hostess and wait tables both."

Four parties were waiting in the tiny foyer, three of them probably from the college in Fairhaven. Miles seated a couple in a freshly cleared booth, then started a waiting list. A waiting list at the Empire Grill? If this continued he'd have to add that damn "e" to "Grill," just like Walt Comeau kept suggesting. Three tables were finishing up at once, so Miles manned the register, then filled Charlene's drink orders. He saw David watching and read his thought: how many of these Cokes and ice teas would have been four- and five-dollar glasses of wine if they had the license?

"That old man takes so much as a dime off one of my tables," Charlene said in lieu of a hello, "I'm going to castrate him."

"I already warned him," Miles assured her, pleased that Charlene's threat so closely paralleled the one he'd imagined. She looked tired but fully capable of carrying out her threat, and, to Miles, as beautiful as the girl who'd already been waitressing for several years when he, at age fifteen, started work at the Empire Grill.

"You got here just in time," she said. "When was the last time we had a rush like this?"

"It's all David's doing," Miles said. "Who knew Dexter County would go for *flautas*?"

Charlene shouldered a large silver tray stacked with plates. "We're going to need that corner booth, Miles," she said. "Those are Tick's friends in there now."

Miles had been too busy to notice the group of seven high school kids crowded into the booth that the girls from the beauty school usually occupied in the afternoon, and his expression darkened when he saw that one of them was Zack Minty. Now that he thought about it, for the last few days Tick had acted like she was on the verge of telling him something.

"How you doin', Mr. Roby?" the Minty boy said in that slow way of his when Miles appeared at the table. Miles knew several of the other kids and liked them well enough. There was also a slightly overweight girl in a unicorn T-shirt and spiky hair of a color not found in nature: this, Miles suspected, must be Candace from art class. "It's good to see you, sir," Zack Minty continued. "You need this booth?"

Why, Miles wondered, were adults so insistent that kids be polite? The ones who were *most* polite always seemed fundamentally untrustworthy. The others at the table were shy and awkward with adults, unable to make eye contact. Young Minty always looked right at adults in a way that made most of them look away first.

"I'd appreciate it," Miles told him. "I think we could manage some free refills over at the counter."

"Sure thing, Mr. Roby. My dad said your business was picking up," the boy said, sliding out of the booth. Standing up, he was nearly as big as Miles, and he seemed to know it. Miles wondered two things. Was he using steroids? And how would his father, who rarely came into the grill, know that business was improving? Okay, maybe it wasn't all that big a mystery. He'd probably driven by and seen more cars than usual in the parking lot lately. Or somebody could've told him. Mrs. Whiting, for example. He still couldn't help thinking that when he'd seen them talking earlier that month outside the Planning and Development office, they'd been talking about him. A crazy thought maybe, but he couldn't shake it.

"You going to the game tomorrow, Mr. Roby?"

Miles nodded. "We're closing after lunch."

"We might actually kick some Fairhaven butt for once," Zack said, the other kids at the table seconding this hopeful prediction. "Make Empire Falls proud."

"Zack's starting at running back," said the girl Miles thought must be Candace.

"Linebacker," Zack said, without looking at her, a hint of contempt creeping into his tone, and Miles could tell it registered on the girl.

"It's my big chance to make an impression, though," he admitted, looking directly at Miles again.

"Good luck," Miles said, his voice as neutral as he could make it.

"Thanks a lot, Mr. Roby. We know the whole town's behind us." Then, as Miles began to clean off the vacated booth with a rag: "See you hired some more help." He nodded in the direction of John Voss as he disappeared through the swinging door into the back room, causing Miles to remember that the Minty boy himself had applied for a part-time job last spring. "He's a good boy, that John."

Miles nodded agreement, though he had no idea whether or not this might be true.

"You think Tick will be finished in time for a nine-thirty movie?" the girl wondered.

"I'll do what I can," Miles said, and was surprised when this casual assurance elicited a smile that was out of all proportion to the circumstance. Miles recognized it immediately as the same smile Cindy Whiting, at her age, had offered in response to even the smallest kindness. The kind that bespoke a miserable existence.

"Too bad John can't come, huh, Candace?" said a skinny boy Miles vaguely recognized.

"*Cut it out!*" the girl yelled, loud enough for everyone in the restaurant to turn and look.

"Hey," Miles said, and he was about to add that yelling wasn't permitted in the restaurant when he saw that the girl's eyes had instantly filled with tears. My God, he couldn't help thinking, how terrible it is to be that age, to have emotions so near the surface that the slightest turbulence causes them to boil over. That, very simply, was what adulthood must be all about—acquiring the skill to bury things more deeply. Out of sight and, whenever possible, out of mind.

"Okay, Mr. Roby," Zack Minty said. "Tell Tick not to worry. We'll stop back by for her. And thanks for the refill offer."

When they were gone, Miles set the booth for five, seated the only party of that size in the foyer, and added the names of three more parties to the waiting list. It was an hour before things slowed down enough that he could go into the back room.

"Your friends said they'd be back," he told his daughter.

Tick's eyes flickered before she could turn away to open the Hobart and extract the plastic tray of steaming glasses. "Okay."

Joining her at the drainboard, Miles selected a few glasses at random to hold up to the light. They weren't as bad as he'd feared, but many of them had tiny, hardened nodes of calcified soap on the outside, which Miles flicked away with his fingernail.

Taking off his outer shirt, he hung it on a peg by the swinging door and grabbed the ice pick from the top of the Hobart, where it was kept for the more or less constant adjustments the fussy old machine required. When its spray jets clogged—the most consistent problem—the glasses didn't rinse cleanly, and the ice pick worked as well as anything for unclogging them.

"I thought you gave Zack Minty his walking papers last spring," Miles said, his head inside the machine, which made his voice sound hollow.

When Tick didn't reply, he turned to look and saw her shrug. "What's that mean?"

"What?"

"That shrug." He knew perfectly well, of course. It meant that this was none of his business.

"Nothing," she said. Further confirmation, if any were needed.

Miles stuck his head back into the Hobart. Several jets were indeed clogged, and it took about five minutes to do a half-assed job of cleaning them out, good enough to get them through until tomorrow and a more thorough cleaning. By the time he'd put in a new load of dirty dishes, his daughter's eyes were full and her body and head had bowed, as if under some great invisible weight.

"Oh, darlin'," he said, drawing her toward him, as much as she'd allow. "It's okay."

"I know how much you hate him," she sniffled into his chest.

"That's not true," Miles said. "He's just a boy. What I *do* hate is the idea that you're afraid to tell me things."

"There isn't anything to tell," she said, pulling away, still not meeting his eye, sullen. "We're just hanging out. The whole gang. Not just me and Zack."

"I gather that was Candace out there?"

"Was she wearing a unicorn shirt?"

Miles said she was. "I think she's got a crush on Zack too."

"What do you mean, *too*? I don't have a crush on him."

"Okay," Miles said, still uncomfortable with the whole arrangement, but figuring he'd questioned her about as much as he could. "It's up to you. You aren't a kid anymore." Though she was. Okay, more than a kid, maybe. A kid with adult intelligence and maybe even some adult experience, brighter and more trustworthy and responsible and grown-up than most kids her age, but still a kid, Miles knew. He only had to look at her to know that. And not just any kid, either—*his* kid. His, far more than Janine's, never mind what the court said. His kid to adore and to protect for a while yet.

"If I'd even got a letter . . ."

Miles was confused until it dawned on him that she was talking about the boy on Martha's Vineyard.

"It hasn't been that long," he said, though it had been almost a month. An eternity at Tick's age. "And be fair. You haven't written him either, right?"

Another despairing shrug. "What for?"

No, the truth was that she was both a kid and not a kid. At sixteen, his daughter already understood that the person who makes the first move stands to be the big loser. If she were to write and the boy didn't write back, that would be even worse. What she was doing, he knew, was accepting the way things were, knowing that she could stand that much but afraid anything worse might be more than she could bear. And he remembered David warning him last week that if he wasn't careful Tick would succeed him as manager of the Empire Grill.

He was about to say something more when he realized the atmosphere of the room had changed, and when he turned he saw that John Voss was standing motionless and silent in the doorway with a tub of dirty dishes. He seemed to have simply materialized there, though more likely he'd come in when Miles was headfirst in the dishwasher. If so, how long had he been standing there, with his long, pointed teeth just visible behind his parted lips, looking like a dog who expected to be kicked? No, not a dog, Miles thought. What the boy really resembled was an android in a science fiction movie, something whose battery had about run out. He wasn't even looking in their direction, but rather off at an oblique angle, his head cocked as if, though his loss of power meant the loss of locomotion, he could still hear. What *was* there about such helplessness that invited cruelty? Miles had to swallow his impulse to tell the kid to get the hell out. What did he mean, standing there listening to a man's private conversation with his daughter? Was it possible that anyone this boy's age could be so completely without social graces that he didn't know enough to clear his throat, apologize for intruding, or failing either of these, set the damn tub down and back out of the room?

"You can put those on the drainboard," Miles told him, setting the boy in motion again, his battery not quite dead after all.

When the door swung shut behind him, the moment seemed to have passed for Miles to say anything further to Tick, though he couldn't help feeling that the boy's intrusion had stolen some chance— he had no idea what—they might never have again. Miles himself had felt on the verge of telling her something straight from the heart, about not to end up getting herself trapped, though there must've been more to it than that. Whatever it had been, it was gone now.

When he consulted his watch, he saw that it was nearly nine and that the only wisdom he was confident of imparting to her concerned the Hobart. "Run these glasses through again without soap," he suggested, since that would finish unclogging the lower jets. "Then you can clean up and go, okay? They said they'd stop back on the way to the movie."

Her eyes brightened a little. "Are you sure? Isn't it still pretty busy?"

"Nothing your grandfather and I can't handle," he assured her. "Go and have a good time."

But he must not have completely banished from his consciousness the sight of the Voss boy standing there motionless in the doorway, because he heard himself say something that surprised him. "You want me to let John off too, so he can go with you?"

She answered almost before he finished asking. "No," she said, her expression urgent, fearful.

"Okay," he said, almost as quickly, surprised at how instinctively he understood that he'd just offered up a really bad idea.

DAVID WAS LEANING up against the refrigerator drinking a diet cola and surveying the dining room floor when Miles, tying an apron on over his T-shirt, joined him behind the counter. It was still hot by the eight-burner stove, and David wiped his forehead with the shirtsleeve on his bad arm.

"Hell of a night," Miles told his brother appreciatively. Every table was still occupied, though no one was waiting to be seated and everyone had been served.

"It was," his brother agreed, though not with the enthusiasm Miles might have predicted, causing him to wonder if David was tiring of all this just when it was about to pay off. That would be entirely in character, of course. Even as a boy David had quickly become bored with things as soon as he'd mastered them. "Good thing you showed up when you did. I don't know what we would've done."

"Bad planning on my part," Miles admitted, though part of his plan *had* been for him to show up in case they got a rush. "I'll hire a replacement for Buster this week, I promise, but it looks like we're also going to need more regular help on weekends from now on. Unless tonight was a freak."

"Could be even bigger tomorrow night after the game," David said. "Did I hear you're closing early?"

Miles nodded. "I thought I'd do breakfast, close around eleven, then open again at six for dinner."

"Sounds okay." David nodded. "I might catch the first half of the game myself."

"Where'd Dad go?" Miles thought to ask, since Max was nowhere in evidence.

"Out having a smoke. I told him he could leave at nine. That okay?"

"Perfect," Miles said. Nothing could be more like the old man than to take his cigarette break ten minutes before he was getting off. On the other hand, his father had helped out. *That* was out of character. "He behave out here?"

"Far as I know. Charlene didn't hurt him, so I guess everything went okay."

Miles nodded. "I'm going to let Tick go, too. She and her friends are going to a movie."

"The Minty boy?"

"I know," Miles said. "I'm not thrilled about it either."

"I didn't say anything."

"You didn't need to."

Right on cue, Tick emerged from the back, pulling a sweater on over her head, the picture of resilient young womanhood. Five minutes before, bedraggled after five hours in the steam, she'd been nearly in tears over the boy from Martha's Vineyard. Now she was not only recovered but indeed radiant and, to Miles's way of thinking, heartbreakingly beautiful. "Can I have some money?" She winced.

Apparently Miles wasn't the kid's only heartbroken admirer, because David magically had a ten-dollar bill in his hand. Miles told him to put it away. "There's a twenty in my shirt pocket," he told his daughter. "Hanging on the peg by the back door." But even as he spoke, he had a bad feeling.

In a minute she was back, wincing again. "There's nothing in your shirt, Daddy."

Which meant that Max, standing innocently outside, had foxed him again, even though Miles had seen it coming back in the car. Telling his father he wasn't going to get the twenty, of course, had been exactly the wrong thing to do. Of course, it wasn't much more than Max had earned, so that wasn't the issue. It was that once again, the old man had gotten his way. Not only was he helping paint the church after Miles had told him he couldn't, but now, in effect, Miles had paid him under the table for working at the restaurant.

This time when David offered the ten, Miles let Tick take it.

"Do you suppose he has any conscience at all?" he asked after his daughter was gone.

"Sure he does," David said, turning his empty soda glass upside down in the nearest tray. Then, after a thoughtful beat: "No slave to it, though, is he?"

"WHY ON EARTH did you want to go and hire that comatose boy?" was what Charlene wanted to know when Miles slid in beside her. It had been Miles's idea that the three of them—he and David and Charlene—celebrate over a drink. When he'd rung out the register in the restaurant, he was stunned by how well they'd done.

There was a half full glass of seltzer-with-lemon sitting next to Charlene's scotch, so Miles supposed his brother was around somewhere. Also, unless he was mistaken, that was Horace Weymouth anchoring the far end of the bar. It had taken until nearly eleven-thirty to close the restaurant, and the Lamplighter was one of the few places still open in Dexter County where they could be reasonably sure they wouldn't run into Max. Unless Miles missed his guess, that probably explained Horace's presence as well.

Certainly it wasn't the ambience. The Lamplighter's lounge reminded Miles of a Midwestern Holiday Inn. There was a small woman with a lot of hair noodling something almost recognizable on a piano on the other side of the dark room. From their half-moon booth only the woman's hair was visible, and her phrasing on the piano suggested that she was determined to get through each song without making a mistake. Was it possible, Miles wondered, that she was related to Doris Roderigue?

He was the last to arrive because he'd given John Voss a lift home. The boy had toiled through a mountain of pots and pans without speaking a word to anyone all evening. His morose silence had thrown

Charlene for a loop. To Charlene, a talker, nothing was more unnatural and perverse. Her secret as a waitress was her ability to disarm people, to get them talking no matter who they were: school kids, the girls from the Academy of Hair Design, long-haul truckers, professors from the college. With John Voss, though, she'd made exactly no progress. "The last man that didn't have any more to say to me than that was the one who tried to rape me in the parking lot, if you recall."

Miles did recall, in fact, though the incident was now twenty-some years old. For years it had fueled a disturbingly vivid teenage fantasy in which Miles, then a busboy and dishwasher, came out the back door with a bag of trash for the Dumpster, interrupting the attempted rape and heroically driving Charlene's knife-wielding attacker off into the night. Actually, the real attacker hadn't wielded any sort of weapon, but Miles had furnished him with one for dramatic purposes. Even at the time he'd known that his fantasy was not entirely innocent, or even decent, despite its moral structure and heroic resolution. His discovery of the struggling pair in the parking lot was always highly precise. He never arrived before Charlene's assailant had made significant progress, enough, that is, to expose her milky breasts. Had Miles actually come upon such a struggle in back of the Empire Grill, of course, he wouldn't have been able to see anything in the pitch-dark parking lot, but in his imagination the scene was sufficiently illuminated for his purposes. The first time he indulged the fantasy, he merely glimpsed Charlene's naked torso, but in each successive reenactment he lingered longer on the sight until, finally, sickened, he gave up the scenario altogether, aware that even though he'd cast himself in the role of hero, he'd in fact come to identify with Charlene's attacker, sharing his heartsickness at the knowledge that no girl this beautiful would ever come to him voluntarily.

Worse than the new busboy's failure to say a damn word, Charlene went on, was that he wouldn't even look at her when *she* was talking. "I swear to God, I could be standing in front of that boy stark naked," she said, "and all he'd look at would be the floor."

This was true, no doubt, though Miles again recalled Zack Minty's overly slick social skills, coming to the same conclusion as he had earlier—that this kid was profoundly untrustworthy. Maybe John Voss had a lot to learn, but the Minty boy had at least as much to *un*learn. Both, it occurred to Miles, were long shots.

"I probably shouldn't have hired him," Miles admitted, and he wouldn't have, but for Tick. According to his daughter, the boy lived alone with his grandmother, and she'd deduced from his ill-fitting, thrift-shop clothes that they were desperately poor. What he was eating for lunch smelled like cat food, and all this week she'd asked Miles to make an extra sandwich for her to take to school. Tonight, the boy had not wanted to accept a ride home, but it was late and Miles had insisted. The ramshackle house the boy directed him to was on the outskirts of town, not far from the old landfill and a good quarter mile from its nearest neighbor. The place had been completely dark when they pulled into the dirt drive, and anyone passing by would've concluded, if they'd even noticed the house so far back off the road, that it must be deserted except, maybe, for varmints under the floors and birds in the rafters. No car was in evidence, and the boy said that his grandmother must have gone to bed early and forgot to leave the light on.

"He worked hard, though," Miles pointed out.

Charlene admitted this was true. "I'll just have to get him to smoke a doobie with me some afternoon. Loosen him up."

David then slid into the booth on the other side of Charlene. "I wouldn't go around corrupting the local youth any more than you absolutely have to, Charlene," he advised, taking a sip of his seltzer. "Officer Minty's got his eye on you as it is."

Charlene snorted. "On you, you mean. Not me."

Miles studied first his brother, then the woman he'd been more or less in love with for twenty-five years. Their quick, easy exchange suggested he was missing something. It was the same way he often felt on Martha's Vineyard around Peter and Dawn, who, like most married couples, had developed a kind of verbal shorthand, a system of quick allusions that required no further referencing. This was just one more way, Miles supposed, that his own marriage had fallen short. He and Janine had always had trouble making themselves understood to each other, even when they spoke in complete paragraphs. It was Janine's position that if they hadn't fucked that dozen times or so, there would've been no reason for them to go through the motions of divorce. They could have just had the marriage annulled, the church's acknowledgment that in twenty years no intercourse of any significance, sexual or even verbal, had taken place between them.

Settling on his brother, Miles asked, "Why would Jimmy Minty have his eye on either of you?"

"Didn't you know?" David grinned. "Charlene here is my distributor."

"I don't get it," Miles said. "Why would Jimmy Minty think that?" If true, this wasn't funny.

"That's not the half of it," David continued. "According to Jimmy, I'm a major grower. I've cornered the whole damn pot market in central Maine. I caught him tramping around the woods behind my place yesterday trying to find my patch."

This really wasn't funny either, though David seemed to think it was. "What'd you do?"

"I suggested he wear orange, this being moose season."

"Miles is right, David. You shouldn't fuck with him," Charlene said, as if, despite this advice, she fully understood the impulse. "He's a cop. It's not like these guys have a sense of humor."

David shrugged. "Actually, we got along fine. I invited him in for a cup of coffee so he could tell me about all his suspicions. Turns out he's fond as hell of us Robys, our families going all the way back to the old neighborhood and all. Hell, his kid's sweet on Miles's kid."

David was good enough at mimicking Jimmy Minty's smarmy voice and obsequious mannerisms that Miles could feel the rage rising from the pit of his stomach. Clearly, the policeman had paid no attention to Miles's warning to stay out of his family's affairs. Worse, to judge from what David was saying, he'd taken the warning as a challenge.

"Hell, the last thing in the world he wants is trouble," David was saying. "That's how come he was out in my woods. Just trying to head off trouble. You know the way he looks at it? He figures his duty is to be a good neighbor first and a police officer second."

Charlene guffawed. "What'd you say to that?"

David shrugged. "I may have told him I thought he was an asshole first, last and in between. I may have hurt his feelings."

"This is not funny," Miles said, meaning it.

"So I guess you didn't see his car parked across the street from the restaurant tonight?" David said, meeting his brother's gaze.

Miles hadn't seen any police cars that night, not that he was sure he'd have noticed if there had been one, busy as they were. "The cruiser?"

"No, *his* car," Charlene said. "The red Camaro."

Miles just looked at her.

"I'm sorry, Miles. I can't help it," she said. "You know I always notice guys in fast cars."

He turned his attention back to his brother. "*Are* you growing marijuana?"

"Mind your own business, Miles."

"It *is* my business, David," he said, feeling a lifetime's worth of resentment welling up dangerously. Every time he allowed himself to imagine that his brother had finally turned the corner, that ingrained irresponsibility would surface again. "Minty probably thinks you're dealing out of the restaurant. Probably that's why the dimwit thinks we've gotten busy."

"We *are* dealing out of the restaurant, Miles," David said, suddenly serious and more than a little pissed, as if he too had just recalled something about his brother's character that he despaired would never change. "What we're dealing is *flautas*. And you know what? I was just talking to Audrey back in the kitchen and she said this place was slow tonight. So was the Eating House out on Ninety-Two. The only restaurant in Dexter County that did any volume tonight was the Empire Grill. Instead of worrying about Jimmy Minty watching the restaurant and me growing weed, think about this. Even on a slow night this place will outgross us, because they've got a liquor license. We did good tonight, Miles, but we'll never do any better, because we can't fit in any more tables, and we can't fit any more people at the tables we've already got. The only way for us to have a real restaurant and make a real living is to sell booze. And don't tell me about Mrs. Whiting, either," he added, eerily anticipating the name that was forming on Miles's lips, "because I don't want to hear it."

"Well, the Empire Grill is her—"

But David had grabbed his coat off the back of the booth and was sliding out. "She summons you two or three times a year to make sure you're right where she left you. You say, Mother May I? and she says, No, You May Not, and then you put your tail between your legs and back out the door, and that's the end of it. All those years of Catholic school have damaged you, Miles. They taught you obedience. Somebody says you can't have something and you just accept it."

"David—" It was Charlene who tried to break in now, but David was having none of it.

"Has it ever occurred to you that every time you return from that woman's house you have scratch marks on you?" To illustrate, he reached down and grabbed Miles's wrist, holding his brother's hand up to the light. The scratch he'd gotten from Timmy the Cat had scabbed over and was even uglier now. It looked like a trench filled in with sand. "Have you ever thought about what that means?"

"That she has a psychotic cat?" Miles ventured.

"No. That's *not* what it means. It means she's toying with you. You're like a moth she's stuck through the chest with a pin. Every now and then she takes you out and watches you flail around for a while, then she puts you away again.

"And don't tell me you're not the only one with scratch marks, either," David continued, which was exactly what Miles had been about to point out. "I know half the town has scratch marks. I *know* she owns most of what's worth owning in Empire Falls. But my point is that she owns you only because you let her. You could wiggle off that pin if you wanted to."

"David," Charlene tried again.

"I mean, it just breaks my heart to watch this. Every year you go off to that island to visit your dreams for two whole weeks. Think about it, Miles. A little island, another world, miles away, at safe yearning distance. Something you can desire without ever being expected to strive for. And you know what? That's not even the sad part. The sad part is that *you* don't love Martha's Vineyard. It was *Mom* who loved it. *She's* the one who went there and fell in love, Miles, not you. You were just a little boy who tagged along, who got to ride in the little yellow sports car. And you're still that little boy."

"David, *please*," Charlene pleaded.

"Don't, Charlene," David snapped. "Somebody should've said all of this a long time ago."

He turned back to Miles. "Yeah, we had a good night, Miles. In fact, we had a great night. The trouble is you're so blind you can't see what that means, so I'll tell you. It means you've finally got a chance to take the wheel. So, take it, Miles. Take the damn wheel. If you crash"—he held up his damaged arm—"so what? Do it. If not for yourself, for Tick. She's soaking up your passivity and defeatism every day. When she's thirty, she'll be saving all year long for a two-week vacation on Martha's Vineyard, because she'll think it was the place *you* loved."

"David," Charlene said quietly, "look at your brother. Stop talking for a second and look at him."

In fact, by now everyone in the lounge was looking at them. Even the big-haired pianist had stopped playing. David's voice had risen until it commanded the attention of everyone in the room, a fact he only now became aware of. "Shit," he said, taking out some money and tossing it on the table. "I'm going home. I'm sorry I spoiled the celebration."

"You don't have to go, David," Miles heard himself say in a voice he barely recognized.

"Actually, I do," he said. "Time I got back and tended to my pot empire."

When Miles said nothing and Charlene just shook her head, David leaned forward until his face was only inches from his brother's. "That was a *joke*, Miles. I've got one plant down in the basement under a heat lamp. Come down and see for yourself, any time you want. Nobody fucks with you over one plant. Not even Jimmy Minty."

"You know," Charlene said when she returned to the booth, "if you and your brother talked to each other every so often, you wouldn't have these blowups. You both store up about a year's worth of shit, and then you explode."

"I didn't explode," Miles pointed out. "He exploded."

"True," Charlene admitted. "But tonight was more words than he's spoken in months, and right now he'd like to have at least half of them back."

"You think?"

"Yes, Miles, I do."

Maybe she was right. Following David outside to his pickup, she'd been gone for about fifteen minutes, and Miles would've concluded that she'd gone home if he hadn't peered through the window slats behind the booth and seen the two of them standing in the parking lot, Charlene giving him hell. While she was gone, Horace Weymouth, who must've heard most of what David had said, sent over a vodka martini, which Miles drank in about three swallows. Then he ordered two more, sending one back to Horace, who raised his glass in grim acknowledgment that the night seemed to call for extraordinary measures. Miles was finishing up the second martini when Charlene reappeared in the booth, noting both the martini glass and the change in his condition.

"Your brother loves you," she now explained. "He wasn't trying to hurt your feelings. He just worries about you, same as you worry about him. You exasperate each other, is all."

"He's got a right, I guess. I exasperate *myself* sometimes," he said, immediately regretting the self-pitying tone.

"That's kind of his point, Miles. He thinks you should get exasperated with someone else."

"Mrs. Whiting."

"Yeah, her, but he thinks you're too nice to people in general. He thinks you eat too much shit."

"You think he's right?" he asked.

"Oh, hell, Miles, I don't know. It's true that you're about the most cautious man I've ever run across. You're kind and patient and forgiving and generous, and you don't seem to understand that these qualities can be really annoying in a man, no matter what the ladies' magazines say."

"I haven't been reading many of those, Charlene," he assured her.

"I know you haven't, hon." She took his hand. "It's just, you know . . . like what David always says about your family."

Miles had no idea that David ever said anything about their family. If he'd come to any conclusions about the Robys, he never shared them with Miles.

"David has this theory that between your mom and dad and him and you there's, like, one complete person. Your father never thinks about anybody but himself, and your mom was always thinking about other people and never herself. David thinks only about the present and you think only about the past and the future."

"I've never heard any of this," Miles said truthfully. "When did he tell you that?"

Charlene ignored his question. "His point is you could all learn something from the others, and you'd be better off. Take the way your father's been left out of you entirely. That's a shame."

Miles tried to consider this seriously. "Charlene," he said, "I can honestly say this is the first time anybody's ever urged me to be more like Max."

"I don't think David wants you to be a *lot* more like your father, just enough so—"

"I wouldn't be such a shit-eater," Miles finished the thought for her.

"Oh, Miles, don't be that way. Don't take everything so much to heart. All David means is that your dad always knows what he wants. And a split second after he figures that out, he's got a plan to get it. Probably a dumb plan, but he's like a little bulldog on a pork chop until you give him what he wants or he finds a way to take it when you aren't looking. David just thinks if you had a little more of that in you, you could figure out what you want and come up with a plan and . . ."

When her voice trailed off, Miles heard the two martinis speak in a voice distantly resembling his own. "Actually," he said carefully, "it's worse than he imagines."

When Charlene didn't say anything right away, he took her silence to mean that it was all right for him to continue.

"When I went to Mrs. Whiting's last week? When I was supposed to come back with a liquor license? David was right. I did leave with my tail between my legs. What he doesn't know is that I didn't exactly leave empty-handed."

Another silence, and Miles could not bear to look up from his martini. "What I came away with—" He sighed, his voice barely audible even to himself. "Was a date with Cindy Whiting. For tomorrow, in fact. We're going to the football game."

Confessing this was so painful that he'd forgotten he was holding Charlene's hand until she gave his a squeeze. "That's really sweet, Miles. That poor woman could use a little joy in her life. I think it's a real nice thing you did."

"To my brother it will be further evidence of my natural propensity for shit-eating."

"He went too far tonight, Miles. I'm sure he'll apologize tomorrow."

"He's wrong about one thing," he said, meeting her eye this time, "if he thinks I don't know what I want."

Though he hadn't intended it, the statement had the effect of making them both aware of the fact that they were holding hands in a dark booth, Miles, a man not yet divorced, and Charlene, a woman divorced many times over. To save her both embarrassment and the need to respond, he let go of her hand, though it would have pleased him to sit there holding it all night. To his surprise, she leaned over and kissed him on the forehead, a kiss so full of affection that it dispelled the awkwardness, even as it caused Miles's heart to plummet, because all kisses are calibrated and this one revealed the great chasm between affection and love.

"Oh, Miles, goddamn it," she said. "It's not like I don't know you've had a crush on me forever. And you know how fond I am of you. You're about the sweetest man I know, really."

He couldn't help but smile at this. "That's another of those qualities that's not very attractive in a man, isn't it."

"No"—she took his hand again—"it's very attractive, actually. And you know what? I'd take you home so we could make love, except I couldn't stand how disappointed you'd be. And you wouldn't be able to conceal it, either, not with that face of yours."

When she reached for her coat, Miles slid out of the booth, then helped her on with it. "If I thought *you* wouldn't be disappointed," he told her as they headed for the door and the waiting night, "I'd insist."

"It *would* be nice if we could get that damn liquor license, Miles," Charlene said when they were outside and she was unlocking the door to her Hyundai. "If I was making decent money, I could put this wreck out of its misery."

"I haven't given up," Miles said, surprised to discover that he hadn't. And it came to him that a smart man might take Cindy Whiting out to dinner at the restaurant tomorrow after the game and make her an ally in this cause. If he was going to go around falling on grenades all the time, there was no law saying some good couldn't come of it.

He was about to get into his own car and drive home when he heard the door at the Lamplighter's entrance bang shut and saw Horace coming toward him.

"Thanks for the drink," Miles said, shaking his hand. "I get stopped for drunk driving on the way home, I'm going to tell the cops whose fault it is."

Saying this, Miles thought to check the parking lot for Jimmy Minty's Camaro, but it was nowhere in evidence. Though this wasn't to say that Jimmy Minty wasn't sitting somewhere out beyond the reach of the parking lot's lights.

"Sorry about the commotion in there, too," Miles said, knowing that Horace was far too well mannered to ask what it was all about, or even to allude to it, for that matter. It was strange, Miles now realized, for a man who instinctively respected people's privacy to become a reporter. Too bad it didn't happen more often.

Horace was groping in his pockets for his keys. "Family," he said, as if this one word accounted for all aberrant behavior.

"Where's yours?" it occurred to Miles to ask. The man came into his restaurant nearly every day, but Miles knew very little about him.

"My family?" Horace looked surprised. "Everywhere. We don't stay in touch. That sounds sadder than it is, actually."

"It does sound sad," Miles admitted.

"I'm not a big believer in all that myself," he admitted. "Blood. Kinship. So what?"

"Home is where when you have to go there, they have to take you in," Miles said, quoting Frost.

The newspaperman unlocked his car, got in, thought for a second, then looked up. "Good fences make good neighbors."

Miles smiled and said good night, then went around to unlock the Jetta. He was about to get in when he heard the passenger-side window of Horace's car roll down and saw Horace leaning toward him. "Speaking of taking people in," he said, "you keep an eye on that new boy you hired."

"Okay," Miles said. "You want to tell me why?"

Horace thought about it. "Not at the moment," he concluded, then added, "Don't ever become a reporter."

I N THE FALL *of Miles Roby's junior year, his father, flush with summer house-painting money, bought a secondhand Mercury Cougar, the idea being that Miles would soon be old enough to get his license. By Thanksgiving, however, Max himself had received three speeding tickets and run over a cat. Miles had been with him for the latter and seen, as Max had not, the animal streak under the wheels, and he'd turned in time to see the cat continue to run frantically around its own head, which had been flattened by one of the Cougar's rear wheels.*

"What the hell was that?" Max said a few seconds after he felt the thump. He'd been leaning forward, one hand on the wheel, the other pressing the lighter to the tip of his cigarette.

"Cat," Miles sighed, disappointed in himself for not seeing the animal in time to alert his father and save its life. When he rode anywhere with his father, Miles always felt a deep kinship with anything alive that couldn't run as fast as Max drove, which, since there were no cheetahs in Maine, was just about everything.

On general principle his father was dead set against swerving to avoid obstacles. If, for instance, they were traveling on the highway behind a semi and the semi blew a tire, throwing a large curve of retread into their lane, Max ran over it, claiming it was more dangerous to try to swerve around it, which for all Miles knew might have been true. What he suspected, however, was that Max enjoyed running things over and seeing what happened to them. Once, the year before, in the car Max had purchased before the Cougar, they'd encountered a cardboard box sitting square in the middle of their lane on a narrow county road. Since no one was coming toward them and no one was following, and since there was plenty of time to slow down and maneuver around the box—indeed, had Max suffered an uncharacteristic fit of good citizenship, there would've been time to pull over, get out and drag the box onto the shoulder—Miles was surprised when his father actually accelerated into it. He braced for something like an explosion, but the box, thankfully empty, was sucked under the car, where it got caught in the drive-shaft and made a hell of a racket for a hundred yards or so before it flapped away, mangled and reduced to two dimensions, into a ditch.

"What if that box had been full of rocks?" Miles asked.

"What would a box full of rocks be doing sitting in the middle of the road?" Max wondered back, pushing in the cigarette lighter on the dash and patting his shirt pocket for his pack of Luckies.

Miles was tempted to reply, "Waiting for an idiot to hit it doing sixty miles an hour," but he said instead, "If it had been full of rocks we might both be dead."

Max considered this. "What would you have done?"

Miles sensed a trap in this innocent question, but at fifteen he continued to play the hand he'd been dealt, confident he had enough to trump with. "I might've stopped to see what was in the box before I hit it."

Max nodded. "What if it was full of rattlesnakes? Then when you opened it, you'd be dead."

Miles had not grown up in his father's intermittent company for nothing. "What would a box full of rattlesnakes be doing sitting in the middle of the road?"

"Waiting for some dumbbell like you to stop and look inside," Max said, causing in Miles a deep regret for having held his tongue earlier.

They'd ridden on in silence for a while until Max observed, like a man who was himself acquainted with regret, at least in its more abstract mani-festations, "Your mother's raising you to be scared of the whole damn world. You know that, don't you?"

Miles chose to ignore this. "What if the box had been full of dynamite?" he said, signaling his belief that their discussion might reach a better conclu-sion if it were a game, and one that didn't feature his mother.

Max must have agreed, because they played it all the way home, filling the box with all manner of imaginary things, from marshmallows to armadillos, and arriving home weary with laughter.

But now, three speeding tickets and a dead cat later, the judge to whom Max tried to explain the tickets (the cat never came up) wasn't laughing. Actually, it wasn't the three original tickets that offended him as much as the two Max had added while waiting for his court appearance, which suggested to the judge a significant learning disability. Max had to surrender his *driver's license right there in the courthouse, after which he was instructed to walk home.*

Instead, Max drove, without benefit of a valid license, to the hardware store out by the highway. There he purchased a small cardboard For Sale sign and stuck it on the Cougar's dash. Then he drove back downtown, parked the car directly in front of the courthouse, and walked home, where he found his son reading a book at the kitchen table. Max Roby generally left matters of moral instruction to his wife, but given the afternoon's events he was unwilling to miss out on such a powerful teaching opportunity. Joining his son at the kitchen table, he said, "Put that down a minute."

Miles, who had been reading The Adventures of Huckleberry Finn *for his English class, the part where Huck has been kidnapped by his Pap, suffered something like a wave of vertigo by coming up out of the story so suddenly and seeing his own father grinning at him across the table. At this time Max still had all his teeth, except for the two that had been knocked out the summer Miles and his mother visited Martha's Vineyard.*

"Always remember one thing about cops and lawyers," Max said. "The worst they can do to you ain't that bad." He paused to allow his son to digest this hard-won wisdom. "They like to think they got you by the balls, but they don't."

All of which, Miles guessed, was a continuation of the discussion they'd avoided in the car when Max had observed that Grace was raising him to be afraid of things.

"You hear what I'm saying?" Max demanded.

Miles nodded, whereupon Max, his moral duty discharged, arose and left. He might have neither a license nor a car, but he had two good legs, and back then there were half a dozen taverns within easy walking distance. After a day like today, he saw no reason not to visit every last one of them. He did not return that night.

So it was *that by the time Miles was old enough to get his license, he had no car to practice on, and consequently he was behind from the start at driver's education, and due to his poor driving skills he was given far less actual driving time than his classmates, when obviously he needed far more. The other kids clearly knew how to drive already. They'd had their learner's permits for months and drove every day, so for them, the purpose of driver ed was to correct all the bad habits already instilled in them by their parents. The experienced boys all wanted to drive with their elbows out the window, and they liked to demonstrate their sure control over the vehicle by steering it* with the palm of one hand. Mr. Brown, the baseball coach and driver's ed teacher, seemed to view these deficiencies as genetic in nature and modifiable only for the duration of his course. Far more significant to Mr. Brown was that they had logged enough time behind the wheel to avoid posing an immediate threat to Mr. Brown's own life as he sat beside them in the driver's ed car, his foot poised above his passenger-side brake.

Unfortunately, the first time Miles drove this car, with Mr. Brown at his right and three other students in the back, he'd gone no more than a block before he began to feel a sense of self-conscious dread descend upon him like a funeral pall. He wasn't afraid that he would wreck the car and kill them all, but rather that he would immediately be revealed as a rank beginner. And indeed the snickers from the backseat were immediate. Having never manipulated an accelerator, Miles had no idea what might happen when he pressed down on it. What he feared was that even slight pressure might send the car rocketing forward out of control, and this reluctance caused him to inch down the street at a speed that didn't even register on the speedometer. When he tried to give it a little more gas, the car bucked.

"Roby," said Mr. Brown, who was staring at him with an expression made up of equal parts fear and incredulity, "don't you know how to drive at all?"

Almost immediately Miles discovered himself to be speeding. Actually, it was one of his backseat drivers who noticed, since Miles, his eyes glued to the road ahead, did not dare risk a glance at the speedometer for fear of losing control of the vehicle, which Mr. Brown stressed was the cardinal sin. A good driver, Mr. Brown maintained, would never be in an accident, because a good driver was always in control, and if you were in control there was no such thing as an accident.

"He's going forty in a twenty-five," a backseat driver pointed out.

Mr. Brown would have noted this himself had he been facing front instead of searching for his seat belt. As a dutiful teacher, Mr. Brown always insisted that his student drivers buckle up before turning the key in the ignition, but he himself seldom wore a belt. His rationale was that he liked to be able to turn around and instruct those in the rear, should an opportunity arise to do so. This was especially true if the backseat happened to be occupied by boys who were members of his baseball team, as was presently the case. Learning that Miles had exactly no experience, however, caused Mr. Brown to reevaluate his position vis-à-vis the seat belt, which had slipped down between the upper and lower seat cushions. By the time one of his ballplayers reported that Miles was speeding, Mr. Brown's forearm had disappeared up to the elbow in the seam, his hand actually emerging on the other side, where another of his ballplayers noticed it blindly groping for anything that felt like a seat-belt buckle. The boy leaned forward, took Mr. Brown's hand, and shook it genially. "How you doin', coach?" he said.

Mr. Brown, sensing the potential for danger, said, "Pull over, Roby." He'd managed to withdraw his hand from the handshake easily enough, but his wrist got stuck between the cushions and he had to peer over his shoulder to check on the progress of his driver. "I said, Pull over!"

Miles did as instructed. Had he been told to slow down before pulling over, he'd have done that too, but unfortunately he hadn't. Therefore, had anyone living on the quiet residential street they were traveling down picked that moment to step outside, he'd have been treated to a strange sight: the Empire High School driver's education vehicle doing forty miles an hour mere inches from the curb, its instructor facing backward, as if his primary concern was the possibility of pursuit, its backseat passengers pressing back against their seats and its driver patiently awaiting further instructions. Meanwhile, only fifty yards ahead, a car sat parked at the curb.

Mr. Brown had a brake on his side of the car, of course, but turned as he was, his right wrist still caught between the seat cushions, he seemed unable to determine its exact location, though he pumped vigorously at what he imagined to be the floorboard with his foot. Had the brake been attached to the underside of the glove box where he was pumping, that would've stopped the car, but of course it was not, and Mr. Brown's inability to locate the pedal now threw him into blind panic. Unable to decide whether it was more important to free his wrist or locate the brake, he went frantically back and forth between the two, succeeding in neither, all the while yelling, "Roby! Roby! Goddamn it!"

As Miles bore down on the parked car, it seemed to him that slowing the vehicle—indeed, stopping it—might be the most advisable course of action, but Mr. Brown's gyrations confused him. Still unwilling to shift his gaze from the road, he assumed his instructor was in fact hitting the brake to no effect, which meant that the car was unaccountably without brakes, which in turn suggested there wasn't much point in him hitting his, so he stayed his course alongside the curb until the last possible moment, hoping for further orders. When none came, he whipped the steering wheel to the right, bumped the car up onto the curb, over an aluminum garbage can and onto someone's lawn. He noticed the address on the mailbox as they sailed by—116 Spring Street—and further noticed that the garage door of 116 Spring Street happened to be open, its bay empty, seemingly in invitation.

The sudden crash into and up over the curb had the salutary effect of painfully freeing Mr. Brown's wrist from the seat, which in turn allowed *him to be flung against the door, his bullet-shaped head spiderwebbing the window glass. Able at last to locate the elusive brake pedal, he was still unable to employ it, having been stunned senseless by the impact. So it was that Miles's old friend Otto Meyer Jr. (the team's second-string catcher) saved the day by lunging forward over the slumped body of the driver's ed teacher and depressing the brake by hand. The car came to a screaming, skidding halt about a foot from the back wall of the garage, looking for all the world as if it had been Miles's intention to park there from the start.*

"Is the car in Park?" Otto asked, his voice sounding strange down there in the passenger-side foot well.

Miles put the car in Park. "Thanks, Otto," he said.

"That's okay," Otto said. "Pull me back up, all right?" The other two boys in the back obliged, and Miles then noticed that the pinky finger on Otto's left hand was bent back at a rather unnatural ninety-degree angle. Otto himself noticed this when he switched the ignition off and the bent finger encountered the turn signal. "Darn," he said, showing it to Miles, without the slightest ill will, before passing out.

UNLIKE OTTO MEYER JR., Mr. Brown did harbor a grudge, and he nursed it long after the impressive knot above his temple had receded. If he'd had his way, Miles would've been kicked out of driver's education, at least until he learned to drive. It wasn't just that he was such a lousy driver, Mr. Brown explained to the principal, or that the damn kid had nearly killed them all. Mr. Brown also had a baseball team to consider, one he hoped to take to the state tournament this year, a squad that now, thanks to Miles Roby, featured a shortstop with a sprained wrist on his throwing hand and a catcher with a broken pinky on his glove hand. Half his damn team was taking driver's ed, and he saw no reason to risk certain injury and possible death or dismemberment by putting them in an automobile with a boy who didn't have any better sense than to jump a curb, fly over a lawn and careen into a stranger's garage. And how could he coach effectively with all these headaches he'd been getting now since the accident? No, he wanted Miles Roby out of the class and furthermore hoped some sensible policy might be enacted to ensure that, in the future, any kid who signed up for driver's education had some vague idea of what to do behind the wheel.

The principal at the time was Clarence Boniface, who was generally disliked because he wasn't from Empire Falls or anywhere near Empire Falls. He'd been hired in preference to several local, in-house candidates, including Mr. Brown himself, because Mr. Boniface could boast (although he didn't) an advanced degree and considerable administrative experience as the assistant principal of a large high school in Connecticut. In his two years at the helm of Empire Falls High, he'd proven himself to be serious, dutiful and competent. He was a good listener and slow to take offense—both excellent and necessary qualities in a high school principal, though they failed to gain him acceptance with the majority, who had determined he was an asshole even before he arrived. In any event, he listened soberly to his baseball coach's solution to the "Roby kid problem," waited patiently until he was sure Mr. Brown had finished making his case and then burst into violent laughter that rapidly became a full-blown fit of hysteria from which he could not be rescued. He hooted, then howled. His face grew red, tears streamed down his cheeks, and he soon was gasping for air. His secretary, greatly alarmed, brought him a glass of water, but he was shaking too badly to drink it.

In the end they had to lay the principal facedown on the carpet, where at first he flopped about like a bass on the floor of a boat, then curled into a fetal position and lay inert, with just enough energy left to whisper, "Oh, God, oh, God. I'm so sorry, Mr. Brown. I never meant . . . I'm so sorry . . . I haven't laughed like that since I was a child . . . my uncle used to tickle me until I wet my pants." Finally he was able to sit up and lean back against the wall. "I must have been suppressing that laugh since the day I moved here," he concluded.

Mr. Brown had no idea what the man had or had not been suppressing, but he didn't like being laughed at in general, and certainly not by someone from Connecticut, and having his principal cleanse his soul at his own expense made him furious. Rising from his chair, he glared down at Mr. Boniface, who remained right where he was, his back against the wall, looking like a man on the wrong end of a firing squad. "You think this is funny?" Mr. Brown said, pointing to his own narrowed right eye. "You think seeing double's funny?"

He had more to say, too, but Mr. Boniface was now holding his aching ribs and pleading with his baseball coach. "Stop . . . please . . . Mr. Brown, I'm begging you . . . I can't take it . . . you're killing me. . . ."

Which left Mr. Brown no alternative but to storm out of the office, having arrived at a firm resolution henceforth to oppose Mr. Boniface in anything the principal favored, whenever the opportunity arose, no matter the cost, a resolution that strengthened over the next month whenever he encountered Mr. Boniface in the corridor and saw his shoulders begin to shake in recollection of the Roby incident. Mr. Brown was in no mood to share his good humor. The note he received from his principal the day after their meeting was curt and unambiguous: You will continue to instruct Miles

Roby in driver's education, a course for which there has never been a prerequisite. In the future I hope you will be able to give him, and every other Empire Falls student who wishes to learn to drive, your complete and undivided attention.

A year later, when Mr. Boniface died suddenly of a massive embolism, Mr. Brown boycotted the funeral, remarking to friends, "Who's laughing now?" He seemed not to understand the significance of the fact that he himself wasn't laughing when he said this.

So Miles, after a poor beginning, was allowed to continue. Mr. Brown let it be known, however, that he was playing the rest of the game under protest, and he actually seemed disappointed that the remainder of the spring term passed without further incident. In truth, he seldom allowed Miles behind the wheel except in the most straightforward situations, nor was he allowed to attempt parallel parking. When the class ended, Mr. Brown informed Miles that he would be receiving a failing grade and further claimed that in all the years he'd spent teaching students to drive, he'd never run into one with less God-given talent. He sincerely hoped that Miles would proceed through life on foot.

Mr. Boniface, aware that of all the vindictive, hateful, small-town morons on his faculty, Mr. Brown was the most lethal, had anticipated this result, so when he received Mr. Brown's grade sheet, he invited Miles to drive him home in his own car. For both parties it was a nervous trip, but they arrived safely at the principal's home, where both realized at the same moment that now Miles would have to walk all the way across town, so they switched places and the principal drove the student home.

"You say you've had no opportunity to practice all term?" Mr. Boniface inquired.

Miles, ashamed to admit there was currently no family car, said this was true.

"Mr. Brown has given you a failing grade," the principal said.

"Well"—Miles shrugged—"I did almost kill him."

"Still," Mr. Boniface said, as if contemplating the long list of extenuating circumstances that might make killing Mr. Brown forgivable, "I'll speak to him."

He followed up on that promise immediately, phoning Mr. Brown at home. "In twenty-five years I've never changed a teacher's grade, but I'm about to change one of yours unless you change it yourself."

Mr. Brown didn't have to ask who they were talking about. "The Roby kid fails," he said. "He damn near killed me."

"I've thought a lot about that," the principal replied wistfully. "Believe me."

Mr. Brown was normally not very quick on the uptake, but he caught this inference immediately. "Yeah? Well, you're stuck with me. And we both know you don't have the authority to change any teacher's grade."

"And you'll be stuck with Miles Roby. If you fail him, he'll have to repeat the course. Have you thought about that?"

Mr. Brown had not. Until now, no one had ever needed to take the course over again.

"And a lot of your ballplayers are frankly marginal in terms of academic eligibility. It'd be a shame if James Minty, for instance, turned out to be ineligible for his senior year. There's a good chance Gladys will be his English instructor next year. In fact, there's a very good chance." Gladys was Mr. Boniface's wife, and whenever Mr. Brown was foolish enough to commit anything to writing, Gladys corrected its grammar and spelling and returned it to him.

"I'll change the grade," Mr. Brown said.

"And you owe Miles Roby an apology."

"Never," said Mr. Brown. Not for a dozen Jimmy Mintys. Not for a thousand.

"Consider what it means to hate a sixteen-year-old boy," the principal suggested. "Consider what it means for a teacher to hate a student."

"What's so bad about that?" Mr. Brown wanted to know. "You hate me, don't you?"

Mr. Boniface, a fair man, conceded the point.

MILES HAD JUST ABOUT given up on the idea of trying for his license anytime soon when his mother returned from work one evening and told him that Mrs. Whiting had offered to serve as his interim instructor. Even more incredibly, she'd proposed they use her new Lincoln to practice with. Miles was so surprised by the offer that he couldn't think of a reason to refuse it, which he would have liked to do. It had nothing to do with Mrs. Whiting, whom he'd met only briefly, and everything to do with her daughter, Cindy.

In matters of affection, the rules of engagement at Empire High were detailed yet unambiguous, an extension of procedures established in junior high, a set of guidelines that couldn't have been any clearer if they'd been posted on the schoolhouse door. If you were a girl and your heart inclined toward a particular boy, you had one of your girlfriends make inquiries from one of that boy's friends. Such contact represented the commencement of a series of complex negotiations, the opening rounds of which were handled by friends. Boy's friend A might report to Girl's friend B that the boy in question considered her a fox, or, if he felt particularly strongly, a major fox. Those experienced in these matters knew that it was wise to proceed cautiously, since too much ardor could delay things for weeks. The girl in question might be in negotiations with other parties, and no boy wanted to be on record as considering a girl a major fox only to discover that she considered him merely cool. Friends had to be instructed carefully about how much emotional currency they could spend, since rogue emotions led to inflation, lessening the value of everyone's feelings. Once a level of affection within the comfort zone of both parties was agreed upon, the principals could then meet for the exchange of mementos—rings, jackets, photos, key chains—to seal the deal, always assuming that the seconds had properly represented the lovers to begin with.

As a cripple, of course, Cindy Whiting had no friends, thus romance could not begin. Had she not been run over by a car as a little girl, she might have been at or near the top of the social pyramid, her parents being rich and her pedigree beyond question, but while no one wished to be unkind, facts were facts and Cindy was a cripple. It wasn't as if anyone was glad she was a cripple, simply that it was impossible to pretend she wasn't when she was. Without a second, she had no choice but to speak on her own behalf, which she did one day in the cafeteria when Miles stopped at her table to carry her lunch tray up to the window. "I love you," she said without preamble.

Miles had a procedural predicament of his own, aside from Cindy Whiting. He did have friends—boys like Otto Meyer Jr., whose pedigree, like Miles's own, was dubious but not impossible—who might successfully, if clumsily, mediate an emotional attachment, but Miles had made the mistake of falling in love outside the system, with a girl named Charlene Gardiner, who worked as a waitress at a greasy spoon downtown and was three years his senior. The system simply wasn't designed to lend assistance to anyone foolish enough to fall in love outside its clearly defined parameters, which meant that Miles Roby, like Cindy Whiting, was on his own.

He knew that Charlene Gardiner was no more in love with him than he was with Cindy Whiting, but that did not stop him from seeking out her company, even if that meant merely watching her forlornly from a booth at the Empire Grill, so nearly every day, he'd convince Otto Meyer Jr. to meet him there after school. Thus he knew that havoc would be wreaked if he accepted Mrs. Whiting's offer of after-school driving lessons. He'd be swept out of Charlene Gardiner's orbit and drawn into Cindy Whiting's. And once in her gravitational pull, he knew he'd be on his own, adrift. His mother would be no help at all. The cutthroat savagery of high school romance inspired in nearly all adults a collective amnesia. Having survived it themselves, they locked those memories far away in some dark chamber of their subconscious where things that are too terrible to contemplate are permanently stored. The more skilled you were at the game in high school, the more deeply your guilty recollections were buried. This was the reason parents so often worried vaguely about their high school children, yet balked at inquiring after the details of their social lives. Heartbreak, they reassured themselves, was "all part of growing up."

Grace Roby was an exception to this rule. For some reason she seemed to have forgotten exactly none of high school's horrors. By this time she'd been working for Mrs. Whiting for several years, and seeing that woman's daughter when she came home from school every day only intensified her natural sympathy. "I can't bear it, Miles," she confessed one evening. "I can't stand to see the way that child has been ostracized, the way her heart is broken each and every day. We have a duty in this world, Miles. You see that, don't you? We have a moral duty!"

Miles could not disagree with his mother's conclusion, though he favored the widest possible definition of the pronoun "we." He was willing to do his share, but according to his calculations, the obligation that was Cindy Whiting, divided among all the citizens of Empire Falls, amounted for each individual to a manageable moral task, one that could be dispensed with by means of the occasional kind word or gesture. He suspected, however, that his mother had something else entirely in mind. Though they never discussed it, he was pretty sure she wouldn't think much of his willingness to shoulder his "share" of the Cindy Whiting burden and leave the remainder to others. The majority, she would remind him, never do their share. Grace believed that those who could see their duty clearly were required by God to do the heavy lifting for the morally blind. Where Cindy Whiting was concerned, when his mother said "we," she really meant "he."

During this same period, something else was also troubling Miles, something he would've been hard-pressed to articulate. Since losing her factory job and going to work for Mrs. Whiting, his mother seemed different, as if she had crossed over into some new place in life. There were few outward signs of this transformation, nothing he could really put his finger on, and though the change had evolved gradually, he sensed it all the same. Grace had come back *from Martha's Vineyard heartbroken, and for a time it seemed to Miles she might never get over Charlie Mayne. But since going to work for Mrs. Whiting his mother had seemed to emerge from her sadness and to inhabit instead some new terrain. She didn't seem happy so much as content, yet that wasn't quite it, either. Nor was "resigned" an adequate description, though she did seem to suffer less now. Rather, it was as if she'd been let in on a secret she'd spent her whole life struggling to understand, and this knowledge, while changing little, made things more bearable. At home she appeared less fretful, both with Miles and with his father (on those occasions when Max graced them with his company).*

To Miles, his mother was no less loving than she'd ever been, but something had changed between them as well. Her hours at the Whiting household were long, and when she finally returned home in the evening, she arrived as if from another universe, sometimes just sitting at the kitchen table for half an hour, looking around their little house, as if life there were completely strange, mysterious and unaccountable. Sometimes Miles caught her regarding him as if he, too, were a mystery, or a stranger, someone she'd once known well but who had undergone plastic surgery so skillful that she could no longer be sure he was who he claimed to be.

That she should regard him curiously was natural enough, he supposed. During his junior year he'd shot up several inches and was now taller than both his parents, so perhaps it was his becoming physically a man that confused her. Whereas his boyish, tree-climbing stage had terrified her, she now seemed less afraid for him. Sometimes, though, her expression suggested an ability to foresee some unalterable destiny, one she herself wouldn't have chosen, and the calmness with which she acquiesced to whatever it was she saw struck him as a little frightening.

If she regarded her family's future with greater equilibrium—Grace no longer fretted about money, even though Max's continued unreliability guaranteed a week-to-week existence—she became consumed with the Whiting family's affairs. Her concern about Cindy, especially, bordered on obsessive, and she questioned Miles every day about how the girl had seemed at school, though she was aware they had only one class together. Over and over she made Miles promise never to allow Cindy to sit alone at lunch, even though he explained there were days that Cindy never appeared in the cafeteria, or came in late in the company of a teacher, or after Miles had already found a seat and eaten half of his lunch. Sometimes, too, she sat with Mr. Boniface.

What he didn't tell his mother was that Cindy often sat by herself at one end of a table designed for twenty students or more, the other end over-crowded with laughing, boisterous kids who seemed purposefully unaware of her existence. To a stranger entering the cafeteria for the first time, it would have appeared that Cindy Whiting was made of different, heavier materials from those that formed her classmates, as if twenty of them were required to balance their end of a teeter-totter. Nor did Miles inform his mother of his own ingenious methods of keeping his promise to her, of leaving the table where he'd eaten lunch with his friends a few minutes before the bell to stop by Cindy's table for a minute or two; sometimes he timed it so that he arrived just as the bell rang and there was nothing to do besides carry her tray. The terrible truth was that such slender gestures seemed even to Miles, at sixteen, both too much and too little, more than just about everyone else was willing to do but far less than conscience dictated. For he did have a conscience. He became painfully aware of it—a dagger through his stingy heart—each time Cindy beamed her hopeful smile up at him.

But it wasn't just Cindy Whiting his mother was obsessed with. Gradu-ally Grace came to dwell on everything that transpired in the Whiting household. She came home worried about bagworms spinning their silky pouches in the hydrangeas. Worried that the shrimp from the supermarket would not be fresh for Saturday's gathering with the hospital planning board. Worried that the house itself was too isolated across the river, where its inhabitants might prove vulnerable to all manner of miscreants sneaking over the Iron Bridge.

Though at times vague and abstracted, his mother was doubly grateful to Miles for being such a help to her. He'd learned to cook dinner for himself and his little brother, and she trusted him with enough money to buy such basics as toilet paper, laundry detergent and milk. "I don't know why I can't seem to focus anymore," she confessed to him, when she forgot something at the store or failed to pay the phone bill. "I swear I don't know where my mind is half the time."

Miles knew exactly where it was, though he loved her too much to point out the obvious: his mother had found another family.

MRS. WHITING SEEMED genuinely fond of him from the start, which surprised Miles, given her views on youth. The woman made no secret of her opinion that teenagers belonged in institutions for the criminally insane, from which they should not be released until the word "cool" had been purged from their vocabulary. She made no secret of her other forceful opinions either. Each afternoon, she pulled up in front of the high school in her Lincoln *at precisely 3:35. Classes let out at 3:20, but then all the school buses lined up outside and students from all four grades stampeded out the quadruple doors—a crush of inconsiderate humanity that an unsteady girl had no business in the middle of. By this point in her life Cindy was accustomed to waiting for crowds to disperse. When she traveled anywhere with her mother, they remained with the frightened elderly, the parents with small children, and the emotionally timid, while the strong and swift cleared the aisles. They avoided sales in department stores, queues for ice cream and popcorn at the lake, anything at all that might involve jostling. Over the years Cindy had come to understand that if she was patient, there would be plenty of popcorn and ice cream left over. She could enjoy the same treats that the fleet and well balanced enjoyed. Just not with them.*

So, only after the phalanx of buses departed, crammed with their cargoes of Empire Falls's Vandals and Huns, Goths and Visigoths, did the Lincoln pull into one of the spaces marked FOR SCHOOL BUSES ONLY. *Though grateful to Mrs. Whiting for helping him learn to drive, Miles immediately understood the cost of the instruction. Now, in addition to any lunchtime kindnesses, he was required to spend another ten or fifteen minutes with Cindy after school, as they waited for her mother. Though both were juniors, they had different homerooms, so Miles, after the first wave of students had left, helped Cindy carry her things to the front entrance. In warm weather they sometimes waited outside, until they discovered they would have to endure less ridicule if they stayed indoors.*

Ridicule was nothing new to Cindy Whiting, of course. During grade school, her classmates' cruel pantomimes of her lurching gait resembled that of the monster in the old Frankenstein movies, holding his arms out from his sides for balance. The Whiting Walk, they called it, and there were contests to judge whose rendition was best. During recess it was not unusual to see three or four boys practicing at the same time, stumbling into the slide or the swing set, bouncing off any objects at hand. The Whiting Walk was such soul-satisfying fun that it carried over into junior high, until the day a girl from the high school, Charlene Gardiner, who was there because her little brother had forgotten his lunch money, came upon a group of boys following the Whiting girl down the corridor, all of them doing their Whiting Walk. When Cindy turned around, they pretended awkward innocence. Seeing this, Charlene Gardiner had become furious and asked the boys in a tone of withering contempt whether they thought they'd ever grow up.

Among the boys at the junior high there was no one whose disapproval carried greater weight than Charlene Gardiner's, since she possessed the choicest set of melons in all of Empire Falls, no contest. One of the boys in the hall that day, Jimmy Minty, having seen her in a bikini at the lake the previous summer, had spent the whole fall semester recounting the experience of watching her bend over to pick up her tube of suntan lotion. To have your maturity questioned by Charlene Gardiner was definitely a scrotum shrinker, and from that moment on, the Whiting Walk became uncool and all its former practitioners were convinced that they had, as requested, grown up.

Which perhaps explained why it came as such a tremendous relief that first spring afternoon when Cindy Whiting and Miles Roby were observed together as they waited for her mother to rescue them. Sure, it was still uncool to make fun of Cindy Whiting by herself, but as part of a couple she was again fair game, even though Miles was the ostensible object of this new derision. Boys who already had their driver's license would roar out of the parking lot, honking their horns and leaning out their windows to shout sexual encouragement to him, as he sat there with Cindy Whiting on a stone bench gifted to the school by the class of '43.

Even more satisfying was to moon them, though this happened only once because the mooners themselves were victimized by bad luck and poor timing. Their intention had been a limited, tactical strike against the two losers on the bench, but no sooner had they framed their pimply asses in the windows of a speeding car than Mr. Boniface emerged unexpectedly from the building, his attention drawn by the honking horn. The view he was treated to stopped him in his tracks, and he watched until the car careened around the corner and out of sight. The wiggling asses might have belonged to anyone, of course, but Mr. Boniface recognized the car and thus quickly identified and suspended the appropriate scholars. Their bad luck was exacerbated by the principal's assumption that he was their intended target, a misapprehension they were hard-pressed to correct. There didn't seem to be an adequate way of explaining that they hadn't meant to moon him, but rather a crippled girl.

Even waiting inside the building did not inoculate Miles and Cindy Whiting against ridicule, of course. One afternoon the entire varsity baseball team—trailed by a grinning Mr. Brown—trotted out of the locker room, chanting "Go, Roby, go! Go, Roby, go!" all the way out to the baseball diamond.

In truth, this jeering had a more profound effect on Miles than on Cindy Whiting, who either didn't understand its import or was pretending not to. "What do they mean, 'Go, Roby, go'?" she wondered innocently, causing Miles, who'd flushed crimson when the varsity trotted by, to glow even more hotly.

Miles, hoping to keep Cindy from reiterating her declaration of love, took to directing their conversations to neutral academic subjects and often helped her with her homework, especially English, which happened to be his best subject and her worst. To Miles, her incomprehension had less to do with stupidity than with stubbornness. For some reason she angrily blamed each and every author in their literature text for her inability to deduce their intention and meaning, and when Miles tried to explain a troublesome passage or concept, her face became a mask of resentment and frustration. Poetry in particular infuriated her. To her way of thinking it was like pig Latin, designed for the sole purpose of allowing those in the know to enjoy the discomfort of those who weren't. Miles suggested that poems weren't really written in code, and that they weren't nearly as difficult as she was making them, but in fact even simple, obvious metaphors threw her for a loop, and more sophisticated forms of figurative language filled her with angry indignation.

"It's simple," Miles said one afternoon. "It's called personification. The speaker of the poem is comparing death to a coachman. 'Because I could not stop for Death, / He kindly stopped for me.'"

"If that's what she means, why doesn't she just say it?"

"She is saying it," Miles said, pointing to the line. The girl's failure to grasp something so simple mystified him. If anyone might be expected to have a feeling for Emily Dickinson, he'd have bet it would be Cindy, but she refused to even look at the page. The poem had made her feel inferior, so she wanted nothing more to do with it. Staring at the line in question would only deepen her conviction that there could be no justification for this or any other poem. "Why doesn't she say it so I can understand it?" she insisted.

Miles thought it might be wise not to answer this question, and so he said, trying to keep the exasperation out of his voice, "Well, do you understand it now that I've explained it?"

"No," she assured him mulishly and, as if to dissuade him from any further attempts at enlightenment, she emphatically closed the book, shoved it into her canvas bag, struggled to her feet, took up her cane and hobbled across the hall to the lavatory.

In her anger and haste, however, she hadn't completely closed the bag, and Miles noticed a thin paperback that didn't look anything like a schoolbook wedged sideways among the texts. He had no business going through her things, but he couldn't help wondering what sort of reading might appeal to someone so militantly resistant to the subtleties of language. The cover, depicting a summer camp setting with two giggling teenage girls sneaking off into the woods after a pair of beckoning teenage boys, looked innocent enough. It resembled those books aimed at seventh-grade girls, the kind read aloud at slumber parties, so Miles was surprised to discover that its contents, *at least on the page whose corner was turned down, were mildly porno-graphic. The passage his eye fell on had two girls, presumably the same ones depicted on the cover, secretly watching half a dozen boys roughhousing in the river. The boys were all naked, and one of them, Jules, was particularly wor-thy of their attention.* "The thing between his legs, so strange and so thrilling, made Pam's pussy pucker," *Miles read. This sentiment cer-tainly required no gloss. He managed to slip the book into the canvas bag just as Cindy stepped back into the hall.*

"And what's more," she said, *apparently taking up the discussion right where they'd left off,* "I don't believe you really understand those poems either. I think you're just pretending."

"Fine," Miles said, *no longer interested in arguing the merits of poetry. The dreadful fact of the matter was that the passage he'd read, its ridiculous alliteration aside, had given him an erection, and there was something about knowing that Cindy Whiting read and presumably enjoyed such books that made the situation worse. When she settled onto the bench next to him, it was as if she was suddenly sitting there naked, and he recalled that her expression when they'd been surprised last week by the mooners, their bare asses and dangling genitals framed in the car windows, had not been exactly what he'd expected.*

"I think you're all *just pretending,"* she continued obstinately. *"And why are you looking at me like that?"*

But at that moment a horn tooted outside, and they saw the black Lincoln idling at the curb. Miles pivoted when he stood and rearranged himself behind his books, but then a strange thought crossed his mind: what the Lin-coln reminded him of was Death's coach in Emily Dickinson's poem.

UNDER MRS. WHITING'S TUTELAGE, *Miles's driving showed steady improvement, much of which was attributable to his very first lesson. After they switched seats, Miles had just pulled cautiously away from the curb when Mrs. Whiting told him to pull over again.* "Dear boy," she said, "are you always like this?"

The question, compounded by the way she was looking at him, caused Miles to feel an inadequacy that transcended automotive matters, as though her question hinted at some larger character flaw. "Like what?" *he heard himself ask.*

"Like paralyzed with fear."

"This is a very nice car," he pointed out.

"Ah, there it *is,"* she replied, *pleased with herself for discovering . . . who*

knew what? She was still regarding him fixedly, causing Miles to wonder if the conversation would right itself soon, or just continue to defy his comprehension. His mother had warned him that Mrs. Whiting would be like no one else in his experience, and now he understood her inability to explain in detail.

Mrs. Whiting was several years older than his mother, he knew, which put her in her mid- to late-forties, but if she looked her age, in some hard-to-define way, she didn't seem her age. Miles was aware that Grace had been a very beautiful woman, and at times, though less and less frequently now, he would be reminded of her former beauty. In the years since their return from Martha's Vineyard she had settled into middle age, as had all the mothers of his friends and acquaintances. Strangely, one had only to glance at Mrs. Whiting to know she'd never been beautiful, probably never even pretty. Her daughter, had she not been crippled as a child and made the transition into young womanhood to the awful cadence of ridicule, would have been far prettier. Yet, from the moment she asked if he'd always been so frightened, what the woman seemed to convey to Miles was a kind of sexuality that, at least in his sixteen-year-old eyes, he'd not witnessed before in any woman her age. It was sexual inadequacy, he realized with a shock, that he'd felt when she looked at him, and that caused his cheeks to burn hot with embarrassment.

"There what is?" he said, regretting the question immediately.

"Your mother," she explained. "I didn't see her at all until you pointed out how nice this car is. Physically you don't look like our Grace, but you share her timidity."

Miles registered the "our Grace" but decided to ignore it.

"It's your father you've got written all over you, of course," she said, as if she imagined this to be a common pronouncement, which it wasn't. "Cindy is her father's daughter too, aren't you, dear?"

This seemed a rather hurtful thing for a mother to say, and Miles glanced in the rearview mirror to see how Cindy Whiting would react to the observation, but her face couldn't have been more blank. Whether she looked like her father or not wasn't a question Miles himself had any opinion on, he supposed, never having met C. B. Whiting. According to Cindy, her father now lived more or less permanently in Mexico, where he oversaw a textile mill like the one that had closed in Empire Falls.

Empire High might have been lacking in many qualities, but it had plenty of parking. There were about a hundred yards of paved parking lot out back, most of it empty by late afternoon. Mrs. Whiting positioned Miles in such a way that the entire stretch lay before him, free of obstacles, nothing beyond the pavement but a gentle, grassy slope, at the base of which was the school's oval, quarter-mile track. "Okay," she said, "floor it."

Miles wasn't certain he heard her correctly. "You want me to—"

"Correct," she said.

"I don't . . ."

"As in, depress the accelerator all the way to the floor."

Miles considered the request. He was pretty sure there was no possibility of misunderstanding, but still. . . . He located Cindy's face again in the mirror, and its expression bore about as much comprehension as he might've expected if her mother had recited a line of Elizabethan poetry.

The only other car Miles had driven was the driver's ed vehicle, which was underpowered by design, so he was greatly surprised when the Lincoln leapt forward beneath his foot like a suddenly uncaged animal. When he instinctively let off the gas, she barked, "No! All the way down!" above the roar of the engine, and so this time he did as he was told, the long parking lot flying past, the force of their momentum pushing them back into their seats, until Mrs. Whiting said, "Now would be a good time to stop, dear boy."

She was right, too. Nearly out of parking lot, Miles ran out of still more between Mrs. Whiting's suggestion and the moment when his foot found and depressed the brake. The Lincoln slowed immediately, its tires squealing horribly. Seeing the car slow was gratifying, of course, but the sound of the tires seemed like a bad thing to Miles, and one the car's owner would surely disapprove of, so he let up on the brake until the screeching stopped, which meant they were still doing about thirty when the pavement ended and they began to bump down the grassy hill all the way to the edge of the cinder track, where they finally came to a complete halt. Miles looked over at Mrs. Whiting, fully expecting her to concur with his last driving instructor that he was indeed a menace behind the wheel, but if she was upset with him, there was no indication. In the back, her daughter was also silent.

"It might have been preferable to stop back up there," Mrs. Whiting observed calmly, "but never mind. This will do fine. Now tell me what you just learned."

"I'm not sure," Miles admitted. In fact, he was not sure whether or not he had wet his pants.

"I am," said Mrs. Whiting. "You learned what would happen if you did something you were afraid to do. You learned how fast the car would go, and then you learned what it would take to stop it again. You were surprised by both, but you won't be again."

Miles nodded, feeling the strange truth of this.

"You can't possibly judge your ability to control something until you've *experienced the extremes of its capabilities. Do you understand?"*

He did. Frightened as he had just been, he now felt surprisingly good about sitting behind the wheel of the Lincoln—a different feeling entirely from losing control of the driver's ed car and ending up in that garage.

"Power and control," Mrs. Whiting insisted. "There will be times when you'll have to put the accelerator down and other times when you'll have to stand on the brakes. Not very many, but some. Now you know the car, and you know that between those extremes there's nothing to be frightened of, correct?"

They were, just then, still pointed downhill, on a piece of high school property not designed for motor vehicles. "Now what?" he asked.

"Now you get yourself out of this situation you got yourself into. Use your best judgment."

Miles nodded, took a deep breath, removed his foot from the brake and coasted out onto the cinder track. Trying to back up the grassy hill seemed like a dicey enterprise, so he simply steered the Lincoln around the oval track, grateful the track team had an away meet that afternoon. He'd nearly completed the entire quarter mile, spotted the tire tracks in the moist grass where he'd descended a few minutes before and was about to follow them back up to the pavement, when he became aware of a voice outside the car, calling, "Hey! Hey! Stop, goddamn it!" and spied in the rearview mirror an apoplectic Mr. Brown chasing the Lincoln on foot. It was hard to know whether he'd been pursuing them all the way around the track or had picked them up at the final turn. In any case, the baseball coach arrived beet-red and winded, and then came around the car and leaned against the hood, blocking Miles's escape route.

"Roby!" he wheezed when he saw who was behind the wheel. "I might've known." Miles obliged him by rolling down the window so Mr. Brown could yell at him better. "Goddamn it! What do you think you're doing? Do you have any idea how much that track cost?"

At that moment Mrs. Whiting leaned across the seat, causing Mr. Brown to start at the sight of her. "I do," she assured him. "I paid for it. Now get out of the way."

"Jeez, Mrs. Whiting, I didn't see you there," the coach cried. "I had no idea—"

"Did you hear what I said?"

When Mr. Brown danced out of the way, Miles slowly followed his tire tracks up the hill until the Lincoln bumped back onto the blacktop and his former instructor fell out of sight in the rearview mirror. Cindy Whiting, who'd lapsed into a comatose silence ever since getting into the car, was still there, of course, and she offered up a tentative, almost frightened smile when she felt his eyes on her. In that moment, seeing only the part of her face that extended from her mouth to her eyes framed in the rectangular mirror, Miles thought he saw someone else, someone vaguely familiar, someone he couldn't quite place.

"Power and control," Mrs. Whiting repeated, a smile playing at her lips.

PART THREE

PART THREE

$$[\quad \text{C H A P T E R} \ 1\,5 \quad]$$

I T HAD BEEN Miles's intention to close the restaurant by eleven. The game started at one-thirty, and he wanted to pick Cindy Whiting up shortly after noon in hopes of saving himself some embarrassment. A bigger hypocrite might've convinced himself it was Cindy Whiting he was trying not to embarrass, but Miles knew better. His thinking was to get to Empire Field before it got crowded so the two of them could find seats in the lower bleachers on the home-team side. Ascending into the upper reaches of the stands with Cindy's walker would not only take forever but also would allow everyone in Empire Falls the opportunity to witness and reflect on the fact that Miles Roby was in the company of that poor crippled Whiting girl who'd once tried to commit suicide over him. Also to speculate on whether he was positioning himself to marry all that money once his divorce became final. By Monday morning he'd be overhearing jokes at the restaurant.

He'd spent much of his virtually sleepless night feverishly climbing and reclimbing these imaginary bleachers, pausing only long enough to replay what Charlene had said to him in the Lamplighter after his brother left, that she'd have let him make love to her except for her fear he'd be disappointed. What he should've replied—this came to him at three in the morning—was that he'd take his chances if she would. But that, after all, had been her point. She wasn't telling him that he *might* be disappointed, but that he *would* be, his own certainty to the contrary notwithstanding. She hadn't offered him a choice accompanied by a stern warning so much as a kind and loving explanation.

Was it possible she was right? In an attempt to resolve the question—and to keep from going back to climbing bleachers with Cindy Whiting—he tried to imagine Charlene following him back to the Empire Grill in her decrepit Hyundai, their slipping in the back door and up the dark rear stairs. That part was easy and delicious in its intimate anticipation. And he had no trouble imagining a kiss there in the dark, or the warmth of Charlene's body against his own. They'd worked together in close quarters for many years, so he knew her smell, even how her body felt, and he was smart enough not to clutter his fantasy with dialogue. Though Charlene might be a talker, it was easier to imagine silence than to imagine her speaking the words he needed her to say. But then the fantasy failed utterly. When it came time to undress her, he discovered that the woman standing before him wasn't Charlene at all. She was Cindy Whiting, and not Cindy at her present age but rather as a young woman, approaching him without reservation even in his middle age. "Dear Miles," she whispered, as if to reassure him it was all right that he'd aged and thickened. "Dear, dear Miles."

So, back to climbing and reclimbing the bleachers for another long hour, his failure of imagination even more disheartening than the endless ascent. At least, he told himself, in the bleachers they were both clothed. He finally fell asleep around four, and the alarm went off at five-fifteen. Dopey with exhaustion, he stayed too long in the shower in a vain attempt to wash the long night away, putting himself behind schedule even before the restaurant opened. Worse, the breakfast crowd, which he'd hoped would be small on game day, was large, steady and talkative, full of anticipation and energy. He managed to run the last customers off by eleven, but he didn't want to leave a mess for David and Charlene and the rest of the evening crew, who'd have their hands full when the Empire Grill reopened at six, so it was past noon before he finished the cleanup, and twelve-thirty by the time he showered off the smell of sausage grease, and one before he picked Cindy up, and one-fifteen before he found a place to park on a side street adjacent to Empire Field, and one twenty-five before they began to climb the cold metal bleachers on the visitors' side of the field, the only place where there were still seats, and those up near the top. At one-thirty, just as Empire Falls kicked off, they finally completed the climb that Miles had begun in bed twelve hours before. Cindy had left her walker at home, content to use a sturdy cane for balance on one side and sturdy Miles Roby on the other. And by the time he'd stared malignantly at a woman in the top row until she moved down so he and Cindy could sit on the aisle, Empire Falls was already behind 7–0, Fairhaven having returned the opening kickoff for a touchdown. Miles sat there, sweating and bushed.

"Oh, Miles, look!" Cindy said. From the top of the bleachers they could see all the way to the river. It was the first weekend in October, and the air was crisp, the leaves approaching their peak, the Knox River sparkling the blue of reflected sky. Empire Falls looked, in fact, like it had been replaced overnight with a better version of itself. Cindy hooked her arm through his, pressing a warm breast against his elbow, and he felt, after too many months of abstinence, a stirring he tried to ignore.

"You know what I feel like?" she wanted to know, and for a moment the question confused him. Popcorn? Candy? Good God, they'd just sat down. "I feel just like a schoolgirl."

Miles knew what she meant. He'd have preferred a schoolgirl too, especially if it meant he himself could be a schoolboy. "Too bad all you have is a middle-aged man for company."

Unfortunately, levity had never had much effect on Cindy Whiting. She gripped the biceps of his left arm with both hands and said, "Dear Miles," just as she had last night in his dream. "There's not a soul on earth I'd rather be with." And with that she pulled herself up his arm and kissed his cheek wetly, holding on to the kiss until it was interrupted by the clanging sound of her cane as it slipped between the bleachers and rattled to the ground below. "Oh, nuts," she said happily. "You see what comes of passion?"

"*This*," Miles said, showing her where Timmy had bitten him half an hour earlier, "is what comes of passion." The puncture marks were still visible, two small white dots. The wound now resembled what it had felt like at the time: a snakebite. In a matter of minutes his whole hand had swollen up like a mitt, though by now the swelling had gone down a little.

"Poor Miles," his companion said, stroking the wound gently with the back of her fingers. "Does it hurt?"

"No," he said, jerking his hand away and rubbing it vigorously against his corduroy knee. "It itches like hell." What it reminded him of, he realized, was the poison ivy he'd contracted all those years ago on the Vineyard, and like that itch, this one returned, worse than before, the moment he quit scratching.

"Stop, silly. You'll make it swell up even worse."

"I don't care," Miles told her, digging at it with his fingernails now. Actually, he did care. He was fervently hoping that the swelling would go down by evening so he wouldn't have to admit to his brother that once again he'd come back from Mrs. Whiting's wounded. It was hard to believe that the animal had managed to surprise him yet again. Miles had been on the lookout, too, dropping his guard only as they were about to leave. Cindy had asked him to hand her a scarf hanging in the hall closet, the door of which was ajar. Reaching inside, Miles saw the scarf on a hook above a tier of shelves and glimpsed a quick movement, too late to withdraw his hand.

"See?" Cindy observed when he stopped scratching. "You've only made it worse."

"It feels better, actually," Miles lied, thinking that with a scalpel he could make it feel better still. "If I need a tetanus shot, I'm going to bill your mother."

That had been one good thing about this visit to the hacienda. Since Mrs. Whiting was away—in Boston, according to her daughter—David couldn't blame him for not broaching the liquor-license issue.

"You'll never guess where I found the little pill last week," Cindy said, in reference to Timmy. "She'd disappeared the day before and when I went to the cemetery, there she was, sitting on Daddy's gravestone."

Miles frowned at her. Did she expect him to believe this?

"Of course I'd brought her with me before, so she knew which one it was. You don't believe me, I can tell."

Actually, Miles wasn't sure which was harder to credit, that the cat of her own volition visited C. B. Whiting's grave or that Cindy herself did. He knew Mrs. Whiting well enough to doubt she ever paid respects to a man whose memory she'd done everything she could to erase, which meant her daughter would have to make the journey on her own. Miles couldn't help admiring the effort if not necessarily the motive. He himself had visited his mother's grave only once, and the experience had struck him as little more than an opportunity for melodrama. What was one supposed to do, standing there at the foot of a grave? Carry on a conversation with its headstone? Plant some flowers? He'd felt more distant from his mother at her graveside than he did standing over the stove at the Empire Grill, or passing by the old shirt factory, or kneeling in her favorite pew at St. Cat's. Even at the Whiting hacienda where she'd finally died, his mother came to him unbidden, and for that reason seemed far more real. Visiting her grave amounted to a kind of summons, and it didn't surprise him that his had gone unanswered. He'd vowed at the time that if it turned out there was life after death he certainly wouldn't linger around his hole in the ground waiting for visitors.

"I put flowers on your mother's grave, too," Cindy continued. "I always do. Did you know that, Miles?"

"No, I didn't," Miles said, feigning interest in what was happening on the field below.

"It's a terrible thing to say, but she was more dear to me than my own mother. When she was sick, and you were away—"

Miles rose to his feet. "I better go down and get that cane before somebody makes off with it."

She looked up at him through moist eyes. "Nobody's going to steal a cane, Miles." Then, noting his distress, "I'm sorry. It's such a beautiful day, and I didn't mean to make you feel bad—"

"You didn't," he assured her. "I'll be right back."

"I'll wait right here, then," she said, with the same self-deprecating laugh she'd had as a girl.

By the time he got to the foot of the bleachers, a roar went up and Miles saw that Fairhaven had scored another touchdown. When the noise subsided, he heard his name being called. The caller turned out to be Otto Meyer Jr., who was leaning up against the chain-link fence. Otto was one of those men who manage to look, as adults, uncannily the same way they had as kids, and Miles never could look at him without seeing a suffering nine-year-old standing all alone on a pitcher's mound. His father was a pushy local life-insurance salesman whose self-importance had demanded that his namesake be a pitcher, even though the coach, Mr. LaSalle, had seen in the boy a natural catcher. A natural second-string catcher (which the boy would later become in high school). But Otto Meyer Sr. was adamant, and so his son had been made a pitcher, though Mr. LaSalle refused to put him into games that were not already decided, and sometimes just for the game's final out, with, say, a seven- or eight-run lead. Otto Meyer Jr., however, made the most of that one out, usually facing at least half a dozen batters in order to record it. Worse, he had to sit on the bench each game and listen to his father heckle from the stands, until the coach finally relented and sent Otto Junior to the mound. Though the old man had died of an embolism almost a decade ago, Otto still looked haunted. His own son, David, was on the football team, and Meyer attended even away games, though he never shouted either encouragement or criticism. In fact, he never even took a seat in the stands, but instead moved from one side of the field to the other and from end zone to end zone. When Miles asked him why he did this, just to see if he knew the reason, Otto explained that he got too nervous in one place. Miles knew better. His attending every game without being anywhere in evidence was a gift to his son, who could then live the game.

"Hello, Meyer," Miles said, the two men shaking hands.

"I just saw Christina over on the other side. She tell you about her painting?"

Miles quickly replayed their most recent conversations. "I don't think so."

"It was one of two selected from the sophomore class to be in the citywide art show."

"Doris Roderigue picked something of Tick's?"

Meyer snorted. "Don't be an idiot. I brought in a professor from the college to do the judging. Christina didn't say anything to you?"

Miles shook his head, at once embarrassed, hurt and proud. Their vacation, he'd come to understand, had represented a brief *glasnost* during which Tick had offered up a few confidences of the sort she'd routinely surrendered as a child. He hoped such openness would continue, but now, a mere month into the new school year, she'd grown remote again. Probably he himself was at fault, at least partly. He'd registered his objection to the Minty boy much too strongly earlier in the week, and as a result Tick now seemed even more reluctant to share whatever was on her mind. "Lately," he told Otto, "she seems to hide where I can't find her. The only way I learn anything is through Q-and-A and then cross-examination. And she tells her mother even less."

"She's in high school, Miles. They all go to ground."

They paused to watch a busted play, then Miles said, "I think she's concluded from the divorce that neither one of us is to be trusted. She could be right."

"Nope. You're wrong. She's a great kid. She just knew you'd find out, eventually."

"You think?"

"Actually," Meyer confided, "I'm afraid I placed an unfair burden on her a couple of weeks ago. I've been regretting it ever since."

"The Voss boy?"

He nodded, looking guilty. "She say something?"

"Of course not."

"I heard you gave him a job. That was awfully good of you, Miles. He's a troubled boy."

"Troubled how?" Miles said, recalling Horace's cryptic admonition.

"The kids all love to pick on him for some reason. I wish I knew more. It seems his parents abandoned him. He lives with his grandmother out on the old Fairhaven Highway."

"I gave him a lift out there last night," Miles said, recalling how strange it had been. No light left on, not a sign of life.

"He was the other sophomore whose work was selected for the art show, incidentally."

Miles nodded, swallowing something like fear. Last night, in the restaurant, he'd felt the same apprehension, an unwillingness to have his daughter linked with this unfortunate creature. Now here he was, grudging the boy's painting being hung next to Tick's in a school art show. Insane. And even worse, a fundamental breakdown of the charitable impulse. Miles could feel his mother's sudden presence at his elbow. No need to visit her grave, either. "He seems to be a good worker. I can't get him to say two words yet, but Charlene's going to work on him."

"I always have a hard time talking around Charlene myself," Meyer grinned. "She makes me stuh-stuh-stutter."

Miles smiled, remembering when as a high school senior, he'd finally confessed to Meyer that he was in love with Charlene, only to have Otto sheepishly admit that he was too, which explained why he'd always been so willing to accompany Miles to the Empire Grill, a decidedly uncool place, to have Cokes after school. There was something touching about his old friend's admission now. Meyer had, as far as Miles knew, a fine marriage. But like Miles, he'd left Empire Falls only briefly, for college, then again years later for graduate school, which meant that Meyer also shouldered the weight of his childhood and adolescent identity—Oscar Meyer, the weiner, he'd been called. Growing up to become principal of the high school had merely confirmed the worst suspicions of his classmates.

"Kind of a shame the rivalry game's so early in the season," he observed.

Miles nodded, noncommittal. "I thought a rivalry was when you win some and they win some."

Fairhaven had won about the last ten. Both high schools had suffered declining enrollments over the past two decades, but Empire

Falls's decline was much steeper, having already dropped from triple-A to double-A, and it was about to drop again to class B. Fairhaven, more stable because of the college and a couple of smaller mills that had somehow managed to stay open, had retained Empire Falls on its schedule but insisted the game be played earlier in the season, as a tune-up for more important contests. For Empire Falls—in the tradition of jilted lovers everywhere— it remained "the game."

Otto Meyer Jr. nodded, watching Empire Falls break their huddle and lumber up to the line of scrimmage. "I don't get it," he admitted. "Our kids are too big and mean and stupid to get pushed around like this every year."

Another roar went up as he said this. Fairhaven had recovered a mishandled snap and was back in business.

"Damn," Meyer said, shaking his head. "Hey, speaking of getting pushed around, will you please stand for school board again? The damn fundamentalists are going to ban every library book worth reading if I don't get some help. You can't leave the good fight to the Jews, you know. This is Maine, and there aren't enough of us to go around. Besides which, some of *your* people are worse than the snake-handlers."

Which was true enough. Many Catholics, Miles hated to admit, *were* trying to out-Jesus their evangelical brethren, though he liked to think Sacré Coeur Catholics were more prone to this than St. Cat's.

"I'll think about it," Miles said. "I swore I wouldn't after my last stint, but—"

"God," Meyer blurted. "Just listen to us. Talking about damn school board. Only yesterday we were those kids out there."

"So long, Meyer," Miles said. "I'd like to chat longer, but my *date* dropped her *cane* under the bleachers."

This provoked a wide grin. "I thought that was Cindy Whiting I saw you with. You want to know the truth? I was kind of surprised to see what an attractive woman she's become."

Miles couldn't help smiling. Meyer was one of the kindest men he knew, and this was his way of suggesting that if Miles was contemplating marrying all that money, it was okay with him. And, as often happened when he ran into Meyer, Miles wondered why they hadn't been better friends over the years. Their mutual fondness hadn't diminished since they were kids, and Miles often got the impression that Meyer could use a friend. One of the odd things about middle age, he concluded, was the strange decisions a man discovers he's made by not really making them, like allowing friends to drift away through simple neglect.

It took Miles a few minutes to locate the right section of bleachers, where it smelled as if several decades' worth of elderly high school football fans had been secretly draining their colostomy bags from above. He was sick to his stomach by the time he found the cane leaning improbably against one of the metal supports. Had someone propped it up like that? Could the thing actually have landed that way? By putting one foot into the crotch of one of the supports and pulling himself up, Miles was just able to tap the bottom of the bleacher seat Cindy was perched on. When she bent over to receive the cane, he could see her face, and it was so full of hope and joy that Miles was tempted to remain where he was. Or, better yet, to bolt. Once the game was over, surely someone would see her sitting there alone at the top of the visitors' section and bring her home.

By the time he returned with a couple of sodas Miles found that his prayer for someone to notice Cindy Whiting had been answered in the way God will sometimes respond to a request that's carelessly phrased. Her companion was Jimmy Minty, and they both waved at Miles as he climbed the bleachers toward them, swallowing hard to keep down the memory of what David had told him last night, that Jimmy Minty had been watching the Empire Grill.

"How come you're setting over here with the bad guys?" Jimmy wanted to know. He was in street clothes and he seemed eager to shake hands, though Miles held a Coke in each. "You ashamed of your own hometown?"

"We got here late," Miles explained, sliding past both the policeman and Cindy, then staring at the same woman who hadn't wanted to budge earlier until she finally moved down again. Fairhaven, he noticed, had added another field goal, making the score 17–zip. "That forced us to *sit* over here with the winners," he added, just barely emphasizing the "i" in "sit."

"I wouldn't say this one was over just yet," Minty quickly countered. "My boy Zack's playing a pretty good game. I never seen a kid so fired up as he was this morning."

"He's on the team?" Miles said.

This time the policeman flinched. He was almost certain Miles knew that, in which case his chain was being pulled.

"Which one is he?" Cindy wanted to know, as innocent as her companion was pretending to be and far more interested.

Jimmy Minty put a hand on her shoulder and leaned close so they could both sight along his extended arm and out past his index finger, all the way across the field to number fifty-six, now on the bench while the Empire Falls offense tried to figure out what to do with the ball.

"What position does he play?"

"He plays linebacker, Miss Whiting," he explained, his hand still resting between her shoulder blades. "That's on the defense. Which is why he's setting over there on the bench just now. It's his job to patrol the line of scrimmage. Make tackles on running plays. Rush the quarterback when he throws. You have to be pretty smart to play linebacker, and I expect there'll be some interest in him if he keeps on like he's going. From colleges, I mean. He doesn't have the size to play pro, and I won't have him eating steroids. I told him, I ever catch you swallowing anything you can't buy at the mall, I'll bust your ass as quick as a kid with a kilo of crack cocaine."

"I didn't know they sold crack by the kilo," Miles said.

"However it's sold," Jimmy Minty allowed. "Zero tolerance is what I'm saying."

"How come you're not working the game today?"

"In uniform, you mean? Well, Miles, I don't work crowd control anymore. Most of the guys you see at the gates and out in the parking lot are rent-a-cops." He took a slender walkie-talkie out of his sport coat pocket and showed it to them. "I am on duty, though. Nothing like the Empire Falls/Fairhaven game to spark a rumble."

A rumble? Miles smiled, trying to recall the last time he'd heard the term. If you could control the urge to kill Jimmy Minty, he was entertaining enough, unless you liked your humor intentional.

"This section seems pretty law-abiding," Miles said, "but I promise to come find you if a fight breaks out."

Jimmy Minty chuckled unpleasantly, confident now that he was being made fun of. "Either that or you could just quell the disturbance yourself." He nudged Cindy with his elbow to include her in the joke. "I wouldn't mind seeing that, would you Miss Whiting? Ol' Miles here, quelling a disturbance?"

Below them, the Empire Falls punter was again trotting onto the field.

"Damn," Minty said. "Another three and out. Our defense is going to be plum tuckered out by halftime."

It was indicative of Empire Falls's team that the thing it did best was punt, and the boy who did all the kicking took this moment to launch one that traveled about sixty yards in the air. Unfortunately, it settled securely into the arms of Fairhaven's punt returner before the first Empire Falls players got more than twenty yards downfield, and before they had a chance to make much more progress in the direction of the ball carrier it became necessary to turn around again because he'd sprinted past while they were trying to shed their blocks. It was the punter himself who finally pushed the returner out of bounds at the Empire Falls thirty, and once again the tired defense trucked onto the field, Zack Minty trying to buck up his teammates by cuffing them on the back of their helmets and barking his signals as Fairhaven's offense broke huddle and approached the line of scrimmage.

Jimmy Minty again put his hand on Cindy Whiting's back and pointed down at the field. "That's my Zack there," he said. "Now we're on defense. They got the ball."

No doubt smelling blood, the Fairhaven quarterback took the snap, drifted back into the pocket and spotted a receiver streaking down the sideline. The pass he threw was a beautiful, arcing spiral, and virtually everyone, including the officials, turned to follow its flight. Miles, however, saw what Jimmy Minty saw. Number 56 for Empire Falls, a full two beats after the ball left the quarterback's hand, put first his helmet and then his shoulder pad into his kidney. Locking his arms around the quarterback's thighs, he lifted the boy off the ground and drove him into the turf so hard his head bounced twice.

The elder Minty leapt to his feet. "Yeah!" he cried, shaking his fist in the air. "Oh, *yeah*! Did you see that hit?" He was pointing excitedly. Cindy, however, as Miles had good cause to remember, was not the best of students. She'd followed the flight of the ball, and even now, despite Jimmy Minty's insistence, she seemed reluctant to look where he directed.

Zack Minty was back on his feet, quickly turning downfield, but the Fairhaven quarterback was still sprawled motionless on the grass, either hurt or aware that his services weren't required just now, the ball having come down in his receiver's arms for a touchdown. The Fairhaven coach, who'd also seen the late hit, now stormed onto the field, pointing alternately at his quarterback and at Zack Minty, who stood with his hands on his hips, staring off at Fairhaven's end-zone celebration and shaking his head. One of the officials farthest from the play trotted up the field, nodding his head and pointing at number 56. The officials held a brief caucus, at the end of which the referee took out his yellow flag and tossed it at the Minty boy's feet.

"Aw, let 'em play, ref!" Jimmy Minty yelled, an unpopular sentiment here in the visitors' stands. "This ain't badminton!"

"Is he hurt?" Cindy asked, since the Fairhaven quarterback still hadn't moved.

"Nah, he just had his bell rung, is all," Minty assured her. "He just needs to set there a minute. Get his bearings."

The celebration over, the crowd now focused its attention on the injured quarterback. After a minute he managed to sit up, then finally stumbled to his feet, his arms draped across the shoulders of his coach and a teammate. When the three of them started for the sidelines, number 56 hurried over and insisted on taking the place of the assisting player. The Fairhaven coach looked like he was going to object, but in the end he allowed Zack Minty to sling the arm of his still woozy quarterback over his shoulder pad and help bear the rubber-kneed boy off the field.

Watching this, Jimmy Minty's eyes filled with tears. "That boy's a class act," he said, nodding at the tableau unfolding below them. "That there's why we have kids, eh, old buddy?"

Miles, too, was moved by the scene, though he was unable to share Jimmy's specific emotion. Once the boy was propped safely on the bench, there was a smattering of polite applause, until Zack Minty trotted back onto the field and was greeted with a thunderous ovation.

"That's the kind of lick that turns football games around," Jimmy Minty told Cindy, his hands cupped at her ear so she could hear what he was anxious that she understand amid the roar.

It was the kind of hit that turned more than games around, in Miles's opinion, and suddenly the policeman's continued presence seemed intolerable. "Is there something you wanted to talk to me about, Jimmy? Or did you just come up here because you were plum tuckered out from quelling disturbances and looking for a place to set?"

It was Cindy Whiting who reacted first. She turned to him and blinked, sorely puzzled, it seemed, to hear Jimmy Minty's phrases coming out of Miles Roby's mouth. Minty also heard—Miles was sure of that—but he stared down at the field for several seconds longer before turning toward him. Miles saw that the emotion that had welled up over his son's "sportsmanship" had drained out of his eyes, which now were hard and empty. "I apologize for your friend here, Miss Whiting," he said, turning back to Cindy. "Miles and me go way back, but for some reason it embarrasses him that we were friends. He always feels better after making a joke or two at my expense. Which I don't mind—not one or two, anyway. A man who goes away to college and comes home with a diploma has earned that right, I guess, and I figure I'm a big enough man to take a little lip, as long as it's not too much."

Miles started to say something, then stopped. There was too much phony sentiment being expressed here to respond to any single part of the speech, though of course Miles knew that for a man like Jimmy Minty trumped-up emotion was indistinguishable from the genuine, heartfelt variety. So he satisfied himself with correcting one fact. "I never got any diploma, Jimmy."

"That's right, you didn't," Jimmy readily conceded, which might've suggested that Miles had fallen into a trap, had Jimmy Minty been smart enough to set one. Too bad Max wasn't with them, Miles thought. The old man was just what the situation called for. He'd be innocently inquiring whether everybody in the police department was issued live ammo or did the dummies get blanks. Where *was* Max, anyway? Miles wondered. It was unlike his father to miss a home game. He usually worked them like a pickpocket, which in a sense he was, putting the touch on every other person he ran into.

"Please convey my best wishes to your mother for me, Miss Whiting," Minty said before turning back to Miles. "You really want to know what I come up here for, Miles? I come up here to tell you I got things all straightened out with your brother, so you don't have to worry. I come up here to say there's no hard feelings. I knew you were mad at me last week, and I didn't want any bad blood between old friends. Because that's what we used to be, Miles. Friends. Used to be. Maybe we aren't friends anymore, but that's because of you, not me. You don't want to be friends, that's okay. But I'll tell you one thing. You don't want Jimmy Minty for an enemy."

A roar went up on the field just then, and Miles looked up to see Zack Minty emerge from a pile of bodies and hold the ball up with both hands, first to the stands on the Empire Falls side of the field, then to the Fairhaven fans, an in-your-face gesture that whipped the home-town fans into an even wilder frenzy. The boy seemed to know right where his father was, and when Jimmy saw what had just transpired, he too raised both arms into the air, a mirror image of his son's gesture, lacking only a second football. Even Cindy seemed to understand that something significant had occurred, and she let go of Miles to join in the celebration, madly clapping her hands together. After all, Miles reflected, there was only her whole life to suggest that this physical abandon might be a mistake. But then again, was it not her whole life that Cindy Whiting was hoping to escape for a few short hours this one particularly lovely Saturday afternoon in early October, lovelier still for the hint of winter in the air? Then Miles saw her lose her balance and pitch forward, and he caught her arm, but Cindy Whiting wasn't a girl anymore, and Miles's grip wasn't good enough to prevent what would've happened had Jimmy Minty not turned back to give Miles one last look and seen her coming toward him in time to catch her. The look of terror on her face remained there even after she was secure in the policeman's arms, where she continued flailing, as if in her imagination she hadn't been caught at all, but was tumbling, head over heels, down to the bottom of the bleachers.

Only when she was seated and calm again, clutching Miles's sore left arm with both hands, Jimmy Minty having disappeared into the crowd below, did Miles recall the clattering sound he'd heard when Cindy pitched forward, and see that her cane had once again fallen to the ground below.

ixty was all Janine Roby—soon-to-be-Comeau—could think. *Sixty, sixty, sixty, sixty.*

Down on the field, the game was stalled because one of the Fairhaven players—their quarterback, she heard somebody say—had been injured. She couldn't see much from where she sat, and she wasn't that interested anyway. She'd sat through most of the first half without really watching. Her only interest in the game was that this was the one everybody turned out for. When she was in high school, she'd missed every damn Fairhaven game because she was fat and her mother made her wear stupid clothes and nobody ever asked her out. She'd been savoring the ironic, vengeful sweetness of this particular event for weeks, imagining it in every detail, praying the weather would stay warm enough that she could wear her new white jeans and halter top, which she indeed was wearing, even though it was a little chilly. Walt, who pretended to be a big football fan, mostly just enjoyed strutting around at any social event that didn't require a jacket and tie; he'd even wanted to get there early, but Janine had nixed that goddamn idea right off the bat. What she had in mind was an entrance, which meant that everybody else had to be in their damn seats. The only problem there was that if everybody had already taken their seats, there'd be no seats left open.

Like most conundrums, though, this one was hardly insoluble, and eventually Janine thought of her mother. For some time she'd been trying to think of ways to get the old bat to like the Silver Fox a little better. She and Walt were getting married, after all, and by the time of the ceremony, she hoped, her mother would at least have stopped referring to him as "that little banty rooster." Maybe if Bea had a good time at the football game, it would occur to her that Walt hadn't spoiled it, and that would be a beginning. An afternoon in Bea's company might do Walt some good, too. The Silver Fox didn't have anything against her that Janine knew of, but he did seem to have trouble remembering Bea's existence. Every time Janine mentioned her mother, Walt's eyes narrowed and he regarded her suspiciously, as if she'd been keeping this person a secret from him. As if he hadn't been keeping the biggest damn secret of all from *her*.

But the real reason for hauling Bea along to the game was so that for once she could be the solution to a problem instead of its source. The plan was, she'd call her mother, say they were running late down at the club, and have her go over to Empire Field early and grab three spots, as close as possible to the fifty-yard line and all the way up at the top, so they'd have a good view. And also so everybody'd have a good view of Janine in her new white jeans and halter when she and Walt climbed up the bleachers filled with men who'd never once asked her out when they were boys, and with the women they'd asked instead. Most of these wide loads now took up the better part of two seats, so let them have a good look too. Janine had learned from all those hours on the Stairmaster that the only time a woman in the right getup is going to look more intoxicating than when she's going up stairs is when she turns around and goes back down them.

But of course everything had conspired to spoil her entrance, which only went to prove what Janine already knew: that no matter how well you planned something, God always planned better. If He was feeling stingy that day and didn't want you to have some little thing you had your heart set on, then you weren't going to get it and that was all there was to it. And today, for some reason, God didn't want Janine Roby— soon-to-be-Comeau—to have the entrance they both knew she deserved. Bea had gone early, but she'd put the three cushions down on seats only a third of the way up the bleachers, because anymore her feet always hurt from standing all day, and so did her lower back from wrestling kegs, and she didn't see any reason to be all the way up there in the nosebleed section anyway. Had Janine thought about it, she would've foreseen all this, but she'd been concentrating instead on the effect of her outfit.

Still, it wasn't really her mother's refusal to follow simple instructions that spoiled the plan. The truth was, Janine was still reeling from this morning's surprise. Sixty! Down at the county clerk's office, Walt

had produced a folded copy of his birth certificate, which he kept trying to smooth out with the palm of his hand, and when the woman at
the window asked him to read the date of birth printed on it, he'd
silently pushed the document across the counter toward her instead.
Janine should've known right then and there that something was up.
Actually, she should have been suspicious already, after all those weeks
she'd been trying to get him down there to file for their marriage
license so that when her divorce finally came through they wouldn't
have to waste any more time on paperwork. His first excuse was that he
couldn't find the damned certificate, and then twice last week he'd
managed to futz around at the club until the clerk's office was closed.
Only today did she understand his reluctance. He'd almost gotten
away with it, too. The woman had silently typed the date of Walt's
birth on the application, then slid his birth certificate back through the
slot in the window. Had she folded it before doing so, Janine never
would have spotted the faded date printed there: April 10, 1940.

1940?

"What the hell is that?" she said, pinning the document to the
counter with the tip of her index finger to prevent the Silver Fox from
folding and returning it to his pocket, a maneuver he seemed anxious
to execute, and when their eyes met, his expression was the same one
he used when he thought he'd pulled a fast one on Horace at gin. "Is
that some kind of misprint?" she demanded. The funny part was, if
he'd told her that it *was* a misprint, she probably would've believed
him, because there was no way Walt Comeau looked any sixty.

Janine located him now, down on the sideline. It was coming up on
halftime, and he was talking to Horace, who was moving a long metal
pole with chains up and down the field. Being down there on the field
was pure Walt, of course. If there was someplace he wasn't supposed to
be, that's where you'd find him. He never went into the Empire Grill
until it was getting ready to close. For some reason he liked the sound
of the door locking behind him and the idea that other people would
want in too and wouldn't be able to get in. He'd swivel around on his
stool and see who it was pulling up outside, only to be disappointed by
the Closed sign. He liked the whole damned concept of "inside," as in
inside information, claiming it was the only kind that was worth anything and letting on that he was in sole possession of loads of it.
Which, now that Janine thought about it, probably was why he never
surrendered any. If you told somebody, you'd just let it outside.

The good news was that Walt didn't even look the fifty he'd

admitted to before this morning. He *looked* mid-forties, a few years older than Miles and Janine herself, and his *being* fifty, so she'd thought, was something to be proud of. Janine had considered it inspirational, in fact. If her future husband could look that good at fifty, then Janine had another solid decade of wearing tight jeans and thin halters without looking ridiculous. But sixty! Sixty was no inspiration. It was a damn deception, and it had occurred to Janine at the moment her index finger pinned Walt's birth certificate to the countertop that what she was doing amounted to trading in a man who couldn't keep a secret for a man who not only could but did. And he wasn't just keeping his secrets from other people, he was keeping them from her too.

Which he denied, naturally, claiming he thought she'd known that he was sixty all along. He even showed her his driver's license, which said the same damn thing. "When did I ever tell you I was fifty?" he asked her on the courthouse steps. Well, it was true she couldn't exactly remember a specific occasion, a direct lie sworn under oath, but she hadn't invented the goddamn thing, either. How many times over the last year had they joked about the decade's difference between their ages, and he'd just stood there grinning—the Silver Fox!—and never once correcting her, never once saying, "I got news for you, darlin', we're not talkin' one decade here, we're talkin' two."

"What's the difference?" he said as they drove home, pretending not to understand why she was so upset. "You know what great shape I'm in. I've got the body of a forty-year-old man. You've said so yourself. Where's the problem?"

"The problem is you lied to me, Walt," Janine said, realizing that of course this too was a lie, and hating herself for it. That he had lied was the reason she *should've* been upset with him, but it wasn't. The reason she was upset was that she'd been looking forward to at least twenty years' worth of spirited, vigorous sex, having largely missed out on the last twenty by being married to Miles. But by the time *she* was sixty she'd be humping an octogenarian, or trying to. Discovering the Silver Fox's correct age also explained why on a couple of recent occasions Walt—who for a small man *was* well hung, God love him—had required considerable manual assistance to get out of the gate. What if in a few short years all her well-hung man *did* was hang? Janine glanced over at her mother, to whom she hadn't breathed a word of this because she knew how hard Bea would laugh. She was, after all, another tragic example of how much God seemed to enjoy frustrating the shit out of women.

"If you're cold, why not put on that sweatshirt?" Bea wanted to know.

Janine *had* brought a sweatshirt along for later in the afternoon, in case it turned chilly, which it had done already. "You see, Beatrice? You answered your own question. I'm not cold."

"Yeah? Well, your nipples tell a different story."

Janine regarded her mother murderously before responding and refused to look down at her thin cotton halter. "Don't trouble yourself about my nipples, okay, Mother? I happen to be enjoying the sun on my shoulders, if that's okay with you. We probably aren't going to see a warm day like this again until the middle of goddamn May, so leave me alone."

Her plan, Janine had to admit, was flawed from the start. She hadn't thought much past her entrance, which—even if it *had* gone as planned—would've lasted no more than five minutes, after which she'd be stuck with her mother's company for three hours. There was some kind of law that applied to situations like this one. The law of something-something. Never mind, it would come to her. Either that or she'd forget the question, which would be just fine too.

Sixty, though. That was going to take a while to forget. Janine knew from experience that it was a lot easier to forget a thousand things you wanted to remember than the one thing you wanted to lose sight of. Again she spotted Walt on the sideline. Since she'd learned this morning that the Silver Fox was sixty, he was beginning to *look* sixty, which was just plain nuts, she knew. How could a man who didn't look fifty yesterday suddenly look sixty today just because of a date printed on a piece of yellowing, folded paper. It wasn't rational. But when Walt Comeau turned around, peered up into the stands to where Janine and her mother were sitting and started waving, all Janine could see was that thing on his neck. What the hell was that—a wattle? Why hadn't she ever noticed it before?

"Who's that woman sitting over there with Miles?" her mother wanted to know. She hadn't noticed the Silver Fox waving up at them and certainly wasn't waving back.

"Where?" said Janine. Miles with a woman? She promised herself not to be jealous unless it turned out to be Charlene.

"Right across from us, except way up top."

That figured, Janine thought. God must have gotten His wires crossed, as usual. Somebody named Roby had wanted seats high in the bleachers, so He gave them to Miles.

"Looks like that Whiting girl," Bea said as Janine scanned the crowd for someone who looked like her soon-to-be-ex-husband. "It'd serve you right, too. You divorce that good man and he marries into the richest family in central Maine and then lives happily ever after and you get the little banty rooster."

"Diminishing returns," Janine said, regarding her mother with undisguised malice.

"What?"

"The law of diminishing returns. I was trying to remember that a minute ago, and you just reminded me."

Her mother squinted at her now, as if, despite her daughter's proximity, Bea was having trouble bringing her into focus. "I swear, Janine. It's not just weight you've lost."

Janine ignored this, having gone back to searching the stands. It took her another minute to locate him, because she was looking for a couple, and instead he appeared to be part of a threesome, the third person being that policeman Miles particularly disliked. The one she'd seen parked across from the restaurant one evening last week, just sitting there. Jimmy Minty. She watched him get to his feet and start to say something, but then a roar went up and Janine saw that there'd been a fumble down on the field. By the time she spotted Miles and the Whiting woman, if that's who it was—Janine had to admit she was going to have to get her eyes checked real soon, since she couldn't see for shit anymore—the policeman had disappeared into the crowd. Was it her imagination, or had they been squabbling right before the fumble?

"I hope Miles hasn't gone and done something to piss off that Minty boy," said her mother, whose eyesight apparently was fine. "He's his old man reincarnated, and William Minty was as purely sneaky and mean as they come. He was the only man your father and I ever eighty-sixed for life."

Janine again regarded her mother, surprised to feel something like fear on Miles's behalf. Fortunately, fending off that emotion wasn't too hard. After all, Miles Roby was no longer Janine's problem, and she forced herself not to look back toward him and the crippled woman, who, if she was seeing right, had hooked her arm through his. She returned her attention to the Silver Fox, who now had an audience of three out-of-work millworkers and was feeding them some line of bullshit or other. She could tell, because he was standing with his feet and arms wide apart, the way he always did when he was telling a story, as if from a pitching deck on high seas. Yes, it was Walt, not Miles, who was about to become her problem—unless she changed her mind in one hell of a hurry, which she was *not* going to do, she decided, for the simple reason that she wouldn't allow her mother the satisfaction of an I-told-you-so. She would marry Walt, all right, just like she'd been threatening, even if it *was* true that he'd planned to keep his old age a secret. Even if he did have a wattle.

It *was* that Whiting girl across the way, though. Now that her mother had identified her, Janine was sure of it. Not that Cindy was a girl anymore. She looked like she'd put on some weight, which for her was a good thing. The last time Janine had seen her she looked like somebody in the last days of a prison hunger strike. It was possible they actually were dating, of course, but the more Janine thought about it, the more she feared that this was some kind of a predicament that Miles had gotten himself into, and she couldn't help wondering how. She knew he was terrified of the woman, who'd been in love with him and even tried to kill herself over him, an idea Janine had always considered comical. In her opinion, being *married* to Miles was what inspired thoughts of self-annihilation. Failing to marry him should've been cause for celebration in any sensible woman. Of course, Cindy Whiting, by all accounts, was not a sensible woman, which was why she'd spent half her adult life in institutions. What in the world could have induced Miles to lower his guard this way? Well, he was a master at trapping himself, of course, but Janine still would've liked to know how he'd managed it this time. In fact, she felt a strong urge to call him up after the game and ask. Since their separation, what she found herself missing most were little things, like listening to Miles try to explain how he'd yet again got himself talked into doing what he'd just sworn never to do again. He wasn't going to run for school board ever again; then, ten minutes later he'd cave in because Otto Meyer had asked him. As if *that* explained anything. As if there were no way to predict in advance that *of course* "Oscar" Goddamn Meyer would ask him. As if Otto Meyer were the sort of man you couldn't say no to, when in fact everybody said no to him, including his staff, who were supposed to do what he told them. Or take American Legion baseball. He was all done umpiring. Never again. That was in the morning. By afternoon, after all the coaches got together and begged him, just until they could find somebody else, he'd agree to one more year. Right. It was pathetic, really, and when Janine decided to divorce him, she'd added watching-Miles-get-suckered-into-doing-things-he-didn't-want-to-do-and-swore-he-wouldn't-do to the long list of things she wouldn't miss. And at first she didn't. It was only lately . . .

Walt was a different breed of cat entirely, of course, never one to draw a line in the sand and then rub it out two minutes later, and this had attracted her from the start. The problem though, she had to admit, was that Walt wouldn't commit either to *doing* or *not doing* much of anything. The secret of his success, he was fond of reminding her, was keeping all his options open. There were times when zigging was called for, but on further reflection you might want to zag. One of his favorite expressions was "You know, a smart man might just . . ." and then he'd explain just what a smart man might do. In the beginning Janine imagined these statements were actually connected in some way to his intentions. Like—they'd sell the house he owned and use the money to buy Miles out of their house. Nobody was going to come out of this divorce with much, but Miles was taking the worse beating, and it embarrassed the hell out of her when Walt just changed his mind. He'd quietly found a renter for his own house and now was consistently vague about how the whole thing would work out, money-wise. Once they were married, was the rent money going into their account or his? Miles, she feared, would never see the first dime.

In fact, now that she thought about it, Walt hadn't said diddly about his finances in general, though of course this would change, by law, the minute they were married. Janine was more than a little curious about how much money there really was, and one of the ways she rationalized their shafting Miles was by promising herself to make sure he got his fair share later, once she could write checks against their joint account. There was the health club, of course, and now the rental house, and she'd gotten the *impression* he owned a couple other properties. She didn't know what they were, exactly, or even where. Lately he'd been talking about building a club in Fairhaven, which despite being twice the size of Empire Falls boasted only two small, seedy gyms. But then he'd also been considering expanding the Empire Falls facility, doubling the size of the fitness section now that area doctors were beginning to send workmen's comp patients in for rehab. A smart man, Walt speculated, might add a few more indoor tennis courts, since the one they had was booked more or less constantly. But in all the time they'd been together, the Silver Fox had not yet turned even one of these *mights* into a *would*.

Janine's reflections were interrupted by the appearance of her daughter, who'd managed to slide unnoticed down the row behind them and sat down next to her grandmother, who promptly gave her a big hug of the sort that she no longer allowed Janine to administer.

"How's life, Tickeroo?" Bea asked.

"Okay."

Her daughter looked, Janine had to admit, positively radiant in the early October sun. The poor child still didn't have much of a chest, and no hips at all, but she was going to end up with a model's build, no doubt about it. Not that she deserved it. Earlier that year when Janine had suggested she take some modeling classes, Tick had sneered that maybe she would, after her lobotomy. Which had pissed Janine off even before she looked up the word "lobotomy."

"Just okay?" Bea said, as if she also had noticed how radiant her granddaughter looked today.

"Well, my snake painting got picked for the art show."

This was news to Janine, as well as the fact that Tick had painted a snake. What was *not* news was her daughter's treatment of her in public. There was an empty seat on Janine's left, the one Walt had vacated, but of course Tick wanted no part of that. For one thing, Walt had touched it, so as far as Tick was concerned it was contaminated. At home she no longer used the upstairs bathroom, for the same reason. She preferred to go all the way down to the basement to shower in the dingy, unfinished bathroom off what had once been the rec room and was now crammed with all the shit Miles didn't have room for in his apartment. About a thousand yard-sale books, basically, which Walt was forever ragging her about, saying how nice it would be to have the use of the room. They could put a stationary bike down there and maybe even a Stairmaster so they—*she*, he seemed to mean—could work out while they watched television at night.

It was bad enough that Tick couldn't stomach Walt, but lately she didn't want anything to do with anything Walt had touched, including Janine. Whenever Janine got too close, she'd wrinkle her nose and say, "Yuck. I can smell his aftershave on you." Which she definitely couldn't smell, not first thing in the morning, after Janine had taken her shower. No doubt about it, they were headed for a showdown, probably before the wedding, for which Tick had refused to be the maid of honor, even after Janine had asked her nicely.

What Janine was gradually coming to understand was that her daughter was a formidable, clever opponent. Naturally, she had her father wrapped around her little finger—that was to be expected. But what baffled Janine was Walt. Even though Tick rarely exhibited anything but contempt for him, she somehow managed things so that he took her side in most disputes.

"I thought that teacher didn't like your snake," Bea was saying. More news to Janine.

"They brought in some professor from Fairhaven to be the judge," Tick explained. "He and Mrs. Roderigue got in an argument out in the parking lot. She told us the next day that Mr. Meyer was just trying to quote-unquote undermine her authority. Like she has any."

"You caused all that trouble by painting a snake?"

"Art's controversial, Grandma."

"Excuse me," Janine said, leaning forward so she and her daughter could glare at each other. "At least say hello, okay? I'm not just some-body you sneak past without so much as a how-do- you-do."

"I didn't sneak past," Tick said. "You weren't paying attention."

"I'm paying attention now, and you still haven't said hello."

"Tell your mother she should put a sweatshirt on," Bea said. "Tell her she looks cold."

"You *do* look cold, Mom."

"Tell her she's got goose bumps," Bea suggested.

Now Janine glared at her mother. "Remind me to invite you to the next football game."

"Your mother's in a pissy mood," Bea explained. "She wanted me to climb all the way up to the top of the bleachers on my aching feet, and I wouldn't do it."

"It's true I'm in a pissy mood, Beatrice. And it's true you aren't help-ing matters, but you're far from the cause, so don't flatter yourself."

"She's also embarrassed because I brought my hemorrhoid cushion to sit on," Bea added.

Also true. What kind of person would announce that particular affliction to the whole damn world? "Mother," Janine said, "you can show the people in the next row your actual hemorrhoids for all I care."

"It'd almost be worth it, just to see the look on your face," Bea snorted, not fooled for a minute.

Her daughter *still* hadn't said hello, of course, but Janine suddenly felt overcome not by anger but by sadness. Her eyes filled with tears, and she had to look away before anyone noticed. That morning, just before she and Walt had left for city hall, the mail had arrived, much earlier than usual for a Saturday, probably so the carrier could finish his route and make it to the game, and among the junk flyers and bills there was a small envelope addressed in a precise adolescent hand to Christina Roby, postmarked somewhere in Indiana. Impatient because Walt was dragging his feet again about going down to city hall, Janine had tossed the letter on the hall table and forgotten about it, though she recalled it when they returned. Now she had only to look at her daughter to know its contents were responsible for Tick's glow.

What called up the tears was the realization that her daughter would share exactly none of this with her. Hell, she wouldn't even have heard of this boy if Miles hadn't said something about him, clearly assuming she knew all about him. Since the separation, Tick had withdrawn all confidences, along with every outward sign of affection. Which hurt, of course, though Janine assured herself that her daughter would tire of this melodramatic attitude. After all, young girls needed their mothers. So far, though, Tick had shown no signs of relenting. Simple civility seemed a strain, and Janine suspected that even this was the result of a promise made to her father.

Janine surreptitiously blotted her eyes on the sleeve of the sweatshirt in her lap and thought, Okay, to hell with it. She'd earned her last chance at happiness and by God she was going to make the most of it. Anybody who didn't approve, well, just too damn bad, and that included her daughter, the little shit. She could just go ahead and keep her secrets. See if anybody cared. To prove she could pull off this posture, Janine turned her back on both her daughter and her mother.

Down below, the Fairhaven and Empire Falls players were trotting back onto the field, halftime over. Janine did her best to act interested and upbeat, yet she couldn't help thinking how soon these limber cheerleaders, now doing back flips, would be married and then pregnant by these same boys or others like them a town or two away. And how swiftly life would descend on the boys, as well. First the panic that maybe they'd have to go through it alone, then the quick marriage to prevent that grim fate, followed by relentless house and car payments and doctors' bills and all the rest. The joy they took in this rough sport would gradually mutate. They'd gravitate to bars like her mother's to get away from these same girls and then the children neither they nor their wives would be clever and independent enough to prevent. There would be the sports channel on the tavern's wide-screen TV and plenty of beer, and for a while they'd talk about playing again, but when they did play, they'd injure themselves and before long their injuries would become "conditions," and that would be that. Their jobs, their marriages, their kids, their lives—all of it a grind. Once a year, feeling rambunctious, they'd paint their faces, pile into one of their wives' minivans and, even though it cost too much, head south to take in a Patriots game, if the team didn't finally relocate somewhere to the south where all the decent jobs had gone. After the game, half drunk, they'd head home again because nobody had the money to stay overnight. Home to Empire Falls, if such a place still existed.

In their brief absence a few of the more adventurous or desperate wives would seize the opportunity to hire a sitter and meet another of these boy-men, permanent whiskey-dicks, most of them, out at the Lamplighter Motor Court for a little taste of the road not taken, only to discover that it was pretty much the same shabby, two-lane blacktop they'd been traveling all along, just an unfamiliar stretch of it that nonetheless led to pretty much the same destination anyhow.

Janine was sitting next to her own destiny, of course, and that destiny was itself perched on a damn hemorrhoid cushion. "Oh, leave the child alone, Walt," she heard her mother say, and she then saw through her tears that her husband-to-be had returned, no doubt sneaking down the row behind her just as Tick had done. Apparently he'd given his stepdaughter a kiss on top of the head and been handed his usual rebuff by way of thanks.

"What makes you think a pretty fifteen-year-old girl wants to be kissed in public by an old goat like you?" Bea asked him.

"'Cause I'm a good-looking old goat," said Walt, whose sense of himself as a desirable male was not easily tilted. After a minute, though, he sensed trouble and came sideways down the row and settled onto the end of the bench next to the somebody whose whole damn world had just gotten tilted, but good. Unless he was mistaken, those were tears in her eyes, tears that she was trying to conceal by pulling her sweatshirt on over her head. The only thing to do was cheer her up, so he began crooning an apropos lyric of Perry Como's.

"The way that we cheered / Whenever our team / Was scoring a touchdown," he warbled, nudging her, in the idiotic hope of getting her to sing along.

Perfect, Janine thought. At last she finally understood her husband-to-be's infatuation with Perry Como, which had nothing to do with the singer's good looks, charm, or silvery foxiness. The fucker was simply Walt's contemporary.

"You know what I wish?" she said without even looking at him. "I wish all of you would just leave me alone."

"Time can't erase / The memory of," Walt continued, not taking her warning seriously, the dumb SOB. "These magic moments / Filled with love."

That was the saddest part of all, Janine thought, now thoroughly awash in self-pity. She couldn't think of a single magic moment filled with love in her whole sorry life, and here she was, trying as hard as she could to deny it, closing in on over-the-hill.

She glanced down when Fairhaven kicked off to Empire Falls, whose kick returner received the ball cleanly and sprinted upfield. When he successfully negotiated the first wave of would-be tacklers and the field began to open up before him, everyone in the stands stood to see if he would go the distance, everyone except for Janine, who knew without looking that he wouldn't, and who, still seated, felt the crush of all the excited people stamping their feet and hollering in the rows above her. Janine understood about her mother's aching feet and why she hadn't wanted to climb all the way to the top as Janine had begged her. But damn, she'd hoped to get farther up than this.

CHAPTER 17

JIMMY MINTY parked the cruiser right across the street from the Empire Grill, where Miles couldn't help but see it when he returned. He'd been sitting there for a while now, pondering the whole Miles Roby situation, but for some reason his mind had wandered onto Billy Barnes, whom he hadn't seen in years. Why Billy should pop into his head, today of all fucking days, he had no idea, since it was Roby he felt like pounding to a bloody pulp. For all Jimmy knew, Billy Barnes could be dead. He wasn't playing pro hockey, that was for sure. Jimmy still followed the NHL closely, and knew his old buddy had never made it, though everybody in Dexter County swore that he would. Of course, even if he *had*, Billy would be washed up by now. Why was it, then, that Jimmy still half expected to see him turn up on the ice some night during a Bruins game?

So what had the kid who couldn't miss ended up doing? Jimmy Minty couldn't help wondering. What did you do when you were good at just one thing, after it turned out you weren't as good as you thought? Well, if you were smart, you probably did what Billy Barnes had done. You disappeared. Why hang around a place where all anybody remembered was that you hadn't made it? So how come? is what everybody would want to know, and who could blame them? Jimmy wouldn't have minded asking Billy Barnes that himself. Sure, there were people who wouldn't ask, but you'd see the question on their faces anyhow. After you said good-bye and started to walk away, you'd see them bend over and whisper something to their kid, and you'd know what it was. That guy back there? That was Billy Barnes. The best from around here to ever strap on the blades. Couldn't miss. Except he did.

"Ambition," Jimmy heard his father say. "It'll kill you every time."

William Minty had been dead for years, but his lectures had survived him. His only son, watching the parking lot and the street near the Empire Grill fill up with cars, could play them back in his mind more or less verbatim. "They got it *all* figured out," the old man would announce from the threadbare old armchair he piloted in the evening. His father was always solemn and silent over dinner, but once in the living room, with Walter Cronkite on the television, he grew talkative. Cronkite, Jimmy suspected from his father's knowing nod, was one of the ones who had it all figured out.

"Figured what out?" he'd found the courage to ask, just that once.

His father regarded his son with curiosity, as if he couldn't figure out how any kid of his could be so stupid. He nodded at the TV again. "All of it," he explained, then stared long and hard at Cronkite. "In school they tell you it's a free country, I bet."

Jimmy couldn't deny that he'd heard this opinion expressed on more than one occasion.

"Yeah, well, don't you believe it. They got the whole thing figured out, believe me, and they've thought of everything. Who they'll let you marry. Where you and her are gonna live. How much the rent's gonna be. How much money you'll make. Which ones are gonna die in their wars. All of it. You think *you* got a say? Think again."

Jimmy thought all this figuring had to be pretty complicated. It would require a lot of organization, and making everything come out right couldn't be easy. You'd have to depend on a lot of the same people his father complained couldn't manage to get you your unemployment checks on time, wouldn't you? He suggested as much to his father.

"Yeah? Well, don't you worry," his father assured him. "If you don't believe me, watch this know-it-all tell you how it is every night for about twenty years, then see if you don't think they've got it all figured."

From where Jimmy sat in the living room he was able to see the Roby house across the driveway. Many evenings Miles's mother would pass behind their living room window, sometimes stopping to pull the curtains shut. At nine years old, Jimmy had thought Mrs. Roby the prettiest woman he'd ever seen, including girls, and he wondered what it would be like to live in the same house as her. He guessed maybe it'd be different if she was your own mother, but he couldn't imagine not having the hots for Mrs. Roby, no matter whose mother she was. He'd caught his father looking across the way a couple times, too. Jimmy had even made the mistake of telling Miles how lucky he was having her for a mother, all to himself, most of the time, Mr. Roby being gone as much as he was home. He'd also asked Miles if he'd ever seen his mother naked, hoping for a description, and Miles hadn't spoken a word to him for a week, until he apologized, which Jimmy was quick to do, because he was afraid Miles would tell his mother that he was a dirty boy.

So Jimmy thought about what his father was telling him about Walter Cronkite and the rest having it all figured out, and he hoped his father was wrong. He didn't like the idea of having somebody else decide who he'd marry. That was a choice he'd hoped to make himself, and he intended to marry someone who looked as much as possible like Mrs. Roby. Or maybe Mrs. Roby herself—later, when he was old enough, if her husband died or disappeared completely. "Nobody can figure out everything," Jimmy ventured hopefully.

"No?" his father said, watching Cronkite carefully, so the other man wouldn't be able to put anything over on him. "Well, maybe not everything. But they got the main things covered, that's for goddamn sure. And don't you ever doubt it, neither."

In a nutshell, his father's philosophy about how to deal with these people was not to appear ambitious. Don't call attention to yourself, was his advice. Keep your eyes open for opportunities, but don't get greedy. Steal small. Make sure if you're caught, they don't catch you with much. Remember "the bother principle," as he called it. "They won't bother you over little things," was the way his father explained his own thefts. Couple loins of venison turn up in your freezer down in the cellar? Who's going to bother you? Two or three big freezers full of hijacked deer? Too much. In fact, the bother principle could gauge the risks of just about any situation. You happen to find a key that opens the lock to somebody's storeroom? Lucky you. You lift the occasional bottle of cheap rye? Who's going to bother you over that? Chances are they don't even count the bottles of the cheap stuff, or if they do and one goes missing, maybe they miscounted. The brand-name booze and case lots? Those they counted. Those they looked for. Better to steal the cheap one. When it's gone, steal another. You got the key, you keep the key. You tell exactly no one. If you don't get greedy, that key stays useful. You steal big, they change the lock, and now you don't have a key anymore. Keys were one of William Minty's hobbies. He made them down in the basement on a machine he'd got for a song when Olerud's Hardware went bankrupt.

Jimmy bolted upright when an old Volvo pulled up alongside the cruiser and proceeded to parallel park in the space behind it. He watched the driver get out, go around and open the door for the woman in the passenger seat. She was nicely dressed, but nothing much to look at. The man was dressed in chinos and a tweed sport coat over a light-blue shirt with a button-down collar, and he was carrying something in a brown paper bag. Jimmy Minty disliked him immediately, probably even before he'd gotten out of the car. Not many men would parallel park if they had to start out next to a cop car. Whoever this asshole was—a professor by the look of him—he was pretty fucking sure of himself. He and his plain-Jane woman crossed Empire Avenue without so much as a glance in his direction, and when they disappeared inside the Empire Grill Jimmy turned in his seat so he could see the inspection sticker displayed on the windshield. Valid, unfortunately.

His watch read six-thirty. Jimmy had figured Roby would be back at the restaurant by now. It didn't take that long to drive across the Iron Bridge, deposit Cindy back at the Whiting house and return. Unless ol' Miles managed to get himself invited inside. Though the possibility was not entirely pleasant, Jimmy had to smile. Mrs. Whiting was in Boston, he happened to know, so maybe Miles and her daughter were going at it on the sofa right now, Roby slipping it to her. *That* experience he was welcome to.

A pickup truck, its horn honking, careened around the corner onto Empire Avenue. Four high school kids were wedged into the cab—no way more than two of 'em could be belted—and three more were standing up in the bed, the tallest blowing one of those long plastic horns. The driver, spotting the cruiser at the last second, stood on the brakes hard enough to cause the boys in the back of the cab to hang on for dear life, and the horn soared out over the side and rattled up the street after them, coming to rest under Jimmy's car. He considered going after them, reading the damn-fool driver the riot act, maybe even issue a ticket, but then decided against it. They were just kids, full of piss and vinegar after the big game. They'd gotten a good scare when they saw him and lost their horn to boot. They'd probably go slow now, at least for a while. Besides, if he chased after them, he'd lose his parking space for sure.

As if to confirm this fear, another car pulled up next to the curb on the other side of the street, and yet another man in a tweed coat got out. Why did they all have to wear a uniform, these college professors? The woman with this guy was a dead ringer for the first one; if they had a plain-looking-woman contest, these two would tie for seventh place, unless there was a swimsuit competition, and then they'd tie for ninth. His father had been right about that part, of course. You didn't get to marry the one you wanted. You married the best of whatever was left. Tweed married tweed, flannel got flannel. As to whether ambition killed you every time, Jimmy Minty had his doubts.

Professors. Maybe that was why he'd recollected Billy Barnes. After high school, Billy had gone off to the University of Maine on his hockey scholarship. He joined a frat house and invited Jimmy up to Orono one weekend for a party, so he could see for himself what he was missing out on. It turned out to be one hell of a party, all right, and it was already in full swing by the time Jimmy Minty got there. Actually he'd arrived earlier in the evening, but then drove around, trying to work up enough nerve to knock on the frat house door. In fact, he'd finished a six-pack before deciding what the hell. When he finally rang the bell, the door was answered by a big guy who had a sixteen-ouncer in his left hand and a passed-out, bare-assed girl slung over his right shoulder, her long dark hair hanging straight down, almost to the big kid's knees, her blue jeans and panties bunched around her ankles. Jimmy, trying to pretend that this wasn't such an unusual sight, explained that he was a friend of Billy Barnes, and the big kid said, "Like I give a shit. Grab yourself a brew. You want a sniff?"

"What?" Jimmy said, feeling angry and confused.

"Dollar a sniff," he explained, and then another guy came over and stuffed a wrinkled bill into his frat brother's shirt pocket, which Jimmy now noticed was full of them. This new kid asked Jimmy to step out of the way, then grabbed and lifted the girl's ankles so her knees rested on his shoulders. Then he leaned forward, inhaling deeply. "That," he said when he'd finished and let the girl's legs drop, "is one sweet pussy."

"So," the big frat kid said to Jimmy Minty, who hadn't moved. "You want a sniff, or are you just going to stand there staring?"

"I was looking for Billy Barnes," Jimmy Minty reminded him.

The kid nodded in drunken comprehension. "Nice ripe pussy and you're looking for Billy Barnes." He shrugged. "To each his own."

Well, it was a pretty wild party. Jimmy drank a beer from one of three identical kegs, wondering if that was all he'd be allowed, not being a member of the fraternity. It was hard to imagine you'd get more than one freebie by dropping Billy Barnes's name, but apparently he was wrong. When he went back to the kegs, one of the frat boys tripped the spigot, without ever looking at him, as if it were the proximity of the empty cup he was acknowledging and not the person holding it. The beer flowed through the tap slowly, and the boy kept talking to a girl (this one fully clothed) without feeling the need to check on Jimmy's cup. When he interrupted their conversation to ask if he'd seen Billy Barnes, the frat kid frowned and said, "Who?"

When he woke up the next morning, Jimmy's head ached so bad that for a long time he just lay still, not even daring to open his eyes. He was vaguely aware of having spent a restless night, chased from one nightmarish dream to another. When he finally opened his eyes, he was in a strange room. Staring at the ceiling was about all he could manage, because even the slightest movement resulted in wave after wave of rolling nausea and pain. It was quiet, though, and from this he deduced that he was alone. Relieved, he closed his eyes and must've gone back to sleep, at least for a while, because when he opened them again the headache, while still nauseating, didn't seem quite as intense.

What worried him was that whoever this room belonged to was likely to show up at any time and demand to know what Jimmy was doing in here. He wouldn't even know who Jimmy was unless by chance this happened to be Billy Barnes's room, and what were the odds on that? He couldn't remember much of what happened the night before, but he did recall asking after his old friend over and over and getting the distinct impression that Billy wasn't held in particularly high esteem by his frat brothers. Not that this surprised him all that much, since Billy didn't have many friends in high school either, except on the hockey team, and that was only because he could skate circles around just about anybody in Dexter County.

At any event, if this wasn't Billy's bed, Jimmy thought he'd better vacate it as soon as possible, so he closed his eyes one last time, counted to three, sat up, and swung his legs onto the floor. Then he closed his eyes again and waited for the crashing waves of pain in his head to subside. When they did, he immediately saw two things in the dim early-morning light. The first was that he was naked, which put him in mind of the bare-assed girl everybody had been paying to sniff the night before, and in a wild intuitive leap he wondered if something of the sort might've happened to him after he passed out. Had he been removed to this bedroom and stripped naked and offered up as a male specimen to curious female partygoers? No doubt he'd have lost the contents of his stomach right then if he hadn't noticed the second thing, which substituted cold fear for nausea. The dingy white sheet he'd been sleeping on was splotched wetly pink all the way up to the pillow, and when close examination revealed the sticky wetness to be exactly what he feared—blood—he vaulted quickly to his feet and backed away from the bed until he bumped into the far wall. This caused another terrific wave of pain in his head, this one so intense that he slid down the wall into a sitting position, where he remained, his knees drawn up to his chest, his hands clasped around his ankles, his forehead resting against his knees. Again he closed his eyes and considered the blessing of darkness, the marvelous way it could subtract the whole world.

THERE WAS A KNOCK on the side window of the cruiser, and when he looked up, Zack had materialized on the other side of the glass. Jimmy rolled down the window and grinned. Lord, the boy was getting big.

He offered his hand. "Hell of a game, son."

They shook awkwardly. "Too bad we run out of time," said the younger Minty. They'd come back in the second half, tying Fairhaven on a field goal late in the fourth quarter. "We would've scored again if we got the damn ball back."

"That's for sure," Jimmy agreed. "And they were all done scoring on you."

"That they were," the boy said proudly.

"Where you off to now?"

Across the street Jimmy Minty's own Camaro idled throatily, double-parked next to the second professor's car, and behind the Camaro sat the pickup that had screeched around the corner earlier. There was no one riding in the back now, and only three in the cab. For show, no doubt. The other kids were probably waiting around the corner to get picked up again.

"Thought we'd drive to Fairhaven for some pizza."

"We got pizza right here in Empire Falls, you know."

"I know," Zack said. "But is it okay?"

"I guess. Who you got with you?" He peered around his son to see who was in the car, but the windows were rolled up, the Camaro's glass tinted.

"Justin. Tick Roby. Girl named Candy Burke."

His father nodded, waiting. There were *four* people in the car. He could see that much, even through the tinted windows. "That's three," he said.

His son seemed reluctant to 'fess up to the last rider. "Some kid named John."

"John who?"

"Voss, I think."

Jimmy nodded, trying to conjure up what he knew about that name. The kid had got caught shoplifting at the supermarket back in July. Jimmy had let him off with a warning. Not worth the bother. Weird kid, he remembered. Not the sort he would've figured his own boy would be hanging around with. "*You* ever get caught shoplifting, I'll kick your ass, you know."

"I won't," the boy promised, ambiguously.

"I still can, you know."

"Maybe." Now the boy was grinning.

"Maybe, my ass," Jimmy grinned back. "You might be able to knock me down, but I wouldn't be like that kid you whacked today. I'd get back up."

"I know you would, Dad."

"You got enough money?"

"Yeah."

Jimmy Minty nodded, then slipped him a twenty anyway. "Take this. You can give it back if you don't need it." Which would be a first. Not that he minded, though. Jimmy didn't want a kid of his to be short, like he'd always been at that age. Getting a bent nickel out of his father had been an all-day job.

"You stay out of trouble. This is a bad night for you to be going to Fairhaven, after that game. You get thrown in jail for fighting, I'll let you sit there."

"I'll remember."

"Do."

"I'm going now, okay?"

"How are you and that Roby girl getting along?"

"Oh, she's being a cunt as usual, pretending she doesn't like me."

Jimmy considered telling him to watch his language, then decided against it. He'd used that word himself, in reference to the boy's mother, who *was* one and who deserved it. Like most of them did, when you came right down to it. "Well, she wouldn't be her father's daughter if she didn't need to come down a peg or two. Don't take any shit is my advice." He was just about through taking it himself, actually.

"I won't be late."

"You wreck that Camaro, I'm not going to give a good goddamn whose fault it was," Jimmy said, feeling the need for one last warning.

"We could switch, if you're worried," the boy said, wiseass.

"Go on, before I give you a ticket for double-parking."

Zack nodded. Before crossing the street, though, he went around the cruiser and retrieved the plastic horn from the gutter, then trotted over and handed it to the driver of the pickup.

THE MOST OBVIOUS EXPLANATION for the bloody bed, he'd figured as he sat there with his eyes clamped tightly shut, was that he was still dreaming. After all, he'd been tormented by one terrible dream after another all night, their fragmented contents coming back to him now in flashes. This must simply be the latest installment. When he opened his eyes again, he'd be back in bed, maybe even his own bed, hungover but safe and sane. Except that when he tested this theory, he found himself still seated at the base of the wall in some stranger's dorm room. The only difference was that he'd begun to whimper. Clearly, a terrible thing had happened here in the night, and since he was alive to witness its aftermath, it stood to reason that the act had not been done *to* him—though he now noticed that his own skin, here and there, was crusted with blood—but rather *by* him. For a long time, probably since he was fifteen or sixteen, he'd been indulging dark, violent fantasies before going to sleep at night, and one of these, it seemed, had somehow come to life. He'd persuaded some girl to come up to this room with him last night, and then she'd pissed him off, and he'd killed her. He vaguely remembered trying to convince several different girls to have sex with him the night before. As far as he could remember, none of them had been even remotely tempted, but one of them must've said yes. Once again he felt his stomach heave.

Despite the psychological plausibility of this scenario, Jimmy Minty took some solace from the lack of supporting physical evidence. If he'd killed some poor sorority girl, then where was she? He got onto his hands and knees and crawled over to where the bedclothes were balled up at the foot of the bed and lifted them up. No girl there. He then padded around to the other side of the bed. Still no girl. Next he checked out the closet, which was full of all manner of shit *except* a dead girl. Was it possible he'd tried to kill her and she'd somehow managed to escape? He poked his head out into the hallway, half expecting to see a trail of blood. There was a large foamy stain on the wall, but that almost certainly was beer. He closed the door again.

Okay, so maybe he hadn't killed anybody after all. But *somebody* had bled like a stuck pig all over the bed. Much of the blood was already dry and crusty, like the spots on his knees and stomach and chest. In other places it was still sticky and moist. Sitting down on the edge of the bed, Jimmy thought for a moment, then reached down and took a clean corner of the top sheet and wiped a spot of dried blood off his knee, surprised that it stung when he did so and that bright beads of blood began forming slowly along what he now recognized as a tiny cut.

How wonderful to discover that the blood was his own, that his whole body was covered by tiny, razor-thin cuts! True, it made him weak to consider that so much blood should've leaked from his own person, but at least he wasn't a murderer. He'd planned on applying to the Maine Police Academy, and it wouldn't look good on his application if he'd gone and killed some girl at a frat party, even if he explained that he was drunk at the time and didn't remember. It had taken him the better part of a year to come up with the police academy idea, and he didn't want to have to start all over, even with the leisure of a lengthy prison sentence to develop other career possibilities. No, if the blood was his own, it meant that he could still be a cop—and what the present circumstance called for, it occurred to him, was some detective work. How on earth had he managed to wake up covered with cuts he didn't remember getting? It was a puzzle.

He'd heard plenty of stories about wild frat parties, about a bizarre ritual called hazing that the older members inflicted on the pledges. Mostly the pledges were just driven out into the country someplace, their clothing confiscated, and left there to make their humiliating way back to campus. Or else they were forced to drink until they passed out. Maybe something along these lines had happened last night. It was his understanding that in order to be hazed, you first had to pledge the frat, but who knew? Maybe he'd been mistaken for a Sigma Nu pledge. Of course no one had forced him to drink until he passed out. He'd done that all on his own. But he'd awakened completely naked, and that was suggestive. Was it possible that all these tiny cuts had been inflicted on him by drunk frat boys playing a prank? Good Lord, there was even one on his dick!

The good news was that his clothes were wadded up among the bedclothes, and Jimmy climbed into them gingerly. Movement of any sort opened the various cuts and made them sting all over again, but there was no help for it. The house was still quiet, everyone drunkenly asleep, he assumed, so the thing to do was slip out quietly before anybody else woke up and wondered who the hell he was and what he was doing there. The question was, Should he take the bloody sheets with him? On the one hand, they weren't his, and he didn't want to be regarded as a thief. On the other, removing them would be a kindness to the owner of the room, who would therefore be spared the shock and mystification of all that blood. Besides, the whole damn fraternity would probably be convinced a murder had taken place, and when they sobered up somebody might remember it was Billy Barnes's weird friend they'd let crash in there. That would take some explaining, and Jimmy Minty doubted his ability to do so convincingly when he only partially comprehended what might've happened himself. So, best to swipe the sheets.

When he began to strip the bed he noticed glinting, as if the bloody sheet had been sprinkled here and there with stardust. On closer inspection it turned out to be shards of paper-thin glass. Jimmy studied a tiny shaving that embedded itself in the tip of his thumb when he tried to pick it up. He sat back down on the bed to think it through and, after a minute, raised his head to look at the ceiling. Directly overhead was an empty light fixture. No, not empty. A ragged piece of thin glass jutted out of the socket, all that was left of the exploded lightbulb. No wonder his sleep had been restless. He'd been sleeping in a bed of broken glass.

The mystery solved, he decided to leave the sheets after all and see if anybody else could follow the clues and solve the mystery. Down the block he found his car right where he'd left it the night before, and he slid gingerly behind the wheel, his buttocks a grid of nicks. Right in front of him was another frat house, with two Greek symbols displayed above the door. This got him thinking. The frat he'd gone into the night before had *three* symbols above the door. "Sigma Nu" was what Billy Barnes had said when he gave Jimmy the address. Would that be two symbols or three? Sig Ma Nu. Three.

The drive back to Empire Falls was uncomfortable, but Jimmy Minty smiled the whole way, confident he'd make a hell of a fine policeman. He was also glad he'd visited the University of Maine. It took most kids a full four years there to discover their true vocation, but he'd figured it out on his own in just one night.

THE POLICE CAR, parked in plain sight across the street, was the first thing Miles saw when he returned from the Whiting hacienda. Ignore it, he told himself. The restaurant looked every bit as busy as it had been last night, which meant they could use his help inside. He drove around back, parked in his usual spot beside the Dumpster, and started toward the back door, then thought again, heading around the building and out into the street. Jimmy Minty had opened the door and gotten out of the cruiser before Miles even stepped off the curb, and he looked pretty surprised when Miles stuck his hand out. Maybe a little disappointed, too, because he was none too quick to take it.

"I'm sorry about this afternoon, Jimmy," Miles said once they'd shaken hands. "I don't know what got into me. I'm tired, I guess."

"Well, it's good of you to apologize. I guess I figured this thing between us was going to get worse."

"I wouldn't want that," Miles said truthfully. "You were right. I don't need any enemies. I certainly don't want to make one of you."

Jimmy nodded warily. It took him a minute to satisfy himself that there wasn't any irony or sarcasm in what Miles was saying. "Why don't you come around and set a minute? Sit, I mean. You were right. I always get that wrong. 'Sit' and 'set.' Old Lady Lampley used to mark it with her red pen. You remember her?"

Miles nodded. "I can't stay long," he said, going around to the other side of the cruiser. "It looks like the restaurant's full."

"You afraid they can't handle things without you?" Minty said when Miles slid in and he himself had settled back behind the wheel.

"No." Miles shook his head. "I'm more afraid they *can*."

Jimmy nodded, as if this wisdom was too profound to swallow whole. After a beat he said, "This is more like it. Me and you, just talking. Not getting bent out of shape."

Miles nodded back. Unless he was mistaken, this was an offer to apologize a second time. Or perhaps to offer a fuller, more satisfactory explanation of their confrontation.

"So what *is* this thing between us?" the policeman asked, confirming Miles's suspicion. "I mean, I understand tired. But that this afternoon? That didn't seem like tired. It was something, all right, but it didn't seem like tired. And before with your dad? That didn't seem like tired either."

"What did it seem like?" Miles asked, both curious and hopeful that whatever Jimmy Minty came up with wouldn't be too close to the truth.

"That's what I've been parked here trying to figure out."

"Look, I shouldn't have corrected your grammar, Jimmy. That was condescending and mean-spirited. You're right to be pissed off."

The other man didn't say anything for a second, but then threw his hands up in the air so unexpectedly that Miles flinched. "Ah, to hell with it. You said you were sorry, right?"

This, Miles noted, was a third opportunity.

"I saw the kids earlier," Minty said, regarding him carefully. "Mine and yours. Bunch of others. Heading over to Fairhaven for pizza. Or so they claimed."

"I'm not so sure that's a great idea."

"Exactly what I said." Minty nodded once more. "Then again, two more years and they'll both be off in college and we won't have a clue what they're doing, am I right?"

"I guess that's true," Miles pretended to agree.

"You ever wish you were young again?"

"Never," Miles said, glad he could answer at least one of these questions with unadorned truth. "It was awful."

"Oh, I don't know—"

"We were stupid," Miles said, surprised by the depth of his conviction. "*I* was, anyway."

"You know what I was thinking before you showed up? I was remembering how Billy Barnes had me come up to UMO that time. Must've been the year after him and me graduated." He went on to tell Miles about the frat party, or at least the part about the boy with the naked girl over his shoulder. "Boy, that made me mad," he concluded. "At the time I didn't even realize."

"Well, it was a horrible thing," Miles agreed, trying not to imagine his own daughter at her first college kegger.

Jimmy Minty looked at him blankly. "Oh, the girl?" he said, blinking. "Yeah, I guess that was pretty shitty, but what really pissed *me* off was those frat boys. How they all knew what was going on. The way they treated you like some fucking idiot because they understood and you didn't. Was it like that where you went?"

Miles couldn't help smiling. "I went to a tiny Catholic college,

Jimmy. You saw more in your first five minutes on campus than I did in three and a half years."

"I don't mean that," Jimmy Minty said, growing visibly irritated at not being understood. "I'm not talking about pussy. I'm talking about the way they all make you feel. Like they belong, and you don't. Like they don't even have to look at you. Was it like that with the Catholics?"

Miles studied him carefully. Dusk was falling, and even in the dim light of the front seat, Miles could see that the man's face was red with recollected outrage. Something about the combination of innocence and urgency in his question suggested the latter stages of intoxication, though the policeman displayed none of the other symptoms. It was as if Minty had posed the question in his mind all those years ago and hadn't had the opportunity to ask it until now. For this reason Miles took his time answering.

"There were times when I felt out of place, I suppose," he admitted. "Times I felt inadequate, especially at the beginning. There were lots of kids from Boston, even Portland, big-city kids who knew plenty of things I didn't. But then at some point you realize you don't feel so incompetent anymore. One morning you wake up in your dorm room and think, this is *my* bed I've been sleeping in. That's my desk and those are my books and this is my world. After that, it's home that starts feeling strange."

The other man had been listening carefully, and Miles realized that, despite his care, what he'd just said had confirmed some dark suspicion Minty couldn't, or wouldn't, let go of. "So I didn't stay long enough, is what you're telling me."

"Well, one night . . . one party—"

"You're saying if I'd stayed longer, I would've become one of those frat boys."

Actually, Miles had no doubt of it. By his sophomore year, Jimmy Minty would have been the boy with the naked girl over his shoulder, but he knew better than to say this. "No—"

"Well, then I'm *glad* I didn't stay."

"Jimmy—"

"No, fuck it, Miles. I'm trying to tell you something here, okay? You mind if I tell you something, or do you know it all?"

Again Miles paused before answering. "There's no reason to get worked up, Jimmy. You asked me a question and I answered it."

"Now, just shut up a minute. Here's the deal. I'm not *getting* worked up, okay? I've *been* worked up since this afternoon. You think you can make fun of me in front of Miss Whiting and a bunch of other people, then come over here and say you're sorry when there's nobody around to hear you, and that squares things. And you know what? It would've, except I saw that look on your face when I mentioned your daughter and Zack. I saw it, all right. Don't tell me I didn't, okay, because that's just insulting me all over again."

Miles put his hand on the door handle. "I'm sorry I upset you, Jimmy."

"No, you just set here a minute. Take your hand off that door 'til I finish."

Miles did as he was told.

"I'm trying to tell you *that's* what's between you and me, not some bullshit like how tired you are. See, this town doesn't seem strange to me. It never did, not for one second. After that night in Orono? When I crossed that bridge into Empire Falls, right then was about the happiest minute in my whole damn life. You can laugh all you want, but it's true."

"I'm not laughing, Jimmy—"

"See, I cared who won that football game today. Maybe people like you think that makes me a nobody, but you know what? I don't give a fuck. Mr. Empire Falls? That's me. Last one to leave, turn out the lights, right? This town *is* me, and I'm *it*. I'm not one of those that left and then came back. I been here all long. Right here is where I been, and it's where I'll be when the sun comes up tomorrow, so if you—"

"I never said—"

"Thing is, Miles, people in this town like you. A lot of people. You got friends, even some important friends. I admit it. But here's something that might surprise you. People like me too. Something else? *I* got friends. Might surprise you to hear we even got some of the *same* friends. You're not the only one people like, okay? And I'll tell you something else. What people around here like best about me? They like it that they're more like me than they are like you. They look at me and they see the town they grew up in. They see their first girlfriend. They see the first high school football game they ever went to. You know what they see when they look at you? That they ain't good enough. They look at you and see everything they ever done wrong in their lives. They hear you talk and maybe they're thinking the same thing you are, except they can't say it like you do and they know they won't ever get any credit. They see you and your buddy the principal with your heads together, deciding how things are gonna be, talking the way you talk and making your little jokes, and they know they'll never get no place with either one of you, not ever. But me? Maybe they just might get someplace with me, and *that's* why they like me. That's why I'll probably be the next chief of police. They like my attitude, I guess you could say. And you know what? An attitude like yours? An attitude like yours leads to things."

Miles had finally had enough. "Are you threatening me, Jimmy?" he asked. "Because you aren't the chief of police yet. Does Bill Daws know who's taking his job?"

Just a flicker of fear registered behind Minty's eyes as he calculated whether he'd gone too far, but then it was gone. "Threatening you?" he said, incredulous. "*Threatening* you. When did I ever want to be anything except your friend? Tell me that. When?"

And of course Miles knew that in the twisted, grotesque way of many true things, Jimmy Minty was speaking straight from the heart. It *was* what he wanted. And he was genuinely mystified as to why he couldn't seem to have it. Which did *not*—Miles had to admit as he got out of the car and crossed Empire Avenue—make him stupid. After all, what was the whole wide world but a place for people to yearn for their hearts' impossible desires, for those desires to become entrenched in defiance of logic, plausibility, and even the passage of time, as eternal as polished marble?

CHAPTER 18

A T FIVE MINUTES TO SIX on Sunday morning a groggy Miles Roby came downstairs to prepare for the breakfast shift and found a man slumped over the counter, his forehead flat on the Formica, as if it had been superglued there. It took a moment for Miles to recognize Buster, his fry cook, back from his annual, heroic bender, which this year looked to have been damn near the death of him. He'd brought along a copy of the Sunday paper, and a fresh pot of coffee was steaming on the Bunn-O-Matic, which suggested that Buster had not entirely forgotten his skills.

Rather than wake him, Miles fired up the grill and filled its gleaming surface with bacon strips, about three pounds' worth. When they started to sizzle, he took up the newspaper, the front page of which was devoted almost exclusively to Saturday's football game, with two photos of Zack Minty: a large one of him brandishing the fumble he'd recovered and a smaller one of him helping the woozy Fairhaven quarterback off the field. The boy had not returned for the second half after the late hit that temporarily knocked him out cold. He'd sat, dazed-looking, on the bench, while Empire Falls chipped away at the score, a field goal here, a touchdown there, until the home team tied the game with a little over a minute to go. No surprise, the *Empire Gazette* saw the game in pretty much the same light as the hometown fans did, as a humiliating defeat for Fairhaven, which had led at the half by a score of 24–0.

There was a surprise on the front page of the paper's lifestyle section. For the last several years, on Sundays, the *Gazette* had taken to running old photos of Empire Falls and its denizens during their glory days. The series was called "The Way It Was," and earlier in the summer they'd run a photo of the Empire Grill, circa 1960, with old Roger Sperry looking like he belonged on a lobster boat instead of behind a cash register, and a lunch counter full of working men extending into the background behind him, and the restaurant's grainy, shadowy booths full of customers. A sign on the back wall advertised a hamburg steak with grilled onions, mashed potatoes, a vegetable and roll for a buck and a quarter. One of the younger men pictured at the counter still came in and always sat on the same end stool, if it was available. For reasons that mystified Miles, the series apparently had a cheering effect on the citizenry. People actually seemed to enjoy recalling that on a Saturday afternoon forty years ago Empire Avenue was bustling with people and cars and commerce, whereas now, of course, you could strafe it with automatic weapons and not harm a soul.

Some characters in the *Gazette* photos were identified in the captions, but others became queries. Can you identify this man? This woman? Who were these people and what did they mean to us? the photos seemed to ask. Where have they gone? Why do we remain? "The Way It Was" always caused Miles to feel as if the town itself was awaiting some cataclysm that would finish them all off.

Today's photo was of the old Empire Shirt Factory's office staff, taken in 1966, the year before the factory closed, and the only person in the second row *not* looking at the camera was a young and beautiful Grace Roby. Miles quickly checked the caption below, relieved to see that his mother was among the identified, because it would have broken his heart to see a "Does anyone know this woman?" affixed to her. Still, seeing his mother so unexpectedly gave Miles a sensation not unlike the one you'd have standing on railroad tracks and feeling, or imagining, the far-off trembling of something large racing your way— not danger, exactly, unless for some inexplicable reason you were duty bound to remain right where you were. Perhaps it was the fact that Grace was not looking at the camera, but rather off at an oblique angle, that suggested she might have been listening to that same distant rumbling. If indeed it was an intimation of her own mortality she was hearing, Miles reflected, it had been closer than she thought.

Several others in the photograph were people Miles recognized, some dead, some living, some still residing in Empire Falls, others long gone. In one case he thought it was a man he knew well, then realized it had to be the man's father. And at the end of the first row stood a small, white-bearded man dressed in a three-piece suit, C. B. Whiting himself, proprietor of the Empire Shirt Factory. If anything grim was bearing down on Mrs. Whiting's husband, he did not as yet seem aware of it. How many years after this photo was taken, Miles tried to remember, did he return from exile in Mexico and put the cold barrel of a revolver against his own pulsing temple? How strange, he thought, that just yesterday he'd stood at the foot of this man's grave.

After the game, once the crowd had dispersed and they'd made their slow, careful way back to Miles's car, Cindy had asked if he'd be willing to take a short walk, and he'd made the mistake of agreeing before asking exactly what she had in mind.

"I think it's the prettiest place in town," his companion said as they followed the well-tended path, Cindy leaning more on her cane now than on Miles, though she did have a firm grip on his elbow just in case. Losing her balance on the bleachers and pitching forward into Jimmy Minty's arms had unnerved her.

At her suggestion they'd parked just outside the east gate, the closest one to the Whiting section of the cemetery. Now in the late afternoon, the sky had clouded over and a chilly wind had come up, rustling brown leaves along the path.

"It *is* peaceful," Miles had admitted, sniffing the air. Was it his imagination or was the breeze redolent of cat piss? Since entering the cemetery Miles had seen several cats darting among the stones. They couldn't possibly be feral, could they? He didn't like to think what would offer them sustenance in a cemetery. The swelling where the Whiting cat had bitten him had gone down, but the hand began to pulse, inviting another round of scratching. This time Miles decided to resist. A police cruiser rolled silently by on the other side of the cast-iron fence about a hundred yards away, too far to make out whether Jimmy Minty was at the wheel. Cindy also tracked its progress until the cruiser turned onto Elm and headed back toward town.

When they arrived at the top of the hill, the river was just visible in the distance, and a shaft of bright afternoon sun from a break in the clouds electrified the blue water. When they stopped before her father's grave, Cindy said, "He brings me here sometimes."

Miles considered this statement. Knowing his companion's lifelong distaste for metaphor, he decided she was not claiming that C. B. Whiting drew her to this place by supernatural means.

"Who?" he decided to ask.

"James."

No help. "James?"

"James Minty." Now it was her turn to regard Miles dubiously, as if he were either slow or not paying close attention. He tried to think whether he'd ever heard anyone else call Minty "James," then gave up.

"I haven't been a very good friend, have I?" he confessed, hating to think that with respect to this poor woman he'd remained as stingy as an adult as he'd been as a boy. After all, how much time would it have taken him to bring her to visit her father's grave on her rare, short visits to Empire Falls.

"Oh, Miles, you were married," she said, apparently reading his thoughts.

There was a large pot of what had once been marigolds on C. B. Whiting's grave. They'd drooped and gone brown, the pot itself filling with brittle leaves. Here the smell of urine was even more pronounced than it had been before. "I put these here just a few days ago," Cindy said, bending over precariously to examine the marigolds. "They should have lasted." She paused. "James works for my mother, you know. I'm sure she paid him for his time."

"Works for her how, exactly?" Miles asked.

"Different ways. He looks after the house when she travels. He helped her put in a security system. Keeps an eye on the old factories."

Miles nodded, suppressing a smile. If there was one person in Empire Falls he wouldn't want to know the intricacies of his security system, assuming he could afford one and had things worth stealing, that person was Jimmy Minty. But perhaps he was being unfair. It was possible Jimmy'd be both grateful and loyal to anyone who treated him decently. And Miles realized too that he'd made a mistake, twice, in provoking him, a mistake it would be either humiliating or impossible to correct.

"Actually," Cindy continued, "she expects poor James to be on call."

"Your mother expects *everyone* to be on call."

"I won't tell her you said that," she said, taking his hand and giving it a squeeze.

"You can if you like," he said cheerfully.

"Dear Miles," she said. "You're the only person she allows to talk back to her. Did you know that?"

"Not that it gets me anywhere."

"She thinks of you as a son, you know."

He couldn't help chuckling at this. "Yeah. A son she's always been disappointed by."

"He was *so* unhappy," Cindy said, as if this new remark flowed naturally from his. Letting go of his hand, she stepped closer to the monument and traced her father's engraved name with her index finger. Compared to the monuments marking the graves of the other Whiting males, C.B.'s was the runt of the litter, though cut in the same style and basic shape as the other, larger stones that marked the nearby graves of Honus and Elijah. Its being significantly smaller gave the impression that his stone alone had not grown after being planted, as if the corpses of his predecessors had already sucked all the nutrients out of the soil. The dead marigolds only furthered this impression. "Mother says he was a weak man who never wanted to be a Whiting but still enjoyed the money and privilege. Did you know he had a whole other family in Mexico?"

"No, I didn't." In fact, he found it fairly shocking.

"After he . . . well, after he died, Mother got a letter from the woman. She wanted money, of course. For herself and the little boy they had. She told my mother they'd been very happy, but I don't believe that. It was Mother who wouldn't allow him to come home."

Miles nodded, wondering if she'd come to this conclusion out of desperate need. As a boy he'd often wondered why Max would disappear for months at a time, leaving him and his mother, and later his brother, to their own devices, so he assumed that Cindy Whiting had probably asked the same questions and perhaps even blamed herself, as Miles had. If she believed her father wanted to come home, it was probably because he told her so in Christmas and birthday cards. At the same time, it occurred to Miles that a man who'd built a hacienda in central Maine might find himself right at home in Mexico. "Did she ever say why?"

"She said he'd been a bad boy. Those were her exact words," she recalled bitterly. "I used to beg to visit him in Mexico, but she wouldn't allow that either. 'Your father's been a bad boy. He didn't want his family and now he can't have one.'"

The smell of urine was starting to get to Miles. "Is it a good idea to be out here in this chill?"

"You mean me?"

Miles gave a faint, helpless nod.

"Dear Miles, you're so sweet to worry," she said, squeezing his hand again, "but I'm past all that now. Even my doctors say so. I want to *live* my life now, not end it. Especially with things looking up." Meaning himself, Miles feared. "We can go back, though, if you want."

They returned to the car, as Miles knew they would, by the path that took them past his mother's grave. There against her headstone sat an identical pot of marigolds, except these were flourishing, their yellow petals bright and healthy-looking.

"It's as if even the flowers know they're marking the grave of a good person," Cindy said sadly. "Do you think that's silly, Miles?"

"Yes, I do," he confessed. "But I know what you mean."

BUSTER SNORTED AWAKE, looking like a man who belonged in one of the *Empire Gazette* photographs, among the missing persons. Miles dug the check he'd been holding onto since the first of September from under the cash register's drawer and handed it to Buster, who studied it for a moment and then asked, "My fired?"

Miles poured him a cup of coffee and another for himself. "I was planning to put an ad in the paper tomorrow morning," he admitted. "You were AWOL quite a while. What's wrong with your eye?"

This was only the most obvious of the many questions Miles might've asked. Buster was pale, emaciated, filthy and looked dispirited, embarrassed and sick as a dog. Moreover, his eye was swollen shut and oozing pus at the corner. Miles felt certain that any number of stories were in the offing by way of explaining his sorry condition. He made a mental note not to let Buster and Max work the same shift until the former had a chance to put himself back together. The sight of either man would give anybody misgivings about the food, but the two of them together would send people running for the parking lot.

"Spider bite," Buster said, gingerly daubing pus onto the corner of a napkin. Miles had to look away. His stomach was never that great in the morning. "There's a weird-looking boy standing outside," Buster said. "Claims he works here."

Miles went around the counter to the front door, where John Voss stood motionless on the steps, hands in his pockets. Yesterday afternoon's warmth seemed a distant memory. This morning it was winter in the air. The boy glanced up when he heard the lock turn in the door, then quickly back at the ground.

"He does work here," Miles told Buster, as he returned to the counter. "He's our new busboy."

"Looks more like a damn serial killer."

"*You're* the one who looks like a serial killer," Miles pointed out. "He's on the quiet side, but so far he seems like a pretty good worker."

Both men looked over at the door, aware that John Voss had not come in, perhaps, Miles surmised, because he hadn't been specifically told to. Sure enough, when he returned to the door, John Voss was right where Miles had left him, apparently awaiting an invitation. "You can come in," Miles told him.

The boy nodded, scurrying inside with surprising speed. Miles followed him into the back room. "You can start on the pots," he said, pointing at the large stack left over from the night before. They'd been understaffed again, and Miles had said just to leave them soaking, knowing the new boy was coming in early. Besides, Sunday was a short day. The restaurant opened only for breakfast, though so few showed up it was hardly worth the effort. With Friday and Saturday nights doing so well, it made sense to close and give everyone a day off. That would also allow him to attend Sunday-morning Mass, which he missed. Most weeks he found a way to slip out long enough to catch the five-thirty on Saturday afternoon, but for an old altar boy, that wasn't quite the same. Yesterday, thanks to his late-afternoon cemetery tour with Cindy Whiting, he'd missed Mass entirely, leaving him feeling slightly unmoored this morning.

Recalling Horace's strange warning on Friday night, as well as Otto Meyer's gratitude for his having given the boy a job, Miles studied John Voss as he filled the sink and began work, trying to imagine what the rest of this strange boy's life would be like. He was off to such a poor start that, to Miles, he seemed destined to become the subject of a future query. *Does anybody know the boy in this photograph?* That is, if he ever made it into a photo. It was the Zack Mintys who got into the newspapers. On the other hand, who knew? The boy might turn out to be the next Bill Gates. "Congratulations, by the way," Miles said. When the boy stopped scrubbing but didn't look up: "I heard you had a painting selected for the art show."

"Tick, too," he said, still without looking up, though Miles could see his eyes darting nervously, as if fearful that volunteering so much information all at once might have dire consequences.

Out front again, Miles flipped the rows of bacon. He always cooked it about three quarters in advance of actual orders, then crisped it to suit his customers. While his stomach was feeling better, the odd feeling of standing on railroad tracks, awaiting an approaching train, was still there—the result, perhaps, of another largely sleepless night. He and David had closed up at ten-thirty, and Miles, exhausted, had gone upstairs and fallen asleep with his clothes on, television remote in hand, before he could even turn the set on. He'd awakened with a start from a nightmare in which he'd been searching for Cindy Whiting's cane beneath the Empire Field bleachers, but instead he found Tick, curled up asleep among the hot dog wrappers and empty Styrofoam cups. Except she wasn't asleep. He realized this in the instant before his violent twitch sent the television remote skittering under a pallet containing boxes of paper towels. His watch said it was midnight, too late to call, but before he could talk himself out of his panic, he'd already dialed his old telephone number. Janine answered on the first ring.

"Did Tick make it home okay?" he blurted.

"Miles," she said, as if she had a long list of people she allowed to call her at this time of night, and he wasn't on it.

"Is Tick back?"

"Not yet."

"It's midnight, Janine."

"I know what time it is, Miles. Is something the matter?"

"Would you mind calling me when she gets home?"

"You didn't answer my question."

"It's stupid," he admitted. In fact, the sound of his soon-to-be-ex-wife's voice, even its cosmic annoyance, was reassuring. "I was asleep. In this dream . . . she was hurt . . ."

Her voice relented a little. "I'm sure she's fine, Miles. Her deadline is midnight. She'll be home soon."

"Call me anyway?" he asked. "And tell Walt I'm sorry about phoning so late."

"You want me to wake him up, or tell him in the morning?"

The annoyance had ratcheted back up a couple of notches, but not, apparently, at him. "Morning would be fine."

"Good," she said. "A man his age needs his rest."

What in the world was *this* about? Then again, Miles reminded himself, he didn't really want to know. And yet. "Is everything okay, Janine?"

"Everything's peachy, Miles. Just peachy. Why do you ask?"

"Call me when she gets in, okay?"

"You don't want to talk to me, is that what you're saying?"

"Are you"—he paused—"drinking, Janine?"

"Maybe a little. Is that all right with you?"

"It's none of my business."

"You got that right," she said. Then, after a beat: "I mentioned it to Walt about the house again. I told him I wanted to buy out your share as soon as we're married."

"What was his response to that?"

"You ever watch a cow chew a cud?"

"You don't have to marry him, you know."

"Yeah, well, I want to, okay?"

"Sure. I'm not saying you shouldn't, just that you don't have to."

"I know, Miles. As far as you're concerned, I can do anything I damn well please—including go to hell, right?"

Conversations like this one, Miles realized, were the price of poor impulse control. "Janine."

"That Cindy Whiting you were with at the football game?"

"Yes."

"If you married her, it wouldn't matter about this shitty little house. You'd own half the damn town. You could pay for Tick's college and move away and never have to see me again."

Unless Miles was mistaken, she was now quietly weeping, her hand over the phone.

"Janine . . ."

Muffled silence for a long beat, then: "They just pulled in, okay?"

"Janine."

"Your daughter's safe. I'm looking out the window at her right now. Go back to sleep."

"Janine—"

But she'd hung up.

"ANYHOW, CAN I have today off?" Buster wondered, as if to suggest that he'd had an even worse night than Miles.

Miles deposited the prepped bacon into a stainless-steel tub. "I insist," he said. "In fact, I really don't want you coming in until that eye quits draining."

"I bet I have to get the fucker lanced," Buster said morosely, as if life offered up little more than a string of such horrible necessities. "I don't know why I keep going up into the Allagash. People think there's nothing going on up there, but they're wrong. There's all kinds of shit happening, all of it bad."

Miles bladed most of the lake of bacon grease into the trough with the side of his spatula, then added some chopped onions to the grill.

"You have any idea how high the rate of alcoholism runs up in The County?" Buster said urgently.

"Normally, or when you're visiting?"

"Normally."

"Pretty bad?"

"Worse," Buster said, as if prepared for a lowball estimate. "Of course, up there near the border, they don't share in the rest of the state's prosperity."

Miles turned around to study his fry cook for the merest trace of irony.

"I guess I could eat a couple strips of that bacon," Buster said. "Maybe an egg."

Miles scrambled two of them and set them on a plate along with some bacon and the toast. Buster dug in with better appetite than Miles would've imagined possible for a man with yolk seeping out of one eye. "You shouldn't have waited for me," he said when he pushed his cleaned plate away. "You should have given my job to some-body else."

"I know that," Miles admitted.

"You're too softhearted," Buster continued. "People take advantage of you."

"I know that, too," Miles admitted, hoping to terminate the analysis.

Outside, he glimpsed Charlene's rusted-out old Hyundai as it turned off Empire into the lot, and for the first time in more than twenty years her proximity failed to cause Miles Roby's heart to leap, as if Buster's exhausted, pus-leaking defeatism had been subtly trans-mitted over the Formica counter and somehow entered Miles's own bloodstream. Buster had set his coffee cup down on the newspaper, which acted as an inky sponge, and by the time Miles moved the cup onto the counter, the ring it left had ruined his mother's face.

"You're a damn fool, is why," Buster said, suddenly angry. He stared as Miles blotted the newsprint with a napkin and then, after a long beat, he began to cry. "I'm sorry, Miles," he said after a minute. Maybe he'd heard the back door open and close and knew that in another minute Charlene would join them. She was far too beautiful a woman to cry in front of. "I don't know what come over me. I really don't."

"Go on home, Buster," Miles said without looking up from the photo, where, though his mother was no longer recognizable, he'd spotted a detail that he hadn't noticed before. There was no doubt about it now. Something *was* approaching. The tracks he was standing on were vibrating with the force of it, yet he was powerless to move away as much as a step. He sensed rather than saw Buster slide off his stool and disappear, and he had no idea how many times Charlene, standing at his elbow, had to say his name before he was able to meet her alarmed, questioning eyes. "Are you all right?" she wanted to know. "You look weird."

Had she gotten there a few seconds sooner, she'd have seen him put the tip of his index finger over the lower half of C. B. Whiting's bearded face, but even then she wouldn't have understood what it meant—that the face now staring back at him was not C. B. Whiting's, as identified by the staff of the *Empire Gazette*, but Charlie Mayne's.

[CHAPTER 19]

BY THE TIME *the bus finally pulled into the Fairhaven terminal, the promise Miles had made to his mother earlier that morning—to say nothing about Charlie Mayne—was beginning to weigh on him. He hadn't imagined that a promise made in safety on a ferryboat docked in Vineyard Haven could grow as weighty as this one had in a matter of hours. In Woods Hole they'd boarded a bus to Boston, where they'd changed to another heading north to Maine. In Portland they'd changed again, this time to a bus whose destination was Fairhaven, which was literally the end of the line. Empire Falls itself, of course, had recently become one stop beyond the end of the line when bus service was suspended the year before, and there was talk now of closing the Fairhaven terminal, which consisted of a window at the rear of the smoke shop and a small designated parking area around back. Grace had parked the Dodge there when they left for Martha's Vineyard a week earlier, though that seemed much longer ago now. Neither she nor Miles was surprised to discover it missing upon their return. To Miles it was as if they'd been away forever, so long that a car left unattended might simply dematerialize, like water in the bottom of a glass. To Grace it meant that Max was out of jail.*

Though a short distance, Fairhaven to Empire Falls was a long-distance call, and Grace had to make several before she was able to reach someone willing to come fetch them. They waited in a coffee shop across the street and, since it was well past dinnertime, Grace insisted that Miles eat something, even though he claimed he wasn't hungry. The fumes from all the buses, combined with the fact that he'd soon be seeing his father again, had made him sick to his stomach, but when the hot dog came it smelled good and he ate the whole thing, Grace watching him sadly as she drank her coffee. When it came time to pay and Grace opened her billfold, Miles saw there was just enough to cover what they'd ordered. Unless his mother had money squirreled away in another compartment, they'd made it back home, or almost home, with only loose change to spare. Which led Miles to wonder what his mother had planned to do if Charlie hadn't showed up and started paying for things.

The woman who came to bring them back to Empire Falls was younger than Grace and very homely, Miles thought, and she drove a car that was in even worse shape than their Dodge. Miles, of course, was relegated to the backseat with the luggage. The trunk wouldn't open, the woman said, and Miles couldn't help thinking how different everything had become in a single day. This time last night he and his mother had been flying across the island in Charlie's slick canary-yellow sports car after consuming a dinner that had cost (Miles had sneaked a look at the check) more than fifty dollars. Tonight, his hot dog had cost thirty-five cents, his mother's coffee a quarter, and even then they'd barely been able to afford it.

Maud—the young woman who'd picked them up at the station—talked pretty much the entire way to Empire Falls, catching Grace up on all that had happened. Once again there was a rumor that the mill was going to be sold, this one fueled by the fact that C. B. Whiting had gone off on Thursday without telling anyone where, causing people to speculate that he'd gone to Atlanta or some other place down south to put the finishing touches on the sale. If true, it meant that some of them wouldn't have jobs at the shirt factory much longer, especially those like Grace and Maud, who worked in the office. New management would bring in their own people for those positions, and it was common knowledge that Southerners worked for even less than Mainers. The fledgling union was already talking strategy. And Max, she added, her voice low so Miles wouldn't overhear, was again a free man. He'd been over to the mill looking for Grace earlier in the week.

Maud seemed not to notice Grace's silence in response to all of this, and they were nearly to Empire Falls before it occurred to the young woman to inquire how their vacation had been. "What's it like being on an island?" she wanted to know, reminding Miles that until a week ago he'd believed islands to be strips of land somehow floating on the water that surrounded them. That's what they looked like on maps, and before arriving on Martha's Vineyard he'd wondered if the ground beneath your feet would feel as solid as it did on "real" land. If everyone on an island were to move to one side, would it tip over? He knew that couldn't be possible, but still he'd been glad to see just how solid everything felt when they stepped off the ferry. It was returning home, he now understood, that made everything so tippy.

His father wasn't home *when Miles and his mother got there, and neither was the Dodge, but there was a note attached to the refrigerator with a magnet. He'd gone to paint a house in Castine and would be back by the end of the week. Miles located the crumpled note in the trash where Grace had tossed it, smoothed it out and read it start to finish, surprised that it said pretty much what his mother had said it did, no more, no less. It seemed to Miles that a man who'd sat in jail for a week while his wife and son vacationed on Martha's Vineyard would've come out with more to say. With so much time to think, he might have grown sorrowful, or angry, or determined, or reformed. His father had apparently rejected all of these options and come out of jail determined to paint somebody's house in Castine. Miles himself was not alluded to in the note—a relief, since it had occurred to him that Max might regard him as his mother's accomplice. Until a few days ago Miles had not suspected the existence of men like Charlie Mayne who might, if given a chance, steal another man's wife, and judging from the note, his father still hadn't tumbled to that possibility either; or if he had, he didn't blame Miles for not being up to the task of protecting his mother's virtue.*

Once back in Empire Falls, Miles and Grace didn't really need either Max or the Dodge. Miles could bike to baseball practice or wherever else he needed to go, and she walked to work in the morning. Like most of the women in the main office, she brown-bagged her lunch to save both money and time. If you ate a quick sandwich at your desk, you could go home at four-thirty instead of five. C. B. Whiting, the mill's owner, still hadn't returned on Monday, so every evening that week the phone rang and rang, girls from the office wanting to know if Grace, who was generally acknowledged to be first among equals at the main office, had heard anything new.

By Friday Max had not returned as promised, and it became clear to Miles that Grace was falling into a deep depression. The reason, he felt certain, had little to do with the possibility that she might lose her job and even less with her husband's continued absence. She was thinking, Miles could tell, about Charlie Mayne and his promise that everything would work out. Each time the phone rang in the evening, Grace leapt for it, her face bright with hope, only to collapse when she recognized the voice of Maud or another of the office girls flush with another rumor. According to one, C. B. Whiting had returned at last, but immediately left again. Twice Miles observed his mother making phone calls herself, then quickly hanging up.

On Monday of the second week, old Honus Whiting, C.B.'s father,

showed up unexpectedly and called a general meeting of all the mill's work-
ers, announcing that for the immediate future he himself would again be in
charge of Empire Manufacturing. He knew there had been a lot of specula-
tion that the mill was being sold, but he wanted everyone to know that the
rumors were untrue. On the contrary, another Whiting mill was being
opened in Mexico, and C.B. would be temporarily relocating there to get the
new operation up and running. Francine Whiting, C.B.'s wife, who recently
had learned she was pregnant, would join her husband in Mexico next
month, once suitable accommodations could be made ready, and she would
winter there, returning in the spring to have the baby, which everyone hoped
would be a male heir to guide Whiting Enterprises International into the
next century. The employees of all three mills listened to what the old man
had to say, and when he was finished they went back to work. Not much of
what they'd heard sounded anything like the truth.

That evening Miles returned late from baseball practice and found his
mother sobbing on the bed in the room she shared with her husband, at least
when Max was around to share it, and Miles immediately suspected she'd
gotten the phone call she'd been waiting for from Charlie Mayne. She called
in sick the next day, and the next. Mornings she was sicker than she'd been
on Martha's Vineyard, and evenings she could barely be coaxed out of the
bedroom long enough to fix something for supper. By the end of the week
Miles was truly alarmed. Grace had such a wild, desperate look in her eyes
that he began to hope for his father's return, something he'd been dreading
because of all the questions that would inevitably get asked. Worse than need-
ing to keep all the secrets he felt entrusted with was the knowledge that his
father would want answers to other questions as well, answers Miles himself
did not possess. But day after day, neither Max nor the Dodge turned up.

On Saturday afternoon of the third week, the door to his parents' bed-
room opened and Grace appeared in a dark dress that Miles hadn't seen her
wear since the funeral of a neighbor who'd been killed on the swing shift at
Empire Paper last spring. She wore no jewelry or makeup, but she'd done up
her hair and would've looked nice, Miles thought, if she hadn't lost so much
weight. An entirely different sort of nice from the nice way she'd looked in
her white summer dress on the island, when all the men had turned to stare,
but nice, still. When she announced that it had been more than a month since
either of them had been to confession, she met Miles's eye meaningfully.

Though it was a sunny afternoon in late August, several nights during
the week had been chilly, and Miles noticed during their silent walk to St.
Catherine's that a few of the uppermost leaves on the elms had already begun
to turn. Grace didn't seem to notice this or anything else; she looked like a

woman marching to her own execution. She'd timed their arrival so they would be the last of the afternoon's penitents. Miles, she insisted, should enter the confessional first and, when he finished, say his penance quickly and wait for her outside. As always, they hoped for the new young priest, but as luck would have it, when Miles slid onto the kneeler inside the dark confessional and the velvet curtain was pulled back on the other side of the latticework, Father Tom's dark silhouette was revealed, and the older priest's stern voice urged him to recount his sins so that they might be forgiven.

Miles had received his first communion the year before, so of course he knew that to conceal one mortal sin was to commit yet another. Since returning from Martha's Vineyard he'd grown certain that he, not just his mother, had somehow sinned there, though he wasn't sure what sort of sin it was or how to explain it to the man on the other side of the lattice. He knew he'd betrayed his father by promising to keep his mother's secret, just as he was certain that if he broke that promise he would be betraying her. In either case it was a sin to try to keep a secret from God, who already knew. Why exactly it was necessary to confess what God already knew had been explained in religious instruction by the very man who now sat on the other side of the lattice, but the delicate logic of it was confusing to Miles at the time and eluded him entirely now. He had come to confession armed with a list of sins he hadn't committed, sins he hoped were equal in magnitude to whatever he was concealing, and he further hoped God would understand that his reticence about coming clean didn't stem from any desire to make himself look good. Father Tom listened to his litany of substitute sins and offered penance with the air of a man who is convinced not so much of the truth of what he's just heard as of the general human depravity in which such behavior has its origins. At the altar railing Miles knelt and said his Our Fathers and Hail Marys and was about to leave when he heard the confessional door open and saw his mother following Father Tom into the sacristy.

He sat on the steps outside for half an hour, and when his mother finally appeared her face was ashen. He guided her home as you might lead a blind woman, and when they arrived she went directly into the bedroom and closed the door behind her. The next morning, Sunday, they went to Mass, but during the sermon Grace became ill and after instructing Miles to stay where he was, she stumbled down the side aisle, one hand over her mouth, and out the side door. Perhaps anticipating this, she had wanted to sit nearer the rear of the church than was their custom, but even so, people turned to watch her stagger out, and it seemed to Miles that Father Tom made matters worse by pausing in his sermon until the church door swung shut behind her. There was an Esso station a block up the street, and Miles suspected his mother had gone there to be sick, but when communion began she still had not returned. Miles waited, then joined the very end of the line, though painfully aware that he should not receive the host. He'd lied in confession yesterday, and knew better than to invite God into his impure body. On the other hand, since he had gone to confession, it would seem strange if he didn't take communion, so he received the wafer on a tongue so dry with guilt and shame that instead of dissolving, it remained there like a scrap of thin cotton cloth. He was still trying to swallow the host when he felt his mother slide back into the pew next to him, looking pale and weak. When she took his hand and squeezed hard, it seemed that what she was trying to convey to him was exactly what he feared most, that she was going to die as a result of what she'd done on Martha's Vineyard. She'd caught something there and brought the illness home with her. Going to confession yesterday hadn't made her better, so Miles wondered if she, too, had lied to the priest, if at the moment she'd realized it was Father Tom, who knew her, instead of the younger priest, she decided to keep her secret. Father Tom must have suspected as much and made her go with him into the sacristy, but even there she must have refused to tell him about Charlie Mayne.

Miles was aware that this scenario was problematic. For one thing, his mother had gotten sick days before Charlie Mayne showed up; but he reasoned that maybe she'd made up her mind in advance to do whatever they'd done, and that was where the sin had begun, in the wickedness of a thought, as he'd learned in religious instruction. Maybe getting sick had been a warning from God that she'd chosen to ignore. This, then, was the price of her short-lived happiness.

When they returned home from Mass, Miles half expected his mother to retire to the bedroom, but instead she told him she had to go out. When he asked her where she was going, she said only that there was something she had to do.

Miles knew it was wrong, but he followed her. Since on Sunday there were few people on the street, Miles was careful lest she turn around suddenly and catch him, but it soon became clear that she was too preoccupied to notice anything. When she got to the shirt factory, Miles thought for a moment that this was her destination, and that she intended to go inside, but after pausing there for a minute, she continued on. At the Iron Bridge, to his surprise, she turned left onto the pedestrian walkway, and there was no way he could follow without making his presence known. When Grace was halfway across, the truth came to him. She intended to jump. He was so sure of it that when she didn't, when she walked right past the place where you'd jump if you were going to, Miles still couldn't banish the idea.

Because what other explanation could there be? After all, there was little on the other side of the river but the country club and two or three houses owned by rich people. On the sloping lawn of one of these, the nearest, was a gazebo where a solitary woman sat staring out across the falls. She was too far away for Miles to be sure, of course, but she seemed to be tracking his mother's progress across the bridge. Perhaps seeing her sitting there had prevented Grace from jumping. Maybe she now intended to jump on the way back.

Miles waited a few minutes to see if his mother, once she reached the far side, would turn back, but she didn't. And by the time he finally left his post at the town side of the bridge, it seemed that the woman in the gazebo was staring at him.

ON LABOR DAY, *without warning, Max returned. Miles, out enjoying the last day of his summer vacation, came home at noon for lunch and found the Dodge parked outside and Max, shirtless and berry-brown from a summer's worth of painting people's windows shut, sitting at the kitchen table, reading the* Empire Gazette *as if hoping to find in it news of what Miles and his mother had been up to during his absence. When Miles walked in, his father finished the paragraph he was reading, then looked up and, seeing his son, grinned.*

Miles could see that he was missing a couple teeth. "What happened?" he asked, immediately frightened.

"What, this?" Max said, sticking his tongue through the new gap. "It's nothing. I just had a little difference of opinion with a guy, is all. He doesn't know it yet, but he's going to pay me about five hundred bucks per tooth."

Miles nodded, not so much reassured by his father's explanation as by his presence. Having dreaded Max's return, he immediately felt how good it was to have him home. His father had only a couple of speeds, which made him predictable, and Miles was ready for things to be predictable again, even if they were predictably odd. Max might not be like other men, but he was always like himself. Other men, for instance, might get upset over minor car accidents, whereas Max saw fender benders as opportunities. If somebody backed into him in a parking lot, which people did with such regularity as to raise suspicions that Max purposely put himself in harm's way, Max took his damaged car to a mechanic he depended upon for an inflated estimate, then he'd offer to settle the matter for half the estimate in cash, in return for which consideration, nobody's insurance company needed to be involved. Meaning the other driver's, since Max himself was never insured. Once the money was in his pocket, he was disinclined to squander it by fixing up the car. Oh, he might replace a broken headlight, since state law required it, and if a side panel was badly dented, he'd pound it out himself, though the results were generally more grotesque than the original dent. The Dodge had been "repaired" so many times that it resembled something built from scrap on a junk heap.

Miles had little doubt that his father would realize his dental windfall, just as he knew no dentist was likely to see a penny. What Miles couldn't know, of course, was that he was witnessing the first stage in the systematic demolition of his father's body, that by the time Max Roby turned seventy he'd look like a '65 Dodge Dart that had been totaled on several different occasions.

At the moment, he had to admit, his father looked the picture of health, his body lean and tanned, and he couldn't help comparing his sturdy appearance with that of Charlie Mayne, who'd looked so pale and concave on the beach. And he couldn't help speculating about what would've happened if Max had gotten out of jail in time to track them down on Martha's Vineyard and found them eating caviar out of a picnic basket on the beach. He tried to imagine a fight between his father and Charlie Mayne, but no picture would form. Charlie Mayne was older and clearly no pugilist. Max was tough and durable, but his specialty, Miles was beginning to understand, was not in punching people but in getting them to punch him, which he was pretty certain Charlie Mayne would never do. More likely, Max would simply have just invited himself to join them, saying, "I like caviar too, you know." In this dramatic scenario, if anybody ended up throwing a punch, it probably would've been Grace.

"Where's Mom?" it occurred to him to ask, since the house didn't feel like she was in it.

"Over at church, she said," Max told him. "She left you a sandwich in the fridge."

"She goes every morning now," Miles said, which was true. Since returning from her journey across the river, she'd been to Mass every day and, moreover, she'd signed Miles up to be an altar boy once school started.

Max grunted. "She must be feeling guilty about something," he ventured, studying his son.

To avoid being stared at, Miles went over to the refrigerator and pretended to look for the sandwich, to put a door between his father and his burning cheeks. Slowly, he went about pouring himself a glass of milk and finally brought it to the table with his sandwich.

"I heard you made a good catch," his father said, causing Miles to wonder whether he'd been told by Grace or by Coach LaSalle. For his father to allude

to the incident now, so long after it had happened, felt weird. It had been a month since he'd put his mitt in the way of that line drive, and it seemed even longer, almost as if it had happened to some other boy.

"Mom's been real sick," he heard himself announce.

His father had gone back to reading the paper and didn't look up. Miles was about to tell him again when he said, "They always are at this stage."

Miles considered whether to ask, Who did he mean by "they"? At what stage?

Noticing this silence, Max lowered the paper again, grinning, his gap-tooth smile no less disconcerting this time, though Miles was more prepared for it. "She didn't tell you?"

"Tell me what?"

"You're going to have a baby brother, is what."

When his father lifted the newspaper again, Miles ate the entire sandwich and drained the glass of milk without speaking. It took that long for the world to rearrange itself, for the facts to realign, for them to convey a new understanding of the way of things. The world, he now understood, was a physical, not a moral order. Nobody got sick and died as a consequence of sinning. He'd been suspecting as much, but now saw it clearly and realized that part of him had known it all along. People got sick because of viruses and bacteria and children—things like that—not as a result of islands or men like Charlie Mayne. What Miles took from this knowledge was mostly relief, and when he spoke he was aware of something new either in or behind his voice, a new attitude, sort of. "You don't know that," he told his father.

"I don't, huh?" Max said, trading sports for the funnies.

"It could be a baby sister."

His father chuckled, probably at Peanuts. *"Mostly boys in our family."*

"Then we're due for a girl," Miles said.

"That's not how it works. It's not like flipping a coin."

"What's it like, then?" It seemed to Miles that it was exactly like flipping a coin, and he didn't see any reason to let his father skate on such dubious logic just because he was a grown-up.

Max studied him, grinning again, though Miles wished he wouldn't. "It's more like rolling dice," he explained. "Except they don't have numbers. There's six sides to a cube, right? In our family 'boy' is written on about five sides of the cube. 'Girl' is only written on one. So, if you had to bet with your own money, which would you bet on?"

Miles did some calculations. After a minute he said, "How many kids does Uncle Pete have?" His father's older brother had moved out west—to Phoenix, Arizona—two decades earlier.

"Four," said his father. "All boys."

Miles nodded. "And you've got me."

"You're a boy too, last time I looked."

"That's five in a row," Miles pointed out.

Outside, footsteps sounded on the back porch: Grace, returning from church. Both Miles and his father glanced up at the kitchen window when she passed. This week her bouts of morning sickness had been less severe, and while she wasn't looking as radiantly beautiful as she had on Martha's Vineyard, neither did she appear as frightened and despairing as when they'd first returned.

"Girl was on the sixth side, right?"

Max considered this while Grace, who'd taken an umbrella with her just to be safe, hung it up in the outside hall. "You're becoming a regular pain in the ass, you know that?"

They were both grinning now, and it occurred to Miles that the strange emotion he was feeling might be pride, though he wasn't positive whether he was proud of himself or proud of his father. He was pretty sure that becoming a pain in Max's ass was an acknowledgment of some sort, maybe even of fondness.

When Grace came in from the hall, she seemed to intuit that father and son were sharing something important, because she sat down between them and reached to put a hand on both of theirs, and for a long moment nobody said anything. It was the first time since they'd returned from Martha's Vineyard that Miles felt that maybe things would be okay, that they would return to normal, or at least what was normal for them. If he felt any regret, it was that Max would never get to see Grace in that white dress, since she'd donated it to Goodwill earlier in the week.

CHAPTER 20

T HE HOUSEKEEPER at St. Cat's, Mrs. Irene Walsh, was finishing up the pots and pans from the Sunday dinner it hadn't even been worth her while to cook. Father Mark, guilty about having eaten so little and feeling the need of a little human companionship, even in the gruff form of Mrs. Walsh, had offered to help clean up, but she'd rebuffed him. He'd just make more work for her by putting things away where they didn't belong, and tomorrow she wouldn't be able to find a thing. She could tell she'd hurt his feelings, which was fine with her.

Mrs. Walsh was not an unkind woman, but she harbored an essentially medieval worldview. Her father had been an army man with a theological bent, and from him she'd learned all about the Great Chain of Being, which, as explained by her father, was not unlike the military's chain of command. God was at the top, and below Him His angels, ranked according to their angelic social class, then the pope, his cardinals, bishops, priests and so on. Mrs. Walsh was comforted by the notion that being a housekeeper to two priests was no closer to the bottom of the chain (occupied by rocks and other inanimate objects) than it was distant from the top. Keeping men of God clean and well fed was honorable if not exalted work, and if others were chosen by God for more exalted work, then there must've been good reasons. To aspire to that which was beyond one's designated station in life was a sin, she believed, and in the end, all the strivers and the enviers would come to know the Truth, that up and down the Great Chain there was but one duty and that was to do God's will. A priest's duty was to be the best priest he could be, just as a housekeeper's was to be the best housekeeper.

Just as annoying as the ones who were always striving to be above their stations in life, to Mrs. Walsh's way of thinking, were the falsely humble fools like Father Mark, who was always slumming in her kitchen, wanting in his ignorance to help out, grabbing dishcloths to wipe down countertops, encouraging her to go home before her work was completed. Poor discipline was what it amounted to, and her father would have agreed. Mrs. Walsh had adored her father, who nonetheless never paid her much mind. A military man, he devoted most of his time to lecturing his sons, whose temperaments were decidedly unmilitary. The more he stressed discipline, the wilder they became, and he died believing that no one had heard a single word he'd said, which was not true. His daughter had been listening. Mrs. Walsh believed, as he had, that society did well to honor distinctions, and she regretted that so many people in today's world seemed intent on blurring them. The young ones like Father Mark were the worst. They put great store in kindness, which was all well and good, but old Father Tom, gone balmy as a magpie, was still more priestly than all the young ones put together, and he'd never once in all the years she'd worked for him felt compelled to lay a hand on a single one of her pots.

"I think that's Mr. Roby who just pulled in," Mrs. Walsh observed from where she stood at her sink.

"How about his father? Is Max with him?"

"Just Mr. Miles. And all he's doing is sitting there."

In the kitchen doorway Father Mark smiled, his first of the day. He could guess what his friend was doing. He was looking up at the unpainted steeple, wondering what cruel code embedded in his genes prevented him from climbing ladders like normal human beings.

"Well, you've been waiting for him," the housekeeper said. "Are you going to tell him?"

Ah, Mrs. Walsh, Father Mark wanted to say. *There is much to learn from you.* She was no great thinker, Mrs. Walsh, but she did like to get things resolved, and you had to admire that. Find out. Do it. Don't turn it around in your hand to examine its many facets. The problem with the contemplative life was that there was no end to contemplation, no fixed time limit after which thought had to be transformed into action. Contemplation was like sitting on a committee that seldom made recommendations and was ignored when it did, a committee that lacked even the authority to disband.

Mrs. Walsh was right. The present circumstance needed to be dealt with, and what's more, it needed to be dealt with by Father Mark, who'd wasted too much time already. The title of the feverish sermon he'd given at the early Mass that morning had been "When God Retreats." He had composed it partly in the car last night on the way home from the coast, and partly during a sleepless night, and partly in the pulpit as he delivered it. It had not gone as badly as he'd feared it might, and his intention had been to repeat "When God Retreats" at the late Mass, but when he returned to the rectory between services he discovered that Father Tom was gone.

Actually, Mrs. Walsh had discovered the old priest's disappearance when she arrived shortly after eight-thirty, by which time Father Tom was usually up and anxious to be fed. On Sundays Mrs. Walsh made him French toast. Then, after the old man's chin began to glisten with maple syrup, she set about preparing the noon meal for the two of them, usually a ham or a roast chicken or, as today, a New England pot roast, a task made no easier by having a sticky, senile priest underfoot. True, she preferred the crazy old priest to the sane young one, but Father Tom did bear more or less constant watching, especially when Father Mark wasn't around. That was one thing the young priest was good for, she had to admit. On Sundays, knowing the other one was across the lawn giving his lame sermons, Father Tom could get mischievous. One morning when he came into her kitchen, Mrs. Walsh had caught a glimpse of him out of the corner of her eye without noticing anything amiss. When she served him his French toast, she did think something was odd about the way he regarded her, as if he was relishing some joke that had escaped her. But Mrs. Walsh found this highly unlikely, she herself being a perfectly sane fifty-three-year-old married woman and the old father being pretty much completely batshit.

Still, since there was nothing in the world Mrs. Walsh despised more than a joke she might be the butt of, she'd stopped dressing her chicken to eyeball him sitting there at the table. He was dressed in a freshly laundered, standard priest-issue, short-sleeved black shirt with a starched white collar, and his usually unruly white hair had been brushed flat. She even noticed that his shoes had been spit-shined and his black linen socks were a match. If a joke was hidden anywhere on Father Tom's person she couldn't locate it, so she returned to cramming handfuls of stuffing into her roasting chicken. Only when the old father rose from the table and brought his plate over to the drainboard—for him an uncharacteristically helpful gesture—did she see that he was wearing no trousers. So today when she'd entered the rectory and the old father wasn't in immediate evidence, she went looking for him, suspicious that more mischief was afoot.

His bedroom door was shut, and when Mrs. Walsh knocked, calling his name and demanding that he open up or else she'd fetch the young one, she half expected a bare-assed, shrivel-dicked old clergyman to open the door and grin at her. While Mrs. Walsh did not look forward to this prospect, neither did it frighten her. At fifty-three she was through with the foolishness of men's genitals. In fact, it had been many years since she *had* cared what hairy things dangled between their pale, scrawny legs. She now considered the fact that she had *ever* cared a kind of temporary lunacy and was thankful that her madness had been short-lived, not terribly virulent, and ultimately cured by marriage, as God intended.

The door remained closed to her threats, which left Mrs. Walsh no alternative but to enter without invitation. The door was unlocked and revealed, when she pushed it open, an empty room. Mrs. Walsh made sure it *was* empty, getting down on her hands and knees, a maneuver she would have preferred not to perform on her inflamed joints, to look under the bed. Her thought was that an aging priest balmy enough to appear pantless in her kitchen might just be playing hide-and-seek. But no one was under the bed and there was no place else in the spartan quarters large enough to conceal a child, much less a full-grown man with the mind of a child.

Neither did the old priest seem to be anywhere else in the rectory. Mrs. Walsh checked every room and every closet in the house, and even took a flashlight down into the cellar, a damp, horrid place that still had coal bins and plenty of dark corners for a demented old priest to hide in. She had just about satisfied herself that Father Tom had risen early and defied orders by going out for a walk, or perhaps sneaked over to the church and hidden in the confessional so he could spy on the young one and listen in on whatever liberal nonsense he was spouting from the pulpit, when something occurred to her and she hurried back upstairs to his room.

He still wasn't there, but more to the point, his bed did not appear to have been slept in. Of course it was possible he'd made it after getting up, as he'd done all his life until his mind began to go, but now he mostly forgot. Yesterday, Saturday, had been Mrs. Walsh's day to change the bedding for both fathers, and when she pulled back the cover and examined the sheets beneath, they felt and smelled freshly of Clorox. Not so much as a hint of stale, flatulent old clergyman.

But it wasn't the bed that provided the real clue. It was the waste-basket, and Mrs. Walsh nearly walked right by it without noticing. The basket she'd emptied just yesterday was now nearly full again, and what it was nearly full of was the small, mint-green envelopes used by parishioners to conceal from other parishioners just how niggardly their weekly offerings were. Every last envelope, no doubt collected from Saturday evening's five-thirty Mass, had been torn open and then tossed into the wastebasket. Also within the metal cylinder were checks that had been enclosed in the envelopes. What Mrs. Walsh registered immediately was the complete absence of legal tender.

When the young one came loping across the lawn after early Mass, Mrs. Walsh was waiting for him, arms folded across her matronly bosom. Where another woman might've been thrown into a tizzy by this point, Mrs. Walsh had remained composed. She now bore the expression of a person who knew that someone's head was going to roll and whose comfort derived from the sure understanding that it would not be her own.

"Good morning, Mrs. W.," Father Mark said in the kitchen door, his excellent spirits no doubt due to the fact that his sermon, at least in his view, had gone well. "Is that your famous New England pot roast I'm smelling?"

To satisfy his curiosity, he went over to the stove and lifted the lid of the kettle she was using to brown the meat. How many times had he been told that such familiarity was not appreciated in her kitchen? Did she poke her head into his confessional and comment upon whatever penance he dispensed?

"Notice anything missing when you rose this morning?" Mrs. Walsh asked, as he replaced the lid on her pot.

"No," said Father Mark warily.

"Notice anything missing now?"

Father Mark took in the entire kitchen, which seemed to be pretty much in order. Was the woman suggesting that they'd been burgled in the night, that he'd failed to lock the door when he came in? Whatever her game was, he had no time for it. Father Mark was, as Mrs. Walsh had intuited, still buoyed by the success of his sermon, but he wanted to jot down a couple small improvements before the ten-thirty Mass—always a more critical audience, since they were actually awake. It was imperative that he make his notes before Father Tom wandered in and created his usual chaos. "I'm afraid I haven't time for guessing games, Mrs. W.," he said, then rooted around in her drawers until he located a pad of paper and a pencil. "If there's something missing, I suggest you talk to Father Tom. He's been hoarding things in his room since he heard the diocese might shut down our humble operation."

Slinging himself into the booth, he paused, the tip of the pencil above the paper, sensing that if he did not write down his first thought immediately, it would be lost forever. In this he was correct. "*What* did you just say?" he asked, looking up, unsure he'd heard his housekeeper right.

"I *said* that what's missing *is* Father Tom."

Father Mark swallowed uncomfortably. "Well, he can't have gone far," he offered, his intended certainty sounding rather wishful. "You're sure he's not around somewhere?"

Mrs. Walsh *was* certain, and told him so.

"Still, let's make sure," Father Mark suggested, rising from the booth.

"Make *you* sure, you mean," she grumbled, but together they searched the house all over again. When they finished, Father Mark returned and searched the church too, aware how fond the old man was of hiding in the confessional.

The mission a failure, Father Mark and Mrs. Walsh stood on the back porch surveying the church grounds, the priest looking gut-shot, his housekeeper smug, their search having revealed nothing but the truth of her theory, which held that the old father had not gone missing this morning between Father Mark's departure for Mass and Mrs. Walsh's arrival, but rather sometime last night. Which meant Father Mark was to blame.

On those rare occasions when he had to leave the rectory in the evening, Father Mark always hired a sitter to watch TV with Tom and make sure he got to bed okay. Mostly he assigned an altar boy to this duty because, after Father Tom had appeared bottomless in Mrs. Walsh's kitchen, Father Mark hadn't wanted to risk a female sitter. The boy who'd done last night's shift had left a note saying the old priest had retired early, at eight-thirty. The boy himself had remained at the rectory until ten, then closed up as instructed and gone home, with the understanding that Father Mark would be home shortly—though, as it happened, the younger priest hadn't returned until nearly midnight. Nor had he looked in on Father Tom, as he now realized he should have. Tom was a notoriously light sleeper, and Father Mark hadn't wanted to disturb his slumber. At least that was the lie he'd told himself at the time and now repeated to Mrs. Walsh. What Father Mark had actually feared was not that the old man would be asleep, but that he would be awake and full of curiosity.

So it was possible, as much as Father Mark hated to admit it, that he'd already been gone for *fifteen hours*! Particularly worrisome was that no one had called to report seeing Father Tom at large. He'd wandered off before, but he was a well-known figure in Empire Falls and, often as not, he was gathered up and returned to St. Cat's even before he was discovered to be missing. That fact, combined with his guilt, preyed on Father Mark's mind, and as they stood there on the back porch, it occurred to him to ask, "Tom *can* swim, can't he?" The possibility that the old priest might've ended up in the river sent a vivid chill straight through him. If he'd gone into the river below the falls, he might travel all the way to Fairhaven, where the dam would stop him. In the previous century, suicides along the Knox sometimes made it all the way to the ocean.

Mrs. Walsh had no idea whether Father Tom could swim, any more than she knew why on earth she was expected to know such a thing. "I'm just glad you had the car," she said. "You know how he used to love to drive that Crown Victoria."

Father Mark looked at her.

Mrs. Walsh looked back at him. "You *did* have the car?"

"Shit," he said, for he hadn't taken the car last night. His companion had driven.

"Bingo," said Mrs. Walsh.

They both regarded the closed door of the detached garage, the one place on the parish grounds they had not checked. Father Mark heard his name called and saw an altar boy waving to him as he entered St. Cat's sacristy door. Father Mark consulted his watch. It was ten after ten, only twenty minutes until Mass was scheduled to begin, and the early birds were already filtering in. What he would've preferred, Father Mark realized, was to postpone further revelations until after Mass. Not possible. Not with the good Mrs. Walsh at his side, her very presence demanding action.

"You stay here," he instructed her, then crossed the drive, paused and finally peered in through one of the garage's square little windows.

On the back porch, Mrs. Walsh watched him lean forward and rest his forehead against the garage door. She counted to ten before he straightened up again. Better to be a competent housekeeper, she thought, than an incompetent priest.

"When God Retreats," so alive and accessible for the early Mass, proved elusive for the late. In fact, as Father Mark ascended into the pulpit, he offered up a quick, fervent prayer asking God to help him recall the main thrust of the sermon he'd delivered so eloquently just two hours before, only to discover that He had indeed retreated, forcing Father Mark to pore desperately over his handwritten notes while the congregation grew curious, then restless, then alarmed. What Father Mark was having trouble locating in his notes was the conviction required to say these things. Two hours before, he had believed them to be true. Now he wasn't so sure.

He had spent the evening before in the company of a young artist who taught at Fairhaven College, the same professor who, though Father Mark was unaware of this, had selected Christina Roby's and John Voss's paintings to represent the sophomore class in the citywide art show. The two men had met a few weeks earlier at the Bath Iron Works at a rally against the commissioning of a new nuclear submarine. Both had been arrested for criminal trespass, then quickly released. During their incarceration, Father Mark had suspected immediately that the young artist was gay.

He was less certain what conclusions the artist himself had drawn, but a few days later Father Mark received a note asking him to visit his campus studio. The letter arrived in Tuesday's mail, and Father Mark, his heart pounding as he held it in his hand, found himself pondering both time, which had just slowed, and how it might be speeded up. Normally he tacked invitations onto the kitchen bulletin board as a reminder, but in this instance he took the note to the desk in his room and put it in the middle drawer among some worthless papers, as if proximity to mundane matters might magically render it mundane as well.

No such luck. He checked the drawer half a dozen times that first day, rereading the letter until he had it memorized. In addition to showing him some work in progress, the artist said there was a spiritual matter he wanted to consult Father Mark about. By Wednesday he was unable to delude himself any further. He was *hiding* the note, and that gesture told him everything he needed to know. Neither did it leave him much choice but to tear the sheet up, which he did, depositing its pieces into the wastepaper basket beside his desk, after which he crossed the lawn to the church, where he lit a candle and knelt at the side altar to offer a prayer of gratitude.

He was about to begin this prayer when he heard a sound behind him and turned just in time to see Father Tom sneak into the confessional. The old man had clearly followed him, and before Father Mark could chalk up his batty colleague's behavior to his dementia, he felt a terrible, righteous rage rising in his chest. He stormed over to the confessional, dragged the old man out, and walked him back across the lawn, dressing him down as they went. When they arrived at Mrs. Walsh's kitchen, the old man was hanging his head in shame and looked so pitiful that Father Mark relented, telling him that of course he was forgiven. He did not, however, return to the church to complete his prayer. A prayer was a prayer, he reassured himself, no matter where it was offered, and Father Mark decided to offer this one in the privacy of his room. Once there, however, it struck him that he was making far too much of the whole thing. There was no reason to believe that the invitation wasn't entirely innocent, and no reason that it shouldn't be innocently accepted. It was not the artist but Father Mark himself who, by his thoughts, had turned this into an occasion of sin. Blessedly, he'd only torn the letter in quarters. He had a roll of Scotch tape right in his desk.

The artist, Father Mark learned when he visited his studio on Wednesday, had been raised in Nicaragua, the son of a low-level American diplomat, who'd died there in a car accident, and a woman from Managua. As a young man he'd come to the United States to study, but after the Sandinistas fell he stayed on. His paintings—Father Mark thought them extraordinary—were expressly religious in theme and imagery, and utterly devoid of irony. American artists were no longer able to paint without irony, the young man agreed, pleased by Father Mark's observation. While there was nothing overt in the paintings he was shown that day in the studio on the top floor of the red-brick building in downtown Fairhaven, Father Mark came away more certain that the artist was gay. Only on the drive home did it occur to him that the spiritual dilemma the man had mentioned had not come up.

That followed two days later, over the phone. Father Mark took the call in the den, purposely leaving the door open. The young art professor began by apologizing for dragging Father Mark all the way to Fairhaven and then not finding the courage to bring up the subject that was troubling him. Not at all, Father Mark said. The paintings themselves had been well worth the trip. The simple truth was, the young man said, that he'd enjoyed Father Mark's company so much that he hadn't dared say something that might very well make him loathsome in his new friend's eyes. At least he hoped they were friends. But now, since Wednesday, he felt ashamed of himself in an even more complicated way, so he'd decided that the best and only thing to do was the honest thing, and confess his sexual orientation.

Yes, said Father Mark, looking up from the phone to find Father Tom in the doorway, and he continued to stand there until Father Mark made a motion for him to move along. If the old priest had any recollection of what had transpired between them earlier in the week, he gave no sign. Listening to people talk on the telephone, to Father Tom's way of thinking, was the next best thing to hearing confessions.

This pregnant silence was exactly what he'd been afraid of, the young artist blurted, sounding distressed. Father Mark hastened to explain that he'd been interrupted and that his silence indicated neither shock nor mortification nor revulsion. He assured the young man that he now had his complete attention, after which he proceeded to talk for half an hour, during which Father Tom found occasion to pass by the open door four more times.

The artist's crisis of faith had been occasioned by the betrayal of a friend who—if you can believe it, he said—also happened to be a priest. He hadn't seen the man in nearly a decade, not since they'd known each other in Texas, where he'd been in graduate school and both had been active in the Sanctuary movement, helping illegal aliens cross the border into the United States, providing them with temporary safe houses and, eventually, forged documents that would allow them to work. Many of these refugees had given their life savings to "coyotes," smugglers who would abandon them to their exhaustion and the hot Texas sun; the majority were rounded up and taken back across the border. The lucky few who slipped through the net wanted nothing more than the kind of hard, dirty labor most American workers spurned, and half of their meager wages they sent back to families in Guatemala or El Salvador or Nicaragua or Mexico.

Both the activists had been arrested on numerous occasions, and it was in jail that the young artist confessed to the priest that as a gay man, he felt as lost and abused in an increasingly hostile church as the illegals did when they were off-loaded from trucks in the darkness and turned loose to find their way, or not, across the Texas desert. If there was no place for him in the Catholic Church, where was he to go?

The priest did more than anyone ever had to put his mind and heart at rest, assuring him that the church was as large and diverse as the world itself. All of God's children were welcome in it. True, there were many who condemned what they did not understand, who made the church seem small and cold as a prison cell. Far better to remember who it was that Jesus Himself chose to befriend during his brief tenure upon the earth. Far better to be an outcast here than in heaven. But the priest was stern, too, reminding the young man that God demanded of him the same degree of fidelity He required of His other children. In His eyes, promiscuity and carelessness were the true offenses, no matter one's sexuality.

When his degree work was finished, the young professor moved on with great reluctance from one marginal teaching post to the next, and it was clear to Father Mark that he'd fallen in love with the priest and had held his memory sacred over the intervening years, which was why it had come as such a shock to get a phone call from him a month ago. His heart had leapt at the sound of his old friend's voice, and his first thought was how much trouble it must have been to track him down in Fairhaven, Maine, of all places. But his joy was short-lived. At first he didn't understand that the priest was calling him to explain that he'd offered misguided spiritual counsel all those years ago, that further reflection and prayer had forced him to concede that while the church was indeed as large as the world it embraced, it could not be infinitely flexible in its doctrine—that is, all things to all men. In matters of faith and morals there could be neither doubt nor dissent, and where its teachings were clear and unambiguous, a true believer had no choice but to accept these as the very will of God. Further, it was the duty of all who were ill to seek the cure.

"You want to know the sad part?" the young man concluded, his voice weak with emotion and on the verge of breaking.

Father Mark, listening both to the voice on the phone and to Father Tom's relentless shuffling in the hall, already knew the sad part. "You suspect he was gay himself, don't you?"

ALTHOUGH FATHER MARK had composed much of "When God Retreats" in his head while lying awake in his bed during an interminable and restless night—during which, he now understood, Father Tom was making his escape—he'd been thinking about the sermon since he'd had a long afternoon's chat back in September with Miles, who told him a story about the week he and his mother had spent on Martha's Vineyard, when Miles was nine and his mother, trapped in the unhappiest of marriages, had, Miles believed, a brief affair with a man she'd met on the island. Father Mark had never met Grace Roby, of course, having arrived in Empire Falls years after she died, but according to Miles, after the affair she'd returned to both her marriage and the church.

Hers was not, Father Mark believed, an unusual story. Most people tried to be faithful, though few could boast an unblemished record. What had struck him about Grace Roby, at least as she was revealed by her son's account, was that by falling in love, she had become an entirely different woman. It wasn't so much that her behavior changed, but rather that she became astonishingly beautiful—so beautiful, in fact, that her beauty could not fail to impress even her nine-year-old son, who'd so taken her for granted to that point that he'd never really seen her as a woman, but only as his mother. For a brief span of a few sun-drenched days, she'd been truly happy, perhaps for the first time in her life, and that happiness had been manifest in a radiance that had turned the head of every man they met.

Though common, it was still a remarkable story, and Father Mark couldn't help being a little in love with Grace Roby himself and, even more disturbing, glad for this woman he'd never met, that she'd enjoyed at least this fleeting happiness. That she had betrayed her marriage and her faith seemed almost too fine a point, perhaps because Father Mark, knowing Max Roby, understood that her married life must've been a trial. That she ultimately returned to both her husband and her faith seemed far more significant, and he said as much to Miles, who confessed his lifelong worry that the intensity of his mother's brief joy had somehow been the root cause of the illness that killed her a decade later. "You're telling me that happiness is carcinogenic?" he'd asked when Miles explained how his mother was never truly the same after their return to Empire Falls, that she'd immediately begun to lose weight, that she became pale as a cave dweller and fell ill several times each winter, that she'd nearly died giving birth to his brother, David. Odd that Miles should've concluded as a child that happiness, not its loss, was what had stricken his mother. Odder still that he apparently hadn't been able to revise his thesis later in life. Was this what it meant to be a Catholic?

But it was only last night, as he lay awake in bed, that the meaning of Grace Roby's story, or one of its meanings, became clear to him. By this time Father Mark's own crisis had passed, leaving him weak and relieved, as if a fever had broken.

They had gone to an opening held at a tiny gallery on a back street in Camden, and afterward the two men had had dinner at a nearby restaurant overlooking the harbor. For the first week of October, the weather on the coast was unseasonably warm, and in the evening it was still mild enough to eat outside under the suspended heat lamps. At the next table a man and a woman were sharing a bowl of steamer clams, which had reminded Father Mark of Miles's story. The man and woman might've been husband and wife, or husband and someone else's wife, but it was obvious they loved each other. When the artist noticed his smile and asked what was so amusing, Father Mark told him Grace's story pretty much as Miles had told it, and in the telling he realized something he hadn't entirely grasped in the hearing. Wondrous! he thought, how the heart leaps when one is chosen, especially later in life, after one would suppose the time for choosing and being chosen has passed. To be recognized as lovely, as desirable—to *feel* lovely and desirable—surely that was precisely what Grace Roby had needed. It was a God-given moment, during which God had mercifully averted His eyes and absented Himself. Hence the title of his sermon.

Some of the paintings in the artist's Camden exhibition had been ones Father Mark had already seen in the downtown studio, but others either were new or had been concealed from him before. The majority of these were specifically homoerotic, and when Father Mark examined them, he could feel the young artist's eyes on him. Later, over dinner, Father Mark explained that his own counsel to homosexual men and women had always been similar to the activist priest's, before, that is, his lamentable conversion to strict orthodoxy. Father Mark also said he wasn't entirely surprised by such a midlife reevaluation. After all, Chaucer had renounced his own *Canterbury Tales*, and surely, as an artist, the young man must be aware of painters and sculptors who in later life disavowed their best work as vain or immoral. Father Mark intended all of this to offer comfort on the off-chance that the young man genuinely needed it, though in truth he was no longer confident that there was either an activist priest or a betrayal. He couldn't say why, but he was suspicious. At the gallery it had also occurred to him that while there might be no single priest, there could've been many.

What was *un*deniable was that Father Mark understood that he was being chosen, and his heart had leapt with recognition, just as he imagined Grace Roby's must have. Was anything in the world truer than that intuitive leap of the heart? Could anything so true be a sin? Even though he now knew, as he had not before, that he wouldn't surrender to this particular temptation, still, how wonderful to be desired! Surely this was God's gift to fallen Man. Both the reason and sweet recompense for the loss of Paradise. How deftly God steps back out of view, as He had done with Grace, as He'd done with Father Mark himself, to let them muddle through on their own. Father Mark understood that he was not to feel virtuous, merely fortunate. Or maybe blessed.

The general thrust of his sermon, which he tried in vain to remember as he stood awkwardly in the pulpit, searching his notes, had been to suggest that while God never abandoned us, neither was He on every occasion equally present, perhaps because His continual presence is what we desire most—that is, to be led away from temptation, away from *ourselves*. We want Him to be there, ready to receive our call in the moment of our need: lead us not into . . . Whereas God, for reasons of His own, sometimes chooses to let the machine answer. *The Supreme Being is unavailable to come to the phone at this time, but He wants you to know that your call is important to Him. In the meantime, for sins of pride, press one. For avarice, press two . . .*

"When God Retreats" had seemed one of his finer sermons as he'd delivered it to his sleepy early congregation. Exhausted and happy, he could find little fault with it as a personal reflection. That God had trusted him to lose and then regain his path had seemed a wise, beneficent gesture. Though now it seemed that what God had actually done was allow him to lose Father Tom.

AND SO FATHER MARK, feeling chastened by the day's events, left the transparently unchastened Mrs. Walsh in her kitchen drying her pots. He crossed the lawn to where Miles Roby's Jetta sat in the back lot. He'd hoped that Mrs. Walsh was wrong when she reported it was just Miles in the car, but she was right and Max wasn't there, which meant that Father Mark could surrender that final hope against hope. The conclusion he and Mrs. Walsh had reluctantly drawn about the old man's whereabouts held up, even though he wanted very much to be mistaken. Being mistaken, after all, was something he could usually manage. But he'd known the truth when he went through Father Tom's wastebasket and found among the mint-green offering envelopes and discarded checks, a rumpled color brochure: *Your New Life Awaits You in the Florida Keys!*

If Miles saw him coming across the lawn, he gave no sign, even when Father Mark waved. He was looking up at St. Catherine's, just as Father Mark had imagined in Mrs. Walsh's kitchen that he would be, but the expression on his face was nothing like what the priest would've predicted. He looked like a man seeing the church and steeple for the first time, almost like a man who'd never seen either one before and was having a hard time imagining what the purpose of such a structure might be.

SUNDAY AFTERNOONS during the NFL season were almost enough to restore a person's faith in the bar business. Of course, if Bea believed her customers, what her own bar needed was one of those wide-screens like they had out at the Lamplighter. Bea's doubts about this need ran deep and philosophical. For one thing, people rarely knew what they wanted. Despite their certainty that they *did* know, she'd never seen much compelling evidence, and since giving her customers what they *said* they wanted would cost her fifteen hundred dollars, she continued to tell them she was considering it. True, her Sunday-afternoon clientele bitched at her more or less constantly about the little black-and-white TV she brought out of mothballs for football season, setting it up on a back shelf usually reserved for bottles of expensive scotches and bourbons for which there'd never been much call, even when people had jobs.

In Bea's view, her patrons' need to piss and moan about something was more profound and real than their need for wide-screen television. The thing about the black-and-white set, they said, was that it created an imbalance. If you were lucky enough to be located on a stool at the good end of the bar, you got to watch the game in color on the regular TV; down at the other end you watched in black and white and the draft beers weren't any cheaper for the inconvenience, either. Plus, on Saturdays and Sundays it could get crowded, everybody elbowing up close to the bar. People's change got mixed up. When you spun off your stool to go to the head, you were liable to spill the beer of the man standing behind you, and by the time you returned he'd have retaliated by claiming your stool. Then he'd tell you to your face he thought you'd left. If Bea would spring for a big-screen TV, they argued, they wouldn't all have to crowd within a foot of one another.

What her customers didn't seem to understand was that deep down they enjoyed being bunched up, just as they enjoyed the jostling and the spilled beer and the stolen barstools. They enjoyed holding their urine as long as they could and then asking the guy on the next stool to save theirs until they got back, knowing full well he wouldn't, even after he promised to. They didn't know it, but they even liked the little black-and-white TV, though they were right, it did have a shitty picture. But there wasn't a damn thing wrong with imbalance. What was life but good barstools and bad ones, good fortune and bad, shifting from Sunday to Sunday, year to year, like the fortunes of the New England Patriots. There was no such thing as continual good fortune—or misfortune, except for the Red Sox, whose curse seemed eternal.

Besides, a new wide-screen TV wouldn't get rid of the imbalance. There'd still be a good television and one shitty one. The only difference was that what people had thought of as the good big one now would become the shitty little one. Worse, the quickest way to beget a new desire, Bea knew, was to satisfy an old one, and each new desire had a way of becoming more expensive than the last. If she was foolish enough to gratify her customers' current demands, who knew what they'd dream up next?

Another reason not to invest in a wide-screen TV was Walt Comeau, who bugged her more than all her other patrons combined. He'd stopped by for part of the Patriots' game today and, as usual, refused to let up. He had a gigantic TV in his health club and said Bea was a damn fool if she didn't buy one just like it. "You like it so much, go watch football there," she suggested. In her opinion, Walt Comeau had altogether too many suggestions for a man who drank seltzer water and never left a tip. She just hoped her idiot daughter wasn't marrying him for his money, because Bea had known her share of Walt Comeaus over the years and she knew how stingy they could be. The way she had this one pegged, Janine was going to have to fight for every bent nickel.

Of course her daughter kept insisting it was the sex she was interested in, her snide tone of voice suggesting that her mother would do well not to even try understanding something so foreign to her own experience. Bea was not nearly as ignorant of these pleasures as Janine imagined, but she thought the sex would have to be pretty much off the charts to offset the Silver Fox's other shortcomings, and somehow she doubted that having sex with a man whose legs were as skinny as Walt's would be all that great. Yesterday, at the game, Bea had wondered if something was wrong between the lovebirds, half hoping there was. Maybe her daughter would see the light before it was too late. But that was wishful thinking, she now realized. Even if Janine did see the light, she'd never admit it. Stubbornness and spite had been the twin linch-pins of her personality ever since she was a little girl, and Bea had given up trying to change her mind years ago. Janine was the sort of person who, by granting too many opportunities, took all the pleasure out of saying "I told you so."

By the time the afternoon's second game wound down to the two-minute warning and the network was threatening another edition of *60 Minutes*, Bea once again had Callahan's to herself. In another hour or so, after they'd had a chance to go home and eat dinner, a few men would straggle back in to watch the night game, though it usually was a piss-poor matchup, attractive to diehards only. The good news was that diehards were Empire Falls's strong suit, and Bea counted herself among them. A sensible woman would've sold the tavern years ago and used the money to move into the assisted-living retirement community that had opened over in Fairhaven and sat three quarters empty be-cause it was so expensive nobody could afford it. Bea could use some damn assistance in her living, and the idea of putting her swollen feet up grew more attractive every day. Someone to rub them now and then would be especially nice. She'd paid a visit to the Dexter Woods open house last spring and while the place was nice enough, what struck her most was that just about everyone who lived there required a hell of a lot more assistance than she did. They needed assistance walking, assistance bathing, assistance peeing, assistance cutting their meat, assistance chewing it, and Bea had a mortal fear of getting out there and becoming like the rest of them. Still, she had half a mind to check the place out again, in case anybody'd moved in who could navigate the empty corridors without the aid of an aluminum walker.

At seven-thirty about the last person she expected to see, Miles Roby, came in with a big bag of Dairy Queen hamburgers and fries. Until last year, when he and Janine split up, Miles had been a Sunday-evening regular, arriving with enough burgers and fries for himself and Janine and Tick and Bea. Max, who had a keen nose for sniffing out anything free, also often turned up regularly. Tonight it looked like Miles brought at least enough to feed that crew, though it was just the two of them and no reason Bea could think of why he should have imagined otherwise. "How'd you know how hungry I was?" she said, setting a tall beer down in front of her son-in-law and drawing another for herself. Actually, she *was* hungry, though she hadn't been aware of it until he started unloading the food. There were half a dozen burgers, as many bags of fries, even some melting ice cream in plastic dishes. "Who else were you expecting?"

"I don't know," Miles sighed.

"Your daughter won't eat beef anymore, and your wife won't eat anything. Ex-wife. Whatever she is besides a pain in the ass. I don't know how she expects her daughter to become an adult woman when she can't manage it herself."

"I think she's a little scared of getting married again," Miles said, "now that it's getting close." His relationship with Bea had always been strange. From the beginning he'd always taken Janine's side with her mother, just as she'd taken his with her own daughter. Miles wasn't sure this lack of loyalty was entirely healthy, though he was relieved she didn't blame him for their failed marriage. Surely Janine had filled her mother in on his every fault, but if so Bea didn't seem to hold any of it against him, and he was grateful for this as well.

"Considering the man she's marrying," Bea said, "I'd say she's right to worry."

"Well," Miles said around a mouthful of burger, "maybe it'll work out."

"You okay, Miles?" she asked, looking him over. He had a haunted expression and paint flecks in his hair, she noticed, and his right hand sported several angry-looking blisters. "You look like you've been rode hard and put up wet, as my late husband used to say."

"Yeah, I'm fine," he told her, though in truth he was feeling a little light-headed, probably because he hadn't eaten anything today. The food would help. He'd spent the afternoon thinking things through as he worked on the church, and that had helped a little too. Since this morning, he'd felt as if he'd been hit by the train he'd sensed bearing down on him when he saw his mother's picture in the newspaper. Now he felt like maybe it had somehow missed him, that it had roared past merely inches away, its thundering force rendering him almost unconscious until it passed. What he was feeling now was the pull of its wake.

"You aren't letting this divorce get you down, are you?" Bea said, wadding up the paper of her first hamburger and opening a second. She'd spoken to her daughter earlier in the day, and Janine had apparently heard from her lawyers that the divorce decree would be issued the first part of the week. She expected she'd told Miles as well—maybe this was what had him looking gut-shot. "You should just enjoy your freedom for a while," she suggested, recalling that she'd seen him with the Whiting girl at the football game yesterday. "Try not to do anything foolish until you're sure you're thinking straight."

"After which I can do something foolish?"

"You know what I mean," Bea said, chewing thoughtfully. "Damn. If I had somebody to eat with every night, I'd weigh five hundred pounds. Most nights I either forget completely or just eat one of those damned eggs." She waved her burger toward the gallon jug of pickled eggs swimming in brine on the back bar. "Your father and I are about the only ones who'll eat them."

"Speaking of Max," he said, "I don't suppose he's been in today."

Bea shook her head, contemplating, Miles could tell, a third hamburger. "When the door opened, I half expected it to be him. He usually shows up Sunday nights."

"Not tonight, I don't think," Miles told her. Before going to the Dairy Queen, he'd stopped by Max's apartment and knocked on the door, to no avail. A woman down the hall said she'd seen him carrying a duffel bag out of the building the night before. That, combined with the brochure Father Mark had found in the old priest's wastebasket, dispelled any doubts about what had become of the two old men. "Apparently he found a ride down to the Keys."

"Who with?"

Miles smiled. "Can you keep a secret?"

Bea snorted. "Did I tell you what you were in for if you married my daughter?"

"No," Miles conceded.

"Well, then," she said, as if that settled the matter.

IN THE MEN'S ROOM Miles examined the five swollen, painful blisters he managed to give his right hand during the course of the afternoon. He had an hour's worth of painting left on the west face, but instead of finishing up, he'd gone around to the south side and begun to scrape, an activity more in harmony with his mood. It felt far more satisfying to be peeling something away, creating ugliness before restoring beauty. He'd scraped until dark, until he could barely see the scraper on the end of his arm, until the blisters formed and filled with fluid, scraped hypnotically until he'd gone beneath the bottom layer of paint in some places, and then deeper still, gouging out rotting wood, half expecting blood to bead up where he'd punctured the church's skin.

As darkness fell, after scraping everything he could reach from the ground he'd set up the ladder and climbed higher than he dared in the daylight. He'd felt strangely serene on the ladder, reaching farther and farther out to where the paint had bubbled and cracked. Even as he moved *up* and *out*, he felt the opposite sensation, as if he were progressing *down* and *in*, through the protective paint and into the soft wood. A powerful and dangerous illusion, he knew, though he couldn't shake the feeling that if for some reason he were to step off the ladder, he wouldn't tumble to the ground but step onto the side of the church, as if its pull had supplanted gravity. Now, standing at the sink of the men's room at Callahan's, his hands shook to think of it.

What he had been peeling back with his scraper, he now understood, was not so much paint as years, all of his boyish misperceptions, most of which he'd never seriously questioned. Charlie *Whiting*. Even with photographic evidence, it was still easier to think of the man in the photo as Charlie Mayne. How many times over the years had he seen photographs of C. B. Whiting in the *Empire Gazette*, yet never recognized the man he and his mother had met on Martha's Vineyard? Of course, the man they'd met there was clean-shaven, but still. Had Grace not been in the same photo, Miles doubted he would've identified him even this morning. He'd simply followed her gaze and finally seen the truth. Or part of the truth. How long had they been in love before Martha's Vineyard? Certainly they had only pretended, for Miles's benefit, to meet for the first time there in the dining room of Summer House, and surely Grace had bought the white dress in anticipation of Charlie Whiting's arrival—itself so magically fortuitous, occurring just as Grace was running out of money. Miles recalled that even at the time he'd sensed his mother was waiting for someone; his father, he'd assumed, because who else was there?

And then, after their return to Empire Falls, she'd awaited the fulfillment of Charlie's promise, only to hear from other employees that C. B. Whiting had been shipped off to Mexico, with his pregnant wife to join him later. Had Grace been shocked to learn—as Miles certainly would have been—that the man who'd exhibited such amazing powers on Martha's Vineyard had none at home? Or did she conclude that he simply hadn't found the courage to confront his wife? Had it occurred to her that Mrs. Whiting would have enlisted the aid of her father-in-law—old Honus—and threatened her husband with the loss of his inheritance? Was the announced pregnancy—no child was born after Cindy—nothing more than a story concocted in order to keep Charlie Whiting from abandoning his family? Was it Charlie's wife or his father who somehow managed to convince him that a solemn oath sworn in private to a desperate woman from the wrong side of the river counted for less than one sworn before family in public? In answer to these desperate questions came nothing but a terrible silence and a second child, since Grace's, growing inside her, was all too real, leaving her to deal with life as she found it, with who she herself was—a married woman, a mother, a breadwinner, a good Roman Catholic.

It was St. Cat's, Miles now understood, that had played the pivotal role in drawing his mother back into the life she'd been trying to escape from with Charlie Mayne. The church in the form of Father Tom had lured her back into what she would've abandoned by offering her eternal hope as recompense for her despair. The old priest might've been mad even then, Miles had realized as he scraped, ignoring the blisters that were forming. Right inside, in the sacristy—the room's heavy air thick with stale incense and its open closet full of priestly vestments, Sunday's golden chalice safely in its nook, surrounded by all the necessary props of religious authority—Father Tom had no doubt explained to Grace the price of absolution. Another priest would have required no more than a full and honest confession before God, but Father Tom would've wanted more. Grace would never have decided on her own to make that journey across the river to humiliate herself before the woman she had wronged, whose husband she'd planned to steal. No, that would have been Father Tom's doing. And of course it *was* Mrs. Whiting his mother had gone to see that afternoon, Mrs. Whiting whom Miles had seen in the gazebo from the bridge. Why had he never made this obvious connection until now? Tracking her rival's progress across the bridge, had Mrs. Whiting also wondered if the journey would prove too arduous, if Grace would make it only halfway before being swallowed up by the swirling waters below? Had she seen what boy it was standing there on the other side of the river? Had their eyes really locked, as they had in his memory?

She'd kept her cold eye on him from the beginning, he now understood, observing this child whose mother had refused to abandon him, even if it cost her only chance at happiness, this child Charlie Whiting would've substituted for his own damaged one, had he been allowed to. On the ladder this afternoon as darkness fell, Miles acknowledged that for all his adult life, even when he was away at college, he'd felt the woman's scrutiny. Sensing for the longest time something behind the mask of her vague affection, he'd never suspected what was concealed there might be the desire for vengeance. Even now he couldn't be sure. After all, what kind of woman wouldn't be satisfied by her rival's death? Was it possible hatred could burrow so deep in the human heart? In a few short hours, after seeing a newsprint photograph, Miles had reimagined the whole world in black and white, but was this, too, a mistake, replacing one oversimplification with another? Perhaps. But now, right now, before he could change his mind again, he felt an over-powering urge to heed his brother's injunction to *do* something, even if it was wrong.

Here in the men's room, having washed his hands, Miles bit through each of the blisters, draining the milky, built-up fluid. Examining himself in the cloudy mirror, it occurred to Miles that maybe that train hadn't missed him after all. The face in the warped glass seemed to belong not to a man who had danced nimbly out of harm's way at the last second but rather to one who had stood his ground between the rails and taken a direct hit.

Or maybe it was just his surroundings. Paint was peeling off the walls of the men's room in strips. Last January the pipes had frozen and burst, and whomever Bea had hired to fix them had cut large squares out of the walls in half a dozen different spots, as if hoping to locate the rupture by pure chance. When they were finished, they'd patched the Sheetrock in some places, left gaping holes in others. This crapper, it occurred to Miles, was his hometown in a nutshell. People who lived in Empire Falls were so used to misfortune that they'd become resigned to more of the same. Why repair and repaint a wall you'd only have to deface again the next time the pipes froze? Leaving the holes as is, more or less, meant that next time at least the plumbers wouldn't have to search for the pipes. Miles quickly calculated what it would cost to make things right, then doubled it, assuming the women's room would be in similar disrepair, then doubled the number again, just to be on the safe side. On the way back to the bar he poked his head into the kitchen, which hadn't been used in years, and did another mental tally, concluding that it would probably be cheaper to paper the walls with ten-dollar bills than to turn it back into a functioning kitchen.

What he was contemplating, he knew, was an act of monumental folly. That he had to do it anyway had come to him an hour earlier on the Iron Bridge. After leaving St. Cat's he'd driven back downtown with the intention of crossing the bridge and finding answers to the questions he hadn't been able to resolve on the ladder. Instead he'd parked in front of the shirt factory and walked to where he'd stood as a boy, staring out across the dark expanse of the river at the dim lights of the Whiting hacienda. His mother had made that long journey alone. And not, he was suddenly determined, in vain.

BACK IN THE BAR, Bea had finally stopped laughing, and the burgers were gone. "Damn, I'm sorry, Miles," she said, wiping her eyes on her sleeve. "But the idea of Max and that balmy old priest stealing a car and running off to Florida's about the funniest thing I ever heard."

"I suppose it is," he said morosely, "if they don't kill themselves, or somebody else."

"So what happens now?"

That was exactly what Miles would've liked to know. Father Tom had blown town in the parish station wagon, it was true, but it turned out the six-year-old Crown Victoria was registered in his name, purchased before he began to slide, at least noticeably, into senility. The last few years it had been understood that he wasn't allowed to drive any more than he was permitted to hear confessions. The problem was that Father Tom dearly loved to do both, and whenever he located the keys Mrs. Walsh and Father Mark had hidden away, he'd take the Crown Vic for a spin, which in his case, was an apt description, because once he tired of his sport and wanted to return home, he was as thoroughly disoriented as a blindfolded five-year-old at a birthday party, which meant he had to be fetched from wherever he was. Sometimes that fetching took a while, inasmuch as *he* had the car.

Just as Father Tom's name was on the wagon's registration, so was he, at least officially, still the pastor of St. Catherine's. While Father Mark had taken over the administration of the parish, he was technically the assistant pastor, which meant that even if he wanted to make an issue of the missing money—no more than five hundred dollars, they'd estimated—it couldn't really be treated as a theft. The money, after all, had been freely given to the church, and its pastor was the church's duly appointed representative. There were virtually no legal strings attached to it.

What Father Mark had been unable to figure out was how an old man who needed reminding that the vented side of his undershorts was designed to be worn in the front had managed to get into the parish safe. The only explanation he could come up with was that his *fingers* must've remembered the combination. The old man no longer recalled it, because for the last year he'd been asking Father Mark what it was and getting angry when he wouldn't tell him. Father Mark could only assume he must've come into the den one day and let his fingers' instinct take over while he sat in front of the safe, dismayed by his inability to remember three little numbers.

At any rate, if Father Tom and his new best pal were presently southward bound in the Crown Victoria, there wasn't much anybody could do about it.

"What I worry about most," Miles admitted to Bea, "is an accident." His father wasn't too bad a driver when he was sober, but of course he wouldn't *be* sober until their money ran out. Father Tom hadn't been too bad a driver when he still had his mind, but now he was easily confused and Miles doubted he had much experience of freeway driving—or any driving, really, outside rural mid-Maine. It was hard to imagine the two men would make it to Florida, but then again, they might. In the Keys, once the money ran out, Max would tire of the old priest's company and probably call St. Cat's and tell Father Mark where to come and pick him up. Miles just hoped Father Tom wouldn't return with an ass full of obscene tattoos.

"By the way," Bea said, reaching under the bar for a folded newspaper and handing it to Miles, "I saved this for you. It's an awful nice picture of your mother."

"That was good of you, Bea," he said, but when he glanced down there were twice as many people in the photo as there had been this morning. There were two of his mother and two of Charlie Mayne, and when he looked back up there were two of Bea as well. "Is it cold in here?" he asked, suppressing a shiver.

Both Beas studied him for a moment, then leaned forward and put a single cool, dry hand on his forehead. "My God, Miles," she said. "You're burning up."

"Never mind that," he said, suddenly feeling the same strong sense of purpose that had come to him earlier on the ladder. "I have a proposal for you."

[CHAPTER 22]

M ILES WAS A *high school sophomore when Empire Textile and its companion shirt factory closed and his mother lost her job. The Whiting family had sold the mill three years earlier to a subsidiary of a multinational company headquartered in Germany. The new owners had very different ideas about how to run the mill, and there were immediate rumors that Hjortsmann International had no real interest in Empire Textile beyond its tax advantages. Under the Whitings, the mill had operated with New England frugality and virtually no debt, whereas the new owners, claiming the need to modernize in order to be competitive with foreign operations, heavily mortgaged every existing piece of machinery in order to expand lavishly. Local workers had questioned the wisdom of this approach from the start. Given the new debt structure, those who knew the operation intimately, including Grace, did not see how the mill could possibly show a profit for many years. Acceptable, perhaps, had the new owners exhibited any signs of patience, but they appeared singularly lacking in this corporate virtue.*

The threat of closure, imagined or implied, sent shock waves through Empire Falls, and when a new labor contract was negotiated, its principal features were longer hours, a new definition of what constituted overtime, the elimination of numerous jobs, pay cuts and diminished benefits. Of course employees grumbled, but they also understood the next year would determine the mill's very existence. When overall productivity indeed rose nearly 28 percent—remarkable, given the mill's deteriorating conditions—the workers congratulated themselves that if the mill wasn't in the black as a result of their concessions, they'd at least managed to guarantee another year or two at their now less personally profitable jobs.

Which was why they were stunned when Hjortsmann announced that both mill and shirt factory would close anyway. In less than a month the mill was completely looted of its mortgaged machinery, which was disassembled and placed on trucks destined for Georgia and the Dominican Republic. In fact, it took less time for the mill to be emptied than for its employees to understand the truth of their situation, that Empire Textile had been bought for this very purpose, and their heroic efforts to make the mill profitable had simply swelled the coffers of Hjortsmann International. This would never have happened under the Whitings, people said, and a delegation was sent to discuss the possibility of old Honus Whiting and his loyal employees purchasing Empire Textile, but by then the old man was in extreme ill health and his son, C. B., remained in Mexico. Only a few understood the new family dynamic, in which Francine Whiting held the real power. She, not her husband or her father-in-law, had brokered the sale of the mill, quite possibly, some whispered, with a complete understanding of Hjortsmann's ultimate intention.

Some employees were offered jobs in Georgia, but few took up the offer to relocate. They had houses and mortgages, and the real estate market was already grim, thanks to the closing of two smaller mills the year before. True, people weren't sure how they'd pay those mortgages now, but they had kids in school and family nearby that might be able to help a little, and many irrationally clung to the possibility that the mill might reopen under new ownership. They stayed, many of them, because staying was easier and less scary than leaving, and because for a while at least they'd be able to draw unemployment benefits. Others remained out of pride. When the realization dawned that they were the victims of corporate greed and global economic forces, they said, okay, sure, fine, they'd been fools but they would not, by God, be run out of the town their grandparents and parents had grown up in and called home. The fortunate ones were older, their modest houses nearly paid off; close to retirement, they would limp to the finish line, then help their less fortunate sons and daughters as best they could.

Grace Roby was one of the few who might've been tempted to head south, but to her the offer was not extended. When Miles's brother was born, she'd taken a year off and then returned to work part-time until he was old enough to attend kindergarten. Though she'd worked at the shirt factory longer than most of the people who were offered the relocation deal, the hiatus meant that she didn't have the required consecutive years of service to qualify. After searching for work for more than a year and exhausting her unemployment benefits, Grace had just about concluded that they would have to move away from Empire Falls anyway, perhaps to the Portland area, when she received an unexpected phone call from a man named William Vandermark.

What Mr. Vandermark, who worked for a Boston firm, begged to inquire was whether Grace would be interested in full-time employment as a personal aide to a woman who'd fallen during the winter and broken her hip. She would be confined, for some time, to a wheelchair, and in this diminished capacity was unequal to the task of managing a large house and garden. What the lady would require, for possibly up to a year, was a reliable person upon whom she might depend for a wide variety of services. She would need assistance keeping the house in order and putting in her spring flower and vegetable garden. Bookkeeping, letter writing, and other business skills would come in handy as well. Also, there was a child who would need attending to. Hours might be long one week, short the next, and if Grace chose not to reside at her employer's house, she would have to be "on call" around the clock. Finally, and Mr. Vandermark was cautious in his phrasing here, the position would no doubt require a certain strength of character, since the woman in question was considered by some to be "difficult."

Grace, then in her late thirties, was confident of her mettle. She'd held down a responsible position for all those years at the Empire Shirt Factory, and of course she'd been married to Max Roby for two decades, a test of character if ever there was one. It was almost as if the job description had been written with her in mind. Still, there was something odd about Mr. Vandermark's remarking on the woman's character, and so Grace, who had already decided to accept the offer, admitted that she had no training as a nurse and wondered why the woman didn't hire a professional. Mr. Vandermark seemed to have anticipated this question, and he reminded Grace that while a professional nurse might be advantageous in some respects, they generally frowned on housework, were indifferent letter writers and unskilled with accounts, and he'd never known one to garden. He didn't entirely conceal his opinion that, indeed, no one person could reasonably be expected to function in so many capacities. Also, he added, a professional nurse would likely have to be hired from someplace like Portland or Lewiston, and his client preferred not to have a stranger in her house.

"Wouldn't I be a stranger?" Grace asked.

"Actually, no," Mr. Vandermark explained. "I believe you are known to the lady, and she to you."

When he paused, Grace intuited in that moment the house, the woman, the circumstances, the entire truth.

DURING THE YEARS *that Grace worked for Mrs. Whiting, Miles saw his mother lose the last bloom of her womanhood. Though not yet forty, she would never again buy a dress like the one she'd worn on Martha's Vineyard for Charlie Mayne, and gradually men's heads stopped rotating to look as she passed them on the street. Before going to work for Mrs. Whiting she had attended Mass every day and in the early-morning light that filtered through the stained-glass windows of St. Catherine's, a hint of her former beauty remained, but she emerged into the gray day looking gaunt, drained of both vitality and desire, despite her conviction that Mass gave her strength and hope for the future. To Miles, his mother was beginning to resemble the handful of other women, widows mostly, in their sixties and seventies, who attended daily worship.*

When it was his turn to serve at Mass, one week every two months, Miles accompanied her to St. Cat's. He disliked getting up so early, but once there, still half asleep as he pulled on his cassock and surplice, he found the experience pleasant enough. For reasons he wasn't able to articulate, the world seemed a better place and himself a better person for beginning each day at church, and before long he began to attend Mass even when he wasn't required to serve. Other altar boys quickly learned that Miles would be there to cover for them if they were sick, and after a while they stopped bothering to ask this favor of him. And it was he whom Father Tom became annoyed with, not the boy scheduled, on those rare occasions when Miles himself became ill.

At St. Catherine's, Miles came to understand that responsibility could be enjoyable. He wasn't sure that what he felt there in the warm church, with the day dawning outside, was exactly a religious experience, but he enjoyed the cadence of the Latin Mass and often was jolted out of some reverie just in time to ring the bell at the consecration. He'd recently discovered the existence of a particularly beautiful girl who worked as a waitress at the Empire Grill, and his thoughts too often drifted from the mystery of Christ's body and blood to the mystery that was Charlene Gardiner, though he tried not to indulge unchaste thoughts during Mass.

Sometimes at the offertory, after taking the cruets of water and wine to Father Tom, who always insisted they be presented to him handles first, Miles caught a glimpse of his mother, often with his little brother either fast asleep or squirming in the pew beside her, and he'd wonder what she prayed for. His father was the sort of man who required more or less constant prayer, augmented, it was often remarked, by a swift kick in the pants, so it was possible she was praying for him, though it was hard for Miles to imagine the exact nature of a Max Roby prayer. If he happened to be gone somewhere, his mother might conceivably offer up a prayer for him to come home and help out. After all, when Max was in residence, Grace could at least leave little David at home during Mass. But no sooner would such a prayer be answered, and her husband returned to the bosom of his family, than Grace would surely begin to offer prayers for his removal again, Max being more trouble than he was worth. When she and Miles returned from morning Mass they were likely to find David standing up in his crib, clutching the railings with his fat little fists, his cheeks beet-red with rage and grief, weighed down by a sagging, fully loaded diaper while Max slept off the night before in the next room.

What Miles suspected, though, was that his mother's prayers had little to do with his father. If she was anything like himself, her prayers sought objects of their own desire much as toddlers chase colored bubbles in the air, and he wondered if his mother's thoughts drifted off in pursuit of long-lost Charlie Mayne the way his own pursued Charlene Gardiner. But that was pure speculation. Grace hadn't mentioned the man once since their return from Martha's Vineyard. In fact, Miles had kept his mother's secret so well that there were times he had to remind himself there was a secret to keep. He began to wonder if he'd imagined the whole thing, and on their way home from Mass one morning—it was probably two or three years afterward— Miles said, "Mom? Do you remember the man we met on Martha's Vineyard? Charlie Mayne?"

He expected her to either be or pretend to be surprised, as he would've been had such a question come out of thin air so unexpectedly. But Grace answered as if she herself had been contemplating that very thing, or perhaps wondering when he'd get around to asking. "No, Miles, I don't," she replied calmly. "And neither do you."

GRACE BEGAN WORKING *for Mrs. Whiting in late spring, a month after the woman had been released from the hospital—much to the relief of the entire staff, who'd had about enough of her. Mrs. Whiting had recently contributed seed money for a new wing, and everyone was aware of just how important a patient she was, but had it been a democracy the staff would've voted as a bloc to take her down to the river at the head of the falls and release the brake on her wheelchair.*

Instead of committing her to the rising waters they gave her into the care of Grace Roby, who trekked across the Iron Bridge above the swift spring torrent each morning shortly after six, rain or shine, to attend two cripples, one temporary, the other permanent. Actually, Mrs. Whiting's broken hip had been occasioned by her daughter, who'd lost her balance, grabbed onto her mother, who happened to be nearby, and taken both of them down. Cindy, thanks to a lifetime of practice, knew how to fall, whereas Mrs. Whiting, whose equilibrium, both physical and emotional, was not easily tilted and who had not fallen once during her entire adult life, shattered her hip, requiring her to cancel at the last moment her trip to Spain, where she'd rented a villa for the month.

The reason Cindy Whiting, then fifteen, had lost her balance and fallen on that occasion was that the operation to repair her damaged pelvis, her fourth, hadn't worked. The doctors had promised that if she underwent the procedure and then worked hard at her physical therapy, her equilibrium would be much improved, and she'd be less dependent on her walker for support. While there were no guarantees, perhaps by spring she'd be able to step unaided onto the dance floor at her junior prom, in need of no more support than the strong arm of some handsome boy. This was the carrot the doctors dangled before her, and Cindy Whiting had followed it bravely, yet again, into the operating room.

The procedure, the chief surgeon later concluded, was neither a success nor a failure. If that most important of medical injunctions was recollected— first, do no harm—then clearly Cindy Whiting was no worse off. In fact, over time, some slight improvement would surely be noted. That it was not more successful, the surgeon admitted, had less to do with the operation than with the patient, whom he hadn't expected to be so easily discouraged, nor so stubbornly averse to physical therapy. The staff reported from the start that neither cajoling nor prodding nor badgering had much effect, that nothing could shake her conviction that the procedure had been a complete failure, that her own efforts would therefore prove futile. Cindy preferred lying in bed and watching television and taking painkillers to being tortured in the physical therapy room. When the distressed surgeon tried to encourage the girl by reminding her of how excited she'd been by the prospect of attending her junior prom, she replied that cripples didn't get invited to dances.

Cindy Whiting's adamant refusal to work at her therapy so frustrated the surgeon that he called her mother in for a consultation. Before the operation, he recalled, one of the things the young woman had most looked forward to was her father's return from Mexico to be at her side, and he was interested to learn why that hadn't happened. Fathers, he hinted, were sometimes *able to motivate daughters in ways that neither mothers nor doctors could imagine. Cindy, he added, seemed particularly devoted to her father, and this just might work in their favor.*

Mrs. Whiting's response was not at all what he expected. She began by admitting that she herself was partly to blame for not preparing the surgeon for the operation's inevitable failure, and then assured him that her husband's presence would only have made a bad situation worse. Her daughter, she explained, had unfortunately inherited her father's fundamental weakness of character. Alas, he himself was a man too easily encouraged, too completely seduced by hope, only to be devastated by disappointment. He'd been born to privilege, conditioned to expect that things would go well, and pathetically unable to cope once they started to go wrong. Mrs. Whiting had done everything in her power to curb these tendencies in their daughter, but nature, it seemed, had overruled nurture. Like her father, Cindy was subject to vivid dreams, which she invariably surrendered without a fight. She assured the surgeon that, no, there was nothing further to be done, and that he was not to blame himself.

The surgeon was not a man who required any such warning. Blaming himself would not, in the normal course of events, have occurred to him. Nor, given his clinical training, was he used to regarding physical failure in moral terms, but as he listened to Mrs. Whiting's dispassionate profiles of her husband and daughter, he found it difficult not to arrive at a moral judgment, though not one he was inclined to share with her, at least not until his services had been paid in full.

IF COLD AND DISPASSIONATE, *Mrs. Whiting's analysis of her daughter's character was not, Grace Roby had to admit, far off the mark. Had Cindy Whiting even a small measure of her mother's willpower, she might, at least physically, have benefited from her most recent operation. As was often the case with children and their parents, this child possessed a trait immediately recognizable in the parent, except that in the child it had become so twisted as to appear completely new. Both women, Grace soon recognized, were equally stubborn, though their stubbornness manifested itself in radically different ways. In Mrs. Whiting willfulness had become a driving force whose relentless purpose was the removal of all obstacles, large and small, whereas in her daughter it took the form of the intractable, doomed obstinacy with which she approached each and every obstacle. To Grace, who'd always been drawn to the heartbreaking plight of the Whiting girl, it was terrible to witness the workings of human nature in the Whiting household and to* acknowledge the all-too-certain outcome of the struggle between mother and daughter.

Grace had never before encountered a woman quite like her new employer, and she quickly realized that to completely withhold her admiration was impossible. After months of close observation, Grace finally discovered her great trick. Mrs. Whiting remained undaunted for the simple reason that she never, ever allowed herself to dwell on the magnitude of whatever task she was confronted with. What she possessed was the marvelous ability to divide the chore into smaller, more manageable tasks. Once this diminishment was accomplished, her will became positively tidal in its persistence. Each day Mrs. Whiting had a "To Do" list, and the brilliance of that list lay in the fact that she was careful never to include anything undoable. On those rare occasions when a task proved more complicated or difficult than she'd imagined, she simply subdivided it. In this fashion, the woman never encountered anything but success, and each day brought her inexorably closer to her goal. She might be delayed, but never deterred.

Her daughter, on the other hand, was forever being deterred. Temperamentally unable to master her mother's simple trick, Cindy Whiting immediately envisioned the entirety of what lay before her and was thus in one deft stroke overwhelmed and defeated by it. She wasn't so much a dreamer, Grace came to understand, as a believer, and what she believed in, or wished to, was the possibility of complete transformation. At some point in her young life she'd come to believe that the whole world, the totality of her circumstance, would have to change if change was to do her any good. Therefore, what she sought was nothing short of a miracle, and it was in these terms that she'd judged her most recent operation. On Monday she would enter the hospital as a caterpillar; on Tuesday she would emerge a butterfly. Not long after the anesthesia wore off, the girl would've concluded that not only had no transformation taken place, none whatsoever was under way.

Did this disappointment make her foolish, even stupid, as her mother suggested? Grace thought not. After all, her whole world had undergone a complete transformation in the terrible instant when, as a little girl, she'd been run over and dragged by that car, an event that had taught her how quickly everything could change and that the stroke accomplishing such change is swift, powerful and beyond human comprehension. She was simply waiting for it to happen again.

BY MEMORIAL DAY, having worked for Mrs. Whiting for just under six weeks, Grace expected every day to be let go. With the garden in and her *employer recuperating faster than doctors had predicted, Grace suspected that before long Mrs. Whiting would see no justification for her continued employment. Not that her salary would make any difference to a wealthy woman, but still. Her employer didn't miss a trick when it came to money, and she seemed to know within pennies how much people needed to survive. The sum she'd offered Grace to come to work for her was so close to the bare minimum she desperately needed that she half wondered if the woman had somehow sneaked into her house and watched her juggling bills at the kitchen table.*

One afternoon in the garden, Mrs. Whiting was leaning on her cane and directing Grace, who looked up from her knees and said, "I hope, Mrs. Whiting, that when the time comes you don't need me anymore, you'll be able to give me two weeks' notice so I can find another job. I can't afford to be without work for long." Even for a day, she thought to herself.

Mrs. Whiting was wearing a straw hat, and she regarded Grace from beneath its broad brim. Was it a smile that played along her lips? "Where will you find work in Empire Mills? There wouldn't seem to be much in the way of opportunity."

"Still," said Grace, who understood that challenge all too well, "I'll have to look."

"Well, that's enough for today," Mrs. Whiting announced. She'd been on her feet most of the afternoon, and although Grace had done most of the actual labor, Mrs. Whiting was clearly tired, having only recently been liberated from her wheelchair. Grace got to her feet and helped her employer back into the chair. "You don't have to worry about looking for other employment just yet. You've been a great assistance to me these weeks."

Grace considered this vague reassurance. "But will there be work for me," she asked, "once you're fully recovered?"

"Let's sit in the gazebo for a few minutes," Mrs. Whiting suggested, causing Grace to regret her decision to raise the issue this afternoon. That morning she'd left David in bed with a severe cold, and she was hoping to return by midafternoon. She'd even mentioned this desire to Mrs. Whiting, who seemed effortlessly to have forgotten it.

The shady gazebo was cool. A temporary ramp made the building wheelchair-accessible, and Mrs. Whiting sat with her back to the house so she could look out over the river. Grace sat at an angle, facing the Iron Bridge downstream. When she heard the patio door slide open, she saw Cindy struggle out onto the patio. It was some seventy yards down the lawn to the gazebo—a journey the girl would not risk, not so soon after her operation, though she regarded Grace and her mother with what appeared to be genuine longing.

"What's to be done, do you suppose?" Mrs. Whiting finally said. She might have been musing about Empire Mills itself, for she was studying the now abandoned mills, their two large smokestacks looming against the late-afternoon sky. Grace heard the sliding door again and saw Cindy Whiting struggle back inside.

Her mother took off her straw gardening hat and placed it on the small round table between them. "You've grown fond of my daughter," she said.

"Yes," Grace freely admitted.

"Would you think me entirely unnatural if I told you I'm not, particularly?" She smiled then. "You don't have to answer, dear girl."

Grace was glad not to have to share her thoughts about one of the sadder human relationships she'd ever encountered. It was as if mother and daughter had somehow managed to disappoint each other so thoroughly that neither one was at all vested in the other anymore. They were like ghosts, each inhabiting different dimensions of the same physical space, so different that Grace half expected to see one pass through the other when their paths crossed. Cindy, coming upon her mother unexpectedly, acted as if she'd just remembered a question she'd been meaning to ask, only to realize she'd already asked it many times over and been given the same dispiriting answer. Mrs. Whiting, when she noticed her daughter at all, seemed merely annoyed. Sometimes they stared at each other in silence for so long that Grace wanted to scream.

"She's such a dear soul," Grace ventured. "Her suffering—"

"Lord, yes, her suffering," Mrs. Whiting agreed, as if commiserating with Grace, not her daughter. "It's positively endless, isn't it?"

"She's not to blame, surely?"

"It's hardly a question of blame, dear girl," Mrs. Whiting explained. "It's a question of need. You'll come to understand that what my daughter needs is not what she thinks she needs. You look at her and imagine she needs sympathy, whereas she needs strength. You'd be wise not to let her cling to you, unless of course you enjoy the sensation. Some people do."

It took Grace a moment to understand that she was being gently chided. "There are worse things than being clung to, aren't there?"

"Perhaps," the other woman acknowledged, as though none came to her off the top of her head. "Tell me. What does your family think of your being away from them so much?"

"David misses me, I think," Grace said. "He's still so little. He doesn't—"

"And the older boy?"

"Miles? Miles is my rock."

"And your husband?"

"Max is Max."

"Yes," Mrs. Whiting agreed. "Men simply are what they are."

Grace looked over the Iron Bridge. After a moment, she said, "Will we ever speak of him?"

"No, I think not," Mrs. Whiting answered, as easily as if she'd been offered some ice cream.

Which did not surprise Grace. They'd barely mentioned him the afternoon she'd first crossed the river to perform her penance. Grace had merely asked Mrs. Whiting's forgiveness and assured her that it was over between her and Charlie, that she was sorry for what she'd done, for what she'd tried to do.

"Will he ever return?"

"To Empire Mills?" Mrs. Whiting seemed to find the question odd. "I hardly think so. As a young man he always wanted to live in Mexico. Did you know that?"

"Yes."

She could feel the other woman's eyes on her now. Yes, of course it would mean something to Mrs. Whiting that her husband had shared his intimate dreams. "He seems quite happy there," she said, as if to suggest that in this happiness they'd both been betrayed.

"Does he ever—"

"Speak of you? I don't believe so, but of course he wouldn't, not to me."

"Does he know?"

"About our present arrangement? Yes. When I told him he seemed to appreciate the irony in it."

Grace took this in in silence.

"Have you any further questions before we put this subject forever to rest?"

Grace shook her head.

"Excellent. If my husband should ever attempt to contact you, I expect you to inform me. Will you do that?"

Grace hesitated for only a moment. "Yes."

"If you fail to keep your word, I will know," Mrs. Whiting said. "One look at you would reveal the whole truth."

"I'll keep my word."

"I believe you," Mrs. Whiting said. She seemed satisfied, as if she'd anticipated both the conversation and its outcome. "You'll work here for the foreseeable future, I imagine," she continued when Grace got to her feet. "You

should know, I've grown quite fond of you, dear girl. Perhaps there's irony in this as well?"

Grace was unable to think of a suitable response. Might it be possible that what Mrs. Whiting had just said was true? If so, did that mean she'd been forgiven? Or was it possible to be genuinely fond of someone you'd not forgiven? Illogical as this last possibility seemed, it was precisely Grace's impression.

PART FOUR

PART FOUR

"DON'T LOOK NOW," David said, looking up from his newspaper, "but here comes the happy groom, back from his honeymoon."

Indeed the Silver Fox was tripping up the front steps of the grill. Though Miles was not particularly pleased to see him, he couldn't help but smile at the fact that he hadn't heard the ticking of Walt's van when it pulled up out front, a sound that had haunted him for nearly a year. One more way his life had changed for the better since his illness.

After the wedding, of course, people kept asking how it felt to be a free man. Actually, to Miles's surprise, it felt pretty good, as if the many delays in the divorce proceedings had exhausted even his capacity for self-recrimination. He'd expected his ex-wife's wedding to take more of a toll on him, to intensify his feelings of personal failure. After all, he and Janine had promised till death do us part before God and family, and now here she was making the same promise all over again to another man. When the justice of the peace asked if anyone here objected to the proposed union, Miles was a little embarrassed to discover that he didn't, at least not anymore. He'd always resisted Janine's naive belief that you could just begin life anew, as if the past didn't exist, but she seemed to be doing exactly that, which suggested that Miles could too, especially now that he'd made his decision.

Of course, the jury was still out on Janine's new life. Miles felt bad that her big day had been such a cut-rate affair. Of course secular weddings always struck him as foreshortened, the ceremony over and done with almost before it began. It took longer to close on a house, and

Miles couldn't help noting that purchasing real estate was viewed, these days, as a more serious occasion, an undertaking with more lasting repercussions. But then, maybe it always had been. It was marriage, after all, that determined the right of inheritance, the orderly devolving of real property from one generation to the next. Perhaps the solemnity that once accompanied marriage was merely a by-product of an even weightier—if not sacred—rite.

The reception afterward was nearly as depressing. Janine had let it be known that what she wanted was a goddamn party, with a kick-ass band and a big dance floor where people could really cut loose. Where *she* could cut loose. The entire event seemed designed to illustrate Miles's many failures as a husband. The whole time they'd been married, she seemed to be saying, she'd been wanting music and excitement and dancing, and now that she was finally shut of Miles Roby, by God she was going to get it.

For this purpose, the biggest room around, if you pushed back the partition that separated the aerobics room from the Nautilus machines, was at Walt's health club, so they'd moved the various instruments of torture—Stairmasters and stationary bicycles and treadmills—out of the way and leaned the yoga mats up against the walls, which suggested that some of the revelers might be driving bumper cars. Judging from the size of the area cleared, Miles had the distinct impression that many more people had been invited than attended.

The band might have been good, for all Miles knew, but they played at a volume calculated to induce the growth of brain tumors. Miles stood off to one side with Bea, whose hemorrhoids were bothering her, and Horace Weymouth, who, as Walt Comeau's reluctant best man, was stuffed into a shiny tux. Miles hated to stare, but he was pretty sure the web of veins in whatever was growing out of Horace's forehead was pulsing in time with the bass guitar. Two hours seemed like a decent amount of time for an ex-husband who hadn't wanted a divorce in the first place to remain at his former wife's wedding reception, so when the band took its second break Miles found Janine and told her that he was leaving, that he wished her all happiness, that she looked terrific, which she did, though not especially bride-like.

"You're not skulking off without one last dance," she said, her face flushed, and she dragged Miles out to the middle of the floor. The band, determined to have equally deafening music fill the room even in their absence, was playing recorded music through their guitar amplifiers. To Miles's additional discomfort, almost everyone at the reception stopped and turned to watch them dance. People somehow seemed to feel that they were witnessing a touching moment.

"I warned you you were going to hate this," Janine said.

"I don't, really," he lied. "The music's a little loud, is all."

She appeared unconvinced. "You should've brought somebody," she said. "Charlene would have come if you'd asked her."

Though Miles could have done without the pitying tone, he was moved to consider the possibility that his ex-wife appeared, somewhat belatedly, to imagine the possibility that he might be lonely. "She's working, actually."

"So you give her the damn night off. You're the boss, Miles. You could close the restaurant if you wanted to." After twenty years of marriage and then some, he was still amazed by how quickly this woman could shift emotional gears from solicitude to annoyance.

"Janine," he sighed, "if you're trying to make me feel better about your being another man's wife, you're doing a good job."

At which her eyes teared up, causing him to apologize as she wept gently onto his shoulder, convincing onlookers that what they were witnessing went well beyond touching. It was damned inspirational. Even the Silver Fox himself got misty-eyed.

These sudden tears on the dance floor had not taken Miles by surprise. The week leading up to the wedding had been full of them, resulting in a series of hellish negotiations, several of which Miles had undertaken from his hospital bed. First, Janine had wanted him to give her away, a notion so bizarre that Miles had a laughing fit before he realized she was serious. She had immediately flushed red with anger and hurt. "I just thought it'd be nice if the whole thing was amicable," she snapped. "What's so wrong with that?"

Amicable. He'd repeated the word, recalling his high school Latin. *Amicus*, meaning "friend," the second noun they'd declined (the first was *agricola*, "farmer," which Miles had found odd, as if it were being suggested that in the normal course of events you'd have more use for the word "farmer" than for "friend").

"How about if I just turn up and smile a lot?" he suggested. "Wouldn't that be amicable enough?"

His ex-wife's eyes brimmed with tears. "Fine," she said. "I'll just give my own damn self away." Which struck Miles as a pretty accurate representation of what had transpired anyway.

If Janine had given in easily on the matter of his participation, it was because, Miles was to learn later, she had a bigger, more important battle to wage, and she needed his help if she was to have any hope of winning it, for her daughter had no more desire to play a dramatic role in her mother's wedding than Miles did. But here Janine was determined. "I swear to God, Miles, you better talk her into being my bridesmaid. I know you can, so I'm telling you right now that you'd better get busy."

Miles tried to reason with her. "You can't force her into doing something she doesn't want to do, Janine."

To which she replied, "I'm not forcing her, Miles. In fact, I gave her a choice. She can either do it or she can wish she had." Then she'd burst into tears right there in the hospital room, bawling her eyes out until Miles caved in and promised to try.

In fact, Janine had sobbed so pitifully that Miles thought she was suffering some kind of breakdown. "You know I don't have a single woman friend in the whole world, Miles." She snuffed her nose, having by now worn herself out with crying. "If she won't be my bridesmaid, I'll have to ask my mother. Don't make me do that, Miles. I know what you must think of me after all that's happened, but if you *ever* cared for me, don't make me stand there between Beatrice and Walt on my wedding day. The judge'll probably get confused and marry the two of them."

The deal Miles had brokered with his daughter was complex, but its principal features were that she would be her mother's bridesmaid and pretend to enjoy herself, provided that afterward, at the reception, she wouldn't be required to dance with the Silver Fox. Also, Miles promised to take her to Boston to see the van Gogh exhibit at the MFA, something he'd have done anyway. He found out later she'd struck a separate deal with her mother to get their computer hooked up to an e-mail server.

"So, are you going to be okay?" Janine wanted to know, confusing him for a moment. Did she mean while she was away on her honeymoon? "Did they ever figure out what was wrong with you?"

They had not. He'd made it back to his apartment that Sunday evening, but later, when his brother came over (after Bea had phoned, asking him to check), Miles was delirious. At the emergency room, his raging temperature and delirium, subsequent to eating fast-food burgers, suggested an *E. coli* infection or, possibly, viral meningitis. He'd been admitted to the hospital and kept there for several days under close observation, even though his fever broke the next morning and by Monday afternoon he was clearly on the mend. By the end of his stay, the half dozen doctors who'd examined him and done his blood work were no closer to a diagnosis. As medical men they'd not sought a spiritual explanation, and Miles was disinclined to ask whether the symptoms they'd been treating might result from his having been visited by ghosts.

As was his custom as a single man, Walt Comeau now burst into song in the doorway of the Empire Grill. "Too many nights," he crooned, his arms outstretched to embrace the world. "Too many days / Too many nights to be alone."

"Can it," suggested David, who had neither gone to the wedding nor sent regrets.

Walt paused briefly, as if this request were the title of a song not in his repertoire. Then he began anew, though at a lower volume, dancing down the counter. "Please keep your heart / While we're apart / Don't linger in the moonlight when I'm gone."

From down the counter came a couple of halfhearted "Pa-pa-pa-payas."

"My *God*, Big Boy!" Walt said, sliding onto his usual stool next to Horace, who'd arrived early enough to eat his bloody burger in peace. "How could you let a woman like that escape?"

Walt and Janine had checked into a bed-and-breakfast on the coast that was running a special off-season rate. Janine, Miles happened to know, had been hoping for Aruba.

"Don't let the stars get in your eyes, Foxy," Horace advised, wiping the counter between them with his dirty napkin in preparation for their gin game.

"Don't let the moon break your heart, either," Buster added without turning around. His first shift since returning to town was nearly over, and he was pouring vinegar onto the hot grill, where it sputtered and foamed and hissed. The air was full of it for a few seconds, enough to get everyone at the counter teared up, but just as quickly it was gone, with an implicit promise that anything so intensely horrible would by design pass swiftly.

"Where were *you* last Saturday?" Walt called down the counter to David. "You missed one hell of a party."

What Miles had heard was that after he left, his ex-wife had danced several strong men into a state of exhaustion, got very drunk, and then berated the band when they finally quit and began packing up their instruments.

David folded his newspaper and rose to his feet, reaching for a clean apron. "Something about the occasion just didn't stir me," he explained.

"Gin," said Horace, laying down his hand and taking up the tablet they used to keep score. "Honest, ain't he?" he said, more to Miles than to Walt.

"Jealous is what he is," Walt said happily, the gin not having registered fully. "He and Big Boy are both jealous. They'd like to kid me that they aren't, but I know better."

"That must be it," Horace agreed. "You going to tell me how many points I caught you with, or do you want me to estimate?"

Walt now stared at the hand Horace had laid down. "You can't have gin already."

"Name one way that isn't gin."

The Silver Fox laid his own hand down and began counting to himself.

"I'll make it easy for you. Fifty-two plus the gin is seventy-two," said Horace, writing it down. "I hope you don't mind me beating you quicker than usual today. I'm driving over to Augusta for the school budget vote, so I don't have time to toy with you."

"Seventy-two," Walt said, completing his own count.

"Open this for me, will you?" Buster said, handing Miles a gallon jar of pickles and rubbing his wrist. Buster's eye had quit draining, but it was still horrible to look at, red and swollen nearly shut. He looked like he'd lost about thirty pounds since summer. Lyme disease, according to his doctor. "I don't seem to have any strength anymore."

Horace shook his head. "Thirty-five years' worth of jerking off with that hand, you'd think he could open a jar of pickles."

"Go home, Buster," Miles said. "I'll finish up here."

The fry cook took off his apron, handing it to Miles without argument. "I'll feel better tomorrow, I promise."

"Give that here," Walt said, meaning the pickle jar. He was already stripping down to his tight, weight lifter's undershirt, as if playing gin with Horace might require a full, unencumbered range of motion. Despite Walt Comeau's professed love of all things sexual, Miles suspected there was nothing he enjoyed more than opening a jar someone else had given up on, so he ignored him, located a rubber snaffler, and twisted the lid off the jar.

"That's cheating," Walt complained. "Anybody can open a jar with one of those."

"Gin," said Horace, who again laid down his cards.

"A damn kid could open a jar with one of those," Walt told Horace, who for some reason was grinning at him. "What do you mean, gin?"

"Sixty-nine plus the gin," Horace explained, writing "89" on the pad between them.

"Eighty-seven," Walt said when he'd completed his arithmetic. He pushed the cards toward his opponent in disgust.

"Count 'em again," Horace suggested, pushing them back.

Walt did, and after a minute revised the tally. "Eighty-nine," he said.

Horace showed him the pad where he'd written that number down already.

"It *could've* been you that was wrong," Walt pointed out. "Did that ever occur to you?"

Horace shuffled and offered Walt a cut, which he took. "Sure it did," Horace admitted. "I always prefer to eliminate the more likely scenarios first, though."

Walt was too busy picking up his cards, one at a time, and arranging them in his hand to consider this insult. "I hear you're going to be getting some competition, Big Boy," he observed, once his hand made enough sense that he could offer up a discard.

David was at the refrigerator, and when Miles glanced over he saw that his brother hadn't even broken rhythm. Miles liked to think you couldn't tell anything from his own demeanor either, but he noticed Horace studying him curiously.

"How's that, Walt?" he asked, trying to keep his voice modulated.

"Janine tells me her mother's opening up for lunches again over at Callahan's," the bridegroom reported, picking up one of Horace's discards. "Next month sometime."

"I wish her luck," Miles said, meaning it. Actually, he'd spent most of the morning over at Bea's tavern with an electrician. The news had not been good. There wasn't an inch of wiring in the kitchen—in the whole building, for that matter—that was up to code, which was fine as long as it was left alone. Renovations, however, as mandated by state law, had to be up to code, which in effect meant that *all* the old, grandfathered wiring had to be brought up to standard. Neither Bea nor Miles could come up with that kind of money without going to the bank, something neither of them wanted to do, since it would make their plans public. Miles, in particular, was determined to keep them a secret, at least until late October, when Mrs. Whiting usually left for the winter.

"They used to serve a hell of a pastrami sandwich over there back when her husband was still alive. Must've been two inches thick. All you could do to eat it."

David lifted a big rack of prime rib, already rubbed with herbs, out of the fridge. When he lost his grip with his bad hand, it dropped the last few inches into the shallow roasting pan and he turned to acknowledge Miles's look. Yes, he should've asked for help; next time he would, maybe. "You actually sprang for a sandwich?" David said, voicing his brother's thought as well.

"Tell you what," Walt said, eyeing his opponent suspiciously. "I'm gonna go down with three."

Horace seemed underwhelmed by this maneuver. "Eight minus your three," he said, showing Walt his hand, then recorded the paltry five points in his own clean column.

"You had my damn gin card again," Walt complained. "How come you never give me my gin card?"

"Because," Horace explained, "that would make you win and me lose."

Miles noticed a police car pass by outside, but couldn't tell if Jimmy Minty was at the wheel. He watched the car move slowly down the street, half expecting it to stop, do a three-point turn and pull over to the curb facing the restaurant. Three times in the last week he'd seen Minty parked up the street, and the last time it had made him so angry he'd called the chief of police.

"Why is Jimmy Minty surveilling my restaurant?"

"He's not. We got a radar trap set up, is all," Bill Daws explained. "These damn kids all think that because nobody lives here anymore they can do fifty through the center of town. If you don't mind my asking, what's all this about between you and him?"

"Hard to explain," Miles admitted.

"Try."

"He seems to remember us being friends once. Maybe we were."

"You aren't anymore."

"I know it."

"Listen, I've been meaning to call you. Unless somebody does something, I'm afraid your ex-friend's going to be made interim chief when I step down."

"You going somewhere, Bill?"

"It appears I am. I've got cancer, though that's not public knowledge."

"My God, Bill."

"Hell, I've had a good run."

"You're getting treatment?"

"Sure. Have been for a while. It's the damn cure that's killing me. Anyhow, Minty's got friends in high places," Bill Daws said, "including a friend of yours. Maybe if you spoke to her. People say she listens to you."

"She does," Miles admitted. "She never does a single thing I ask her to, though."

"Still," Bill Daws said, "you'd be doing the town a favor if you'd try. There's nothing worse than a bad cop."

"Sure there is," Miles said. "And I'm sorry to hear about it, Bill. Is there anything I can do?"

"Don't tell a living soul."

This was the first cruiser he'd seen since their conversation, and at the bottom of Empire Avenue it hung a left and disappeared just as Tick turned the corner and headed up the hill toward the restaurant. Maybe it was Miles's imagination, but lately his daughter appeared to be walking a little straighter under her heavy backpack. The best part of the last couple days, with Janine and Walt honeymooning on the coast, was that he'd stayed with Tick at the house so she wouldn't be alone at night. He'd slept on the sofa and returned to his apartment before showering, but even so it had seemed pretty strange to be back in what had been his home for so many years. He did his best not to feel bitter about his loss of the place, to simply enjoy his daughter's company, and most of the time he'd been successful. Tick's companionship, alas, had been divided unequally between her father and her computer keyboard, which she clicked away at feverishly, the boy she'd met on Martha's Vineyard clicking back at her from Indianapolis. When he'd written her two weeks earlier he'd included his e-mail address, and apparently it was possible for them to talk to each other directly, simultaneously, keyboard to keyboard. Such intimacy. Every now and then, Miles, reading a book in the next room, would hear his daughter chortle at something the boy had typed, and when he looked up, her face would be aglow before the computer screen, a girl clearly in the throes of cyber romance. Could such a thing be called real? Miles decided it could, at least if it lightened the load of her backpack.

Loping along at her side this afternoon was the tall, awkward figure of John Voss, who was busing David's private party tonight. They were an odd pair—his daughter and John—but it appeared they were actually conversing, which shouldn't have seemed odd, but it did. In some ways it was odder that she should be talking to this strange boy at her side than that she should converse nightly with a boy over a thousand miles away by means of a keyboard. When they arrived at the restaurant, John Voss, mute and nervous as always, headed straight for the back room to his dirty pots and pans. He'd been working at the Empire Grill for three weeks now and, as Miles had predicted, had become a good, reliable busboy. There were times on weekends that Miles wished the kid had one more gear, but he worked steadily and efficiently, if not urgently. He followed orders well, and Miles had even taught him how to clean the caked soap out of the Hobart's spider mechanism. But though he responded when spoken to, it remained impossible to engage him in normal conversation. When Miles gave him his first paycheck, the boy looked at it as if he had no idea what use it might be, and only later did Miles intuit that he had no idea how to convert the check to cash, so Miles escorted him down to Empire National, helped him open a savings account, and showed him how to record his deposits. The boy had managed to convey, however awkwardly, his gratitude, but when he reported for work the next day, he offered Miles neither a smile nor an acknowledgment, as if the day before had not occurred. In the three weeks of their acquaintance, John Voss had not once met Miles's eye, and even Charlene had made little progress.

Tick gave her uncle a kiss and slid her heavy backpack to the floor with a thud that rattled glasses and coffee cups, then gave her father one of her quick, sideways hugs.

"Hey, there, Littabit!" Walt bellowed, rotating on his stool and holding out his arms. "How about giving me one of those?"

Tick acknowledged neither the man nor the noise he'd made. Apparently Walt's installation of e-mail onto her computer hadn't earned him any affection points. "New Empire Moment," she announced to her father. "Have you seen the sign at the Lamplighter?"

Miles tried to recall whether he'd driven by in the last couple of days, then shook his head.

"Their new special's 'chicken smothered with barbecue sauce.'"

Miles chuckled, wondering if he would have caught this one himself. "Kinder to just chop their heads off, huh?" Then a different thought, since the Lamplighter was out by the Fairhaven Highway. "When were you out there?"

"A lot of my friends have their licenses now," she said, pouring a tall Coke for herself and another, he supposed, for John. "Don't worry. I wasn't at the motel."

"I never thought you were." He had to smile at the phrase "a lot of my friends." Not so long ago she'd been telling him she didn't have *any* friends. Now she had all kinds, some with driver's licenses, some as far away as Indiana.

"Is there any chance we could go to Boston next Sunday? The van Gogh's only there two more weeks."

"I'll see if your uncle's willing to flip eggs next Sunday morning." He paused. "Hey, is there any chance Indiana Jones is planning a trip to Boston anytime soon?"

"Next Sunday," she admitted, trying not to smile. Apparently she was as pleased with him for figuring this out as he'd been with her for the smothered chickens.

"He's another van Gogh lover, this kid?"

"Donny," she said, before disappearing into the back room. Before the door swung shut, Miles glimpsed John Voss kneeling in front of the dishwasher, its door flung wide open and leaking thick clouds of steam. The boy was peering up into its innards, ice pick in hand.

"THAT'S A HUNDRED-DOLLAR VALUE, Big Boy," Walt hollered down the counter. The Silver Fox had progressed, all too predictably, from another whipping at gin, to urging Miles to arm-wrestle him. As an inducement he was offering a free three-month membership at his health club, which he maintained would change Miles's life by improving his self-esteem. Having married Janine, Walt now seemed more determined than ever to compensate her ex-husband for his loss. "Nobody in his right mind would turn down that kind of offer."

"Could I convince you to do next Sunday morning?" Miles asked his brother.

David sighed—with good reason, since he'd had to work double shifts when Miles was in the hospital. Now this. "What's wrong with Buster? He was just complaining he needs more hours."

"I could ask him," Miles said. In fact, if David said no, he'd have to. "I'm not sure he'd be able to answer the bell after one of his Saturday nights, is the thing." Buster's doctor had warned him to lay off the booze until he got his strength back, but not drinking on Saturday night ran contrary to all of the man's natural inclinations.

"You know how I hate breakfasts, Miles."

"I promised Tick I'd take her to the Museum of Fine Arts," Miles explained, his voice low so Walt wouldn't overhear and volunteer his services. "The show she wants to see is ending pretty soon."

"Okay."

"Unless you wanted to take her yourself. She'd love that."

"No, you go," David said, opening the oven door and peering at the prime rib roasting slow inside. He'd also prepared a pan of red potatoes in herbs, which Miles picked up and slid onto the rack above the beef. If he hadn't been there, David somehow would have handled it, using the crook of his arm to cradle one end of the pan, his good hand to grip and guide. His awkwardness was one reason his brother didn't like to drive long distances, Miles knew. Actually, freeway driving would be easier than the in-town variety, but with only one good hand, David didn't trust himself in an emergency, especially with Tick in the truck.

"Since we're whispering," David said, "how much longer do you expect to keep Callahan's a secret?" According to plan, they'd be out of the Empire Grill by Thanksgiving, Christmas at the latest. The problem was that plan was already falling apart, the news from the electrician this morning being only the latest example.

"As long as possible," Miles said. "Let it come out in its own time." He knew what his brother meant, though. It was getting harder and harder to conceal the amount of time they were spending over at Bea's. And then there were all the phone calls, which Miles tried to conduct in a low voice, because there were usually customers within earshot, but of course nothing attracted their interest more than a confidential tone.

"I don't understand," David said. He'd been cheered by Miles's unexpected change of heart but troubled by his refusal to explain how it had come about. And his insistence on secrecy made no sense at all. "It's not like she can *do* anything, even if she wanted to. For all you know, she'll be delighted to be shut of this place. You'd do better to come clean. Plus you owe her that much."

"Aren't you the one who's always telling me what I *don't* owe her?" Miles reminded him. "Besides, I'm not so sure there's nothing she could do, not if she put her mind to it."

"If that's true, wouldn't you rather know sooner than later?"

"I'd rather she went away and stayed away for a month or two. I don't know why she's hanging around, and I keep thinking maybe it's us."

"More likely it's development office business," David said, reasonably enough. "Somebody said she had a bunch of visitors out to her place this week."

"Black limos with Massachusetts plates again?"

"Okay," his brother conceded. "But if you're right, and if she's suspicious and means to cause problems, find out *before* you start borrowing money and making commitments. When she sees how things are, maybe she'll relent on that liquor license and you won't even *have* to move."

"I couldn't do that to Bea."

"No, I suppose not. My point is, the whole thing's going to come out soon anyhow. You're no secret-keeper."

Miles let this go. Since recognizing "Charlie Mayne" in the newspaper, Miles hadn't said a word about it to anyone, including his brother, even though his discovery had changed everything. That Sunday morning, he'd felt the knowledge taking root somewhere in his gut and imagined its tentacles probing outward into other parts of his body. Was it that he and his brother had never spoken easily that prevented him from sharing this secret? Of all the subjects they'd been tight-lipped about over the years, their mother had always been right at the top of the list, so maybe that was it. Or maybe it was the possibility that David already knew—that if Miles blurted out the story, his brother would say, Good Lord, Miles, you're just figuring *that* out?

It would've been easier to confide in Father Mark, but for some reason Miles hadn't told him either. In fact, he hadn't even been back to St. Cat's since that afternoon he'd scraped the south face and imagined Father Tom sending his mother across the Iron Bridge to perform her penance. Now he wasn't sure he'd ever go back, not even to the Rectum. For some reason the secret's tentacles had wrapped themselves around his easy friendship with Father Mark and squeezed all the enjoyment out of it. The priest had visited him in the hospital, but he didn't stay long and seemed distracted. Their conversation had been as uneasy as it was the afternoon Father Tom had gone missing, when it had seemed that each man was aware of having failed the other by not imagining what these two old men were capable of. If this was a matter of simple embarrassment, in time it would surely go away, but Miles feared it was something more complex. For the moment, he'd concluded that the church—or at least its representative, Father Tom— had been worse than no help to his mother when she desperately needed it, and for now he'd decided to steer his own course, much as Grace had.

"I shouldn't butt in," David said, "but I'll tell you one more thing. You ought to call that woman."

Miles sighed, aware that his brother wasn't talking about Mrs. Whiting anymore but rather her daughter, who'd called him at the hospital last week and twice since then at the restaurant. He'd managed to fend her off with vague promises of dinner at the Empire Grill as soon as he was recovered, a promise he'd not kept.

Yet more tentacles here. Was it conceivable that Cindy already knew the truth? Was that the reason she'd taken him to the cemetery, to stand before the two lovers' graves? Would he even have made the connection in the newspaper the next morning if Cindy hadn't foreshadowed it? Miles found himself recasting their entire past in light of the cruel possibility that Cindy had known more than he did from the start. He recalled in particular the high school afternoons when they'd waited together for Mrs. Whiting's black Lincoln to pull up, and how willful the young Cindy had been in her disdain for Emily Dickinson. Out of dark necessity had she become expert at not understanding things she didn't want to be true? Miles could almost imagine Mrs. Whiting whispering, *This woman who's been so kind to you? She's the one your father loved, the one he wanted to run off with. This boy you like so much? The very child he preferred to you.* Miles remembered, too, that book of Cindy Whiting's: "How it made her pussy pucker!" Was this, in its own cheap way, helping the poor girl understand how such things could happen between men like her father and women like Grace? Was it possible Cindy herself had fallen in love with Miles because she'd been told he was her father's preference?

He tried to reason through these questions toward logical answers, but reason seemed to lead him instead to further questions. Probably, he'd concluded, Cindy's devotion to her father's memory suggested that she didn't know the truth. She seemed to blame his desertion on her mother, not on Grace, whom she remembered with genuine affection. If the two were linked in her mind, it was in their love for herself, not for each other. On the other hand, what was more mysterious and confusing, to child and adult alike, than love? Yes, he should call her. His brother was right. But he wouldn't, not yet.

"Listen," David said, when Miles greeted his recommendation with silence. "Forget I said anything. It's none of my business, I know."

"No," Miles told him. "It's good advice. In fact, you've been giving me good advice right along. I should've been listening."

"Well, I never listened to you when I needed to. I just hope you don't have to hit a tree doing fifty like I did."

"Maybe that's exactly what I need," Miles said, feeling that in a sense he already had. "You've been the one on the ball lately, not me."

David shook his head. "It's not the tree that did it. I was so fucked up for so long that by the time I got straightened out, not many people had any expectations left. I'm not so much on the ball as off the board. No, hitting the tree isn't a strategy I'd recommend. There are too many people who'll never really forgive you."

Miles would've liked to deny the truth of that, at least for himself, but he couldn't. He'd meant to forgive his brother, maybe even imagined he had. He'd also meant to learn to trust him, but instead merely fell into the habit of waiting for him to fuck up again, even though he hadn't for a long time.

"Why don't you go up and take a nap?" his brother suggested. "You look beat."

"Maybe I will," Miles said. "You need me tonight?"

"Well, I'd be a fool to turn down the offer." David grinned, an offer, Miles understood, in return.

As he trudged upstairs, the phone in his apartment was ringing. Because they'd just been speaking of her, Miles expected it to be Cindy Whiting, but he was wrong.

"You done with that church yet?" said the voice at the other end.

"Hello, Dad," Miles said. "Where are you?"

"That job probably ain't going so quick with me gone and you afraid to climb a stepladder."

"I've been out of commission, actually."

"How come?"

"I got sick. They had me in the hospital for a couple days."

"I wondered where the hell you were. I been calling."

"Then Janine and Walt Comeau got married this weekend."

"Good for her."

"Thanks, Dad," Miles said. "Listen, did you say where you were? Did I miss that part?"

"Florida," Max said, as if everybody knew that much. "You should come down. Good place for a single guy."

"Where's Father Tom?"

"Down the other end of the bar. He won second place in a Hemingway look-alike contest. He's got a beard now. Came in all white."

"How could you do it, Dad?"

"Let him grow a beard? Why shouldn't he?"

"You know what I mean. How could you take money from a senile priest and run off to Florida and drink it all up?"

"I never took a dime."

"No, you just let him pay for everything, right?"

Max didn't deny this.

Miles rubbed his temples. That these two geezers had made it all that way was truly astonishing. How had they managed to avoid being spotted by the troopers of every state from here to Key West, all of whom had been put on the lookout for a purple Crown Victoria driven by two old men who looked like escapees from a mental hospital? "Is the car still in one piece?"

"Should be. We left it at the public landing."

"What public landing?"

"In Camden."

"Congratulations. Now you've lost me."

"We come down here on the *Lila Day*. Me and Tom crewed."

"Wait a minute. You want me to believe you and Father Tom crewed a *schooner* all the way from Camden, Maine, to the Florida Keys?"

"Not just the two of us, you dummy. Cap'n Jack and four other guys. I'm an old salt, you know."

You're an old something, all right, Miles thought.

"Tom fell overboard once, but we went back for him. After that he was more careful."

Miles tried to imagine the old priest, trussed up in a life jacket, bobbing on the rough water, cold and uncomprehending. He could even appreciate the justice of it, given that the old man had been heartless enough to send Grace on that walk across the Iron Bridge. So why wasn't he able to take much pleasure from it? "Dad," he said, "do you have any idea what'll happen to you if Father Tom gets hurt?"

"Yep," his father said, confident he knew the answer to this question better than the man who'd asked it. "Not a goddamn thing."

Okay, he was probably right.

"Why shouldn't he have a little fun?" was what Max wanted to know, since they were asking questions. "Old men like to have fun too, you know. Down here, people *like* old men."

"Why?"

"They don't say," Max admitted. "Tom hears confessions every afternoon at the end of the bar. You should see it."

"That's terrible, Dad."

"Why? Think about it."

"It's sacrilegious."

"Your mother really messed you up, you know that?"

And that was all it took, just the one mention of Grace, and suddenly the question was out before Miles could consider the wisdom of asking it. "How come you never told me about Mom and Charlie Whiting, Dad?"

Max reacted as if he'd been expecting the question for years. "How come you never told *me*, son?"

CHAPTER 24

"So what are we *doing* here?" Justin Dibble whined, causing Zack Minty to regret, for about the tenth time in the last half hour, inviting him along. Inviting him by promising to kick his ass if he didn't come. Zack had his reasons for wanting company, but damned if he could remember them, and now here was Double Dibble wanting to know the exact thing Zack couldn't really explain.

"Waiting for it to get dark," Zack told him. Which was true. He'd parked the Camaro on the shoulder of the old landfill road in the gathering dusk. The house the Voss kid lived in with his grandmother was just visible through the trees, though. You couldn't see the car from the house unless you were looking for it.

"You're just pissed off 'cause he showed you up," Justin said, rolling down his window to toss out an empty Cheetos bag.

"That's a two-hundred-dollar fine," Zack pointed out. One of the good things about being a cop's son was that over time you learned what all the consequences were. That didn't mean you wouldn't take a chance anyway, but at least you knew how big a rod they'd stick up your ass if you got caught. To Zack's way of thinking, some crimes were worth the risk, but it was hard to imagine anybody dumb enough to risk a two-hundred-dollar fine over a sixty-cent bag of Cheetos.

"How would anybody know it was me?" Justin said, licking his orange fingers.

"You wipe your hands on my dad's upholstery, he'll fuck you up good."

Double Dibble kept on licking, the clean fingers glistening, the others still Cheeto-orange. "Nah, your dad likes me."

"Not as much as he likes this car," Zack reminded him. "Not even close."

Just one orange finger, the middle one, was extended now. Justin sucked on it provocatively.

"John Voss showed me up when, dipshit?"

"Playing the game."

Zack knew this was coming, of course. He'd put off responding to the remark so it would seem like it didn't mean shit to him. "How the fuck do you figure that? I'm the one that taught him."

"Yeah, but he's better at it. You flinch."

"The fuck I do."

"You flinch, every time."

"Right. Like you'd know. You're too chicken to play, even."

Justin shrugged, wiping his fingers on his pants.

Zack would have liked to drop the subject, but couldn't. "The reason he doesn't *flinch* is he doesn't have a *brain*. He's too stupid to be scared."

"You're the one who's always saying there's nothing to be scared of," Justin reminded him, examining the orange streaks on his baggy chinos with mild regret. "That's why we're all supposed to play, right?"

"It's a rush, okay? What I'm saying is, he's so fucking stupid he doesn't even get the rush." Justin didn't look convinced. "Anyway, fuck you. You don't play, you don't get to criticize."

"I played once. It's a dumb game."

"A dumb game that made you piss your pants," Zack snorted.

One thing was for sure. Zack was going to have to sit down and reevaluate his whole friend situation, which was going from bad to worse. It wasn't that long ago he'd had pretty cool friends. Now he was surrounded on all sides by losers. This was what happened when you didn't pay attention.

Some of it couldn't be helped, of course. Zed and Thomas had moved away with their parents, and they'd been the best of the bunch. Then a couple other friends decided they wouldn't have anything to do with him anymore, though they never said why. Like he couldn't figure it out when they started hanging out at the country club pool and playing fag sports like tennis and golf. Which left him with pretty slim pickings, like Justin Fucking Double Dibble. He'd actually been pretty cool in junior high, but now it was like he didn't give a shit anymore. He'd been a pretty decent basketball player, but he wouldn't even try out for the team, which was fucking stupid because he probably would've made it. Anymore all he wanted to do was eat junk food and play video games and whack off to that porn shit he was always downloading off the Net.

Next year would be better. As one of the few sophomores on varsity, Zack had been admired, if not completely accepted or welcomed by the older guys, especially the seniors. At times it almost seemed like they'd heard something about him before they even met him, something that made them suspicious. He'd thought it'd be different after the Fairhaven game, but Coach had fucked him over by giving the starting linebacker job back to Billy Wolff after his ankle healed. Like that was all it took for him to forget who made the hit that turned the whole fucking game around. Coach hadn't come right out and said it, but Zack was pretty sure he blamed Zack for all the bad publicity. The Fairhaven quarterback hadn't played since, and in the paper last week it said his parents were taking him to Boston to see if they could find out why his headaches wouldn't go away. Zack could've told them why. The headaches wouldn't go away because then the pansy would have to play again. One good shot had separated the kid from his desire to play football.

A late hit, they were calling it now, after they'd watched the game film, which didn't even really show it, since the camera had followed the flight of the ball. Coach got asked about it in an interview and said the tape wasn't conclusive, but in the locker room before the last game he'd given a speech about wanting all good clean hits, and a lot of the guys had glanced over at Zack, and then down at the floor. Which had pissed him off so much he'd immediately gotten into a shoving match with a kid on the opening kickoff, resulting in offsetting penalties. He'd spent the rest of the game at the very end of the bench. Coach hadn't even looked his way, except to shake his head. So maybe things would be better next year, and maybe they wouldn't.

Zack studied the house, now visible in silhouette through the trees. Which was weird, if you thought about it. The Voss kid, who at first hadn't wanted them to give him a ride home the other night, and then didn't want them to turn down the dirt drive, claimed his grandmother was sick and shouldn't be disturbed. But the house had been dark, just like it was now. Was the old woman so fucked up she couldn't get out of bed to switch on the light, or so completely out of it she didn't know when it was night?

"So what's the deal with Tick?" he said, without looking at his passenger. "She got something going with this John Voss?" The reason he wanted Justin along, he now recalled, wasn't just to have somebody keep watch. He wanted to think this whole situation through one more time. Double Dibble was in art class and sat at the same table with Tick and John Voss—and that fat pig Candace—so maybe he could help Zack out a little.

Justin shrugged. "She just feels sorry for him."

Zack considered this possibility. True, Tick was like that, big-hearted when it came to losers. She had this idea she was going to be an artist, but unless Zack missed his guess, she'd probably end up opening a home for three-legged dogs. He'd recently seen a story on TV about some shit-for-brains woman in California who took in wounded animals of every description, even big fuckers that ate like fifty pounds of dog food a day, and let them limp and hop around her ranch like an army of spastics. Instead of begging donations to feed them, what she should've asked for was enough bullets to put them out of their misery. "So how come she got him a job at her old man's restaurant?"

Justin shrugged, clearly thinking he'd just answered that question. Getting the kid a job was something you might do if you felt sorry for him. "She's in love with some kid she met on vacation, is what I heard," Justin answered instead. "He lives in Indiana or someplace."

"Or *someplace*? Like, one or the other? If not Indiana, then *someplace*? You sure about that? You sure it's not, like, *someplace else*?"

"I'm just saying what I heard."

"Heard from who?"

"Candace."

"The blow-job queen."

"Hey," Justin said, "she wants to give *me* a header, I'll take it."

"That's because you got no standards," Zack explained.

"You telling me you wouldn't like to nuzzle those tits?"

"She's a fat cow, is what I'm telling you."

"Big tits isn't the same as fat." Justin appeared to have strong, confident views on this particular subject. "Fat is stomach and waist and thighs. Big tits is a whole different thing."

Zack wasn't terribly interested in this abstract physiology argument, or any of Double Dibble's other opinions, either. So what if Tick was in love with some faggot from Indiana or Someplace? Like he was supposed to care? Zack was fast coming around to his father's point of view on the subject of girls, who seemed to inhabit this earth for the sole purpose of fucking with your head. "They're not happy unless they get under your skin," was how his father had explained it, back when he was trying to make Zack understand about his mother and all the trouble and why she left. "They never come at you straight," his father went on, "like a man would. They just nick away at you, a little nick here, a little nick there. At first you don't even think you're bleeding, then the next thing you know you're a quart low, maybe two." But they had you over a barrel too, his father always added. What could you do, turn into a fag?

"What do you bet we find a bunch of queer magazines under his bed?" Zack said. This possibility had come to him last night, and he'd been turning it over in his mind all day. Until they'd played the game, Zack had figured the kid for a total wimp. Now he didn't know what to think, because Justin was right—the kid hadn't flinched. He'd held the barrel right to his temple and pulled the trigger, like it was nothing. Of course, if he was a queer, that made sense. He probably figured he was better off dead anyway, so what the fuck.

"What do you mean *we*? I already told you I'm not breaking into any house."

"It's not breaking in if you have a key. If we get caught, we'll just say the door was unlocked and we just stopped by to see if our buddy John wanted to hang out. No big deal."

"He's gonna freak when he finds out."

"Why? What's he so afraid of?" This fucking kid who didn't flinch.

"He's probably, like, ashamed or something."

"Ashamed or something? What's that, like Indiana or Someplace?"

"Maybe his grandmother's this crazy lady who pisses in her stockings or talks in tongues and shit. I don't like anybody meeting my parents, either. My old man raises up on one cheek to fart. His corduroy chair's got this smell you wouldn't believe. My mom sleeps till noon and wanders around in her robe all day."

"I'm sure they're real proud of you, too," Zack said.

CROUCHING LOW, they crept along the treeline toward the dilapidated house in the pale light of an almost full moon. In the car, Zack had doubted both his purpose and his resolve, but being on his feet and moving made him feel strong and sure. Justin, the pussy, had wanted to wait in the car, but Zack had insisted he come this far. If a passerby stopped and asked Justin what he was doing just sitting there in the dark, he'd piss his pants and blow the whole thing.

"What if she's got a shotgun or something?" Justin whispered, when they'd made it as far as the stand of pine trees twenty yards from the back porch.

"The same crazy old woman who pisses her stockings has a fucking shotgun?"

"I lived all the way out here with no neighbors, I'd have one."

"Why are you *such* a pussy?"

He shrugged. "What am I supposed to do while you're in there?"

"How should I know? Think about Candace's tits and jerk off."

"Okay," Justin said, and with that he pretended to do as instructed.

This was the dangerous part, Zack thought as he moved out across the weedy lawn toward the back of the house. For twenty yards he'd be in the open, visible in the moonlight from both the road and the house. Maybe girls were a mystery, like his father said, but to Zack fear was an even bigger puzzle. The way it came and went. The way it made no sense. That's what the game was all about, really, and the reason he'd invented it in the first place. If the gun was empty and you knew it, if you'd taken the bullets out yourself and you'd double-checked to make sure you hadn't missed any, then the fucking thing couldn't shoot you. If you knew anything in the world at the instant you pulled the trigger, you knew that. Why, then, was it so hard to do? Why, if you weren't this fucking Voss kid, did you flinch?

He wished now that he'd never introduced him to the game. Almost wished he'd never invented it. In the beginning it was fun, watching people freak out when they saw you do it. Tick had been the worst. He'd known better, even at the time, than to play the game with her, but he'd gone ahead and done it anyway—though he never expected her to go completely ballistic. Afterward, showing her all over again that the gun was empty, that there hadn't been any danger at all, only seemed to make her madder, and she'd refused to speak to him until he promised never to play again.

Now he wished he'd kept the promise. In breaking it, he'd hoped the news would get back to her and she'd realize it was because of how she was treating him. Except the whole thing had backfired. He knew it made no sense, but seeing this Voss kid not flinch had fucked him up somehow. Two nights in a row he'd lain awake thinking about it, knowing this fucking kid had upped the ante to the point where the next step was to spin a real bullet in the chamber, and then they'd see what they were really made of. He could feel that awful necessity growing inside him, and part of him was glad. The other part, the late-at-night part that couldn't sleep, was scared, probably even more scared than that shit-scared Fairhaven pansy who kept pretending to have headaches. But maybe, Zack thought as he scurried across the lawn toward the porch, there was another way, because there was something inside this house that John Voss feared more than any gun.

He was almost at the back porch steps when the ground suddenly dipped, which sent him lunging forward to regain his balance, and with his next step he tripped over what felt like some kind of iron rod sticking out of the ground. He went down hard, narrowly avoiding impaling himself on the spike. His shin burned, and through the ripped denim of his jeans he could feel warm blood.

His first thought was that he'd stumbled into a horseshoe pit, but then he discovered that a thick chain was attached to the top of the spike, the sort of chain that you might find a large dog on the other end of. Or in the house. The possibility of a mean-assed dog hadn't occurred to Zack until that very moment. He'd just about concluded that this whole idea was too fucked up when his foot brushed against something wooden, and he found there on the ground, against all laws of probability, the very thing he needed if there *was* a dog: a baseball bat.

He went up the porch steps as quietly as he could, and when the top riser groaned under his weight, he cringed in anticipation of a volley of barking, but none came. He paused at the back door, listening, but the house was silent, and after a minute he leaned the bat in the corner and took from his pocket the set of keys his father was always boasting would open any door in Dexter County. The third key on the ring worked, and the door swung open into darkness.

AFTER A FEW MINUTES, it occurred to Justin Dibble that the suggestion his friend had offered in jest wasn't such a bad idea, so he unzipped his fly and went to work. It took a while, and he had to stop once when a car slowed at the sight of the Camaro parked there on the shoulder, but then sped off in the direction of Fairhaven. Justin had barely finished when he heard a sound and saw a dark figure trotting back across the lawn, and he only just managed to tuck himself in before Zack arrived back at the stand of trees. Justin was afraid that his friend would guess what he'd been up to, but his thoughts were clearly elsewhere. Even in the pale moonlight Justin could see his eyes were gleaming with excitement.

But all he said was, "This is *SO FUCKING GREAT!*"

TICK HAS LEARNED several interesting things about Mrs.
Roderigue. For instance, that her favorite painter is Bill Taylor, who has a show, *Painting for Relaxation*, on the local access
channel. Taylor's specialties are old rowboats and the rocky Maine
shoreline, and most of his paintings contain both of these features.
Amazingly, he manages to complete a painting, start to finish, during
his one-hour time slot, and when he's on location instead of painting
from a photograph or postcard, that hour includes the time it takes
him to set up his easel. He prefers to work in watercolors, freely admitting that oils slow him down. He always keeps a battery-operated hair
dryer on hand so he can blow-dry the freshly applied paint and save
precious seconds.

In truth, Tick does like to watch him work on TV, and she can't
help but admire the way he attacks the canvas—Taylor's own phrase—
something she knows she has to learn. Where her own strokes are
tentative and often fearful, Bill Taylor's brush never seems to do anything that causes him regret or even misgiving. To Tick it seems as
though his arm, wrist, hand, fingers and brush are all an extension of
his eye, or perhaps his will. When he does make a mistake, he just
chuckles and says, "Never mind. We'll fix that later," and sure enough,
he does.

Tick knows there are many secrets she has yet to discover, and she
looks forward to the day when she, too, will have dozens of good tricks
with which to magically transform mistakes. But what she'd most like
to acquire is the whole *attitude*. Nothing in her experience suggests
that mistakes rectify themselves in the fullness of time, and certainly

not in an hour. Quite often, it seems to her, there's good reason to be alarmed by them, the most indelible things on her canvas.

For instance, she's made the mistake of being Zack Minty's friend again, an error in judgment based in part on his insistence that he'd changed, which he has—for the worse. Zack always had a frightening, smoldering quality, as if he might at any moment burst into flame, but lately he seems already on fire, someone to step back from, though Tick seems to be the only person to notice the difference. John Voss is another mistake, though befriending him was the principal's idea, not hers. In some ways John is the exact opposite of Zack, a boy whose tiny flame is flickering for lack of oxygen. At first his job at the Empire Grill and their lunch arrangement seemed to be doing some good, but over the last few days he's become even more suspicious and darkly silent than before. He shows so few signs of life that Tick half expects to look across the Blue table at him and find that he's stopped breathing.

Between these two and Candace, who as usual is driving her crazy, she doesn't like to think what her life would be like if Donny hadn't finally contacted her with his e-mail address, or if she hadn't convinced Walt—who she'd have to start being nice to, eventually—to get hooked up to a server. She'll actually *see* Donny in less than a week, and when she thinks about this her throat gets full and happiness comes over her so powerfully that she has all she can do to conceal it from her friends. Love is what this happiness feels like.

What she suspects but would like to know for sure is whether Mrs. Roderigue's in love with Bill Taylor. Tick has met Mrs. Roderigue's husband, who is also named Bill, a man who resembles a human bowling ball. The reason their marriage has been so successful, Mrs. Roderigue tells anyone willing to listen, is their shared devotion to the Lord, but Tick imagines Mrs. R. has a secret devotion to Bill Taylor, who is tall and lean and somehow elegant with a full head of unruly hair. To Tick, he resembles one of his own paintbrushes, and she can't help wondering whether Mrs. Roderigue regrets ending up with a bowling ball when there was a paintbrush not so very far away on the coast of Maine. If so, she's made a mistake that has not rectified itself in the fullness of time.

To Tick, Mrs. Roderigue's love life is not that pleasant to contemplate, but neither is the possibility that there is no such thing as love for certain unfortunate people. She would like to think it's a possibility, if only as a long shot, for everyone. Mrs. Roderigue certainly *speaks* of Bill Taylor as if she were in love with him. She says she wonders every year if there might be a budding Bill Taylor among her young apprentices, and yes, from time to time she sees potential, but then in some way or other all of her students seem to fall short. His style, she adds dreamily, may in the end be unique.

Last week Mrs. Roderigue gave her students the Bill Taylor assignment of watching *Painting for Relaxation* in order to discuss the great man's technique in class on Monday. To the teacher's grave disappointment, Tick alone had watched, though she'd forgotten it was homework and saw the program only because she usually did. Bill Taylor's show, despite its title, contained more genuine suspense than anything else on television. At times—say, with only ten minutes left—it didn't seem possible he could finish the day's painting, but you were always wrong to wager against a man who wielded a brush with such vigor. Sometimes he finished with only seconds to spare, without even enough time for a proper good-bye to his television audience, but somehow he always completed his painting. Tick isn't sure how to feel about this. The fact that he always finishes adds to the suspense each week, but sometimes Tick finds herself hoping something will happen to prevent him, like a gust of wind tipping over his easel and scattering his brushes; but then she feels guilty for wishing failure on this poor man, which is sort of like going to an auto race hoping to see an accident. Tick would've been interested to know John Voss's thoughts on Bill Taylor, but she doubts there is a television at his grandmother's house.

"So, Christina," said Mrs. Roderigue, clearly disappointed to have to carry on this important conversation with her least favorite student, "how would you describe Mr. Taylor's style?"

Tick knew the correct answer, of course. The word Mrs. Roderigue had in mind was of the sort that might've been printed on one of those scenic postcards that Bill Taylor painted from. A word like "sublime." Why not give it to her?

Instead, she said, "Fast."

THE MOST DISTURBING THING Tick has learned about Mrs. Roderigue is that she's related by marriage to the Mintys, which may be why Zack always has a hall pass bearing her signature. This allows him to leave his study hall once or twice a week to join her and John Voss in the cafeteria. Ever since Tick made it clear that she's not interested in being his girlfriend, Zack has intensified his ridicule of the other boy to such a degree that she's considering telling Mr. Meyer what's going on. Even *with* a pass Zack has no business being in the cafeteria or having a key to let himself in, and she knows that if the principal got wind of it, Zack would get in trouble, maybe even be suspended from the football team. She's also debated telling her father, except she's afraid of what he might do, given how much he despises Zack's father.

She should do *something*, she knows, for John Voss's sake, but at times he almost seems to feed on the abuse, and if he won't do anything in his own defense, why should she? And so, for now, she has decided on a policy of appeasement, feeling that even though her influence on Zack is greatly diminished, she still has some, and she fears, too, that if she told him she didn't even want to be his friend anymore, he'd be capable of far worse.

Tick is fully aware of the dangers inherent in this policy, since they're studying World War II in European History, and the consensus seems to be that Hitler should've been confronted sooner. Tick doesn't disagree, exactly, but she's mystified why her classmates seem so blind to the costs of open hostility. Last week they were shown a movie that began with the D day invasion of Normandy, and even before the first American soldier, a boy not much older than Tick, had been shot in the head when the big doors to the amphibious troop transports were lowered into the surf, Tick felt her left arm growing numb and she had to rest her forehead on the cool desktop to keep from being ill. Ten minutes into the film Mr. Meyer had come in and helped her out of the classroom.

So, for now, anyway, appeasement. And if she's wrong? At the bottom of her backpack is the stolen Exacto knife she hasn't yet returned to the supply closet, though she's had countless opportunities. Sometimes, when Zack's tormenting John Voss in the cafeteria or, like today, visiting art class on some flimsy pretext so his friend Justin Dibble can join in the sport, Tick imagines pulling out the knife and swiping it across his wide, stupid forehead.

"So, John," her former boyfriend is saying, "how's your grandmother? She doing okay?"

The boy doesn't acknowledge this question or even look up from his painting. The class is now working in watercolor, Bill Taylor's favorite medium, and Mrs. Roderigue, apparently weary of her students' subject matter, has brought a vase of flowers and set it up in the center of the room, temporarily rearranging her color-coded tables into a large U so everyone has a good view of the floral arrangement. In this new symmetry, since all of the tables are identical, there's no differentiating Blue from Red until someone sits down, thereby establishing the table's identity for the day. Every day this week Tick and the Voss boy have arrived early and established a different table as Blue, today choosing the one closest to Mrs. Roderigue's desk. This was Tick's idea, actually. She was curious to see what lengths the woman would go to in order to avoid paying Blue any attention. So far—and the period only has ten minutes to go—Mrs. Roderigue hasn't even looked in their direction except when Zack entered a few minutes ago and sat down next to Candace.

Though obviously Zack doesn't belong here, Tick is just as glad to be ignored by their teacher. She finds it difficult to paint anything with someone watching over her shoulder, and of course she'd feel duty bound to ignore any artistic advice of Mrs. Roderigue's, anyway. Since she described Bill Taylor's style as fast, she's sensed that the woman's opinion of her, never high, has fallen precipitously. "Is that a smart-aleck answer?" she'd demanded. Tick assured her that it was not, but the teacher continued to look insulted on her idol's behalf.

What Tick wonders now is whether she'll be accused of doing a smart-aleck painting. At the center of the bouquet is a monstrous peony, probably purchased on sale at the supermarket. By Tuesday its curling petals had begun to collect at the bottom of the vase, infusing the room with the faint but unmistakably sweet odor of corruption and imminent death. Tick knows that what Mrs. Roderigue intended is for her students to paint the peony as it had appeared on Monday when it was still beautiful, at least to her way of thinking. In Tick's opinion there was something extravagantly excessive about the peony from the start, as if God had intended to suggest with this particular bloom that you could have too much of a good thing. The swiftness with which the fallen petals began to stink drove the point home in case anybody missed it. As a rule, Tick leans toward believing that there is no God, but she isn't so sure at times like this, when pockets of meaning emerge so clearly that they feel like divine communication. She realizes it's entirely possible that this is simply Tick communicating with Tick, but she is willing, largely in deference to her father, who believes in God and wishes she did too, to keep an open mind.

Her apprehension about the watercolor has to do with her decision to depict not the peony's beauty but rather its rancid decay. The other smart-alecky thing is that she's painting the shapes of her fellow students, the ones who are facing her as they paint the flowers, into the background. While this hasn't been strictly prohibited, Tick's pretty sure Mrs. Roderigue hasn't intended for anyone to see beyond the flowers themselves. She will also not be pleased to see that Tick has painted one of the tables green, the one next to it brilliant red, or that behind them is the boxy, hovering shape of the teacher herself.

"You're one lucky dude, John," Zack's saying. "Having a grandmother to take care of you, I mean."

Tick cannot help but turn and stare at him, though she doesn't indulge this need for more than a second. With John Voss sitting there, of course, there's no way to say the obvious—that if he weren't spectacularly *unlucky*, his parents would be taking care of him. In fact, for the last few days, for reasons Tick doesn't understand, Zack has been taking every opportunity to insert the boy's grandmother into every conversation. Saying what a fine woman she must be. And how he'd like to meet her sometime. Didn't they think she'd make a good subject for *Community Heroes*, a monthly feature on the local TV channel? Earlier in the week, when Zack first suggested this in the cafeteria, John Voss had looked up from the sandwich Tick had brought for him, and the expression in his pale, watery eyes had confused her, even frightened her, though she couldn't say why. Now he seems to have removed himself and gone to a place even farther away.

"Hey," Zack says, nudging Candace, off on a new tack now. "I've thought of a good name for Tick's new boyfriend."

Except for the fact that there's a boy she likes who lives in Indiana, Tick has revealed nothing about Donny, not even his name, so in retaliation for her secrecy, Zack has come up with this new name game.

"Hickman," he says, snorting loud enough for everyone over at the Red table to hear. "Get it? I mean, the boy's from fucking Indiana!"

For the last few days he's been openly flirting with Candace, trying to make Tick jealous. Strange, when Zack did this with other girls last year, she simply couldn't control her own feelings of hurt and betrayal, even rage. Not giving a shit, she's decided, is like the defrost option on a car's heater that miraculously unfogs the windshield, allowing you to see where you're headed. It's now Candace, poor girl, whose windshield's all foggy. She broke up with Bobby, the boy who may or may not have been in jail, even citing Zack as the reason why. According to Candace, Bobby's "out" now, and rumor has it he's coming to Empire Falls to find this Minty asshole who stole his girl and kick his ass.

Clearly, she can't quite believe her good fortune to have Zack Minty interested in her—which shows she's not entirely stupid, Tick thinks, since he isn't. What he'll do is continue flirting with Candace until he's sure that Tick really doesn't care, and then he'll tell people it was all just a joke. What Tick's coming to realize is that in some way Zack's never been interested in her either, though not, she suspects, in the same way he's not interested in Candace. While part of her would like to understand this better, the other part is glad she doesn't.

"Oh-my-God-oh-my-God . . . I've *got* it!" Candace shrieks. Whatever she's got is just too great. She can hardly stand it. "Is it okay if I say it?" she asks Tick. She'd like to be forgiven in advance of her disloyalty. She's been asking her all day if it's okay that she and Zack are maybe going to start hanging out. Now she'd like to be sure it's okay if she participates in this new "Let's Make Fun of Tick's New Boyfriend" game.

"Knock yourself out," Tick tells her, not wanting to deny Candace pleasure. If her windshield weren't all fogged up, she'd see heartbreak speeding right at her, its high beams on.

The bell is going to ring in just a few minutes and what Tick would like to know is whether her painting is finished. That's one of the many things Bill Taylor is always so sure about. She'd also like to know whether Mrs. Roderigue will recognize herself looming out of focus behind the Red table.

"Goober," Candace says with a peal of laughter. "Goober Hickman."

Zack Minty turns to regard her, deadpan. "That's really funny. Laugh, I thought I'd die," he says, and the girl's laughter dies in her throat.

"It's as funny as what *you* said," Justin Dibble offers, causing Tick to glance in his direction. She catches his eye for a split second before he looks away. She has long suspected he's fond of Candace, that his teasing her has been intended as a courtship ritual. Since Zack began flirting with Candace earlier in the week, Justin has been wearing an expression of hurt and betrayal, though he hasn't openly broken ranks until now. Tick wonders what the cost of his doing so will be.

Zack may be pondering the same question, because he does not register his friend's challenge except to include him when he turns his attention back to silent John Voss. "Let's let John Voss decide," he suggests. "Hey, John. The subject is Tick's new boyfriend. Which is the funnier name? Hickman or Goober?"

John Voss raises his eyes to look at Tick, and it occurs to her that this may be the first time he's heard about Donny. He quickly drops his eyes again, but before he does, Tick sends him a look she hopes will suggest that it doesn't matter if he wants to answer.

"Okay, how about this?" Zack says, when the boy doesn't respond. "Which do you think your *grandmother* would think is funnier?"

The bell rings then, and Minty shoves his chair back and stands up, pausing for a moment to tower over John Voss, who seems not even to have heard the bell. Candace quickly gets to her feet too—girl on a string—and after a beat they head for the door together, Justin watching them go through narrowed eyes.

"Ask her for us, okay, John?" Zack calls over his shoulder.

Her painting, Tick decides, is finished. For the same reason that Bill Taylor's paintings are always finished. Because the hour is up.

H E RECOGNIZED HER VOICE *immediately, though it had been nearly four years, at his high school graduation, since he'd heard it last.* "Hello, dear boy," *she said, and the "hello" was all it took, the "dear boy" merely confirming and intensifying his visceral reaction. Was this what criminals in the Witness Protection Program felt like when they were recognized on the street by a former associate?* "I've been trying to reach you for days. I'm afraid you'd better come home."

Just that quickly, everything in his life changed. How long had it taken to make the arrangements? Fifteen minutes? Had he spoken or merely listened? Later, he was unable to reconstruct much of the conversation, but he had not resisted. Of that much he was sure. After all, he wasn't in the Witness Protection Program. He was Miles Roby, and his mother was dying.

The reason Mrs. Whiting hadn't been able to reach him was that his roommate, Peter, and his girlfriend, Dawn, had convinced him to join them on Martha's Vineyard over the long Columbus Day weekend. It was Indian summer in southern Maine, and it would be even warmer in Massachusetts. Besides, wasn't it Miles who was always telling them how beautiful the island was? (He'd told them about the Vineyard so that they'd understand that he'd been somewhere besides Empire Falls.) Except that he couldn't really afford it, there was no reason not to go. He'd already made an excuse not to go home over the long weekend, telling his mother that between his regular classwork and his editorial responsibilities at the school literary magazine, he was swamped. It occurred to him now that when they'd spoken on the phone last week, she'd sounded almost relieved.

He'd gotten good at coming up with excuses to avoid Empire Falls and, since his sophomore year, had managed to spend very little time there. Peter's parents owned a seafood restaurant on the Rhode Island coast, and the last two summers Miles had worked for them—in the kitchen the first year, out front as a waiter the second. It wasn't a fancy restaurant. They served mostly clam and shrimp baskets to tourists, but the money was good and Miles had very few expenses. He'd been allowed to stay for free in a spare bedroom that had been Peter's older brother's, so he was able to save nearly all of his earnings for tuition. Peter's parents seemed to like him, and he liked them too, especially their easy affection for each other and their common cause when it came to doing things in the restaurant, always making each other's tasks lighter, their eyes constantly feeling out the other from across the room.

His experience at the Empire Grill stood him in good stead, and he'd made himself indispensable, unlike Peter, who seemed determined to convince his parents that he was entirely dispensable. He was always wanting days off to go to the beach or to visit the three different girls he was stringing along, one of whom was Dawn. If Peter's parents hadn't forced Miles to take a day off now and then, usually a slow Monday or Tuesday evening, he would've worked straight through the summer from Memorial Day to Labor Day. When they offered him time off to go home, they accepted his excuses without actually believing them. Peter, Miles suspected, had explained that his parents were poor and that the money he was earning was nothing short of a godsend.

The truth was that Miles had come to dread even the rare, brief, unavoidable visits to Empire Falls. He hadn't been a college freshman for more than a few weeks before deciding that this was where he belonged, among people who loved books and art and music, enthusiasms he was hardpressed to explain to the guys lazing around the counter at the Empire Grill, talking the Bruins and the Sox. Even harder to accept—did he even understand it himself?—was his increasing sense of estrangement from his own family. Getting to know his roommate's parents so well, witnessing how much they loved each other, he'd seen clearly for the first time that his own parents' marriage, far from a sacred union, was a kind of sad mockery, a realization that made him especially angry with his mother. He'd have been angry with his father, too, except there wasn't much point, since Max wouldn't notice, for one thing, and wouldn't care, for another.

Grace's feelings, however, could be hurt, so Miles hurt them by suggesting in various subtle ways what a fool she was for not leaving a man like Max. Anyone so foolish, he implied, probably deserved what she got. Could leaving have resulted in more misery than staying had? He was even prepared to tell his mother she'd have done better to run off with that Charlie Mayne fellow they'd met when he was a boy. At least the two of them might've been happy, instead of everybody *being miserable. Except for Max, of course, who remained Max in any scenario.*

The problem was that Grace hadn't obliged him by saying what he'd expected her to, never once claimed to have sacrificed her own happiness for his and his brother's—a claim he felt sure he himself would've made, had the shoe been on the other foot. Stranger still, Grace had simply smiled at his characterization of her "not leaving" Max. "I wonder what you mean by that, Miles," she'd asked him, and of course he immediately saw what she meant. How do you go about leaving a man who was so seldom around to begin with? Why would you? "Do you mean that I didn't divorce him?" Well, yes, that was what he'd meant, though his shrug was intended to suggest that he'd meant that and a lot more. She responded by regarding him patiently until he finally saw the truth, then concluded the issue for him. "Have you ever seen a husband and wife more completely 'put asunder' than your father and me?"

She also seemed to want him to understand that what she'd done was precisely what he'd blamed her for not doing. She not only had walked away from the life he considered her to be trapped in but also had acquired another new whole family, or hadn't he noticed? And it was the second family, he realized, not the first, that was the true source of his confusion. On each dreaded vacation from St. Luke's he'd witnessed his mother's increasing absence from their own home, even when she was present in the house. It was as if they'd both gone off to college, not just him. And just as his real life was now at St. Luke's, his mother's real life now lay across the river with Mrs. Whiting and her daughter. Miles had seen all this coming even back in high school, but he'd looked away, because on the surface, things weren't so very different. His father, as far back as Miles could remember, had always been either gone or on his way to the nearest pub.

The difference now was that Grace no longer cared. Nor did she seem to comprehend the difficulties her own absence was causing. Right before her eyes David was turning from a sickly, sweet-mannered child into a healthy, angry, troubled adolescent, a transition that appeared to puzzle and sadden Grace without moving her to action. With each visit to Empire Falls it became clearer to Miles that his brother was, in essence, an abandoned child who was developing his own survival strategies, one of which was to ape his father's careless indifference and self-sufficiency. Miles could tell just by looking at David that he was one of those kids who featured in faculty negotiations each fall. The teacher who got stuck with David Roby would want to be compensated with two or three good students of his or her own choosing. "He's just trying to get attention," Grace told the high school principal when David got into *trouble, and then more trouble, and then worse trouble. She said the same thing to Miles when she explained over the phone what his brother had done this time. She seemed genuinely lost and brokenhearted about the boy, but in the rueful way you might worry about a niece or nephew you'd always been fond of, but who was, after all, your sister's child and not your responsibility.*

But Grace also seemed unaware of what was happening to herself. With each passing season, she grew more gaunt, more ghostlike. When he asked if she wasn't feeling well, she told him she was just going through the change early. Some women did. Far from being troubled by this, Grace seemed almost grateful. Was it possible that only a dozen years ago this same woman was still in radiant bloom, that in her white summer dress she'd turned the head of every man on Martha's Vineyard? That Grace seemed to have no recollection of that woman was enough to break his heart. Enough to make him find excuses to stay away. Enough to enter, had the opportunity been offered, the Witness Protection Program. It hadn't yet occurred to him that this was precisely what college is.

"SHE'LL BE FURIOUS," *he warned Mrs. Whiting on the phone, after it was all decided. First thing in the morning he would see the dean of students, explain the situation and take a leave of absence. Mrs. Whiting would send a car for him, and by midafternoon he'd be at his mother's bedside. Grace would remain at home for the time being and continue with her chemotherapy and radiation treatments—was it possible that these had begun nearly six weeks ago and Grace hadn't told him?—but eventually she would be moved to Mrs. Whiting's single-floor house, where it would be easier to care for her. Neither Grace nor anyone else in the Roby family had had health insurance since she lost her job at the shirt factory, but Mrs. Whiting told him not to worry about medical bills. Old Roger Sperry, it so happened, was also ill, and needed help at the Empire Grill. If Miles was willing to gradually take over and run the restaurant for a year or so, until they could find and train a new manager, Mrs. Whiting would see to it that Grace had what she needed. Eventually, of course, he would return to school and finish his degree.* "She'll hate us both, Mrs. Whiting. You do realize that?"

"*You always did worry about the oddest things, dear boy,*" *the old woman replied nostalgically. Miles had no idea what she meant by this remark and was afraid to ask.* "Your mother will no doubt be angry at first, but she will never find it in her heart to hate you. Whether or not she hates *me* is rather beside the point, don't you think?"

"What about—?"

"My daughter?" Mrs. Whiting guessed, rather uncannily, Miles thought. "She'll want to be here, of course. You know how devoted she is to your mother. Far more than to her own, I dare say. And when she finds out you'll be here . . . . Still, I suppose she might be kept in Augusta for the most part, if you'd prefer."

"Mrs. Whiting," Miles said, "why would I want that?"

In response to this, silence. Meaning that he shouldn't ask questions he didn't want answered.

"I understand she's doing better?" Miles ventured. The summer before last he'd received an envelope at the restaurant in Rhode Island, addressed to him in his mother's small, neat hand. Folded carefully inside a single sheet of Grace's pale green note paper—Cindy is not doing well, she'd written. A card from you would mean the world—was a newspaper clipping. C. B. Whiting's obituary from the Empire Gazette stated that Mr. Whiting, who had recently returned from Mexico, had died at home as the result of an accidental gunshot wound, the weapon having discharged while he was cleaning it.

Miles would not learn the truth for nearly two months. He'd come home on Labor Day for the briefest of visits—registration at St. Luke's started on Tuesday—and mentioned C. B. Whiting's accident to his father. "What accident?" Max had snorted, then chuckled. "You put a loaded gun to your head and pull the trigger, the hole the bullet makes is no accident."

Which caused Miles to think back. Some part of his brain had registered that something about the obituary and his mother's note was odd. It was unlike her to have so little to say about such a tragedy, especially one that touched her second family so directly. And had he thought about it, he might have noted another curious thing. The obituary was long, as befitted an important man, its details filling two columns. At the top of the second was "C. B. WHITING," in boldface type that resembled the caption to a photo. It hadn't occurred to Miles when he opened his mother's letter, or later when his father revealed that the "accident" had been a suicide, to wonder why Grace had clipped around the photo. After all, Miles had never met the man, and wouldn't have known him, to borrow one of Max's favorite phrases, from a bag of assholes.

"And on what basis do you understand that she's doing better?" Mrs. Whiting said flatly.

"My mother wrote—"

"Yes, of course. But then, your mother is as devoted to my daughter as Cindy is to her. If wishing made it so, people the world over would visit our Grace instead of Lourdes."

Miles couldn't help smiling ruefully. The woman still had the ability to nonplus him. In three and a half years at St. Luke's, he'd never met anyone remotely like her.

"Mrs. Whiting," he said, "I owe you an apology."

"Whatever for, dear boy?"

"I haven't been back home much these last couple years. But when I was there, I should've come to see you."

"Well, never mind that," she told him, without, he noted, denying the truth of his assertion. "You're going to be home now. Aren't you, dear boy?"

OF COURSE, *part of the reason that Miles hadn't realized in high school that his mother was undergoing a transformation was that he attributed her increasing vagueness about their own family to years of disappointment and exhaustion and too much responsibility. He noticed—as Max did not, or didn't appear to—that she was no longer vested in her husband, and he was troubled that Grace was so forgetful about his brother. But she was only rarely vague or distant with Miles himself. More often her concern for his future, far from abstract, bordered on mania. In fact, during Miles's junior and senior years, Grace had two obsessions, equally powerful. She was determined that Miles would go to college and that Cindy Whiting would attend her senior prom. Each goal seemed like a long shot to Miles. Together, they might be seen as evidence that Grace was purposely setting herself up for some sort of emotional train wreck.*

And it wasn't just college she had in mind for Miles. He was to go out of state, which rendered the difficult virtually impossible. Gaining admission to the University of Maine presented no particular problem, and paying for tuition, board and books there was relatively inexpensive. The problem was that word "relative," because Miles had no idea where even that small sum would come from. Add out-of-state tuition on top of such expenses and the idea became laughable. When he pressed his mother about why distance was so important to her, she surprised him by saying, "So you won't be able to come home whenever you want to." The Farmington branch of the U of M was less than forty-five minutes away, the main campus at Orono about an hour. Kids who went there, she explained, often flocked home on weekends, and this, she was determined, he would not do. "I don't cross that river every day of my adult life so my son can come running back to Empire Falls."

He'd heard the phrase "crossing the river" so often during high school that it no longer truly registered. "Why do you think I cross that river every day?" she often asked him when they argued. "Why do you imagine I do that,

Miles? I do it so that you won't have to." Or, "Do you think I enjoy crossing that river every day? Do you?" The way she asked such questions, her eyes wild, her voice shrill, was not without its comic aspect, at least to a high school boy. She spoke, it seemed to Miles, as if there were no bridge, as if she daily forded the Knox River's strong current at the risk of being swept over the falls and dashed upon the rocks. But strangely, not crossing the river seemed unthinkable, and when Miles suggested that she look for another job, she reacted as if he'd suggested something not just naive—a job? in Empire Falls?—but also unprincipled, as if hers were the only honest work available. It was as if she'd come to see crossing the river each morning as a deeply symbolic act, and his failure to see the necessity of it illustrated just how little he understood about her, the river and life itself.

But she was no more obsessed with Miles's going off to college than she was with Cindy Whiting's attending her senior prom. The two events were linked in her mind, of equal weight and significance. When his mother began to talk, a full year in advance, about making sure that Cindy had a date, Miles didn't object because as yet he had no idea how much it meant to her or of the lengths to which she would go to ensure that it came to pass. What he thought Grace had in mind was to use her knowledge of Mrs. Whiting's friends and acquaintances to locate a suitable date for the poor girl. Surely there must be some second or third cousin somewhere who might be apprised of the situation, convinced of its gravity and pressed into service. Only when his mother asked him to keep an eye out for some shy classmate who might betray any small sign of affection for the girl, did Miles comprehend the precise nature of her delusion: that a date for Cindy Whiting might be found at Empire High, a notion that struck him as only slightly more ridiculous than the idea they might "find" money for out-of-state tuition if they just looked hard enough. Only gradually did the basis for his mother's confidence dawn on him, and when it did he set about the task of finding some other girl to fall in love with and ask to the prom. If he could manage this, his mother would have to come up with a new strategy, and when she failed, at least he would seem to be blameless. Falling in love, he noticed, was something people accepted as natural, something they couldn't blame you for.

The problem was, he already was in love.

It didn't do him any good, either, because Charlene Gardiner was a full three years out of high school and the odds of her accepting his invitation to the senior prom ranked right up there with his mother's wishful thinking about out-of-state tuition and a romance for Cindy Whiting. Still, Miles continued to hope for a miracle. During his junior year he'd taken a job as busboy at the Empire Grill so that he might be near Charlene, and during his senior year he even worked a few hours after school, three or four days a week, for the same purpose. On afternoons when he wasn't working, he talked his friend Otto Meyer into accompanying him to the restaurant for Cokes and later coffee, which they hoped might make them look older. What confused Miles enough to keep his hopes alive when he might have been more productively engaged in trying to get some other girl to like him was that Charlene Gardiner acted genuinely fond of him, despite the fact that she always had at least one boyfriend her own age or older. Being in high school, Miles had no idea there were girls in the world who might be nice to some boy who'd suffered the misfortune of falling in love with them, even when they couldn't return the favor. Charlene Gardiner was such a girl. Instead of seeing Miles's crush on her as an occasion for ridicule—by far the most effective cure for a crush—she managed to convey that both Miles and his infatuation were sweet. She didn't encourage him to persist in his folly, but neither could she bring herself to treat his devotion as something shabby or worthless. Mockery and contempt Miles would've understood and accepted as his due, but affection and gratitude confused him deeply. Gratitude for her kindness clouded his judgment, and the proximity she allowed him was simply too intoxicating to give up, so he convinced himself that her fondness was merely the beginning, that if given the opportunity it would metamorphose quite naturally into love. He made no connection between Charlene Gardiner's kindness to him and his own kindness to Cindy Whiting, an analogy that might have proved instructive.

Although his dilemma deepened with each passing day—no closer to finding a girl to ask to the prom, while inching ever nearer to having one "found" for him—Miles took some slender comfort in the fact that Otto Meyer wasn't making much headway either. He too had family problems. His father, an angry, aggressive man, had recently suffered a stroke, and he returned home from the hospital madder than ever, except that he was no longer able to express his fury. The stroke-flattened side of his face placid and unmoving, the unaffected side red and contorted, about all he could do was shake his huge head with rage and toss strands of spit through the air like a St. Bernard. Though Otto was also smitten by the charms of the beautiful Charlene Gardiner, he was not, like Miles, prone to unrealistic fantasies. Neither was he blind to the charms of girls his own age, so one gray afternoon in early February when they were sitting across from each other in a booth at the Empire Grill, he informed Miles that he'd asked a girl from their class to go to the prom with him and she'd accepted. Miles tried hard not to appear *crestfallen. The girl Otto had asked, who years later would become his wife and the mother of his son, was exactly the sort Miles himself should have been looking for. She was pretty, smart, shy and full of fun without knowing quite yet how to express this latent side of her personality. Neither popular nor unpopular, she wore unfashionable clothes at her mother's insistence and somehow intuited, as certain remarkable young girls will, that there were worse things than not being popular, that life was long, that she would one day have perfectly adequate breasts, that in fact there was nothing wrong with her, never mind what others seemed to think. During the days that followed Otto's bold invitation, about a dozen boys told him how lucky he was, that they'd been about to ask her themselves.*

Once he was over the shock, it was not hard for Miles to feel happy for his friend—but Otto's unexpected announcement happened to coincide with another that same afternoon. When Charlene Gardiner stopped by their booth to refill their coffees, she accused them both of not being very observant. She then wiggled the fingers of her left hand in front of them provocatively. They were enchantingly lovely fingers and one was encircled by a tiny ring, the significance of which Miles still hadn't grasped when a motorcycle pulled up outside with a low, throaty rumble and Charlene made a beeline for the door. The young fellow on the bike—he had longish, windblown hair, a leather jacket and a chin that required frequent shaving— barely had time to unstraddle the bike before Charlene was in his arms, and then he was twirling her in the air and they could hear her whoop through the plate-glass window. Around and around the young man spun this girl that Miles would continue to long for well after she was married—first to this biker, then to two other men—even after he himself was married. When the twirling out in the parking lot finally stopped, it was Miles who felt dizzy.

When Charlene came back inside to ask if she could get off her shift a half hour early, Roger Sperry nodded to her from behind the counter, and before the restaurant door could slam shut, she was on the motorcycle, which had throbbed back to life in anticipation of her return, and just that quickly Charlene Gardiner and her new fiancé were gone. "You'll never guess who my mother wants me to ask," Miles said to Otto. They weren't looking at each other, but at the space outside the restaurant window.

"Cindy Whiting?" Otto said, and when Miles looked at him he just shrugged. "Your mom called mine last week. I thought maybe you'd suggested me."

Miles closed his eyes and let the humiliation of what his mother had done wash over him.

"It's okay," Otto assured him. "I mean, it wouldn't have been so bad. Cindy's actually kind of pretty, don't you think?"

To Miles, this seemed completely beside the point. All he could think of was the chant he'd lived with since last spring when he was learning to drive: Go, Roby, go! Go, Roby, go!

"Plus she's a nice girl," Otto said. Which was true, and when Miles didn't deny it, he added, "Plus she likes you. Better than anybody."

"That's the worst part," he admitted, meeting his friend's eye.

"No. The girl you love just rode off on the back of a motorcycle," Otto said. "That's the worst part."

"Screw you, Otto," Miles suggested.

"Plus we could double," his friend continued. "Anne wouldn't mind." Anne Pacero was his date. "I bet she'd like to get to know Cindy better. It'd be okay."

Imagining all of this, Miles had to look down. "What if she thinks I like her or something?"

"You do like her."

"You know what I mean."

Now it was Otto's turn to look down, and Miles tried to think if anyone else his own age had ever suggested doing the right thing because it was the right thing. Under different circumstances, Miles thought, he might've been grateful to Otto for risking a moral point of view. Maybe he was grateful even in the present circumstances. What he would have liked to explain to his friend was just how needy and hungry this girl was, how she lived in a dream world, how the smallest kindnesses engendered and sustained her fantasies. But as he struggled to find a way to express this, he saw how close he was to describing his own yearning for Charlene Gardiner, who indeed had ridden off into her future without saying good-bye to him or scooping up the quarter he always left for a tip.

After dinner that evening, once his brother had gone to bed and Miles had gotten out his homework, Grace came into the dining room where he'd spread his textbooks across the table. "I want you to go to St. Luke's," she said.

A small Catholic college not far from Portland, it was the most costly of the schools he'd applied to. In addition to St. Luke's he'd sent forms off to the University of New Hampshire and the University of Vermont and, without his mother's knowledge, the University of Maine. He remained convinced that when the time came, she'd be forced to acknowledge reality. "Mom . . . ," he began.

"I went to St. Cat's this afternoon," she said.

Miles sighed deeply. My God, he thought. She's praying for out-of-state tuition.

"Father Tom knows people at the college," she said, reassuring him at least a little. "He thinks with your record there's a good chance of a scholarship. He said the parish might even be able to help with your books. And it's where you want to go."

What he felt like asking—no, screaming—was, What does wanting have to do with anything? Instead he simply nodded. It was what he wanted.

"We'll find the money," she insisted, taking his hand. "Do you trust me?"

Is it possible to say no to such a question? "Okay, Mom," he said, almost too brokenhearted by her faith to speak.

"Good," she said. "And now I have a favor to ask of you."

And it occurred to him that perhaps wanting something really badly might not always be the most foolish thing a person could do in this world. Because that afternoon when he returned home from the grill, at about the time his mother was crossing back over the Iron Bridge into Empire Falls, he'd called Cindy Whiting. "Oh, Miles," she'd said, her voice immediately rich with tears. "Dear, dear Miles."

CHAPTER 27

OTTO MEYER JR. listened to the recorded message that told him the number he was dialing was no longer in service, hung up, and reached for the big plastic bottle of antacids he kept in the lower right-hand drawer of his desk. Every principal he knew kept *something* in the lower right-hand drawer, something to get him through the day, and Otto comforted himself that there were far worse things he could be hiding. Unscrewing the lid, he shook four or five tablets into the palm of his left hand and chewed them somberly. Before replacing the bottle, he counted how many remained through the wide round opening. Nineteen, it looked like. Not enough to last the week, not the way this week was going. Which meant a trip in to the Fairhaven Wal-Mart, where he could buy another family-size bottle of generic equivalents, five hundred a batch for practically nothing. The pharmacist swore they were identical to the national brands, but Otto had his doubts. More and more of the damned things were required to settle his stomach.

No longer bothering with the recommended dosages, for months he'd been "nuking" his problem stomach at the first sign of a flare-up. The number of antacid tablets he chewed these days was based on the size of the problem that was making the acid in his stomach churn and then rise in his throat until he could taste it on the back of his tongue. Last week, after learning that one of his best teachers had gone home after school and beaten his wife so badly she had to be hospitalized, he'd recommended about a dozen tablets and followed his recommendation to the letter. When he went to visit the man's wife in the hospital the next day and she looked out at him from between the slits of eyes swollen nearly shut, he went downstairs to the gift shop and bought a roll of the national brand and recommended to himself that he eat about half of them right there in front of the cash register. The next day he paid a visit to the teacher at his home, where he found the man sitting in his kitchen staring at a handgun that lay on the dinette table—which suggested that the correct dosage was the other half. Now this John Voss thing.

The third note had appeared in his mailbox this morning, though there was no way of knowing whether it had been put there today or late yesterday afternoon, after the staff had gone home. Like the others, this one consisted of a single sentence, typed, then printed out, he had no doubt, on a machine in the media center. *Where is John Voss's grandmother?* No salutation. No signature.

The first had appeared in his box on Friday, and Otto had paid no attention, assuming it to be the work of a crank, several of whom worked regular hours under his jurisdiction. The second appeared in the center of his desk on Monday morning, and at first glance he thought it was the same one, until he remembered wadding the original up and throwing it away. When he asked Gladys, his secretary, who'd put it on his desk, she shook her head and said, "What note?" In response to the second note Otto ate an antacid and asked for John Voss's file, and now—with the third note and the file spread out before him—he asked Gladys to find out where the boy was during sixth period.

The answer—in the cafeteria, eating lunch with Christina Roby— Otto might have remembered if he'd thought about it. He himself was responsible for this arrangement, which, Allah be praised, seemed to be working. Well, actually, he had no idea whether it was working or not, except that he generally heard about it when things *didn't* work, especially when what wasn't working was something he'd instigated, in which case he heard about it over and over. The only new development he could recall was the boy's dishwashing job at the Empire Grill, certainly a positive sign. True, the kid remained generally unresponsive to teachers and other external stimuli, but Otto had noticed an improvement in his appearance these last few weeks. He seemed cleaner, his hair less matted, his thrift-store wardrobe less bizarrely mismatched. Was it possible he'd fallen in love with Christina Roby? Otto supposed it was. After all, the link between romance and personal hygiene was well established, and he remembered how he himself had begun to bathe after falling in love, back in tenth grade, with the beautiful

Charlene Gardiner. So, maybe. They were working together. They were in the city art show together. They had lunch together all by themselves. Might all of this have caused a romantic constellation to form in the boy's otherwise comatose mind?

Poor Christina, he couldn't help thinking as he swallowed the last of the chalky antacid and then went directly to the cafeteria, where he found not just these students, but also a third, Zack Minty.

THE BIG BOTTLE of antacids that Otto Meyer kept in his desk drawer at school did not represent his entire stash. He kept an additional three or four rolls in the glove box of his Buick, and of course he also had a jar on his nightstand at home. Parked in front of the ramshackle house out on the old landfill road, chewing a couple of tablets in preparation for his interview with the boy's grandmother, he noted that the air was almost cold enough to bear snow.

In another month the four o'clock mornings would begin again. On days when snow was predicted, Otto and the principals of the elementary and middle schools would be up early, groggily watching the weather channel and listening to the state weather service on the radio. By five-thirty they would have to decide whether it was too dangerous to put the buses on the road. Parents, for the most part, were eager for their kids to go to school, because otherwise they would have to figure out what to do with them. Before attending to these necessary arrangements many parents liked to call Otto Meyer Jr. at home and convey their impression that he was a fucking idiot, a lazy, no-good bastard angling for a reason to take a day off of work, as if it weren't enough he had the whole summer. If Otto was in the shower and his wife answered, they told her instead. The parents who were the angriest and most abusive on snow days were generally not the ones who had to worry about missing a day of work to attend to their children. Rather they were the same parents who signed their kids up for the free-lunch program and sent them to school inadequately clothed, but who *could* afford answering machines so they never had to waste time talking to principals and bill collectors.

Actually, even these were not the worst. The very worst, Otto Meyer thought as he studied the dilapidated house, were the ones you never saw, the ones who seemed to exist only as narratives prepared by state caseworkers for files that followed kids from school to school in a feeble attempt to prepare teachers and administrators for what they were up against. According to the file he reviewed before driving over here, John Voss's parents, who'd disappeared beneath the bureaucratic radar nearly five years ago, had been small-time Portland drug dealers and habitual abusers who discovered after having children what a nuisance they could be when serious business was being transacted. When John was a little boy, it had been their habit to stuff him into a laundry bag, pull the string tight and hang him on the back of the closet door, where he could kick and scream to his heart's content. After a while he always calmed down, and then they could have some peace. The trouble with the silence was that sometimes they'd forget all about him, fall asleep and leave him hanging there all night.

Otto did not normally think of himself as philosophically or politically confused, but after rereading this file he found himself deeply conflicted about whether or not John Voss's parents should be summarily executed, assuming they could be located. On the one hand, he had never favored capital punishment, reasoning that it didn't really solve the problem it was intended to address, but in this instance the problem it *would* solve—quite elegantly, he thought—was the disgust he felt at the idea of sharing the world with these two particular people.

Not that he considered himself an ideal parent. Far from it. He and Anne had indulged their son, Adam, beyond reckoning, and as a result the boy was showing signs of a distinctly unrealistic worldview. He seemed, for example, to believe the world was kindly disposed toward him as a matter of course. Otto had been ineffectual in the area of discipline for too long, but now, he suspected, it was too late to start doing things differently. Earlier in the year when he'd caught his son at a party that featured both alcohol and drugs, he'd told the boy he was grounded until further notice. Adam nearly busted a gut laughing on his way out the door. The word Adam himself applied to his father's parenting skills was "clueless," and Otto had come to accept this as his due. He didn't like to think where his failure had begun, because whenever he tried to, he could taste that failure commingling with minty antacid on the back of his tongue. The simplest conclusion was that he'd gone into parenthood with an overly modest game plan, by promising himself he would never be the living torment to his son that his own father had been to him. In this, apparently, he'd succeeded. Adam seemed genuinely fond of both his parents without feeling the slightest obligation to listen to anything they said. His customary "Right, Dad" did not, Otto now understood, connote agreement or even comprehension.

Anne was of the opinion that all this was quite natural, that what her husband was always trying to explain to her as he lay in the dark unable to sleep—that they'd somehow failed to prepare their son for the real world—was silly. Adam suffered from nothing more serious than adolescence, a disease that would eventually pass, like a particularly virulent episode of chicken pox: ugly to look at but temporary and certainly not life-threatening. The boy knew he was loved, she reminded him, which struck Otto as the last feeble hope of the truly clueless parent. They'd made every mistake in the book.

No, Otto thought as he climbed the rickety porch steps and rang the bell. Somehow he and Anne had managed to raise their son without stuffing him into laundry bags or bringing him up in a house as haunted as this one.

The boy had warned him that he might have to ring the bell several times. His grandmother was hard of hearing and her bedroom, which she seldom left anymore, was all the way in the back. The principal had lied, of course, in explaining that he had some papers she needed to sign. The boy had offered to get her signature that evening, but he'd said no, he wanted to speak with her personally, in case there was anything the school could do to help—a terrible lie, now that he thought about it. The boy's eyes had darted here and there nervously, never making contact with his own, but he seemed more anxious and embarrassed than panicked. Yes, it was true, he confessed, his grandmother had disconnected the phone last spring, to spare the expense; the only calls they ever got were nuisance ones anyway. When Otto asked whether she'd considered how unsafe it might be to live so far out of town without a telephone for emergencies, he'd replied, "That's what I'm for. Emergencies."

Of the two interviews, the one with the Voss boy had been less disturbing than the one with Zack Minty.

"How did you get into the cafeteria?" the principal asked once they were back in his office.

"It was open."

"No, it's locked after fifth period."

"They must've forgot."

"Shall I call Mrs. Wilson?"

"Go ahead. Anyway, it was open."

"Did you get your friends to let you in?"

"It was *open*."

"It was not open."

Sullen, then. Just sitting there, this boy who would clearly make it through his entire adult life without resorting to antacids. Smug. Self-satisfied. A Minty, through and through. The boy's grandfather William kept his freezer full of illegal deer and moose meat, and was a wife beater back when that particular crime was still considered a private matter. A shifty, brutal, lifelong scofflaw, in and out of jail for the sorts of petty crimes that suggested more a lack of imagination than an unwillingness to commit more serious offenses, he was also, according to rumor, the man the Whitings had turned to when one of their mills was in danger of going pro-union and they'd needed a couple of key heads cracked. As for the father, the shady Jimmy Minty, now rumored to be the town's next police chief, he collected two paychecks, one official, the other under the table from Francine Whiting. And now this late hit artist, young Zack, another apple that hadn't fallen far from the tree. In Otto's opinion, he would wind up a lawbreaker like his grandfather or a corrupt enforcer like his father, but he'd be trouble either way. Unless the unlucky girl he married shot him—as Jimmy's wife had threatened on several occasions, before she ran off—he'd escape justice entirely.

The principal picked up the hall pass the boy had flourished. "What class do you have with Mrs. Roderigue?"

"I don't have one with her."

"Then why would she give you a pass?"

"I guess she likes me."

"Why would she do that?"

"Why would she like me?"

Actually, that was exactly what Otto wanted to know, but he decided to rephrase the question. "No, why would she give you a hall pass?"

A shrug. "We go to the same church. Plus she's my aunt or something. My mother's sister is her brother's wife. Whatever that is."

"What that *is*, is no reason to give you a hall pass. Did you forge her signature?"

"No way I'd do that."

"Why not?"

"Because you could find out."

"Not because it would be wrong?"

"That too, I guess."

"I don't want to see you in that cafeteria again during sixth period. Agreed?"

Another shrug.

"Do you understand? I'll be checking." Suddenly, he had a brainstorm. "Did you write this?"

Zack Minty leaned forward, took the page and read it, then handed it back with what might have been a trace of a smile. "No."

Of course he had. Otto was suddenly certain of it. John Voss's grandmother had a name, Charlotte Owen, and whoever wrote the note didn't know this and either had no idea how to find out or was too lazy. A kid, then. This kid. "Not the kind of thing you'd do?"

After expressing great perplexity at this question, he shook his head, "No."

"Because it would be wrong, or because you'd get caught?"

"How would I get caught?"

"Why do you and your friends torment John Voss?"

"We don't."

"What do you get out of it?"

"I said we don't."

As Otto started out of the building, the class bell rang and he saw Doris Roderigue standing in the doorway to her classroom. "Don't ever let me catch that Minty kid with another hall pass signed by you," he told her, not caring particularly whether any students overheard or not. When she began to say something, he handed her the hall pass. "Never again. Is that understood?"

Outside, he just sat in the Buick until he calmed down. He didn't give a hoot about Doris Roderigue, but the Minty boy's last words were still ringing in his ears. When he was told he could leave, he'd gotten to his feet slowly, as if disappointed that their conversation had come to an end. He was limping, Otto noticed—no doubt to remind the principal that he played football and had been injured for the greater glory of Empire High. At the door the kid stopped and looked off at an oblique angle. "Where is John Voss's grandmother?" he said, as if the odd nature of the question had just occurred to him. "Huh."

THE BACK DOOR, like the front, was locked. Otto shouldn't have tried it, but he did. After all, what would he have done if it was *un*locked? Enter without invitation? After knocking several times, loudly, he went back down the porch steps and stood in plain sight, calling up to what he hoped was the old woman's bedroom window, identifying himself and trying to look harmless and unthreatening in case she was peering out from behind the curtains. It occurred to him that perhaps she *had* heard him ringing the bell out front, perhaps had even looked out from behind the thick curtains that shrouded the front windows and, seeing a stranger there, become terrified. He even imagined her lying in a heap just inside the door, a stroke victim, and himself the cause. How would he go about explaining *that*? After all, there were no papers for the old woman to sign, simply his cold, intellectual curiosity, the need to know the answer to a question posed by a cruel prankster: *Where is John Voss's grandmother?* As if that were any of Otto Meyer Jr.'s business.

Standing in the middle of Charlotte Owen's weedy lawn and staring up at the dark, curtained window, Otto could feel, despite the cold air, clammy perspiration tracking down his right side from his armpit. His nerve failing him, he was about to leave when he noticed the rusty iron stake. Because of the contour of the ground, only the top of it was visible from the base of the porch, but coming closer he could see that attached to it was a sturdy chain and at the end of the chain a metal clasp. Otto Meyer looked around for the canine suggested by these details, but there was no doghouse nearby, no water bowl back on the porch. And, of course, no dog had barked when he rang the bell. He kicked aside a clump of something that might have been an ancient, fossilized dog turd, or perhaps just a clod of earth. Otherwise, the ground was bare.

Funny how the mind works, Otto considered. This time when he turned back to the house and stared at the curtained second-floor window, he was sure he hadn't given Charlotte Owen a stroke by ringing her doorbell and pounding insistently on her back door. Charlotte Owen was not home, and hadn't been for some time. The boy was living in the house alone. A stake in the ground with a chain attached didn't prove any of this. Probably, Otto had to admit, it didn't even suggest it. But he was certain all the same.

At the foot of the porch he found a stone that was about the right size. The thing to do was call the cops, of course, but that might mean Jimmy Minty, and Otto had had enough of the Minty family for one day. If it turned out he was wrong and the whole thing backfired, he could always claim he'd heard the old woman inside, calling for help. A wind had in fact sprung up, and the moaning it made in the surrounding trees did sound a little like an old woman's lament. Feeble, but it would have to be his story. If he was wrong. Except he wasn't. Strange, too, that being sure had settled his stomach.

Once again he climbed the back steps. At the door he didn't hesitate before breaking the small pane of glass nearest the doorknob and reaching through the jagged opening to let himself in.

THE EMPIRE GRILL had a Closed sign hanging in the window, but when Miles saw it was Otto Meyer he went over and unlocked the door. "All right, all right," he said. "I'll stand for school board, but I'm telling you right now I don't have time to campaign."

"Thanks," Otto said as Miles closed and relocked the door behind them. "You won't have to campaign, I promise. When people see you're on the ballot, they'll make their mark right by your name."

Over at the counter Otto recognized a couple of the regulars Miles allowed to hang around drinking coffee after the lunch crowd cleared out. Horace Weymouth, the reporter who usually covered the school-budget wars was there, and Walt Comeau, who owned the club out by the strip mall and who'd just married Miles's ex. It was a little on the chilly side in the restaurant, but Walt had stripped down to his white cotton T-shirt. Maybe it was warmer over by the grill.

"Big Boy!" Walt Comeau bellowed. "Get back over here. Let's settle this right now. No more running away."

Miles ignored him. "You want a cup of coffee, Meyer?"

Otto laid a hand over his stomach. "Have a heart, will you?"

"Glass of warm milk?"

He started to say no, then reconsidered. "You know what? I hope you weren't joking, because that sounds wonderful."

"Grab a seat."

"Okay if we sit over there?" He motioned to the far booth, which a group of girls with large, elaborate hairdos was just vacating.

Miles nodded. Otto said hello to the girls, one or two of whom he recognized from their thinner high school days, then slid into the booth. While Miles took care of their check and let them out, he consolidated their plates and coffee cups, wiping the table clean with a lipstick-smudged napkin.

"That was quick," he said when Miles handed him his milk, warm in its glass.

"The beauty of the microwave," Miles admitted, sitting down.

"Big Boy!" Walt bellowed again.

Miles sighed. "Be right there."

"What's all that about?" Otto couldn't help asking, since the very idea of Walt Comeau in Miles Roby's restaurant was strange enough.

"He's always trying to get me to arm-wrestle him."

"Why?"

"You'd have to ask him. It seems to have something to do with his belief that one of us isn't a real man. You know what? You don't look so hot."

Otto shrugged. "Your new busboy working today?"

"John? He was supposed to come in for a couple hours to clean up the lunch stuff, but he hasn't turned up. Until today he's been real reliable."

"If he shows up, I'd appreciate your giving me a call."

"Okay," Miles said. "Is he in some kind of trouble, Meyer? None of my business—except for Tick."

"She here?"

"At home. I just talked to her."

"Good," Otto said. "I just feel sick about this, Miles. I'm the one who asked her to be nice to the kid."

Miles sat up straighter in the booth. "You better tell me, Meyer."

Now Otto sighed. "I don't know. Maybe everything's all right. I'm going to have to get to the bottom of it, though."

"Big Boy! Name that tune." Walt spun off his stool and danced his crooner's jig as he came toward them singing:

> Never dreamed anybody could kiss thataway,
> Bring me bliss thataway,
> What a kiss thataway!
> What a wonderful feeling to feel thataway,
> Tell me where have you been all my life.

"Go away, Walt," Miles said. "I'm having a conversation here."

"Okay, I'll give you one hint," Walt said. "Who do I always sing?"

Miles just stared at him, and what occurred to Otto Meyer was that if Miles had worn that expression while talking to *him*, he by God would have done as he was told.

Instead Walt slid into the booth on Otto's side. "You know something? I'll admit it. I might give him shit all the time, but I love this guy. That's the truth. Can you believe he actually came to my wedding? Pure class is what that is. But I'm still gonna whip his ass arm wrestling." And with that he reached across the table and gave Miles a friendly cuff on the side of the head. Then, noticing that Horace Weymouth was making for the door, Walt called after him, "Where you sneaking off to?"

Horace, ignoring him, nodded to Miles. "No court in the land would ever convict you," he said.

FIVE MINUTES LATER they had the place to themselves, and since there was nothing to do but address the situation, Otto Meyer explained that the boy's legal guardian was not in residence at the house out on the old landfill road. That the old woman's clothes were hanging in the bedroom closet, the house was full of furniture, the kitchen with pots and pans. That there was nothing to indicate that Charlotte Owen had abandoned the boy, as his parents had done. And yet she wasn't there. "I think the boy's living out there by himself," he concluded. "I think he has been for some time."

"Could she be in the hospital?"

"I thought of that," Otto Meyer said. In fact, before coming to the Empire Grill he'd returned to his office and made several phone calls. "Charlotte Owen was admitted to Dexter Memorial in Fairhaven last April with pneumonia, released two weeks later. She hasn't been read-mitted since."

"Still, there's—"

"That's not all. There hasn't been any electrical power or telephone service since the end of March, and when I turned on the tap in the kitchen, the faucet was dry."

"Well, good God, Meyer, she can't have died. It's the sort of thing people hear about. It makes the newspaper."

"I know, I know," Otto admitted, finishing the last of his warm milk. That had been another of his calls, to the county courthouse. No death certificate had been filed in the name of Charlotte Owen. No elderly woman's body awaited identification at the morgue. "Keep talking. You're making me feel better."

"There has to be some explanation."

Otto pushed the empty glass over to where he'd stacked the girls' dishes and cups. "I know that too. The problem is, the one I keep com-ing up with is that Charlotte Owen died last spring after she returned home to a house with no heat, and that boy hasn't told a soul."

"Then where *is* she, Meyer?"

For a moment Otto considered telling his old friend about the three letters he'd received asking this very question, but he decided against it. Odd how the meaning of the question changed entirely depending on whether it referred to a living woman or a dead one.

But there was one thing Miles *did* have a right to know, and that was about the laundry bag. "You didn't hear this from me," he began, aware that he was violating the confidentiality of a student's file. By the time he finished, Miles had gone as white as his apron.

IT WAS AFTER MIDNIGHT when Otto Meyer got home. The first thing he did was go into his son's room, where Adam lay asleep. As usual, he'd gone to bed without turning off his computer. The screen saver he'd chosen some time ago was a human skull that grinned out at the world before fragmenting, then dissolving, then coming back together to grin anew. Otto, exhausted and suddenly on the verge of tears, shut it off and then sat there in the dark for a few minutes, watching his son breathe by the light that filtered in from the hall.

Later, when he entered the bedroom he shared with his wife of twenty-two years, Anne was asleep with the television on, tuned to one of the Bangor stations now off the air, but where the story had run on the eleven o'clock news. Tomorrow? He didn't even want to think about that. In a few short hours the lawn outside would be crawling with reporters. He undressed quickly and slid into bed next to his wife, who woke up and took his hand. "I'm sorry," she said. "I meant to stay awake."

"Tomorrow," he said, "if you think of it, will you call David Irving and see if you can get me an appointment?"

"Your stomach?"

No need to answer this.

"They still haven't located the boy?"

"They will tomorrow."

"What will happen to him?"

"I have no idea."

"What will happen to us?"

"We'll survive," Otto told her. She was right, of course. This was the sort of thing high school principals lost their jobs over—and probably, though he would never say this to Anne, *should* lose their jobs over. "It'll start early," he told her, giving her hand a squeeze before reaching up to turn out the lamp. "We should sleep if we can."

What he meant was that *she* should. Sleep was pretty much out of the question for him, exhaustion or no exhaustion. In the dark bedroom the events of the afternoon and evening grew even more vivid.

It was Bill Daws he had called with his suspicions, even confessing that he'd broken into the old woman's house. When he'd finished, the police chief said simply, "Meet me there."

He'd waited out in the car while Daws and Jimmy Minty and another policeman searched the entire premises. Otto had not himself gone into either the attic or the cellar, of course, but even taking into account that there was no light in the house to search by, it had taken a very long time to ascertain officially what everyone seemed to know from the beginning. Bill had had a radiation treatment that morning and when he came back out of the house with Minty, both men silent, he did not look well. Minty went over to his cruiser and talked on the radio.

"Well," Bill Daws said, "I suppose the good news is that we don't know for sure that she isn't off visiting her sister or something."

Otto was grateful to hear this possibility given voice. It was the very straw he'd been clinging to.

"I got a bad feeling, though," the police chief added.

"Me, too, Bill, me, too."

"Anyway, neither one of them's here, so why don't you go on home?"

He nodded, understanding that the only reason Bill Daws had wanted him there at all was in case the boy turned up. "I was thinking I'd go back in to school."

"Whatever."

"Did you notice that stake out back?"

"I did."

"What do you make of it?"

"I'm trying not to think about it," Daws admitted. "Listen, if this thing turns out bad, like I think it's going to, we won't be able to keep it quiet."

"I wouldn't ask you to."

Dusk had fallen completely, and the two men heard the vehicles before the headlights cut through the darkness into the driveway. The first was some sort of police SUV with a German shepherd pacing anxiously in back. The other was Jimmy Minty's Camaro, and when Zack got out Meyer noticed again that he was limping. His father went over and they exchanged a few words, the boy glancing over at the principal and shaking his head. Then he got back in the Camaro and drove off, back toward town.

"What was all that about?" Bill Daws wanted to know when Jimmy Minty joined them.

"I asked him if he wrote those notes," Minty explained, looking at Otto. "He didn't."

Bill nodded, said nothing.

"How come you people want to blame my boy for everything?"

"What people are those?" Otto said.

"At the school. You. Coach Towne."

Otto turned and looked Bill Daws in the face. "He wrote the notes."

"Yeah?" Minty said. "Prove it."

"All right," Bill said in a way that made it clear he'd had enough of this. "See if you can get ahold of somebody at Central Maine Power," he told Minty, effectively dismissing him. "We'll need some temporary power at this house."

The officer who'd driven the SUV now had the German shepherd on a leash. "Where do you want to start?" he called over. "Here at the house, I guess," Daws said, his voice dispirited. "It's over across the way we'll find her, though."

Which meant the police chief had thought of it too, and this relieved Otto's fears that he might be the only one to whom such a horrible notion had occurred.

CHAPTER 28

JANINE GOT THROUGH her midday step class, after which she was supposed to work the desk, checking members in and making the pain-in-the-ass protein shakes they served in the Fox's Den, the small lounge of half a dozen tables where the workmen's comp guys—assholes and scam artists every one—liked to hang out after their physical therapy. Janine hated to look at them even on a good day, which this certainly was not, not anymore, not after going to the bank. She was still wobbly about the knees, truth be told—and not because she'd done her advanced step class on an empty stomach, either. The idea of food, normally a sweet, forbidden fantasy, made her stomach roil—with what, she couldn't imagine.

"Still no sign of that Voss boy, is there?" Mrs. Neuman, a short woman, had to peer around the cash register to see the TV hung from the ceiling in the Fox's Den while she waited for Janine to key in her membership number. The noon news broadcast was signing off now, urging viewers to stay tuned for the soap that followed.

It had been five days since the woman's body had been discovered at the old landfill, though it wasn't really a body anymore. More of a skeleton, really, according to the newspaper, so little left after six months' exposure that positive identification would have to await dental records, wherever they might be. Charlotte Owen had outlived not only her friends but also three Empire Falls dentists; the fourth, who apparently had her files, had retired somewhere in Florida. The boy, John Voss, had simply vanished.

"Just goes to show," Mrs. Neuman intoned, "life is one big secret. You never even know who's living right next door." Which was not entirely apropos, Janine almost told her, since the old woman and the Voss boy hadn't had any neighbors.

And anyway, never mind about not knowing who's next door. Half the time you don't even know who you're marrying until you go to pick up your license and happen to see by pure chance how old the fucker really is. Then—talk about your secrets—just when you think you've straightened out the whole age thing and go ahead and marry the old fart anyway, against your better judgment, plus the advice of everybody you know, then you go to the bank and try to write a check on your joint account—and whammo! There you are, wondering all over again, just who *is* this son of a bitch anyway?

Not that Janine would say any of this to Mrs. Neuman. No more than she'd tell this human medicine ball to stop wasting her time and money at the club. Five days a week Mrs. Neuman showed up at one o'clock, a busy time in the exercise room, and did her leisurely stroll on one of the three working treadmills, reading the free magazines and pissing off the members who were interested in real workouts. At the rate Mrs. Neuman walked the goddamn treadmill, she could get as much good out of sitting in a chair and flipping through *TV Guide*.

"Imagine that?" Mrs. Neuman said. "You live to be eighty-some-odd-years old, and one day the good Lord decides you're all done, and your own grandson takes you out to the dump and leaves you there. I swear to heaven, I just don't know anymore."

"Me either, Mrs. Neuman," Janine said, picking up the phone to dial Amber, who was always looking for extra hours.

"Must've just slung that poor old woman over his shoulder," the woman said, slinging her own workout bag over her own round shoulder, where it slipped off again halfway to the women's locker room door. "Probably what'll happen to me if it's that one grandson of mine that finds me."

"Not unless he rents a forklift," Janine muttered, as the door swung shut behind her. "Get here as quick as you can," she snapped into the phone when Amber agreed to come in and finish Janine's shift, "before I do something I'll regret."

This exact opportunity presented itself the moment she hung up, when the workmen's comp table called for another round of light beers, which they believed they could drink all afternoon without getting drunk or gaining weight, this despite the fact that they left drunk every afternoon, their heavy beer guts sloshing. The worst of the lot was Randy Danillac, who had been a year ahead of Janine, though he had no recollection of her in high school, though she'd stared at him dreamily for two straight years. She suspected that not one of these goldbricks was actually injured, but most at least had the decency to pretend. Danillac just preferred working two or three days a week instead of the full five, so he collected comp from one Empire Falls contractor and worked off the books for another in Fairhaven. According to medical affidavits, he was supposedly unable to stand up straight, a condition that didn't prevent him from playing racquetball whenever he could find an opponent who didn't mind being called names after every point.

"Why, thank you, darlin'," he said when she delivered their round of light beers. He looked her over good, too, something she normally wouldn't have minded, then gave her one of his crooked smiles. "Married life seems to agree with you. Nothin' like gettin' it regular, is there?"

When he said this, Janine finally glimpsed the appeal of the irony her ex-husband was always trying to get her to appreciate while she was trying to get him to appreciate sex. Irony was one of the many things wrong between them right from the start. Janine simply wasn't the sort of woman—and she freely admitted this—who benefited from constantly having the concept of irony explained to her. Yet in the present instance the irony of her high school devotion, through her entire sixteenth and seventeenth years, to a man who grew up to become about the worst cheating rat bastard in town—well, it was inescapable. No, that wasn't ironic. It was the fact that he'd finally noticed her and wanted to screw her that was ironic.

"You know what, Randy?" she said. "You can just eat me, okay?" And she was out the door before it occurred to him to take her up on the offer.

THE SAD TRUTH, Janine had to admit as she drove over to the Empire Grill, was that she'd gone and divorced a man she could talk to and married one she couldn't. Her need to talk to somebody right this second probably qualified as yet another irony. As was the realization that she missed Miles's calm, quiet ways. Since the separation she'd grown nostalgic about them, and since marrying Walt, she'd begun to recall her old life with Miles with a wistful fondness, which she had to remind herself was simple lunacy. Sure, Miles had been a good listener, and a listener was exactly what she needed at this particular moment, but what they never told you was that good listeners could be maddening as hell. He had to *weigh* everything you told him, as if making sure that he understood every last nuance was the only thing standing between him and offering a perfect solution. Either that or he'd treat her like she was just talking to hear herself talk, which also drove her batshit. She'd tried explaining all this to her mother once, which was a mistake. For a bartender Bea wasn't much of a listener, as quick with a diagnosis as Miles was slow. "What you don't realize," her mother told her, "is that it's really *you* driving your*self* batshit. You can't ever be content with anything, even for a minute. Miles doesn't say anything because there isn't a damn thing *to* say."

Which was why she was driving over to the Empire Grill instead of to Callahan's. Better to talk to a man with no answers than a woman with all the wrong ones. Miles was also far less likely to say I-told-you-so, her mother's favorite words. "Well, for heaven's sake, Janine," she could hear her mother say after she'd explained her discovery this morning that the Silver Fox, who was forever rubbing his chin in contemplation of his next move, whose only concern seemed to be timing, didn't even have enough capital to invest in a week's vacation out in Arizona, where they had all those good-looking Latino masseurs to rub you down with oil. "Whatever made you think that Walt Comeau *did* have two nickels to rub together?" her mother would ask, pure know-it-all that she was.

At least Miles could be counted on to sympathize with a person, to register surprise at the fact that Walt didn't even own the building that housed his health club but rented it from that damn Whiting woman who owned the Empire Grill and half the town. Her husband also rented most of the equipment in the exercise room. Hell, there wasn't a single aspect of the operation that wasn't leveraged to the hilt. There were even two mortgages on that little piece-of-shit house he was renting out since he'd moved in with her. And if he actually owned that parcel out on Small Pond Road, where he was always thinking out loud they might build a camp one of these days, when the time was right, then Harold DuFresne down at Empire Fidelity didn't know a damn thing about it—and he would, too, since everything else the Silver Fox "owned" was held by Harold as collateral on the health club. Walt had even borrowed money for the ring and the half-assed weekend honeymoon on the coast, during which it should've occurred to her, if she'd had a brain in her head, why Walt liked sex so much. It was free.

How in the world, she wanted to know, had she managed to put herself into a situation where the person she most wanted to unburden her soul to was the man she couldn't wait to leave so she'd be free to create the mess? These were all ironies, no doubt about it, and she hated every one of the fuckers, even before she turned onto Empire Avenue and saw the Silver Fox's van parked in front of the restaurant. Which meant she couldn't very well have her talk with Miles, not with her husband sitting there at the counter. Life *was* secrets, as the horrible Mrs. Neuman said, and for better or worse—stupid words she'd said not once but twice—she was wed to both the Silver Fox and secrets she *had* to keep. He'd known all along, of course, that when Janine found out she'd just have to swallow everything whole. Worse, she knew the time to begin was right now. Just park next to her husband's van, go inside and pretend that "getting it regular" agreed with her. Stand next to Walt and watch him lose their pennies to Horace at gin, then slip her hand in his trouser pocket and reassure herself of the one thing the dumb son of a bitch did have to offer.

Maybe tomorrow she'd be able to. In fact, she'd have to. But not right this minute, she decided. No, she knew where the steak knives were kept, and if she went in there right now, she might race around the counter, pull one out and cut off her nose to spite her face. Janine drove on past the restaurant.

Since the town's only unmarked police car wasn't in its usual spot in the alley next to the closed Firestone shop, Janine did a squealing U-turn and headed back up Empire the way she'd come. She'd gone about four blocks when she noticed the tall, skinny figure of her daughter making her solitary way up the street, leaning forward as usual under the weight of her backpack. When Janine tooted and pulled over to the curb, her daughter regarded the Jeep suspiciously, as if the Silver Fox might be scrunched down in the backseat somewhere. She came up to the car reluctantly.

"Where you headed?" Janine said when she'd rolled down the window and her daughter tentatively bent forward to peer inside.

"Grandma's."

"Climb in." Janine leaned across to open the door, ignoring her daughter's expression, which suggested that she'd just been ordered to push the vehicle up the street. Opening the rear door, Tick turned and backed into the opening, resting the bottom of her backpack on the seat and then walking out from under it, a maneuver so graceful and practiced that Janine's eyes filled with tears. At that age, she hadn't simply been overweight, but also clumsy, always tripping and bumping into things. Tick had the kind of grace you were born with, that you couldn't starve or Stairmaster yourself into, that you probably didn't even recognize unless you lacked it. "What's at Grandma's?" Janine asked.

Well, sure, the kid also had a knack for looking at her mother in a way that inspired violence. Grandma, her daughter's expression now seemed to convey, was at Grandma's. "It's quiet there, okay? I can do my homework," Tick finally explained when it became clear that Janine wasn't going to pull away from the curb until she got a straight answer. "Nobody bothers me," she added.

Nobody like Walt, was what she was saying. Nobody like Janine herself, probably. And no sooner did this thought occur to her than she was visited by a horrible mental picture of her daughter walking down the roadside at night, weighed down as usual, but not by her backpack. This time the load was Janine herself, and her daughter was headed for the dump. Every day this week she'd been meaning to talk with Tick about the Voss boy, who was all over the news and all anybody could seem to talk about, but somehow she'd managed not to. She knew Tick worked with the kid at the grill and they were in the same art class, where they had both been picked for some show. Which she'd been meaning to visit so she could see this snake picture she kept hearing about, but which her daughter hadn't ever even mentioned. True, Janine had been preoccupied with the wedding, but that wasn't much of an excuse. On the other hand, it wasn't much of a reason to imagine Tick hauling her carcass to the dump, either. Still, it was time to start making some of this shit between the two of them right.

But as Janine began to formulate a question that would broach the subject of the Voss boy, she heard herself ask something easier. "So how come you never tell me any of those funny things you see on signs like you do with your father?"

Apparently the answer was easy, too. "You never think they're funny."

"Try me."

"Nooooo," her daughter said, making it a multisyllable, singsong word.

And just that quickly Janine was pissed off again. "I'm not smart enough to see what's so damn funny, is that it?"

The little shit actually considered this question seriously before answering. "You always get them. You just never think they're funny."

"Maybe they aren't."

"Then why do you want me to tell you one?"

"Maybe I don't. Maybe I'd just like us to be friends, okay? Maybe I might like to take you to Boston for an art show sometime, if you'd ask me instead of your father. Maybe it would cheer me up to know my own daughter liked me."

"Walt isn't cheering you up?"

Janine pulled over, three blocks short of her mother's tavern. "Out."

"What?"

Well, at least *that* got the kid's attention. She was looking at Janine, scared now, aware she'd gone too far. "Out," Janine repeated, not wanting to follow through, but feeling she had to. "You want to treat me like shit, you can damn well walk."

What she was hoping was that her daughter would *not* do as she was told—not a lot to hope for, since she almost never did. But of course this time she would. Tick opened the door and got out, leaving Janine fresh out of options, trapped as usual. Rather than watch, she looked away, as if she couldn't care less, and when she heard the door slam she glanced quickly over her left shoulder to make sure no traffic was coming down Empire Avenue, then jerked the wheel and stepped on the gas, hearing at the same instant her daughter yell, "Stop!"

Her first thought was that her bluff had worked, that Tick wanted to apologize, but it was a more urgent scream than that, and when she looked back over her right shoulder she took in what had happened in an instant. At the same time Tick had closed the front door, she'd opened the rear one to retrieve her backpack, hooking one of its straps in the crook of her elbow, all of this just as Janine had pulled out—and somehow the pack had gotten wedged between the seat and the floor, yanking Tick off her feet. Only the back of her daughter's head was visible through the open door, but when Janine got around to the other side of the Jeep, she could see that Tick hadn't been seriously injured. In fact, thanks to the height of the vehicle, her daughter's behind was suspended an inch or two above the pavement. To Janine, she looked like a cartoon character whose parachute had failed to open. Nothing about her daughter's expression was comic, though. Her face had fragmented, then come together again in a mask of pain and fear and struggling rage. "Get away from me!" she screamed when Janine stooped to help unhook the backpack. "Don't touch me!"

"Stop this right now, Tick!" Janine snapped, frightened herself. "You're all right. I'm just trying to help."

Then, somehow, her daughter was free and on her feet and walking away, rubbing her shoulder, sobbing as she went.

"Tick," Janine called, trying to sound stern, her voice cracking in betrayal. "Come back here. Please, sweetie."

Nothing. She just kept on walking. There were maybe half a dozen people on the street, no more, but Janine was sure they'd all witnessed what had happened and now were watching the scene play itself out.

"Tick!"

Her daughter whirled then. "*Leave . . . me . . . alone!*" she screamed, loud enough to be heard the length of Empire Avenue.

The Jeep was still running, of course, her daughter's backpack still wedged between the seats, and when Janine tried to close the door, it wouldn't, and then, after she'd given the backpack a swift kick it still wouldn't, and then Janine herself was sobbing her frustrated heart out and kicking the door of the Grand Cherokee as hard as she could, the only pleasure left to her that of seeing the dent grow and grow.

And for how long did Janine Roby—no, Janine Comeau—sob and rage and kick in the door of the Cherokee? Until it latched. Not completely, of course, because it couldn't, not with her daughter's burden wedged in so tightly, but at least tight enough that it wouldn't fly open.

Janine was still shaking when she got back in behind the wheel. What she needed to do was to catch up with her daughter and make this right, by force if necessary, set all of it right, somehow, some way, she didn't yet know how, but by the time she pulled out onto Empire Avenue again her daughter had disappeared, and it was too late, she realized, with one last sob, too goddamn late.

"WHAT DO YOU FIGURE all that's about?" David wondered when they passed the old shirt factory. They were returning from Bea's tavern in his pickup, and he slowed as they approached the corner of Empire Avenue. For the first time since the factory closed, at least as far as Miles could recall, the big iron gate was open. Just inside sat a white stretch limo with Massachusetts plates—behind it, Miles caught a glint of red metal. On the steps of the old brick building a group of men in dark suits were listening to a woman Miles immediately recognized as Mrs. Whiting.

"You don't suppose the rumors could be true?" Miles said. For weeks now the grill had been alive with talk that a buyer had been found for the textile mill. As usual, Miles had dismissed this as needful speculation. Now, Mrs. Whiting's presence in the company of these suits would be enough to fuel foolish optimism through a long Maine winter.

"Be nice if something was going on," David admitted, turning onto Empire Avenue. "It would also explain why she's left us alone, if she's got bigger fish to fry."

It was still a bone of contention between them that Miles had not formally notified Mrs. Whiting of their intentions. From the start Miles had allowed that his brother was probably right, but since that morning last month when he'd recognized Charlie Mayne in the newspaper photograph, he'd grown even more reluctant to confront Mrs. Whiting, as if *he* had been the one who betrayed her all those years ago on Martha's Vineyard. And even though it was crazy, he couldn't shake the conviction that Mrs. Whiting would be able to tell just by looking at him that he'd stumbled onto the truth at last. It had always seemed to Miles that she'd searched his face for signs of some particular under- standing whenever they met; then, finding none, she would allow things to proceed as usual. Intellectually, he knew his brother was right, that it was better to have everything out in the open, but his intu- ition counseled a more furtive course.

Not that it was much of a secret anymore. He and David were now spending every free minute at Callahan's, Miles working late into the evenings, doing as much as possible himself, not wanting to start out any further in debt than they absolutely needed to be—especially since Bea was on the financial hook for the renovations, which on an hourly basis were threatening to spiral out of control. Today Miles got Buster to cover both the breakfast and lunch shifts while he struggled to repair the ancient gas stove at Callahan's, which hadn't been fired up in twenty years. David, who had to prep and serve Mexican Night at the grill this evening, had spent most of the afternoon setting up accounts with distributors and doing whatever tasks could be managed by a man with one good hand. Neither was trying to conceal his involvement in the reopening of Callahan's kitchen, though the story for public con- sumption was that they were just lending an old friend a hand.

One thing was certain. Mrs. Whiting, who knew everything, couldn't possibly *not* know this. Though maybe David was right and she was too busy with development office business to sweat the small stuff.

Somehow Miles didn't buy it.

THEY PARKED BEHIND the Dumpster and entered the grill, as always, through the back door. Every day this week, whether coming or going, Miles had half expected to see the Voss boy pacing the lot, staring down at his feet and looking expectant and wary, hungry and lost. When the news of the boy's grandmother broke and he disap- peared, Horace Weymouth, feeling guilty about having kept the secret and no longer seeing that much harm could be done, finally told Miles what he'd witnessed out at the old house last month. The howling dog had been chained to the stake, and the boy himself had also been emit- ting terrible, throaty noises, as he beat it with a stick. The animal, try- ing desperately to escape, raced around in ever-shortening circles of panic, the chain bunching up around the stake until it was completely gathered in a ball and the side of the dog's head was held flat to the ground. Even then the poor thing had tried to get away, strangling itself in the process. Only when it finally understood the hopelessness of flight did the boy toss the stick away and begin trying to soothe the terrified creature, staying well clear of its frightened, snapping jaws until it began to calm down and whimper pitifully. Then the boy himself got down on all fours, crawling closer and closer, cooing at the animal, gently stroking its wounded flanks, until the dog finally forgave his attacker and licked his face. Horace realized that the boy was weeping and begging the animal's forgiveness, still careful, though, because it was bewildered and conflicted, and something would cause it suddenly to quit licking and snap. Then it would resume its whimpering, the boy all the while cooing, "I know, I know," as if in perfect understanding.

It was, Horace said, the most horrifying and heartbreaking thing he had ever seen. His first impulse was to report what he'd witnessed—and knowing what he knew now, he wished he had. But he'd seen the boy around town, and knew something of his family and his standing at the high school, and Horace himself knew what it felt like to be considered a freak. Had he reported what he'd seen, the boy probably would've been removed from his grandmother's home and sent to the juvenile correctional facility in Sunderland, a truly gruesome place.

Horace also told Miles something that had not made it into the news reports: that in the same area of the landfill where Charlotte Owen's decaying remains were uncovered, they'd also found the bodies of several dogs, each exhibiting signs of having been tortured or beaten to death.

Miles had shared none of this with his daughter, of course, knowing how upset she already was by the boy's disappearance, but he did tell her about the laundry bag and made her acknowledge, for her own safety, what he believed to be true—that John Voss was a tragically abused boy, that something in him was broken and that simple kindness might not be enough to fix it. Tick had nodded in something less than complete agreement and in the end he wasn't sure how much of it had taken root. The whole conversation reminded him of the one earlier that year about the separation that would ultimately end in his and Janine's divorce. In both cases his daughter's greatest need had seemed to be for him to stop talking.

Horace and Walt were playing gin when Miles and David came in. Walt had already stripped down to his white-ribbed muscle shirt. How many of these, Miles wondered, did the man own?

"Hello, Walt," he sighed. "Hi, Horace. Buster."

"No more double shifts," Buster said. Though his eye had cleared up almost completely, he looked like a man who'd spent every last nickel of his strength and energy.

"You want to go home?"

"And never come back," Buster added, stripping his apron off over his neck.

"Just let me take a quick shower," Miles said. "Then you can split."

"You see that white limo, Big Boy?" Walt wanted to know. "The one with the Mass plates?"

Miles nodded.

"Drove right down the middle of Empire Avenue all the way to the mill. Don't tell me there isn't something in the works, neither. Go outside and sniff. You can still smell the money in the air."

Through the front window, Miles saw Charlene's Hyundai, its signal blinking while she waited to make her turn into the lot. There would be six on tonight, Miles serving as host and floater, David at the stove with an assistant for salads and desserts, Charlene and another girl working the floor, plus the new busboy he'd hired to replace John Voss. For the Empire Grill, a full crew. At Bea's, with nearly three times as many tables, they'd have to double or triple their staff. David would have to train at least one other person how to cook noodles twice, and Charlene had already volunteered. That was fine with Miles, though he hated to lose her on the floor, which she owned like no one else. Ironically, Charlene was the one who'd been looking forward to hustling drinks, which would double her tips. Still, he understood that at forty-five, after twenty-some years and God knew how many miles up and down the floor of the Empire Grill, she wanted and possibly needed a change.

That wasn't the only thing he'd come to understand about the woman he'd loved since high school. He also knew that she and his brother were lovers and probably had been for some time, having agreed to keep this secret in order not to hurt his feelings. David would've argued for honesty, but Charlene would have said no, not yet. The realization had come to him in stages, beginning back in September at the Lamplighter when he came in and saw Charlene sitting alone in the half-moon booth. Right next to her draft beer sat David's glass of tonic, the two drinks forming a tableau of intimacy, even in the absence of one of the drinkers. Later, when she'd followed his brother outside, Miles had watched through the window, and something about the way they'd stood together in the parking lot registered without him even knowing. He glanced down the counter at him now, as he, too, followed Charlene's turn into the restaurant, smiling until he felt his brother's gaze, then meeting Miles's eye. Yes? Miles asked by raising his eyebrows. Yes, his brother nodded.

They might have had more to say on the subject, but the phone rang just then. "Miles Roby?" said a voice Miles didn't recognize.

"Yeah."

"Did you know your wife's on upper Empire Avenue screaming obscenities and kicking in the side of your Jeep?"

"Here," Miles said, handing the phone to the Silver Fox. "It's for you."

WHEN HE GOT OUT of the shower, the phone was ringing again, his private line this time. Janine, he thought. He'd not wanted to divorce his wife, and as their final dissolution drew nearer, it had occurred to him that he might actually miss hearing her piss and moan and rant and rave and sob her heart out. For as long as he'd known her, Janine had kept up a pretty constant head of steam, and in truth he'd been looking forward to having Walt Comeau assume the responsibility for releasing her valve. He had no idea what had caused Janine to stop in the middle of Empire Avenue and terrorize her own car, but he was certain her new husband deserved first crack at it. Unfortunately, all Walt had done was grow pale and set the phone back down.

But this time he was wrong, though he almost would've preferred it to be Janine on the phone.

"You finish painting the church yet?" his father demanded once Miles had accepted the charges. Had Max lost his mind completely or simply forgotten he'd begun their last phone conversation with this precise question?

"No, Dad, I haven't."

"Good. You don't want to work for those people."

He knew better than to ask, but couldn't help himself. "What people, Dad? What are you talking about?"

"Those Vatican goons come right into Captain Tony's and lifted Tom right off his barstool by the elbows."

"Vatican goons?"

"Right," Max said, apparently relieved that they had a good connection. "That was yesterday. I haven't seen him since. The sissy one find his station wagon?"

Miles told him he had, for once refusing to be baited. Earlier in the week, Father Mark had bummed a ride to the coast to retrieve the parish's Crown Victoria.

"Right where I told you it was, I bet."

"Do I understand this, Dad?" Miles said. "You want credit for telling me where you left the stolen car?"

"I didn't steal anything."

"No? How about that twenty you took out of my shirt pocket?"

Max ignored this. "So, where do you suppose they took him?"

"Someplace safe, where he can be looked after."

"He was safe right where he was. *We* were looking after him. I thought this was supposed to be a free country. Or don't you Catholics believe in freedom?"

"Did you want something, Dad?"

"You could send down some money if you felt like it. You wouldn't believe the price of beer down here. Ain't even the season yet."

Translation: with Father Tom gone, he'd lost his meal ticket. And immediately following this, another thought. "How'd they know where to find him?"

"Who?"

"Your Vatican goons."

"The sissy one must've told them."

"I don't think so. Do you want to know what I think? I think when the money ran out, *you* called the diocese."

"You just don't want to send me any money," Max said.

"How come I'm always the one you ask? How come you never ask David?"

"I do better with you. Some people are a soft touch, others got harder bark on 'em. You're like your mother. David's more like me."

"For a man who couldn't stay home, you put a lot of faith in genetic logic."

"I never doubted your brother was mine, if that's what you're getting at. Any more than I doubted you were."

That *had* been what he was getting at, he realized.

"A man knows what's his, you know," Max said. "Tick yours?"

"Yes."

"How do you know? Blood test?"

Outside on the stairs leading to the apartment, Miles could hear footsteps. Charlene's, unless he was mistaken, though it wasn't that hard to imagine them as belonging to his mother, as if she'd somehow been summoned by this conversation to resolve their dispute.

"How much do you need, Dad?"

"I'm okay for now," he said, as if he also had wearied of the present conversation. "I'll let you know. First of the month, go over to my place and pick up my check and send it down here, okay?"

"Okay."

Miles hadn't completely shut his door, so Charlene tapped a warning before poking her head inside. Normally, he knew, finding Miles with nothing but a towel wrapped around his middle, she'd have had some smart-ass remark to offer. Not this time. "You better come down," was all she said before pulling the door closed.

"BIG BOY!" Walt was calling excitedly. It always bothered him when something was going on at one end of the counter while he was at the other. It seemed to him not entirely a coincidence, perhaps, that Miles and David and Charlene had all gathered down there out of earshot.

"If I'm not back in an hour," Miles told Charlene, his voice low and more under control than he felt, "call Brenda. If she can't, try Janine." His ex-wife would hostess in a pinch, assuming she'd finished trashing the Jeep.

"Someone should go see Bea," David said. "She sounded pretty upset."

Not five minutes after Miles and his brother had left Callahan's, two state inspectors had appeared and within half an hour had shut the place down. The long list of code violations included wiring, which Miles already knew about, filthy, inadequate bathroom facilities—no argument there—and rodent droppings in plain sight in the kitchen area—in plain sight only because Miles had pulled both the refrigerator and the stove away from the wall, something nobody'd done in more than a decade, so he could work on them. The transgressions against health and safety codes continued down the page, some minor and inexpensive to correct, others more substantial and costly. Under "Recommended (But Not Required)" the inspectors had suggested a new roof, noting flashing along the interior walls, and estimating that the cost of the "Required" repairs might run as high as a hundred thousand dollars—twenty thousand more than Bea and her husband had paid for the business thirty years ago.

"Can you take half an hour?" Miles asked Charlene. At this point David was the one person who couldn't leave the restaurant.

She nodded.

"No more than that," David warned her. "Thursday's crowd comes early." Then, to Miles: "You're the one who should go see Bea, not Charlene."

"I'll go over there as soon as I finish talking to Mrs. Whiting."

"I've been begging you to go see her for—"

"And I just realized you were right," Miles told him.

"I'm right now, too," his brother assured him. "To hell with her. I've seen you when you get like this, Miles. You should wait till you've calmed down. If I had two good arms, I'd make you."

"Be glad you don't," Miles heard himself say, then closed his eyes and shook his head, realizing what he'd just said. "I'm sorry—"

"Until you do something like this to yourself"—David lifted his ruined arm—"you have no idea what sorry is."

"David—"

But his brother had already turned away. "I've got a hundred and fifty seafood enchiladas to make," he said. "Do what you want."

Charlene took him by the elbow. "Miles, you don't even know for sure she's behind this. It could be a coincidence."

Miles shook his head. "A surprise health inspection the same week as the Liquor Control Board?"

That had been on Tuesday, the state Liquor Control agent showing up late in the afternoon in response to allegations that Bea was serving minors. A second violation, he warned her as he sat at the bar filling out the paperwork on his clipboard, could result in the loss of her license. When she asked what the first violation was, he'd pointed over to the booth where Tick sat doing her homework. She'd come in just a few minutes earlier, slid into her favorite booth and pushed aside two half-full glasses of beer that Bea hadn't had a chance to clear away. "You aren't going to tell me that girl over there is twenty-one, are you?"

"No, I'm going to tell you she's my granddaughter and she's not drinking beer, which you can see for yourself."

"She's sitting at a table with *glasses* of *beer*. You know the law, Mrs. Majeski," he said, initialing the report. "You can appeal, of course. Otherwise, you'll want to take care of this fine within sixty days."

"Where's Curtis?" Bea said, referring to the regular state guy.

"I believe the man has retired," he said on the way to the door. When he got there, he stopped. "Oh, Mrs. Majeski? Good luck on your new restaurant."

"No," Miles now told Charlene. "That's no coincidence. And next week, when she gets an offer on the place from some stranger, that won't be a coincidence either."

"I know," Charlene conceded. "I do. It's just . . . I don't know what I'll do if I don't have a job."

"Don't worry about that," Miles said, giving her hand a squeeze, sure of this much, anyhow. "Mrs. Whiting isn't going to close the Empire Grill. She wants it open. She wants us all right here. Or me, at least."

Charlene shook her head. "I don't understand."

"I do," he said, meeting her eye. "It took a while, but I do."

"Big Boy!" Walt called again. "Come on down here! Today's the great day, my friend! No more running!" He had his elbow planted firmly on the counter, his hand open, fingers wiggling.

He was seeing *everything* clearly, it seemed to Miles, even Walt Comeau. In marrying Janine, Walt had no doubt hoped to enhance his reputation as a man's man and a smooth operator. The Silver Fox. Now, a week into his marriage, he was beginning to realize that Janine could very well be his *un*manning. Behind all the bravado, Miles could see—almost smell—the man's panic, which increased noticeably when he saw Miles coming toward him with a stool, which he set down right across from him on the other side of the counter.

"Jesus," Horace Weymouth said, as if he'd just been dealt a hand of gin the likes of which he'd never seen before.

"Say go, Horace," Miles commanded without looking at him.

"Go," said Horace, and Miles slammed the back of Walt's hand onto the Formica so hard that three water glasses leapt off it and shattered on the floor, so hard that the Silver Fox's legs shot straight out and, for a split second, his whole body was parallel to the counter, a victim of a sudden levitation, the stapled hand his only connection to Mother Earth. At that moment Miles released him, and it was his hips that struck the hard linoleum floor first, then the back of his head, then both feet, which bounced just once. Then the Silver Fox lay still, his eyeballs having rolled up in their sockets.

Miles was already out the door.

THE GATE WAS STILL OPEN, but Miles parked outside on the street and walked between the stone pillars. In all the years his mother had worked at the shirt factory, he'd never passed beyond the arch, a fact that now seemed astonishing. After Grace's death, of course, there'd been no reason to come, but as he entered the courtyard, he couldn't help feeling that he was finally attending to some long-ignored obligation.

The white limo was still parked there, and on the other side of the brick wall sat Mrs. Whiting's Lincoln, invisible from the street. Motionless on the shelf behind the backseat was what Miles thought at first glance must be one of those mechanical animals that nodded rhythmic agreement when the vehicle was in motion, but he then realized it was Timmy the Cat. The animal was regarding him curiously, marking his progress along the courtyard and smiling, it seemed, if cats other than the Cheshire variety can be said to smile. When he heard a car door open, Miles saw that the flash of red he'd noticed earlier was Jimmy Minty's Camaro, which had been blocked from view by the limo.

Mrs. Whiting and the limo men had made their way from the shirt factory down to the adjacent textile mill that overlooked the falls. The group was clustered just outside the main entrance, sighting along Mrs. Whiting's extended arm, first looking up at the old building, then out across the river. What was she pointing out? Her own house, a quarter mile upstream? Was that, too, for sale?

At the end of the courtyard a brick walkway led around the shirt factory and down the slope to the mill, and it was here that Jimmy Minty had planted himself. "You're on private property, Miles," he said.

"I thought all this belonged to the town."

"We won't argue." Jimmy Minty shrugged. "It's posted, anyhow."

He wasn't wearing the plaid sport coat he usually wore while on duty. Still, Miles thought he'd check. "Who am I talking to here, Jimmy?"

"Come again?"

They were face-to-face now. "Are you on duty?"

"Sort of. I do a little private consulting."

"Like your father used to."

He nodded. "Old Mr. Honus Whiting hired my dad now and then.

I saw him beat the tar out of a fella one night not far from where we're standing. I was the only witness, in fact. Stubborn little fucker. It was a beating he could've avoided."

"How about your mother? Could her beatings have been avoided?"

Minty took a moment before answering. "No," he said sadly. "I don't think so. You all probably heard a lot of that over in your house, huh?"

"We should've called the cops."

This seemed to stimulate a memory. "I ever tell you about the time your mom came over? You must not have been there. Hot summer afternoon, all the windows open. My old man was going to town on Ma like he did sometimes when she pissed him off, then all of a sudden he turned around and there was your mother standing right in the middle of our living room, like she paid rent. Told my old man he was going to stop what he was doing 'right this instant' and wasn't ever going to start up again. 'Right this instant'—her exact words. She had a hammer in her hand, turned around so the claw end faced the front."

Miles had no trouble conjuring up the scene. "Right this instant" *had* been one of her pet phrases. He'd only seen Grace mad once or twice, but he could imagine her there with the hammer, and could also imagine William Minty backing up a step when he saw her.

"Hard to say what would've happened if Ma hadn't spoke up," Jimmy chuckled. "She's settin' there on the floor with a busted lip, takes one look at your mother standing there with that hammer and tells her to go fuck herself and mind her own business. See, your mom, being so pretty, was what my mom feared most, even more than my old man." He paused. "She never told you about that day, huh?"

"Not a word."

He shrugged. "Ah, fuck the past, right?" And when Miles offered no opinion on whether this was either possible or advisable, his eyes narrowed. "My boy Zack's thinking about quitting the football team, did you know that? I keep trying to talk him out of it, but I don't know. Coach won't play him no more, so maybe he's right. What's the point? All that shit in the newspaper about him being a dirty player. I guess everybody figures he's a bad kid now. Your friend the principal's trying to blame him for what happened to that old woman they found."

Miles had no desire to hear any of this. "I'm here to see Mrs. Whiting, Jimmy. It won't take long."

The other man seemed almost grateful for the change of subject. "She said for me to tell you tomorrow."

"She knew I was coming?"

"There ain't much that lady doesn't know, Miles. Several steps ahead of people like you and me. She's kind of disappointed in you, is my impression."

"I'm sure she'll tell me all about it," Miles said and started around the policeman, who grabbed him by the left elbow.

"Except not today."

When Miles hit him, as hard as he could, Jimmy Minty held on to his elbow for balance, but finally had to let go and sit down on the curb that bordered the walkway. His nose was broken, that much Miles could tell. It took the blood a moment to start, then it began to flow freely, soaking the front of his white shirt. Miles could see from where he stood that Timmy was racing frantically around inside the Lincoln, from window to window, as if she had a fat wager on the outcome of these hostilities.

Down at the mill, Mrs. Whiting and the limo men had gone inside. Miles stood over Minty, unsure what was supposed to happen next. The policeman was leaning back on both hands now and staring up at the gray sky, probably in the hope that his blood wouldn't flow uphill. He sniffed four or five times, then sneezed mightily, dappling both Miles and himself.

"Well, how about that?" he said. "Ol' Miles Roby committing a violent act. Won't people be surprised."

Miles stared down at him, recalling his father's advice about cops: the worst they could do to you wasn't that bad. Miles found it more than a little disconcerting to be following his father's counsel in an important matter, but he was still a very long way from regret, which he had a feeling there'd be plenty of time for later on.

After a minute, the worst of the nosebleed having stopped, Jimmy Minty got to his feet. He was wobbly, but also, Miles saw, determined. "Come on over to the car," he said. "Let me put the cuffs on you."

"Not until I've talked to Mrs. Whiting."

"I have my orders."

"Well."

Minty drove his fist into Miles's midsection, doubling him over. Another punch he didn't even see dropped him to one knee. He was still trying to get his breath back when Jimmy hit him behind the left ear, setting off an explosion in his skull. He slumped onto the brick path then, and when no further blows followed, he rolled over and saw that Minty had returned to the Camaro and was rooting around in the glove box, which suggested to Miles that he must've blacked out, at least for a few seconds. By the time the policeman had located the handcuffs, Miles had managed to get back to his feet.

"You'd do better to just *set* back down, Miles," Minty advised. His nose was swelling and turning gray. "You created your disturbance, and now I've quelled it."

It occurred to Miles that despite his broken nose, this was a richly rewarding experience for Jimmy Minty. He easily slipped the next punch Miles flung, and then Miles was back on his knees, cradling his stomach, retching onto the bricks.

"Now straighten up and put out your wrists," Minty said, but instead, twice more Miles struggled to his feet, and twice more found himself back on the ground.

By the time Mrs. Whiting and the limo men returned up the walkway, one of Miles's eyes was completely closed, the other a mere slit. Both men were seated, facing each other, on opposite curbs, looking like they'd been on the same losing side of a fight, the victors having unaccountably run away. The handcuffs still dangled from the policeman's fingers, and Miles could tell it embarrassed him. "You go on along, Mrs. Whiting," Minty said, his breathing sounding strangled. "I'll finish up with this after I've caught my breath."

The businessmen, clearly nervous, gave the two locals a wide berth, walking well off the brick path onto the grass to circle around them.

"You amaze me, dear boy," said Mrs. Whiting. "What was so important that it couldn't wait until tomorrow?"

Across the courtyard, Miles could hear the limo's doors open and close, the solid, well-made sound of money sealing itself off. Since she was probably expecting him to say something about Callahan's, he decided to disappoint her. "I just came by to give you my notice," he told her. "You'll have to find someone else to run the Empire Grill."

Jimmy Minty quit fingering his broken nose to listen to this.

"You appear to have been visited by some sort of revelation, dear boy," Mrs. Whiting observed. "Here's my suggestion, though. Why not think things over? Passionate decisions are seldom very sound."

"When did you ever feel passion?"

"Well, it's true I'm seldom swept away like those with more romantic temperaments," she conceded. "But we are what we are, and what can't be cured must be endured."

"What can't be cured must be avenged," Miles said. "Isn't that what you mean?"

She smiled appreciatively. "Payback is *how* we endure, dear boy. Now, before you say another word in anger, for which I should have to punish you, you'll want to stop and consider not just your own future but your daughter's. She may require assistance with her university expenses in a couple of years, much as *you* did." She paused to let this sink in. "And of course there are your brother and the others who depend upon the Empire Grill for their admittedly slender livelihoods. In the end, though, it's up to you, just as it always has been."

"Power and control. Right, Francine?"

It was the first time he had ever called her by her first name. In fact, over the years he'd nearly forgotten it. Strange that it should return to him at this moment.

If being addressed so intimately offended Mrs. Whiting, she took pains to conceal it. "Ah!" she said, in mock delight. "You *were* paying attention to my little lessons, weren't you, dear boy! I could never be sure." And with that she turned and stepped nimbly around and toward the Lincoln.

"He preferred my mother, didn't he, Mrs. Whiting?" Miles called after her. "That's what all this is about, right?"

She stopped—stock-still for a moment—then returned to where he sat. "And am I not a model of Christian forbearance, dear boy? Did I not forgive your mother her trespass? Did I not welcome her into the very home she destroyed? Did I not offer her every opportunity for the expiation and redemption you Catholics are forever going on and on about?"

"Redemption? Wasn't it really retribution?"

"Well, as I once explained to my husband, there was a little something in the relationship for each of us." She started away again, then stopped and turned back. "Having said that, I wouldn't want to leave you with the wrong impression, dear boy. I was *very* fond of your mother, just as I'm very fond of you. In the end I think she was glad things didn't work out quite as she'd hoped. I like to think she came to understand life's great folly."

Then she looked down at the policeman. "Do you think you can manage to lock up, Jimmy? The padlock on that gate is a little stiff. It requires no end of coaxing."

"I'll take care of it, Mrs. Whiting."

Miles couldn't help but smile, having made more or less this same promise to the woman for twenty-five years—the precise destiny his mother had feared above all others. When the Lincoln glided out between the stone pillars, followed by the limo, Miles felt something rub against his elbow, and when he looked down there was Timmy, who must've escaped when Mrs. Whiting opened the car door. The animal seemed satisfied with the damage already inflicted on Miles and offered no additional malice.

Jimmy Minty got to his feet and offered Miles a hand, which Miles accepted and then held out his wrists to be cuffed. Jimmy led him over to the Camaro, kicking the cat out of the way, hard, when she tried to follow.

Miles tried without luck to remember the last time he'd been in a sports car. The engine growled like a caged animal directly beneath his feet. Charlene had once confessed that she considered this a sexy sound. Human folly indeed. Outside the gate, Minty put the Camaro in Park and went back to close and lock the gate. As Mrs. Whiting had predicted, this was not an easy job, and Miles could hear him swearing at the lock.

"You never should've come back here, old buddy," Jimmy Minty said when he got back in the car. "Your mother was right about that. I'll never forget how she screamed at you. I guess that's what I was trying to say before all this started." By "all this" he seemed to mean everything that had happened since he'd found Miles parked outside his boyhood home back in September. "I felt real bad when I heard her screaming at you like that, all those things she said when she was dying, and you just trying to help."

Miles closed his eyes and listened to her, the memory still fresh, horrible. *Go away, Miles. You're killing me. Can't you understand that? Your being here is killing me. Killing me.*

"Not that you cared if I felt bad or not," he added.

"Do me a favor, Jimmy?" Miles asked when he eased the Camaro out onto Empire Avenue.

"Sure." He seemed anxious to demonstrate that despite being habitually and cruelly misused, he wasn't the sort of man to withhold a favor if asked nicely.

"Ask my brother to make sure Tick gets down to Boston on Sunday."

His promise to his daughter was the thing he'd forgotten, the thing that, had he remembered it, might have kept him from heading down this very wrong road. He remembered thinking a few minutes earlier that there'd be plenty of time for regret later. How quickly "later" had arrived.

CHAPTER 30

T HE BLUE TABLE has the blues. Is it even remotely possible, Tick wonders, that this is somehow due to the continued absence of John Voss, who'd been more absent than present back when he was still sitting there? Even Candace, who usually could be counted on to talk from one bell to the next, is quiet today. What Tick's trying to fathom is not the girl's silence, which she understands, but how things work: more specifically whether they happen fast or slow. She knows from recent experience that the whole world can change in what feels like an instant, but she suspects that the swiftness is really just an illusion.

Take Candace, for instance. Did they become friends yesterday, or has their friendship been growing since September? Clearly it's caught both of them off guard. The expression on Candace's face yesterday afternoon, a mixture of gratitude and disbelief, was vivid testimony to how surprised she was to see a swollen-eyed Tick on her doorstep. For the last month she'd been suggesting that Tick stop by some afternoon after school so they could take a walk along the river, but her offhanded manner implied that she didn't really expect this to happen.

Tick had no trouble finding where Candace lived with her mother and her mother's boyfriend of the moment—a three-story building on Front Street. Front ran parallel to the river, below the falls, the worst neighborhood of Empire Falls, settled by the poorest of the French Canadian immigrants back when it was a company town. Houses had been built only on the north side of the street, and for good reason. In the glory days of Empire Textile, the solvents and dyes used on the fabrics were dumped directly into the river, staining the banks below the falls red and green and yellow, according to day of the week and size of the batch. The sloping banks contained rings, like those in a tree trunk, except these were in rainbow colors; they recorded not years but the rise and fall of the river. Even now, fifty years later, only the hardiest weeds and scrub trees grew south of the pavement on Front Street, and when the brush was periodically cleared, surprising patches of fading chartreuse and magenta were revealed.

The apartment was on the second floor, its entryway at the top of a rickety exterior staircase. The woman who answered Tick's knock was big and braless and dirty-haired, and didn't look old enough to have a sixteen-year-old daughter. When she pulled the door open, Tick felt a blast of unhealthy heat and saw a man who looked about her father's age, wearing a fishnet tank top and seated at a dinette, concentrating grimly on the flyer from the Fairhaven Wal-Mart. "Hey, Moron!" the woman called over her shoulder, without bothering to say hello to Tick, "Candy! You got company!" Then she walked away from the open door, leaving Tick to either come in or not, as suited her. To remain outside suited her best. The sight of this awful woman had the effect of putting Tick's recent argument with her own mother into a whole different perspective.

When Candace saw her from the kitchen doorway, her face lit up and then darkened with perplexed embarrassment at the presence of a girl like Christina Roby in their shabby neighborhood. The last time she'd been this surprised was back in September, when the same girl took up residence in art class with herself and the other Boners.

"Hi?" she offered, apologetically.

"Could we maybe take that walk?" Tick said.

"Sure." Candace's face quickly brightened again, as if at the opportunity of a lifetime.

"ANYWAY," CANDACE SAID after they'd climbed down the bank, "I'm in love with Justin now."

At the end of a dry October, the river was running low and they were able to leap from rock to rock pretty far out into the current. From shore it had seemed like they might be able to hopscotch all the way to the opposite bank, but Tick now saw that the farther out into the river they got, the farther apart the rocks actually were. The wind was also more bitter away from the sheltered bank, so they changed direction and headed downstream toward the bend. There the indented shoreline would provide a windbreak.

"Justin," Tick repeated when they found a couple big rocks to rest on. She couldn't help smiling at the idea of Candace and Justin Dibble, who'd spent most of the term tormenting her by describing the monster crush he claimed John Voss had on her. She also suspected that Candace didn't realize that by flitting, emotionally if not physically, from boy to boy, she was imitating her mother.

"He really loves me," she explained, as if the boy's feelings for her were the deciding factor, as opposed to her feelings for him.

"What about Zack?"

"There'll probably be a fight when he gets out of the hospital," Candace admitted fatalistically.

Strange, but fights over Candace appeared to be backing up. Earlier in the week, Bobby, the girl's former boyfriend from Fairhaven, who Candace claimed had been in jail, showed up at the high school, just off school grounds, looking for Zack Minty, whom he didn't know by sight, unaware that the boy whose ass he'd come to kick had been admitted to the hospital that morning with an infected gash on his shin. For some reason he'd waited a long time to have the injury looked at, claiming he didn't even remember how he'd got it but speculating it must have happened at football practice. It hadn't looked like a football injury to the emergency room physician, who immediately put him on antibiotics. For a long time Zack's fever had refused to come down, and yesterday the doctors still wanted to keep him under observation, though they'd promised both him and his father that unless his fever spiked again, they'd release him on Friday and wouldn't stand between him and playing on Saturday, the last home game of the season.

"Do you think Justin would win?" Candace wondered idly, as if this were a conundrum, on the magnitude of Superman versus the Incredible Hulk.

"Against Zack or Bobby?" Tick asked, though it made no difference, since Justin stood no chance against either.

"Zack," Candace clarified. "I don't think Bobby'd fight Justin. He just wanted to get it on with Zack because he heard Zack's tough."

Even sheltered from the worst of the wind, it was still cold—and getting dark too, though it wasn't yet four o'clock. Still, coming here had been a good idea. Tick could feel her spirits gradually picking up.

Her shoulder still hurt from being dragged by her backpack, but what happened had frightened more than injured her. And, as was often the case, talking to Candace buoyed her spirits, though she did wonder if the mere fact that somebody was worse off than you was a proper basis for friendship. Both girls were silent for a while, listening to the water slide by at their feet.

"When you and Zack were together," Candace finally said, "did you ever play the gun game?"

Tick studied Candace's expression and saw the fear in her eyes. "Once," she admitted.

"He said you used to play it all the time. He was trying to get me to."

Zack called it "Polish Roulette," which was supposed to be a joke. He'd broken one of his father's revolvers open and shown Tick there were no bullets in the cylinder. Then you were supposed to put the barrel of the gun against your head and pull the trigger. The idea, as he explained it to Tick, was to see how rational you were. If you knew by the evidence of your own senses that the gun wasn't loaded, then you had nothing to fear. Except it was still a gun and your mind couldn't forget that. "It's a rush, though," he admitted, grinning at her, "'cause, like, what if you were wrong and there was one bullet in there you missed?"

"Don't you hate it when you find out people are lying to you?" Candace said, apparently referring to Zack's claim that he and Tick had played the game all the time.

"Candace," Tick said, "promise me you'll never do it?"

"Okay." She shrugged, her fear apparently evaporating the instant she shared the story with her friend.

"No, I mean it," Tick said. "Promise me right now, or we're not friends anymore."

"Okay, okay," Candace said, more seriously now. Then: "We're friends? I can tell people we're friends?"

"Sure. Why not?" Seeing how badly Candace wanted that made Tick wonder whether it would have made a difference if she'd told John Voss the same thing. What if all everybody needed in the world was to be sure of one friend? What if you were the one, and you refused to say those simple words?

It was nearly dark now, and when they started back toward the riverbank a movement on the shore attracted their attention. About fifty yards upstream, right where the river began to bend toward

Empire Falls, stood a group of men in suits, huddled and shivering but attentive. They seemed to be listening to a woman Tick recognized as Mrs. Whiting, who owned the Empire Grill and, according to her father, most everything else in town. Just barely visible through the bare autumn trees, a white limousine idled on the roadway, and it was this that had caught Candace's eye. "Wow," she sighed. "How'd you like to ride in one of those someday?"

What Tick noticed, however, was that the woman had noticed *them* as well. And even though she and Candace were standing close together on a big rock, somehow she was certain that Mrs. Whiting was smiling not at Candace but at her.

SLOW, TICK DECIDES. Things happen slow. She isn't quite sure why this understanding of the world's movement should be important, but she thinks it is. It could even be the reason that guy Bill Taylor isn't a very good painter. His art happens fast, and he's always talking about how swiftly light changes, about how important it is to "attack" your painting, to get a record of what you're seeing, because you'll never see that exact thing again. Tick understands what he means, but can't help feeling that the opposite is equally true.

Take her parents. At the time, their separation had seemed a bolt from the blue, though she now realizes it had been a slow process, rooted in dissatisfaction and need—in their personalities, really. Maybe the whole thing had come on *Tick* suddenly, but in reality her mother's slow march from eye contact to flirtation to infidelity to divorce to remarriage was a Stairmaster journey whose culmination was probably the beginning of another climb that would prove just as slow and inexorable.

And that's the thing, she concludes. Just because things happen slow doesn't mean you'll be ready for them. If they happened fast, you'd be alert for all kinds of suddenness, aware that speed was trump. "Slow" works on an altogether different principle, on the deceptive impression that there's plenty of time to prepare, which conceals the central fact, that no matter how slow things go, you'll always be slower.

The art room has a long bank of windows facing the rear of the school and a huge parking lot that's never filled except during boys' basketball games. This afternoon only the first four or five rows of parking spaces are occupied, and from her seat at the Blue table Tick can see straight down a corridor between the third and fourth rows of cars, which means that eight or ten drivers have actually respected the yellow lines painted on the blacktop. Beyond the lot is a gentle, sloping bank and the oval cinder track her father once told her a funny story about. Beyond that, open field runs to a line of trees where the wetlands begin. Here Tick spots an almost imperceptible movement off in the distance between the rows of cars. What it looks like is a small ball bobbing in a gentle breeze on a placid lake, except there's no water where she's looking.

Tick idly watches whatever it is bob up and down and then sideways before returning to her still life, which she completed two days ago but still feels is unfinished, she's not sure why. Maybe it's because she can't see how anything so poorly executed could be considered finished. It also bothers her to think that what's wrong with the painting could be the result of a bad decision made early on. Worse, she's not sure whether the bad decision was Mrs. Roderigue's in selecting the ugly peony in the first place, or her own. Her decision to paint the peony in its ugliness is defensible, she thinks, but now she realizes that she's painted the surrounding flowers as if they were corrupt by association. If making things seem prettier than they are is a lie, then making them seem uglier must be another. She can tinker with the painting, improve it in small ways, but it won't change the lie at its heart. Only starting over could do that, and it's too late. Next week they begin a new unit.

She steals a look at Candace's painting, and is surprised to see that it's not bad. Up to this point she'd simply recycled last year's efforts, not a strategy Tick would have recommended, given that Candace took and failed this same class last year on the basis of this very same work. But Mrs. Roderigue appears to have no memory of any of it, and none of Candace's work so far has received the grade it got the year before—a fact Tick thinks Mr. Meyer, the principal, might be interested to learn. That Mrs. Roderigue's grading corresponds rather chillingly to the income level of her students' parents has—according to her father—already been brought to Mr. Meyer's attention, which might explain why Candace is faring better this year.

What impresses Tick most about her friend's effort is that she's accomplished exactly what Mrs. Roderigue requested—that is, to remember the peony's beauty and paint that memory. In a way, the big gaudy pink flower of love is the perfect subject for Candace. Seeing what a good job she's done, Tick at once feels both happy and sad for her friend. Yesterday, on their way home from the river, she and Candace cemented their friendship with a genuine exchange of secrets.

Candace, of course, had used Tick as a repository of secrets all term, but this was the first time Tick reciprocated.

The secret Candace shared is that she and Justin had sex, which explains why he's been so quiet in class today and why they exchange shy, scared smiles, full of gratitude and wonder and regret each time he looks up from his work. What Tick told Candace is that she's the one who picked up the Exacto knife back in September and that it hadn't been found in all that time because it was tucked snugly in a side pocket of her backpack. Further, she's admitted to Candace that the reason she hasn't returned the knife to the supply closet is that she likes the idea of possessing a weapon, which of course is absurd for a pacifist, as Tick believes herself to be. In truth, every time she takes it out and feels its cool surface, her left arm starts to go numb and she has to put it away before she becomes ill. The thing to do, she knows, is return it to the supply closet at the end of today's class, but Tick knows she won't, and she knows the reason is that Zack Minty was released from the hospital late this morning. She passed him in the hall between classes and saw the way he looked at her and Candace. For the last ten minutes she's been expecting the classroom door to swing open and for Zack to join them at the Blue table. Tick can't help anticipating bad things, especially after what happened yesterday between her father and Zack's dad.

It's still hard to believe, her father going to jail. According to Uncle David, that's where he'll end up once he's well enough to be released from the hospital. Zack's dad had wanted to throw him in a cell yesterday when they arrived at the station, but the chief of police had sent them directly to Empire General, where Tick hasn't been allowed to visit him yet. According to her uncle and Charlene, who'd been waiting for her at the house, the lawyer they hired didn't think he'd be locked up for long. There was little doubt he'd be arrested, though, and he'd have to post bail. More than anything, according to Uncle David, her father was embarrassed. He didn't want Tick to see him in his present condition. And he wanted her to know how sorry he was to have botched their trip to Boston on Sunday, though David and Charlene would take her instead. Before she knew it, everything would be back to normal.

When Charlene and her uncle rose to leave, it occurred to Tick to ask where her mother was. She'd delayed coming home in fear of the inevitable scene. After their altercation on Empire Avenue, her mother would be a basket case, swinging back and forth between anger and worry, and Walt would be lurking in the background, making everything worse.

The two grown-ups exchanged a clumsy glance that said that this was the very question they'd been hoping she *wouldn't* ask. "She'll be home soon," Charlene told her. "She's over at the hospital."

"She can visit Daddy, and I can't?"

Then they told her that it wasn't her father Janine was visiting, but Walt, who'd been admitted with a concussion and a broken arm. Reluctantly, they explained how this had come to pass.

Then another question occurred to her. "Who's running the restaurant?"

"We closed it for tonight," David admitted. "No way around it. You want to come over with us and eat an enchilada? I got about a hundred and fifty of them in the oven."

And that's what they'd done, the three of them. They'd sat in a corner booth with all the restaurant lights off, silently eating enchiladas and watching cars pull into the parking lot, see the sign on the door, and drive off again.

Meanwhile, Tick did a tally in her mind. In one day her mother had nearly dragged her down Empire Avenue by her backpack; she'd become best friends with Candace Burke; her father had broken Walt Comeau's arm in a wrestling match, then gotten into a fight with a policeman and ended up in the hospital, from which he'd be taken directly to jail; and a sign had been posted on the Empire Grill reading CLOSED UNTIL FURTHER NOTICE. And that wasn't counting the horrible events earlier in the week.

But everything would be back to normal before long?

WHATEVER'S BOBBING OUT THERE, Tick notices, is still bobbing, but closer now. What it looks like is a human head, though of course that makes no sense. She watches curiously to see whether it will resolve itself as sense or remain nonsense, and she's just about to bet on the latter—an acknowledgment, perhaps, of the irrational world, where people she knows, like her father, become people she doesn't know, where the whole world tilts and solid things become as liquid as objects in a Dalí painting, where human heads disassociated from their bodies are borne along on waves of windblown grass—when this particular bobbing head resolves itself before her eyes, tilting the world back again, though not completely. Because the head, she realizes, belongs to John Voss, and in fact it's not bobbing on water or waves of grass, but rather on his shoulders. What she's been observing is the boy's natural, loping stride as he approaches the school, crossing the distant field, and then the cinder track, his body hidden below the curvature of the land. Only when he reaches the gentle incline where her father once lost control of Mrs. Whiting's new Lincoln do the boy's neck, shoulders and torso become visible, a recognizably human form. And then just as suddenly he changes course and vanishes entirely behind the rows of cars, gone so completely that Tick wonders if she's imagined him there.

The best evidence that what she's seen is real is that her left arm has gone numb.

WHAT SHE REALIZES when he enters, a sixteen-year-old boy with a grocery bag folded under his arm, is how relieved she'd been by his disappearance. Though terribly ashamed to feel this, she can't deny it. One look at him now—head down, shoulders hunched forward, resolutely silent, as if he thinks he can walk into art class and take up where he left off—brings back to her the thought she'd tried so hard to ignore last week, which she was too embarrassed to admit even to her father: that everyone is better off with this boy gone.

Not that he is the *cause* of all this trouble, because she knows he isn't. He's not even really to blame for what happened with his grandmother. In a way, John Voss is like Jesus—blameless, perhaps, but nevertheless the center of all the trouble. If Jesus had gone away, things in Galilee would have returned to normal, just as her father promised they soon would here in Empire Falls. So, as Tick sees John again— and she's the first to, because she's been watching the classroom door, waiting for it to open—a wish escapes before she can call it back, that he should disappear again, this time for good. Dead? Is that what she means? She hopes not. No one could want this boy, this child who had dangled from a laundry bag inside a dark closet, not to exist. Merely for him not to exist *here*, because here has proven to be the wrong place. She feels like Jesus' disciples must've felt. They never wanted him crucified, of course, but what a relief it must have been when the stone was rolled across the entrance to the tomb, sealing everything shut so they could go back to being fishermen, which they knew how to do, rather than fishers of men, which they didn't. No wonder they didn't recognize him later on the road to Emmaus. They didn't want to, any more than Tick wants to welcome this poor boy back into their midst.

Except for being blameless, John Voss is not, of course, at all like Jesus. What has he ever been but a silent, sullen, angry burden that no one, including Tick, has wanted to shoulder? Outside of her father, who'd given him a job, and Tick, who'd given him the bare minimum of kindness, the only person who'd showed him any generosity was his grandmother, and he'd repaid that kindness by tossing her lifeless body onto the landfill as if it were a threadbare rug. No, his disappearance *has* been a blessing, allowing the whole horrible story to recede from public consciousness. True, for the last five days everyone in Dexter County was looking for him, but the truth is, nobody hoped to find him. Is there a term for that? Tick wonders. The thing everyone is searching for and hoping not to find? The thing you're secretly glad has made a clean getaway, lest you yourself be blamed should it ever be located?

John Voss moves deliberately across the room to the Blue table and stops just a few feet from Tick, no doubt confronting the fact that there's no place for him to sit. In fact, starting the day after his disappearance, there'd been one less chair at this table, representing, Tick realizes, everyone's secret wish. Mrs. Roderigue, she notes, has risen from behind her desk and actually seems to be contemplating a journey across the room. Everyone else is just staring, dumbfounded.

Without looking at anyone, John sets his folded grocery bag down on the table with a dull thud. Now that he's close, Tick can smell him. It's the same rancid smell he'd had back in September before he started working at the restaurant. His clothes are wet and caked with dirt, his hair knotted with bits of leaves and twigs. The room is silent. Tick can feel nothing on the left side of her body. She reaches down to her backpack, where in one of the side pockets there is, in addition to the Exacto knife, the extra sandwich she's brought along every day this week in case the boy showed up.

Justin Dibble is the first to speak. "Hey, John," he says, as if this were a normal day, just another class. "What's in the bag?"

At first he doesn't appear to hear. When he finally reaches into the bag and takes out the revolver, it seems to Tick that he may have done so in response not to Justin but to a voice in his own head. The revolver looks like an antique, or maybe a stage prop, with its wooden grip and long barrel. He points it and pulls the trigger without hesitation, and then Justin Dibble vanishes in the roar. He simply isn't sitting there anymore. Mrs. Roderigue, halfway across the room, stops next to the vase of still-life flowers, unable to move forward or back or even to scream, and before the echo of the first explosion dies there are two more and Mrs. Roderigue drops to her knees, a large peony blooming on her bosom, the vase tumbling off the table and shattering on the floor.

"Oh-my-God-oh-my-God," Candace whimpers, and Tick reaches out to the boy just before the fourth deafening shot. She isn't sure if she has actually touched him, but apparently she has because John Voss slowly turns to look at her. Both of them are standing now, though she cannot remember rising to her feet. Behind her she hears or imagines hearing the classroom door open and other kids running out, something she wishes her own legs would allow her to do. She can feel her vision narrowing the way it does when she's about to lose consciousness. She looks over at where Candace was sitting, but the girl is no longer there and she hopes this means that she has either fled or ducked under the table. She wants for Candace not to be harmed, now that they're friends.

It occurs to Tick that Zack Minty's stupid game has prepared her for this moment. She faces John Voss as bravely as she can, knowing it will all be over soon. Her vision has now narrowed to the point where she can barely make him out, his face bloody, his eyes almost sad. When he speaks, his voice comes from a long way off. "*This* is what I dream," he tells her, in answer to the question she asked him so long ago. Then he squeezes the trigger, and she hears what she is certain will be the last sound she will ever hear, and feels herself thrust backward into blackness.

ACROSS TOWN, Miles Roby was sitting at the edge of the hospital bed compiling a mental list of all the people to whom he owed an apology when one of them, his former mother-in-law, walked in, sat down in a chair just inside the door and burst out laughing. Miles studied Bea through his good eye, the other still fused shut with mucus and blood and swelling. Finally she stopped and caught her breath. "I'm sorry, Miles," she sighed. "I'm not laughing at you."

As lies went, this one seemed particularly feeble to a man dressed in a hospital gown so threadbare it verged on transparence. He had a room designed for two all to himself, so it wasn't like there was anybody else for his former mother-in-law to be laughing at. At first the other bed had been occupied by none other than Jimmy Minty, causing Miles to wonder if some sort of perverse hospital policy required men who'd beaten each other up to share lodgings afterward. Actually, it was more Jimmy Minty who'd beaten Miles up, which was why the policeman had been released, and Miles, with bruised kidneys and a cracked rib, two broken teeth and blood in his urine, was left behind, still groggy with medication, to be laughed at by visitors. He'd had half a dozen between last night and this morning, though the visits were a little hazy, thanks to the painkillers the night before. David and Charlene had been to see him, of course, and Father Mark had brought the news that it was at last official: Sacré Coeur and St. Catherine's would become one parish. He himself was awaiting reassignment, he didn't know where; someplace even colder and farther north, he was guessing. Even Janine had stopped in briefly. It was just like him, she said, to finally go and do something interesting after she divorced him. She also asked if he realized that with his two broken teeth, he was beginning to look like Max. At least she'd kept Tick away, for which he was grateful.

An hour ago he'd asked the nurse for another of the yummy painkillers he'd been given last night, but she'd smiled and said, "Oh, no, I don't think so," as if she knew perfectly well that he'd been a very bad boy to enjoy it so much. By way of compensation she provided him with two entirely inferior Tylenol Threes, but his head still felt like a yo-yo suspended on the end of a malicious child's string. A few minutes before Bea entered the room in a gale of laughter, three ambulances housed in the garage directly below his room—a design flaw, surely—screamed out of the hospital en route to God knew where—their sirens loud enough to explode his head. All of which, he knew, was pretty much what he deserved.

"I just stuck my head in down the hall," Bea finally explained. "You should see the goddamn rooster."

Walt Comeau's name was near the top of the list of people Miles owed apologies to, of course, and the reason he was sitting on the edge of the bed rather than lying down was that he'd been contemplating whether, if he took it slow, maybe with the aid of the walker he'd used earlier to go to the bathroom, he might be able to make it down the hall to where David and Charlene had told him the Silver Fox was convalescing. Miles thought it might cheer Walt to view the sorry condition of the man who'd broken his arm and given him a concussion.

On the other hand, why undertake such an arduous journey to apologize to one person when there was another candidate right there in front of you? "Bea," Miles said, hanging his head, "I can't even begin to tell you how sorry I am."

"Don't be," she said. "He had it coming."

"Not that," Miles assured her. His voice had a strange echo inside his head, like an overseas call being bounced off a satellite. "The tavern. I should've seen it coming. What she'd do, I mean."

Bea took his hand then, studying his still-swollen fingers. "Speaking of the bar, I got an offer on the place this morning." She looked up at him. "You don't seem that surprised."

"Mrs. Whiting?"

She shrugged. "It came from a law firm in Boston, by way of a local realtor, but yeah, that would be my guess."

"Good deal?"

"Probably thirty or forty grand more than it's worth."

"You should take it."

"I know. Maybe I will." She looked him in the eye, long and hard.

"Do."

She nodded. "Still, I'm thinking, fuck her."

Now there was something going on out in the hall. First shouting and then a doctor, two nurses and an orderly went by at a dead run.

"I'm not sure F. Lee Bailey could win a pitched battle against that woman," Miles said, feeling a terrible exhaustion set in at the thought of her. "Not in Dexter County, anyway."

"How do you know?" Bea said. "It's been twenty years since anybody tried."

"For good reason."

Bea got to her feet then, clearly disappointed. "Well, I better go before I tire you out. Just tell me one thing, though. Wouldn't you rather go out in a blaze of glory?"

He couldn't help but smile. "Look at me, Bea," he said, though she already was. "I just did."

WHEN SHE WAS GONE, Miles went over to the window and stood there looking across the parking lot and through a line of bare trees to where the gray river flowed.

He'd had one other visitor. Last night, sometime. He couldn't remember exactly when. Maybe early this morning. He'd drifted off into a narcotic sleep and awakened with a start to find Cindy Whiting sitting at his bedside. Her appearance had stunned him almost as much as her presence. She looked, Miles couldn't help thinking, astonishingly like her mother. Or rather the way Miles imagined Mrs. Whiting might look after a long illness, assuming there existed a virus with the temerity to use her for a host. It was hard to tell how much weight Cindy had lost since the football game—what, three weeks ago? Her face was pale and gaunt, the flesh along her upper arms sagging.

"You're awake," she said.

"How long have you been here?"

"A while," she admitted. "Do you know what I was just thinking about? How strange it is that you and I happened to be born on the same day in this very hospital."

"Almost the same hour."

"For a long time I thought of it as a sign. That we were meant to be together. And that almost happened, didn't it, Miles?" When he didn't respond, she continued. "Do you remember the time we kissed?"

He did. It had been an impulse born of confusion, but still, impossible to either call back or erase from memory. God knew, over the years he'd tried. It had happened the night before Grace, in the final stages of her illness, was moved from the Whiting home to the hospital, where she would live another forty-eight hours, most of them in a coma. June was hot that year, and at Grace's insistence Max, newly returned from the Keys, had taken David to the coast with him two weeks before, ostensibly to help on the house-painting crew, but in fact so he wouldn't have to watch his mother die. Roger Sperry's illness had already killed him, and Miles, who'd been home since the previous October, was working long hours at the Empire Grill. He was grateful for the distraction, and lengthened the hours whenever possible, though he was ashamed of himself for leaving school to be with his dying mother, only to hide out at the restaurant, no more prepared at twenty-one to watch his mother die than David was at twelve. What little strength Grace had left she used to express her anger—it was rage, really—about his decision to leave St. Luke's. Even though the academic year was finished—he'd driven down for Peter and Dawn's graduation the month before—and though it was pointless for her to be angry over something that no longer pertained, Grace, in her confusion and pain, clung to her anger as if that alone might keep her alive. Didn't he realize, she kept asking, that the mere sight of him only increased her suffering? As her condition worsened, he delayed his visits as much as possible, often arriving at the Whiting house at a time when, according to the rhythms of her illness, she was likely to be asleep or heavily sedated with morphine.

It was Cindy Whiting—having returning to Empire Falls herself from Augusta—who had been his mother's constant nurse and companion. Miles often found her crying quietly at Grace's bedside when he arrived after closing the restaurant. On the night Cindy was now recalling, his mother was awake when he appeared, and upon seeing him in the doorway she'd simply turned her head and looked away, a gesture so eloquent in its futility that it had backed him out into the hall. Cindy had risen to follow him, leaning heavily on her cane in order to close the door quietly behind her. Her eyes were swollen with her own suffering, and it hadn't seemed so wrong for him to take her in his arms. When she raised her head to his, they'd kissed, and where was the harm in a kiss so full of need? He should have broken it off, of course, but he hadn't, the moment proceeding recklessly until he slid his hand up under her sweater, then under her brassiere, cupping her breast, feeling her shudder against him. They'd remained like that until there was a moan of pain from inside the room, and Cindy whispered, "I'll be right back," and returned to his mother's bedside.

Poor, crippled girl, she could do nothing quickly, however, and by the time she returned, he was gone.

"Yes, I remember," he told her, blinking at the memory.

Then she said something that surprised him. "You *do* know I've had lovers, don't you, Miles?"

"I'm glad, Cindy," he said, feeling himself redden with embarrassment, because, no, he hadn't suspected this.

"I wanted you to know, because I'm leaving tomorrow. The truth is, I don't do very well at home. I never have. There's a man in Augusta who cares for me, and I like him well enough. It's not a wonderful life, but I can see clearly there, and it's important for me to see things clearly. I want you to know about this man, because you always imagine me unhappy, and that hurts my feelings. It's like you decided a long time ago that someone like me is incapable of joy. It hurts you to think that my life is a misery, so you don't think of me at all. You don't call me to find out how I'm doing, because you think you already know. It doesn't occur to you that I might be happy . . . that I might like to share it with you."

"I'm sorry, Cindy."

When it was clear he was unable to choke out any more than this, she said, "Is it so terrible for you to know I'll always love you?"

"No, of course not. It's just that I've been such a poor friend to you, Cindy, right from the start."

"It's true you always managed to hurt my feelings worse than all the others, but that was only because I *had* feelings for you. You never meant to hurt me. Not ever. I know that."

She got to her feet then.

"Remember how you used to try to get me to understand poems?" He nodded.

"Actually, I understood a lot more than you thought. It was just so much fun watching how frustrated you'd get."

"Thanks a lot."

"I'm more like my mother than you know."

"No one's like your mother."

At the door she stopped, then turned back to regard him. "She's not finished with you, Miles," she said.

He nodded. "I know."

IT TOOK HIM A WHILE, but he managed to dress, not wanting to traverse the corridor, which was strangely deserted, in his hospital gown. The door at the near end of the hall had just slammed shut, and the sound of people running and shouting still echoed in the stairwell. The nurses' station was abandoned, and somewhere nearby a two-way radio barked loudly, but with too much static for the words to be comprehensible. He'd made it about halfway down the corridor when the double doors at the end swung open, and Bill Daws, the chief of police, looking pale, stepped through them. "I was down in radiology when the call came in, Miles," he said.

This explained why a man who was usually so meticulous about his appearance now stood before him with his shirt only half tucked in.

"You better come with me," he added.

MILES WOULD RECALL many of the details only later. Over long weeks and months, they returned the way flashes of lightning illuminate a nocturnal landscape, eventually coming together to form a narrative: the boy, John Voss, statue-like, his face bloody, locked alone and unattended in the backseat of the police cruiser; then, inside the modular addition that housed the art and shop classes, much of the horror visible from the doorway; in the studio itself, a small empty wooden table in the center of the room, at the base of which Doris Roderigue was sprawled, facedown, her legs splayed, her forehead resting in a puddle of water and broken glass; under a nearby table, the body of a boy Miles recognized from the grill, part of Zack Minty's crowd, with a gaping wound in the head; and finally, slumped up against the wall near the door, one hand resting on his stomach and looking as if he were stricken by a severe attack of dyspepsia, the body of Otto Meyer Jr.

Miles took in, really took in, none of this at the time, any more than he'd registered the crowd of students outside, some dazed, others crying, interspersed with shell-shocked teachers. Bill Daws had been waved through a blockade hastily set up at the street entrance to the school, but already the first frantic parents were arriving, abandoning their cars in driveways, on lawns, in the middle of the road, anywhere, and then running through backyards and across the school grounds from all directions, heavy, middle-aged women, many of them, some slipping and falling in the wet grass, then grunting back onto their feet again and moving forward, almost completely blinded by tears and a fear the likes of which they'd never known, never even imagined. Miles both saw and did not see any of this, nor did he really see any of the living once he and Bill Daws entered the room where Justin Dibble and Doris Roderigue and Otto Meyer Jr. lay dead. Several policemen and county officials were conversing quietly, as if they had no wish to be overheard by one another or the deceased. Jimmy Minty was among them too, with two black eyes and a metal protective plate over his nose, trying to talk to his son, who kept turning away and finally pushing his father hard with both hands, one of which was wrapped in a bloody bandage.

Miles was only vaguely aware of the officer who grabbed his elbow to keep him from tromping through the blood and glass and water, or of Bill Daws's guiding hand on his shoulder—amazingly strong, he would marvel later, for a man so ill. It was Bill who finally asked, his voice filling the room, this man who would himself be dead by Christmas, "Where is this man's daughter?"

In the tormented aftermath, what Miles found hardest to forgive himself for was the fact that when they'd entered the room, he walked right past her. She was huddled in the corner, behind the classroom door, he kept reminding himself, trying to be rational about it, though his guilt was too profound to admit reason. He had walked right past her. Wasn't there something in a father, he asked himself, some extra sense, that should've told him right where she'd be? Wasn't she his only daughter? A better father would've been able to find her blindfolded, in the dark, attracted by the invisible beacon of her suffering. How long did he stand there in that room, his back to her, as if to suggest to this beloved girl that the rest of them were the important ones? This thought would wake him in the middle of the night for months, long after he'd come to terms with the other horrors.

The young policeman stationed at the door, the same one who'd given Miles a hard time back in September in front of his childhood home, was the one who tapped his chief on the shoulder and said, "Here, sir." He seemed to notice Miles only after he'd taken a step toward his daughter, urging him, "Be careful."

The girl in the corner didn't look much like Tick, though of course he knew it was. Her expression was one he'd neither seen before nor imagined she was capable of forging. At first he didn't realize what she was clutching to her chest: an Exacto knife held tightly with both hands, as if its blade were three feet long. And when Miles, perhaps not immediately recognizable with one eye swollen shut and two broken teeth, offered that first movement toward her, his daughter made a flicking motion with the knife, warning him away, and from her throat came a gargling hiss.

Sinking to his knees before her, he said, "Tick," his own voice sounding only slightly less strange than hers, the stern voice he rarely used, only when he really wanted her attention. He wasn't sure it was the right tone or that kneeling there saying her name again and again was the right thing to do, because he had no idea how far into herself she'd withdrawn. He wouldn't remember later how many times he called to her before her eyes flickered, or how many more before they came into something like focus and she saw him for who he was. In that instant she was suddenly back, and her expression first relaxed, then came apart, and she was sobbing, "Daddy, Daddy, Daddy," as if she had no idea how far away he might be or else, wherever she'd just been, she'd been counting the number of times he'd spoken her name and was now counting them back to him.

David Roby would wonder later how a man in his brother's condition was able to do what he did, to gather up his daughter into his arms and in that none-too-gentle bear hug of his, carry her out the door and away. Later, Miles himself would remember Jimmy Minty's comment as they were leaving. "We gonna let him just walk out of here?"

And Bill Daws's response. "You tend to your own kid, Jimmy. Let's all just tend to our own kids, okay?"

CHAPTER 32

I N EARLY APRIL it turned warm, and Miles could see from the weather map in the newspaper that the unseasonable temperatures extended all the way up into Maine, which had endured a particularly brutal winter, one nor'easter after another, dropping a foot of new snow every week. He'd spoken to his brother after the last of these, and David reported that as of April Fool's Day half the residents of Empire Falls still had little red flags attached to their car antennas so they could be seen as they backed out their driveways between towering snowbanks. The town's budget for snow removal had been exhausted in late January.

"Business will pick up soon," David added. It had been slow most of the winter, partly due to the weather, partly because after the Empire Grill closed, a lot of their customers, especially those from the college in Fairhaven, were slow to follow them to Bea's tavern, despite the ads they'd finally taken out in the school paper. "We could use you, sooner than later."

"Sorry," Miles told him, "I don't think so."

"How's Tick?" his brother asked, both men aware that this hadn't really changed the subject.

"Good," Miles told him. "Better every day."

"She doesn't want to come home?"

The truth was, she did. Just last week she'd asked if they could visit during Vineyard High's spring break, and had she claimed to miss her mother, Miles might've given in. But what she had in mind was to visit Candace, who remained hospitalized, and John Voss, who only last month was declared incompetent to stand trial and remanded to the state mental hospital in Augusta. Miles wasn't sure that either of these visits was a good idea just yet.

In the months since the shooting, Tick had come to terms with the broad outline of what had happened that last afternoon. That John Voss had shot and killed Justin Dibble and Doris Roderigue, that he'd also shot Candace Burke in the neck, the bullet nearly severing her spine. She understood, too, that he'd then turned on Tick and would've shot her too if Otto Meyer Jr. hadn't stepped between them. She even knew that the boy had then turned the gun on himself and pulled the trigger several times but that only one bullet remained in the chamber—a bullet as old as the gun itself, his long-dead grand-father's service revolver—and it had not fired.

This much Tick understood, but what Miles didn't know was how much of this understanding was reinforced by memory. Though she'd had terrible nightmares for nearly two months, she wouldn't talk about them, so he didn't know if it was remembered horror she was experi-encing or dream analogies. Over time he told her what he thought was important for her to know. He told her that Candace was alive as soon as he heard this news from his brother. And much later he told her about Otto, who once had lunged from the backseat of the car to save the baseball team from Miles's inexperience at the wheel, and who had now saved Tick's life at the cost of his own. Other things he kept silent about. Even now, in April, his daughter had given no indication of recalling that when John Voss had pointed the revolver at Candace, Tick had reached out and cut him from eyebrow to ear with an Exacto knife. Nor what happened when she returned to consciousness and saw Zack Minty leaning over her, how she'd sliced open his palm with the same weapon.

No, if she'd managed to repress these details, they could stay repressed. Coming back from the abyss had been a long haul, and he refused to risk a relapse by returning home too soon. He hadn't even wanted to enroll her at the high school on Martha's Vineyard in mid-January—and still wasn't sure he'd done the right thing. Her new teachers, like everyone else, knew of the events in Empire Falls, but somehow didn't connect them to her. They seemed fond of Tick and suspected she was intelligent, but didn't know what to make of her vagueness and lapses of attention. Miles chose not to enlighten them.

Having devoted the last five months to her recovery, he only recently had begun to feel confident that she would make it all the way

back. The part of the island where they were staying was mostly unin-
habited during the winter, and rather than walk on the deserted beach
or along the windy bike path, on weekends Miles had taken to driving
into Edgartown, where they took long walks among the narrow, quiet
streets, stopping at shops and galleries and the library, anyplace there
were people and distraction. The shooting, he understood, had rendered his daughter's world dangerous, and it was his belief that only
the repetition of bad things *not* happening would restore her former
relationship to it. Progress had been so slow at first that he'd started to
doubt the wisdom of his plan. An angry conversation overheard in a
restaurant would sometimes be enough to set her sobbing and shaking.
But gradually she began to stabilize. One day in late February, they'd
stopped in at the fish market, where a hand-lettered sign was affixed to
the lobster tank: DON'T TOUCH THE MALE AND FEMALE LOBSTERS. "So,"
she asked the man behind the counter, "exactly which lobsters *can* we
touch?" It had taken all of Miles's willpower not to seize her in his arms
and dance a jig out the door and right up the middle of the street.

So when she asked last week why he was so dead set against going
up to Empire Falls over the break, he'd lied, reminding her that he
might very well be arrested. The dread possibility of being separated from him was still sufficiently scary for her to drop the idea
immediately. He felt guilty playing on this fear, but what choice did he
have? Predictably, his brother had been a tougher sell. The last time
they spoke on the phone, David asked point-blank if they were remaining on the island for Tick or for himself. "Have you thought about
Janine?" he asked. "This hasn't been all that easy on her either, you
know."

Miles couldn't dispute that fact. Not after putting their daughter in
the Jetta and speeding away from the shooting as if he had legal custody, as if the child's mother had no right to a voice in the decision. At
the time, of course, he'd thought of nothing but escape. During the
long, bleak Vineyard winter, though, he'd had the opportunity to think
everything through, and the thinking had changed exactly nothing. It
wasn't that he didn't feel bad for his ex-wife, who didn't deserve this,
and of course he was grateful to her for not coming after him with cops
and lawyers. Six months after their flight from Empire Falls, he still
hadn't spoken to Janine, nor had Tick. In fact, he'd told only David
where they were, though he assumed Janine knew. Once things had
calmed down, she'd have figured it out, and if she'd called Peter and
Dawn they'd have told her.

That had been their sole stipulation. Of course, they said, he could have the house for as long as he needed it. They'd seen the news, and agreed with Miles that the best thing for Tick might very well be to get her out of there, away from the school, the reporters and all the rest of it. But they'd both refused to lie to Janine. Fortunately, she hadn't called, and neither had anyone else, like Horace Weymouth or Father Mark, both of whom were likely to have figured out where they'd gone. Maybe not exactly where, but it was a small island, especially when emptied of tourists.

He couldn't help smiling at the idea of David, who'd barely spoken to Janine since she took up with Walt, being the one to point out his arrogant disregard for her. According to David, she'd gone through a transformation of her own, quitting her job at the health club and coming to work as a hostess and waitress at her mother's restaurant, where she'd put back on most of the weight she'd Stairmastered off during the previous year. She had little to say about her marriage, which David suspected was already rocky. The Silver Fox had made the transition from the Empire Grill to the new Callahan's smoothly enough, but he no longer stripped down to his muscle shirt and wouldn't play gin with Horace anymore. If he was tempted to observe that his wife was gaining weight, he controlled the impulse, which was smart.

"I can't get used to you siding with Janine," Miles told his brother.

"Don't be a jerk," David said. "I'm siding with Tick. I think you enjoy having her all to yourself. You like having her need you. Keep it up and she always will."

"She's never going to get her hands on my daughter," Miles told him.

Silence on the other end for a beat. "I assume we're now talking about Mrs. Whiting?"

"We are," Miles said, not so much embarrassed by his vague pronouncement as by how easily his brother could translate it.

"Miles, I have to tell you, I think you've gone a little crazy on this subject. She left town a week after you did. She's been gone all winter. Her house is for sale."

"Let me know when it sells."

"She's already unloaded most of her commercial real estate, right down to the Empire Grill. She's made a fortune on the Knox River project, and since Bea turned down her offer and got a lawyer, she's left us alone. She's pulling out, Miles."

"You could be right," Miles said, though he didn't believe it for an instant.

"If it's Jimmy Minty you're worried about, don't bother. He'd have to sober up to cause any trouble, and he's shitfaced over at the Lamplighter every night."

Actually, Miles was aware of this development. Among the many newspaper clippings his brother had sent him through the winter, most having to do with the new Knox River Restoration Project, there were several detailing Officer Minty's travails, and they came with annotations in Charlene's small, careful hand. Not long after the shooting, which was national news until an even worse incident had occurred out West, Jimmy's wife showed up in Empire Falls with her new fiancé and a downstate lawyer, who served her husband with divorce papers containing allegations of emotional and, in one instance, physical cruelty, the exact nature of which she threatened to make public if he chose to contest either the divorce or the custody arrangements detailed in the supporting documents. A week later, when she returned to Seattle, where she now lived, she took her son, Zack, with her.

Minty might have fought this had another problem not presented itself simultaneously. Bright and early one morning, before he'd even finished shaving, the county sheriff arrived at his door with a search warrant and a team of uniformed officers who apparently knew exactly what to look for. In record time they found several items—expensive stereo speakers, a new microwave, a VCR—for which Minty could provide no proof of ownership, and from which the identifying serial numbers had been expertly removed. He claimed he'd paid cash for the items in question down in Portland and hadn't saved receipts, and he was highly insulted by the suggestion that items of identical description had disappeared in a series of nocturnal thefts from several local merchants. This story might've worked if he hadn't missed one I.D. number on the inside of a laser printer, the very one stolen from Knox Computer a couple of months earlier. Investigators also confiscated the key-making machine they found in his basement, along with a key ring bristling with what were described as master or skeleton keys. While he hadn't been indicted, the allegations turned up in the newspaper, after which he resigned from the force. According to David, he'd put his home on the market in hopes of covering his legal fees and was presently living as a caretaker at the Whiting hacienda.

"He came into the tavern a couple of weeks ago, actually," David added. "Said Zack had written wanting to know how Tick was. He also said to tell you no hard feelings."

Again Miles had to smile. "That's awfully good of him. He kicked the shit out of *me*."

"True," David conceded. "His nose didn't heal right, though. He looks like he misplaced his own and borrowed the one he's got now off a corpse. It's kind of gray. Still, I think if you were to lie and tell him you're sorry, that'd be it."

"I *am* sorry," Miles said, though he had reservations about Jimmy Minty's capacity for forgiveness. "I keep telling you, it's not Minty. I *know* her, David. Maybe it's taken me a lifetime, but I do."

"Okay, then," David said, "explain it to me."

Miles had no intention of doing so, well aware of how paranoid it would sound. Among the other clippings he'd received from his brother was a story about the purchase of St. Cat's by a Massachusetts investment group, which planned to convert the church into four three-story condominiums. The most extravagant of these featured a Jacuzzi in the steeple Miles had never worked up the courage to paint. Architectural plans illustrated the future purpose of the building where Miles and his mother had attended Mass, and there were small photos of Father Tom (pre-dementia) and Father Mark, both of whom were now residing at Sacré Coeur. Perhaps there was no justification for Miles's belief that the real buyer of the church was Mrs. Whiting, or that she would maintain a residence in one of the condos, so as to spend at least part of the year living in the heart of something he'd loved before she managed to seize and corrupt it. Power and control, again. And no matter how little basis he could claim for this belief, he truly did believe it.

"Look," David said, "I'm glad Tick's getting better. But has it occurred to you that you're getting worse?" When Miles didn't respond, he continued. "It's not going to be much of a victory if you save her and destroy yourself."

"It's a trade I could live with," Miles told him, aware that it was this precise bargain that his mother had made, or attempted.

"And I could understand that—if you had to. But what if this martyrdom *isn't* necessary? Tell me who's won then—you or her?"

"I'm not trying to be a martyr, David."

"Really? You wouldn't shit a shitter, would you?"

"David—"

"Because I've been down that road, brother, then off the road and into the fucking trees, and all I have to show for it is a busted flipper."

"Actually, you've come out of it rather nicely," Miles pointed out, meaning Charlene, and knowing his brother would catch his drift. The silence on the line suggested he was right, and Miles immediately felt bad about the low blow. "Look, can we leave this alone?"

"Fine." Then, after a pause: "Bea wanted me to say hi. Also to remind you that you're still a fully vested partner in the new Callahan's."

"Tell her thanks for me."

"You're missing out, Miles. That's all I can say. You wouldn't believe what's going on down by the river. The new brew pub's going to open by the Fourth of July. The credit-card company's sunk millions into renovating the old mill. The shirt factory's going to be an indoor mini-mall. Even a few houses are starting to sell."

"You sound like a real booster."

"Well, there's no law says good things can't happen every now and then."

If what David had described was an unalloyed blessing, then Miles would be glad. For his brother, for Bea, for Charlene, for all of them. He didn't expect anybody to share his resentment about the way it was coming about, that once again the lion's share of the wealth generated would never reach the citizens of Empire Falls. The houses they couldn't afford to sell last year would be houses they couldn't afford to buy the next. And it was Francine Whiting, of course, who'd pulled it off, in essence selling the same thing twice, first the mills themselves, then the parcels of riverfront land she'd cleverly retained. And, too, there was an irrational feeling he couldn't quite dismiss, that all of this new hope and confidence was built on the foundation of a loss everyone was far too anxious to forget. His friend Otto Meyer was a large part of that loss, and the dead boy, Justin Dibble, and, yes, even Doris Roderigue. If Candace Burke survived, perhaps a few years down the road she'd be grateful for a job doing phone solicitation for the credit-card people, a job she could handle from her wheelchair. And there was John Voss, now returned, in a sense, to the dark closet he'd been forgotten in as a child—a loss no one would ever wish to recall.

But his brother was right, of course. Mrs. Whiting hadn't shot anybody, and all of the world's ills could not be laid at her doorstep.

"You okay for money?" David wanted to know.

"For now."

"What about for later?"

"Later, David, will just have to take care of itself."

MONEY WAS THE ONE THING he'd promised himself early on that he wouldn't think about. His debts were mounting, naturally, and had been since the afternoon they'd fled town. They hadn't stopped at either Janine's house or his own apartment. It would've been smart to pack a hasty suitcase, but Miles was afraid that even a brief delay would result in their detention, so they'd left with nothing but the clothes they were wearing, bound for a destination that Miles was able to define only as "away." And since Tick hadn't asked where they were headed, there was no need to explain.

By the time they'd gotten onto the interstate at Fairhaven, heading south, her convulsive weeping had stopped and she'd retreated into herself again, her blank silence ghastly, frightening. By the time he pulled over in Kennebunk to gas up, she'd stopped responding to his questions, and he'd had to go around to her side of the car, open the door and forcibly turn her head toward him while he explained that everything was going to be okay, that he was taking her away from that place, that she had to trust him. When he finished, she had nodded, but she looked like she was concentrating as hard as she could just to remember who he was, and her nodding in agreement had the appearance of a guess.

Back on the highway, it occurred to Miles that they were headed to Martha's Vineyard, to Peter and Dawn's summer house. Being able to replace the word "away" with "Martha's Vineyard" buoyed his spirits irrationally, and so did the notion that the two of them would be hiding out on an island, as if anyone who pursued them would have to swim there. Thinking that the idea of the Vineyard might also improve Tick's spirits, he told her, but again he suspected it hadn't truly registered, and when they reached the New Hampshire tollbooth and he looked over at her, she was crying again. A moment later he understood why. She had released her bladder onto the seat.

Just over the Massachusetts line he pulled off the interstate at one of the Haverhill exits and drove around until they found a strip mall with a Kmart. Only when he told her he'd be inside for just a minute and Tick began to shake in terror did he finally understand. She'd had to use the bathroom all the way back in Kennebunk, but she'd been afraid to go inside by herself, afraid for Miles to be out of her sight. "It's okay," he reassured her. "You can come with me."

And so they'd gone inside together, Tick clutching his hand. The store was nearly empty, an hour or so from closing, but they still attracted considerable attention, what with Tick reeking of urine and Miles with his bruises and one eye still swollen completely shut. In addition to a package of underwear and a pair of cheap jeans—he made sure of the size by checking the tag on the back of the pair Tick was wearing—he also picked up a roll of paper towels, a package of sponges, some upholstery cleaner and a big bottle of generic ibuprofen. Since leaving Maine, his head and body aches had returned with a vengeance, and he knew he wouldn't make it all the way to Woods Hole without some relief. He chose the men's room over the women's, found it to be empty, and locked the door behind them. Inside, he opened the package of underwear, bit the tags off the jeans, opened the paper towels and wet a handful, instructing Tick to use one of the stalls and clean herself up as best she could. He promised to stand right in front of the door where she could see his feet beneath the partition, and he talked to her the entire time, stopping only to chew a disgusting handful of the ibuprofen.

At the register he got an extra plastic bag for Tick's soaked jeans and then paid for everything, having had the presence of mind to save the wrappings so they could be run through the price scanner. This foresight didn't seem to impress the checker, who regarded Miles with unconcealed disgust and Tick with heartfelt sympathy, as if to suggest that she understood what *this* was all about.

Out in the parking lot again, Miles half expected the cops to arrive before he could finish sponging urine out of the passenger seat. He was about to pull away when he noticed a bank with an ATM kiosk. There he took out three hundred dollars, the maximum allowable for one day. That left about another three hundred in the account. After that, who knew?

TWO DAYS AFTER the phone conversation with his brother, Miles found himself nursing a cup of coffee in a window booth at a chowder house in Vineyard Haven. Thanks to a teachers' in-service, Tick had only a half day of school, and when he looked up from the dregs of his coffee, he was visited by a startling hallucination. Stumping up the street toward him, looking for all the world like a man who knew where he was headed, was Max Roby, who couldn't possibly know anything of the kind, since Miles knew for a fact that he'd never set foot on the island. His father was on the opposite side of the street, but when he was about half a block away, the old man suddenly tacked across the street, giving the impression that he knew his son was not only on this island (improbable) but in this building (impossible). Since there was no way he could've known, it followed that he didn't, but Miles was still surprised when Max passed by the chowder house entrance. In fact, his father stopped only when Miles rapped on the window.

A moment later Max Roby, late of Key West, Florida, slipped into the booth opposite his son, late of Empire Falls, Maine.

"You've *got* to be shitting me," Miles said, staring at him.

"I figured I'd run into you," Max said, looking pleased with himself.

"You did?"

"Maybe not this quick," Max allowed, though he seemed not to fully appreciate, as Miles did, the long odds involved in the present circumstance.

"We're staying on the other side of the island, Dad," Miles explained, exasperation already creeping into his tone in a conversation not yet one minute old. "Most weeks I don't even come into town except to buy groceries. This is the first time I've ever been in this restaurant, and I just happened to be sitting in the only window booth."

"I've been lucky lately," Max said, as if to suggest there was no reason he shouldn't be, given the general tenor of his life to this point. "I tell you I won the lottery down there in Florida?"

This was the kind of question Max loved to ask, one for which the answer was obvious to both parties, and one it was best just to ignore—a trick Miles had never mastered. "No, Dad. We haven't spoken in six months. You didn't know where I was. So, how could you have told me?"

"Oh, I knew where you were," Max assured him. "Just because I'm sempty doesn't mean I'm senile. Old men got brains too, you know."

Miles rubbed his eyes with his knuckles. "You're telling me you actually won the lottery?"

"Not the big one," Max admitted. "Not all six numbers. Five out of six. Pretty good payoff, though. Over thirty thousand."

"Dollars?"

"No, paper napkins," Max said, holding one up. "Of course dollars, dummy."

"You won thirty thousand dollars."

"More. Almost thirty-two."

"You won thirty-two thousand dollars."

Max nodded.

"You personally won thirty-two thousand dollars."

Max nodded, and Miles considered whether there might be yet another way to ask the same question. Usually, with Max, phraseology was crucial.

"Me and nine other guys from Captain Tony's," Max clarified after a healthy silence.

"You each won thirty-two thousand dollars."

"No, we each won three thousand. Ten guys go in on a ticket, and you have to divvy up the winnings."

Now, it was Miles's turn to nod. Wheedling the truth out of his father was one of the few pleasures of their relationship, and Max took equal pleasure in withholding it. "How much do you have left?"

Max took out his wallet and peered inside, as if genuinely curious himself. "I got enough to buy lunch. I'm not cheap, like some people. I'm not afraid to spend money when I got it."

Which was why he so seldom had any, Miles might have pointed out. Instead he said, "So, Dad, what are you doing here?"

"I come up with the *Lila Day* as far as Hilton Head, but they were laying over for a month or two, so I caught a bus to Boston, then another to Woods Hole, then the ferry to here," he jerked a thumb back over his shoulder. "My duffel bag's in a locker down at the wharf."

"That's *how* you got here, Dad," Miles said. "You sort of left out the *why*."

Max shrugged. "There some kind of law against a man visiting his son and granddaughter?"

Miles, who on many occasions would've voted for such legislation, had to admit there wasn't any yet.

"I thought maybe I could cheer her up," he said. Miles must have looked doubtful, because he added, "I *do* cheer people up sometimes, you know. There was a time when I even used to cheer your mother up, believe it or not."

"When was this?"

"Before you were born," Max admitted. "She and I had a lot in common there at the start."

"And I spoiled it?"

"Well," Max said thoughtfully, "you didn't help any, but no, it wasn't you. Not really."

"What, then?"

His father shrugged again. "Who knows? I'll tell you one thing, though. It's a terrible thing to be a disappointment to a good woman."

"I know a little something about that myself," Miles admitted, since they seemed, for the first time ever, to have entered confession mode.

Max lip-farted. "What—Janine? She was born unhappy. There's no comparing her and your mother. Give Grace anything to be happy about, and by God she *was* happy. If she'd met that woman's husband first, instead of me, everything would've been different."

Miles couldn't help smiling. That had long been his own estimate of the situation, but even so he was surprised that his father had come to the same conclusion.

"'Course, then there would've been no you."

"Not a tragedy."

"And no Tick."

Right, no Tick either.

"Well, I'd have missed the both of you." Max was grinning at him. "Her especially."

"If we walk up the street," Miles said, glancing at his watch, "we can meet her bus. After that, you can buy lunch for the both of us."

"You look like you could stand a good meal," Max said as they rose from the booth. "How much weight you lost since I seen you?"

"I don't know," Miles said. "A lot, I guess."

"You don't have the cancer, do you?"

"No, just a kid. Some people worry about them."

"You think you can hurt my feelings, but you can't," Max assured him, not for the first time.

As he and his father headed up the street, it occurred to Miles that the unlikely event he'd feared over thirty years ago had at last come to pass: his father had come looking for him on Martha's Vineyard.

TRUE TO HIS PROMISE, Max *did* cheer them up. Tick had always enjoyed her grandfather's company and he hers. Watching them together had always fascinated Miles, and now, belatedly, he began to understand their mutual ease. Like Miles, his daughter would point out Max's offenses against hygiene, but her tone was different, and for the first time Miles saw that the same observation from him sounded more like a moral statement. Trailing behind was always an implied imperative—that Max should do something about it—that would, of course, provoke a man like his father to dig in his heels. When Tick said, "You've got food in your beard, Grandpa," it was clear she was merely providing a service. If he *wanted* food in his beard, that was his business. When he said, "So what?" she just shrugged. Or, if what was stuck in his beard was particularly grotesque, like that morning's crusted egg yoke, Tick would merely grab a napkin, instruct her grandfather to hold still and gracefully remove it, a gesture that never failed to make Max smile beatifically. His father, Miles had long suspected, was basically a lower primate. He enjoyed being groomed.

A few days after Max's arrival, after Miles had walked Tick up the dirt lane to where she caught the school bus, he returned to the house and wrote his sleeping father a note saying he was spending the morning reading in the Vineyard Haven library, something he'd been doing since Tick got settled into school. It was a beautiful little building, and he'd find a quiet corner near Special Collections, read until he grew hungry, pick up a sandwich at a restaurant nearby and then return for as much of the afternoon as remained until school let out. Before long he knew the names of all three librarians, one of whom had confessed that she'd taken him for a professor or a writer researching a book. He'd smiled and told her no, he was by trade a short-order cook, but her remark burrowed deep because what she'd mistakenly imagined was indeed what he'd once hoped to be, and was preparing to be when Grace fell ill. He and Peter and Dawn had been the most talented writers on the literary magazine, and while those two had no more reason to think they'd end up writing TV sitcoms than Miles did to believe he'd graduate to flipping burgers at the Empire Grill, at least his friends now occupied the same quadrant of the galaxy they'd dreamed that they'd one day inhabit. But to be told, at forty-three, that he looked like what he'd meant to be only increased Miles's sense of personal failure.

Here on the island, especially once Max showed up, it was impossible not to think of his mother, and the Grace he found himself remembering was still angry with him for betraying his destiny. Many days, only the sight of his daughter stepping off the bus, looking and acting more like her old self every day, had kept him from sinking into a profound depression. Thankfully, seeing Tick alive and well was enough to confirm his sense that his best destiny in life was as this child's father.

Still, his feeling that his mother was resting uneasily in her grave caused Miles's lie, on this particular morning, in the note he'd written to his father. Instead of driving into Vineyard Haven, he pointed the Jetta across the island toward Summer House, where he and his mother had stayed so many years ago. Though it was only a ten-minute drive from Peter and Dawn's place, he'd never returned there, neither during the long winter, nor on the many vacations he and Janine and Tick had taken over the years. In fact, the first time they visited Peter and Dawn, he'd told Janine that Summer House didn't exist anymore, lest she want to see it.

But it did exist, and as he drove through the village, virtually deserted in the off-season, the details flooded back over him. The Thirsty Whale, where he'd greedily devoured clams, was still a restaurant, but under another name and closed until Memorial Day. The village itself was somehow both larger and smaller than he remembered it. There were more buildings, and they seemed closer together, and the epic distance back to their cottage when he was sleepy and full of buttery clams wasn't much more than a hundred winding yards.

The gate was down across the dirt road that wound up the bluff among the beach shrubs, so Miles had to park and walk. The main inn, with its sweeping, wraparound porch, was exactly as he remembered it, and so, too, the cottages below, their rose trellises already greening in the warmer weather. He quickly found the one they'd stayed in, the name "Sojourner" above the door, the strange word returning to him across the decades on a wave of memory. Peering in the dusty window at what had been his tiny bedroom, he half expected to see his mitt sitting on the nightstand where he'd left it. Indulging such nostalgic emotions made him feel more than a little foolish, and they probably would be of little use in explaining why he'd ignored the NO TRESPASSING sign at the gate. Still, having come this far, he decided to complete the journey, which meant following the path down to the beach. Here, too, the beach grass was greening up, spring here already in full stride, nearly a month ahead of central Maine. The beach itself was still deserted, so he sat down for a while where he thought his mother had spread their blanket, and studied a fogbank resting a couple hundred yards offshore. Whose ghost did he expect to encounter here, he wondered—his mother's, or that of his boyhood self?

He didn't become aware that the fog had moved in until he turned around and saw it had nearly engulfed the bluff, which now was visible only in vague, blurry outline. By the time he located the path again, the mist was so thick he was able to orient himself only by watching the ground at his feet, and once up the cliff he found "Sojourner" again by literally blind luck. From its front porch neither the main house nor the nearest cottage, where Charlie Mayne had stayed, was visible. As he rested there on the step—a grown man now, whether he felt like one or not—he realized it was Charlie Mayne's ghost he'd come to commune with. Miles and his mother had left the island together that morning thirty years ago, returning to their lives in Empire Falls, and she now lay buried in the town cemetery. It was Charlie Mayne they'd left behind on the dock as the ferry steamed away, so of course it was appropriate that he should be here still. Even recognizing his face in the photograph of C. B. Whiting couldn't change that. It was *Charlie Whiting* who lay buried up the hill from his mother, but *Charlie Mayne* was a different sort of man entirely, and it was he whom Miles wished to summon for questioning.

So when the man emerged through the mist and sat down next to him on the porch step, Miles looked him over carefully and saw that it was indeed clean-shaven Charlie Mayne and not bearded C. B. Whiting. Still elegant and silver-haired, Charlie had not aged at all, nor was there a bullet hole in his right temple from the day that other fellow took a pistol he'd purchased in Fairhaven down to the river with him.

When Miles saw the man's familiar sad expression, he said, "My mother died, Charlie." He didn't want him to think she was inside "Sojourner" putting on her white dress so they could all go out to dinner.

Charlie Mayne nodded, as if to suggest that, of course, this is exactly what would've happened.

"She waited for you," Miles said, when he didn't speak.

"I meant to come. I wanted to."

"Then why didn't you?" Miles asked, having wondered for over thirty years.

"When you're older, you'll understand. There are things that grown-ups intend and *want* to do, but somehow just can't."

This explanation made Miles feel like a boy again, and when he spoke it was with a ten-year-old's whine. "But you got steamer clams in a restaurant that didn't even have them on the menu."

"Well, steamer clams are different," Charlie Mayne explained.

Which made Miles even more petulant. "You killed her," he said. "You killed my mother."

"No," Charlie Mayne said. "I'm afraid your mother died of cancer."

"How do you know? You weren't there. You never came. You made her happy, then you broke your promise, and she died."

"What was I supposed to do?"

"What you said."

"I tried."

"No, you didn't." He was crying now, as he hadn't since he was a boy, the kind of crying that did some good. "She never stopped waiting for you."

"You're wrong about that. She did stop. Don't you remember? You're the one who never forgot." Charlie Mayne reached over then and tousled Miles's hair.

When Miles looked down he saw he *was* a boy, that he'd never been anything else, that his life as a husband and father had been a dream. "I hate you," he sobbed.

"And I you," Charlie Mayne replied kindly.

"Why? I'm just a boy."

"Because if it hadn't been for you, your mother and I could've run away together like we wanted to. You were the reason."

"It's not true," he cried, knowing it was.

"So, now do you see the way it really was?" Charlie Mayne nudged him. "You're the one who killed your mother, not me."

HE AWOKE A MAN, with no idea how long he'd slept on that crooked porch. The fog was still thick and there were voices in it, though he couldn't tell where they were coming from. At first whoever was talking seemed to be over at the next cottage, but then the voices shifted in the direction of the main house.

"Probably just somebody fishing off the point."

"In this?"

"It's a beater with Maine plates. Who around here's got Maine plates?"

After a while the voices receded, and Miles, embarrassed, walked quickly back to the Jetta. Another car was parked by the gate, but whoever it was had chosen not to block him in, so Miles did a three-point turn and headed toward home. Not just across the island, either, for he suddenly knew that his brother was right. It was time to return to Empire Falls, to his life. Better to be a man there, his "Sojourner" dream had shown him, than a boy here.

Max was standing in Peter and Dawn's kitchen in his undershorts, scratching himself thoughtfully. "That was David," he said.

"Who was David?"

"On the phone."

"I wasn't here when it rang, Dad."

"I know," Max said. "That's why I'm telling you. David said to tell you the Whiting woman died yesterday. The old one, not the cripple."

"Francine Whiting?"

"That's right. Drowned."

Miles had to sit down. "That's crazy."

"You don't believe me, call your brother. I'm just telling you what he said."

"Drowned?"

"In the river, he said. Call him back if you don't believe me."

Miles shook his head, trying to imagine the world without Mrs. Whiting in it. Who would keep it spinning? he wondered.

"Anyway, I should go back for the funeral," his father declared. "You hear what I said?"

"Why?"

"Because you look like you didn't."

"No. Why would you go to her funeral?"

Max was grinning broadly now. "You never listen to me. Just 'cause I'm sempty don't mean you can just ignore me, you know."

"Why do you want to go to that woman's funeral, Dad?"

"Because we're related. The Robys and the Robideauxs. Like I been telling you. I bet you she left me a little something."

THEY PACKED THEIR THINGS that night and closed up the house next morning, having called Peter and Dawn about their change of plans. Miles also called Callahan's, hoping to speak to his brother, but it was Janine who answered. "We're on our way back, if that's all right with you."

"There's plenty of room at the house," she told him, sounding weary. "Walt's moved back to his own place."

"I'm sorry to hear it, Janine."

"Don't be. I'd take him for everything he's worth, if he was worth anything. Has Tick forgiven me?"

"What for?"

No response to this. "Have *you* forgiven me?"

"Again, what for?"

"Just so you won't be surprised when you see me, I've gained a lot of weight."

"I've lost a lot."

"Just to piss me off, or what?"

"See you soon, Janine."

They'd just turned out of the driveway—Tick in the backseat with her headphones on, Max up front in the passenger seat—when the glove box door flopped open.

"You never got this fixed, huh?" Max observed, proceeding to rummage through its contents.

"I don't think it can be," Miles said, smiling to think how long ago it seemed that Max had broken it.

"Don't be an idiot," his father said, confident in his opinion that anything could be fixed, and only mildly disappointed that the glove box had yielded no currency.

W HEN *C. B. Whiting was summoned back to Empire Falls after living more or less happily in Mexico for nearly a decade, he was determined to fulfill his destiny as a Whiting male, or, more precisely, to be the first in his male line to get that destiny right. His grandfather Elijah would've have died a happy man had he succeeded in beating his wife to death with a shovel, but he waited too long, and by the time he realized that this homicide was his true destiny, he was no longer up to the task physically, whereas the old woman was still spry. Though he gave her a good chase, she kept eluding him, and after several wild swings with the shovel he sat down exhausted, she disarmed him, and that was that.*

His grandson was well aware of his intentions, because he'd never made any secret of them. "Young Charles, if you only knew what went on in that carriage house," the old man confided when the boy was still young enough to spend his days climbing trees on the Whiting estate. "If you had any idea how awful a bad woman can be, you'd become a priest rather than take any such chance." When C.B. pointed out that they weren't Catholics, Elijah allowed that this was true, but noted that the Romans were always eager for converts.

Honus Whiting never attempted to murder his wife, so far as C.B. knew, though he did admit on his son's wedding day that he'd denied, on average, one homicidal impulse every day of his married life. That very day, in fact, he'd already been visited by three particularly strong ones and it wasn't noon yet. When C.B. asked if his mother's extensive travel didn't help, his father shook his head. Knowing that she was alive somewhere was enough to sour everything. In later life the old man got some relief when his wife took up residence in their Back Bay apartment, but then one day, without warning, she announced her intention to quit Boston and return to the Whiting estate, which filled her husband with terrible grief and even worse trepidation. "I can't help feeling it's her or me," he confessed one night after several brandies—prophetically, as it turned out.

Actually, Honus was naturally inclined to prophecy. For years he'd been saying his wife was going to be the death of him, though everyone understood him to mean his financial death. For most women, he was fond of explaining, contemplating a purchase of something extravagantly expensive was a process that consisted of several stages, and for which there could conceivably be more than one outcome. Whereas his wife went from "Oh, isn't that pretty" to "It would look wonderful over the mantel" to "Ship it very carefully" in a single breathtakingly fluid motion, skipping entirely, for efficiency's sake, the notion of its cost.

One afternoon not long after Honus, then deep into his seventies, had suffered a minor stroke and was released against his will into the care of his wife, he got up from a chair too quickly and, suddenly feeling woozy, grabbed on to the nearest piece of furniture to steady himself. This happened to be a tall mahogany cabinet with glass doors, the shelves of which displayed many of his wife's prized globe-trotting purchases. Since he was alone in the house, no one ever knew exactly what happened, but C.B. suspected that when his mother's treasures began to topple from their shelves, his father, excited by the prospect of destroying in one stroke so much of what his wife held dear to her acquisitive heart, might've held on to the cabinet longer than was absolutely necessary to restore his equilibrium, and that his weight finally brought the entire piece down upon him, crushing what little of his life remained. He lay there for hours, buried in the shards of his wife's extravagance, until his failure to answer the dinner bell resulted in a search.

So when C. B. Whiting was summoned back from the life he'd made for himself in Mexico, where he'd had as much money as he needed—far more, really, given the value of the peso—and a beach nearby, not to mention a woman who for five years had lived with and loved him, and a little boy who was his son in all but name, and the leisure to write a poem should the idea for one ever come to him, he understood that his best self was about to be taken away for a second time. He had little doubt that he would eventually adjust to its loss, as he had before; no, the difference was that now he was less inclined to make the sacrifice. The first time he had trusted that what his father wanted him to do was probably for the best, whereas now he was simply being informed that he was no longer permitted to be happy. And informed not by someone he loved but by the one person he loathed above all others in the world, the woman he'd promised to love, honor and obey all of his days, till death did they part. On the flight home he considered his grand-

*father and his father and then concluded, so be it. Meaning death. Namely
hers.*

*In Boston he was met by a limousine driver, an agreeable fellow who
didn't at all mind waiting in Fairhaven while C.B. shopped for a present for
his wife. If the driver thought it strange that he should have chosen a pawnbroker for the occasion, he kept his misgivings to himself.*

*His deliberations did not take long. When the shopowner asked what sort
of handgun he had in mind, C.B., having developed over his fifty-nine years
a healthy respect for his own incompetence, replied, "Something foolproof."
The pawnbroker produced a clean, basic revolver, showed him how to load
and unload it, then watched him practice with dummy cartridges, until he
was certain C.B. had the hang of it, and finally reminded him that the gun
wouldn't fire with the safety on unless you were counting on the safety being
on, in which case it just might. It also wouldn't fire without bullets, so C.B.
put a small box of them in one jacket pocket and the revolver in the other.*

*"Where to now?" the driver wanted to know when C.B. Whiting climbed
into the back of the limo.*

"Home," C.B. said, loading the revolver. "I'm anxious to see my wife."

So what prevented him?

*When the limousine pulled up in the driveway of his former home, C. B.
Whiting was neither conflicted about his intentions, nor doubtful of his ability to fulfill them. He had not waited too long, as his grandfather had, nor in
his father's manner had he grown so accustomed over the decades to denying
homicidal impulses that he no longer recognized them for what they were.
When he stepped out of the car, he felt as certain of his purpose as he ever had
about anything in his life, and when he reached into his jacket pocket for the
gun—heavy and reassuringly solid in his hand—he felt not the slightest
revulsion at the actuality of taking a human life. That what he'd determined
to do would be considered a crime by the vast majority of his fellow citizens
seemed irrelevant. For one thing, the act he intended was not motivated by
malice. Not really. He didn't want his wife to suffer, as she had caused so
many others to suffer. Nor did he want her to feel pain. He merely wanted an
end to her existence. He hoped only for a steady hand, so that a single shot
would do the trick.*

*Again he asked the driver to wait. If he was lucky, they might make it
back to Boston before Francine's body was discovered. If he was very lucky, he
might make it all the way to Mexico, where he could disappear with the woman and the boy. But getting away mattered less than making sure he didn't*

somehow botch the job. When he opened the door to the house he'd had built so long ago, which had turned out to look so little like a hacienda, really, he could feel his father and his grandfather smiling down upon him.

NO ONE HAD HEARD *the car pull up, and of course C.B. didn't ring the bell. He had simply let himself into his own house, as men do the world over. Inside, it was so quiet that when he flipped the gun's safety off with his thumb, he half expected the resounding click to be followed by an explosion, but it wasn't. Luck, it began to seem, was finally going to smile on a homicidal Whiting male. No doubt he would find his wife outside, probably down at the gazebo. If he quietly slipped out the patio door, he might even be able to make it across the broad lawn before she became aware of his arrival, and he would remove her from the mortal coil without her ever knowing what hit her. The limousine driver, listening to the radio with the windows rolled up, wouldn't hear the report. Afterward, he surely would wonder why they were returning immediately to Boston, but limo drivers were trained to obey, not question, people who paid them.*

But luck was not on C. B. Whiting's side any more than it had been on his father's or his grandfather's, so when he rounded the corner of the living room and saw the tableau that had been prepared for him, he knew at once that only God—the same God with whom he'd gone to war over the moose—could have arranged it and at the same time have blinded him so completely to the possibility of these three women standing just a few feet apart.

Cindy was not in Augusta, as he'd imagined, but just inside the patio door, one hand on the handle, as if she intended in that frozen moment to slide the door open and join life on the other side, as if such a thing were possible. He knew, of course, that she was clutching the door handle for support and that this scene bespoke her entire life on the wrong side of one barrier or another, ever since the day so long ago when he'd risen up in impotent rage against his wife, packed a suitcase, tossed it into the trunk and gunned the Lincoln in reverse even before the automatic garage door had raised completely, not caring in the least if he tore it off on the way out. He'd heard nothing and felt only a small bump—not for the first time either, since the child was forever leaving things in the driveway. She liked to rest all of her dolls up against the closed garage door, pleased with how many of them there were, and that was exactly what the bump felt like, except that the doll must've gotten caught up under the car. When he pulled out onto the road and felt the second bump, he looked and he saw her in the rearview mirror and thought, indeed, that he'd again run over one of his daughter's dolls.

Except this one was too big. C.B. himself had bought every one of her dolls, and he couldn't remember any that looked like this.

How could something like that happen? The question was no sooner asked than answered. C. B. Whiting might have been a weak man—well, in truth, he knew he was a weak man—but he'd never mastered the fine art of self-deception as most weak men do, so when he asked himself how it was possible to forget all about his beloved daughter, he realized that of course this wasn't the first time, but merely the first to bear consequences. This time it was hatred that had clouded his vision. In the past he'd been just as blinded by love.

Exactly when had he fallen in love with Grace Roby, now standing outside the patio door? He had noticed her, naturally, at the shirt factory, and then her pregnancy had proceeded in lockstep with Francine's, but perhaps it was that moment at the hospital, when he saw Grace cradling her baby at her breast, when he was truly lost. It wasn't simply that she was so tired and beautiful. There was something about her joy in the child, her happiness and gratitude, that allowed him to glimpse the possibility of another, better life and to wonder what if? Both women were kept in the hospital for three days after they gave birth, the maternity ward so full that even a woman with the name Whiting couldn't get a private room—Thank God! he recalled thinking—and by the time they were released, he would've made the trade right then and there, his wife and baby daughter and all his wealth for the opportunity to return with Grace and her infant son to the little rented house she shared with her husband, a fellow who was always flecked with dried paint and seemed to have no idea how lucky he was. The intensity of his passion for this woman—and the shocking vividness of his vision of another life, so tangible and yet remote in what was now the beginning of middle age—made C.B. wonder if he was losing his mind, or if surrendering both Grace and the possibility of happiness might not be too much to bear. Worse, when he drove Francine and his own newborn daughter, writhing and twisting at her mother's meager breast, across the Iron Bridge and saw the swift water running beneath, he recalled his war with God over the moose and he realized for the first time that God had won, that as an arrogant sinner the only course left to him was penance. Unable to surrender his newfound hope, he knew now that the only way to win Grace Roby would be with God's permission, and that would be denied until he was worthy of her, which he resolved forthwith to become.

How long he courted Grace without her even knowing! Weeks into months into years, watching her at work from his glassed-in office on the top floor, seeing her on weekends along Empire Avenue with her little boy in tow, her husband always off somewhere painting houses. Grace was the sort of woman whom sorrow actually made more beautiful, and C.B. knew instinctively that except for the little boy, Miles, she had precious little joy in her life.

He also sensed that when other people experienced sorrow, her heart went out to them, as if the weight of her own burden allowed her to shoulder even more. It was after the accident that left his daughter a cripple that Grace seemed really aware of him, and although he was suffering the torments of the damned, not just over what he'd done but for the lie he'd allowed his wife to tell the police—how coldly and competently she'd invented that speeding green Pontiac!—deep in his heart he was thrilled by the knowledge that at last he'd made contact.

What an astonishing fantasy his love for Grace Roby had become in the years that followed! How it at once filled and absorbed his days, as her little boy grew healthy as a weed and his own child bravely endured one complicated, unsuccessful operation after another. Grace became for C. B. Whiting a dream not only of love and happiness in life but also of redemption, for he began to see in her the very principle of human compassion, the one person in the whole world to whom he might one day reveal his terrible secret, who would not just understand but forgive. If he were able to tell her, and if she were still able to love him, then wouldn't this be his salvation? And if such forgiveness were possible in a mortal woman, could less love and forgiveness be expected of God Himself? There were times when such fevered reasoning struck C. B. Whiting as sheer lunacy, and others when it seemed divine truth.

Regardless, by slow, steady degrees he could feel this woman beginning to fall in love with him. First glances, then gestures, then words and solemn professions, and then, finally, a plan. Francine knew, of course; she probably had suspected from that first day in the hospital. Incapable of anything like love herself, she was expert at sniffing out the disease in others. His and Grace's plan, which his wife had nearly succeeding in thwarting completely, had been to spend the entire week together on Martha's Vineyard. He'd imagined it might take that long to convince her, even though he knew her heart now belonged to him. Of course, it was the boy who complicated things. Taking her son away from his father was something Grace would not do lightly, even though the man had done little enough to earn such consideration—and she would never, ever, leave without him.

Ah, two days on that magical island offered almost enough beauty and happiness to justify one's existence. And how close they'd come to making it work! It still took his breath away, imagining it, a lifetime with this woman. Even now he would've jumped at the chance, though the drawn, emaciated woman standing with his wife on the other side of the patio door, apparently examining the garden, was almost unrecognizable as the one true love of his life. A single glance was enough for him to know what his years in Mexico had been like for her. The penance he'd once assumed for himself, he'd allowed her to perform in his stead. His wife, he was shocked to acknowledge, was now by any objective standard the more attractive woman.

Of the three women, Francine became aware of him first, and in her thin smile he understood his folly in believing he would succeed where his father and grandfather, both better men, had failed. It was as if she knew all about the gun in his pocket, knew, too, how useless it had become.

Then Grace looked up, and in her expression was the understanding he feared the most: that he had not suffered terribly these years since Martha's Vineyard, that he had found a way to be happy with another woman, another little boy. No doubt she'd sensed it that final night on the island, when she had come to him in his cottage and they'd made love and talked about the future, and about the past. As he'd always imagined, she heard his confession and took what he'd done to his own child into her wonderful, forgiving heart and redeemed him. Only later, when they made plans to flee their lives and begin another together, and when she realized he meant for it to be just the three of them—himself, Grace and Miles—and had thought to leave his daughter behind or, worse, neglected to think of her at all, did he manage to ruin everything. He tried his best to cover the mistake, suggesting that he'd had no idea Grace would be willing to take Cindy with them, but the damage was done. In that moment she'd seen him as a man prepared to abandon a child. Maybe she didn't immediately understand what effect such knowledge would have, but C. B. Whiting did.

The child he would've left behind, who so many years before had to be convinced that her memory of the crippling accident was incorrect, was the last to notice his homecoming, perhaps seeing some movement reflected in the glass. Cindy alone was glad to see him. She spun, nearly losing her balance, and lunged toward him crying, "Daddy!" And in that word he heard a second, far better purpose for the weight in his pocket.

BY TAKING HIS OWN LIFE when he did, C. B. Whiting robbed himself of the opportunity to become, in his remaining years, a somewhat less deluded man. Had he lived, he might gradually have learned that his wife was not quite the monster he believed her to be, that for her, affection was not impossible so much as unnatural and difficult, that she resembled the soil her family had tended for so long before selling out: blighted, but not entirely barren. And had he lived long enough to see his beloved Grace grow ill and die, had he found the courage to help her along in this journey, he might have come to understand that he'd expected too much of her good heart, which being human was fragile, imperfect and destined to fail. That his poor opinion of himself would have changed is unlikely, however, and it might have been this realization that compelled him to quit the earth.

One thing is certain. By ending his life when he did, C. B. Whiting died in the mistaken belief that like his forebears, he had failed to kill his wife, which wasn't entirely true. Had he lived, it would have surprised and perhaps even cheered him to learn that he actually had sealed her doom the year he proposed to her, not long after the dead moose washed up on his bank. That was the summer his engineers warned him that dynamiting the Robideaux Blight and cutting a new channel might increase the severity of floods, to which the river was already prone. In fact, afterward the river did become less manageable, though none of its previous floods came close to matching the one that occurred the spring that Miles and Tick Roby were still living on Martha's Vineyard. More snow had fallen that winter than the previous three combined, and when an early thaw came that first week in April—temperatures reaching into the seventies all the way to Canada—the snow melted in torrents and the Knox River roared through Empire Falls ten feet above flood stage, halfway up the tall first-floor windows of the old textile mill, which was in the process of being converted to a brew pub on the ground floor and the lavish offices of a credit-card company above. At the river's crest, half of downtown was underwater, including the old Empire Grill.

There was less damage on the other side of the river, where the bank was steeper. While the water never reached the Whiting hacienda, it did wash the gazebo clean away. Why Francine Whiting was in it at the time, of course, was impossible to know. Perhaps she imagined that so long as she herself commanded this stage, the river would never have the temerity to approach. She was not, like her daughter, a believer in swift, powerful, life-changing forces, and she might not have recognized this one when it arrived. Or perhaps she simply got trapped, a sudden surge of water cutting her off from the house.

The day the river crested was warm, with a high blue sky, the kind of afternoon, after a long gray winter and several days of warm spring rains, when she could have fallen asleep, the rays of the sun warming her skin. Though no one actually saw her get swept away, downstream in Fairhaven, where the flood damage was even worse than in Empire Falls, an emergency worker on a sandbag brigade near the dam saw what he believed was a woman's body glide by in the raging water. The corpse hung up briefly at the dam, but out there in the middle of the torrent, lodged at the top of a dam that might collapse at any second, and nothing could be gained by attempting a rescue. Besides, whoever this woman might have been, she was dead now, and under such circumstances the workers would not have been inclined to risk their own lives, even if the spectacle before them hadn't revealed a ghoulish aspect. For astride the body, crouched at the shoulders of the dead woman, was a red-mouthed, howling cat.

Together, dead woman and living cat bumped along the upstream edge of the straining dam, as if searching for a place to climb out and over. Bumping, nudging, seeking, until finally a small section of the structure gave way and they were gone.

ALSO BY RICHARD RUSSO

MOHAWK

Mohawk, New York, is one of those towns that lies almost entirely on the wrong side of the tracks. The leather tanneries that once supported it are closing. Its citizens have fallen on hard times. Dallas Younger, a star athlete in high school, now drifts from tavern to poker game, losing money, and, inevitably, another set of false teeth. His ex-wife, Anne, argues bitterly with her mother over the care of her sick father. And their son, Randall, deliberately neglects his schoolwork—because in Mohawk, it doesn't pay to be too smart. Out of derailed ambitions and old loves, secret hatreds and communal myths, Russo creates a richly plotted novel that captures every nuance of America's backyard.

Fiction/Literature/0-679-75382-6

STRAIGHT MAN

In *Straight Man*, Russo performs his characteristic high-wire walk between hilarity and heartbreak. His protagonist is William Henry Devereaux, Jr., the reluctant chair of the English department at an underfunded college in the Pennsylvania rust belt. In the course of a week, Devereaux will have his nose mangled by an angry colleague, imagine his wife is having an affair with the dean, wonder if an adjunct is trying to seduce him with peach pits, and threaten to execute a goose on local television. At the same time, he must come to terms with the dereliction of his youthful promise and the ominous failure of certain vital body functions. In short, *Straight Man* is classic Russo—side-splitting, true-to-life, and impossible to put down.

Fiction/Literature/0-375-70190-7

ALSO AVAILABLE

Nobody's Fool, 0-679-75333-8
The Risk Pool, 0-679-75383-4
The Whore's Child, 0-375-72601-2

VINTAGE CONTEMPORARIES
Available at your local bookstore, or call toll-free to order:
1-800-793-2665 (credit cards only).